Anton Bruckner

a genius emerges

Gordon L. Thomas

Published by SellMy Books

A CIP catalogue record for this title is available from the British Library

ISBN 978-0-9956778-6-9

Cover design by Rohan Renard (www.RenardDesign.com)

First published 2024

Printed in the UK

SellMy Books   contact: www.gordonlthomas.com

About The Author

Gordon L. Thomas is retired and lives with his wife in London, England. He began his career lecturing in physics at King's College, London. He then worked in the UK Home Office as a scientist and also as an administrator. Latterly, his responsibilities were in police science and physical security. Since retiring he has become a keen writer and this is his sixth novel.
His previous works are;

The Harpist of Madrid, published in 2011
The Emerald of Burgos, 2013
Expulsion, 2016
Return to Madrid, 2019
It Began in Florence, 2021

For more information please visit www.gordonlthomas.com, which you may use to contact him.

Acknowledgements

There are a number of people whom I must thank for helping me with the writing of this novel. First my darling wife, Janet, who gave me so much support while writing it.

A number of others read the first draft and commented. I am therefore also grateful to fellow author friends, Loretta Proctor and John Chamberlain, and my other friends Chris Forkan and Steve Browne, all of whom gave me helpful feedback and suggestions for correction and improvement. I also thank another friend, Dot Keogh, for suggesting the blurb.

I am also thankful to our daughter, Mel Hartley, her husband, Guy, and our son, Greg, and his wife, Sue, for their constant encouragement and for pressing me to complete this novel.

I am deeply indebted to the biographers and writers of books and articles, about Bruckner and his music, whose works I have studied. Without them it would have been impossible to give this novel such a strong factual basis.

Foreword

This is a biographical novel based on the life of the nineteenth century composer, Anton Bruckner. It deviates only slightly from the facts, principally in the dialogue between Bruckner and the many people he interacted with. It begins in 1837 with his reaction to the death of his father and its consequences for the young Anton, or 'Tonerl' as he was then known. The novel concludes in 1892 with his determined and complex struggle for the premiere of his Symphony No. 8.

There are several purposes of this novel. First, as much as words will allow, to share the greatness, the challenges, sheer emotion and otherworldliness of Bruckner's music. Second, to bring attention to many other of Bruckner's works. While he is most famous for his symphonies, he wrote over a hundred other works, some commissioned by others, many of which are referred to in this novel.

Thirdly, and most importantly, the novel attempts to dispel a number of the myths which still engulf Bruckner. Some of his biographers say he had had few to no friends. This is far from true. He maintained good terms with many he had met through his life. Richard Wagner was a good and supportive friend as was Arthur Nikisch, and Hans Richter, both well-known conductors who championed his symphonies. The von Mayfields, a couple in Linz, were good friends as were the Weinwurm brothers, his former landlady in Linz and, up to his dying day, his housekeeper, Frau Kathi.

An early biographer claimed he was simple minded and childlike. This is far from the truth. In changing career, first from being teacher at St Florian School to being the principal organist at the Linz Cathedral, he shrewdly negotiated an arrangement with St Florian, to return to the school if the post as organist did not work to his satisfaction. He struck a similar deal when he moved from there to being a lecturer in organ play and music theory at the Vienna Conservatorium. While less interested in other branches of the arts, he was a skilled mathematician, an accomplished physics and Latin scholar and, of course, probably the best organist in Europe. He certainly made no effort to change his Upper Austrian dialect to something more akin to the accepted one in Vienna, and this may have affected some scholars' impressions of him.

Another misconception is that he weakly agreed to his university students changing his symphonies to make them more acceptable to the then modern audiences and orchestras. There is little firm evidence for this. In all cases, the various versions of his symphonies available in his lifetime, were the products of his mind alone and what he regarded as improvements, or simplifications of earlier versions. He did authorise some performances of a symphony of reduced size, provided the score was not altered. In one case, that of his seventh symphony, although the premiere was almost certainly performed as he wrote it, two students and Arthur Nikisch, the conductor, might have made some unauthorised changes before its performance and later publication, but this remains in doubt. The classic case of rejecting the opinions of others concerns his fifth symphony. Two of his students wrote a two piano version of it and, without consulting Bruckner, arranged to have a public performance of their version. When they told him what they had organised, Bruckner insisted they cancel the concert and rearrange it for when he was totally satisfied with their version. He succeeded in his demands. A possible exception is over Bruckner's eighth. On being invited by Bruckner to examine and perform his first version, the conductor Hermann Levi made a number of critical comments and said he could not perform it as written. Over the next three years, Bruckner revised it and made a considerable number of changes. However, his alterations bore little relation to what Levi had said about it. It is likely, as in many of his symphonies, that he would have revised it anyway, despite Levi's comments.

Part of Bruckner's appeal is his eccentricity. He enjoyed wearing lose fitting baggy trousers, boots and wide collared shirts, even during public performances. Unusually, he was clean shaven and had short hair, when longer locks and beards were more the fashion. So he could look a little strange. He elevated his composing above his need for a wife. He made numerous attempts to persuade young women, many in their late teens, to marry him but they all failed. This was due to his inexperience and clumsiness in his attempts at seduction. He died celibate because he would never indulge in sexual intercourse outside of marriage, which was against his intense Catholic beliefs, even though he sometimes doubted the existence of a God.

Lastly, a further purpose of this novel is to celebrate the 200th anniversary of Anton Bruckner's birth, which was on 4 September, 1824.

To the memory of Graham Tiller.

Chapter 1
1837 Death in the family

The classroom door opened. The headmaster appeared. He walked over to the young lad who was teaching arithmetic.

'Tonerl, you have to go home. Now. Your mother wants you.'

'What's the matter? I can't leave now. I'm in the middle of a lesson.'

'Go, I tell you. Your father has not many hours left. I will take your class. So, go!'

The giver of life shone brightly through the classroom windows, that morning of 7 June. Tonerl placed his stick of chalk in the headmaster's hand and went. His heart beat faster. His father had been ill for many months but seemed in good spirits that morning as Tonerl left. What had changed since?

Tonerl was thirteen years old and took over his father's teaching at the Village School when his father began to suffer from tuberculosis which forced him to stop work. Somehow, and under an almost unbearable strain, Tonerl combined teaching at the school, ringing the church bells at five in the morning and attending classes. How he found time to sleep, God only knew. Tonerl had three younger sisters, Rosalie, Josefa and Maria Anna, and a younger brother Ignaz. Without Tonerl working, the family would have been reduced to begging or dying of starvation.

He ran the short distance to the family house in less than two minutes. It stood proudly on the corner of a short street in the tiny village of Ansfelden, in Upper Austria. As he stepped in, the eerie sound of crying greeted him. It came from his father's bedroom. He knocked and entered. What he saw frightened him.

A priest was leaning over his grey-faced father, uttering a formal prayer, '...commend you, my brother, to Almighty God, and entrust you to your Creator. May you return to Him who formed you from the dust of the earth.' From the dust of the earth, thought Tonerl, what a strange expression. He looked into his father's eyes. They looked in no direction and certainly not at him. He heard a rattling, croaking noise coming from his father's mouth. Then silence. He'd gone. Tonerl collapsed on the floor, completely overcome by the death.

A few minutes later, he felt a gentle slapping on his face. The priest was bringing him out of a faint. 'What was that?' said Tonerl. Then he suddenly realised. Father is dead! He then flooded with tears and went to hug his mother who was crying, too.

His mother was the stronger and stopped her sobbing to comfort the young lad. 'We must think about what we do now,' she said. 'Thank you, Father, for being with us. We can manage, if you want to go.'

'God bless you all,' said the priest. 'Please let me know if I can help before Anton's funeral.'

'Of course,' she said.

The priest crept towards the door and gave the sign of the cross before he turned and went. Mother lifted the bedsheet and placed it over her husband's still warm face. 'Let's go to the kitchen,' she whispered.

***

'I have been expecting your father's passing, and have a plan for our future,' she said, unfeelingly, and only minutes after he died. By then she had gathered together the children, and instructed them to sit around the family dining table, with her at the head, in what used to be their father's place. 'We will be much poorer without your father's income. So, I cannot afford to keep you in this house. We are going to move to Ebelsberg, where I have friends, but not all of you will come with us. You are the oldest, Tonerl, so you must leave.'

'That doesn't seem fair, Mama. So what do I do? Live on the streets?' he said, almost in tears.

'I have an idea. You can go to St Florian. You've been there many times. You enjoy playing the organ and you'd have three to choose from there.'

'I suppose that isn't so bad, Mama,' he said, thinking there were worse options. 'So when do you expect me to go? Will I be able to stay there?'

'We'll find out this afternoon. I'll ask our neighbour to look after you children while we are away. We'll go there in our cart.'

After a modest lunch of bread soup and goat cheese, mother and son set off for the ancient monastery of St Florian. It stood majestically on an escarpment in the Austrian hills, about five kilometres to the east of Ansfelden. Neither could erase the thought of the father's death from their minds. They each reflected on what a caring man he had been. He doted on his family and had been severely affected by the deaths, close to childbirth, of three of the couple's first four children. Along with reading, writing and arithmetic, just like any other Austrian teacher, he taught his pupils to play musical instruments, such as the violin, the organ and the spinet as well as a range of wind instruments. Austria led the world in teaching music, so it was not surprising to them that Mozart, Schubert, Haydn and Strauss were their outstanding sons. He was the family's sole breadwinner, until Tonerl helped out.

'Here's the main entrance,' said Mother. She pulled a bell chord by the giant door. Within moments, a clean shaven, squat monk, who seemed breathless, as if he had been running from inside this massive structure, appeared.

'Can I help you, meine Frau?'

'You can. I would like to see the prior, whose name is Arnett, I believe.'

'His name is Arneth. May I ask you why you wish to see him?'

'I would like to ask if my son here could join your boys' choir. He is a good singer and can play some musical instruments.'

'I'll see if he's available. But be warned, he may well be busy and you may have to return in some days' time.'

'We can return, if necessary.' The monk turned on one heel and vanished, leaving the door open but them outside. He seemed to be gone an age but it could only have been a few minutes.

'Come in. You are fortunate. Prior Arneth will see you.' He led them in, through the entrance hall and along a corridor to a door which he knocked. The word 'enter' sounded from within.

'This lady and her son would like an audience with you, Reverend Prior.'

'First, welcome to St Florian. I think I have seen you here before, young man. Please sit in those chairs. I have an important meeting in thirty minutes so please be quick. Start by telling me who you are.'

'My name is Frau Theresia Bruckner and this is my son, Anton. We are from Ansfelden.' She said she wanted Prior Arneth to accept Anton as a chorister. She explained why.

'I am sorry to hear about your husband's passing. May he rest in peace. Tell me, Anton, what do think of your mother's suggestion?'

'It is a new idea to me. I like it. I am interested in music and sing in the church choir.'

'What instruments do you play?'

'The violin, the organ and the spinet. I play the organ at our church.'

'Very interesting. Do you have any other interests?'

'Not really, but I have composed some small pieces.'

'Really?'

'Yes, four small pieces for the organ and a *Pange Lingua*, which I composed first.'

'Tell me more about your composing. How did you learn?'

'Be quick,' interjected his mother. 'The prior hasn't got all day.'

Anton glanced at her while thinking how to summarise what he would say. 'I am nearly thirteen. When I was eleven, my parents sent me to live with my godfather and cousin. His name is Johann Baptist Weiss. He lives in Hörsching. Along with my father, he showed me how to play the organ.

3

Johann taught me how to compose. It was his idea for me to write the *Pange Lingua*. I suggested I write the four organ pieces.'

'Would you like to be a composer, as a career?' said Arneth.

'What?'

'A composer. To earn a living writing music?'

'No fear. I want to follow my father into teaching. That's my ambition. But I need to improve my musical skills to be a good teacher.'

'Well, Frau Bruckner. I am impressed by your son, especially with what he has told me. I will accept him as a chorister. He will live here and I will ensure he is fed well. Bring him along in two weeks from today. With all his clothes and things, his instruments and so on. We will continue with his education so he can go on to be a teacher.'

Frau Bruckner burst into tears. 'Thank you! Thank you, Reverend! I cannot thank you enough. You have solved a big problem for me and Anton.'

'I thank you, too, your Holiness. I look forward to living here.'

'I think you will fit in well. Please go now or I'll be late for my meeting.'

On the way home, Frau Bruckner couldn't stop talking. It was as if some internal force made her speak continuously. Her husband's death and the meeting with the prior had filled her head with thoughts, which had to escape from the prison of her mind. She first spoke about the prior and his decision to take in Anton. It was difficult for her to believe that he had so willingly accepted her son, without even asking him to sing. Anton said, probably rightly, that it was because he had told the prior he sang in the church choir. Then she began to speculate about what would happen to him at St Florian. Would they turn him into a monk? Could they abuse him in some awful way which would affect him for the rest of his life? She had heard of monks beating children to punish them for sins they had yet to commit. What if they gave him some menial duties, like washing the dishes after the monks had dined, or peeling potatoes every day? Tears ran down her face at the thought.

'Please don't cry on my behalf, Mama. I can look after myself. Don't you remember how I padded my pants when I played that robbers game with my pals? When they whacked me, I couldn't feel a thing!'

'Oh, I remember, Tonerl,' she said, stifling her sobs.

Then a blood red cloud of panic descended upon her. Or was it anxiety? So many tasks had to be completed when they arrived home. The first was to arrange the funeral. Whom would they invite? Who needed to be told? Would they write or speak to her husband's friends and relatives directly? How would she choose the coffin, the flowers, and the hymns? Then the question of food and drink. Would they have a wake and, if so, where would they hold it? What would she do with the children?

In his youthful way, Anton tried bravely to comfort her. 'I can help you, Mama. You've said nothing that I can't do. After all, I am now the senior man in our family.'

Next she ranted about the move to Ebelsberg. How long would the authorities allow her to stay in the house? When would the new teacher, who would replace her husband, move in? Would they throw her out? The family could become homeless. Dare she commit herself to renting in Ebelsberg before someone moved into their house? How would they move there? Would they need help and, if so, from whom? And how would she and the children survive in Ebelsberg?

***

Like all funerals, Herr Bruckner's was a sad event. This unhappiness was much amplified by the presence of his young children. Rosalie was eight, Josefa seven, Ignaz four and Maria only one year old. The beautiful, tall-spired church, just metres from the family house, provided the service venue. His friends, along with the Weiss family, except Johann, congregated outside, waiting for the coffin to arrive. Mourners came from as far away as Linz where Herr Bruckner had played the violin at a number of different celebrations, helpfully for cash on the day. Most knew each other and chatted noisily while waiting. The school had closed for this sombre occasion, so the teachers could attend. Most touchingly, nearly all the pupils from the school were there. Many had been taught by Herr Bruckner.

As the church clock chimed eleven o'clock, the horse-drawn hearse appeared. Six bouquets of carnations adorned the plain oak coffin. Frau Bruckner, with Maria Anna held tightly in her arms, walked behind the hearse. Anton, hand-in-hand with Josefa, and Rosalie, holding hands with Ignaz, followed. They entered the church on the heels of the pallbearers. The crowd of attendees followed, until the church filled to overflowing. The organist played and the tiny choir sang Johann Weiss's Requiem, as Weiss himself conducted. With the family in the front row, the congregation assembled behind them. The priest appeared and stood facing those present.

The service began with a threnody in Latin. Anton placed his arm around his mother's waist to comfort her, and to minimise his feeling of loss. She sat with Maria Anna on her knee. The other children sat on the pews in the order they were holding each other and looked on, blank faced. It was as if they were not aware of the loss they had suffered. The choir sang a further mass, accompanied by the organ. Halfway through the Credo, Ignaz burst out laughing. Frau Bruckner looked sternly at him and put her forefinger to her lips. 'Shut up,' said Rosalie. 'I can't help it,' said Ignaz. 'Shut up or go outside!' said Josefa. That stopped him.

After the mass, the priest led a hymn, gave a reading from St John's gospel and a homily.

'Is someone present delivering a eulogy?' he shouted. No one answered. 'In which case we shall continue with the committal.' He stepped towards the coffin, which stood on a red draped catafalque.

'I am giving the eulogy!' yelled a man's voice from the back. 'I was outside when you shouted and someone told me.'

'Oh, headmaster, it was you!' said the priest. 'Please take the stand.'

The headmaster poured praise on the memory of Herr Bruckner. He said what a good teacher he was, how well he played the violin and the organ and how much he was loved by his pupils. The school had made a collection for the Bruckner family, he said, so they would be giving Frau Bruckner twelve florins to keep her and her children out of poverty. A welter of applause filled the building.

The priest led the coffin, held high by the four pallbearers, out of the church. The family and others followed to a freshly dug, expectant grave. While still holding Maria Anna in her arms, Frau Bruckner let out a piercing scream as her husband's coffin was lowered into its final resting place. The other children began to cry, with the exception of Anton who bravely held back his tears. Some of Herr Bruckner's teacher colleagues, each on the verge of crying, dropped earth on the coffin. This was a moment of unbearable sadness, which no one wanted, but had to be endured.

The wake was a totally different event, led by Frau Bruckner, who had transformed herself into a welcoming and jolly host. The fears and anxieties she had expressed on the way back from St Florian had vanished, like a mist dissolved by the rising sun. Their tiny house and garden thronged with guests. They hesitated to eat the almost tasteless semolina pancakes she provided, but gladly drank the fresh apple juice.

'You should not have laughed during the Mass,' said the gravedigger to Ignaz.

'Sorry, but I couldn't help it and I don't know why I did,' he said.

'I'm so grateful for the twelve florins,' said Frau Bruckner, smiling at the headmaster's wife. 'That will keep us going for at least six months!'

'It's a shame we couldn't collect more. I was in the same position after my first husband died. I had to do housework for all manner of people, some of whom failed to pay me. With my five children, it was a horrible time. You'll do better, I'm sure.'

Johann Weiss spoke to Frau Bruckner. 'I'm so sorry for your loss, Aunt. Your husband was a great man, as testified by his headmaster. We will all miss him terribly. Please let me know if there is anything I can do to help you.

Anton tells me he's been accepted as a choirboy in St Florian. What an honour. I'm certain he will do well there, especially as he's a bright young lad and keen to learn. He wants to follow in Uncle's footsteps and become a teacher. Is that right?'

'He certainly does. The prior asked him if he wanted to be a composer, but he said he wanted, as you say, to become a teacher. He wants to qualify, when he's old enough. Thank you so much for offering to help me. He is due to start at St Florian in a week's time. Could you take him, please? I dread leaving him there myself. I'm sure I'd become quite tearful!'

'Of course, Aunt. Nothing would please me more.'

Chapter 2
1837 - 1840 St Florian

After a tearful farewell from his mother, Anton and Johann sat on the front seat of the family cart. With their two horses in harness, they were on their way to St Florian. They had known each other for a long time, since before Maria Anna was born. Despite the ten-year age difference, they became good friends, and had developed a strong, student-teacher bond. Anton looked up to him in the same way he admired his own father.

'So what do you hope to get out of this?' said Johann.

'I'm not really sure, but, if I can improve my education and become a better musician, then I might do teacher training. That would be perfect. It would be good to make some friends there, too!'

'Do you know where you'll be staying?'

'No. Not a clue. Could be in some dormitory or even sharing accommodation with a few other students.'

'How do we get in?' said Johann.

'Just pull that bell cord over there.'

Johann did so and, a minute later, the same lugubrious, out-of-breath monk appeared, who had opened it before. Anton explained their purpose and, without uttering a single word, the monk led them in. Johann carried a sack of Anton's clothes and things on his shoulder. Anton held his violin. As previously, the dour monk led them to the prior's office.

'I'm glad you've arrived here,' said Reverend Arneth. He stood to shake Anton's hand. 'Who's your friend?' Anton introduced Johann and reminded him of what he said before.

'Of course,' said Arneth. 'You have clearly been of significant influence on this young man. I'm grateful to you for giving him a solid grounding on which we can build.'

'My father was also a great help,' said Anton.

'Naturally,' said Arneth. 'My first duty is to show you around this beautiful building, so you can leave your things here until we return. Would you like to join me and Tonerl?'

'I'd be delighted.'

Prior Arneth could not conceal his love for St Florian and its chequered history. As he led them along the lengthy corridor outside his office, he proudly explained that it was the largest monastery in Upper Austria. It rivalled Melk Abbey and Klosterneuburg as the most impressive examples of baroque architecture in the whole of Austria.

'So when was it built?' said Johann.

'I'm glad you asked. The monastery, named after Saint Florian, was founded in the eighth century. Since 1071, it has housed us Augustinian monks. None of us here is that old, of course! In the late seventeenth century, they completely rebuilt it in the baroque style, as this huge, closed rectangular construction. This wing is nearly a hundred metres across and has a parallel wing, about fifty metres away. We'll walk right around on the ground floor. You, Tonerl, can explore the upper levels later. This entire structure, including the Basilica, was the masterpiece of the architect Carlo Antonio Carlone. Sadly, he died before its completion, but Jakob Prandtauer finished the work.

'The monks, nearly five hundred of us, live in these rooms,' he said, pointing to a door. 'This one is unoccupied at present, so I'll show you inside.' He opened the door with what appeared to be a skeleton key. 'We call them cells. See how bare they are. A crude bed, a small wardrobe, a prayer station, and a bookshelf. Nothing else. We'll continue around the wing to the library, which is one of the largest in Austria. We have over seventy-five thousand items, which include some rare manuscripts. The one lying open in that cabinet is the Saint Florian Psalter, which contains all the psalms, written in German, Latin and Polish, and is decoratively illuminated. It is one of our most treasured artefacts.'

'Amazing,' said Johann.

'I've seen nothing like it before,' smiled Anton.

'Now we'll look at the gallery,' continued Arneth.

What they saw staggered both Anton and Johann.

'You will never have seen such a display of art in your lives before. It is all European, some from the Netherlands, but most from Germany and Austria. We are most proud of these colourful pictures by Albrecht Altdorfer, a fifteenth century German artist of the Danube School. He is most famous for the intense colour in his paintings and the use of landscapes. These are spectacular, but just wait a few minutes!'

They worked their way around to the glorious, impressive, almost overwhelming Basilica. Anton had been there before, but with no guide. They entered through a side chapel, which brought them close to the altar. 'There's the most spectacular of our Altdorfers. We call it the Saint Sebastian Altar. When closed, it shows four pictures of the martyrdom of the saint. When open, it shows the Four Stations of the Cross. It is now in its closed state. But you will see it open one day, Anton.

'What will please you most, gentlemen, are the three organs here. That one is the largest and most impressive. It has four manuals, 103 stops and 7,343 pipes. We will have you playing each while you are here, Anton.'

9

'Could I play one of them now?' said Johann.

'Yes, you may, but you, Anton, will have to operate the bellows around the back. Be the calcant.'

'I can do that,' said Anton.

Within moments, Johann was playing the organ part in the Sinfonia to Bach's Cantata Number 29. He stopped after about five minutes.

'Brilliant,' said Arneth. 'Well done! You are a virtuoso.'

'Not really,' said Johann, looking at the floor. 'You flatter me!'

'Would you like to try, Anton?'

'Certainly, soon, but I would be too nervous to play now. I'm not that good,' he said, in due but justified modesty. 'The quality of the sound is better than our organ at Ansfelden.'

'I don't blame you for declining,' said the prior with a smile. 'Let's go back to my office. The next step is to show you where you'll be living and introduce you to the headmaster. I hope you will like him! My reason for saying that will soon become clear!'

The prior led the way back. Johann said he had to leave. He shook hands with Anton and wished him good luck, saying that they would stay in contact. The prior shook hands with him and he left.

***

'Now I'll take you to the headmaster, Anton. I'll carry the sack of your things and you can carry your fiddle.' They stepped out of the Monastery the same way that Anton and Johann came in, then walked a few hundred metres to a modest house in the village of St Florian. A bearded, smiling gentleman, wearing a short, light grey frock coat, let them in. 'This is headmaster Michael Bogner, Herr Bogner to you!'

'I'm pleased to meet you, Anton. Prior Arneth told me much about you. Has he said you will stay in my house?'

Anton frowned, and his eyebrows dropped. 'No. I expected to stay in some dormitory so I am surprised! And pleased,' he added, after a pause.

'And there are two other choristers staying here. You will meet them soon. One is also called Anton, so we will call you by your nickname, which is Tonerl, I believe. The other is Wolfgang. Let me show you to your room,' said Herr Bogner.

The room faced south so was light and airy. Anton smiled broadly the moment he entered. A wooden desk with a chair placed underneath it faced the window. The small wardrobe stood next to the door and the bed alongside an adjacent wall. A jug of water sat on the side of a washstand, against the wall by the door. The curtains and carpet were a bright shade of red. This cosy room was small, but felt homely to Anton.

'I'll leave you to settle in,' said Herr Bogner. 'We have supper early, at six o'clock sharp, and you will hear a gong when it's ready. So you come down then. You'll soon find the dining room!'

So this is what the prior meant, when he said he hoped I would take to the headmaster, thought Anton. I would stay in his house! I wonder what the other choristers will be like. I wonder where they are now. Practicing for the choir, perhaps? He soon unpacked his things. Carefully putting his clothes in the wardrobe, he realised they would have to last him a long time. His mother couldn't afford to replace them, and he couldn't rely on the prior for clothing.

While he was lying on the bed, half asleep, the gong sounded. He knew what it meant, but felt apprehensive. Even though he quite liked him, or did so far, he hardly knew Herr Bogner. The other boys were totally unknown to him. He took an inward breath and went downstairs. He gingerly opened a door and looked in. 'This is the kitchen, son,' said a woman dressed in a long white dress and a floppy white hat. 'The dining room is straight ahead, if that's what you're looking for.'

'Thank you,' said Anton.

He slowly opened the door. All he could see was a table laid out for five people. He sat there and waited. He daren't sit at the head of the table, so sat at the end, furthest from the door. He then heard the voices of two boys. They entered and halted as they saw him. One was fair-headed and tall. The other dark and shorter. They each wore a blue and white surplice.

'Hello. Who are you?' said the taller one.

'My name is Anton Bruckner. I've just joined as a chorister. I'm from Ansfelden, not far away. You look like choristers, too.'

'You don't look like one,' replied the taller.

'He won't, not yet anyway,' said the more sympathetic, shorter one. 'My name is Wolfgang. I've been here two years now. I'm from Enns, which is not far away, either. Welcome to the choir, Anton.'

Realising how abrupt he had been, the taller one introduced himself in friendlier terms. 'My name is also Anton and I'm from Styer. I joined at about the same time as Wolfgang.'

'So you will join the school, as you are staying here,' said Wolfgang.

'Certainly. I'm only thirteen, so I have a lot to learn. Not just arithmetic, reading and writing. I suppose the school is in the monastery.'

The blond one laughed. 'So you don't know much about this place. No. There's a separate school in the village, just down the road from here. We only go to the monastery to do choir practice.'

'I see,' said Anton. 'I also want to improve my skills as an organist, and in playing the violin.'

11

'Call yourself an organist?' said the blond one. 'How can a kid like you be an organist? You're not tall enough to begin with!'

'Don't be so unkind,' said Wolfgang. 'If he says he plays the organ, I'm sure he does. So leave him alone. I'm sorry about this one,' he said, pointing to the other Anton.

Moments later, the door swung open, and Herr Bogner walked quickly in. 'I'm sorry I'm late, lads. I've been delayed at a finance meeting. But don't worry. It was about the monastery, not the school.'

The lady dressed in white followed him in, carrying two plates, one of which she placed in front of Wolfgang and the other in front of Anton Bruckner. 'So feeding him before me?' the blond one said. 'He hasn't been here five minutes!'

'Don't be rude,' said Herr Bogner. 'You'll get yours in a moment.' The cook said nothing. Once they had a dish in front of each of them, the headmaster said grace. Then they tucked into their meal of sausage, boiled potatoes, and cabbage.

'We have a problem with your names,' the headmaster said, during the meal. 'Our new Anton has agreed that we should use his nickname of Tonerl. That's right, isn't it Anton?'

'Of course.'

***

It took Tonerl several weeks to settle into the school. Life there was so different from Ansfelden. There he knew everyone, including the teachers, who admired him because he was helping them. At the St Florian School he found it hard, at least to begin with, to relate to the other pupils. He felt the odd one out, especially as he was the only one from Ansfelden. Most had been born in the village of St Florian, so knew each other well. Not only that, he was still grieving over the death of his father and, when feeling low, cried himself to sleep at night.

At one point, he wondered whether he should be somewhere else, at a school in Linz perhaps, or with Johann Weiss in Hörsching. Yes, that would have been better. There was a good school there he could have attended and an organ at the church. It was too late. He could hardly change then. It would upset too many people, but mainly his mother. Press on he must, and accept he was there.

He felt more in control when it was one of those days on which he could spend time at the Monastery. While he gradually felt at home and happy at the Bogner residence, he felt even better in the Monastery. Especially in the Basilica while he was sitting at an organ, at first, one of the smaller ones. The magnificent, main one cast a spell over him every time he looked at it.

After Tonerl had been at St Florian School for just over a month, Herr Bogner told him at breakfast that he was wanted in the Basilica and to be there by 9 o'clock. Chuckling to himself, Bogner said, 'You will meet someone who will be helping you. I won't tell you the name of the person or what he does. But you will find him to be of great value. He may even influence your future career!'

By then, Tonerl had settled in well enough to take some teasing, especially from Herr Bogner, whom he was growing to like. 'I don't mind a little mystery!' he replied.

All the way to the Basilica, Tonerl wondered who this person could be. How could he change his future or even give it direction? As he entered the church, he heard the most beautiful sounds coming from the organ. They were so sublime they made the hair on the back of his neck rise. Tonerl walked up to the console where a bearded, brown-haired man was playing. To Tonerl, he appeared old, but he was probably in his thirties. He must have seen Tonerl in the mirror, so nodded his head to acknowledge him. Then he continued playing until he reached a place to stop. He stepped towards Tonerl.

'I'm pleased to meet you, young man,' he said with a glowing smile. 'My name is Herr Anton Kattinger. I'm the head organist here and I understand you want to improve your organ playing. You are Tonerl Bruckner, aren't you? Are you him? I don't want to be teaching the wrong person!'

'Yes, I am Tonerl Bruckner, Sir,' he said, and they shook hands.

'First, tell me about yourself and why you are here.'

With his friendly approach, Herr Kattinger had made Tonerl feel relaxed, so he spoke freely. He told him where he was from and about his family. Holding back a tear, he explained what great admiration he had for his father. He spoke about Johann Weiss and what he had taught him. Then he said he was at St Florian because his mother could no longer support him. Finally, he told Kattinger that he was right. He wanted to improve his organ playing.

'Thank you for that, Tonerl. You've given me a clear idea of what you want from me. Do you have any long-term ambitions?'

'Yes, I want to be a schoolteacher, like my father.'

'At some point, I'll allow you to play this magnificent beast, but for now, I'll teach you on one of our smaller, choir organs. That one over there.'

They walked over to it.

'I'd like to start by getting some idea about how you play. Is there anything in particular you would like to play me?'

'Not especially,' said Tonerl, hesitating.

'Can you read music?'

'Quite well,' he said. 'My father and Johann Weiss taught me.' Then, after a moment's thought came out with, 'I've written a couple of pieces for the organ. Would you like me to play them? I can remember them, so I won't need to read anything.'

'What an excellent idea! Yes, play one, to begin with. Just relax and make yourself comfortable at the console. By the way,' he grinned, 'one of our apprentice monks is behind there on the bellows pump, so it will make plenty of sound!'

Tonerl shuffled himself on the bench. 'Shall I start?'

'Yes, when you are ready.'

After about ten seconds, Tonerl took a deep breath and started. The main theme of the piece was a march, which started softly, as if it was an army in step in the distance. He pressed the swell pedal to increase the volume and used other foot pedals to bring in some lower notes. Then the second, dainty tune appeared in which Tonerl used the flute pipes. This he followed with some variations on each of them and brought the piece to a close in about four minutes.

'Bravo! Bravo!' Kattinger said, applauding. 'That was good. What a nice piece of composition. I enjoyed the contrast between the two themes. And each is quite new. Now, I want you to play a piece for which you have to read the music. Here we are. It's on the stand.'

Tonerl hesitated while he read it through a few times. 'I'll play it now,' he said.

He found the piece more of a challenge than his own composition and made several mistakes. He had to use two manuals when he had only used one before. 'I'm sorry,' he said. 'I didn't do well on that one.'

'It was much more difficult than your piece. That was deliberate, so I could see what areas we need to work on. Let me tell you something, Tonerl. You are good for your age. There is much to do to improve your play, your touch on the keys, for example, and the timing by which you should release them. But you are far from a beginner and, by the time we're finished, you will become an accomplished organist. I can't guarantee it, but with my instruction and your practice, that's what you'll be.'

Tonerl was so pleased, he was almost in tears. 'Thank you!' was all he could say.

'We need to arrange a timetable, so seeing me doesn't clash with your school lessons, singing, and your violin lessons. Don't worry about that. That's my job, working with the other teachers. I know that Herr Gruber wants to see you tomorrow, here in the Basilica. He will be your violin teacher.'

***

That evening at dinner, Tonerl spoke about his meeting with Herr Kattinger.

'I knew you would like him,' said Bogner.

'I thought so, too,' said Frau Bogner, who had frequently joined the group for the meal. Tonerl adored this plump, heavy-breasted lady, who seemed to want to mother him.

'Hmm,' said the blond Anton. 'You must have made flattering remarks to him, so he had to like you or seem to.'

Wolfgang stood up and pointed at blond Anton. 'Why are you always so nasty to Tonerl? He's never as much said a cross word to you. If you can't think of anything nice to say, just keep your mouth shut.'

The blond one stood. 'Why should I take any notice of you? I can say what I like.'

'Sit down, both of you, and stop this nonsense. As for you, Anton, don't be unpleasant to Tonerl. He doesn't deserve it. Next time you do, I'll give you a severe reprimand. You pupils are supposed to work together and be friends, not sworn enemies.'

They followed this exchange by a few minutes' silence before Herr Bogner restarted the conversation. 'So what did Herr Kattinger get you to play on the organ?'

'A couple of preludes for organ I wrote about a year ago and a piece I had to sight read.'

'I'm amazed,' said Frau Bogner. 'You wrote the preludes yourself? How did you learn to compose?'

Tonerl wished he hadn't mentioned his composing for fear of appearing immodest. He quietly told them about Johann Weiss and what he had learnt from him.

'Incredible,' said Frau Bogner. 'You were lucky to have such an excellent teacher and cousin as well!'

'So you will meet Herr Gruber tomorrow,' said Herr Bogner. 'He is a superb violinist and he was a friend of a friend of Beethoven.'

'Really?' said Frau Bogner.

***

Tonerl hardly slept that night, wondering what Herr Gruber would be like. Oddly, he felt a sense of dread. After breakfast, and carrying his violin, he made his way to the Basilica. He suddenly realised when he arrived he didn't know what Herr Gruber looked like. He then thought that may not matter, as he may well realise, when he saw him carrying a violin case, that he might be his new student.

'Good morning, young man. Do you happen to be Anton Bruckner, known also as Tonerl?'

'Yes, Sir. That is me.'

'I'm pleased to meet you. My name is Herr Max Gruber. I shall teach you the violin.'

'I'm pleased to meet you, too,' said Tonerl. 'I've brought my violin with me.'

'I can see that. I didn't need telling. I'll tell you about myself. I am a virtuoso violinist and have been for many years. Not only do I teach, I also play in some of the most prestigious orchestras in Upper Austria. I play in the St Florian orchestra and in the Theatre Orchestra in Linz, to name but two. Ignaz Schuppanzigh, a famous violinist of our country, who taught the great Ludwig van Beethoven and became a great friend of Beethoven, taught me. He founded the famous Razumovsky Quartet, the first of its kind. I, too, was a friend of Beethoven. So I'm more than qualified to teach you, young man.'

Tonerl could, even at his age, detect an arrogance in this character. He wondered how being well-known made him so fit to teach. The fact he'd played in an orchestra was far more relevant.

'How well do you play?'

'Reasonably well, I think. I've been playing since I was four. I also play the organ.'

'I know that! I know that! I'm only interested in your violin playing.'

Tonerl's head went down at his remarks.

'Get your violin out. I want to hear you. Play anything you like.'

Herr Gruber's abruptness made him feel nervous. He thought for a moment about what he would like to play. He settled on some rhythmical music he had often played on dance nights. So he said nothing but played the jolly piece for about five minutes.

'Hmm,' was Gruber's reaction. 'You clearly enjoyed playing it. It's a pity it was so poor. Your violin is out of tune by about half a tone. Flat on all strings. You don't hold the bow properly and you often lose your rhythm.'

Tonerl couldn't hide his disappointment. He felt he played better than Herr Gruber had said. Nor did he think he was out of tune. He'd tuned it with a set of tuning forks before breakfast. Should he give up on the violin and concentrate on his singing and the organ?

'You look unhappy about what I have said, but it's true. Any other teacher would have said the same.'

'Yes, I am upset, but only with the way I played. I thought the violin was in tune. But if you say it's not …'

'It isn't. So do you want lessons or not?'

Tonerl raised his eyebrows at this unexpected question. 'Yes, I do. I hope you will teach me,' he said, not believing he wanted him as a teacher. He really didn't like the man.

'In which case, I will. I don't know when I'll see you again. From what Herr Kattinger is saying, we need to work out a timetable for you. This will include choir practice and the rest of your education. I'll let you go now, and I'll see you at your first actual lesson. Goodbye.'

'Goodbye, Sir,' was all Tonerl needed to say. He took the strong hint and went. He had no more work that morning, so went back to his room in the Bogner's house. As he was lying on bed half asleep, he heard a knocking on the door. It was Frau Bogner.

'Hello, Tonerl. How did your meeting with Herr Gruber go?'

'Not that well. I was nervous and didn't play my best. He said the violin needed tuning when I didn't think it did.'

'I thought I heard you tuning it this morning.'

'I was.'

'I shouldn't say this, but he can be quite difficult. Mind you, if he says you're good, you are. Did he say he'd accept you as his pupil?'

'Yes, but he let me decide.'

'He does that with all of his pupils the first time they meet, unless he thinks they are so bad, he doesn't want to teach them. So you did well, if you ask me!'

'Thank you, Frau Bogner. I feel better now… the best I've felt all morning! Please could you let me have some writing paper, a pen and some ink? I haven't got a lesson until 2 o'clock this afternoon, and I would like to write a letter to my mother.'

'Of course, Tonerl. I'll get some. You can write at your desk or here, if you prefer.'

Tonerl sat down at his desk, pen in hand and a blank sheet of paper in front of him. He looked up at the ceiling and half closed his eyes. He needed to think of his experiences up to then. Not wanting to worry her, he was positive on all fronts, even if that meant exaggerating a little. There was not one even slightly negative point he would make. As far as the blond Anton went, he would say he had two good friends there and shared digs with them in the headmaster's house. The headmaster and his wife liked him, he would say, and that he liked them. He would tell her about the room and the meals, but not mention the violin teacher.

***

Tonerl gradually became familiar with the complex timetable that the staff prepared for him. No two days were the same, so it was helpful that they gave

17

him a copy and did not expect him to memorise it, even though he soon did. After about a month of complying with the complex, demanding schedule, which meant he was fully occupied from 8 o'clock in the morning until 6 o'clock at night, Prior Arneth summoned him to see him. He was terrified. What could he want? What had Tonerl done wrong?

Tonerl knocked on the prior's door. 'Enter!' came from within.

He sheepishly went in and stood by the door. Arneth approached him and shook his hand.

'Tonerl, I'm pleased to see you. Come in and sit in that chair. Generally speaking, you are doing well in your studies. You have proved that the first impressions you gave me are accurate. You are improving on the organ, Herr Kattinger tells me. So he's got you improvising then?'

'Yes,' said Tonerl. 'I've only just started that and have a long way to go.'

'You are too modest, my friend.'

Interesting, thought Tonerl. So he regards me as a friend, so I must think the same of him.

'I enjoy playing the organ. It gives me a strange feeling of homeliness, as if I belong on the organ console.'

'That means you love playing it. I'm pleased for you.'

'Thank you.'

'You are not making such good progress on the violin. I know Herr Gruber is a very demanding teacher, but says you need to do much better. More practice, maybe?'

'Yes.'

'Thank you. I just wanted say how well you are progressing, except on the violin. Go away and work on that. You have the talent but lack the skill. We'll see each other again before long. I hope so.'

'So do I, Prior Arneth.'

It was good to know he was doing reasonably well at St Florian. He had not achieved much success on the violin but would work on that.

***

The weeks at St Florian School passed with surprising speed. The weeks turned to months and the months to over two years. By then, Tonerl's voice had broken, so he no longer sang in the Basilica choir. Instead, he played one of the two smaller organs in choir practice, and occasionally his violin in the small Basilica orchestra. Over this period, pupils came and pupils went. Much to Tonerl's delight, the unpleasant, inimical, blond Anton left. A lad called Karl Seiberl replaced him in Herr Bogner's house. He and Tonerl soon became friends and met each other regularly. They often went for walks in

18

the fields surrounding the town. They talked about their respective families and what they themselves wanted to do when they left St Florian.

'What did your father do?' said Karl to Anton, one chilly autumn morning while they were strolling in the town.

'He was a schoolteacher in Ansfelden. I learnt a lot from him because he was an excellent musician. He was a wonderful father to us children, but especially to me, as he taught me so much. And to play the organ and the violin. I was so upset when he died.' Tonerl was almost in tears.

'So you could play some instruments before you came to St Florian?'

'Yes. My cousin, Johann Weiss, also helped me to play and understand music.'

'Johann Weiss, did you say?'

'Yes, he's about ten years older than me and, would you believe, he was my godfather, too!'

'They say it's a small world, and it is! My brother, Josef, knows Johann Weiss. They have been friends for years. That is the Johann who plays the organ in Linz Cathedral sometimes, isn't it?'

'Yes! That's him!'

'What a surprise. Maybe, you'll meet my brother sometime.'

'I'm sure I've met him! He was having a conversation with Johann when I went to see him about composing a piece he was keen for me to write.'

'It's a smaller world than you think. He's always going to see Johann Weiss. They have a lot in common.'

'So, what does your father do, Karl?'

'Mine is a headmaster in St Marienkirchen, so not too far from here.'

'Do you want to become a teacher when you leave school?'

'No. I want to be a lawyer! I wouldn't like to teach! What about you, an organist at a cathedral?'

'No, I want to be a teacher. That way I can help my family with the finances. My mother is struggling to keep herself and my sisters and brother. She has to do some lowly work on farms and in people's houses.'

'You'd be better off as a musician, especially with your natural talent.'

***

Not many days after this interesting discussion with Karl, he was again called to see Prior Arneth. He had seen him and spoken to him many times over the intervening years and, as usual, felt quite relaxed.

'I have two new ideas for you, Tonerl. First, I have been talking about your organ playing with Herr Kattinger. Thanks to your dedication, you have become competent, especially for a young lad of fifteen. So we would like to give you the opportunity to play on the main organ at the Basilica.'

19

Tonerl's face lit up like a burning beacon. 'Surely, I'm not good enough for that?'

'You certainly are, my friend. And if you'd like to, we would like you to play the organ during the day when parishioners come and go. They would love it.'

'What would I play?'

'We'll give you the music and you can improvise to your heart's content.'

'When can I play it? I am dying to!'

'As soon as you are free and want to. Let Herr Kattinger know and he'll find a bellows pumper.'

'Thank you, Prior. I'll go now and see you again soon.'

'Just a minute, my friend. Do you remember, I said I had two new ideas for you? Don't you want to know about the second?'

'I'm so sorry, Prior. I was so excited about playing the main organ.'

'My next idea is this. I first have to ask you a question. Over the time you have been here, you have consistently said you want to become a schoolteacher. Is that still your ambition?'

'Indeed, it is.'

'The idea is this. There is a teacher training college in Linz. The course lasts for ten months. Assuming you pass the final exam, you will have a certificate that will qualify you to teach anywhere in Austria, at any junior school. I would like to write to the college and ask them to accept you. What do you think?'

'I would be grateful and very pleased, Prior Arneth. But who would pay?'

'St Florian would pay for the course and for your lodgings in Linz. That would include your food and upkeep.'

Tonerl didn't know what to say.

'Well?'

'I'm delighted. I cannot thank you enough. I would be more than pleased to go. Would that mean I would have no more connection with St Florian?'

'Not at all. You would still be officially on our books. You are a valued pupil here and we might even think... only think... of you teaching at St Florian School. But let's not get too far ahead of ourselves!'

The following day, after his lesson on the choir organ with Kattinger, Tonerl said he would like to take up the offer, made to him by Prior Arneth, to play the main organ. 'Of course,' said Herr Kattinger. 'I anticipated you wouldn't be able to wait much longer, so I've told our bellows man to move up to that one, as soon as you are ready.'

'I'm ready now,' said Tonerl.

As Tonerl walked up to the main organ, its glory and magnificence almost overcame him. He saw it as an instrument of overwhelming splendour and felt quite small in relation to its enormity. 'Just sit on the bench and play,' said Kattinger. 'Anything you like and can remember.'

Tonerl played a piece that Kattinger had taught him and soon improvised freely. He had never felt so powerful in producing sound. It filled the whole Basilica, and reverberated around its structure. Like nothing else he had ever experienced before, playing it gave him a sense of pleasure and excitement. He fell in love with it, as if it was alive with human qualities. After this mind shattering encounter and after about a quarter of an hour, he stood up from the instrument and gazed at the manuals.

'I do believe you are shaking,' said Kattinger.

'I am. It is so powerful.'

'Do you know the Bach Toccata and Fugue in E minor? He was only two years older than you when he wrote it!'

'Yes, I've heard my cousin Johann play it. I love it. I know it as I've played parts of it with him, but not very well!'

'I have the music here if you'd like to play it now.'

He took the score, put it on the stand and read it, so thoroughly he even flicked back through the pages to check his understanding. He patiently took all the time he needed to remind himself of the piece. Then he launched into it. The sheer volume of sound he created inspired him to play it at his utter best. It was not a brilliant performance, and he slightly lost rhythm in some of the tougher stretches. He lifted his hands high at the end.

'You did well with that, Tonerl. It won't be long before you are playing in our Sunday services! But you have a training course to concentrate on first!'

Chapter 3
1840 - 1841 Teacher training

Tonerl had a few weeks to spare before his course began, so badly wanted to be with his family. But he had no money. He spent some hours deciding what to do. He'd muster up enough courage to ask the prior. They were friends, after all, even though seriously different in age. Walking to the prior's office, he wondered what his reaction would be. He knocked on the door. The usual reaction sounded.

'Enter!'

'Tonerl, it's good to see you.'

'I won't delay my question, Prior Arneth. I have no money and before I start at Linz, I would like to spend a couple of weeks with my family. As you know, they have moved to Ebelsberg. Could you please lend me enough to get there? Somehow, I would find enough to get myself to Linz, so you need not worry about that.'

'My dear Tonerl. I will lend you nothing... I will give you enough to travel to Ebelsberg, and from there to Linz. I think we have not thought your situation through properly. We should have ensured you had sufficient money, at least for your travels. And a little in addition, so you could attend the occasional concert and have some to spend on yourself. I am going to put that right.' He took a purse out of his surplice pocket, opened it and handed Tonerl six one florin coins. 'This should be ample for your transport and to keep you for the ten months of the course. If you need more, don't be afraid to ask!'

'I cannot thank you enough, Prior Arneth... and am so grateful. I shall take care of it and spend it wisely.'

'I know you well, Tonerl, so have no doubts on that score!'

That evening, Tonerl packed. In the morning, he thanked Herr Bogner, and his wife profusely for all they had done for him. After breakfast, he shook hands with Wolfgang and Karl, said he hoped to see them all again, and left for the town centre. As he was just about to hail a cabriolet, he saw a cart heading toward the road to Linz. The driver wore a dented tri-corn hat with a feather stuck in the band. He held out his hand to stop it.

'Good morning, Sir. Where are you going?' said Anton.

'I'm heading to Ansfelden.'

'Could you give me a lift, please?'

'Of course, young fella. Chuck your stuff in the back and climb on.' Anton could see much of his load was pork joints and cabbages.

The driver was one of those people who, in the presence of another being, had to talk. He related to Tonerl much of his life story from his birth in Emms to doing delivery work, as he was then for a local farmer. Tonerl had to reciprocate and said he was actually heading for Ebelsberg. Much to his delight, the cart driver said it was not far out of his way, so he'd go to Ebelsberg first, and then to Ansfelden. He knew a shorter route than the usual one.

As he climbed out of the cart, Tonerl offered the driver five kreuzers from the change Herr Bogner gave him for a florin.

'Don't be daft, young man! I can't take money from you. And if you want a lift back to St Florian, I leave Ansfelden's market square, Tuesdays and Thursdays, at one o'clock in the afternoon.'

***

Carrying his violin case and with the sack of his other things slung over his shoulder, Tonerl soon found his mother's new abode. It was one of the smallest, scruffiest houses in the village. He knocked on the door.

'It's you, Tonerl,' said Josefa, as she opened it. 'Come in and put your things down.' She gave him a hug and a kiss on each cheek.

'It's so good to be home,' said Tonerl, 'especially as I've never been here before.' He felt sorry for them as he glanced at the thread bare mats and dilapidated furniture. The house was in poor condition, compared with their home in Ansfelden. 'How are you all?'

'We are not doing well. Mama is working all hours to keep us in food and clothing. She isn't very well. The others are alright. While Mama is working, we have to look after Maria Anna. She is three now. Come in and see the others. They are in the back room. Mama is at the farmer's, helping with the ploughing. She'll be back before dark.'

The other three greeted him like a long-lost brother, which he was. Rosalie and Ignaz kissed and hugged him, both at the same time, while Maria Anna slept in her cot.

'It is so good to see you! You are taller now,' said Ignaz.

'So are you,' said Tonerl, smiling.

'Aren't I?' said Rosalie.

'Wow! You are so much taller, I didn't recognise you!'

'You're teasing me, Tonerl!'

'You've taken us all by surprise,' said Josefa. 'We thought you were still at school in St Florian. So why have you come today?'

Tonerl explained the background and told them about his time at St Florian.

'So you are going to be a teacher then?' said Rosalie. 'You'll have to come here to teach us!'

23

'I'd love to, but I need to make a living at it, to help you all, as well as me.'

'Why haven't you been here before?' said Ignaz. 'We have missed you.'

'I was studying nearly every day and had no money for fares.'

'You could have walked it. It's not that far,' said Josefa.

'It was mainly because I didn't want Mama to have to feed me. Her idea for me going to St Florian was so that she only had you four to look after.'

'We'll have to look after you now!' said Rosalie.

'I can pay my way. I have some money!'

'Show us,' said Ignaz.

Tonerl took his purse out of his sack. 'Here you are.' He poured the contents onto the floor.

'I've never seen so much money before. Where did you get it from?' said Rosalie. 'Did they pay you for any work you did?'

Anton was in the middle of explaining when their mother walked in. She flopped herself into a well-used armchair.

'My God, it's you, Tonerl! What are you doing here?'

Tonerl was quite surprised at the state of his mother. Her clothes were dirty and worn, but she had been working in a field. He noticed her hair was greyer than when he left home and her face showed signs of ageing. But she looked well fed and not at all unwell, so not as he expected from what Josefa said. He leant over and planted a kiss on her lips. Then he told her why he was there and that he would pay for his keep.

'It's so good to see you, my eldest. Of course you can stay. As long as you like. And you won't pay me. Your cousin Johann has been so good to us. What I earn keeps us just above the poverty line. But Johann improves our lives by giving me a florin every month from his school salary. He is a lovely man. You'll probably see him while you are here. What's all that money doing on the floor?'

'It's what Prior Arneth gave me for my food and lodgings, and anything else I need at Linz. Ignaz wanted to see it. I'll pick it up now.'

'How much did he give you?'

'Six florins.'

'Take care of it. If someone robs you, you are in trouble.'

His mother regularly left him in charge while she went to work. He often practiced his violin and enjoyed playing it most while entertaining his brother and sisters. Nearly every day, to the sound of it, they would dance around their house, laughing as they did.

'Mama, the day I arrived, Josefa said you were not at all well. Are you?' he asked, one evening when they were alone together.

'I sometimes give the impression I'm not well when I'm simply exhausted. Especially when I come home.'

'Are you sure you are telling me the truth, Mama?'

'Yes, my son, you need not worry about me, especially as I have Johann's support. He is so good to us.'

It was as if she wanted to change the subject.

***

The fortnight passed surprisingly quickly, so it was soon time to head for Linz. Much emotion flowed at his departure. The only ones who didn't cry were Ignaz and little Maria Anna. She was too young to understand. Tonerl tried to make his departure easier by saying he would visit them more often, provided his money didn't run out. Johann came to the fore, paying for a cabriolet to take him there, that morning of 30 September.

'You are a headmaster, Johann,' said Tonerl as they sat in the back. 'So what can I expect at the college?'

'It's an incredible place. It produces the best teachers in Austria, not just Upper Austria. They will teach you a range of subjects you will need to teach, including how to teach. They will also improve your ability as a musician and tell you how to teach the violin, piano and, of course, the organ. I assume you have passed the entrance examination.'

'What exam?'

'The entrance exam!'

'No. Prior Arneth didn't mention any exam. What will they be testing, do you know?'

'Your basic education and your ability to become a teacher. You should be fine. You stood in as a teacher for your Papa, didn't you?'

'Yes, I did. I taught reading, writing and arithmetic.'

'Where will you be staying? You won't be able to stay at the college.'

'St Florian has arranged for me to stay with a landlady at Bethlehemstrasse 37, so I have to find it.'

'Driver, not the college! Take us to Bethlehemstrasse 37 instead,' shouted Johann to the driver, as he leant out of the side.

'Will do, Sir!' he shouted back.

'So where is the college?'

'In Elisabethstrasse, at the northern end, about as far as you can go.'

***

'I've been expecting you, young man,' said a pretty, young blond lady as she opened the door to number 37. 'Do come in. Let me take your violin case.'

'I'll just say goodbye to my friend,' said Tonerl. 'Thank you so much, Johann, for helping me and for being so kind to my mother.'

'It's nothing, Tonerl. Now I know where you live, I'll come to see you. Say, next Saturday morning?'

'Please do.'

'Goodbye then, until Saturday.'

'Goodbye.'

The main front window of the house allowed a golden stream of light to pour in, even in the autumn when the sun was low. It was a three-bedroomed house, two for single beds and one for a double. The landlady used the double and showed Tonerl to his, which was at the back. It looked over a tiny garden which was planted out with a variety of late season vegetables. His bed was tucked up against the side wall, the opposite side of which sat a desk and a narrow chest of drawers.

'I hope you like it here,' she said. 'My name is Irene Planck. You can call me Irene. St Florian is paying your rent direct to me. For that you get this room, breakfast, an evening meal, and any washing you want done.'

'I'm sure everything will be fine, Frau Planck... um Irene. I'm looking forward to my stay here.'

'You are my only lodger at present, so feel free to come and go as you please. You can sit with me in the lounge, if you wish.'

'Thank you for that. Is it alright if I practice my violin in my room?'

'Of course. If you want an audience, you can play it to me!'

Tonerl wasn't sure what she meant by this and felt disinclined to entertain her. He soon unpacked and set the room to his satisfaction. Rather than sit there for the rest of the day - it was only 12 o'clock - or in her lounge, he decided he would explore the city and locate the training college.

Tonerl had never been to a city before and its sheer size and complexity dumbfounded, almost frightened, him. He mentally noted his every move so he could easily find his way back to Bethlehemstrasse. The streets thronged with people, going about their errands or heading to meet others. Just after he turned right into Elisabethstrasse, he saw a man sitting on the pavement outside a shop. The man was holding out a bowl, a begging bowl. He'd never seen a beggar before. As he passed him, the man raised the vessel towards Tonerl.

'Give me a kreuzer, Sir,' he said. 'I'm crippled, and begging is my only way to stay alive.'

Tonerl stopped. He didn't know what to do. It wasn't his money. Prior Arneth gave it to him to spend, not to give away. He thought again. What would the prior do? Surely he would give something to the beggar. So he dropped a kreuzer into the man's bowl.

'God bless you, young man.'

Further along Elisabethstrasse, Tonerl saw a sign pointing to the cathedral. Feeling excited, he followed it. Turning first to the left, then to the right, then left again, he saw it, towering above him like a double-headed giant. There he was, looking up at the 'brother' of St Florian. He urgently needed to see inside. So, he pushed the huge door open and walked in. He knelt and crossed himself at the sight of the altar. Individuals, men and women, were sitting on the pews, apparently in prayer. A priest came towards him.

'What do you want, son?' he said, suspecting Tonerl of looking for trouble.

'I wanted to look around the cathedral,' he said.

'Why?'

'I've been studying at St Florian and this is the first time I've been here. Its similarity with the Basilica struck me.'

'Oh, you know St Florian. Do you know the prior?'

'Yes, Prior Arneth. I know him well.'

'In which case, I'm happy for you to look around. I can tell you a about it and give you a tour, if you wish.'

'Yes, please, Reverend.'

'It is similar in design to St Florian because the father of the architect who designed St Florian designed it. It's called the baroque style. The Jesuits built it between 1669 and 1683. Come in further and look up behind you. There you can see the organ loft. Franz Krismann built the organ. He designed the one in St Florian.'

'I am learning to play the organ.'

'Wonderful! I'd love to show you more, but I am already late for a meeting. Go up to the loft and have a closer look if you wish.'

'I'll do that.'

'Oh, while I think of it, the picture over the altar is by Antonio Bellucci. And three pieces by Beethoven, his Equales, were first performed right here! I hope to see you again, young man.'

'I hope I see you, too.'

The cathedral impressed him as he walked inside its enormous structure. Its beauty and silent sanctity enthralled him.

His next challenge was to find the college. He took the route Johann had told him and was relieved to find it at the north of Elisabethstrasse. Should he enter this inviting façade or wait until tomorrow, the day he was due to start there? He had to take an entrance exam, if Johann was right. So he walked a few hundred metres further north, only to be confronted by the most impressive stretch of water he had ever seen. With eyes wide open, he gazed in awe at the quiet, deliberate flow of the Danube. It must have been at least sixty metres wide. A small sailing boat was tacking its way upstream. He

27

wondered where it might be heading and for what reason. Was it simply for the pleasure of being on water? Then several rowing boats came from the opposite direction. Each had a cargo hidden it its depths, some form of merchandise for here or elsewhere?

He turned to explore more of this huge, bustling city. It was nothing like the peaceful atmosphere of village life in Ansfelden or Hörsching, and not remotely akin to the religious calm of St Florian. The only place he could experience such tranquillity was in the cathedral. He wondered if he could settle in a city as crowded and as lively as Linz.

***

After a hearty evening meal, enjoyed in the company of his landlady, he slept well, so well that she had to knock on his bedroom door to wake him.

'It's gone 8.30,' she shouted through the closed door. 'You need to be at the college by 9 o'clock!'

Tonerl rushed to wash and get dressed. Missing breakfast, he was out of the house by 8.50 and ran to the college as fast as his young legs would take him. He entered at one minute to nine.

'You're out of breath, young man,' said the plump lady at the reception desk. 'How can I help you?'

'I've come here to enrol. I'm due to start my teacher training course today.'

'And your name?'

'Joseph Anton Bruckner.'

The lady took a notebook from a drawer and opened it. She slid her finger down a list of names. 'I can't see… Oh, here you are. You are being sponsored by St Florian. Is that right?'

'Yes, meine Frau.'

'You must pass the entrance examination before we can admit you. Would you be happy to have it today? There is an exam at 9.30. An interview would follow. Is that too short a notice?'

Johann was right. 'No, meine Frau.'

'You should be fine. You have good references.'

'When will I know if I've passed?'

'Tomorrow. At 9 o'clock. If you've passed, the course starts at 9.30. I'll show you to the examination room.'

Anton counted ten other students about to take the exam. A heavily bearded invigilator placed the papers upside-down on each desk. Then he went to the front and said they each had one hour to complete the test. Anton was amazed how simple the questions were. He finished in thirty-five minutes and put the scratchy quill pen back into its inkwell. Wondering whether to stay at the desk or leave the room, he stayed put and read through his answers. They seemed alright to him.

He had to queue up for the interview. There were three interviewers, none of whom he recognised. The chairman appeared much older than the other two. He started and asked the first question.

'Thank you for applying, Herr Bruckner. Your references from St Florian impress us. Herr Kattinger and Prior Arneth wrote them. Do you know these two gentlemen?'

'Yes, well.'

'That's good. Why do you want to become a teacher?'

'I've taken so much from others who have helped me. I want now to put something back into the world. I especially want to support my mother, sisters and brother.'

'How many sisters do you have?'

'Three. The family lives in Ebelsberg.'

'Have you any relevant experience?'

Anton was delighted with this question. 'Yes, mein Herr. A few years ago, before I went to St Florian, my father, a schoolteacher, was taken ill. The headmaster at the school invited me to take most of my father's lessons, especially the ones in arithmetic and music. So I taught at the school for about eight months.'

'Good. I now want to hand over to the professor to my right.'

'You said you taught music and maths. Exactly what music did you teach?'

'Mainly some basic music theory, piano playing and the violin. I sometimes took students to the church to teach organ play.'

These seemed the crucial questions to Anton. Others followed about where he was staying in Linz and whether he intended to see his family while on the course. After half an hour of questioning, the chairman confirmed that the exam result would be available at 9 o'clock the following morning at reception. His stern face betrayed nothing to Anton. He couldn't detect if he passed or failed.

He hardly slept that night, wondering what the outcome would be. He was so early for breakfast he had to wait for Frau Planck to appear.

'Why are you so early, Anton?'

'I want to be at the college reception before 9 o'clock, so I get my results earlier than the others.'

'I'm sure you have no reason to worry! Don't rush your breakfast or you'll get indigestion!'

Anton ran to the college and was first in the results queue. The other ten stood behind him. They were there for nearly a quarter of an hour before the reception lady came with a handful of letters. With the surname 'Bruckner', Anton's was at the top. She handed it to him. He tore it open. A pass!

Moments later, she made an announcement. 'Those of you who succeeded, please follow me to your first lesson.' Only six of them trailed behind her. There were already at least thirty other students in the class, who presumably had passed the entrance exam earlier, or were exempt.

A tall, thin teacher stood at the front and explained the content of the curriculum. Anton was pleased, and at the same time, disappointed. They limited the desk subjects for training to reading, writing, arithmetic and history. There was no mention of geography or any of the natural sciences. However, there would be, as was traditional in Upper Austria, much work on music, including theory and practice, as well as training in how to teach music. The instruments he mentioned were the piano, the organ, and the violin. That enthused Anton to his core. The man then announced that there would be no more lessons for that day, and told them to reassemble the following morning at 9 o'clock.

Assemble they did in front of the same tall lecturer. He started by asking each student to introduce themselves by name, say where they were from, and what they wanted to achieve from the course.

'I'm from Styer,' said a dark-haired, slim boy with untidy hair. 'I don't know why I'm here or what I want to do.'

'You what?' glared the lecturer.

'I told you once. Do I have to tell you again?'

The entire class erupted in laughter, but the boy stayed calm. The lecturer kept his composure. He shouted, 'Order, order! That was not amusing! In which case, I don't want you in this class. I've dismissed you.'

'You can't do that because I've paid.'

'I can and I have. Go to reception. Tell them I've expelled you. They'll give you your money back. Is there anyone else who doesn't know why they are here? If so, put up your hand.' Not one hand arose.

'That's good. I hope none of you changes their mind.' He restarted the introductions. All were uncontroversial except when a student called Joseph Beckstein introduced himself. Someone asked him a question.

'Are you a Jew?'

'I am proud to say, I am.'

'I don't want to study in a class with a Jew.' He stood to walk out. Then stopped.

'I'm a Jew as well!' said another pupil.

'And me,' said one more.

'So am I,' said the lecturer. 'At least one Jew will teach you. Are you still going?' He pointed to the objector.

'Yes. Does anyone want to join me?' No one stood up.

What happened shocked Anton. He was new to people acting this way, just because they didn't approve of a person's religion. Was this a feature of cities because he'd not encountered anything like it in Ansfelden? He could not possibly treat anyone so badly. When the lecturer spoke again, Anton was still thinking about it.

'You, yes you! You over there!'

He looked up, only to see the lecturer pointing at him. 'Yes, you!'

'Oh, me?' he said.

'It's your turn!'

Anton stood up. He'd never spoken to such a large gathering before. He felt nervous for a few seconds, then settled himself. 'My name is Anton Bruckner. I'm from Ansfelden. Just like my father was, I want to be a teacher. I'm especially keen to teach the violin, piano and organ, as well as other subjects you train us to teach.'

It took a full hour to complete these introductions. Then they had a break before the lesson proper began. Afterwards, the tall lecturer - he was at least two metres tall - gave a lesson in teaching arithmetic. He actually taught some basic arithmetic himself. Then he told the class to make notes of how he did it. Anton found him uninspiring. He learnt nothing to add to his own experience. The one useful point the lecturer made was that each of the students, over the ten months of the course, would have to give a lesson. This would be to all the other students, treating them as if they were elementary school pupils.

Anton found the afternoon session equally disappointing. A short, bald lecturer with a *pince nez* introduced the class to history teaching. He unenthusiastically spoke about the history of the Habsburgs. Anton hoped that the college would provide better sessions than this.

The lectures continued in the same monotonous style for the whole of the first week. On the Saturday, as expected, Johann appeared at number 37.

'So you passed the entrance exam, Tonerl. Congratulations! How is the course going?'

'Thank you. It was a much easier exam than I expected and the interview went well. I was still doubtful about passing though, and pleased that I did. I'm disappointed with the course. All they have done, so far, is to teach some subjects we are to learn to teach. We've had to do some arithmetic, some writing and have had to read to them. Listening and waiting for the other students has been boring. There hasn't been a sign of a music lecturer yet.'

31

'I think you have misunderstood, Tonerl. Let's think about the arithmetic first. They want to see how you do your arithmetic, how you add up and take away. Do you count on your fingers? Do you know your tables? That sort of thing. As for history, there are various topics in the curriculum. The subject of the Habsburgs is one of them. On writing, they want to see how you write. That is, how you hold the pen and whether you are a good writer. And the same goes for reading. If you don't read well, they'll probably improve you. On all these topics, they'll teach you how they are best taught.'

'I'm glad I told you. I'm keener now!'

'On the music, they probably want to focus on the other subjects for a few months and then bring music into the course.'

'That doesn't help me. I can practice my violin playing while here. The landlady doesn't mind at all. But my skill in organ playing is dying.'

'I can help with that, Tonerl. Hörsching isn't far. I can take you to my church and you can practice on the organ there. Come and play in the Sunday services. I'll come here to take you.'

Tonerl accepted Johann's kind offer. He played regularly in the church services. Sometimes he would play the organ in all the hymns or Johann and he would divide them between them. When Johann played, Tonerl would sit spellbound, such was the quality of his performing. Tonerl could only aspire to such heights.

***

'Have you ever heard any orchestral music?' said Johann at one of their Saturday encounters.

'Yes, we had a small orchestra at St Florian and a much smaller one at our church in Ansfelden.'

'No, I mean at a concert hall, played by a full orchestra of around seventy players.'

'In which case, no.'

'Well, there is a concert at the Linz Music Association next Wednesday. They are playing Beethoven's fourth symphony at five o'clock. Would you like to come to the concert?'

'Yes, that's a great idea.'

'I'll meet you here.'

Anton listened intently to the symphony. While he enjoyed it, he felt guilty about spending the time there when he could study or be practicing.

'What do you think of that?' said Johann.

'Hmm. I quite liked it. I found some of it too repetitive, so not bad, but not as good as I expected.'

***

Johann was right about the musical part of the course. For at least three months, it concentrated on all the other subjects such that the students' proficiency in teaching gradually improved. Then, unexpectedly, after a lesson in teaching pupils to write, a softly spoken, shaven gentleman appeared in front of the class. The lecturer asked the class to listen to him for a moment.

'My name is August Dürrnberger. I will teach you to train students to play the organ, but my main job will be to improve your skill on the instrument. This I will conduct individually. I will start with a student called Anton Bruckner because he is first in alphabetical order. Are you in this class, Herr Bruckner?'

Tonerl raised his hand. 'I am, Sir.'

'Excellent. May we meet at reception at 2 o'clock for a discussion?'

'Of course, Sir.'

Anton didn't know what to expect. As he was sitting alone in the student refectory, he wondered why a lecturer or teacher wanted to meet him at reception. Surely, a meeting room would be more appropriate. Perhaps there was more to this than Anton could see.

'Good afternoon, Herr Bruckner,' said Herr Dürrnberger. 'I have a little surprise for you. I have an arrangement with the Cathedral under which I can use the organ to teach students. You are the first in your class. So I hope you give me a good report when you see your colleagues!'

They soon reached the Cathedral and climbed up to the organ loft.

'Sit on the bench,' said Herr Dürrnberger. 'Now play me something, anything you wish.'

'But there are people here who may not like what I play.'

'Don't worry about that. I have full permission to teach you here, so I must listen to how you play. In fact, I'm the director of music,' he said with modesty.

'Alright. I'll play a few pieces for organ I wrote myself,' he said, looking down. 'Shall I start now?'

'Yes, go on!'

Anton launched into the first of his organ preludes, stopped for a couple of seconds, and then played the second. At the end of it, he raised his hands a little, in a dainty flourish.

'I'm surprised,' said Dürrnberger. 'You are a good player. What age are you?'

'I'm sixteen. My birthday was only a few months ago.'

'You are good for a lad of your age. Can you read music? If I give you something on music paper, will you play it?'

'Yes, I read music, not well, but I should be able to play it, if it's not too difficult.'

Herr Dürrnberger took some sheets of music from a briefcase. He sorted through them. 'Try this piece by Bach.' He placed it on the music stand.

'Do you mind if I read it through first?'

'Not at all. Take as much time as you need.'

Anton leant forward to read the piece. It was Sonata No. 2 in C minor. Anton had never seen it before. It started vivace and looked difficult. He turned the first page over, and another. Then started. He found himself straight into the rhythm of the piece. He like it and it inspired him to play well.

'Stop there, please. You are a good organist, Anton. I've not heard any student as good as you for many years, if at all, and especially at the first lesson. And I've heard some brilliant players, I can tell you!'

'Thank you, Herr Dürrnberger. You've made me very happy.'

'You've made me think about where we go next. We can improve your play to make you close to being a virtuoso. That will take quite an effort. We will also teach you figured bass notation. You need to be so familiar with any figure, you can translate it straight into your hands and play it!'

'I'm aware of figured bass but have not learnt it yet.'

'Are you familiar with the techniques of improvisation and playing fugues?'

'I can perform limited improvisation, but I've never played a fugue.'

'Over the coming months we'll work on refining your play… because that's all you need… improvisation and playing fugues. If it all works well, you could become a top organist!'

'That would be excellent, Herr Dürrnberger!'

'And another thing. Those two organ preludes you played were impressive. How old were you when you wrote them?'

'Twelve.'

'Have you thought of becoming a composer?'

'No. I want to become a teacher, just as my father was.'

'You said you wrote four preludes, and you played only two. Do you remember the other two?'

'Yes, note for note!'

'Well, please let's finish by you playing those!' Dürrnberger looked and listened, open mouthed.

***

The remaining months of the course were highly intensive. Anton had to cope with teacher training in reading, writing, arithmetic, and history. The lecturers no longer expected students to demonstrate their own skills in these subjects but to show their ability as teachers.

Anton spent many hours practicing his organ playing and being taught by Herr Dürrnberger, who had written a book on music theory which Anton studied intensely. After a month of organ lessons, Dürrnberger gave him much needed instructions on the violin and, to improve his music reading ability, gave him some copying to do. It took him an age to write down Bach's 'Art of Fugue', which was a useful exercise for him to complete.

'Have you heard of the composer, Albrechtsberger?' asked Herr Dürrnberger, some weeks later.

'No. Is he famous?'

'Not as famous as some, but he was a composer of preludes, fugues and sonatas, mainly for the piano and organ. One of his best-known works is a Concerto for Trombone and Orchestra. He taught Beethoven and was a good friend of Joseph Haydn. It's his work on fugues I think you could learn most from. So I want you to study the scores for six of his fugues and copy them out. Are you happy with that?'

'Just give me the scores, and I'll start straight away,' he said. Such was his enthusiasm for learning anything connected with the organ.

Anton and Herr Dürrnberger, stimulated by Anton's willingness to learn, became good friends, in a similar relationship to his with Prior Arneth.

The ten months of the course passed at great speed. On 30 July, Herr Dürrnberger congratulated Anton on his success. He presented him with a teaching certificate of education and a certificate, signed by himself, on music theory and organ playing.

Chapter 4
1841 - 1843 Windhaag

Anton wanted to go home. He went straight back to number 37 to pack. Frau Planck greeted him at the door.

'I see from what's in your hand you've passed! Congratulations!'

'What I am so pleased about is that, as well as the teacher training certificate, they presented me with one for organ playing and music theory. That allows me to teach up to high school level. I'm delighted, Irene, let me tell you!'

'They may get damaged, the way you are carrying them, so I'll give you a document case.'

'You are kind!'

'Oh, and what's the book?'

'My organ teacher gave it to me. It's about music theory. He wrote it and he signed this copy. Although he's twenty-five years older than me, we became good friends and we said we would keep in contact.'

'That's very good. So when are you leaving, today or tomorrow?'

'I think I'll leave today. If I get a cabriolet this afternoon, I shall be home well before dark.'

'So let me get you a meal before you go.'

As she kissed him farewell and wished him a successful career, Frau Planck placed a five kreuzer piece in his hand. 'This will go towards the fare,' she said. He wondered if she rewarded others of her lodgers in the same way, or whether he was the only one to be so privileged.

***

The well-worn, old vehicle pulled up outside his house at six o'clock that evening. He couldn't pay the driver quickly enough.

'That'll be fifteen kreuzer, son.' Tonerl counted it out and gave it to him. 'We usually get a tip.'

'Oh, here's a two kreuzer piece.'

'Thanks.'

With his sack of things slung over his shoulder, and carrying his violin and the document case, he dashed up to the front door and rushed in. 'Tonerl, it's you!' shouted Josefa, who ran up and kissed him. Then she called out to the others. 'Tonerl's back from his college!'

'Good to see you!' said Ignaz. 'How did you get on? We've missed you since you last came, in April was it?'

'Yes, on April fool's day!'

Then Rosalie appeared. 'You're home! But for how long this time? It was only two days in April!'

'Yes, but at least I came home for longer at Christmas! Where's Mama and Maria Anna?'

'Mama is doing a house cleaning job a few doors away. She should be home soon. And Maria Anna is sound asleep in her cot. She'll wake up to be fed soon,' said Josefa.

'You haven't said how you got on,' said Ignaz.

'Well, I've got something to show you. Just a minute.' He went back up the hall to fetch his new document case. 'Look at these!' He pulled out his two certificates and held them up on display, one in each hand.

'They look smart and in lovely print. What are they then?'

'My certificates from the college! I'm so pleased.'

The three of them clapped in unison. As they were doing so, their mother entered. 'What's all the noise for?... Tonerl, it's you! How lovely to see you.' She stepped up to kiss him.

'Mind my certificates, Mama! I was showing them off to the others. I can now teach in an elementary school and teach the organ up to high school level!'

'I can't tell you how proud I am, my little boy! Seeing those makes me feel fifty centimetres taller. You've proved that St Florian made a good choice in sending you to the training college. Did you do well in all subjects?'

'All except writing. The teacher told me the written word was my weakest subject. Although he said I was not good at expressing myself in writing, I was good enough to teach it.'

'That's a relief, to me and you, Tonerl!'

'Probably more to me, Mama.'

'We've missed you so much since we last saw you,' she said.

'What I want now is a job. I'm going to see Prior Arneth and ask him. He's in charge of all the schools in St Florian's area of responsibility.'

'Please don't go yet! Spend some time with us first.'

'I will, Mama. At least a fortnight. I can't see myself starting as a teacher before the autumn term. I'm dying to become one because I want to help support you.'

'You are a good boy, Tonerl. We all love you!'

Tonerl thrived on the time he spent with his family. Again, he spent hours entertaining his sisters and brother. One of his favourite activities was to play gigs on his violin, and have them dancing around the house. Little Maria Anna giggled and dribbled as he picked her up and spun her around in the air. Then she would chuckle as they all laughed together. They were the happiest of times.

Life was still hard for their mother, but along with Johann's assistance, they kept above, but not far above, the poverty line. Surviving on bread, potatoes, cabbage, corn, and offal was not a luxury. Somehow, it made them a closer family, like goldfinch chicks, huddling in their nest.

Anton wrote to the prior to tell him about his results and to ask for a meeting to discuss his future. The prior replied promptly and asked to see him at 10 o'clock in the morning, the following day. Anton decided he would walk to St Florian. All he had left, jangling in his pocket, was less than a florin, so he needed to economise. He could not even think of asking his mother for money. He started early, in good time for the meeting.

'In general, you did well on the course,' said the prior. 'The college wrote to me to tell me. Not so good on the written word, I understand but sufficiently well to teach it. And you've improved your violin play.'

'So they said, Prior Arneth. I'm pleased, overall. I'm so grateful that you paid my fees and lodgings.'

'So you are looking for a teaching post?'

'Exactly.'

'Well, since you wrote, I have been considering several possibilities. Some good ones are too far from your home. But the one I've selected is also some distance away. It's in a village called Windhaag. It's tiny. The population is only a few hundred. There are about forty properties there, including a church, and it's the only school there.'

'It sounds good. Where is it and how will I get there?'

'Because it is so far away and because your family is poor, we will pay for your transport there. In fact, one of our cart drivers will take you to Linz from Ebelsberg. You will then catch the train to Grünbach. From there it's about seven kilometres to Windhaag.'

'How will I get there from the station, carrying all my luggage?'

'I'll write to the schoolmaster... his name is Franz Fuchs... to ask him to meet you there. You'll have to leave on the first of October to start on the first day of the autumn term, which is the third. You will find the winters much colder, because it's a lot higher than Ebelsberg. From here, it's on the other side of the Danube. It's near the Maltsch which flows into the Vlatava. So you will be right on the border with Bohemia. How exciting!'

Tonerl gave him a straight look. 'You are surer than me.'

'Well, I think you'll enjoy it. It'll be an adventure, especially for a young lad like you. We will also pay for your end of term journeys home.'

While none too sure about this distant assignment, Tonerl thanked the prior profusely and headed back home.

***

'Where?' said his mother.

'Windhaag.'

'Never heard of it.'

'Nor had I until the prior told me about it.' He related what Prior Arneth had said and about how he would reach it. The other children, except Maria Anna, listened intently, their eyes wide open.

'My God, it's in the middle of nowhere!'

'Not quite,' said Tonerl. 'Nowhere is a kilometre further north, in Bohemia!'

'Not funny,' said Rosalie.

'How much will they pay you?'

'I don't know,' he said. 'However much it is, I'll give you at least half to help you and the children.'

She hugged him tightly. 'You are a wonderful son, Tonerl. Truly dutiful,' she said, with a tear rolling down her cheek. He took out his handkerchief and wiped it away.

Tonerl thrived on the two months and more with his family. On some days, when he knew his mother was working on a farm, picking the crop of potatoes or beetroot, he would help her. He would bargain with the farmer to be paid at least something, perhaps just a kreuzer, which he would give to his mother.

Towards the end of the break, a letter arrived addressed to him. He wondered what it could be about. Had the tax officials discovered he was working, or was it an offer of a different job? He ripped it open. He breathed a sigh of relief. It was from the prior, telling him to be ready at 9 o'clock the day after to be picked up by the cart from St Florian.

After their tearful goodbyes, Tonerl loaded his sack of things onto the cart, as well as his violin in its case. He made sure he included Herr Dürrnberger's book.

They soon arrived at Linz station. Tonerl had never seen a horse-drawn train before. A railway official was tethering a team of eight horses to the front of the eight carriage vehicle which ran on a pair of rails about a metre apart. The St Florian driver bought Tonerl a return ticket.

'Here you are, son. You can come back with this. Don't lose it, and hang on up there until the end of term.' He loaded Tonerl's bag onto a carriage while Anton tightly clutched his violin case.

'I hope it all goes well,' said the St Florian man.

'Thank you. Me too!'

The train set off at a snail's pace, so Tonerl could hardly detect its motion. He heard the driver in the front carriage crack his whip at the horses. They soon escaped the clutches of the busy city and entered the quietness of the countryside. He had never seen such spectacular scenery. The beautiful trees

39

bordering the fields seemed to be urging him to his magical destination in the clouds. Fairies were playing, some chasing each other, while others were riding on the backs of strange creatures with scaly skin. He could hear a celestial organ playing, but could not see it. Some gnomes danced around a bonfire in full flame.

'Ticket, Sir?' a man said, looking into his carriage at the train's first stop. Then said it louder. 'Ticket, Sir?' Tonerl woke from his dream. He fumbled around in his pocket.

'Here it is,' he said, still half asleep.

'So you're going all the way, Sir?'

'Yes... I suppose I am.'

It took a full three hours for the horse train to reach Grünbach. He clambered onto the platform with all of his luggage, then walked to the station entrance to find Herr Fuchs. Apart from those meeting two other passengers, there was no one in sight. He sat on a bench in the mid-afternoon chill, wondering what to do. A porter came to ask if he needed help.

'Yes, please. Could you kindly tell me the way to Windhaag?'

'Are you walking there, young man, with all that luggage?'

'I'm supposed to be meeting someone here, but he hasn't turned up.'

'It's about seven kilometres, and nearly all uphill. You just follow that road over there,' he said, pointing. 'A young lad like you will only take a couple of hours. Good job you're wearing a thick coat. It'll be colder up there.'

'Thank you,' said Tonerl. He picked up his luggage and set off, hoping Herr Fuchs might just be late, and that he'd meet him on the way.

He arrived in Windhaag exhausted, with no idea of where Herr Fuchs lived. Prior Arneth was right. There were only about thirty houses. He'd knock on a door and ask if anyone knew where Fuchs lived.

'I know he's the schoolmaster,' said a lady with a straw hat who answered the first door he knocked. 'But I don't know where he lives. Ask next door. Three of their kids go to the school.'

Tonerl left his luggage in the street and walked up to the door.

'Yes, he lives at house number 24.'

'In which road?'

'It's just house 24 in Windhaag. You come out of here and go left for about two hundred metres and it's on your right, near the school.'

'Thank you,' he said, on the point of exasperation and exhaustion.

After struggling the last few hundred metres, he knocked on the door of number 24. A man with a long beard answered.

'You must be Anton Bruckner,' said the man, not looking Anton in the eye.

'I am,' he said. 'I was expecting to see you at the station at Grünbach.'

'I wasn't available,' he said.

Anton frowned. Not the best start to a teacher-headmaster relationship, he thought.

'You'd better come in,' he said, without a hint of welcome. 'Bring your luggage.' As they walked in, Fuchs said, 'You'll be sleeping here.'

'In which room?'

'Here, in the hall, on that bed.'

It looked more like a bench to Anton. Pushed against the wall was the narrowest bed he had seen. 'And where do I put my things?'

'I'll show you,' he said, as he led the way to the kitchen. 'In there,' he said, pointing to a cupboard halfway up the wall, as a frightened looking young girl looked on. 'This is a servant,' said he, without expecting her to speak.

'Hello,' said Anton. 'What's your name?'

She looked straight at Fuchs, as if she doubted her right to reply. With him glaring at her, she said, 'No one uses my name here. I'm just the skivvy.'

Anton didn't know what to say. He half smiled at her, then looked at Fuchs. 'You will get to know her better as you will have your meals with her here, in the kitchen. What are you cooking tonight?'

'As it's Saturday, just vegetables. Herr Anton has had a hard day of travel, so I will prepare a millet porridge and a cabbage broth.'

'I'll see you in the morning,' said Fuchs. 'Sundays will be busy for you and me. Be up by half past four and I will take you to the church. I am assistant to the pastor, so much has to be done in there, starting at 5 o'clock with the ringing of the church bell, which will be your job.'

Anton stayed in the kitchen and tried to start a conversation with the maid. 'I'm busy doing your meal, so not interested in talking.'

Feeling disappointed with his first hour there, he unpacked then sat at the kitchen table to study his copy of 'The Art of Fugue'. He and the maid ate their mediocre meal in silence. His mother, by the force of economy, had to produce some basic meals, but this was the crudest food he'd ever eaten. From the muddy colour of the cabbage soup, she must have cooked it at least five times before.

On the walk in the dark to the church, they did not exchange a single word. The two of them entered and Fuchs lit a candle for each of them.

'I have to show you around,' he said, as if it was an obligation, which he wouldn't perform unless absolutely necessary. First, he showed Anton into the sacristy. 'You must help me change in here, into that surplice.' He held up his candle and pointed to the dirty-looking garment, hanging on a door hook. Then he showed him the organ.

'I play this during Mass and other services. I expect you to share that duty.' Anton's face shone. It was his first smile since arriving in Windhaag. Presumably, he would be playing it at weddings and christenings. What joy! His mind refused the thought of funerals. At least, it seemed, Fuchs wouldn't expect him to lead a service.

'I'll show you the bell tower.'

They stepped out of the nave into the belfry. The headstock, carried a single bell, which swung from the rope in front of them. 'By the clock it's just on 5 so ring it now.'

Anton did as instructed.

'That's enough. Stop. Now we go back for breakfast and return for Mass at 7 o'clock.'

Anton had never spent so much time in a church. Devoted Catholic and strong believer that he was, he found the day quite tiring. While waiting in the vestry, he thought he might compose a Mass.

He started at the school on the Monday morning. By then he had: tolled the bell at 5 o'clock, helped Fuchs into his surplice and attended 7 o'clock Mass. He'd also been to a field Fuchs owned to dig potatoes and returned to swallow down some millet soup. If Fuchs thought Anton would find all this excessively daunting, he was mistaken. Anton had carried out bell ringing and teaching duties for his father that began at 5 o'clock and even at 4 o'clock in the summer months.

**

'Look! It's our new teacher, Mama!' said a girl.

'Our new teacher looks so young!' said a little boy.

Both expressions, with grinning variations, welcomed Anton into his new post. He couldn't stop smiling as this merry band of children poured into his classroom, while he stood by the blackboard at the front.

'What's your name, Sir?' shouted a little girl.

'My name is Anton Bruckner,' he said in breach of Windhaag tradition, which did not permit the pupils to know teachers' Christian names.

'Where are you from? Not from around here!' said a boy.

'I'm from a village called Ebelsberg, which is near Linz, the capital of Upper Austria. Ebelsberg is about the same size as Windhaag! I'll show you.' He quickly sketched a map of Austria on the blackboard and labelled Windhaag, Ebelsberg, Linz, and Vienna.

'I'm from this place which is about thirty kilometres from here.'

'What's that drawing?' said a boy from the back. Anton then explained what a map represented and drew the scale. The exchange with the children continued in the friendliest spirit. They laughed and stood up, sat down again, and clearly liked their new teacher. Anton could not conceal his look of joy at having such a cheerful class.

'It's break time now, Herr Bruckner,' said a voice from the back.

'Do you go outside, even when it's cold like this?'

'Yes, we kick a ball around to stay warm,' said one. 'Come out and join us!' said another. He spent the entire break playing with the children. At one point, he noticed Herr Fuchs scowling at him from a window.

'Right,' said Anton, after the break. 'I need to know how good you are before I can teach you. How many of you can write your name?' Of the twenty or so, six raised their hands.

He then investigated their ability at reading and arithmetic. From what the children said, it was vaguely similar to their writing skills, so he had quickly discovered that he had much work ahead of him. He liked a challenge.

Using the blackboard, he taught the class adding up. He had lost himself in his work when one child raised his hand and shouted. 'Excuse me, Sir!'

'Yes, my boy. What is it?'

'The morning class finishes now, according to the clock.'

'Well, thank you for telling me! I'll see you all this afternoon.'

'No, you won't, Sir. It's a different lot this afternoon.'

He could hardly believe what he heard, but accepted what the little girl had said.

As the parents met their children, he stood by the door. 'I've never seen my child so happy coming out of school,' said one.

'Nor me,' said another.

'It must be the new teacher,' said a third.

Anton smiled with vicarious satisfaction.

He made the afternoon session equally successful. Again, he discovered he would have to work hard on their basic learning. Again, the mothers noticed their children were happier than usual. Surely, this couldn't last, he thought, as he walked the few steps back to number 24. Fuchs challenged him as soon as he entered.

'I saw you playing ball with them in the morning break. You should not engage with children in that way.'

'Do you mind explaining, Herr Fuchs?'

'You must stay aloof and be superior to them.'

'I shall, of course, do as you direct. But that is not what I learnt on the training course.'

'I don't give a whistle for what you learnt there. Just do as I say and you won't come to any harm.' Anton could see this as a possible physical threat. He didn't reply.

'You must now accompany me to one of my fields. You will hoe to prepare the ground for ploughing, ready for next year's crop.'

'I'm more than willing!' he lied. He wasn't letting this ogre get the better of him.

He finished his labours at sunset, about 7 o'clock, and went back to 24 for a miserly dinner in the company of the miserable maid. So he had, with a success recognised by the parents, completed his first day as a teacher. He had enjoyed the teaching and even getting up early, but loathed the menial tasks demanded by Fuchs. He felt exploited, which he was. Every day he had a routine that included ringing the bell, attending to vestry duties, working in Fuch's fields, teaching the two classes, doing more work after school, and having dinner with the girl servant.

The increasingly popular Anton soon became well known to the entire population of the village. He was invited into many homes, particularly those with a love of music and where he could enjoy playing his violin, either solo or with others. The family of Franz Sücka, a weaver, made him especially welcomed, as did his wife Zäzilia. In his free time he taught music to their children, Franz, Maria and especially to Rosalia, the youngest. At Franz Sücka's request, he helped prepare young Franz for the entrance exam for the teacher training college in Linz.

'You play the violin well, Rosalia, but I will teach you to play faster tunes so you can play quick, dance music with the rest of us.'

'I'd like to do that, Herr Bruckner. I feel quite left out when you all play!'

'It won't take long, but you'll need to practice.'

'You can play your violin as much as you like, Rosie, as long as it doesn't interfere with your studies,' said her mother.

Anton showed her how to practice some fast scales, moving her fingers quickly and bowing pairs of strings. He wrote some scales and practice tunes on a piece of music paper and gave it to her. He improved the techniques of the others, too.

One night, at their house, while he was enjoying an evening meal of roasted pork, mashed potatoes and beans, Franz asked him a question. 'Are you still drinking that awful soup for breakfast at Fuchs' house?'

'Yes, and it's horrible. I don't know how I stomach it.'

'Well, you can stop drinking it now. Every morning, at 8.45, I or Zäzilia will bring you a malted coffee. You've done so much to improve the kids' violin play and taught them so much about music, it's the least we can do.'

'That's not necessary, Franz. I can put up with the ghastly soup. But very kind of you to offer!'

'No, we are doing it, just for you.'

So every school day, Franz or Zäzilia walked into his classroom with a hot coffee in a jug wrapped in a tea cloth.

Herr Fuchs soon demanded that Anton play the organ during the Sunday services. Anton could not believe his luck. For the initial weeks, he played conservatively, mainly to respect the unstated wishes of Fuchs. He expected that anything out of the ordinary would cause trouble. His enjoyment of playing was boundless. How it contrasted with his relationship with Fuchs. He would arrive at church early, so he could play it while the parishioners were coming into the church and stay late, so he could play to them on their way out. Some enjoyed his playing so much, they would stay until he finished.

Anton soon became more adventurous and played some secular music there, including the four preludes for the organ he had written when living with Johann. Then he remembered the idea he had soon after he arrived, which was to write a Mass. So he composed a short one in the classic six parts. Not wanting to stretch the singer or players beyond their experience, he wrote it in C major, for a contralto voice, two horns and organ. His choice of soloist and instruments was based on knowing one of the congregation was a brilliant contralto and two of the men were horn players. He would play the organ. Wisely, he thought he should tell Fuchs about his composition, if only to avoid upsetting him.

'That's ridiculous. Why bother with that? Our parishioners like the Masses we have and perform. You should spend your time preparing lessons, not wasting it on amateur compositions.'

Anton was not to be intimidated and pushed him further. 'I thought I would let you into this as Bertold Meyer, Franz Sücka, and Maria Jobst have asked if we can rehearse it at the church. This is so we can play it as Mass on a Sunday, but only when we have it ready for performance.'

'Are you asking me if you can rehearse in the church?'

'Yes, I am. So please may we go ahead?'

Fuchs must have felt cornered. If he refused, Anton would have to tell the other potential performers, which would damage his already waning popularity. If he agreed, he would be giving in to Anton, who, much to Fuch's annoyance, was gaining in popularity.

'Yes, but do not overdo the use of the church. Keep rehearsals to a minimum.'

Anton concealed his delight and, with a blank face, simply thanked him.

Rehearsals began with intensity. Anton had written out the individual parts and given them to the performers. He was pleased that he had chosen Maria Jobst as he loved her dark voice and her delightful personality. He wondered if she might show any liking for him.

'I think we need a conductor,' said Maria, after they had played it through without one. 'It sounds disjointed and uneven.'

'I think you are right,' said Anton. 'It shouldn't be me at the organ. I'll be facing the wrong way!'

'I'll do it,' said Franz Sücka. 'It will be quite easy, as I'll wave the horn up and down. You'll see me through the organ mirror!'

'Perfect,' said Anton.

So that's what they did. It took only two rehearsals to make their efforts fit for public performance. They would play it at the 8 o'clock Sunday Mass and, depending how it went, again at later services that day.

Anton had never heard a Mass applauded before. The congregation took pleasure from the uninhibited joy of the piece and the high quality of the performance. It was more like a celebration than a supplication. So they played it three more times that day.

***

Winter in Windhaag was rapidly approaching. From their early flurries, the snow falls were becoming heavier and more frequent, such that by mid-December, it was over a metre deep in places. Anton found it difficult to walk and fell over several times. Prior Arneth was right in what he had said about the winters. He had fallen again on his way to the Sücka household for an evening meal and entertainment afterwards. Fortunately, his violin escaped any damage.

'Anton, you are covered in snow,' said Zäzilia. 'Come in quickly, out of the cold. Take off your coat and go in by the fire. I'll shake it by the door.'

'You look cold, Anton,' said Franz, sympathising. 'You're not dressed for winter.'

'You're shivering,' said Franz junior.

Zäzalia entered. 'Anton, you need more clothing for this weather. Do you have more at Herr Fuch's place?'

'Not really. Another pair of trousers and a shirt. That's about all.'

'Franz, could you lend Anton an under coat and a few jumpers? Also a pair of strong walking boots and a scarf. He could do with one of your leather hats, too.'

'Of course I will. We'll send him back to Fuchs much better equipped for this weather.'

The Sücka family became fond of Anton. Franz or Zäzilia not only brought him coffee and gave him winter clothing, but also involved him in family activities such as parties, and gatherings with friends from the village. Fuchs could not fail to notice how well integrated Anton had become in Windhaag. Envy became the driving force in Fuchs' attitude towards him. He decided he would try to humiliate Anton, so challenged him one morning at the church. Snow still covered the ground, so they could do nothing in the fields.

'I'm not at all happy with some aspects of your teaching. You are too informal and vulnerable to class misbehaviour. So I will teach your class this morning and you will sit and observe me.'

The children seemed surprised to see Herr Fuchs at the front of the class, and Herr Bruckner sitting at a table to one side.

'This morning is going to be different for you. I will teach you, not Herr Bruckner. He will observe my methods. Boy, you with the light brown hair at the back, stand and recite the nine times table.'

The lad stood up and gave a faultless rendition.

'Sit down.' Then he picked on a girl sitting at the front. 'You,' he pointed, 'Come up here and write your name on the blackboard.'

She unhesitatingly wrote her Christian name and her surname. 'Is there anything else you'd like me to write, Sir?'

The whole class laughed loudly.

'Just you all be quiet,' said Fuchs as he slapped a cane on the girl's desk. 'And don't you be so insolent,' he said, pointing at her. The girl went back to her desk, head held high.

He then picked up a book from the class bookshelf, opened it and told one boy to read from the first paragraph on the page. The boy read it perfectly and sat down.

All Fuchs had achieved in his attempts to humiliate Anton was to prove how effective he had been as a teacher. He left the class at the morning break.

***

Anton did not go home for Christmas. Windhaag was cut off by snow and the horse train from Grünbach was suspended. However, he managed to go home for Easter. His family greeted him like the Prodigal Son. His mother was the first to welcome him.

'I love you, Anton. I'm so pleased to see you. Thank you for your letters. You are doing well. It's a shame that Herr Fuchs is so unkind. And what hideous food you have to eat!'

'It is so good to see you, Anton,' said Rosalie. She kissed him on both cheeks. 'Mama has let us read your letters. It sounds as if you are a good teacher, even if the headmaster is not a nice man!'

'I get on so well with nearly everyone else, especially the parents of my pupils. I've been welcomed into many of their homes. I even give some of their children extra lessons for which they pay me.'

'And I can't understand the meanness of the man. Paying you a mere twelve florins is ridiculous,' said Mother. 'Couldn't you have asked for more?'

'I did, but he refused, telling me it was from his money, not the authorities, and that was all he could afford.'

'What nonsense! Especially from a man who owns a farm. He's not poor.'

'While we are on the subject, here are six florins.'

'But you can't afford that, Anton. I can't take it. You've only earnt a little more in the two terms you've been there.'

'I have, not just from private lessons, but also from playing my violin in a small group at the village tavern.'

'Not with Herr Sücka? What a lovely family.'

'Yes, with him and his son. So you must take this money, Mama.' Almost in tears, she did.

***

Anton enjoyed the break with his family and on the way back, on the horse train, wondered what Herr Fuchs might have in store for him. He looked forward to seeing his class of bright and cheerful children, but dreaded his encounters with Fuchs and working in his fields. As promised, Franz Sücka was at Grünbach station to meet him and save him that uphill walk to Windhaag.

Anton soon settled back into his daily teaching and work routine, frequently varied by visits to the Sücka family. He often played late into the night with young Franz Sücka and his father on the horn, at taverns, festivals, carnivals, and wedding receptions. It was always a pleasure for Anton to go home for the end of term break.

One morning, after harvest time, and at 4.30 in the morning, Fuchs had a new instruction for Anton.

'I want you to take the cart and go to the houses in Windhaag. Ask them if you can shovel the shit from their privies into the cart. Then bring it back and spread it on the fields.'

'You want me to what?'

'You heard me. Do you want a repeat?'

'Yes, in case I misheard you.'

So Fuchs said it again.

'Listen to me, Herr Fuchs. I'm not your damned slave. You have made life here as difficult for me as you can. This is the last straw. I won't shovel anyone's shit. Do it yourself. And you can shove any more of your work straight up your ass.'

Fuchs face turned red. 'Don't you dare speak to me like that, you scum of the earth!'

'I just have. And I meant every word,' said Anton. He turned, walked out of the kitchen, out of Fuchs' unwelcoming house, and went to the church.

It was still early. Anton sat on the organ bench. He felt in control when sitting at an organ. He had created this fissure with Fuchs and needed to think about what he would do. Would he continue living at Fuchs' house or would he ask one of his friends to take him in? Fuchs wouldn't dare throw him out or even tell the maid what Anton had said to him. So, after the day's teaching, he would go back there and see what happened. He looked at the clock. It was time to ring the bell, so he did. Then he went back to the organ bench and sat on it again. He remembered that Franz and Zäzilia had invited him to breakfast, which was at 8 o'clock. Wondering what to do until then, he checked that the resident calcant was there. Good luck shone upon him, and he was. Anton asked him if he would start pumping earlier than usual. He said for Anton he would. So Anton sat at the organ, thumped the keys, and pushed the pedals continuously for almost two hours. He played Fuchs out of his system.

He couldn't wait to tell Franz and Zäzilia about this confrontation.

'I'm firmly on your side, Anton,' said Franz.

'I am, too,' said Zäzilia. 'But you may have provoked him into getting rid of you.'

'Can he dismiss me?'

'No, because the central authorities appointed you,' said Franz. 'Only they can do that. You are such a gifted teacher and are so popular in Windhaag, they have no grounds for doing that. But he may persuade others to take you out of the job. If so, we will miss you terribly.'

'My worry,' said Zäzilia, 'is that he will throw you out of his house. I'm sure Franz will agree to you staying here, at least until things cool down.'

'I agree. Here's an idea. I'll come back with you to his house. You can pack your things and I'll bring them back here. You can then go to the school.'

'You two are so kind to me. Yes, let's do that Franz.'

'I may ask you to do some crap shovelling while you're here!' said Franz.

'Take no notice of him, Anton. I hope you don't mind sharing a room with young Franz.'

'Not at all. I can help him even more with his music and preparing him for the Linz training course.'

Anton had removed all his things from the house by a quarter to nine. He saw no point in leaving a note for Fuchs. He taught in his usual ebullient style. No one, not even the parents, would know that anything was amiss.

His second winter in Windhaag was nothing like as bad as the first, so he could easily travel home to Ebelsberg for the festivities. He enjoyed a wonderful time with his family during Christmas, even though it was a simple celebration, and was excited to resume teaching, especially since he was comfortable living in the Sücka family home.

He had almost completed an arithmetic lesson when a man appeared at the classroom door. At first, he thought he was dreaming. Then he realised he wasn't.

'Prior Arneth, it's good to see you! Do come in.' The children looked around with raised eyebrows. 'Come in and take a seat. I will have finished in a few minutes.'

With the lesson over and the children out in the playground, Anton spoke to Prior Arneth. 'So why have you come here, Prior?'

The prior stood up. 'Tonerl, I've mainly come to inspect the school. I see each school eighteen monthly and it's your school's turn today. I've talked to Herr Fuchs and I hate to tell you this, but he is not happy with you.'

'I know, Prior, but please tell me more.'

'Neither Fuchs nor the canon like your teaching methods. Fuchs says you don't understand discipline. According to him, you are totally obsessed with your music, and have annoyed the congregation with your adventurous organ playing. You are too popular with the villagers when a teacher should blend into the background.

'Before you tell me your side of the story, I'll tell you what I think. The reason, in my book, is jealousy. Fuchs is not a popular man. His teaching methods are antiquated and yours are new. And he cannot cope with that. I know you well. You are a good teacher. He's wrong and so is the canon. And I have a solution, Tonerl. I'm going to transfer you to another school.'

Chapter 5
1843 - 1845 Kronstorf

Anton bade farewell to his class and his friends in Windhaag. Zäzilia Sücka shed many tears as she embraced him. 'Will we never see you again, Anton?' 'I hope I will see your family in the future. We have spent some wonderful times together and I thank you for making me so welcome, especially during my hour of need.'

'It has been a pleasure, Anton,' said Franz. 'My parting gift will be to take you to Grünbach station.'

Maria Jobst, to whom he had dedicated the Mass, came to see him go. 'I hope we meet again, Anton. I hope to become a famous singer one day. Maybe we will meet in Linz.' She kissed him.

News of Anton's dismissal surprised his family and Johann Weiss.

'Will you never teach again?' said his mother.

'I will. Prior Arneth is finding me a new post, nearer to here, he thinks.'

Within a week of his return, a letter arrived from Arneth. It appointed him as an assistant teacher at a school in Kronstorf, not fifteen kilometres from Ebelsberg.

'Read this, mother,' said Anton, smiling with joy.

His mother grabbed the letter.

'Unbelievable, and so close. I can take you there.'

'I can walk it myself in a few hours, Mama!'

'You'll have to run to make it in two hours! Pity about the pay. Only twelve florins, but living in and all expenses paid. A good result, Tonerl. And you will be home every weekend and on holidays.'

'I truly hope so, Mama,' he said, knowing he would surely spend some weekends at Kronstorf.

Rosalie, Josefa and Ignaz were equally pleased and so was Maria Anna who, by then, was seven years old and could well understand what was happening.

***

Kronstorf was even smaller than Windhaag. With only a hundred inhabitants, mostly wealthy and peasant farmers, only about forty children attended the school.

Anton took up his mother's offer of a cart ride there. She left him, his violin and two suitcases, outside the schoolhouse, where, according to Arneth's letter, the headmaster, Franz Lehofer and his wife, Theresa, lived.

He banged on the door which was promptly opened by a slim, fair-haired lady dressed in a long, pink dress.

'Ah, come in. You must be our new assistant teacher, Anton Bruckner.'

'Yes, I am the same.'

'My husband has gone to see the prior at St Florian and will be back soon. I'll show you to your room.'

'Thank you, Frau Lehofer.'

She took his violin while Anton carried his cases. They climbed the narrow stairs.

'Your classroom is in there,' she said, pointing to a dark green door. Anton put down his things and looked in.

'It looks nice and I'm so looking forward to teaching!' There were only fifteen desks, a blackboard and a small table at the front. Some Christmas paper chains still decorated the walls.

'Next to it is your room, so you won't have far to go to work!'

Anton looked in. The tiny cubbyhole measured about two metres by three. The Lehofers used it for the storage of items for the school. They had piled boxes almost up to the ceiling, just inside the door. A small bed sat below the window, a narrow chest of drawers stood against the wall, with a small table opposite. Anton was pleased to have his own space, tiny though it was, but one he didn't have to share. Best of all, they didn't expect him to sleep on a bench in the hall.

'Sorry about the boxes, but we'll move those to give you more space. You can only just stand to play your violin in there! Let me leave you to settle in. Our rooms are along the landing. We eat at about six o'clock. I'll knock on your door about then. Is that alright, Herr Bruckner?'

'That'll be fine.'

He was amazed at the contrast between his welcome here and the ghastly reception at Windhaag. Frau Lehofer seemed very pleasant. He wondered what her husband, Franz, would be like.

Sure enough, there was a knock on his door at the time he expected it. He stood up to answer it.

'Hello, Anton. I'm your new headmaster, Franz Lehofer. I'm pleased to meet you. Our dinner is ready now, so come and join us!' he smiled. Anton noticed that Franz Lehofer gasped slightly to breathe, as if he was suffering from some chest complaint.

The dining room was much bigger than Anton's room, but still not large. The table was laid for just the three of them, so there were no other teachers living there, and no children. As the two of them were sitting there, with Franz Lehofer at the top of the table, his wife arrived with two plates of smoked ham, semolina dumplings and cabbage.

'My goodness,' said Anton, grinning. 'How did you know this is my favourite meal?'

'I didn't,' said Frau Lehofer. 'What a delightful coincidence!'

'Tell us about yourself,' said Franz, as they ate.

Anton enjoyed telling them about his past, which, for a seventeen-year-old, could only be recent. He related his time at St Florian, the training college, and told them about his family and friends. In conclusion, he said he was extremely keen on music, played the organ, violin and piano and had composed a few pieces, mainly for performance in church.

'It's a small world, Anton. I was trained at the same college. I only did four months there as I became ill with a lung problem which I still suffer from, but much less now. They still gave me a certificate... about fifteen years ago,' said Franz.

'I'm so pleased you love music, Anton. I play the violin. Franz plays it too, and he's a good organist. I can see we'll have some great musical times together!' said Theresa.

'I'm fascinated to know about your composing, Anton. When did you start and what pieces have you written?' said Franz.

'I started when I was twelve, with some organ preludes and a *Pange Lingua*. My latest piece is a short Mass which a small group of us played in the church at Windhaag. The congregation loved it. The contralto, Maria Jobst, was brilliant. She made it a success. So I dedicated it to her!'

'So when you become famous, she will be famous too!' said Theresa.

'Not me. I don't know of any famous teachers.'

'One thing I should tell you, Anton. It's about your salary,' said Franz, hesitating slightly. 'I've been told by Prior Arneth to pay you the same as Fuchs paid you in Windhaag, namely twelve florins. He didn't want Fuchs to find out you had been dismissed from his school only to start on a bigger salary here. But once you've settled in, in say a couple of months, I'll increase it to twenty.'

'That will be fine, Franz. Thank you.' He didn't say he already knew it would be twelve florins but smiled when Franz mentioned twenty.

***

Anton slept well that night, already feeling relaxed in the company of Franz and Theresa. The following day was a Sunday, so the three of them attended Mass at the church, only a few yards from the house. The organ impressed Anton. For a small village and a relatively small church, it was larger than he expected and had two manuals. He thought then that he would love to play it and said so to Franz, who said he probably could, anytime, but not during a service. He would speak to the parish priest, Alois Knauer, and seek his permission.

Term started the following day. He introduced himself to his class and explained he lived in Ebelsberg, not far from Kronstorf. Following the example of the tall, thin lecturer at the Linz training college, he then asked the children where they were from. Some were from Emms, Styer or from farms quite some distance from Kronstorf. Only about half were from the village itself. As at Windhaag, Anton tested the children on how they performed in reading, writing and arithmetic. They surprised him by showing him they were better than those he started with at Windhaag.

***

Anton liked his job in Kronstorf. He soon settled in to the local community and became well known and popular with the small population. His mother and siblings were pleased. On the first of his regular weekend visits home, Anton gave his mother the first florin that Franz Lehofer paid him. She sobbed with joy, as he had overcome her doubts about Anton ever being a success as a teacher. A local landowner and music enthusiast, Michael Födermayr, lent him a piano which he installed in his classroom. The children in his class loved to hear music, so he often played it to them and their parents, after lessons had finished.

After he had been there for a time, and at dinner that night, Franz Lehofer asked him a question. 'Anton, are you interested in sport?'

'Yes, very much. I play ball games and swim a lot.'

'Are you interested in bowling or curling? We bowl in the summer and do curling when the lakes freeze over in winter.'

'These would be new to me, but I'm more than willing to try either or both.'

'That's good, Anton. I can imagine you would be good at them. With your build.'

'Which lake freezes over?'

'A lake on Michael Födermayr's land, right next to the river Enns. In some winters the river freezes over and we skate and do curling on that. Usually, it's Födermayr's lake. Lots of village people play as well as families who live on farms or other villages whose children go to our school. Födermayr plays both.'

Anton enjoyed the bowls. He took to it like a cat to chasing mice. They had set up the bowling alley in the church hall.

'It's your turn, Anton,' said Theresa, who had just bowled.

Anton took a ball, swung his arm back, and threw it as hard as he could down the alley. It missed every skittle and ended up in the side gulley.

'I thought you'd be better than that, Anton,' said Franz.

'It's only my first attempt,' he replied, looking down the alley. 'Don't forget. I've never played this before!'

His turn soon came around again. 'Better luck this time!' said Michael, who had all but cleared the alley.

Anton decided on a different tactic. He would take the ball back slowly and take aim for the skittle in the centre. To his surprise and satisfaction, he cleared them all.

'We call that a strike,' said Theresa. 'You get another go for that!'

Anton did the best he could to match what he'd done before. Good luck shone on him again. Another strike!

'Fantastic, Anton. Only your second attempt and two strikes already. Set them up again, Franz. See if he can get another,' said Theresa.

Anton tried the same again. All but one skittle fell. It shook on its base but stayed upright. Anton laughed. 'Very nearly,' he said. 'Not bad, eh?'

'I'm amazed,' said Franz. 'You are a true sportsman!'

'You are teasing me!'

***

Alois Knauer insisted he hear Anton play at the church before giving him permission to use the instrument unattended. Because he was so impressed, he made Anton assistant to the resident organist, who generously shared the Mass performances with him.

Anton made the most of these opportunities and, as he had in Windhaag, played some of his organ preludes and other pieces he knew well. Improvisation became his speciality which he so enjoyed. He played Bach's Toccata and Fugue in D minor, which raised the hair on the back of his neck. The parishioners who heard his playing loved it. No one objected to his modernity. On the back of his successes, he told Alois about the Mass he had written in Windhaag. Alois immediately said he wanted it played in Kronstorf.

'I know a wonderful mezzo soprano who would be delighted to sing for you. Her name is Terweide Böhmer. I don't know any horn players so would a couple of trombonists suffice?'

'Yes, of course.'

'I'll ask them.'

Within a matter of days, four players were deeply engaged in rehearsals. The trombones made life difficult. They drowned out the singer as well as the organ. 'We need to play at a different level,' said Anton.

'I'm not sure we can do that,' said one of the trombonists.

'Can we try?' said Anton.

'Yes, certainly,' said the other.

They started again. 'No, that's still not working,' said Anton. 'I have another idea. You trombonists can stand at the back of the church. You, Terweide, could conduct me and our trombone men. Alright?'

'Good idea,' said the men.

'I think I can,' said Terweide. 'But you'll have to show me how, Anton.'

'We'll follow you,' said Anton. 'Just raise your arms like this, and bring them down to start. Then, as you know, you can just move one arm, in time to the music, which is not fast.'

The first time they tried it, it was almost perfect.

'That's it! The congregation will love it!' said Anton.

They played it at the Sunday service. The canon explained that it was a new Mass and hoped they would enjoy it. It met with a mixed reception. Most of the congregation, of about eighty people from Kronstorf and the surrounding areas, appreciated it. But some hated it and stormed out of the church. The canon's face went blank, and he shook. Anton wondered what in the Mass could upset them. He concluded it was simply new, not of style, nor of content, but a new Mass, different from any Mass they would have heard before. It was vaguely similar to a piece by Palestrina, whose works some of them could be familiar with. Despite those who walked out, he took much satisfaction from those who stayed and clearly liked it.

Terweide shed a tear at the unexpected reaction. Anton and the trombonists comforted her. 'I find it totally incomprehensible that those people walked out,' she said. 'Your Mass is a homage to our Lord and not one word or note could offend anyone. Many enjoyed it. All I can suggest is you write another one. Maybe for a choir? I'd love to sing again in another of your works, Anton, I really would.'

'Do you know, I was thinking of writing another one? The reaction of the minority is best forgotten. It was simply new to them. Someone told me that one of J S Bach's religious works almost caused a riot at its first performance.'

The strange reaction was the first thing talked about at dinner that night.

'I'd forget it if I were you. No new piece of music is liked by all who listen to it the first time,' said Franz. 'But it's a good idea to write a new one, if you can find the time. We'll call it The Kronstorf Mass! Let's change the subject somewhat. You said you enjoyed swimming, Anton. So do I, and Michael. Want to have a swim in his lake tomorrow?'

'Yes, but I have no swimming costume here.'

'You're about the same size as me, so I'll lend you one, unless you want to swim, naked!'

'I'd only swim naked if I was alone,' said Anton.

Michael was keen to join them at the lake. He said he had a little office work to do first, but he'd be there in about thirty minutes. So Anton and Franz set off on their own from Födermayr's large, luxurious house. Anton had never seen such an impressive residence before and wondered, on the way to the lake, half a kilometre away, if he would ever own anything like it. He soon concluded he didn't want such a property.

Anton could see the beautiful expanse of water, close to the river Enns, which flowed steadily through a shallow valley. He felt part of nature as he smiled and gazed at the lake and noticed their isolation from any other sign of human activity. The two men were soon breaking into a swim. 'You're a powerful swimmer,' said Franz.

'You're a pretty strong one yourself,' said Anton. The lake was longer than it was wide. They were happily gliding at a good pace along its length, which was about three hundred metres. 'Let's swim back, shall we?' said Franz, as they reached halfway. 'By the time we reach the shore, Michael will be with us.'

They turned simultaneously and went back. Michael had not arrived, so they sat on a log and chatted for a while. 'Do you know, Anton, in the six months since you came here, you have become popular? The children in your class, and indeed their parents, like you. And I can see how the children have progressed since your arrival. I can't speak for the whole of Kronstorf, but your musicianship has impressed many people. You should extend your influence by playing the organ in Styer. There is a magnificent instrument there. If you agree, I'll ask Knauer to contact the Styer pastor, Joseph Plersch, for his permission. I guarantee you will love the organ. It is far better than ours!'

'Yes, please, Franz!' said Anton with a smile.

'Hello men,' said Michael, as he arrived at the lakeside. 'So how about a race?'

'From where to where?' said Franz.

'We've done it before and you beat me! From here to the far end and back. But you have to get out, touch the tree and return!'

'I only asked, so Anton would know!'

'I'm willing,' said Anton, grinning. 'What does the winner get?'

'We rarely have a wager, but the losers could buy the winner half a stein of beer,' said Michael. 'What do you think, Franz?'

'I'll take some beating so I'm for it!'

The three of them splashed in to waist depth. 'Go!' said Michael.

He dived in and took the lead. After about a hundred metres, Anton found himself between the two of them. Franz overtook them both, hopped out of the water, touched the tree and came back in. He was leading by about twenty metres and smiled at the other two, as he passed them on the return leg. Anton decided he would try a higher gear, so changed from a breast stroke to the crawl. It took him almost two hundred metres to catch Franz. They had left Michael about forty metres behind. Franz heard Anton and saw him alongside, so put on a spurt. Anton responded to the challenge. They exchanged the lead several more times before Anton just beat Franz and won.

'My God, Anton, you can certainly swim. Well done!'

'I've been river swimming since I was a kid, often against the flow, so I've become quite strong in the water,' he said.

Michael eventually finished, almost totally out of breath. 'I don't know how you two did it,' he said, 'especially as you had swum out and back, not half an hour before the three of us swam together!'

They soon dried out in the sun and walked the kilometre to the Kronstorf village inn. 'Thank you, fellows, it's an excellent beer here, as good as in Ansfelden.'

'I didn't know you were partial to a beer!' said Franz. 'We ought to come here more often! I'm going to ask the pastor at Styer if he can let Anton play on the organ.'

'That's a good idea. You'll love it' said Michael.

Anton was soon on his way to play the magnificent Krismann organ in Steyr. It was only an hour and a half's fast walk away, so he managed it with ease. The sight of this magnificent instrument made him smile from ear to ear. It was huge with almost a thousand pipes, three manuals and twenty-six registers. Immediately, he fell in love with it. After climbing up the steps to the loft, he sat at the bench and played the organ part from his C major Mass. He played it full volume so filled the church with sound. Then he spent a full half hour improvising on the main tunes, playing them at a high speed with contrasting sound levels. Word must have reached the local population that a stranger was playing this wonderful music on their organ. Within an hour, there must have been fifty people listening. A round of applause greeted every piece he played. After he felt he had played enough, and started collecting up his music sheets, a lady came to speak to him.

'Thank you, young sir, for entertaining us so well! Please could you tell me whether you are familiar with the works of the composer, Franz Schubert?'

'I can't say I know many of his. I remember hearing a piece at a concert I attended in St Florian but that's about all.'

'I play the piano and am very fond of Schubert's music. In fact, I heard him play the piano at my home when I was younger. I was just wondering if you would like to play some Schubert with me. I hope you don't think I'm being unladylike. By the way, my name is Karoline Eberstaller. What's your name?' 'Mine is Anton Bruckner. I'm a teacher from Kronstorf. Yes, I'd like to play some Schubert with you. Shall we say, Saturday afternoon?' 'Yes, that would be fine. I'll see you then. Could we meet here at midday?' 'Of course.' This strange request from the woman with the long brown hair protruding from her colourful bonnet puzzled Anton. He thought she was at least ten years older than him, but she seemed a gracious lady. She looked aristocratic, with smooth skin and unblemished hands. Surely, she wasn't looking to him as a potential husband. He would soon discover her intentions.

Saturday came around and Anton walked to Styer in the pouring rain. He was soaked as he walked into the church. Karoline Eberstaller was waiting for him. 'You are very wet, Herr Bruckner. I live only a few yards from here. You can share my umbrella.'

They sped to her house and dashed through the front door. 'I'm soaked,' said Anton. 'I can't possibly play this wet.'

'I can lend you some of my father's clothes. I'll take you to a spare room so you can change. I'll find you a towel, too.'

Within a quarter of an hour, Anton was sitting with Karoline at her piano in the borrowed clothing. 'Here is a piece Schubert wrote for four hands,' she said, placing the music on the stand.

'I must read it through first. I'm not that good at sight reading!'

The piece sounded wonderful to the extent that several members of the household appeared to listen. Anton was relieved. He was not interested in spending much time alone with the lady, pleasant though she was. They played several other pieces by Schubert before concluding. They agreed to meet again in two weeks.

That night, at dinner, Anton told Franz and Theresa about his afternoon with Karoline Eberstaller.

'I'm confident she won't be interested in a deep relationship with you. She is another music fanatic. I'm surprised she hasn't tried her hand at composing,' said Theresa.

'Oh, that is good to know. I'm going back for another session in two weeks' time.'

'Did you ever know Leopold Zenetti, when you were a pupil at St Florian?' said Franz.

'Yes, but not very well. I believe he played the cello in the little orchestra.'

'He plays a range of instruments, including the organ,' added Franz.

'He lives in Enns,' said Theresa. 'I'm sure he would be pleased to see you if you wanted to go there. We've met him several times. He is a composer in his own right and a music theorist.'

'I think I have a free day next week, so I'll go to see him then.'

Anton liked the idea of meeting a composer, other than Johann Weiss, who knew much about music theory. This was a subject he felt he could usefully know more about, despite learning much on the intricate subject from August Dürrnberger. On receiving no response from knocking on his door, Anton realised he should have written to Zenetti about seeing him. I shouldn't have spent that hour walking here without an agreed time to meet, he thought. He turned to go back when he heard a man shouting from the side of the house. 'Hello! Who are you? What do you want?'

Anton told him Franz had recommended they meet. Zenetti looked at him with a frown. 'That's strange. He usually asks me if I want to meet someone. And I haven't heard from him.'

Anton struggled to persuade Zenetti to talk to him, and eventually Zenetti invited him in. They soon became relaxed in each other's company. Anton explained his interest in music and his wish to understand more, especially as Franz had told him about Zenetti's expertise in theory.

'But, having studied organ play under Johann Dürrnberger, you must have a good understanding of the theory.'

'Not really. It was only at a basic level. I concentrated on becoming a reasonably good organist with Dürrnberger, so learnt only basic music theory. It was more about notation and becoming familiar with writing it and studying some pieces. That's why I copied out Bach's "The Art of Fugue" and some of his fugues and fugues by Albrechtsberger.'

'Albrechtsberger? How interesting. So August concentrated on what you needed to become a competent organist, including improvisation.'

'Exactly! And I'm keen to learn more. I should have said, I have written some pieces, mainly religious works.'

'Really? What have you composed?'

'A *Pange Lingua* of one verse, some preludes for organ, a short Mass in C major for contralto and two horns, and a few other pieces. I've just started on another short Mass.'

'And how old are you?'

'I'm coming up to nineteen.'

'I'm surprised that you have written all this. And you are so young! Please bring me the music, so I can see at least some of it.'

'Of course, on my next visit!'

'So you want to be a composer, then?'

60

'Not at all. I just enjoy writing music. I have no intention of composing for a living and just want to remain a teacher. But improving my knowledge of music will make me a better teacher.'

'I will help you by becoming your teacher. You are so enthusiastic I won't even think of charging you, but in return, you will have to adhere to a strict timetable. What hours do you teach?'

'Unless I stay late to play the piano to my pupils, I'm finished most days by one o'clock.'

'In which case, come to see me on Monday, Wednesdays and Fridays. Try to be here by three thirty.'

'Can you spare me all that time?'

'I'll give you an hour a day. Take this book back with you and look at the first couple of chapters. That's where we'll start. And like August, I'll have you studying J S Bach, but his "Well-Tempered Klavier" and keep looking at "The Art of Fugue".'

All the way back to Kronstorf, Anton thought about the exchange with Zenetti. He would hate the uncertainty of life as a composer, especially the insecurity. As a teacher who loved music and composed in his spare time, he felt comfortable. The certainty of a regular income was a major factor in his life. He would try to improve, but compose only as a hobby. His final thought was to start again by composing a new Mass, another in abbreviated form, for choir and organ, not just for a contralto soloist. He would enjoy the challenge.

Chapter 6
1843 - 1845 A new love in his life

Anton had not been busier since working as the headmaster's slave in Windhaag. He often had his breakfast early and started his piano practice at 7 o'clock in the morning, which was the time Franz and Theresa got up. He didn't want to disturb them by starting any earlier, but even then could be their alarm call. Before his class came to school, he would prepare his lessons. At the end of his teaching, if he wasn't seeing Leopold Zenetti, he would entertain his class and often the parents by his boisterous piano playing. He would then walk to Styer and spend an hour or more playing the organ. He enjoyed this part of the day the most. Filling the church with a tornado of sound gave him a feeling of power that nothing else could provide. Most weekends, he would visit his family and, if time permitted, go to Styer to play piano duets with Karoline Eberstaller. Occasionally, he would visit Johann Weiss in Hörsching, where they would talk about Anton's experiences as a teacher and what he had learnt from Leopold Zenetti.

***

Most winters in Upper Austria are cold, but that one was so cold the Enns froze over, as did Födermayr's lake. Anton anticipated the question he dreaded.

'Now the lake and the river are solid ice, would you like to try your hand at curling?' said Franz Lehofer, with a wry smile.

Anton looked directly at him. 'Umm... I'm not so sure. Before I do, please show me the technique. I have never seen it done, but I have spoken to a few in Ansfelden who have attempted it without success. They ended up black and blue!'

'I'll show you how to do it without falling over. There are several of us going to the lake this afternoon, including Theresa, Terweide and Michael. So there will be five of us.'

'Alright, I'll come and, if it doesn't look too dangerous, I'll try it.'

They all assembled by the lake at the spot from where the swimming contest began. Terweide and Michael were already there when Anton, Theresa, and Franz arrived. Michael and Franz struggled to carry the stones on a stretcher like contraption. Franz walked on the ice and expertly marked out the course.

'Anton is new to this, so I'll show him how to throw the stone, and could you please do the brushing, Theresa?' said Franz.

Theresa walked onto the ice, keeping her balance so well she could have been walking on dry land. Franz launched a stone from his right hand. It landed almost silently on the ice and skidded towards the target he had drawn.

Theresa moved to the front of the stone and frantically brushed the ice in front of it. It landed just short of the centre of the target.

'Would you like to try now, Anton?'

'Yes, why not?' Anton moved onto the ice. Being as careful as he could, he inched his way onto it. His feet went their separate ways, so he promptly fell, hitting his side on the ice. He tried to stand up, but the more he tried, the less he succeeded. His arms and legs flailed out. Whatever effort he made, he remained flat on the ice, struggling like an upturned tortoise.

'Let me help you,' said Franz, as he tried not to laugh. He moved onto the ice and lifted Anton by the arms. The other three grinned and watched. 'Now, bring your legs together and try to stay upright.' Anton did what he was told and remained in one place like a statue. 'Now move your feet gradually and centimetre by centimetre, back onto the bank.'

'I've made it,' said Anton, triumphantly. 'That wasn't very successful, was it? And I didn't even pick up a curling stone!'

'I think we are asking Anton to do too much. We need to get him to walk confidently on the ice before expecting him to play curling,' said Terweide.

'You are right,' said Theresa. 'We all learnt from someone holding our hands as we stepped onto it. I'm not strong enough, so could you do it, Michael?'

'Let's try, Anton,' said Michael.

Michael walked backwards and held Anton's hands in his. Anton moved with him. He stumbled but stayed upright. His ability to balance came into action and he walked, still hand-in-hand, with a little confidence.

'I'm going to let go of your hands, Anton, but you can grab mine if you feel you are going to fall.'

Anton managed this stage well and kept his balance.

'Now walk back to the bank,' said Michael.

Anton succeeded with a half-smile.

'Would you now like to try curling, Anton?'

'Yes, I'll try again.' He stepped onto the ice and picked up a stone. He lobbed it towards the target and fell again, this time onto his back. With difficulty, he eventually stood.

'You are nearly there!' said Terweide.

'I'm not comfortable with this sport,' he said. 'So, as I'm preventing you all from playing, I'll stop while I'm not injured and watch you four. I may try again next winter.'

'You are probably wise,' said Franz. 'I don't want to lose a good teacher, not from a silly accident!'

Anton enjoyed watching the others who split into two teams, Michael partnering Terweide and Franz with Theresa. Anton cheered on the Lehofers and felt a little less embarrassed when they won.

**

Nothing could stop Anton from composing, even if he had to work late, in the light from a flickering candle. He enjoyed writing as much as playing the Krismann organ in Styer. At the suggestion of Alois Knauer, he wrote a piece called *An dem Feste*, the festive but religious words of which the priest himself had written.

'I'm totally enthralled that you have composed this wonderful piece for me,' said Alois, as he read through Anton's score. 'We must get it performed! Would you mind conducting it, if I can find the singers? So it is for two tenors and two basses. I have some truly excellent singers in mind and I'll speak to them. The only slight complication is that they all live in Enns. I'll ask the priest there if we can use his church. He has a very receptive, warm congregation and we'll get it played at the end of a service as an added extra!'

A few days later, Alois went to see Anton at the schoolhouse. 'Good news! The priest at Enns is happy to have your piece performed at his church, and I've recruited the singers!'

'That's good news, Alois. I'll copy out the parts so the singers have one each.'

'Unnecessary, Anton. I've already done it! But I have a special favour to ask of you. Could you please dedicate the work to the priest at Enns? His name is Josef Ritter von Pessler.'

'I will, Alois. It will be my pleasure!'

'Thank you. You are a hero!'

They performed the piece in the September, after a midday Mass. The four tenors and basses sang the work with energy and enthusiasm to such a degree that the parishioners erupted into applause. Alois called Anton towards him and announced him as the young composer, to which they cheered and applauded again.

'I'm going to ask another favour of you, Anton. Could you please come to my house for dinner tonight? My sister is an excellent cook. I'm sure she would love to meet you. I don't think she's met a composer before!'

Anton laughed. 'I call myself a teacher. I'll never be a composer! But yes, I accept your kind invitation. I shall tell Franz and Theresa I won't be dining with them tonight. I'm sure they won't mind. They'll probably be glad to dine alone!'

'Wonderful. I have my pony and trap, so I'll give you a ride back to Kronstorf. You won't have to return by the means you came!'

The priest's house stood next to Kronstorf church and glowed in the summer sun. The steep sloping roof protected it from the heavy winter snows.

'Martha, this is my new friend, Anton Bruckner. He's a teacher next door. He's the man who wrote the festive piece we played this afternoon at Enns. As you suggested, I've invited him to dinner.'

'Pleased to meet you, Herr Bruckner. We haven't met before, but I have listened to some of your wonderful organ playing in our church. You have definitely brightened up Kronstorf! Thank you for putting my brother's festival verses to music. I would have come to Enns to hear it, but I had an engagement at Michael Födermayr's house.'

Martha stepped towards Anton with her arm outstretched. She wore a long, amber coloured dress with a white, ruffled collar. It surprised Anton that she looked so much younger than her brother. She seemed to be about the same age as Anton, while Alois appeared to be about twenty-seven. Her blond hair and stunning smile captivated Anton. He looked into her blue, sparkling eyes. His heart missed a beat and then hammered against his ribcage. Was he falling in love with this beautiful woman? At first, he failed to speak. Then all he could say was 'Hello' in a tone which did not reveal his sudden onset of feelings towards this woman, who almost caused him to faint. I must quickly get a grip on myself, he thought. Alois glanced at him, then vanished into an adjacent room. Anton did not want to appear embarrassed in front of Alois' sister. He gained control and then spoke firmly.

'I'm equally pleased to meet you, Fräulein Knauer. It was so kind of you to invite me for dinner.'

'Do come into the lounge. You can converse with Alois while I prepare dinner.' She escorted Anton into a large, homely room. Light blue mats were scattered randomly on the polished wooden floors. Two settees faced each other in front of an open fireplace. 'He won't be long. Come and make yourself comfortable.'

Anton sat on a settee wondering what to do about his sudden attraction to Martha. He liked her open personality and lack of shyness, as well as her sensitivity in ensuring he was content before going to cook. He had never felt this way about a woman before. Although he was friendly with Karoline Eberstaller, and enjoyed playing the piano with her, he felt no emotional connection with her. This was different. He felt strongly that he'd like to know more about Martha and possibly have a long-term relationship with her. How could he develop this friendship when he had so little experience in this complex area? He might be a qualified teacher, but he possessed no expertise in the love of a woman.

'Ah, sorry I took so long. Anton. I had some papers to sort out. How are you feeling? You seemed quite speechless when you met Martha, as if you were becoming unwell.'

Anton thought a moment about how to respond. 'I was awestruck by her beauty and her friendly welcome. She is a very attractive woman,' he said, keeping his tone, if not his words, flat so as not to betray his stronger feelings.

'Please don't fall in love with her! She is the only support I have. She cooks, looks after the house, buys our food and maintains the home finances. So please leave her with me, otherwise I'd have to buy someone in!'

Anton wasn't sure whether to take him seriously. 'But if she fell for someone, you couldn't expect her to stay here, could you?'

'No, of course not,' he said, sounding unsure.

'You can now come into the dining room. Our meal is ready.' Anton expected nothing extravagant in the home of a priest. He sat at the table with Alois at the head. The place opposite was for Martha, who appeared with a steaming dish of stew, which she served while talking. 'I hope you like beef cooked like this, Anton. There are some chopped carrots in it and some basil and thyme. I have made some dumplings which I'll fetch in a moment, and some mashed swede.'

'It sounds delicious to me, Martha. And I'm so grateful to you two for inviting me.'

After Alois said Grace, the three of them started eating together. Anton enjoyed a beer with the meal, which Alois poured from a large jug. 'You said you had an appointment today with Michael Födermayr. May I have the audacity to ask why you went there?'

'You are impertinent, Anton!'

'No, he's not, Alois. I give Michael's children private bible lessons. He wants them brought up as strongly religious people and I teach them for an hour every week. They are bright, intelligent children. I must tell you about a question the lad asked me when we were doing the creation. He said, "Where did the light come from on the first day when God didn't create the sun, the moon and the stars until the third?" I said I didn't know because I wasn't there and maybe it all came from the light created on the first day. He said, "What nonsense! How can you expect me to believe anything else in this book?" So I don't know to this day whether he believes it!'

'You never told me that, Martha! What a story!'

'Can you explain it, Alois?' said Martha.

'No. It is one of those unexplained mysteries in Genesis. Like Eve being created from a rib of Adam. Genesis is a book of myths and makes no claims for actuality. It's surprising how many Christians believe it, word for word, and don't question it, in the way that Michael Födermayr's son did.'

The conversation between the three of them continued into the evening, long after they had finished the meal. Both Martha and Alois asked Anton about his past and what had brought him to Kronstorf. Anton asked them similar questions about their backgrounds. Unsurprisingly, they had a number of mutual contacts, including Prior Arneth, Karoline Eberstaller and, of course, the Lehofers who were virtually neighbours of theirs.

'How do you know Karoline Eberstaller?' said Martha, as if she was wondering about the nature of Anton's connection with her.

'I go to her home in Styer occasionally to play piano duets with her. She introduced me to Schubert's music for piano. I usually combine my visit to her house with an organ session at the church there. I have official permission to play it, granted with the help of Alois, for which I'm grateful.'

'I could be quite jealous if there was more to the relationship than that!' Anton's eyes opened wide at this unexpected reply. So there could be some future in a friendship with Martha, if he could believe what she said.

'I think I should go now,' said Anton. 'I don't want to outstay my welcome!'

'In which case, could you take Anton to the door?' said Alois.

'Of course.'

'Well, thank you for coming to dinner, Anton,' he said. 'Let me know how you get on with the new Mass you are composing. I'd be delighted to present its first performance in our church.'

'Let's plan for that,' said Anton, as he stood up and followed Martha, who closed the door to the lounge and led him along the hall.

'Before you go, Anton, let me tell you something. I really like you and would like to know you better. Are you free on Thursday afternoon?'

'Yes, after my lessons have finished, at about 1 o'clock.'

'I'd like to invite you here then, if only for a hot drink and a slice of my cake.'

Anton's smile filled his face. 'I would love to see you then, Martha. We have a date!'

She lifted her head to his face and kissed him on both cheeks before showing him out.

He slept erratically that night, wondering how things would develop between them, if they could develop at all. He found her attractive. Could they have a loving relationship which would eventually lead to marriage? If they saw more of each other, whom should he tell? His mother? The Lehofers were sure to find out anyway, as it would be on their doorstep.

Thursday soon came around. Anton knocked on her front door at 2 o'clock by the church bell. Martha beckoned him in. 'It is good to see you, Anton. I've been thinking about you a lot,' she said, while holding both his hands. She wore a plain white, belted dress that almost reached the floor.

'I've been thinking of you,' he said. 'I don't know where this friendship is going, but we'll just have to see!'

'Quite right,' she said. 'We'll have to find what we have in common and what we can share. Sit in the lounge while I prepare a drink. What would you like?'

'A coffee would be nice. Black, please.'

He stepped into the lounge and sat on a settee. He didn't have to wait long before a smiling Martha entered with two cups of coffee. She put them on the table between the settees and sat next to him.

'You told us a bit about yourself at dinner, Anton, but I'd like to know more. Where did you learn to compose?'

He told her about Johann Weiss and his stay with him, about Anton Kattinger, at St Florian and August Dürrnberger at the Linz College.

'What a coincidence. I attended that college probably around the same time as you. But I gave it up after two months because I wanted more on religious studies than what they taught.'

He told her about his time at St Florian and his difficult time at Windhaag.

'So they didn't dismiss you, just moved you to Kronstorf.'

'Exactly,' he said, as she moved closer to him on the settee. She turned her face towards him and kissed him firmly on the lips. He put his arms around her. She kissed him again, her tongue working its way into his mouth. He took great pleasure in doing the same, just as she locked her arms around him. They stayed in this tight embrace, as if the one had captured the other. Anton experienced a feeling in his groin, which he'd never had before.

'That was gorgeous!' she said, as they gently separated. 'I'm falling in love with you, Anton. There is no doubt in my mind.'

'I feel exactly the same, Martha. We must meet as often as we can.'

'I agree. I'm a very busy person, like you. I teach bible studies from Monday to Wednesday and Fridays. So I'm free on Thursdays. Would that suit you?'

'That's perfect. I see Leopold Zenetti on Mondays, Wednesdays and Fridays in the afternoons, and I'm back late because I walk to his house in Enns and back.'

They agreed to meet at Martha's house on this basis, and work out whether to go out somewhere or stay indoors. Neither wanted to say goodbye, but they hugged each other in a passion laden embrace.

***

Not long after *An dem Feste* was performed, Anton returned to working on the short Mass that he'd discussed with Terweide and the Lehofers, all of whom wanted it played at the Kronstorf church, as did Alois Knauer. He decided to write it as a Mass without Gloria or Credo, but to compose an outrageously audacious Agnus Dei at the end.

'It looks a brilliant piece to me,' said Franz, at dinner one night. 'I like the idea of scoring it for a choir, a small group of players and the organ. We'll see if we can attract a group of choristers who will appreciate a new piece to perform in.'

'May I be in the choir?' said Terweide, whom Theresa had invited to the meal.

'Only if you agree not to cry if anyone walks out,' said Anton.

'Oh, alright!'

'I'll ask Alois Knauer about performing it in the church,' said Franz.

'May I come along, too? I've become friends with his sister Martha. I know he has mixed feelings about us, but it might just help if I came. He said he'd like it performed in his church.'

'Good. Then we'll see him together.'

The following day, Franz and Anton met Alois, just after a Mass he delivered.

'It's unusual to see you two together, gentleman! To what do I owe this unexpected and most welcomed pleasure?'

'Anton has written a *missa brevis* which has not yet had its first performance. He has called it the Kronstorf Mass, in honour of our little village. Can we perform it at your church, Alois? Anton thinks you said we could.'

'I don't recall that, Anton. And I'm not really sure. I'll need to have a look at it first. I can read music, as Anton knows. But I don't want to risk upsetting my parishioners with a piece of unacceptably modern music. You will recall the upset that Anton's Windhaag Mass caused when we played that.'

'Come on, Alois. You are being a little prissy, aren't you?' said Franz. 'Only very few disliked that earlier work. Surely, you can accept it will be fine. No one objected to Anton's work based on your poem.'

'It's my church and my responsibility for what happens there! As you are being unreasonable I refuse,' he said, with a glaring look and his eyebrows at full height.

Anton wondered if, for some unaccountable reason, he was jealous of his relationship with Martha. He remembered the ambiguous conversation he had with Alois while Martha was preparing dinner, the day he first met her. His attitude toward Anton had certainly changed since he was seeing her regularly. She admitted she had told him about their developing relationship.

'What's upset Alois?' said Franz, as they walked back to the schoolhouse.

'I think it could be me, or rather my friendship with his sister, which he doesn't like at all. He told me when I first met her, he didn't want her to marry.'

'That's ridiculous. Every girl has the right to leave home at some time in her life.'

'I'd rather you tell him than I do!'

'So what do we do about a performance?'

'Leave it to me. I'll have a word with Martha. She might persuade him.'

***

Undeterred, and to fulfil a request from Joseph Plersch, Anton embarked on another, very special Mass. The priest wanted a new one to celebrate Maunday Thursday. While sitting at the small table in his room at the schoolhouse, he wrote a plan. He would begin with the gradual *'Christus factus est'*, taken from St Paul's Epistle to the Philippians. A Credo would follow in a different key. He would omit the Kyrie and Gloria, but instead insert an offertory based on the *Dextera Domini* from Psalm 117. He was just writing the word 'Sanctus' as the next section in the plan, when he heard a knock on the door. It could only be Franz or Theresa. 'Come in, whoever you are and whatever you want!' he shouted, put his pen back into the inkwell and looked around.

'Good afternoon, Tonerl!' Michael Arneth stood at the door.

'It's good to see you, Prior Arneth. How are you?' he said, stunned at the sight of him.

'Well, thank you!' he said, as he shook Anton by the hand. 'I've just been speaking to Franz Lehofer, and he is pleased with what you have done, and are doing in Kronstorf. As he is pleased I am, too! Good work!'

'Thank you,' said Anton, who told him about his teaching and organ playing, what he had composed at Kronstorf, and the audience's reaction to the performances. He also mentioned his sporting activities and lastly spoke about the new Mass he was then writing.

'You must try curling again, Anton. Better luck, next time! Apart from coming here to inspect the school and to see how you are progressing, I have some interesting news. You did well in the examinations at the teacher training college. So I would like you to take a further examination. If you pass, it will equip you to teach up to senior level, just short of undergraduate lecturing. You'll have to go back to the teacher training college to take it.

They will examine you in classroom subjects and on your musical skills, both theory and practice.'

'That sounds good news to me, Prior Arneth. Thank you,' he said, sounding none too sure. He was fully occupied, but to have to revise for another examination would put him under more pressure. Then there was the relationship with Martha... 'When will the exam be held?'

'On the twenty ninth of May, so you will have time to finish your Maunday Thursday Mass... and get it performed!'

***

Anton worked hard in every department of his existence. The Maunday Thursday Mass took much of his time, but it too would be a *missa brevis*. So he hoped that it would last no longer than ten minutes, which still meant a major piece of composition. His lessons with Leopold Zenetti were consuming, especially the walk to Enns and back and the range of exercises Zenetti gave him as 'homework'. He still found the time on a Thursday for Martha.

'Good afternoon, my dearest. How are you?'

'I don't know now how I survived the week without seeing you, Anton,' she said, as she opened the door. This was their first encounter after the awkward conversation he and Franz Lehofer had with her brother. She placed her arms around him and kissed him on the lips.

'I don't know how I survive, either. The only thing that keeps me going is being so busy. I seem to be occupied from five in the morning to nine at night! But it is lovely to see you, my sweetness!'

They went into the lounge and sat next to each other on a settee. Martha told him about the bible lessons she had given, one of which was for a senior administrator who worked in Linz. His wife was a nurse who worked only one day a week, so Martha looked after their four children then, which included taking them to school in Kronstorf.

'There are a couple of interesting things I must talk to you about. Do you remember me talking about the Mass I was to write to be performed here?'

'Yes, of course. We discussed it the first time I met you.'

'Well, your brother has decided it won't be performed here. I don't quite understand why when he seemed so keen before.'

'I think I know the answer, Anton.' She looked at him with a tear in her eye. 'It's because of us. He is jealous of you. From his various hints, although he hasn't said as much, he doesn't want me to marry a schoolteacher. He might feel differently if you were a composer.'

'But I'm not a composer and never will be. I love music with a passion and will continue composing, but as a pastime only. I want to be a senior schoolteacher.'

'I understand completely, Anton and I shall defy him. I'll speak to him about your new Mass. I love you intensely and you are my true love.'

Martha squeezed up to him kissed him. He clasped her and kissed her with equal fervour. They remained in each other's arms until Anton spoke. 'I said I wanted to become a senior teacher. Well, my mentor at St Florian came to see me a few day ago to tell me he wanted me to take an exam to qualify me as one. It will take place at the teacher training college we both attended in Linz.'

'That is at least worth another kiss, Anton! I'm sure you'll pass!'

'I'm not that sure, but will do my best, of course. My weakness is the writing. If I fail, I don't know what I'll do. Much as I love teaching children up to ten years old, I would like to teach at a more senior level.'

'You'll be fine, Anton.'

Sadly, Martha's attempt at changing her brother's mind failed. The Kronstorf Mass was not performed in Kronstorf.

***

That weekend, as always, his family welcomed him with hugs and kisses.

'Another exam, Tonerl. Surely, you are well enough qualified already?' said his mother.

'It's essential for my career, especially as I'm keen to teach at a more senior level.'

'But will you need to move to a different school?'

'Probably.'

He then handed his mother three florins which was more than usual because, as he said, he had been paid for playing his violin in a dance group at the local tavern in Kronstorf on a Friday and Saturday night. Tears of gratitude ran down her face. She said she'd spend it on clothes for the children. By then Josefa and Rosalie were in their teens and were becoming interested in what they wore. Maria Anna, by then nine, was sure to follow.

Working on the Maunday Thursday Mass gave him much pleasure, so much he couldn't stop. He quickly settled on the plan and immediately launched into the composing. He decided to show the completed manuscript to Joseph Plersch, in effect its commissioner, before even thinking of rehearsals.

'It's superb, Anton. No one could have made a better job of it. I have an excellent choir at Styer. It will be easy to rehearse, if you can play the organ part. They are familiar with the words. So we won't need to write out the parts for them. Some of the older ones can't read anyway!'

Anton played the Mass on the organ to the assembled choir, who sat and listened, as Joseph Plersch sang it. They agreed to return to the church the following day for the first rehearsal. Anton waited and waited but none of them arrived. He spoke to Joseph, who said several lived near the church and he would go to see one of them, to ask what had happened.

'They are just terrified of the idea of a Maunday Thursday Mass. I said there is nothing strange about it and others have been written before. The choir member I spoke to said he'd convince the others to be here in an hour. First, he wanted to arrange it for tomorrow, but I told him you lived in Kronstorf and you didn't need to walk there and back again tomorrow.'

'Thank goodness for that!' said Anton.

They tried not to look at Anton as they individually entered the church. Anton welcomed them with a smile and they rehearsed the piece well, much to Anton's surprise.

Maunday Thursday soon came around. Anton felt unusually nervous. He was particularly concerned about Joseph Plersch's ability as a conductor. He need not have worried. Nobody walked out, quite the opposite. It was the second time Anton heard applause for a Mass. He and Martha walked back to Kronstorf hand-in-hand, smiling as they went.

***

Anton spent many hours preparing for his examination. There was little he could do about the classroom subjects, but he practiced improvising on the church organ until his fingers were sore.

'Hello Anton, I'm taking you to Linz for your examination,'

'How did you know, Johann?'

'Your Mama told me a few weeks ago. She gave me the date and here I am in my pony and trap!' Johann laughed. 'It is tomorrow, isn't it?'

'Yes,' said Anton. 'The twenty-ninth of May! I was about to go to Styer to arrange a cabriolet!'

'No need! Just put what you want to take in a bag and off we go! Where are you staying, near the college?'

'I was thinking of staying with Irene Planck, my landlady while I was there. Last week I wrote to her but haven't had a reply yet. I hope she is well.'

'We'll go there first, but find a hotel, if she doesn't have a room.'

Franz and Theresa wished Anton good luck as he climbed into the trap, and off they went. Anton and Johann could always find much to talk about and spent the entire journey chatting about their common interests in music, especially organ play and composition. Anton told Johann about the

73

successful performance of the Maunday Thursday Mass and the problems he'd had with Alois Knauer over his Kronstorf piece. He explained what he thought the reasons were.

'So you are in love, Anton?'

'Yes, I'm very fond of Martha. I'm not sure where it will lead, but we enjoy each other's company. Her brother and I were good friends for a time. In fact, until his sister and I started seeing each other.'

'Take care, Anton. Blood is thicker than water. I'd hate to see you hurt. You won't know what her brother could do to end your relationship, even though she sounds a strong-willed girl.'

'She is, and she can stand up to her brother.'

Anton knocked on the door of Irene Planck's house.

Her broken appearance shocked him. She cried at the sight of him.

'What's happened to you, Irene? It looks as if you've been in a fight!'

'Almost right, Anton. A drunken student wanted me to let him lodge here. I didn't like the look or smell of him, so I told him I was full. Then he punched me in the face. That was yesterday and it still hurts.'

Anton hugged her gently. 'I'm so sorry. Have you reported it to the constabulary?'

'Yes. I always ask the person's name. He said he was Erich Fischer, so the constable has at least a name to go on.'

'Please let me know if they arrest him. I'm going to ask you the same question. May I please stay two nights? I have to take an exam tomorrow at the college.'

'Anton, I would give up my own bed for you, so yes, of course.'

Johann and Anton said their goodbyes, and Anton settled into number 37.

Chapter 7
1845 - 1848 Back to St Florian

Anton did not know exactly what time the examination was to take place, so made sure, after Irene had provided him with a bread and cold ham breakfast, he was at the college by 9 o'clock. He recognised the plump lady at the reception desk from the time he first enrolled there, some five years before. She had become plumper.

'Good morning. My name is Anton Bruckner. I have an examination today but I don't know at what time.'

'Ah, I recognise you, young man. You were here about five years ago! Yes, your exam is at 9.30. Then you have a set of musical tests at 11.30. I'll show you to the room. You are the only candidate today. Follow me.'

The lady took him to a small room on the first floor. It was completely bare except for a desk and a table at its centre. 'Sit there, please. The examiner will be here shortly.'

A tall, thin man appeared holding a folder. Anton recognised him, too. It was the Jewish lecturer who had taught him before. He had extended his beard by at least ten centimetres, so looked somewhat different from then. He didn't seem to recognise Anton.

'Good morning. Please take a pen and ink from inside the desk. Here is your examination paper. You have an hour and a half to complete it. I shall be back at 11 o'clock.' He then left the room.

The exam took a totally different form from the first one. It expected the candidate to write a series of essays about teaching techniques in different subjects, how to plan a lesson, how to manage a rowdy class, and what the candidate would do about a particularly difficult, disruptive individual. Realising essay writing was a weakness of his, Anton was concerned about having to write so many of them, especially as he had not practiced for the tests. So he took extra care with how he expressed himself, put the pen down at about 11.15 and read through what he had written. The tall, thin man came in at exactly 11.30. Anton handed him his answer papers, and the man went. He did not say where Anton needed to go next, so he returned to ask the lady at the reception desk.

'You just wait here until the examiner arrives,' she said, pointing to a chair. He thought he'd mistaken the time, so was about to go back to the receptionist when he heard someone calling him.

'Anton, it's so good to see you after more than four years!'

Anton smiled, stood and held out his arm. August Dürrnberger shook hands with him. 'I am so pleased to see you, Herr Dürrnberger. May I assume you are my examiner today?'

'You may, indeed! I'm hoping you are at least as good as you were four years ago and hopefully even better. Again, we go to the Cathedral and I examine you there.'

On the way, Anton told him how much he had used the textbook Dürrnberger had written and that he was taking lessons from Leopold Zenetti. He said what he had composed and stressed that he played various organs, including the Krismann at Styer.

'What I want you to do is to start off by improvising on this theme from a piece by Michael Haydn. It's an Offertory called "Tres Sunt". You probably haven't heard or seen before.'

'No, I haven't.'

'That's good!' He placed a sheet of music paper on the music stand. Anton briefly looked at it and started. First, he played the theme, then varied it, inverted it, and reversed it. He played it in different keys and in various instrument stops, at changing volumes, diverse speeds and in conflicting shapes. He concluded with a flourish.

August Dürrnberger could hardly believe his ears. He'd heard nothing as stunningly brilliant in his life. He couldn't speak, so he applauded. 'I am completely beside myself, Anton. That was outstanding. I will give you the highest possible grade for that. Congratulations!'

'Thank you.'

'Now I want you to complete a written test. Here is a theme by Joseph Preindl. I want you to create a fugue from it. You've got one hour!'

With the hour ended, Anton handed him several sheets of ink filled sheets of music paper. Dürrnberger sat on the organ bench and read it. 'There are a few minor errors here, Anton. But otherwise it's a work near to genius. Well done!'

'You are too kind to me, Herr Dürrnberger. Thank you again!'

'We must keep in touch, Anton. I'd hate this to be our last day together.'

'We will, I promise.'

***

A week later, the post delivered a tubular parcel to Anton's house in Ebelsberg. He knew he had passed the music theory and practice, but was unsure about the written examinations in teaching. Using a sharp knife to open, it he saw two certificates. One was for his musical skills and the other for classroom teaching to senior level. He had passed on all subjects. He breathed a sigh of relief.

His mother and siblings were delighted.

'Does this mean you will have to leave Kronstorf, Tonerl?'

'No, Mama. As far as I know, I stay at the school there, at least for now. But I will be applying for more senior jobs. That will help us all, as I'll earn more money.'

His weekend over, Anton made an early start and walked back to Kronstorf. He went straight to the schoolhouse and looked at some papers to prepare his lessons.

'Well, how did you get on?' said Theresa, as he stepped into the kitchen to greet her.

'I passed!'

She hugged him tightly. 'Well done, Anton. We felt sure you would. In fact, we are happy and unhappy at the same time. No one wants you to leave us for a job somewhere else. Franz would rather give you his job and exchange it for yours.'

'I'm happy to stay here until something arises,' he said, deliberately not revealing his true intentions, so diluting any affect they may have on this woman. She had, for nearly three years, treated him with such kindness. 'Is Franz in?'

'No, he's gone to St Florian to see Prior Arneth. I'll tell him about your result!'

'I must go to my class.' He treated his pupils in the way he always had, even though he felt more qualified as a teacher. Staying for a half hour after the class, he played the piano to the children and their parents. He could easily recall the tune from Haydn's Tres Sunt so improvised on it once more. It met with a round of applause from the parents, in which the pupils gladly joined. He then packed his document folder and walked as quickly as he could to Enns to meet Leopold Zenetti.

'What a result, Anton. I hope my lessons had something to contribute. You have been so successful, I'm wondering if you need more help from me!'

'I'm certain they did, Leopold. We are not halfway through The Well-Tempered Klavier yet. I really would like to continue!'

'Of course we will. I was merely jesting.'

***

Anton felt compelled to tell Martha. He would have to tell her about his ambitions and what Theresa had said about taking over from Franz. Thursday soon arrived and he knocked on her door. As usual, she greeted him with a loving kiss.

'The week is so long without you, Anton. This is the best day of the week only because it means spending time with you. Let's go in and you can tell me about your exam and how it went.'

Anton sat on a settee and waited for Martha to bring him a coffee. She brought in two cups and put them on the table between the settees.

'Martha, why have you changed?'

'I decided we could be more intimate with each other if I wore this shorter dress. And I'm wearing nothing underneath!'

Anton put on a false smile. He did not want to get close to intercourse. Fond of her though he was, he had no intention of making her pregnant. He might follow her, but stop before anything deeply intimate occurred.

'So how did you get on, Anton?' she said, cuddling in closer, and looking up into his eyes.

Anton told her in detail, so as to delay as long as he could any closer interaction. He spoke about the state Irene Pascal was in when he saw her. Playing the long game, he said he had to take special care in writing some essays, which he knew was not his best skill. Then he explained how August Dürrnberger made him so welcomed and was impressed by the improvements he had made in the theory, and in playing the organ. Eventually, he concluded by telling her he had passed.

'A million congratulations, Anton!' She pulled up her dress, almost to her waist, and placed a naked thigh over his leg. 'You can put your hand on my thigh, Anton. It will do us both good!'

'I'm less sure than you, Martha. Where will it lead?'

'It will just be innocent fun. Go on, just stroke me. I'm not asking you to touch me more intimately, not now anyway!'

Anton said nothing but, with some reluctance, lifted his hand, placed it gently on her leg and started stroking it. As his fingers reached her upper thigh, the door to the lounge opened. Her brother Alois, stood there and immediately saw Anton's hand on Martha. His face reddened. With his eyebrows raised, he shouted.

'What ever do you think you are doing to my sister, you disgusting creature?'

Anton took his hand away. Martha pulled her skirt back down. 'Don't you dare refer to my friend in such appalling terms,' she yelled. 'What contact we have with each other is nothing to do with you. So get out of this room.'

'I'll do no such thing. And it is much to do with me. If you become pregnant with this ogre, it will be my reputation which suffers. I will be the laughingstock of Kronstorf. I will have to resign and then what would I do?'

'There is no chance of Martha becoming pregnant,' said Anton, coolly. 'Our intimacy would go nowhere near that far until and if we wed. It's not just your reputation we are protecting. It's ours as well! My reputation as a schoolmaster, especially in this tiny village, would suffer. The authorities would force me to move to a much bigger town, such as Styer or even to Linz. And Martha. As a teacher of bible studies, she would have to stop, not least to give birth, but by reputation, too.'

'He's right, Alois. We aren't stupid. So calm down.'

Alois' face became even redder, almost purple. He pointed his finger towards Anton. 'Get up and get out of my house!'

'I shall go now, before you explode,' said Anton.

'I'll come to the door with you,' said Martha.

They dashed out of the room. Alois followed them to the lounge door to see that Anton went.

'I apologise for my brother, Anton. His behaviour was outrageous. We must both be strong and defy him. We must not allow him to affect our relationship because it is so beautiful. We were so unlucky he came in when he did. I could easily have locked the door. That would have given us time to disengage. And I would have had time to straighten my dress. So shall we meet again next Thursday?' she said, standing outside the front door, while holding it almost closed.

'Certainly, Martha. Let's let him cool down for a few weeks and meet in the schoolhouse. Theresa and Franz will be pleased to see you. I've not had a lady visitor before, and I'm sure they won't object. My room is so small, one of us will have to sit on the bed and the other on the chair. It will be fine!'

'I'll come around to yours, then. Usual time!' They parted with a kiss.

***

Anton hankered for something different. He seriously wanted to have a more challenging post. While he liked the school, and living with the Lehofers in the schoolhouse, he had no interest in taking over Franz's post.

Two months after he succeeded in the exams, he received a letter from an unexpected source, Friedrich Mayr, of St Florian, who was Prior Arneth's deputy. It appointed him to the post of 'first official teaching assistant in the parish school of St Florian for the second big classroom.' The news delighted him, so his ambition was at last fulfilled. At first, the strange wording baffled him, but that didn't matter. He needed to tell Franz and Theresa, followed by Martha.

'I already know!' said Franz.

'How?'

'I had a letter from the provost two days ago. But he told me not to discuss it with you until you received the letter,' said Franz.

'And Franz told me!' said Theresa.

'Congratulations!' said Franz. 'You've given me a problem, as we will have to replace you. According to the letter, Prior Arneth is already working on that. We must give you a good send off, Anton. Your class will be very sad to see you go. Oh, and here are two important documents for you. They are testimonials from me and Alois Knauer.' He handed Anton a large envelope. 'Read then now, if you like!'

Anton read the one from Knauer first. 'I'm amazed at the praise he heaps on me, especially as he's not at all happy with my relationship with his sister.'

'He's clearly been able to separate his thoughts on your work from your feelings for her. It's an excellent report. You should keep it with your certificates.'

'I'll read yours now!' He took it from the envelope. 'Thank you so much, Franz, I could not have wished for a better testimonial. I shall certainly keep them both... for ever!'

Anton then walked the few yards to the house where Alois and Martha lived. Alois answered with a frown. Anton attempted to diffuse any possible awkwardness. So, he immediately thanked him for the positive and helpful testimonial.

'Oh, thank you, Anton. I assume you want to see Martha. She already knows you will move soon. I told her.'

For a moment, Anton didn't know what to say. 'Thank you, Alois. That saves me a few sentences!'

'You'd better come in, I suppose.'

She and Anton hugged each other before a word was exchanged. Martha spoke first.

'I'm sad and happy, Anton. My brother has told me your news. I will be sad to see you go!'

'We can easily keep in touch, Martha. And I'm sure we will.'

Franz was right. The children in his class were upset when he left. His last day was wet with the tears they shed. Even their mothers were unhappy. One student, a girl of about six, told him through her tears, and holding her mother's hand, she really liked him as he was 'so good, slender, and pretty'. Anton was almost in tears himself on hearing her touching words.

***

Johann Weiss collected him from the Lehofers to take him the twelve kilometres to St Florian. He loaded up Anton's luggage on the back of the trap while Anton said his thanks and goodbyes to the Lehofers, promising he would always be their friend.

'Those were the best years of my life, Johann. I will never forget the love the people of Kronstorf showed me. Never. And I've learnt so much while I lived there. I'm sure I'll be going back to Styer as often as I can. I've become good friends with Joseph Plersch, the priest, and I just love playing on that Krismann organ.'

'I know him well, Anton. He is a special person with a great interest in music. I can understand you wanting to go back. And what about Martha? How will you keep in touch with her?'

'Do you know, Johann? Because I don't. My days at St Florian will be so full. She might be better off finding a husband who is not as busy as I will be. I've thought a lot about her and my latest thinking is to leave it to her to decide whether she wants to continue with a relationship with a teacher. If she did, it would be totally against her brother's wishes, as you well know.'

'I cannot advise you on that front, Anton. She is very fond of you, I'm sure.'

They came to a halt outside the St Florian Basilica. Anton pulled the bell chord by the enormous door. He recognised the clean shaven, short monk, who had let him in before. He explained who he was and asked to see Prior Arneth.

'He asked me to instruct you to go straight to Herr Bogner's house, where you will be living. Apparently, you lived there when you were just a student, so you know where it is. Prior Arneth will see you in due course.' He didn't quite close the door in their faces, but wasted no time in saying goodbye.

'Do you remember where it is, Anton?'

'Down in the town. There's a tavern there. I've never been there before but if you've got the time, I'd like to buy you a drink, the least I can do.'

'Good idea, Anton. Tell me the way.'

The Sparrow Inn stood between two shops in the town centre and overlooked the square. Anton led the way in, onto the sawdust scattered floor. They were soon sitting in a booth supping at a fresh, frothy stein of Pilsner.

'This is good, Anton. Do you drink a lot of beer?'

'Not a great deal. I went to the village inn with Franz Lehofer occasionally. Usually, just before closing time to get one in after dinner. His wife, Theresa, didn't mind as long as we were home by midnight. I used to play my violin in a group there sometimes, usually at dance nights.'

'So where do you see your career going? You are developing into a skilful composer and a brilliant teacher.'

'I intend to stick to teaching. I can't see myself supporting my family from an income composing.'

'I wouldn't rule it out completely, Anton.'

With that, an older gentleman with a beer stained tri-corn hat and well-worn clothes came up to them. 'I know you, sonny,' he said to Anton.

'Really?' he replied with his eyebrows lowered.

'Yeah. I gave you a lift from here to Ebelsberg on my cart, my Christ, about five years ago.'

'I remember!' he smiled. 'You are a kind man. Let me buy you a beer.' Anton realised that the man was one of those who could never stop speaking. He had chatted with Anton all the way to Ebelsberg. Anton thought Johann wouldn't want to speak for long to this individual, so he went up to the bar and left the drink he bought with the barmaid.

'I've left it at the bar, as I didn't know where you were sitting,' he said on his return to the booth.

'No problem, Sir. I wish you well. Anytime you want a lift!'

Anton and Johann gulped down their beers, virtually to the dregs, and made their way to the Bogners' house.

'Welcome back,' said Frau Bogner, as she opened the door. 'Come right in!'

'My friend is just unloading my things. I must help him.'

Johann left Anton with a shake of the hand. 'Good luck my godson! We'll stay in touch.' He climbed into the driving position and went.

'It is so good to have you back in our modest home,' said Frau Bogner. 'So this will be your third teaching job! Come in and see Michael.'

'I'm delighted you've got this job, Anton. You were the first choice, even though I had no say. But you need to settle in before we discuss the work. We're putting you in the room you had before, so I'll give you a hand with your things. And you can call us by our first names! You're not a kid now!'

While he was organising his belongings, Anton wondered how many other candidates they considered for the job. It was strange, as he hadn't even applied for it.

In the few days before the start of the autumn term, Herr Bogner explained the post.

'Unlike your job in Kronstorf, you will teach three classes. From 8 o'clock until 12 you will teach the older children. We've organised them into two separate classes so that will keep you busy! Then, from 1 o'clock until 4, the younger ones. Your predecessor, Hans Schläger, loved teaching both the older and the younger groups. Nearly all are from the town, but a few are from the local villages. One or two can be a little boisterous, but on the whole they are well behaved and keen to learn. You will like them.

'You will also repeat the lessons for the older ones which you will take on Sunday afternoons. And, whenever you can organise it, you will be giving singing and violin lessons to three boys' choirs. So carrying on where Hans Schläger left off! You can do that on Saturday or on Sunday mornings. You will want to practice organ playing so you will have a couple of hours to play in the Basilica after school or in any free time at weekends. Elise and I now dine at 7 o'clock, so, assuming you will be dining with us, you should be home by 6.45.'

'Goodness me, Michael, I won't have much time for anything else! Oh, and how much will I be paid?'

'More than you were. I hope 36 florins a year sounds good. By the way, we provide board and lodgings at no charge.'

'Unbelievable, Michael. I was expecting about twenty-five! And to pay my own way! My family will be pleased because I can provide more support for them.'

'So we are both happy, then!'

On the Sunday, the day before term started, he went alone to see 'the second big classroom'. It surprised him that he was not aware of it as a pupil. It was enormous. The desks were set out in two rectangular groups of about thirty desks each with a gap of about two metres between them. So teaching two classes of the senior children would be easier here than in two separate classrooms. It would be straightforward to talk to one group while the other children were writing an essay, or whatever they were supposed to do. He smiled the moment he spotted an upright piano at the front of the room. The thought of starting there thrilled him. Although he much enjoyed teaching at Kronstorf, he would be working on a much larger canvas at St Florian. Here the standards of teaching, in all aspects, were the highest in Upper Austria, if not in the whole country.

His first day with the older children started at precisely eight o'clock. He stood at the front of the class while they all came in. Each was wearing a school uniform of blue and white.

'We are all here now, Sir,' said a boy at the back. 'We would like to welcome you, our new teacher.'

On hearing the words 'new teacher', every pupil in the class stood, smiled and applauded. Anton was amazed. Nothing like that had happened to him before. How could he possibly do wrong, he thought.

The moment the applause stopped, a clean-shaven gentleman came into the classroom and walked to the front. He was about fifty, thought Anton, and was dressed impeccably. Anton wondered what was happening. Not another teacher or an assistant, surely.

'My name is Hans Schläger. I am your predecessor and thought it would be a friendly gesture to introduce you to your new class,' he said, speaking face to face with Anton.

'Thank you,' said Anton, smiling.

Herr Schläger then turned to the class and told them about Anton, where he was from, where he had taught, that he was an excellent organist, a violinist, singer and sportsman. 'Now, over to you, Herr Bruckner,' he said. 'I'm sure they will love you and you will soon love them!' He turned and left the class.

Anton was unprepared for such a welcome, which he thoroughly appreciated. No one had mentioned his skills as a singer before. He presumed it was to make him appear well qualified to teach the three choirs. Nor had he any idea what Herr Schläger would be doing next, retire perhaps, or be promoted to a higher post?

Michael Bogner had given Anton a copy of the week's timetable. The rest of the first period would be on geography and the time after the morning break would be on music.

'Could you please play us something on the piano?' said a girl, sitting at the front, right at the start of the music lesson.

'I'm supposed to be teaching you! I'm not here to entertain.'

'Go on, Sir. Please!' said the boy sitting next to her.

'I will, but only because you have asked me politely. But I'm going to turn this into a lesson. I'm going to play you a piece by Schubert in which he flips from minor to major keys. Listen and see if you can spot the changes.'

In this simple way, Anton was demonstrating his piano version of a string quartet by this master composer whom Anton admired, much more so since playing piano duets with Karoline Eberstaller.

Michael Bogner appeared to introduce Anton to the smaller children in the afternoon class. So both schoolmasters, Hans Schläger and Michael Bogner had done their best to give Anton a welcoming start to his new post at St Florian.

On his first evening, rather than play an organ in the Basilica, and partly because he had spent so much time on the piano, he did some composing. A month before he left Kronstorf, Franz Lehofer, had handed Anton an interesting, patriotic poem and asked Anton whether he had seen it before. Anton had not, but liked the words so much he would set them to music. So before dinner, he started the piece he would call, *Das Lied vom deutschen Vaterland*. He would score it for four male voices, two tenors and two basses. He took out a sheet of music paper, dipped a pen in his ink and started composing it, with a bold octave leap between the first two notes. Nothing like Palestrina, he thought. I'm developing my own individual style.

That night over dinner, Anton had plenty to tell Michael and Elise. The thought of the senior children giving him a round of applause staggered them. He admitted he was almost in tears, and it was the appearance of Hans Schläger that settled him down.

'You have a difficult act to follow, Anton. You may not know that Hans started up the St Florian choirs, including the three boys' choirs which you will be training. He contributed hugely to the culture here.'

'That's incredible. Some achievement. I'm puzzled where Hans is going and what he's doing next. He's too young to retire!'

'He's going to Vienna to study composition. He has his eye on becoming the director of a choral society there. I won't tell you which one in case you apply before him!' he chuckled.

'No chance! I've just started writing the music for a patriotic poem Franz Lehofer showed me. It will take me a week or two to finish it. Do you think Hans would mind me dedicating it to him?'

'What are you calling it?'

'Das Lied vom deutschen Vaterland.'

'You'll never meet anyone as loyal and patriotic as Hans. So yes, go ahead Anton. We'll arrange to have its first performance here, in the Basilica, even though it's far from religious!'

'Thank you!' said Anton. 'I'll tell you when it's finished!'

Anton was looking forward to the Sunday when he would start teaching the choirs. This would be a novel experience, even though he had conducted choirs before. He'd first have to find out how good they were, whether they could read music and whether there were any amongst them who could be soloists in their own right.

By 9 o'clock, all three choirs had assembled in the choir stalls at the Basilica, the one with the most senior boys, in front of the altar, and the other two on each side of the quire. These two comprised the one of the middle range of ages, from seven to eleven, and the one of the very youngest.

'I know many of you are in the classes I teach and some are from elsewhere but near St Florian,' he said loudly so everyone could hear him. 'There are sixty of you and in a short time, I want to get to know you individually. To that end, I want each of you to tell me your names and I will write them down. By next week, I will have made up a label with your name on it I want you to pin to your chest so I know who you are. So starting with you senior lads from my left, please give me your names.'

It took quite a time for the boys and Anton to complete the list of those present. 'Are there any boys who usually attend who are not here?' Four boys gave him some other names.

'Right. I now want to hear you sing. Turn to hymn number one hundred and eight. At the count of three, start from verse one. One, two, three!' They began. 'No, no, no! You are all out of rhythm! I will conduct the start. When my hand is at its highest. Then start!' He moved his arms while counting to three. 'Perfect! Just keep singing. When you get to the end, start again from the beginning. I will come around and listen to each of you individually.'

He did exactly that. Having reached the last boy of the youngest, he stopped and spoke. 'Well done, lads. I'm really impressed. You and Herr Schläger clearly worked well together. My key job will be to make some minor improvements where necessary and to break in any new members. I'd like you to reach a standard so high we can hire you out for public performances.'

As he had admitted, the quality of the singing was high. Some of the lads were exceptionally skilful and others slightly less so. There were obvious potential soloists amongst them, especially in the oldest group.

'Next Sunday morning, I will deal with you as three separate choirs, starting with the youngest,' he said, smiling and in the same augmented voice. He gave them the times he wanted to see them. By then, he would have produced the labels.

***

Anton was content with his first week. For him, it could not have gone better. He liked the children, especially the little ones, those from five to seven years old. None has presented him with any problems: quite the opposite. They were almost too good to be real. He soon became confident that he had mastered the complex timetable. One of the most attractive features, to him, was to have the choice of which organ to play in the evenings, after school.

One such evening, after a few months there, he was sitting on the bench of the main St Florian organ, the Krismann. While totally absorbed in playing Bach's Prelude and Fugue in A minor, he suddenly became conscious of someone standing close behind him. He decided not to interrupt the ecstatic experience of playing this masterpiece, so continued until the end.

'You have reached an unbelievably high standard, Tonerl. You are brilliant. Near to virtuoso!' Anton Kattinger patted him on the back. Tonerl stood, and they shook hands vigorously. 'And you are much taller now than you were when you left here, what six years ago?'

'I'm so pleased to see you and that you enjoy my playing, Herr Kattinger.'

'I could stop here and listen to you all day, Tonerl. You are that good. I'm not even sure I could teach you anything!'

'I'm sure you could. I'm still weak at counterpoint and harmony.'

'So you might be, but your improvisation on that fugue, as you did towards the end, was totally staggering. If Bach was listening, I'm sure he would have applauded!'

'You are too complimentary.'

'How have you improved to such a degree?'

'I'm not totally certain. I practice a lot. And I love improvising. I do that far more than I should, probably. Do you remember me mentioning my cousin, Johann Weiss? He's a good organ player and I've had great encouragement from him!'

'You stick to improvising, Tonerl. That is where you shine. Yes, I remember your cousin. You told me about him, but I'm not sure I met him. Is he the cousin who taught you how to compose those pieces for the organ?'

'Yes, that's the one!'

'We ought to get him along here and play with him. We'd play an organ each!'

'I'll ask him.'

***

As Anton walked into the Bogner's house that night, Elise greeted him. 'You've had a long day. I'm just about to serve dinner. There's a letter for you on the hall table.'

Anton opened the letter. It was from Martha.

Dear Anton,
I haven't heard from you since you left Kronstorf.
Is it all over between us?
If it is, good luck and goodbye.
Martha

He took several seconds to recover from the shock. Then he felt a strong pang of guilt at not having made any contact with her, even though he had left it to her to contact him. He wasn't sure what to think or do. It did not indicate that she wanted to continue with him. If she did, she would not have written the third sentence in such abrupt terms. It expressed no hope for their future. Had she struck up a new relationship while he had been at St Florian, he wondered. Should he reply? How much had he missed her? The new job had kept him so busy, he had to admit, he had hardly thought of her. He concluded that, although he was fond of her when in Kronstorf, his feelings for her had all but vanished. He did not love her. If for no other reason than to allow her to find someone else, if she hadn't already, he would definitely reply. In response, he said:

87

Dear Martha,
Thank you for your letter. It seems the strength of feelings
we had for each other, have diminished since I have been here.
I feel it is over between, us but hope we can remain friends.
Good luck for the future.
Anton

He did not expect a reply and didn't receive one.

***

Anton's contentedness with life intensified while at St Florian. He became completely enveloped in its culture and seemed accepted there. As he did in Kronstorf, he regularly visited his family in Ebelsberg. His mother was so delighted with his regular payment of two florins a month, she suggested that Johann Weiss need not supplement her any more.

'I'm doing no such thing. You are hardly living a life of luxury. So I will continue giving you what I have been giving you since Uncle Joseph died,' said Johann, when he and Anton were both visiting.

Anton's mother kissed him on both cheeks. 'You are both so kind,' she said through her tears.

'Ignaz, Rosalie and Josefa are well into their teens and Maria Anna is now ten so they take more feeding and clothing, too. Mama, you need all we can give you,' said Anton.

While mother went to the kitchen to prepare a meal, Anton and Johann talked about their music.

'I want to try an idea on you, Johann. I'm thinking of setting up a men's choral society in St Florian, to sing in the Basilica.'

'What? You must be mad, Anton. Don't you know Metternich has banned them? They've been outlawed for years now. He doesn't want any popular movements set up because he feels so vulnerable. He's a dictator, an arch-enemy of democracy. He opposes what people all over Europe want now.'

'I know that, but a small group in St Florian won't upset anyone.'

'You'd be surprised. There are things going on in this country causing trouble. Students at Vienna University, bankers, farmers and ordinary workers who feel over-run by Catholicism are on the verge of revolution.'

'I don't feel over-run. In fact, I've never been happier! But I am aware of some unease, from what August Dürrnberger told me when he did my exam. I will take your advice, though, Johann. I won't set up a society, just a small men's choir.'

'You'll get away with that, especially if they only sing in the Basilica.'

'I have another question. A week ago, I was playing the Krismann organ there when my old organ teacher at St Florian, Anton Kattinger, came in to listen. He asked if the three of us, him, you and me would play a concert of organ music there.'

'Great idea, Get him to put a programme together.'

'Of course!'

Kattinger and Anton collaborated on assembling a concert programme. It would include the Introduction and Spring Chorus from Haydn's Seasons and a session of improvisation on a theme Kattinger would write. They would draw up a flyer to put in shop windows, at the town hall, in the tavern, in the school and in the Basilica.

'I have a surprise for you, Anton,' said Kattinger, just as a friendly face appeared at the door.

'I didn't expect to see you here, Franz,' said Anton, smiling and looking Franz Sailer in the eye. 'You've been a friend of our family for years! And I'm grateful for all the support you've given me. Along with your companionship. Why are you here?'

'Well, I work here on various things, mainly as a copyist and that sort of thing.'

'So when do you find the time? Your job in the Linz Judicial Office must keep you busy!'

'I just do, Anton. I'm sure Anton here will tell me about when you'll be playing the organ in the Basilica, and I hope to see you then!'

'Excellent, or at my mother's house, maybe.' Franz turned and left Anton with Kattinger.

'What a surprise!' said Kattinger. 'And a pleasant one!'

***

Anton made the time to establish the men's singing quartet. He would be a member and find three others. His persistence eventually paid off. He convinced Ludwig Ehrenecker, one of his main teacher colleagues, to join. Ludwig was gifted with a wonderful tenor voice. A monastery administrator, Franz Schäffler, became the second tenor, and Anton appointed a monastery gardener, Johann Huebler, as second bass, with Anton as first.

'They've asked us to sing in the Sparrow Inn tomorrow night,' said Anton, as they assembled one Sunday afternoon for rehearsals.

'Will they pay us?' said Johann Huebler.

'Yes, but in beer. Not cash!'

'Even better,' said Franz Schäffler. 'As long as they keep it flowing!'

'I don't usually drink,' said Ludwig. 'But I'll make an exception that night!'

The landlord welcomed them to their first performance in the inn. He had advertised the event in the window and at the town hall, so the tavern was crammed with spectators, who, by the time they were ready to perform, were all holding steins of beer.

They started with a few well known drinking songs, just to get their audience in the listening mood. Then they moved on to a serenade, the *Ständchen*, which Anton had completed only days before. The audience applauded loudly at the tune and the cheery lyrics. The mayor stood on a bench and shouted out. 'Hear Ye, hear Ye! I want to praise the group and especially Herr Bruckner who wrote the music for that great song!'

'Hear, hear!' shouted many.

Anton stood on a chair and shouted out. 'Thank you, Herr Mayor. I've been wondering whom I should dedicate this piece to. So I hereby dedicate it to your wife!'

A further round of drunken applause greeted Anton's announcement. 'Let's drink to the mayor's wife,' shouted one. 'Didn't know he was married,' said another to a peel of uncontrolled laughter.

'He had to marry her,' bawled another.

'Careful what you're saying!' shouted the mayor. 'Or I'll have you for slander!' Another tremendous burst of laughter.

Next they sang *Das Lied vom deutschen Vaterland*. The whole inn erupted into chaos. Beer glasses were smashed on tables. Hats were thrown into the air. 'Austria's in the shit,' shouted someone. 'We're all in the shit,' shouted another. 'We're all going to bloody starve,' shouted a red faced individual. 'You're right! This damned potato blight is going all over Europe and there'll be no spuds for any of us!' screamed yet another.

Anton wanted to restore order to this disruption, if he could. 'Let's play my *An dem Feste*, shall we? That'll calm this lot down.' So they sang it as loudly as they reasonably could. Fortunately, it had the desired effect. Most stopped their arguing to listen.

While sitting at a table enjoying their well earnt drinks, they chatted about their performance. 'We should never have played your *Vaterland*, Anton,' said Johann Huebler.

'We weren't to know it would cause such strife! We won't rush to sing it here again!' Anton said.

'Too bad. But I thought we sang well. We're becoming a good group. We ought to try some other venues, further from here. Not just for the money but for the beer!' said Ludwig.

'I think we are legal, lads. We aren't a choral society, merely a small group of singers. We'll see what we can do,' said Anton, feeling confident.

They drank up, left the tavern, and made their way to their homes.

***

Anton, Johann Weiss and Anton Kattinger enjoyed playing their 'three organ recital' at the Basilica. Kattinger played the main organ, while Weiss and Anton played the choir organs. At least three hundred locals attended. Many were familiar with the Haydn, which attracted muted applause. The improvisations on the theme that Kattinger had written attracted huge appreciation and shouts of 'encore'.

'Thank you so much,' said Kattinger loudly to the audience. 'I would like now to introduce you to Anton Bruckner who will play you his latest work, *Prelude and Fugue for Organ*. Over to you Anton.' They had planned for him to play it instead of embarking on further improvisation, in response to any 'encore' request. Anton played it and improvised like a master. Anton Kattinger was not surprised and Johann was delighted.

They concluded with Anton's quartet singing *Stänchen*, its first official performance. At the end of the song, with the mayor and mayoress present, Anton announced he had dedicated it to His Honour's wife. She burst into tears.

Chapter 8
1848 Revolution

'Would you like to attend a concert with me, Tonerl? I'm going to see Mendelssohn's St Paul in Linz next week,' said Johann, as the two of them were looking again at pictures in the Monastery gallery.

'What an interesting work to hear. It can't be performed very often because it's so long. Yes, I'll come. How will we get there?'

'Not sure yet. The concert is an evening one, so we'll have to stay the night.'

'I have a new friend at my school. Would you mind if I ask him to come with us? His name is Franz Schäffler. He's a senior administrator and member of my choir.'

'By all means. The concert is on Saturday at 5 o'clock. We can meet here at midday. I'll borrow a wagon to take the three of us. I may bring a friend, too.'

The very thought of listening to this oratorio enthralled Anton. Its intense religiosity could, he thought, inspire him to write other holy works. He was aware his masses were comparatively short, as were his other religious works. Listening carefully to the Mendelsohn could help him in the development of his own style of composition. Not that he would want to emulate the master, but he could learn, even so.

Anton easily convinced Franz Schäffler to come along with them. They all met up on the Friday and set off in a friend of Johann's wagon. When they reached halfway, it shocked Anton and Franz to see small groups of soldiers patrolling the road. Each soldier carried a long musket, and wore a uniform topped off with a brimmed hat. As they approached the city, they could see more groups of soldiers.

'What is happening?' said Anton.

'You wouldn't know, of course, cooped up in your ecclesiastical surroundings!'

'I know there is a revolution under way, but I thought it was confined to Vienna, Budapest and Prague,' said Franz.

'I'm afraid not,' said Johann. 'The government is trying to maintain this country as a totalitarian state. These troops are here to ensure no revolutionary activities occur… especially among large gatherings of people. I'd be surprised if the concert hall isn't crawling with them.'

They booked themselves into a hotel in good time to arrive at the concert hall. Johann was almost right. The venue wasn't exactly seething with troops, but there were pairs of them standing outside, by the main door, and inside at the entrances to the hall. The three of them made their way to their allotted seats.

'Are there any other pieces on the programme, other than the St Paul?' asked Franz.

'No,' said Johann. 'But it's long enough to more than fill most programmes!'

Anton rapidly became intoxicated by this enthralling masterpiece. He failed to see how he could write anything so brilliant. Nor could he contemplate finding the oceans of time which he would need, both to write the libretto and the vast amount of music to support it. During the first interval, the three of them stood at the bar at the back of the hall and had a drink.

'Well, what do you think, Anton?' said Franz.

'I am enjoying it. How long did it take Mendelssohn to compose it?'

'About three years, I think. It could have been less. I don't know,' said Johann.

'I can't ever imagine composing anything as lengthy, elaborate, or as complex myself,' said Anton.

The performance continued towards a second interval, then to its conclusion. A generous round of applause greeted it, to which the performers and conductor bowed deeply.

'Thank you so much for asking us to come with you,' said Anton.

'I also thank you,' said Franz Schäffler.

'It has been a pleasure,' said Johann.

'I have enjoyed this so much. It's been a few years since I heard Beethoven's fourth symphony, but I think this is a far more important work. And I have learnt a great deal from it. The way he uses the orchestra to compliment the choir and the soloists. It's as if he's guiding them along their path of song. I love the enormous range of dynamics he employs from the almost silent where you have to listen for any sound, to the very loud which threatens to split your ears. I must keep these points in mind when composing,' said Anton.

'You bastards should fuck off from here and jump into the river!' a man shouted at the soldiers, as the three of them stood up to leave. This unexpected outburst from a fellow concert-goer shocked them. The two soldiers patrolling the door said nothing, but simultaneously clicked their heels. The man said nothing else but left.

The three walked to their hotel. Many troops were patrolling, more than they had seen before. It was getting dark, so the numbers had probably increased because of the greater threat at night.

They stopped in a tavern on the way. 'What are your views on the troops?' said Anton to Johann.

93

'Those soldiers were not looking for trouble. They seem well disciplined. They impressed me by the way they handled the man who swore at them.'

'Me too,' said Anton.

***

A week after the Linz concert, Anton was working alone in the 'second large schoolroom' when there was an unfamiliar knock on the door. Nothing could have surprised Anton more than to see the mayor of St Florian standing there.

'Please excuse my interruption, Herr Bruckner. Your headmaster, Michael Bogner, told me I could find you here. Before I tell you the official reason I came, I thank you for dedicating your lovely song, *Ständchen*, to my wife. She is so grateful and so am I.'

'It was a pleasure, Your Honour. It was to reward your generous comments about the piece.'

'I'll continue. I am on a mission to make a special request to selected staff. Therefore, I have a question for you. We've had an official petition from Vienna to recruit some of our people into the National Guard. You know there is a revolution going on in the country. At present, it is mainly happening in Vienna and in some other large towns. The university and colleges have been the most active, as have farmers, bankers and groups of peasants and civil servants. The military activity has focussed on Hungary, which has declared itself an independent democracy. They are, of course, part of the Habsburg Empire, centred on Austria. Emperor Ferdinand has negated the various laws they have illegally put in place, and we are effectively on a war footing with them.'

'So what is your question, Mayor Schlager?'

'I am asking you, one of the staff nominated, if you would like to join the National Guard. I'm sorry to thrust this question on you, but I would like to give the government in Vienna a positive response.'

'Hmm. I wasn't expecting anything like that. You've taken me completely by surprise. I need time to think about that and to discuss it with Michael. Do you know what the duties would be? Would I be sent to fight the Hungarians or Czechs?'

'No, you would not. You are not a trained soldier and only the fully trained go to war. According to Vienna, you would be a guard on duty here in St Florian. Your job would be to prevent people of this town and the surroundings from causing a revolt.'

'How would I do that?'

'You would have the power of arrest and be able to detain any offenders.'

'And if they refused?'

'You would be trained to use a musket. And approved to shoot to kill. I must go, Herr Bruckner. I will give you three days to decide. Good day.'

Anton was almost shaking at the proposal. He felt undecided. On the one hand, he had been selected as one of the chosen few to join the troops. On the other, he was not prepared to risk his life. He would discuss it with Michael at dinner.

***

'Only you can decide, Anton,' said Michael.

'Before I can, I need to ask some questions. For one, would you replace me as a teacher? And second, for how long would I be doing it?'

'When he spoke to me, the mayor was talking about two years.'

'That's a lifetime at my age!'

'I've also spoken to the prior, who says they would replace you as a teacher on a purely temporary basis. They have someone in mind, apparently a monk, who would revert to the priory when you finished your time in the guards.'

'Hmm. I'll reflect on it for a day or two, then let you know. Which one of us would tell the mayor?'

'I think that's for me, Anton. If you decide to do it, you can continue staying here, if your duties are in St Florian. I cannot think they will expect you to stay in some barracks somewhere!'

'Thank you. That's useful to know.'

He still didn't know what to do, so the following evening, straight after school, he walked home to discuss the proposal with his family.

His mother's response surprised him. 'Tonerl, accept it. I would be so proud to have a National Guard in the family. What do you think, Ignaz?'

'So would I, Mama. I'd join myself if they asked me. At fifteen, I'm probably too young!'

'I'm still not sure, but you are beginning to persuade me,' said Anton.

He stayed the night and walked back to St Florian, with whether to join constantly on his mind. He arrived just in time to start his class. During the day, he decided. That night at dinner, he told Michael Bogner that he would like to become one of the troops. Six days later, he received a letter from the mayor giving him instructions on his training. It told him to go, as soon as possible, certainly before 10 o'clock in the morning, to the town hall in Styer and ask to speak to the National Guard recruitment officer. Before he went, he explained to his classes that he would be away from St Florian for a time, but didn't know how long, possibly up to two years.

'We hope you survive, Herr Bruckner, and come back in one piece,' said one of the older boys.

'I will miss you badly,' said one of the young girls. Then she shed some tears.

'Please don't cry,' said Anton. 'I'm sure I'll be alright. So don't worry.'

***

He walked to Styer carrying a case in which he'd put a change of clothing, some music paper and a copy of the Well-Tempered Klavier. He knew the town well, so soon located the town hall and walked in. The recruitment officer handed Anton a sheet of paper.

'Can you write, son?' was the unnecessary question.

'As a matter of fact, I can.'

'Then fill in this enrolment form.' Anton started completing it, but the officer interrupted him. 'Not here, son. That desk over there.'

Anton obeyed and soon gave it back to the officer.

'Now go to that room through there where someone will measure you up for a uniform. Then come back and I'll tell you what to do next.'

'I have quite a good memory, so you can tell me now, if you wish. I'm sure I won't forget.'

'No insolence, please,' he said in a raised voice.

Anton didn't reply but went into the room the officer was pointing to. It smelt of male perspiration. A man in a white pinafore with a fabric tape-measure round his neck told him to stand with his arms pointing outward. He then used the tape to do the necessary. Anton then returned to the recruitment officer.

'The next step is to train you to use a musket,' he said. 'You need to go to Eisvogel Farm, which is just outside the town on Kronstorfstrasse. You will be given further instruction when you arrive.'

'I know where it is,' said Anton.

'I don't remember asking you if you did,' said the man.

Anton took his luggage to the farm. He knocked on the door to the farmhouse. A soldier answered it and directed him to a large barn about two hundred metres behind the house. As he approached, he could hear a gunshot. I must be in the right place, he thought.

'Who are you?' said a soldier, stationed just inside. Anton saw several men holding muskets with a soldier standing beside them, apparently teaching them to fire. He told the man his name.

'Good. We are expecting you. Have you fired a musket before?'

'No.'

'We'll train you. It's not as difficult as it looks,' said the man.

Anton was standing there watching the others under instruction when a uniformed soldier approached him. He wore exactly the same type of uniform as the guards he, Johann and Franz saw in Linz, and carried a musket.

'Herr Bruckner. I'm your instructor. There's a space for us over there, at the end of that group being trained. Let's go there and begin.'

'Thank you,' said Anton, not knowing what else to say.

'Have you ever handled a musket before?'

'No.'

'Take it,' he said, handing it to him.

'It's quite a weight.'

'Yes, but you look strong, so you'll be fine. We'll make you into a good musketeer! First, I'll tell you how it works, then I'll show you how to load it.' He explained the flint striking, ignition mechanism, and how the exploding gunpowder created enough pressure to push the speeding ball out of the barrel.

'This is how you load it. Hold it more or less horizontally. Then open the pan here. Take a cartridge of powder, open it by tearing it with your teeth. Spit out the paper and pour half the gunpowder into the pan. Close the pan and pour the rest of the powder down the barrel. Now put the ball in, then the rest of the paper cartridge. Take the ramrod out and ram the paper in hard. That will stop the ball from dropping out. Then put the ramrod back into its holder and you're are ready to shoot. This is how you fire it. Are you right or left-handed?'

'I'm right handed.'

'Put the butt of the stock against your right shoulder and hold the barrel half way up. Cock it like this. Raise the barrel, aim at that target at the back of the barn and fire! I'll show you!'

He fired the musket and hit the target, just off centre.

'Here, now you do it!' He handed Anton the musket and gave him a gunpowder cartridge. Anton tore it open with his teeth and spat out the piece in his mouth. He took his time in pouring the powder into the pan, then into the barrel, pulled to cock it, and then completed the task by putting the ramrod back into place.

'Not bad,' said his instructor. 'You just need to speed up or the enemy will kill you first. Now fire it at the target.'

Anton aimed and fired.

'At least you hit it,' he said. Anton had successfully hit the outer ring. 'We'll get you to load and fire five more times. Then I'll make an assessment.'

Anton followed his instructions. He hit the centre, the inner ring and the outer ring once, but missed the target completely twice.

'You've done well, Bruckner. Just be a bit more relaxed with your hand on the barrel and you'll do better still.'

'Thank you, Sir.'

'We need to train you in self-defence now. That's not my job, so you'll have to go to the large shed over there,' he said, pointing to a wooden structure some hundred metres away.

Anton went there. A short, bearded soldier, also wearing full military uniform, greeted him. 'So you're here to learn how to defend yourself,' the man said. 'Have you had any previous training?'

'No.'

'I'll show you.' He went to kick Anton in the crutch but, as fast as lightning, Anton grabbed his foot and pulled him to the ground. 'Bloody hell, I wasn't expecting that,' said the man. 'Looks like you don't need much instruction. Where did you learn that?'

'At the teacher training college in Linz. I attended about eight years ago, and they taught me how to deal with unruly pupils.'

'So they taught self-defence.'

'You could say that.'

'So, all I need to show you is how to attach a bayonet to a flintlock musket. You'll be fully equipped then.' The man took a musket from a rack and showed him. 'See. Straightforward, isn't it?'

'Quite easy.'

'Now go back to the recruitment officer at the town hall and he'll tell you what the next part of your training is. Good luck!'

'Thank you.'

On the way back to the centre, Anton wondered what he had let himself in for. None of the National Guards he had seen patrolling the roads to Linz, or in the city, appeared to fire their weapon, even when provoked. What were they training him for, to take a more attacking role perhaps, or to send him to an area where they expected greater trouble than in Linz or its approaches? He'd find out soon enough.

'The next step is to send you on an exercise. It's late in the day now and I want you to go to this address to stay the night. It is an army barracks on the edge of the town. They will give you an evening meal and, after breakfast, instructions on the exercise. Here is a map showing you how to get to the barracks.' He handed Anton a crumpled sheet of paper, which someone had used before him.

The conditions in the barracks reminded him of the sleeping and eating arrangements in Windhaag. They told him he had to sleep in a dormitory with some twenty other men. From their accents and behaviour, most were from peasant stock. The dinner consisted of overcooked cabbage soup and suet dumplings. The noise in the dining area was deafening, with most of the men, by their rowdiness, acting like regular soldiers and not like timid trainees. They continuously shouted abuse to each other across the tables. Breakfast was no better.

'Could the trainees assemble outside in five minutes?' said another instructor, also dressed in military uniform.

Having left his belongings in a wooden locker, Anton went out and could see he was one of about twenty. Some he recognised as men who had musket training the day before.

'There are going to be two military exercises for you today. On the first, you will go into Styer, fully armed with muskets and bayonets fixed. You will patrol the streets looking for suspect gatherings. If you see groups of more than five, you will ask them to break up. You will threaten to arrest them if they refuse. If they persist in refusing, you will bring them back here and hand them to the jailer who will lock them in the cells. You will defend yourselves if any are violent towards you. If you have to shoot, you will aim at their limbs. Unless they threaten you with a potentially dangerous weapon. In which case, you may shoot to kill.

'Before you go, you will be fitted with a uniform and given your musket. You will depart from here in groups of three and spread yourselves around the town. I want you all back in the canteen for debriefing by one o'clock this afternoon. I will then instruct you about the second exercise. You are now dismissed.'

Dressed in a uniform that fitted well and which, by its smell, had been worn several times before, Anton joined up with two other new recruits and set off for the town centre. He couldn't believe he was now a soldier. It felt strange to be walking in public, carrying a musket fitted with a bayonet. Anton had never felt so self-conscious in his life. He hoped he wouldn't see anyone he knew.

The three made no attempt to walk in step, as no one asked them to, nor trained them for such military display. On the way, they talked about which part of the town they would patrol.

'Not near the church, please,' said Anton. 'I know several people there.' He thought he would be intensely embarrassed if Joseph Plersch saw him. Even more so if he invited Anton into the church to play on the organ, dressed in his uniform. They agreed to patrol outside a tavern near the town hall. If the National Guard recruitment officer spotted them, it could work to their advantage.

The three of them positioned themselves outside the inn, with Anton and another close to the door and the other on the road. Most passers-by looked at them with suspicion, even though they represented the state. Most drinkers going into the tavern wished them a good day. Some just chuckled at the sight of them. A passing dog urinated on the leg of one of the other two. Anton noticed and had difficulty suppressing his laughter.

'Good morning, Anton. I can't believe I'm seeing you.' He looked around to see the smiling face of Karoline Eberstaller, wearing the same, head covering scarf she wore when they first met.

Anton visibly blushed.

'That is you, isn't it, inside the soldier's uniform? Is that some form of fancy dress, or are you a soldier now?'

He didn't know what to say. 'Yes, I've been volunteered for the National Guard, Karoline. I've signed up for two years and this is my first military exercise.'

'But what about your teaching, Anton, and your composition? Does that mean you'll be doing neither for two years? And your wonderful organ playing?'

As she finished the sentence, one of the recruits approached them. 'Are you supposed to chat to members of the public while on duty?'

'I don't see why not. Members of the constabulary do,' said Anton. The man returned to where he was standing.

'I'm not sure about the organ playing, Karoline. But I won't be teaching. There's nothing to stop me from composing, so I'll be doing some in my spare time. I may even play the organ at the church, if Joseph Plersch allows me!'

'That'll please him, I'm sure. But don't go there in uniform!' They both laughed. 'I must go now, Anton, as I have shopping to do. But I'll keep an eye open for you.'

'I hope to see you soon,' said Anton, thinking that he'd rather not be in uniform on the next occasion.

The three of them continued standing at the tavern until it was almost time to go. 'How much longer have we got?' said the recruit nearest to Anton.

'About ten minutes by the town hall clock,' he said.

'Good. I'm bored to madness here.'

Seconds later, two men emerged from the inn and started swearing at Anton. He said nothing. One of them clenched his fist and held it in front of Anton's face. He might need to defend himself. First, he would try reasoning with the man. 'Put your fist down and get away from me,' he said.

'What if I damned well don't?' the man said.

'I'll have to arrest you for threatening me.'

The man continued his intimidating behaviour. Anton's two colleagues came to help. 'What game do you think you're playing?' said one of them. 'This idiot has been abusing me,' he said.

'Well, I'm threatening you now. Get away from him and put your fist down or I'll smack you in the legs with the butt of by musket.'

'No, you bloody won't,' said the man's companion. He moved to punch the soldier in the face but missed. The third soldier lifted his musket and put the point of the bayonet onto the man's neck. Anton shoved the butt of his musket into the body of the aggressor, who fell to the ground clutching his chest. The three of them had brought the awkward situation under control.

'What should we do with them?' said Anton.

'They are not a revolutionary group, just two thugs. So I suggest we just let them go,' said the one with the bayonet on the man's neck.

'I agree,' said the one who the punch missed. 'They did no harm to any of us.'

'I agree. Let's release them with a warning,' said Anton.

The two men drifted away with their heads hung low.

***

On arriving at the barracks, the three of them joined the group of new recruits.

'Why are you three so late?' said the instructor.

'We had to deal with a couple of drunks who wanted to assault us,' said Anton.

'Why didn't you arrest them?'

'They weren't a big enough group to qualify,' said one of the others.

'I see,' said the instructor. 'This afternoon you will be engaged in a more realistic exercise. You will go back to Eisvogel Farm and form two groups. We will arm you with blank cartridges and you will attack each other in a musket fight. You will be judged by two of us. Go to the canteen and have something to eat and drink first.'

The food was just as awful as the night before, but Anton was so hungry, he had to eat something. All twenty or so made their way to Eisvogel Farm. They reassembled in front of the barn where they had been trained in musket fire. The instructor split them into two groups and armed each of the recruits with a musket, a bag of blank balls and cartridges of gunpowder. He sent one group with another instructor away from the barn towards some woods about three hundred metres away and ordered about ten recruits, with Anton among them, to stay close to the barn. He explained that, on the sound of a shot from a pistol, the groups should start attacking each other. Moments later, a gunshot sounded.

'Load your muskets and fire,' said the instructor.

All could see and hear the shooting from the other side. The trainees showed great enthusiasm for what they regarded as a game. Anton did better than most and reloaded and fired at a good speed. Only two of the men on his side were quicker than him. With more than twenty firing their weapons as frequently as they could, the noise was almost continuous as well as loud. Along with the flashes from the muskets, it was like a Chinese firework display. Anton noticed the instructor taking notes, presumably about how each of them was managing. Firing continued until each trainee had run out of blank musket balls.

'Now return to the barracks,' said the instructor to Anton's group. 'You will receive further instructions there.' He walked back with the two who patrolled outside the tavern.

'Any idea what happens next?' asked one of them.

'No,' said Anton. 'But I imagine they'll tell us where we are to be posted. Where we live or somewhere else.'

'Sounds like you're right. The question is when, and will they expect us to stay in those awful barracks until they make their minds up?'

The recruitment officer told them to go to the canteen to wait for the promised details. Gradually, all twenty or so of the trainees assembled there. The officer then made an announcement.

'Thank you for enrolling in the National Guard. We expect you to consider your appointment as a great honour. For it is an honour to serve the Empire. Based on your performance here, the military has accepted each of you. The next step is to inform you about your posting. You will therefore return to your normal place of residence and await the details, which we will send as soon as we have made the allocations.

'You will wear your uniform and we will supply you with two dozen rounds of live ammunition. You will retain your muskets.'

Anton bade his farewells to his two tavern guarding colleagues and headed back to St Florian. He felt less self-conscious than he had before while walking the streets of Styer, but it seemed strangely incongruous to be in uniform and carrying a musket and his suitcase.

He knocked on the Bogners' door, rather than scare them with a military intrusion. 'Goodness, Anton. You look good as a soldier!'

'Thank you, Elise. I'm glad you like it!'

'I'm less sure about the musket, though! Come in. You are just in time for dinner. Speak to Michael while I prepare a few more vegetables. First, change into your civilian clothes!'

'Thank you. I'll do that.'

Anton was soon discussing his military future with Herr Bogner.

'So you will certainly be a guard on our streets, then.'

'As far as I know. They will write in a few days to let me know. I've asked them to write to me here.'

'That's fine, Anton.'

***

Anton went home for a day or two to tell his family about the training and what the military expected of him.

'I'm so proud of you, Anton. You will make a wonderful guard,' said his mother. 'You are a reasonable man and will treat people fairly and with respect. If they deserve your respect, that is!'

'Tell us all about it,' said Ignaz. 'I may want to be a soldier myself!'

On his second day at home, Anton's family had a surprise visitor. His mother opened the door to Franz Sailer.

'I didn't expect to see you, Franz. Do come in. Anton is staying with us for a few days while he waits to hear about his guard posting,' said mother.

'I hope he gets something here or in St Florian,' he said. 'I didn't know he was staying here.'

'He's in the lounge with the others. Go through while I make you a drink.'

Anton was surprised and pleased to see this family friend, whom he had known for many years, and who often helped out at St Florian.

'Good to see you, Anton, but I have a duty to my godson before I shake your hand!' said Franz, before hugging Ignaz.

'Thank you, Uncle Franz,' said Ignaz. 'It's good that you've visited while Anton is here. He's often said how good you have been to him, mainly as a musician friend.'

'So you've been giving me praise, Anton?'

'Yes, and well deserved.'

Anton was telling them about his training exercises, some of which Ignaz had heard the day before, when his mother appeared with some cups of juice. The conversation about Anton's new career and Ignaz's thoughts about joining the army continued. The girls joined in and laughed together when Ignaz said what he wanted to do.

'You can be quite unkind,' he said, grimacing at them. 'It's good to have an aim in life.'

'Sorry, Ignaz. We shouldn't have teased you in front of Uncle Franz,' said Rosalie.

'Now peace is restored, I must go,' said Franz. 'Give me some dates to hear you play that Krismann again, Anton. I'll enjoy it.'

***

That evening, Anton walked back to St Florian. He was not in uniform, so let himself into the Bogners' house.

'Good to see you, Michael. Any letters for me?'

'Nothing. Just as well! They may have wanted an immediate response!'

Just a few days later, the expected and dreaded letter arrived.

Herr Bruckner,
You have been appointed as a National Guard reservist in
the town of St Florian.
As such, you will have no military duties, unless notified.
Commandant, Styer

Anton was shocked and delighted. He rushed to tell Michael Bogner.

'I don't believe it, Anton.'

'Read it for yourself, Michael.' He handed him the letter.

'So it does. You'd have thought they would say more, but maybe there's not much more to say. What do you think, Anton?'

'This strange episode has shaken me, but only slightly. It has made me wonder what I want to do in my life. I'm wondering whether I should become a full-time composer. I don't know. But it will be good to get back to school. I'm sure that will help me.'

'The children in your classes will be delighted.'

'I really look forward to seeing them!'

'I'll have to speak to the prior about you replacing the monk. Assuming he agrees, you'll restart the Monday after Easter Monday, the first day of the summer term. If you want to go back home, you can.'

'I'll stay with you, if I may.'

'Of course.'

Chapter 9
1848 - 1851 Indecision

Before starting to teach again, Anton often played the Krismann organ in the Basilica. He felt entranced and secure, sitting on the bench playing and improvising. His favourites were organ pieces by Bach, Michael Haydn and Albrechsberger. Local people, as well as staff at the monastery, came to listen to him. At the conclusion of a piece, the Basilica would echo with their applause.

Late on one such day, Michael Bogner surprised him by appearing and standing beside him, next to the instrument. Anton looked around smiling, but Michael was not smiling. He looked sad and his eyes looked as if he was on the point of weeping. Several in the Basilica were still listening to his wonderful outpourings, so he closed the piece he was improvising on, as quickly as he could.

'Hello, Michael. It's unusual to see you here. Is something wrong?'

'I have some terrible news, Anton. Prepare yourself for a shock. Franz Sailer has died suddenly of a heart attack.'

'No! I'm staggered. That is a terrible tragedy. Awful,' he said, almost in tears. 'I loved the man, and so did my brother, Ignaz.'

'Ignaz?'

'Yes, he was Ignaz' godfather. He will be so upset. So will my mother and the girls.'

'I didn't know he was a family friend.'

'Yes, he was very close to my family. He came to our house only a week or so ago. What luck I saw him then. You would never guess he would have passed on so soon. I'm upset, devastated.'

'I must go, Anton. I'll see you at dinner.'

'I cannot play anymore after such sad news. I'll tidy up here and lock up. I'll be back soon.'

The conversation at dinner that night focussed on the death of Franz Sailer. All three agreed he was an exceptional man. He could play the piano well and even dabbled in composing.

'Did you know he owned a Bösendorfer piano, Anton?'

'Yes, I've been to his house several times and played it. It is a piano of excellent quality, probably the best in the world. He loved pieces for four hands. We even played it after we'd had a few beers. We'd play as fast as we could and collapse into laughter at the end!'

'That's typical of the man. His main job at the monastery was to copy documents. They were mainly papers they had to send to the authorities. And official letters for which copies had to be kept. But he would also copy out parts from scores for the choir and orchestra. This was an example of his love for music.'

'We must attend his funeral,' said Elise.

'Absolutely,' said Michael.

While lying in bed that night, Anton's thoughts turned to the idea of writing a Requiem Mass in memory of Franz Sailer. He spent some time thinking about it. It would be loosely based on Mozart's Requiem but be completely different. It would be more modern in structure and content and be a highly individual piece. Albrechsberger's works for trombone inspired him as he decided on the score. It would be for three trombones, a horn, three soloists and a mixed choir. In writing it, he would not attempt to emulate the genius of Mozart, but would do his best to make it a work of quality, befitting of a Mass in memory of Franz. He recognised that all his works, up to then, were fairly short, from a minute or two to ten minutes. But this would be a substantial piece of a size he had never even contemplated before. It might even make him consider a career change. But he would keep that to himself.

***

Anton did not settle into the teaching work as well as he hoped. Could it be the uncertainty he had brought upon himself by thinking of leaving his current profession? The death of Franz Sailer had affected him badly, and he wondered if that was a contributing factor. However, he still enjoyed teaching the three classes, especially the younger ones, who still seemed fond of him. And because of its musical content, he enjoyed working with the choirs. He still liked practicing on the Krismann and on each of the choir organs. Not long after he had restarted his teaching, Anton Kattinger came to see him.

'Have you a moment to spare, Tonerl?'

'Of course.'

'I need to tell you something important. I'm having to leave St Florian. As you know, I have duties as a minor tax official here. In his infinite wisdom, Emperor Franz Joseph is closing this office and I'm having to move to Kremsmünster. It will mean a minor promotion to tax inspector, so it has a good side and the bad one of leaving St Florian. I shall come back for various events, of course, but it's over thirty kilometres away, so it won't be often. I shouldn't speculate, but you are the obvious choice to replace me.'

'Anton, I am deeply shocked. We have become great friends, and that includes my cousin, Johann Weiss. I will miss you. I hoped you would continue to help me improve my organ play, but now that will not be so.' Anton's face collapsed into sadness at this, a musket shot to his head.

'You don't need me, Tonerl. Of the three of us, Johann is the best, but only slightly better than you. I am far behind both of you!'

'So when will you be leaving, Anton?'

'I don't know yet. I expect to receive a date soon... and there is work to finish here. You are one of the first I've told, so please keep it to yourself. But you can discuss with Michael Bogner if you wish, and Prior Arneth, who is responsible for replacing me.'

'Thank you for telling me that, Anton. You've given me something to think about.'

The possibility of becoming Kattinger's replacement did not excite Anton. Quite the opposite. It unsettled him even more. If he took the job, would he lose his teaching post? If not, would they restructure it in some way that may not suit him? Were they going to push him out of teaching?

***

Partly to take his mind off his confusion and uncertainty, Anton spent much of his spare time composing the Requiem. It was important to be clear about the structure before he started putting notes on paper. It would start with an introduction in the same way as Mozart's, but he would not include a Kyrie. Then he'd launch into a Dies Irae followed by an Offertory which would be in three parts, concluding with a double fugue. Then he'd write the Sanctus, the Benedictus and a three part Agnes Dei. So it would be in six movements, in contrast to Mozart's, which was in five, but his would have fewer parts overall. It would be in the same key as the Mozart: D minor. He had been writing it, on and off, for some time when he heard a soft knock on his bedroom door. 'Enter,' he said. It was so late, it had to be Michael or Elise Bogner. It was Louise, their daughter.

'Hello, Anton. You don't mind me calling you Anton, do you?'

'Not at all.'

'What are you doing?'

'I'm writing a Mass in honour of Franz Sailer.'

'I didn't know that!'

'Few people do. So what do I owe the pleasure?'

'My Papa has asked me to see you.'

'Really?'

'Yes. To give you some good news. The details of Franz Sailer's will were released a few days ago. He's left you his Bösendorfer piano.'

'That's incredible! I could kiss you!'

'You can if you like!' So he kissed her on both cheeks.

'I'm totally stunned. Your news has really excited me. They are the best pianos in the world! I think there could be a problem in where to put it. There is already a piano in my classroom at the school. And your father wouldn't want it in the house.'

'Papa was thinking about putting it in the Basilica so you could play it there.'

'Excellent idea!'

'You could lock it up, like the Krismann, and only you could play it, unless you gave someone else permission, that is. It would stay there until you wanted it removed.'

'Your father has thought this through. Please tell him I'm utterly thrilled. You've brightened my day, Louise.'

'Thank you. I'd better go now.' She kissed him on the chin and left.

It took Anton some time to recover, as if he'd been struck by an arrow. He could not see how, even from saving his teacher's pay for ten years, he could afford one of these magnificent pianos. It would remain in his possession for the rest of his life. A second arrow, Cupid's, penetrated his heart. It hadn't beaten faster since he fell for Martha Knauer. His mind drifted into confusion. He didn't know what to think about Louise. She was an attractive, jolly young woman. She could not have been more than fourteen, so hardly of marriageable age. Any concentration he had on composing had evaporated, so he went to bed.

***

A few evenings later, Anton was dining with Michael Bogner, Elise and Louise.

'I know Anton Kattinger has spoken to you about him having to take up a tax inspector post in Kremsmünster,' said Michael. 'You may not be surprised to know that Prior Arneth and I have also discussed it. In short, we would like to offer you the post of Provisional Organist, as Kattinger's temporary replacement. While you are thinking about it, let me tell you about the consequences for your current post. You would play the organ on Sundays, at various times throughout the day. So would no longer teach the choirs on Sunday mornings. We haven't solved that problem yet but are thinking of asking one of your colleagues, Petrus Schärschmidt, to take over the teaching. That's confidential information, so please don't tell anyone. I mention it so you know your pupils will still be taught well... so what do you think?'

'I'm confused and not sure. Isn't there someone else who could do it? My cousin, Johann Weiss, for example. He's a genius at the organ. He was best at that recital the three of us gave, what a year ago?'

Anton was stretching Bogner's patience. 'You don't have to decide now, Anton. But this will be a tremendous breakthrough for you. You will have a double career... that of teacher and professional musician. I can't understand your reluctance!'

'You would if you were me. Let me explain. What I need most is security. That is more important to me than being a professional musician. It's because I need to support my family.'

'Right. I'll tell you what we'll do. If you accept, we guarantee you will have your job as teacher back, if things don't work out for you. Oh, and by the way, St Florian will pay you eighty florins a year as Provisional Organist. This is on top of your salary of thirty six florins for teaching, as well as staying here for nothing. And we will make the post permanent within three years. So there is no risk at all.' He raised his voice to say the last sentence.

'Alright, Michael. I gratefully accept. I'll do the job or jobs to the best of my ability, I can assure you.'

Michael came around the table to congratulate him. 'I'm so grateful, Anton. You will be brilliant, I'm certain. When you get the chance, could you please speak to Kattinger and he will tell you exactly what the job entails.'

'Congratulations from me, too,' said Elise who, up to then, had sat quietly and listened.

'And from me,' said Louise.

After dinner, Anton resumed work on his Requiem Mass. He was thinking this piece would be his most important work by far. Writing it was a pleasurable challenge. By then he had finished the Introduction and Dies Irae and was working on the first part of the Offertory.

Despite his agreement to accept the position of Provisional Organist, Anton was still unsure about his future. Up to then, his sole ambition was to follow in his father's footsteps and become a teacher. In becoming the Provisional Organist, he would still have a foot in his career in teaching. He felt as if he was at a crossroads where the signposts pointed in three different directions. One to being an organist, the second to being a teacher, and the third to being a composer. So he would strive to become a first rate organist and combine that with composing. Eventually, he would abandon his career as a schoolteacher. The important point was to take his time. He'd always been a patient and determined person, so would take as long as necessary, but be utterly diligent along the way. The restless feeling of uncertainty, indecision, and confusion had suddenly evaporated. Happiness had returned.

'There are several points I have to make, Tonerl. You are a better organist than me, so you have an excellent start,' said Anton Kattinger, when they met to discuss the hand over. 'I'm sure you know by heart the most popular hymns we sing at the Sunday Eucharist. Some are ancient and some are newer. Here is a special hymn book with the organ parts included.' He handed Tonerl a large, leather bound volume. 'Take care of it, as it is one of the Basilica's treasures. I know you love to improvise, but in playing these hymns, you must stick closely to the written themes. Otherwise, the congregation will feel uncomfortable. But there is some scope as long as the main theme is always present. Try out and practice these hymns before your first Sunday Mass.'

'That's sounds like good advice to me.'

'I'd follow it carefully, if I were you. Towards the back of that volume, there are other hymns you need to familiarise yourself with. These are for weddings, funerals and memorial services. You may be asked for advice on what music to play on these special occasions, so you will need to become familiar with a wider range of organ music. You may even be asked to transpose other pieces for the organ. So there is a great deal for you to do!'

'Thank you, Anton. When do you start in Kremsmünster?'

'In just over a week. So that gives you just a little time to come back with questions.'

Tonerl had no questions but continued working on the Requiem, which he had all but finished when he started the combined post. He struggled for the first few months, but like any other function that has a weekly routine, he gradually became quietly competent in both roles. His peers respected this, as did Michael Bogner and Prior Arneth. The Basilica's congregation also began to enjoy his slightly different approach.

***

He regularly visited his family, all of whom were delighted with his increased responsibility. On one of his visits home, Johann Weiss was there. Anton told him all about his new job as Provisional Organist and how he combined it with his teaching duties, even though they had been reduced.

'How do you manage all that work?' said Johann.

'It's not as difficult as it sounds. There's not much time for leisure activity, but I still compose. I was uncertain about taking all of it on, but I'm feeling quite happy about it now. This is because I'm getting good reports from Prior Arneth, who is my boss for the organ playing.'

'Well done, Tonerl. I half expected you to become a professional musician. But you are both!'

'It sounds strange, but it's true!'

'I also have some good news! Like you, I've taken on additional responsibilities. They differ greatly from yours!'

'Tell me more!'

'I've accepted responsibility for managing the collection and maintenance fund at my church.'

'You must have the time to do it, or you wouldn't have taken it on. How long have you been doing it?'

'About two months. I have the time, Tonerl, I can assure you!'

Anton was nervous about the Sailer memorial service. It would include the first performance of his Requiem. He lived in fear that something would go drastically wrong, but he didn't know why. He regarded this work as his best, so wanted to ensure it would be performed to the highest standard, both for his benefit and for the memory of Franz. The service was to take place in the September, a year after Franz's passing. Anton spent much time in organising it. Prior Arneth agreed to write the programme. Since Anton would be the organist, he needed a conductor. Over a few beers in the Sparrow Inn, he persuaded Petrus Schärschmidt, who had taken over his choir duties, to accept the role. Similarly, and in the same venue, he convinced his singing quartet members, Ludwig Ehrenecker, Franz Schäffler and Johann Huebler, to be the soloists. Petrus himself recruited members of his choirs to sing. The St Florian orchestra would play in it.

'So how many rehearsals do we need?' said Petrus, when they met to discuss the plan.

'Hard to say,' said Anton, frowning and raising his hands. 'This is a new work and I'm the only person familiar with the thing! Let's start with three. That will tell us if we need more.'

'Perfect. We also need to copy out the parts.'

'I've asked the man who was assistant to Franz Sailer, and he said he'd do that and have them ready in a week,' said Anton.

'Good work. So we'll hand the parts out, give the performers say three days to become familiar with theirs and have the first rehearsal on the fourth day. That'll be the Thursday after next. Say, after lunch?' said Petrus, looking at his diary.

'That shouldn't be a problem. I'll ask Michael Bogner to take my teaching duties for the afternoon.'

With all the arrangements in place, the Thursday came around with frightening speed. By two o'clock in the afternoon, all the performers had assembled in the Basilica. Most were peering at the part they were to perform.

'I'm now ready to start,' said Petrus, after striking the music stand with his baton. 'I will raise my hand at the count of three and we'll begin.'

The strings made a beautiful and convincing start, but the choir were uncoordinated and their sound was poor.

Petrus struck the music stand and shouted. 'No! Sorry choir, but we can do better than that!'

'My fault,' shouted one. 'It was my fault. I started too early and many others followed me!'

'The best thing to do is to count the beats, four to the bar. You come in on the seventeenth beat! So we'll start again!'

111

Petrus spoke as the players performed. 'Perfect. Nice. Very good.'

So they continued into the Dies Irae. The lady mezzo-soprano missed her point of entry in this quick starting movement. Again, Petrus struck the music stand and held up his hands to stop play. He didn't know the lady's name. 'No, Madam!'

'I know! The speed of this movement threw me, so I wasn't ready. Sorry.' Her head hung low and she was almost in tears.

'Please don't worry. We all make these kinds of mistakes. So don't be upset. It could be any of us. We are so grateful to you for agreeing to sing this piece with us. It's not like a more familiar piece. It's never been played before, so we are bound to make mistakes. I'm sure I'll make some on the way.'

'Thank you, Herr Schärschmidt. I feel I can continue now.'

'We'll begin the Dies Irae again then. One, two, three! Beautiful. Perfect entry, Madam. Exactly on the beat.'

The rehearsal continued with Petrus making several more stops and giving instructions to the players as they were in action. He directed the choir to be quieter or increase the volume by speaking out or by gesture. He reduced the volume of the alto trombone several times as the enthusiastic player became too loud. It took them four attempts to achieve a virtuoso performance of the third movement of the Offertory, the '*Quam olim*', because of its double fugue structure. After about an hour and three quarters, they came to the end.

'Bravo, bravo,' shouted Petrus. 'You can congratulate yourselves on a really excellent first rehearsal. Come over here, Anton. Tell us what you think!'

'I'm so excited to hear my longest work yet rehearsed so well, I can hardly speak. But you, Petrus, and this wonderful assembly have performed it nicely. I wondered what it would sound like and now I know! Thank you, everyone, for playing so well!'

'So how many more rehearsals do you think we need?'

'Let's have one more. If it goes well, we won't need a third.'

'I agree,' said Petrus.

Apart from a few minor blemishes, the whole assembly played well in the second rehearsal. 'What do you think?' said Petrus to Anton, sufficiently loud to enable all the performers to hear.

'I'm extremely happy,' said a smiling Anton. 'I think we can all applaud ourselves! We can all look forward to the fifteenth of September!'

Petrus led the applause and all the performers joined in, especially the mezzo-soprano who made the late entry and whose entire face smiled.

While Anton and his colleagues were rehearsing, Prior Arneth was preparing the order of the service he would lead. He decided on a short, welcoming introduction, the playing of the Requiem and then the eulogy.

'I know you have a major role, Tonerl, but would you like to give the eulogy?'

'I would willingly read it, Michael, but I have a better idea. Franz Sailer was godfather to my brother, Ignaz. I think we should ask Ignaz to do it.'

'How old is he?'

'Fifteen.'

'He's only a lad.'

'But a very mature one. He is a man now, and the person who protects my mother and sisters. I could help him prepare it.'

'In which case, you win! Please ask him and offer help from either of us.'

'I can go home on Saturday, if you can find someone to take my afternoon class that day.'

'I will, of course, if you can be back here for the Sunday Eucharist.'

'Agreed!'

After greeting his family members, Anton asked Ignaz the question.

'I'm not sure, Tonerl. I'm too young, surely.'

'But you are his godson and he loved you dearly. I can help you prepare something. We will need to write to the Judicial Department in Linz to ask his colleagues there what they would like us to include and whether you should deliver it. We can invite them to be represented at the service.'

'I'm still hesitant, Tonerl, but I'll do it if they agree.'

'Good man!'

'What are you two scheming?' asked their mother as she stepped into the lounge.

Anton explained.

'That sounds a good idea to me. You have my blessing, Ignaz.'

'And mine!' said Rosalie, who was standing behind her mother.

Anton wrote a letter to the lawyers in Linz. It asked for an early reply to be addressed to their home in Ebelsberg. He asked Ignaz to read it carefully, take any necessary notes from it, and post it to him at St Florian. That way, they would both know what the Judicial Department wanted and, in particular, whether they were happy with Ignaz delivering it.

In their reply, the office had no objections to Ignaz giving the eulogy. They said he could mention only that he worked for the Judicial Department but, even if Anton or Ignaz were aware of any details of his job, they should not mention them. This was a surprise and disappointment to both Ignaz and Anton. So, between them, they wrote a eulogy based on Franz's relationship with Ignaz. They included his work as a copyist at St Florian, with only a passing reference to his judicial activities.

Having lost his sense of uncertainty, Anton became more confident, especially in his ability to form relationships with young women. So he attempted to befriend Louise. He could hardly pursue her at the dinner table so tried other methods. So he wrote a series of little love songs and posted them under her bedroom door. His expectation was that she would find them intriguing and reply to him. She might even invite herself into his bedroom, as she had when she told him about Franz Sailer leaving him the Bösendorfer.

His songs had no effect. Louise ignored them. So he tried another tactic. He would invite her to join the choir, which sang on Sundays, and which had only a few female voices.

'So what do you think, Louise?' said Michael, after Anton had asked the direct question in front of him and Elise.

'I'm not interested.'

'Why not? You've a beautiful singing voice,' said her father.

'Yes, it would be a good outlet for you,' said her mother.

'I'll tell you both something. Anton has been trying to become a friend of mine. I'm not sure how friendly he wants to become. He's written about ten different love songs for me. And posted them under my bedroom door. Why he can't ask me straight, I don't know.'

Anton could feel his face going from almost white to bright red. He didn't know whether to stay at the dinner table or escape from his embarrassment. It took him a good ten seconds to decide to remain.

'Let me explain, Louise. I'm very fond of you and would like to know you better. Since you are only fifteen, I can have no other intentions. So I'll leave you alone, if you are uninterested.'

'You could do worse than Anton,' said Elise.

'And I could do better,' she said, as she stood and left the room.

'I'm sorry about that. I just wanted to know Louise better.'

'No need to apologise. You've done nothing wrong,' said Elise.

Michael said nothing but, with the trace of a frown, looked straight into Anton's eyes. Anton abandoned efforts to become friendly with Louise, at least for a time, maybe until she was a year or two older.

The fifteenth of September was soon upon him. Even though the rehearsal went well, he still felt apprehensive about the service. He walked alone to the Basilica, accompanied only by his thoughts and fears. While Petrus had conducted well in the rehearsals, how would he perform in front of possibly a thousand people? The orchestra was used to performing publicly, but the choir was not. He shouldn't worry, he thought. It's too late to do anything now.

He met his own family in the Basilica. His mother beamed to see him, as did Ignaz, who held a couple of folded pages close to his chest. The girls, Rosalie, Josefa and Maria Anna came, too. Anton was always happy in the presence of his family. They exchanged hugs and kisses. Johann Weiss had accompanied them and Anton had paid for the cabriolets for their journey, there and back. The large number of people there, from the mayor and his wife, to many of Franz's monastery colleagues, surprised them all. Michael Bogner had declared this an official school holiday. Many of Anton's teaching colleagues were present, as were many parents and children.

'I didn't expect this many people, did you?' said Petrus.

'I thought there would be a good number,' said Anton, as the orchestra, choir and soloists were taking their places. 'I'll sit at the organ bench. Good luck with the conducting. You'll be fine!'

'I hope so,' said Petrus.

The service started exactly on time. 'Let me welcome all present here to this memorial service in honour of our great friend and colleague, Franz Sailer,' said Prior Arneth. 'We remember him with affection and have all missed him in the year since his passing. This is a special occasion and we are underlining it with the first performance of the Requiem Mass by our Provisional Organist, Herr Anton Bruckner. Petrus Schärschmidt, also one of our colleagues, will be the conductor. So I hand over to you, Herr Schärschmidt.'

'Thank you, Prior Arneth.'

Petrus started, not by a count of three but by pushing up his baton twice, then exaggerating a third movement on which the string section came in. The choir began exactly on the seventeenth beat. Anton was feeling less anxious. As he played, he listened for the trombones. The alto produced exactly the level of sound which Anton had written and Petrus had demanded. The next possibility for an error was the double fugue in the '*Quam olim*' of the Offertory. They could not have performed it better. Anton glowed as the piece concluded with the '*Cum sactis*' of the Agnus Dei. He breathed an audible sigh of relief.

Much to Anton's amazement, the congregation applauded. Prior Arneth thanked them. He then introduced Ignaz and escorted him to the pulpit.

'Ladies and gentlemen,' he began. 'It is an honour for me to be giving this eulogy for my godfather, Herr Franz Sailer, or Uncle Franz, as us Bruckner children called him. We loved him. He was not only generous, especially at Christmas, but he was funny, too. I remember him telling me he used to enjoy horse racing until he fell off and broke a leg. "Not the horse's but mine", he said. One day he said, "I walked into a door once and that's why I've got a flat nose". "I've never got married because I prefer to sleep outside and not many women like that, especially if it's dark", he told me. His job was in the Judicial Department in Linz. I know no more about it because no one there will tell me.' Several people chuckled. 'He did much voluntary work at St Florian. With much keenness, he would copy musical scores and produce parts for members of the orchestra or the choir. We will always remember him for this great work. My brother, Anton, who wrote the Requiem Mass, will always be grateful to him because he left him his Bösendorfer piano. Thank you.' Ignaz stepped down from the pulpit to the sounds of the congregation, discussing what he had said.

Prior Arneth brought the service to a close by again thanking everyone who attended, and saying what a fitting service it had been for his friend, Franz Sailer.

'Well done, Ignaz,' said Anton as he met his family and Johann outside. 'What a nice eulogy. Congratulations, especially for the bit about the Judicial Department not telling us what Uncle Franz did for them! You must have written that bit yourself!'

'That made people laugh. A good thing for such a solemn event. Lightened it up a little,' said his mother. 'Yes, well done, Ignaz.'

'I agree,' said Rosalie. 'And you held back your tears.'

'What tears?' said Ignaz.

'Didn't you feel you could cry?' said Josefa.

'No!'

'I cried when you were doing it,' said Maria Anna, pretending to wipe tears away.

'Congratulations to you, Anton,' said Johann. 'Your Requiem is excellent. You might have based it on Mozart's, but you've ended up with something distinctly Anton Bruckner. Well done, my godson!'

'Thank you, Johann. I'm so glad you like it.'

'Your colleague Petrus conducted it well, too,' said Johann.

'Oh, thank you,' said Petrus, as he joined the group. 'But the credit should go to Anton for writing it and the incredible group of players who performed it. They did well, don't you agree, Anton?'

'You all did. I was so relieved it went so well.'

The family members and Johann walked the short distance to the cabriolet stand, just outside the St Florian town hall. Johann gave Anton a manly hug and a handshake. His mother, the girls and Ignaz bade their farewells and off they went.

***

Anton regarded the performance and reception of his Requiem Mass as a major triumph, previously unequalled for any other work of his. On his way

116

back to the Bogners', he thought again about his future. He felt he was on the right path. He would concentrate on his organ playing for the present and continue with his composing when he could spare the time.

His responsibilities as the 'Provisional Organist' and teacher gave him a strong sense of being needed in St Florian. To show his commitment to being a highly competent teacher, he took a correspondence course in Latin and physics at the teacher training college in Linz. It lasted nearly a year and, having applied himself with great diligence, he passed with distinction, and treasured the certificate they awarded him.

***

He often visited his family, the more so after Michael Bogner handed his Saturday duties to Petrus. The unofficial reason was to give him more time to rehearse his organ music for the Sunday Eucharist. He burst into their home in Ebelsberg, three weeks or so after the transfer, and shouted out that he was there. He was met by his mother, who immediately cried into his chest.

'Whatever is wrong, Mama?'

'We've had some awful news today, Anton.'

'Tell me! Has something happened to one of our family?'

'No, it's Johann Weiss. He's committed suicide,' she sobbed.

'I can't believe it,' he said, trying not to cry. 'How do you know?'

'Our priest came to tell me, first thing this morning.'

'Did he say why?'

'He didn't. He said he didn't know.'

They both hugged each other and cried. Anton couldn't remember shedding actual tears, except tears of joy, since his father died. Johann had acted like a father to him when he was staying in Hörsching. He wondered how he could live without this great friend and teacher, the man behind his love of music, his adviser and constant mentor. They eventually stopped their sad embrace.

'May I borrow the horse and cart please, Mama? I shall go to Hörsching today to find out what happened.'

'Of course, Tonerl.'

'I'll go now and be back before nightfall.'

While driving there, he couldn't stop thinking about Johann, who was not the type of man to kill himself. He was outgoing, personable and enjoyed the company of his many friends. Whatever made him take such irreversible action? A sense of grief and melancholy overcame him. He could hardly see the road through his tears.

'Good day, Reverend,' he said to the priest, as he entered the church.

'My goodness, it's you, Anton. I haven't seen you since you were so tall.' He put his hand out. 'I'm so sorry about Johann, your cousin and godfather.' The priest put his arm around Anton's shoulder.

'What happened? You must know.'

'Yes, I do. I'm not sure if you are aware but, just over a year ago, Johann volunteered to take responsibility for our maintenance and collection fund. It has to be audited by the church authorities regularly. When this was last conducted, a few weeks ago, the auditor discovered that a sizeable sum of money, nearly a thousand florins had been embezzled. A police officer went to his cottage to interview him. This terrified him and he came to the church. He went to the bell tower, took a spare bell rope, and hung himself from a tree. I'm so sorry, Anton. The sad thing is we are sure the money was taken before he took over. We should have had it audited before.'

'Yes, you should. You are blatantly incompetent. I'm disgusted with you. He took over this job in good faith and look what you've done to him. You're a murderer! He was an honest man who did nothing wrong in his life.' Anton sobbed. Tears ran down his face. 'I'll never come back here again!' The ride back did nothing to ease Anton's seething anger.

His mother cried when Anton related this tragic tale. Johann had meant so much to her. They could hardly have survived without him.

'Do Rosalie, Josefa, Maria Anna and Ignaz know?'

'Yes. I told them after you had gone. I said he'd died in an accident. They were upset, but not as much as us two. Should I tell them the rest of the story?'

'Not unless they ask, Mama. I must go back to St Florian.' They hugged again, and he walked back.

***

'I'm so sorry about your cousin and close friend,' said Michael Bogner at dinner that night.

'I am, too,' said Elise. She came around the table and gently hugged him.

'Same here,' said Louise.

None of them knew what to talk about, so the dinner was an unusually quiet one. Michael thought of asking Anton about Johann, but decided it might not be a welcomed question, even though he had met him occasionally. Once the meal was over, Anton drifted into his room and sat on the bed, feeling sad and still in a state of shock. There was a soft knock on the door, which Anton recognised. 'Come in, Louise!'

'I am truly sorry, Anton, about your cousin. I didn't know what to say at dinner. So I thought I'd see you now.'

'You are kind, Louise. It was my fault. I didn't feel very sociable at all. I'm still in a state of shock. I could cry now, but I won't because you are here.'

'I mainly came to offer any help I can give you.'

Anton pondered for a moment. Was she trying to rekindle the relationship she broke off nearly two years ago? Did she think more of him now, or was she just sorry for his loss?

'You are a really nice person, Louise. And kind. Maybe I could see more of you. Perhaps to go for a walk, occasionally. Do you have a male friend?'

'Not at present. So yes, we should go out together. Did you have any day in mind?'

'Saturdays are my best days because I have no teaching duties then.'

'Let's go out next Saturday then.'

'Excellent!'

Chapter 10
1851 - 1854 A new direction

The death of Johann had its effect on Anton. He wondered if his plan to become a composer was the best way forward. So rather than change course, he would try a few other drastically different options. He was still busy with his teaching, but Michael Bogner could readily find a substitute, possibly Petrus Schärschmidt.

'I have a request to make,' said Anton, when Michael visited him in his classroom at a lunch break.

'Go ahead, Anton.'

'Believe me, I am fully committed to all I do here, being Provisional Organist, my composing and my teaching duties. But I have to confess, the death of Johann has made me think. I would like to try some voluntary legal work. Just to see if the profession has any appeal. So I would like your permission to do some work at the law court in St Florian. I would be happy for you to reduce my salary accordingly. Would that be alright, Michael?'

'First, let me tell you why I am here.' He put the stress on the 'I'. 'It is to say that your position of Provisional Organist is no longer provisional. It is now permanent. Congratulations! You will receive a document from Prior Arneth confirming it and a rise in pay.'

'Thank you, Michael. I'm so pleased, I can't find the words. That takes me nearer to being a full-time musician, which contradicts what I would like to try next.'

'You don't need time off to do voluntary work in the courts. They have hearings on Saturdays, when you are free anyway. So yes, of course you can try it out! And you don't need my approval.'

One Saturday morning, when he had no other commitments, Anton visited the court and spoke to a senior lawyer there.

'I know you, don't I? You're the organist at the Basilica!'

'Yes, I am actually,' he said, looking at him with his eyes half closed, regretting that he didn't recognise the lawyer.

'Presumably, you have a legal issue we can help you with. Is it contractual? If so, we have people here who can deal with it.'

'No, not at all. I saw a notice on the board at the town hall which said you were looking for volunteers, so I thought I would offer you my services.'

'That is kind of you, Herr Bruckner. That is your name, isn't it? Yes, I'm sure we can find you some work. When would you like to start?'

'Next Saturday?'

'Yes. Would eight o'clock suit you?'

'It would, indeed.'

***

At lunch time, he asked Louise if she'd like to go for a walk. She agreed, so they strolled into the town. Neither knew what to say to the other or what they thought of each other. Louise spoke first.

'So where are we going?'

'Wherever you like. Would you like to go to the park?'

'Why not? We can walk around or sit on a bench.'

'Alright, we will.'

They walked to the park. At first Anton didn't know what to say and Louise seemed nervous. As they entered the park, Anton spotted a covered cart with a man inside, apparently selling food and drinks. So he started a conversation with a question.

'Would you like something to eat? I can buy something from that wagon over there.'

'No thank you. I've only just had my lunch.'

'In which case, let's sit on that bench,' he said, pointing to a seat overlooking a stream.

'Good idea,' she said.

'I wonder if there are any fish in it,' he said, as they sat down.

'I can't see any,' she said, smiling. 'Not that means there are none there!'

Anton could feel she was more relaxed, so he told her how happy he was, teaching at St Florian and living with her and her parents. She said she was glad and it was good to have him staying there. Her response prompted him to seek her views on a relationship, possibly with him.

'So, how do you see your future, Louise? Will you marry and have lots of children or will you stay single and help your parents in their old age?'

'Don't make me think of such things, Anton. I don't know. I'll probably get married some time, but I'm happy as I am. What about you?'

'I've already lost one nice girl when I was in Kronstorf. That was my fault for neglecting her while I was here. But I would like to get married and have children.'

'Are you actively looking for a wife?'

'That's a tough question. I often think of such things. Would you see me as a potential husband, for you or someone else?'

'I'm not sure, Anton. From what I know of you, I'm certain you can love a wife. I'm not sure if I would be the one for you. We would need to get to know each other better. Living in the same house doesn't help. Maybe we should do this sort of thing more often. I'm sure my parents wouldn't object to us meeting in your room, or mine provided we didn't... '

121

'Yes, I agree. My room next time!'

They chatted on the bench for a half hour about their respective futures. Anton said he would always compose music and play the organ. Louise said before she married she would like to try teaching and asked Anton about his experiences at the teacher training college in Linz. He gave it a good report, saying she would enjoy it there. Anton then escorted her back to the Bogner house. He thought of holding her hand but decided he wouldn't. He couldn't work out whether she was interested in him or not.

**

'So what work would you like me to do today?' said Anton on the Saturday to an officer of the law courts.

'Do you know much about property law?'

'Not much, but I can usually understand legal documents.'

'We have a case of a farmer claiming that a neighbour has put up a fence, which encloses part of the area owned by the farmer. Would you like to look at it?'

'Yes, please.'

'I'll get the papers.'

Anton spent the morning in an office, studying the documents and eventually reaching a conclusion. The official shared the same office, so Anton could tell him what he had found.

'The farmer is right. The neighbour claims the fence has been there a sufficient time for the land to be his. But the fence has only been there two years.'

'That agrees entirely with what we think. Could you please draft a letter for us to send to each party?'

'Of course,' said Anton. He soon gave the official his text.

'Nice work,' he said. 'Do you have time for another case?'

'Not now,' he said, 'but I'll be back on my next free Saturday.'

This experience gave Anton an idea of what the legal profession would be like. It seemed boring to him. One more visit wold be enough for him to make a final decision.

**

Many people in St Florian had praised his ability as a composer, but few had any idea about the profession. An interesting thought occurred to him. Some years ago, Prior Arneth had introduced him to a composer called Ignaz Assmeyer, if he had remembered his name correctly. Anton recalled this character boasting about being a friend of Schubert and being taught composition by Michael Haydn. The prior introduced him as the conductor of the Court Orchestra in Vienna, as well as a former Imperial Organist and a choirmaster to the Court. He thought he would head for the Court Orchestra, find him and show him some of his work, especially the score of the Requiem. Despite this earlier, brief meeting, Assmeyer could not really know Anton, so he would give a purely objective view of his ability as a composer. He'd go to Vienna by train.

Anton took two days to find him. He was unaware of the location of the Orchestra but eventually discovered them playing in the Imperial Court Chapel, which Anton found in the Swiss Wing of the spectacular Imperial Palace. The substantial size of the Chapel, its airy brightness and intimacy impressed him. He immediately realised they were rehearsing Mendelssohn's Reformation. Assmeyer, who was conducting, appeared to be much older than Anton expected or remembered. He had a full head of hair, piled on top like a small haystack. Anton sat and watched until he finished. He approached him after he fulsomely praised the orchestra and stepped down from the rostrum.

'I do like your style of rehearsing.'

'Oh, thank you. Are you here for a special purpose?'

'Yes, my name is Anton Bruckner,' he said, hesitatingly. He reminded him about their meeting previously at St Florian and explained why he was there.

'Leave your best work with me and come back tomorrow, at the same time, young man, and I'll tell you what I think.'

'Thank you, Herr Assmeyer. I shall be eternally grateful. Your opinion will influence how I decide on my future.'

Reflecting on what Assmeyer might say kept him awake nearly all night. Would he tell him his Requiem was poor and suggest he try another profession? What a waste of sleep, he thought, as he enjoyed a German sausage and egg breakfast in the hotel restaurant.

Assmeyer gave him a friendly greeting. 'I am flattered that you asked for my opinion. I read the complete score of your Requiem and suggest you continue working diligently towards your planned aim. I'm sorry I can't spare you more time. We are rehearing Beethoven's Ninth this morning. Good to meet you.'

He was unsure when he left, but the more he thought about it, he could only take what the great man said as encouragement to be a composer. That was important.

'So you're going to become a professional composer are you, Anton?' said Michael at dinner, the first night he was back from Vienna.

'Not exactly, or not yet. I'm still looking at other options, but you could say I'm reassured by what Assmeyer said. He is one of our best living composers, so he should know.'

'So what are you going to try next?' asked Elise.

'I'm not certain. I may try the civil service. They are always looking for trainee officials in Linz.'

'You need to think about that. Once you have one of these permanent, secure jobs from which they can't sack you, unless you are stupid enough to take money from the till, you'll be there until you die. And your composing will stop.'

'I'm not so sure about the composing coming to an end, Michael!'

Straight after dinner, Louise came to his room to see him. 'Lovely to see you, Louise, and not at the dinner table!'

'You look busy, Anton. What are you writing?'

'A little piece, mainly for my amusement. It's a setting of the Magnificat.'

'You really intend to become a composer!'

Anton smiled but didn't comment.

'I've come here to make a particular point, Anton. I really like you as a person and as a professional teacher and organ player. You have a lovely personality, too. However… '

'Please go on.'

'We've discussed the possibility of getting married. I've thought a lot about it, but I've decided not to marry you. You are coming up to thirty and I'm only sixteen. I need more time as a single girl and I hate to say this, but you are too old for me. Sorry.'

'No need to apologise, Louise. You'll never know what you are missing.' He smiled.

'I'll go now,' she said, and she left, gently closing the door behind her.

His thoughts became a series of contradictions. Admittedly, he liked her but, not sure that he loved her. He felt attracted to her, but not in the same way as he was to Martha. How could he continue living here, now she had rejected him? Should he find somewhere else? No, he'd stay here. He'd see what else might happen in his quest to find a good woman. It was not urgent.

He went home that Saturday and told his mother about his visit to Vienna.

'Assmeyer? I've never heard of him.'

'He's one of our best composers and that's why I went to see him. The clever man has written an enormous number of works, mainly religious, and he's the conductor of the Imperial Court Orchestra. My Requiem impressed him.'

'I'm not surprised, Tonerl. So you will become a composer then.'

'I'll tell you, Mother, but keep it to yourself. Yes, that is my ultimate aim. I'll always play the organ. But the main thing is, I will give up teaching. All in good time!'

'I have some news, too! Rosalie has got married.'

'Really? Is she pregnant?'

'No. She's married to someone you know!'

'Who?'

'Johann Huebler, a gardener at St Florian.'

'He's a member of my quartet of singers.'

'He was. I doubt he is now.'

'Why not?'

'They've moved to Vöklabruck.'

'That's fifty kilometres away! If not, further. I must go to see them, at least to give her a wedding present! I imagine you really miss her.'

'Of course, Tonerl. But I've still got Maria Anna and Josefa. And Ignaz of course!'

It was the summer term break, so Anton had time to visit the happy couple. His mother had given him the address, so he had no difficulty in finding the pretty, white-walled property. It was a small, two storey house with a bright green front door and green window frames.

Rosalie opened the door to him, and immediately apologised for not letting him know about the wedding.

'Johann wanted to move here quickly, partly because he had made an offer on this house. We debated whether he should move here first and get married later. But we went ahead, and here we are!'

Anton couldn't bring himself to complain about the hasty move. 'If you are happy, Sis, then so am I! Here is a small present.' He handed her a little purse in which he had put ten florins.

'You are kind, Tonerl,' she said, and put the purse on a sideboard without opening it.

Nor did he want to upset Johann Huebler. 'I tried to find you, Tonerl, to tell you I'd be leaving the choir,' said Johann. 'You were teaching or at the Bogners' house. I didn't realise Rosalie is your sister!' Anton didn't believe him but said nothing. He just thought his excuses were pathetic and unsubstantiated.

Anton felt he didn't want to stay too long with the newly wedded couple so spent only two nights there before exchanging fond farewells and a promise to return when he could.

The day after his arrival at St Florian, he asked Prior Arneth if he knew about Johann Huebler's wedding.

'I did not know, Tonerl, but he left his gardening position only two weeks ago. All he said was he wanted to be with his family and friends in Vöklabruck.'

'I'll need to find a replacement in my men's singing quartet.'

'Not that easy. Ludwig Ehrenecker, is taking up a job in Enns and Franz Schäffler is very ill. He's not well enough to sing.'

'I'm surprised Ludwig hasn't told me about his move. I thought he and I were good friends.'

'Please don't hold that against him, Tonerl. He is a good friend of both of us, but he asked me to say nothing until his new job is confirmed and it isn't yet. So please don't say anything to him.'

'I'd like to see Franz.'

'Please don't. He is highly contagious and I wouldn't like you to contract any nasty illness of the kind he's got.'

'Thank you, Prior Arneth. I understand.'

Despite his strength of character and individuality, Anton felt lonely. Ludwig Ehrenecker confirmed to him he was leaving for a better post in Enns. Anton didn't say he already knew. Poor Franz Schäffler died of whatever horrible illness he was suffering from. So, with Johann Huebler leaving St Florian, the quartet had completely collapsed. He had few friends in St Florian or anywhere else, except Petrus Schärschmidt, and the brothers Karl and Josef Seiberl, who lived a considerable distance away in Marienberg, and whom he hadn't seen for years. He felt he needed to tell someone what was happening in his life and, putting his thoughts on paper, he believed, would help him see things in a clearer perspective. So, as he hardly knew Josef, he wrote to him.

Anton penned a lengthy letter, setting out his plans for the future, even citing his thoughts about leaving teaching behind and becoming a professional, full-time composer. Writing as he thought, he told him about his promotion to Organist at St Florian and what Assmeyer had said about him continuing to press ahead with his composing. In conclusion, the letter said, 'You can see how everything has altered. I sit in my small room, all alone in the deepest melancholy.'

Anton thought hard about the last sentence, but wrote it to reflect his state of mind after another attempt at romance had failed. It was with another sixteen-year-old, an Antoine Werner, who worked as an assistant to a tax collector in St Florian. His sister had introduced them while the tax official employed Rosalie as a cook.

Despite these setbacks, he continued to play the organ and to compose. Not only did he complete the *Magnificat*, he put *Psalms 22* and *114* to music. He scored *Psalm 22* for mixed choir, soloists and piano. This was the first work in which he'd used this instrument. His idea was to play the first performance of the piece on the Bösendorfer which Franz Sailer had left him. He wrote *Psalm 114* for his often used combination of three trombones, along with a mixed choir of soprano, alto, tenor and bass.

Anton noticed that, with the dissolution of his quartet, St Florian was becoming less interested in music. No one other than him was interested in resurrecting the quartet, so he didn't. He put his frustration into writing to Assmeyer, complaining that 'St Florian is treating music and musicians with great indifference'. He enclosed a copy of the score of his *Psalm 114*, saying he would be delighted if the master would accept Anton dedicating it to him. The idea, as he said in his letter, was to show the Court Conductor that he had taken his instruction 'to continue working diligently towards your planned aim' seriously, and that *Psalm 114* was one of a number of works he had composed since seeing him the previous year. Assmeyer wrote a short reply, thanking Anton for the dedication, and inviting him to contact him again if the need arose.

***

Having lost his friends, Johann Weiss, Franz Schäffler, Ludwig Ehrenecker and, in effect, Johann Huebler, Anton was totally devastated to hear from a friar that his friend and supporter, Prior Arneth, had died. The prior lived to the creditable age of eighty-three and many at the Monastery, including Anton, had for some time, because of his failing health, expected his passing. A long life of the departed is no compensation for those left to mourn. The number of years of a human being's age has no real meaning, other than arithmetical. The prior's death added another layer of loneliness to Anton, who always tried to resist feeling sorry for himself. This awful news saddened him greatly.

'We are as upset as you, Anton,' said Michael, at dinner that night. 'I've known him for over thirty years. He was my first contact at the monastery.'

'He was mine, too, Michael, but I've only known him for about seventeen years, since my mother brought me here and begged him to take me in,' said Anton.

'He's been a good friend to us,' said Elise.

'Apparently, his funeral is in three days' time, so the friar who told me said.'

'I imagine they would like some of your compositions played there,' said Elise.

'As Organist, I've already discussed the service with his successor, Friedrich Mayer. As part of my job, I've written two pieces especially for his funeral, and we will perform my Requiem there, too.'

'Can you tell us about these pieces, Anton?' asked Elise.

'Yes. One is called *Vor Arneths Grab*. It's an elegy. I've given it a mildly festive feeling rather than making it too funereal. The other piece is called *Libera me*. It's a motet written in five parts for choir, three trombones, organ, cello and double bass. It uses the well-known text. I've tried to be original in writing it, so I think it's quite modern.'

The death of Prior Arneth had a profound effect on Anton. He continued to think what an incredible help he had been to him, from his first acceptance of him at St Florian, to entering him into the teacher training college At Linz, finding him posts at Windhaag, Kronstorf and at St Florian, as well as appointing him Organist. He had given Anton direction in his life, more than any other person he knew. Almost in tears, he knelt by the side of his bed that night and prayed for the soul of his close friend, a man he would never forget.

***

Friedrich Mayer directed the funeral, which he made a combination of sadness and celebration. A vast number from Upper Austria came. Prior Arneth's responsibilities as Director of Education gave him contacts in many schools at tens of kilometres from St Florian.

'I can't believe you are here,' he said to Alois Knauer, after the service. 'Are you still a priest, or have you retired?'

'I'm still there, but Martha isn't.'

'Really?'

'No. She married three years ago and is living in Linz.'

'Wonderful. I'm glad she is happy. I feel bad that I neglected her so much when I came here.'

'Please don't, Anton. She is as happy as she could be.'

'How are you enjoying your job as Organist?' asked Anton Kattinger.

'Good question, Anton. Since Prior Arneth rightfully handed over some of his duties, interest in music and musicians here has diminished. It's sad really. But I'm pressing on and perform organ recitals in the Basilica and compose for special occasions.'

'Did you write those two new pieces played earlier?'

'Yes, they are mine.'

'Well done. I liked them a lot.'

'How is life in Kremsmünster?'

'Not as good as here. I'm bored by tax work. You've got the job I loved most!'

'Sorry about that!' said Anton, not meaning it at all.

Anton enjoyed reunions with the Lehofers from Kronstorf and Hans Schläger, his predecessor in his teaching post. He spoke to August Dürrnberger, his teacher in Linz, and Leopold Zenetti, whom he only rarely saw because they were both so busy.

'Did you write that Requiem and those shorter pieces?' said Zenetti.

'Yes, I wrote them all.'

'Your Requiem is as good as any composer's.'

'Not true,' said Anton. 'Mozart's is better.'

'Hmm. Not so sure but yours is up there. Especially the double fugue of the *Quam olim.*'

'I did enjoy writing it, I must admit.'

'You should become a full-time composer, Anton.'

'I'm looking at several options at present.'

The option he wanted to try, which most annoyed those close to him, few though they were, was to apply for a post in the civil service. The post of secretary at court interested him. He'd compare it with composing for a living. It would not stop him from writing music: quite the opposite. He'd almost certainly be able to devote more time to this extraordinary hobby of his which, up to then, hadn't earnt him a kreuzer.

'You're totally insane,' said Petrus Schärschmidt. 'You are a composer with the top post of Organist here. Everyone respects you as a teacher, and you want some dreary job as a low grade administrator doing tedious work that no one else wants to do. And the pay is poor. You'd be wasting your life.' He held out his hands, frowned and left Anton, before he swore at him, tempted though he was. Instead, he wrote to Anton, saying he should forget the idea and continue working in his current role.

So, undeterred, he wrote to the Organising Committee of Linz and asked for the job, giving all the details of his qualifications. He told them about the multitude of certificates, which he promised to show them, if needed. They refused to consider him for a post.

That refusal probably benefitted him. He would try a different approach. Many had praised him locally for his accomplishments as a musician. He thought he would value an independent Viennese opinion, especially if it was from professional sources. He would take up Assmeyer's offer of help. So, he wrote to ask if he could, as a special favour, test his ability as an organist by arranging a panel of specialist musicians to listen to his organ playing. He knew he had taken a risk in asking, so felt none too optimistic about the outcome.

It was about three weeks later, as Anton walked into the Bogner's house after playing until late that night on the Krismann organ, when Elise gave him a letter, with a stamp showing it was from Vienna. He ripped it open.

'You'll never believe this, Elise. One of the country's top musicians has granted me a special request. He has organised a panel of three experts to listen to my organ play in an examination.'

'Why has he done that? You are brilliant as an organist, Anton. You don't need any examination!'

'I agree,' said Michael, who heard the excitement and came into the hall.
'I wrote to Ignaz Assmeyer to follow up on the meeting I had with him last year. I took a chance and asked if he and his colleagues would assess my organ playing... and he's agreed. I'm so pleased. He will be a member, as well as a Simon Sechter and a Gottfried Preyer, neither of whom I've met.'

'But you are so good, Anton.'

'Yes, maybe. But you need to understand. I'm now a professional organist and teacher, right? But, except for my early examination at the teacher training college, and Anton Kattinger's assessment, I've not taken any high-level examination in organ playing.'

'There are times like this, Anton, when I totally fail to understand you,' said Michael. 'When does this unnecessary assessment take place?'

Anton re-read the letter. 'Not until the ninth of October, so not long to wait. At least it doesn't clash with the instalment of Prior Arneth's successor.'

'What is happening at the instalment?' said Michael.

'I've written a new work, a *Missa Solemnis*, especially for it.'

'I hope I'm invited!'

Anton and Jodok Stülz, the deputy provost, planned the inauguration ceremony for Friedrich Mayer. It would take place in the Basilica. The main work to be performed would be Anton's *Missa Solemnis*. They would also perform his *Magnificat*. After the service, which Jodok would lead, there would be a banquet, held in the main dining hall of the Monastery. Anton would play the organ and would ask Petrus Schärschmidt to be the conductor.

With everything in place and two successful rehearsals completed, the inauguration would begin. Anton, as usual, felt nervous beforehand. However, between them, Jodok, Petrus, the orchestra and choir did exceptionally well.

'I regard it as a great honour that you wrote your *Missa Solemnis* especially for my enthronement, Herr Bruckner. It is a magnificent piece of composition,' said Friedrich Mayer. 'There are many musicians in Vienna who would love to know about it. Do you know Simon Sechter there?'

'No, but strange you mention him. I am going to Vienna in a few weeks' time. I'll be seeing him then.' He had no intention of telling Mayer about the actual reason for his forthcoming visit.

'Show him the score! And thank you for all your work here as Organist and teacher. I'm sure we will continue to get on well.'

Anton walked to the main dining room in the Monastery, along with many others who had attended the inauguration ceremony. He was about to walk in when a friar held out his hand in front of him.

'Excuse me, Herr Bruckner. I don't see your name on the list of invitees. Do you have an invitation?'

'No, not an actual document. But I've assumed all along I could attend, official invitation or not.'

'I'm sorry, Herr Bruckner, but the banquet is strictly for the ecclesiastical staff here and their guests. So I have to ask you to go.'

Anton's face dropped. He could feel the pain. If he couldn't attend the banquet, he'd go to the Sparrow Inn and celebrate on his own.

He stepped up to the bar and picked up the menu, which was written in chalk on a black tablet.

'What would you like, mein Herr?' said the pretty barmaid, who had served him before.

'I'm here to celebrate a certain event which was held at the Basilica, just half an hour ago.'

'Not the enthronement of the new provost?'

'Exactly that.'

'What would you like?'

'I'll have a five course meal today with a bottle of your best red wine and a bottle of Alsace white. I'll start with the asparagus tart, then I'll have the lemon sole followed by the smoked ham, semolina dumplings and cabbage. Then I'll have a beef schnitzel. I'll finish with an apple strudel and a large pot of your best coffee. Are they all still available?'

'Of course, mein Herr.'

'I'll take a beer to the booth while I wait for my first course!'

'Certainly,' she said as she took a half stein glass from the shelf.

Anton took his drink to where he was to sit. He still couldn't understand why they hadn't asked him to the banquet. Was it something he'd said or done? His relationship with Jodok was excellent, so he could have invited him. The wretched experience increased his sense of disillusionment with St Florian. It became worse as he sat there. Somehow, it gave greater purpose to his assessment by Assmeyer and his colleagues. He would need a testimonial from top professionals if he was to seek work elsewhere.

'Here you are, mein Herr, the asparagus course. I hope you like it. Which wine would you like first, the red?'

'No, the white, please.'

Anton gradually ate and drank his way through this colossal meal. As he was enjoying the apple strudel, he felt a tap on the shoulder.

'Hello! I know you, mate,' said an older gentleman, with a stained tri-corn hat. 'Remember me? We met here some time ago, and you bought me a beer. I once gave you a lift to Ebelsberg.'

'Yes, I remember you!' Anton welcomed some company, having sat there alone for several hours.

'You had one of your pals here last time. It's not good to be drinking alone,' he said.

'Go on, buy yourself a beer.' He gave the man a two kreuzer piece.

He brought the beer back and sat in the same booth opposite Anton. 'So why are you on your own?'

Anton explained.

'The bastards! You did all that for the fuckers and they ignored you. Those priests can be arrogant shits.'

'You could be right,' he said, not actually agreeing. 'So I came here to celebrate on my own. That Mass deserves it!'

'Good for you!' The two of them clinked their glasses together.

***

Anton enjoyed the train journey to Vienna. He went straight from the station to book a hotel for the night and then to the Court Chapel in the Imperial Palace. He arrived just in time.

'I'm glad we could agree to your request, Herr Bruckner,' said Ignaz Assmeyer. 'We will test you here on the Chapel organ. First, let me introduce you to Gottfried von Preyer. He is the former Director of the Vienna Conservatory and still Professor of Harmony and Composition. This is Simon Sechter. Simon is one of the world's most prolific composers. He is a teacher of music theory and composition at the Conservatory and taught Schubert for a time.'

'I'm pleased to meet you, Herr Bruckner,' said Sechter. He was clean shaven, wore glasses with small lenses, and a medal on his jacket.

'Likewise,' said von Preyer, who wore similar spectacles and was also clean shaven but had a rapidly receding hairline.

Anton felt unusually confident as he sat at the organ bench to play the pieces which the three had given him. As usual, he took his time in reading the scores before he started. His instructions were to play the pieces, as written, and then improvise, as freely as he wanted.

The three of them sat in quite different places. Assmeyer sat the back of the Chapel, von Preyer in about the tenth row from the front, on the left, and Sechter about halfway back, on the right. Anton enjoyed playing and could have carried on for longer, but stopped after about fifty minutes. The three listeners gathered at the front and beckoned Anton towards them.

'That was utterly brilliant,' said Assmeyer. 'I've never heard our organ played so well!'

'I totally agree,' said von Preyer.

'It was stunning,' said Sechter. 'You should examine me!'

'That double fugue you improvised on the Bach was extraordinary. Not many organ players in the world could do better,' said Assmeyer.

'You are good enough to teach organ play at Conservatory level,' said von Preyer. 'We should create a post here for you!'

'I'm delighted you all liked my performance. I have to say I loved to play for you. It gave me as much pleasure as I hope I gave you.'

'Good,' said Assmeyer. 'We have a document prepared to take with you. It is a testimonial and we will each comment on it and sign it. Please wait here.'

A few moments later, Assmeyer emerged with a rolled document. 'Here it is, Herr Bruckner. Congratulations. You passed with distinction and honours. Keep up the good work. We wish you every success.'

'Many thanks, Herr Assmeyer. I am pleased and delighted. You are very high in my estimation, and I fully appreciate all you have done for me.'

'Let me know if you need me again. Have a safe ride home.'

Anton had not felt so happy for a long time. His plan, conceived after the passing of Johann Weiss, was coming to fruition. How could he become a full-time musician and leave the teaching behind him?

Chapter 11
1854 - 1855 A Change

'How did that pointless examination go?' said Michael Bogner, as the four of them, Anton, Michael, Elise, and Louise were having dinner.

'It wasn't as pointless as you make out, Michael,' said Anton, smiling broadly. 'The most significant musicians in Austria, if not the whole of Europe, examined me.' He told him their names and professions.

'I've only heard of Assmeyer. Is he the one who visited us some years ago?'

'Yes, that's the one.'

'I didn't like him much.'

'I won't criticise him. They each gave me a distinction and honours for my organ play.'

'I still don't understand how useful that could be.'

'The diploma is signed by all three, so if I applied for a job elsewhere, I could show them the diploma. It's a professional qualification. And a rarity at that! No other organist in the whole of Europe will have anything approaching it. So it sets me above all others, at least in writing!'

'Do you know, Anton? I now understand you!' Michael smiled.

'So do I,' said Elise.

'I'm still not sure,' said Louise. Her response didn't surprise him.

'But I'm not yet ready to give up teaching, Michael. I'm off to Linz in a few days to take my exams to qualify me as a high school teacher.'

'So you may remain a teacher?' said Elise.

'I'm a teacher now, and who knows what my future has in store?'

'What subjects are you to be tested in?' said Louise.

'Latin, physics, geography and mathematics plus anything else they want to examine me in.'

'Which have you studied?' said Elise.

'Latin and physics, on a correspondence course.'

***

Anton arrived in Linz the day before the two days of examinations took place. He hadn't booked a place to stay in advance, so thought he would try Irene Planck.

'It must be ten years since I saw you last, Anton. What brings you here this time?'

'Another examination. This time to be qualified as a high school teacher. Could I stay with you for two nights, please?'

'As I've said before, I'd give you my bed if I had no rooms. But I have one you can take. And we'll have dinner together, if you'd like that.'

'I'd love it!'

It was late in the day, so Irene went to her kitchen to prepare the meal. Anton followed.

'Last time I was here you had been punched by some angry student. You were badly bruised. You said you reported it to the constabulary. Did they catch him?'

'Yes! They charged him and took him to court. Luckily, a neighbour saw him, so was an independent witness. The judge sentenced him to two years in prison and six lashes.'

'What an excellent result. I'm pleased for you!'

'And you, Anton? The last time we met, you took some exams to qualify you for senior school. You went home to wait for the certificates. I assume you got them?'

'Yes, two rolled up in a cardboard tube! They gave me good results, I'm glad to say!'

'Well done, young man! So what have you done since then?'

Anton told her his tale in some detail, from leaving Kronstorf to getting the teaching job at St Florian, being promoted to Organist, and listed many of the works he composed. He didn't tell her about his failed love affairs to avoid any embarrassment.

'You have been fully occupied. So you want to be a composer then?'

'That's my plan. I've tried legal work, was turned down for the civil service, so have abandoned looking at other options.'

'So why do you want more qualifications in teaching?'

'It's a kind of insurance. If you are in a job, there is no guarantee that you will find a better one. So you get the best qualifications you can for the profession you are in.'

'That all makes sense to me. So, what is the best piece of music you've written so far?' she said, wanting to change the subject.

'Interesting question. I think my *Missa Solemnis* is my best, followed by the *Requiem Mass*. I've written so many pieces, some only half a minute long!'

'You keep composing, Anton. You could push Beethoven off his perch if you carry on!'

'You are joking!'

The examinations were just as challenging as Anton expected. The most difficult was the physics exam. First, he had to work out the efficiency of a heat engine. Once he had thought through the system of units, he completed it. He then had to apply the simple lens law to designing a telescope. He found that quite easy, as he had carried out a similar calculation before. Then he had to work out a resistance in Ohms from measurements on a Wheatstone bridge, a device invented in London not long before. He struggled a little until he could remember the exact circuitry and the balancing condition.

He then sat the examination in Latin. He had to translate a passage from Latin into German, another from German into Latin and to write an essay in Latin on ancient transport.

After lunch, he returned to complete some tests of his mathematical skills. These included solving some quadratic and simultaneous equations. Then some trigonometry and algebra. He found the algebra more difficult, but succeeded just inside the allotted time.

Having finished for the day, he returned to Irene exhausted.

'You look tired,' she said.

'I am. My brain has turned into beetroot soup. I'm looking forward to tomorrow lunchtime when the exams are over. I don't care if I never take another one again, in whatever subject.'

She hugged him tightly and kissed him on the cheek. 'There,' she said. 'Just a little affection to make you feel better.'

Her reaction surprised him. She must have been at least fifteen years older than him, almost old enough to be his mother. Surely, she didn't want a relationship with him. Nor did he want anything other than friendship with her. He far preferred women younger than himself, even though his attempts to attract one had come to nothing, at least up to then.

'Oh! Thank you, Irene. You are kind! You took me by surprise!'

His exams resumed at 9 o'clock the following morning. He felt he had completed the geography examinations successfully. But he was less sure about the human biology, and an essay they set on modern teaching methods. The examiner told him he would receive the results by post, hopefully within a month. He could only wait and see.

He went back to number 37 to collect his things, and say goodbye to Irene.

'I don't know when I'll see you again, Irene. Thank you for looking after me so nicely. I'll make a point of dropping in when I'm next in Linz, if only to say hello.'

'I'll welcome you, Anton.' She kissed him on the cheek.

He took a cabriolet back to St Florian.

'So did you pass them all?' asked Elise, as he walked into the lounge.

'I honestly don't know. They said they'd tell me the results in a month, so I'll find out soon enough. The Latin, the physics and the mathematics seemed alright, but I was less sure about the human biology and an essay I had to write. I'm not good at essays.'

'You've probably done well,' she said, reassuringly.

***

His work at St Florian continued at its usual hectic pace. The children in his infants' class loved the way he taught, and his friendly attitude towards them. Their parents often complimented him on his way of dealing with them. There was no doubt in his mind that, if he stopped being a teacher, he would miss them. These thoughts were passing through his mind during a lunch break when he heard a knock on his classroom door.

'Please enter!'

It was Provost Mayer. 'Good afternoon, Anton. I want to discuss something with you. Do you have a moment?'

'I do, Friedrich.' He felt sufficiently senior to use his first name. Mayer didn't raise an eyebrow.

'I'm speaking to you in your capacity of Organist. Do you know of a composer... and organist... called Robert Führer?'

'Vaguely. Somewhat controversial, I believe.'

'Yes. He once sold a Stradivarius which wasn't his. But that crime is long forgotten, it seems, and he's one of the most popular composers in Germany and Bavaria.'

'So what are you saying, Friedrich?'

'He has written to me to invite himself here to hold a recital in the Basilica. He wants paying for it.'

'If he's that popular, we could charge a ticket price and make more than we paid him. I hope he doesn't want an orchestra as well.'

'That's what I was hoping. No, he only wants to play solo but you could, if you wanted to, play one of the other organs in a duet or play before or after him on the Krismann.'

'That sounds fine to me. Let's sort out a programme with him when he arrives.'

'Good. I'll write to him. Bye for now.'

Anton vaguely remembered, or thought he did, that Führer was the composer who had made some disguising changes to a Schubert mass and claimed it as his own. He wasn't sure, so decided not to mention it to Provost Mayer.

***

'There's a large letter for you, Anton. It came in the post today,' said Louise as Anton came in after a solid day's work.

Anton realised it was probably the certificate with his exam results.

'How did you get on?' said Michael.

'Give me a chance, I'm trying to open it without wrecking the contents! Here we are... Yes, I passed... It says, "Very good" for all except the human biology for which it says, "pass". I'm especially pleased with the physics result! That was a difficult paper, as was the Latin!'

'Good man. And what about the teaching essay?' said Elise. 'That must be important.'

'Yes, I have to say I'm pleased with that, too!'

***

Robert Führer had a better reception than he probably deserved. Provost Mayer and deputy Jodok met him at the monastery's main door. Having refreshed him with drinks and food, they brought him to meet Anton, who was ready for him and waiting in the Basilica by the main organ.

'I'm pleased to meet you, Herr Führer.'

'And I am to meet you, Herr Bruckner. Let's go to first names, shall we? I'm Robert.'

'I'm Anton.'

'So you are a composer, too?'

'Yes, I have composed quite a few works.'

'What's your best?'

'Probably this *Missa Solemnis*.' He passed the score to him.

Führer took his time in reading it. He didn't read the complete score but read some parts in full and skipped through some others.

'Let me play some of the organ line,' said Anton. He played the first two parts, the Kyrie and the three sections of the Gloria. Führer listened intently.

'That verges on being a masterpiece, Anton. It is well up there close to the best Solemnis written. Congratulations!'

'Thank you so much!'

'Let me make a suggestion, Anton. What I think you need is to develop your skills in counterpoint and harmony. You could do worse than having some lessons with Simon Sechter, in Vienna. Do you know him?'

'You're the second person to recommend him to me. Provost Mayer recommended him after we played the *Missa Solemnis* at his inauguration ceremony.'

'We can't both be wrong!'

'I met him a few months ago. He, Ignaz Assmeyer and a Gottfried von Preyer gave me a testimonial confirming my ability as an organist. It's the only advanced qualification I have for organ.'

'You'll have another when I can find a piece of manuscript big enough to write it on!'

'That is kind of you. Thank you!'

It didn't take the two of them long to devise a programme. Anton took great care in avoiding the use of an orchestra or a choir. He made one minor concession in that he would play the Bach Toccata and Fugue in D minor but add parts for three trombones.

'You can't mutilate a piece by Bach!'

'It's not mutilation! It's making it different. So I will play my *Prelude and Fugue for Organ* as the audience enter. I'll then introduce you. You can play whatever you like, but you should decide before we print the programmes and fly sheets. Then we'll finish with the Bach. Does that sound alright?'

'Frankly, no. In what you propose, they would leave remembering your corrupted Bach. I want them to leave with my work in their heads.'

'That will be fine, Robert. You are the guest, after all!'

Führer didn't want to rehearse his work because he claimed to know it so well. But Anton decided on two rehearsals for his modified Bach. The three trombone players were delighted with the idea. It took him a couple of evenings to write the parts into Bach's score and three days for the copyists to produce the new sheet music for the trombonists. Because he was giving the trombone even more prominence, the players committed to playing as well as they could, and each performed brilliantly in the rehearsals.

Anton was staggered at the number of people who came. While the posters advertising it had only been put on walls and in shop windows in St Florian, many arrived from towns and villages from tens of kilometres away, as he could judge from the number of carriages, with their horses still tethered, parked outside the Basilica.

After Anton finished playing his *Toccata and Fugue for organ*, Jodok Stülz introduced Führer who introduced Anton. He and the three trombonists then played the modified Bach Toccata and Fugue. A satisfying round of applause greeted its ending. Anton then introduced Robert Führer, who started to play the Mass he had written and transcribed to an organ solo. Something went drastically wrong. To Anton, it sounded terrible. Wrong notes sounded, as did mistaken rhythm changes. But Führer continued as if everything was perfect. A trombonist looked at Anton with eyes wide open and his arm outstretched. Another looked over with raised eyebrows. Members of the audience spoke to each other, wondering what was happening. Many left the Basilica while Führer played on. By the time he'd finished, half the audience had gone. He stood up from the organ bench and bowed. Fewer than a dozen applauded. Anton thought they must be deaf.

After the rest of the audience had gone, Anton, Führer, and Jodok met in a side chapel.

'So what went wrong?' said Jodok.

'What do you mean?' said Führer.

'They loved Anton's modified Bach, but when you took over, half the audience left.'

'Really?' said Führer.

'Afraid so,' said Anton. 'You played dozens of wrong notes and lost your place several times. Didn't you realise?'

He still couldn't admit to making any errors. 'In that case, there's something wrong with your organ.'

'Or your ears,' said Jodok. 'We've got the best tuner in Upper Austria, so there's nothing wrong with the organ. It was you.'

'It was your choice not to rehearse,' said Anton. 'Bit of a mistake.'

'You are too polite, Anton,' said Jodok. 'It was a fucking stupid mistake! Only an idiot could make it!'

Anton had never heard a priest use such shocking language. 'Let's disperse shall we. I can't see much good coming from further discussion,' he said, trying to calm the situation.

'I've never been treated so badly in my career,' said Führer. 'Here's that document I promised. He handed Anton a rolled up manuscript. 'I'm packing my bags and going!' He turned and sped from the chapel.

'I'm glad to see the back of the man,' said Jodok. 'He let us all down. When one performer does a poor job, it reflects on the entire ensemble.'

'You have a point there, Jodok.'

Führer was never seen in St Florian again.

***

Anton wanted to take up the suggestion to seek lessons from Simon Sechter, so he wrote to ask for a meeting.

'Another letter from Vienna, Anton.'

'Really?' he said, as he took it from Louise. He opened it and quickly scanned it. 'Excellent!'

'Not another examination, Anton,' said Michael.

'No! Another course in composing. It will probably be a correspondence course with a brilliant teacher there… if he'll take me on!'

'But you are a brilliant composer, Anton. You don't need lessons!' said Elise.

'I do. There are aspects of composing I need to improve on and that's what it's about.'

Anton had no difficulty locating the Vienna Conservatory. Its wide, orangey, sand coloured façade, of perfect symmetry, compelled him to stop abruptly and admire this striking piece of neoclassical architecture. A lady at the reception desk instructed him on locating Sechter's office. He knocked on the door.

'It is such a pleasure to see you again, Anton!' said Sechter, as he opened it. 'Come in and sit down. I'm completely baffled. What can I do for you this time?'

'Several people have recommended that I enrol for your course of study in counterpoint and harmony.'

'Really? May I ask who?'

'The new provost at St Florian, Friedrich Mayer, and the well-known composer, Robert Führer.'

'He's well known for several things,' he said, not wishing to elaborate.

'I've brought a few references and the score of the *Missa Solemnis* I wrote about a year ago. It was first performed at Provost Mayer's installation.'

'I'm less interested in the references because we've met before and I know you well enough, but give me the *Missa*.'

He sat at his desk and read it. 'So it's for a string orchestra, trombones, a horn, soloists, choir and organ... You go straight in with the choir. What a good start. Good transition from the tenor in the Gloria and change of tempo. Very emphatic Credo. Nice double fugue...' and so he commented, as if he was actually listening to it being played. 'What a superb work. It has a confident, thrusting feel about it. I like it. Yes, I'll take you on as a correspondence pupil, Anton. Would that work for you?'

'Wonderful. I'm so grateful, Simon. I must pay you. What is your rate?'

'Nothing. You are so promising, I won't charge. But I'll give you some advice.'

'That is kind. What are you advising?'

'You'd be a better musician if you concentrated on music, your organ playing and composing. You need to stop being a schoolteacher. So my advice is for you to leave St Florian and get a job as a musician elsewhere.'

Anton's face dropped.

'Don't look so miserable. It's only advice. You don't have to take it!'

After thinking for a few moments, and while still doubtful, Anton could see some merit in this suggestion. It fitted well with his plan conceived at what he called the crossroads.

'I'll think about it. I have a good job at St Florian... but, as you say, there is much teaching there and my plan is to leave the school behind. So, how will the lessons start and when?'

'I'll give you some exercises now.' He stood, took a couple of steps to a filing cabinet, and opened it. Then he located a file from which he removed some sheets of paper. 'Here you are. Some exercises you can take with you. Complete them in your own time and post them back to me. Oh, and take this book on counterpoint and harmony.'

141

While on the train back, Anton thought about what Sechter had said. He decided he would apply for some other jobs, especially if they didn't involve teaching a class of children. He showed little interest in local news or politics, but, because he wanted to look at alternative posts, he subscribed to a local newspaper. Within a few weeks of reading only the advertisements, he spotted one for a cathedral organist in St Wenceslas Cathedral in Olmütz, Bohemia. So he applied for it. He waited weeks for a response and felt quite guilty that he'd applied without informing Provost Mayer.

A week or so later, while Anton was practicing on the Krismann, Mayer came to see him. 'I want to ask you something, Anton. You haven't been looking very happy of late. Is something troubling you?'

'I don't think so. I've just started a correspondence course in harmony and counterpoint with a well-known teacher in Vienna. I'm busy teaching but, I'm not doing any composing at the moment, because my teacher there has told me not to do any.'

'That's an odd thing to ask. It's a bit like teaching mathematics and telling your pupils they mustn't do any algebra.'

'I know, but I must do as instructed.'

'I'm still not happy with your answer, Anton. You have avoided my question. By the way, we haven't been working together very long, but we are getting along nicely. You are a good colleague as well.'

'Now you are making me feel guilty and I have a confession to make.'

'Really?'

'Yes, I've applied for another post. That of organist at the cathedral in Olmütz.'

'What! You've applied for a job working for the Czechs? Have you ever heard that a Czech has done something good for us Germans? And you have done it without my knowledge. I'm furious with you, Herr Bruckner.' Unlike Jodok Stülz, thunder at him he might, but at least he didn't swear.

'I'm not sure what to say, Provost Mayer. I'm lucky to have such a good job here. But I cannot guarantee a life of service in St Florian. But I will keep you better informed in future.'

'That's all I can ask, Tonerl.'

'Thank you, Friedrich. The more I think about it, I'd be surprised if they saw me.' He was right: he'd wasted his time.

According to his plan, Anton had to escape from classroom teaching. While still contemplating a new position, Wenzel Pranghofer, the organist at Linz Cathedral died. Anton knew they had advertised the post and the examination date of 13 November. He decided not to apply for fear of causing another upset with Provost Mayer.

'I didn't expect to see you here today, Anton?' said the St Florian organ and piano tuner the morning of the exam.

'Why not?'

'Don't you know the tests are being held today for Wenzel Pranghofer's job?'

'I do.'

'Why haven't you applied? You are the best organist in the country!'

'I have an excellent, highly prestigious post here.'

'Not as prestigious as Organist at Linz Cathedral!'

'Now you've raised my curiosity... but only my curiosity. I'll go to Linz, if only to see what's happening!'

He took a cabriolet to the Cathedral in Linz. On the way, his head swam with thoughts. Perhaps he should have applied and told Provost Mayer his intention. He still didn't know how to approach this without offending the provost. So he'd head to see August Dürrnberger first.

'Driver, I've changed my mind,' he shouted. 'Please, take me to the Teacher Training College.'

'Will do, mein Herr!'

'Anton, it's so good to see you. So you are here to compete for the organist post?' said August, as Anton walked into his office.

'No, not at all!'

'Why ever not?'

'How can I? I haven't told them anything about it at St Florian... and what do you think they would say if I applied for the post behind their backs?'

'I see what you mean. But let's go to the Cathedral. I'm on the selection panel. There's nothing to stop you from listening in!'

They walked the short distance to the Cathedral and entered.

'I know him,' said Anton, nodding towards the two candidates who were waiting to perform.

'Which one?'

'The one on the left. It's Engelbert Lanz, a teacher and composer who lives here. He visit's St Florian occasionally to stand in as a teacher. I'm quite a good friend of his.'

'I think I know the other candidate, Anton. He is Raimund Hain, an assistant teacher who lives in Linz. Like you, I taught him. There are only two being examined, it seems.'

Anton sat in the pews as August joined the five other examiners. He listened intently as Lanz attempted to improvise on a theme and play a fugue. The man played moderately well, but to Anton produced a short, mediocre fugue.

Hain then took to the organ loft and began playing the same piece. From the poor job he did, it was barely identifiable. He then spoke, half way through his attempt at the fugue. 'I'm not very good at improvising, so I'll stop there.' He stepped down.

Anton could see the reaction of the examiners. They bent themselves forward and mumbled along the line to each other. It sounded like a combination of compliments and derogatory remarks.

August stood and came back to Anton, who appeared, at that moment, to be in prayer. He tapped him on the shoulder. 'Get up there and play, Anton. Go on. Now!'

After a momentary pause, Anton stood, walked up to the organ loft, and began. He started by playing the theme, exactly as intended. Then he improvised, simply at first, then with greater and increasing complexity. He concluded with one of the most grandiose fugues he'd ever conceived.

Every member of the examining board, except two, applauded. August smiled and clapped vigorously. So did other people who were in the Cathedral and who had come to pray or to listen to this public examination. Someone shouted, 'Bravo'. Another, 'Encore'. It was as if Anton had just completed an organ recital.

He stood and walked back to the pews. Engelbert Lanz came over to congratulate him. 'What a superb performance, Anton. You've killed off the opposition. Well done!' He shook hands with Anton and left along with Raimund Hain, who said nothing but turned and smiled at Anton.

Anton stayed where he was and could hear some heated discussion by the board. They mentioned him several times, and the names of the other two candidates. A priest, whom Anton didn't recognise, mentioned Engelbert as if he favoured him. So did one of the other four members. Their decision was yet to emerge. Discussion continued. Anton wondered if it would ever end. Then August seemed to make an important point to which they all agreed. The church official then said the word 'decision.' He then led August back to Anton.

'My name is Johann Schiedermayr. I'm the canon at Linz Cathedral. Congratulations, the job is yours if you'd like it, Herr Bruckner,' he said with a broad smile.

Anton thought for a moment before he spoke. 'Thank you so much, Canon. Can I accept it provisionally? I need to settle certain issues before I can give you a final decision.'

'Let me explain. The decision we have made is provisional. If you take the job, we will re-test you again in January. Although I cannot guarantee your success then, I cannot see how anyone in Upper Austria could improve on the performance you gave us today. So in effect, we are both taking it you will accept provisionally. It's for you to decide if this is the job you really want. And for us to decide if you are the best candidate for permanent appointment.'

Anton thought for a moment. 'I'm happy with that.'

'Good. We agree, then. You are officially in post from tomorrow. I can accept some delay, especially as you live in St Florian. But please may we meet here as soon as you are available? There is much we need to discuss.'

'Of course.' The canon and Anton shook hands on their deal.

August and Anton walked back to the College together. 'What a fantastic result, Anton.'

He was almost in tears. 'I owe it to you, August. I'd never have gone to the organ loft if you hadn't insisted! So I owe you a huge thank you.'

'Don't even think of it. We must spend more time together when you are back in Linz!'

'Need I ask what the discussion with the board was about?'

'No. It shouldn't concern you at all. By the way, you must make a friend of Bishop Rudigier, as well as the canon. The bishop could be your best ally, apart from me, of course!'

While it was provisional, the post fitted perfectly with his long-term plan to escape from school teaching. He didn't want to cause any problems at St Florian, which he held close to his heart. In the cabriolet, on the way back, he decided to see the provost as soon as he arrived.

With great trepidation, Anton confessed that he had taken part in the competition and that they offered him the post.

The provost patted him on the back. 'That is a different matter and I don't, for one moment, blame you!' he said. 'I could not possibly hold you back from such an improvement in your position. Go to Linz and go with God's and my blessing!'

'Thank you, Friedrich. You are so understanding. Canon Schiedermayr wants me to start as soon as possible.' Anton explained the terms he had agreed with the canon.

'You will win the second set of tests, Anton, the way you play. But let's not worry about that until January. Go now to Linz and start working there. Do exactly what he wants. For now, you can stay in the Florianerhaus in the Landstrasse, which we own. They will cater well for you there. Don't worry about your job here. I shall do nothing about finding your successor until they offer you the job permanently. Good luck.'

145

***

'Oh, we will miss you,' said Elise at dinner that night.

'I can only wish you well, Anton. It's a big step up for you. You have been a brilliant teacher here and I will find it difficult to replace you. And that will also apply to the post of Organist. I imagine Provost Mayer is furious!'

'Not true, Michael. He is really supportive. He told me to go with God's and his blessing.'

'Well, he's gone up in my estimation. Good for him!'

'So I'm afraid I will leave, if only temporarily.'

'You can come and go from here, as you please. As long as we know what you are doing!' said Michael.

'I shall go to see the canon in a few days. He will tell me more. But with Advent just around the corner, I can't see I'll be playing the organ much until the Feast of the Immaculate Conception. Then again, on the twenty-third of December. And start again after Christmas.'

'You'll need to find somewhere to stay in the city. Use a hotel, or at least somewhere where you don't have to prepare your own food,' said Elise.

'Don't worry, the provost is allowing me to use the Florianerhaus in Landstrasse. Apparently, the food is good there. I imagine it will be a little basic! I'm busy here for a few days, but I'll let you know when I'm going.'

'Good luck, Anton,' said Michael.

***

Having dealt with his immediate commitments at St Florian, he packed sufficient items for his time in Linz. The following morning, he took a cabriolet to the Cathedral but went via Ebelsberg.

'What are you doing here, Tonerl? We weren't expecting you today,' said Ignaz, as Anton entered the house.

'I had to call in to tell you my news.'

'Tonerl, it's you. What a lovely surprise!' said his mother.

'I've called in on my way to Linz, Mama, with some news. I can't stop for long. There's a cab waiting for me outside!'

'Come on, out with it!' said Josefa.

'I'm leaving my teaching and organ work in St Florian to become the Organist at Linz Cathedral. I'm on my way there now.'

'You must be insane,' said his mother. 'You have a lovely job at St Florian and you are good at it as well as being popular. And the money is good. Come to think of it, I'm cross with you because you never told me you were applying for it.'

'Let me quickly explain, Mama.' He briefly summarised what happened and what was going to happen, stressing that he hadn't actually applied.

'That's different, Tonerl. I couldn't expect you to tell me before you went to see what was happening. So congratulations! What are your chances of the job becoming permanent?'

'It depends who applies. If it's just the two who lost to me, I should win again, but if someone very good applies… you never know.'

'Everyone I speak to reckons you are the best organist in Austria so you'll get it, my son. Don't you worry! Off you go now. Don't keep the cabriolet waiting any longer!'

***

'It is good to see you again, Herr Bruckner.'

'Likewise, Canon Schiedermayr.'

'There are several things you need to know about, besides what I told you when we offered you the job. The first is we need to swear you in. I shall organise that for later. Second, you must apply for the permanent post. Your application has to be submitted by the end of December. Third, we must introduce you to your new colleagues. That means a visit to the parish church to meet the priest. I'm not sure if I told you this, but you will also be organist at his church.'

'No, but that will make life interesting!'

'We don't expect you to be in two places at once! You will need a deputy. Between us, we'll arrange that. So, do you have any questions?'

'Just one. Can't you just assume, by the fact I shall be in post here that I have by default already applied?'

'I would like to agree, but the system doesn't work like that.'

'I see,' he said, slightly raising his eyebrows.

'Let's begin by taking you to the parish church.'

The two of them walked the short distance to the church. Its beauty touched Anton. Its white baroque tower proudly dominated the whole building, as if it was in control of the entire structure, which shone in the welcoming sun. They met the parish priest in the transept. Canon Schiedermayr introduced them.

'I am pleased to meet you, Herr Bruckner. My name is Pieter Prinz. I'm the pastor here. Congratulations on winning the competition for Organist, here and at the Cathedral. I read all about it in the local news. I'm sure we will get on well together. Do come and look at the organ. Play something on it, if you wish.'

'I'd be delighted. I'm sure we will become good friends, especially if my position becomes permanent!'

The three of them walked towards the organ. 'This is a new instrument. It's only been here for three years. Ludwig Mooser designed and built it.'

Anton climbed up to the organ loft. He repeated what he played in the competition. To Anton's perceptive ear, its sound did not match the superb quality of the organ in the Cathedral.

'Brilliant,' said Prinz.

Schiedermayr applauded as Anton stepped down.

'What do you think?'

'I'm not sure how to put this, Pastor Prinz, but there are a couple of issues here.'

'What do you mean?' said Schiedermayr, frowning.

'The manuals and the pedals are in need of repair and the wind flow is not good, so the intonation is not what it should be.'

'I'm shocked,' said Prinz. 'But if it needs attention, then attention it will receive. Would you mind putting your findings in writing to the parish council?'

'Not at all.'

'That wasn't the best start,' said Schiedermayr, as they walked back to the Cathedral.

'What do you mean?'

'You are only the Provisional Organist, and you should have kept your critical comments to yourself, at least until, and if, you are appointed permanently.'

'I'm sorry, but I don't want to be playing a faulty organ. So the sooner they put it right, the better,' said Anton, sounding firm and convincing. They walked the remainder in silence, which was broken only at the Cathedral.

'I want you to attend a swearing in ceremony tomorrow,' said Schiedermayr.

'I haven't brought a suit or anything like that.'

'Don't worry. Come as you are. Then your next task will be to play on Saint Mary's Day. You are then free until the twenty-third of December. But send in that application or one of the other applicants will step into your shoes. You've got until the end of December.'

Anton felt awkward attending the swearing in ceremony in an old overcoat with a button missing and in his galoshes. But 'come as you are' was the instruction. A priest told him to put his hand on the bible and say, 'I do' after he had read a statement. This obliged him 'to act with propriety at all times, to be conscientious in his duties, to maintain his good reputation, and that of the church.'

Saint Mary's Day soon came around. Many of the congregation approached Schiedermayr to praise Anton's playing of the Mass. They clearly recognised Anton's talents and his position as the new Organist. They left Schiedermayr in no doubt that they wanted him confirmed in the post. Schiedermayr seemed less sure.

Chapter 12
1854 - 1855 A Competition

Anton procrastinated over submitting his application. He had no intention of satisfying those who persisted in pushing him to apply and saw advantage in applying late. By then, he was back in St Florian, carrying out some residual duties, practicing his organ playing, and working on the examples Sechter had given him.

'Have you sent off your application yet, Anton?' said Provost Mayer, as they met in the Basilica.

'Not just yet.'

'Don't you want the job?'

'I do.'

'Good. We will be sorry to see you go. Could we have some sort of celebration? Maybe, you could write a farewell piece we could play in the Basilica. I'm glad you haven't yet applied.'

'Really?'

'Yes, to help you, Jodok and Franz Schäffler's replacement, Ignaz Traumihler, have written you testimonials which we'd like you to include. Here they are, if you'd like to read them.'

Anton felt quite emotional as he read the boundless praise they heaped upon him.

'I can't send these, Friedrich.'

'Why in heaven's name not?'

'They exaggerate my worth and ability.'

'Sometimes you make me angry, Anton. They reflect only the truth as they both see it. Jodok, Ignaz and I will be furious if you don't send them, exactly as written.'

'Sorry, Friedrich. I didn't mean to offend anyone. I will send them. While we are speaking, may I ask you a favour?'

'Go ahead. Anton.'

'As you know, even though the post is permanent, I don't know whether they will accept me on that basis. I know I am a good organist. But I already detect some opposition there. If they dismissed me, it could only be because of the politics.' He told him about the exchanges over the organ at the parish church. 'So, I wondered if you would, please, keep my job open here, in case I want to return.'

'Yes, Anton. We will fill it temporarily, probably with someone already here. Let's say for two years. Is that alright?'

'Excellent, Friedrich. More than I was hoping for.'

As he walked into the Bogners' house, Louise handed him two letters, both postmarked Linz. He opened them quickly. They each complained about the clothes he wore for the swearing in ceremony. One said that if he passed the next examination, he should respect the occasion. This would be by not wearing an untidy overcoat with a button missing, nor overshoes and a scarf. The second letter made the same points but was more strongly worded. He didn't recognise the names of the senders, but kept them. Becoming a little anxious about the competition, he applied with the two references. He also sent a letter to the parish council about the unacceptable condition of the church organ.

They held the competition on 25 January. Anton raised his eyebrows at the sight of the other candidates. He was now one of four, one more than he expected. Raimund Hain, himself, and two others, who were strangers to him. Engelbert Lanz had apparently lost interest. A mixed choir was expectantly sitting in the chancel.

'Who are the others?' he asked August, as they waited for the competition to begin.

'I have their details in these notes. One is called Georg Müller, a private music teacher from here. I don't know him. The other is Ludwig Paupie, an organist and composer from Wels.'

Unlike the confidence he showed at the first competition, Anton felt edgy. They called Müller up first. He played the theme given to him, but could barely improvise on it. Implicitly refusing to accompany the choir, he stepped down. Not that good, thought Anton.

Then it was Paupie's turn. He rejected the tune given to him and went his own way with a theme he had invented. Accompanying the choir was totally foreign to him. They couldn't anyway accompany a tune they didn't know. His mediocre performance pleased Anton. Hain, to everyone's surprise, took up the tune that Paupie had rejected and at least made its improvisation sound interesting. The choir sang but he failed in his effort to accompany them.

Anton stepped forward anxiously. This all seemed too important to take lightly. His only positive thought was how poorly the others had performed. Sitting on the organ bench had its usual effect. As he played the set theme and improvised, he was in another universe, one of perfect sounds. He performed the choral accompaniment with unsurpassed skill. Like any competent musician facing away from the audience, he could detect their enjoyment of his playing.

A round of applause greeted him as he returned to his place.

A few minutes later, August came and patted him on the back. 'This time there is no contention, Anton. We unanimously agree your success over the others! Congratulations.'

'Once again, I'm grateful to you, August. I'd never have won without your encouragement. Like anyone about to change career, I'm excited and a little nervous, but I think I'll be fine.'

'I'm totally sure you will be. And don't forget who your friends are! Now go back to St Florian to say your goodbyes!'

***

He raced out of the Cathedral and ran into the Domgasse to catch a passing cabriolet. The instruction to the driver was first to stop at Ebelsberg, wait outside his house for about ten minutes, and then go to St Florian.

'Brilliant news, Anton,' said Maria Anna, as Anton blurted out the result. 'Mama is in the kitchen. Tell her!'

His mother smiled. 'I knew you'd win, Tonerl. I told you! So, you must say goodbye to St Florian.'

'Not really, Mama. I won't be working there, but I have such close connections there. And I'll go back for a swim occasionally!'

'You're mad, my son! And we want you to see us whenever you can!'

'Don't worry, Mama. I'll always do that. And I'll be able to improve your lives here by giving you more of what I earn.'

'Have they told you about your pay?'

'Not yet, but I'll soon learn. It will be more than at St Florian, I can assure you. The only thing that worries me is I'll be looking after myself. So I have a question.'

'What's that?'

'Could you come to look after me there? Please! With two women here and a man, they shouldn't need you to attend to them.'

'I'm not moving to Linz, Tonerl. At my age, I could never settle in the city. I couldn't change from village life. So sorry, Tonerl, but no!'

'Don't worry, Mama. I'm sure I can cope! I must go. The cab is waiting outside.'

'Can't you stay for dinner?'

'Sorry, Mama, but no. I have so much to do back at St Florian before I go back to Linz.'

'Understood!'

They parted with affection. He stepped into the cab and arrived at the Bogner's by a quarter to seven.

'Fantastic news, Anton. So you won in the end,' said Michael, pleased to congratulate him.

152

'I knew you would,' said Elise. 'It couldn't have gone to a better person!'

'I can't tell you how pleased I am,' said Anton. 'What made me feel reasonably confident was the others did so badly. I was the only one of the four who played the accompaniment to the choir. The others gave up on it.'

'You have no trouble accompanying other singers, Anton. You've proved that a hundred times over!' said Elise.

***

Canon Schiedermayr wrote to him to confirm the appointment. The letter comprised an official document written in similar terms to the text of the swearing in ceremony. In a separate informal letter, he suggested a meeting at the Cathedral to discuss details which needed settling. Anton took this as an urgent request and travelled there as soon as he could.

While entering, he spoke to a priest who was standing by the impressive front door between the two baroque towers. 'Good afternoon. Could you take me to Canon Schiedermayr's office, please? I have a meeting with him shortly.'

'Hello, mein Herr. I think I vaguely recognise you. Did you come here about fifteen years ago to look at the organ?'

'Yes, I did! I remember you!'

'May I ask why you wish to see the canon?'

'I'm the new Organist here and I start soon.'

'Incredible! You have made a success of yourself!'

'It's early beginnings, but thank you!'

The priest led him in.

'Congratulations, Herr Bruckner,' said Schiedermayr, in a more friendly tone than at their previous encounter. 'We were delighted you submitted yourself to our re-assessment. You were magnificent, I can tell you. You blew away the opposition, as if they were leaves in the wind!'

'Thank you, Canon Schiedermayr. That's kind of you to say.'

'I must tell you more about the post. I will start with a relatively minor issue. We have taken to heart your written comments about the organ at the parish church. They will complete the remedial work by the end of the month. So, on reflection, I'm pleased you made those observations to Pastor Prinz.'

Anton responded with a smile.

'Then there is the question of hours. Obviously, we need you to play at the usual services. We want you to make the Cathedral an attractive place for worship, and for people to attend. We would like you to spend as much time as you wish in practising here, and at the parish church, but mainly here. You can play religious and secular work in whatever proportion comes to mind.'

'That all sounds wonderful to me.'

'Then there is the question of your salary. We will pay you a stipend of five hundred and twenty florins a year. Does that sound alright?'

'That's more than fair. I'm grateful.'

'We would also like to contribute to your accommodation. The diocese owns a property at Pfarrgasse 162, not two hundred metres from here. The apartment on the second floor is vacant. It's clean and tidy, with some nice river views. There is a kitchen, and three other rooms. Would you like to have it?'

'I have a grand piano that I need to find a home for. Would it take my piano?'

'I think so. Bit tricky to get it up the stairs, but yes.'

'Assuming the piano fits then, yes please!'

'We won't charge you for the rooms, of course. Here are the keys. Any questions so far?'

'No questions I can think of at present, but I have a commitment in that I am working on a correspondence course with a teacher in Vienna. That won't affect my work here, but I thought I should make you aware of it.'

'What is the course on?'

'Counterpoint and harmony.'

'You are, from what I've heard, a brilliant composer and organist. Why do you want to be taught more?'

'You exaggerate my ability. I'd like to become an excellent composer, among the best. To do that, I need to improve drastically!'

'I think I understand. At some point, I'd love to hear some of your music. I gather you have written a *Requiem Mass* and a *Missa Solemnis*.'

'I have, indeed.'

'We must play them in the Cathedral!'

Anton wasn't sure whether he should take this as an instruction or simply a suggestion. He would take it as a suggestion, but remember it, if he could.

'I'll move into the Pfarrgasse as soon as I can and start work,' he said with an irresistible smile.

Walking away from the Cathedral, Anton glowed with the early success of his confirmed appointment. He had never worked in a city before and remembered how strange it felt to him when he first stayed there for his teacher training. Having August Dürrnberger as a friend and ally was certain to make his transition from teacher to full-time musician easier. And it was now looking as if he could count on Johann Schiedermayr as an ally. Before going to the Pfarrgasse, he would call on an old friend.

'My God, Anton, what are you doing back here? It was only a few months back you came to sit the high school teacher examination!' said Irene, as she opened the door to him.

'I've something great to tell you, my dear friend. I've been appointed Organist at the Cathedral here!'

'No! I'm stunned, Anton! So after becoming fully qualified to teach at a high school, you drop teaching completely to become a musician! What's happened?' She stepped forward to give him a kiss. Then put her arm out to beckon him in. They sat in the lounge and he told her the full story.

'You were very shrewd in getting the provost to agree not to fill the job permanently until you are settled here. I imagine he wasn't too keen on that.'

'He surprised me. I don't know if he changed career before, but he was very understanding.'

'You look really excited at living and working here. Where will you live and when do you start? I'll have to come to the Cathedral to listen to you play!'

'I am in the post now and they've officially confirmed it. I'm here to sort out the details and then start. I'll be living in the Pfarrgasse... in a house the church owns. Number 162.'

'I still can't get over it! Would you like to stay here, Anton? I'd love it if you did!'

'Sorry, Irene, but I must stay at the place in the Pfarrgasse. They wouldn't like it if I stayed here, even though I'd much prefer to.'

'That's fine, Anton. But we must keep in touch. By the way, I know many people here, and can introduce you to them, so you won't be short of friends. If you would like to eat with me tonight, come back, but by 5 o'clock!'

'You are too good to me, Irene. Must go, but I may be back later!' He kissed her on the cheek, walked the short distance to Pfarrgasse 162, went up to the second floor and entered his apartment. It had an odd musty smell about it, as if the windows needed to be left open. The size of the rooms made him smile as they were certainly large enough to meet his needs. He'd have his piano placed in the room at the back with a view of the Danube. A bare table sat next to the side wall and a couple of chairs were dotted at random in the room, as if someone couldn't decide where they should go. He chuckled audibly as he realised it would be a difficult task for the removals men to lift the piano up the stairs and into the room. Anton swung the windows open to admit fresh air from the direction of the river.

He would sleep in the larger of the two bedrooms. The kitchen was well equipped but the larder was bare. I won't start cooking here today, he thought. I'll take up Irene's offer.

***

'You're back, Anton! I'm delighted. I'll do your favourite dish! Pork, dumplings and cabbage. So what did you think of the apartment?'

155

'I had to open a few windows to let out the fetid smell, but apart from that, I liked it. It is as big as I need. My only doubt is about getting my grand piano up the stairs!'

'The one Herr Sailer left you?'

'Yes. It will be a novel experience for me, cooking my own meals and looking after myself.'

'You can come to me for a meal. I wouldn't charge you!'

'But I would certainly pay you. I could afford it on my huge salary. Five hundred and twenty florins a year and free accommodation.'

'My God, Anton. A fortune. Or I could go to your apartment and help look after you.'

'That is so kind, Irene. But you have students to look after. You have always been a good friend to me, as well as my landlady!'

'Talking about friends, as I said, I will make some introductions for you. I know a couple you must meet. They will love you. They are Moritz von Mayfield and his wife Betty. He is a senior government official. He is well-educated, and definitely a great lover of music. Betty is an accomplished pianist and admired by Clara Schumann, she says, and I believe her. They live just along the road. I'll take you to meet them or bring them to see you at the Cathedral.'

'That's a brilliant idea. At present, and apart from you, I have no friends here, except professional colleagues. Only August Dürrnberger and Canon Schiedermayr.'

'We'll soon make your life here really pleasant!'

'I couldn't wish for a better friend than you, Irene.'

'Don't be silly! What are you doing for breakfast tomorrow?'

'I haven't decided. I'll be going back to St Florian tomorrow. Top of my mind is organising the delivery of my piano, apart from all my other things.'

'Sleep well in your new bed and get back here at about 8 o'clock.'

***

'Please, take care,' said Anton, as the removal men struggled to lift the main body of his piano from the cart. This was the last of his possessions they took into Pfarrgasse 162. 'It's the most valuable thing I have. I'd die if you damaged it.'

'Don't worry, mein Herr. It couldn't be in better hands than ours!'

Anton watched as they turned it on its side and, with two at the back and one at the front, eased it up the two flights of stairs.

'How are we going to get it through this door?' said the one at the front. They all stood on the landing and looked at it.

'Take the door off its hinges. It might just go through then.'

'There's a screwdriver in the cart. Get it, please,' said the one in the front to one of the others.

They soon had Anton's front door standing further along the hall, and the main part of the instrument in the room he had chosen.

'That's it, mein Herr. All done,' said the apparent boss, as they finished reassembling it.

Anton gave them ten kreuzers and told them to have a beer on him.

'Thank you very much. Oh, we've just got to put the door back. Mustn't forget that.'

He then sat on the stool and played a piece on it. It must be a superb piano, he thought. It was in perfect tune. As he finished, he heard a knock on the door.

'Just coming!' he shouted, wondering who it could be.

'Hello. My name is Karl Zappe. I live on the floor below. You are Herr Bruckner?'

'Yes, that's me. Pleased to meet you. Sorry if I made too much sound.'

'We could only just hear you, so I thought I'd come to meet you. It wasn't too much at all. You play the piano as well as you play the organ.'

'Thank you. I presume you also work at the Cathedral.'

'Yes. I was on the panel that examined you at the re-assessment. Many congratulations. The other contestants were nowhere near as good as you! My boss is August Dürrnberger, who is the director of music. I'm his deputy and the director of music at the Linz Theatre.'

'Very interesting! Thank you for appointing me! I know August Dürrnberger well.'

'In that case, we will all be working closely together. Come down to my apartment and meet my family.'

'That would really please me!' He went down with Zappe.

'This is my wife, Nora, and those two terrors are my son and daughter.'

'I'm pleased to meet you all.' Anton was soon sitting in their drawing room playing with their children, whose toys were scattered across the floor, while Nora went to the kitchen to brew a pot of tea.

'That man has got baggy trousers,' said the boy.

'No need to be rude,' snapped Karl.

'He's right. My trousers are very wide. I like them like that. It's just my style,' said Anton, laughing. He knelt on the floor and played with the little boy's toy soldiers. 'Bang, bang,' he said as he held a soldier and pointed its gun towards the boy. The lad laughed and pretended to fire back.

'I was a soldier nearly ten years ago,' he said, standing back up. 'Then they dismissed me for good behaviour!' Karl didn't ask so Anton didn't explain.

157

The little girl had gone to the kitchen with her mother but soon came back. He fell to his knees in front of her and said, 'Jesus, little Fräulein!' The girl ran back to the kitchen crying.

'Sorry about that, Anton. She'll soon become friends with you. Not many of our visitors do what you just did.' He laughed.

'I love little children. I used to teach them and the older ones when I was at St Florian.'

'Would you like to dine with us this evening, Anton? We'd be delighted if you did.'

'Thank you, Nora, but I really need to settle into my apartment. My piano has spent more time there than I have! That is kind of you, though.'

'Another time, perhaps.'

'I'd love that.'

Anton had never had to look after himself like this before. He had to buy food and drink, cook, make his bed, do laundry, keep the place clean, and passably tidy. And that was on top of all his other commitments.

Within a few days, he had settled in. He'd prepare himself an evening meal four days a week, and eat out the other three, either in a local tavern or with friends and neighbours, if invited. The Zappes were a good possibility along with Irene, whom he only had to ask.

Life for him in Linz became hectic. He spent up to five hours a day playing the organ either at the Cathedral, or the parish church. He laboured up to six hours on the material Simon Sechter had given him. And he became popular as a piano teacher.

One afternoon at the Cathedral, he was totally immersed on improvising on a bright sounding theme from a Michael Haydn Mass. He toyed with the theme in so many ways that he must have been playing for at least three quarters of an hour before he stopped. It was only four o'clock in the afternoon, so thought he would play on for a few more hours. But he needed to stretch his legs before starting again, so he climbed down from the organ loft to the nave. As he reached the bottom, a large man wearing a purple cassock with red cuffs stood about five metres away, looking at him strangely.

'Good afternoon, Herr Bruckner. I'm utterly intoxicated by that beautiful piece you have just played. It was absolutely stunning, one of the best pieces I've ever heard.'

Anton recognised the standard dress of a bishop. 'I'm delighted you liked it, Your Grace.'

'I've been here several times while you have been playing, and I very much enjoy listening to you. Your music takes me to places deep in my mind, and I feel nearer to our Creator.'

'No one has said anything like that to me before. If that is the effect, then I am even more pleased.'

'I'm so glad that Johann Schiedermayr has asked you to play a good proportion of secular music. I am quite an enthusiast. I love Mendelssohn's music and Beethoven's, especially his ninth symphony.'

'I've not heard that one, but I have the fourth.' He hesitated to say it didn't impress him, so he didn't.

'I hope you don't mind, but I will come to listen to you whenever you are here and I am free.'

'Of course not, Your Grace. I'm just about to play a piece by J S Bach, if you'd like to stay and I'll be improvising on that too!'

'I have to go now, Herr Bruckner, but I'll be back, certainly within a day or two.'

Anton was pleased that the Bishop enjoyed his music. He seemed a likeable, educated and interesting man. Getting to know him better would be a pleasant challenge. He would think of something that he might do especially for him, such as to write a new composition or to organise a concert at the Cathedral.

**

He soon took a further step to integrate himself into the community. It happened by coincidence, late one afternoon, while he was with Pieter Prinz at the parish church.

'So when would you like us to sing it at your church? We need one or more exact dates,' said a heavily bearded man to Prinz. Anton didn't know what the man was talking about. He turned towards Anton. 'Oh, I recognise you, don't I? I was on your re-assessment panel. I'm Anton Storch. I run the Linz Men's Choir.'

'Not another of my judges!' said Anton, beaming.

'Another?'

'Yes, I've also spoken to Karl Zappe and met his family!'

'Marvellous!' said Storch. 'How are you settling in?'

'Quite well. I've played here and at the Cathedral many times and for many hours! I've never been busier!'

'So, you wouldn't have time to be a member of our choir then?'

'Why not? I love to sing!'

'In that case, please join us. We are rehearsing Handel's Messiah here tomorrow morning. Could you be available? At around ten o'clock?'

'I have to play for morning Mass, but yes. It will be a pleasure.'

'Great to have you in the choir, Anton,' said Pieter Prinz. 'Especially in the Messiah, which doesn't need an organ.'

'I could always improvise an organ part, and sing from the bench! I'll see you tomorrow, then.'

He left Prinz and Storch to agree some dates, presumably to perform the Messiah. Irene had kindly invited him for dinner that night, so headed for her house.

'I've no students at present, so I've invited some guests you must meet, Anton,' she said, after giving him a hug.

'Really? Not the Mayfields?'

'Yes!'

'Good. I've been looking forward to meeting them.'

'So what do you think of the job now you've been in it a month... since the second assessment?'

'I like it, Irene. I wondered how I would react from moving from the cloistered environment of St Florian to working in a busy city like Linz. I'm doing well, I think. And I've made some friends.' He told her about the Zappes, about joining the Linz choir, and how much time he was playing on the organs at the Cathedral and at the parish church.

'You mustn't take on too much. You have your health to think about.'

'Don't worry, Irene. I'm quite strong!'

'I must get started with the meal. We can chat in the kitchen.' Then there was a knock on the door. 'You go, Anton.'

'Good evening. You must be Herr Bruckner,' said a well-dressed gentleman. 'I understand you will dine with us tonight!' A man and woman entered and introduced themselves to Anton.

'Come through. Irene is preparing a meal.' Anton led them into the lounge, where they began to converse.

'So you are a composer and an organist, Anton. I imagine you thought a great deal before leaving St Florian to come here,' said Moritz.

'I did, indeed. But the move fits well into my plans. I really want to do more composing and I'm still studying composition.' He told them about Simon Sechter and his course.

'You must come with us to some concerts,' said Betty. 'There is so much music played in this city. They are playing Beethoven's Ninth here soon. The Linz Choir is singing in it.'

'Goodness!' said Anton. 'I've only just joined it, so I might be performing myself!'

The conversation became wide ranging, the more so when Irene had served up the main course and she could join in. Irene told them how she had met Anton, who spoke of his experiences at the teacher training college and about his family. Moritz explained what he did as a senior civil servant.

160

'I'm not sure if you are aware, but the Government brought into law the Gendarmerie Act in 1850. Before then there was no formal structure for the police. Emperor Franz Joseph was behind it. He appointed one of his top generals from the imperial army to be Inspector General of the Gendarmerie for the whole of Austria. The model the Emperor used was the French one. I'm responsible to the Minister in Vienna for the administration of the act in Linz. I work with the Inspector General's military officer here.'

'What a colossal responsibility, Moritz. I imagine you are extremely busy.'

'Fairly. I have some good people working for me, and that helps.'

Anton told him about his brief time in the military and that he was made a reservist after intensive training.

'You were lucky. Many of our troops were killed in Hungary and in the riots in Vienna,' said Moritz.

'I must admit, I felt let down, but was quite pleased in the end. At least I could get back to my job at St Florian,' he said, smiling. 'And what about you, Betty? Irene tells me you are a good pianist.'

'I do play to a reasonable standard. I've played Clara Schumann's piano concerto at our concert hall. She was present and was thrilled! She said I played it better that she did at its first performance. That was under Mendelssohn with the Gewandhaus Orchestra in Leipzig. I was nearly in tears!'

'I can imagine. I'd love to hear you play it. That's what I've really missed at St Florian. I hardly heard any music there. I must listen to more.'

'We'll soon put that right,' she said.

Chapter 13
1855 - 1861 Linz

Anton travelled by train to Vienna to stay with Simon Sechter. He had already posted several exercise books to him. They met at Vienna West Station.

'It's good to see you, Anton. Did you have a pleasant journey?'

'Yes, fine! I was late this morning, and nearly missed the train, but here I am. It's good to see you, too!'

'Let's go to my apartment. I'm so pleased you can stay. Have you seen much of Vienna?'

'No. I've only been to the Imperial Court Chapel for you and the others to test my organ play. And, of course to the Conservatorium, for you to approve me as one of your pupils!'

'We'll catch a horsecar tram to my place.'

It surprised Anton that Sechter lived in such a modest apartment. It was in a back street, off Kolingasse, near the university. Surely, as a professor, he could afford something larger, with more of a garden, thought Anton. He must have earned a substantial salary, supplemented by fees from teaching.

'Let me show you to your room.'

Anton followed him up the narrow staircase into a tiny room. It had a single bed, a narrow wardrobe and a small washbasin, with a jug of water beside it. 'Unpack your things and then come down for a drink,' he said.

Sechter was pouring two cups of tea as Anton stepped into the kitchen.

'Tell me more about yourself, Simon. All I know is that you are the Professor of Composition at the Conservatory. You are a composer and you give private lessons. And you live here!'

'Correct. I have a wife, who is staying with her mother at the moment. We have a son who lives in his own apartment on the other side of the city. He runs his own business, but, sadly, he's not doing well. I have about twenty students, but you are the most committed, judging by what you've sent me in the post. You may not know that I am a quite prolific composer. I've written over four thousand fugues and write one every day. One of my interests is to apply numbers to music. I've written one piece I call "104 variations on a theme of 104 bars".'

'I'm amazed,' said Anton. I've only written about forty pieces up to now. Only two of any length. What is the significance of the one hundred and four bars? That's one lengthy theme!'

'Yes. I composed it as a numerical challenge, to see if I could make a sensible theme that long!'

'Could you play it to me sometime, just the theme? I wouldn't want you to play the 104 variations. That would be ten thousand, eight hundred and sixteen bars at least!'

'How do you get that?'

'Well, 100 times 104 is 10,400 plus four times 104, which is 416, so 10,816. Easy. That assumes each variation is at least the length of the 104 bar tune, yes?'

'You are more of a numerologist than me, Anton. I've never worked it out before. But it is a gigantic piece of music.'

'It must be. Say two second a bar. That works out at 21,632 seconds, which is 6 hours and 32 seconds.'

'I'm amazed at your numerical skills, Anton. Stunned, in fact.'

'Oh, it's nothing. No skill in that calculation. It is 21600 divided by 3600 which is six; plus thirty-two seconds! I've always been interested in numbers, ever since I studied arithmetic as a child. So what other music have you composed?'

'I've written several operas, one a burlesque called "Ali hitsch-hatsch", many pieces for piano, some waltzes, some songs, and a few masses. Plus other odd works.'

'You are certainly prolific. How do you find the time, along with your teaching at the university and private tuition?'

'It's not difficult. I set specific times during the day for my composing, and I do some every day. Tell me more about your life.'

Anton summarised what he had achieved up to when they last met, about a year before. He explained in greater detail his work at the Linz Cathedral and at the parish church.

'So how do you manage playing two organs?'

'Ah, I have a deputy who is excellent and reliable.'

'You are leading a very interesting life, Anton. Let's go out to eat, and I'll show you around the city.'

They walked to a tavern near the city centre. Simon bought two steins of beer and ordered a ham and cheese sandwich each. Anton felt he needed to reciprocate so bought the second round.

'The beer here is not as good as in Linz,' he said.

'Don't believe you. You can't beat a Vienna Pilsner.'

They soon finished their lunch and started the tour. It surprised Anton that the city was better spaced than Linz, in that there was a large open area between the buildings. Simon took him to where he worked at the Conservatory. Anton remarked on the number of rooms with a piano.

'We use them for teaching composition,' said Simon. 'Students use them for trying out thematic material they have written.'

'Can't they imagine what the tune sounds like in their minds? That's what I do. I have a piano on which I play music I've composed, or others have. I don't sit at a piano and use the keys to write a tune.'

'We use them not as the chief means of composing, but to supplement their mental efforts to compose.'

'I may even try that technique myself. I have a Bösendorfer piano in my apartment in Linz.'

'A Bösendorfer?'

'Yes. Our family friend, Franz Sailer, left it to me when he died. He was a justice official in Linz, who did some voluntary work in the St Florian Monastery.'

'You're lucky. That's one of the best pianos ever made.'

'Yes, I know. I played it after the removals men took it apart, struggled up two flights of stairs with it, and re-assembled it in my flat. It was in perfect tune!'

'Now for a few other sights. I'd like to show you the Piaristenkirche. You'll love it. It's built on similar baroque lines to your cathedral in Linz. There's a superb organ there. Do you know about the Piarists?' said Simon, in the horsecar tram they took from the Conservatory.

'No, I'm not aware of them.'

'Beside their vows of chastity, poverty and obedience, they protect and care for youth. It's an amazing order. They have been so successful in Vienna... and elsewhere. But you will be most interested in the organ there!'

Half an hour later, they were standing in front of the organ, at least as it was. 'It's still being built, Simon. Why bring me to a partly built organ?'

'I'm sorry, Anton. I forgot they hadn't finished building it! What a rarity, to see an incomplete instrument. Don't you think?'

Anton soon overcame his shock at seeing the half built console, and hundreds of pipes laying on the ground. 'It looks as if it will be a magnificent organ... when it's complete!'

'I'll show it to you again when it's finished! You might even want to play it!' They both laughed.

He then took Anton to see the Josefstadt Theatre, only a few hundred metres from the Piaristenkirche, on the corner with the Piaristengasse. 'This was one of the best in Vienna. Beethoven composed a work to play at its opening, The Consecration of the House overture.'

'I didn't know that.'

'He conducted the performance.'

'Incredible!'

They walked back to the apartment. By then, it was late in the evening, so Simon started preparing an evening meal for them. While they were waiting for some potatoes to cook, the two of them conversed in the kitchen.

'Try some of this beer.' Simon turned the tap on a barrel, having placed a stein glass beneath. He handed the frothing stein to Anton, who took a deep draft.

'Exceptionally good. Better than the one we had in that tavern.'

'I'm glad you like it. I'll have one, too.'

They each finished their first beer, and had virtually consumed a second stein, before Simon served the meal of boiled beef, cabbage, dumplings, and potatoes.

'Let me get us another one each,' said Simon, before they were halfway through the meal. 'There's plenty left in the barrel. I only had it delivered yesterday, and it won't keep until tomorrow.'

'Yes please. Great idea.'

They downed another stein each. 'I'm so enjoying this meal. It's so Austrian. Just the kind we have in Linz. And washed down with some exceptional beer. Do you buy this type often?'

'All the time, especially when my wife is away with her mother!' He laughed.

By the time they had gulped down the rest of their beer, they were both unsteady on their feet and slurring their speech. The conversation turned to their experiences with women.

'I just don't understand how a man like you could have failed, Anton. It was a mistake to neglect that one in Kronstorf who fancied you. You should have gone further when she tried to seduce you!'

'I couldn't. Her brother appeared, so we had to stop. I was pleased because there are things I could not do outside of marriage. My moral code doesn't permit me.'

'You don't have to go all the way to enjoy physical contact. You could have started up again when he was gone, or when you had another chance.'

'You could be right. We were both fond of each other, but she's married now. Apparently, she lives in Linz. I must see if I can call on her.'

'Why not?'

They chatted well into the early hours of the morning and eventually retired.

After a light cheese and bread roll breakfast, Simon told Anton he wanted to work through the exercises he had set.

'I'm staggered by how much work you have completed, Anton. You are my best student. And you have produced some work of a high standard. Not all of it, but most of it is of excellent quality. Have you been composing while on my course?'

'No, just a few tiny pieces. I've virtually stopped in favour of working on it.'

'That's excellent. Keep it that way until you finish. My theory is that, if you stop the use of your skill for the length of the course, you will be a better composer at the end. So don't even write any small pieces. Otherwise, I shall castigate you!'

The two of them spent many hours discussing and analysing Anton's 'homework'. It was clear to Sechter that Anton had committed himself fully to studying harmony and counterpoint. He could quote word-for-word passages from a three-volume treatise Sechter had written on musical theory: The Principles of Musical Composition. Having started at the beginning, he was gradually working his way through.

This was Anton's first stay with Sechter, so, in case he did not get on with him, thought he'd stop there only for two nights. Because they seemed to become friends, Anton would ask to stay longer next time. He hoped to go there regularly, especially during Advent and Lent, when the demands upon him as organist were minimal.

'Before I leave, I have a favour to ask of you, Simon.'

'Go ahead!'

'I am a great believer in having a record of my achievements, should I need it in applying for other jobs, or to support a case for promotion. So could you please produce a document of few words that records my performance on the exercises you have set me up to now?'

'Of course. I intend to give you a mark. I do for all my students.'

Anton returned to Linz with a piece of paper upon which Sechter had written the markings he had given Anton, along with the simple comment 'Good work'. This satisfied Anton, but he realised he could improve. So he would spend more time on the new exercises Sechter had set.

Anton's job in Linz continued apace. He was as busy as he had ever been at St Florian, if not more so. He was constantly required to play at both the Cathedral and the parish church. While his deputy, Ferdinand Edelhart, was a highly competent player, Anton's skills at the instrument were vastly higher, so he was in greater demand than Ferdinand. Anton was popular, no more so than with Bishop Rudigier, who often appeared unannounced at the Cathedral to listen to him playing. He spent many hours a day working on the exercises that Sechter had given him and studying Sechter's treatise. As time passed, he felt an increasing desire to compose. He was dying to put some of his new ideas on to paper but he dared not do so for fear of upsetting his master. He felt frustrated because Sechter's teaching methods were retrospective. They were based on conventional, established rules which Sechter adhered to rigidly, like a priest delivering the Eucharist. Anton wanted to be a modern composer, who would exercise his own unique style and originality and smash these rules to pieces. But, he would, until the end of the course, comply with Sechter's methods and wishes.

Anton laboured up to seven hours a day on the exercises. After one intense period, he sent seventeen filled, sizable notebooks to Sechter, who became quite concerned about his friend and pupil overworking. He wrote a letter to Anton which said,

Dear Anton,
I really must implore you to take more care of yourself and to allow yourself more relaxation. I can assure you that I am fully convinced of your thoroughness and eagerness and I do not want your health to suffer under too great a mental strain. I feel I have to tell you that I have never had a more dedicated pupil
Regards to my dear friend,
Simon

The letter seemed to have little effect on the diligent and enthusiastic Anton, who carried on as before. He visited Simon every Lent and Advent for three years until he had to take an examination. He had to demonstrate his skills, yet again, in organ playing and did so with unmatchable success on the then completed Piaristenkirche organ. Sechter wrote a testimonial about Anton's performance in which he said,

Bruckner shows much versatility in improvisation and in developing a theme and may therefore be regarded as one of the finest of organists.

By one of those unusual coincidences, a critic from the Weiner Zeitung attended and wrote a piece in the paper which praised Anton in fulsome terms. After his successful completion of two further tests, Anton and Simon were enjoying a coffee in a café, situated in one of Vienna's gracefully designed parks.

'My dear Simon,' he said, after taking a sip. 'I am so grateful for all you have done to improve my skills as a composer. You have revolutionised my thinking on the subject, and I'm itching to compose again!'

'Don't forget, Anton, you have passed with flying colours in elementary and advanced counterpoint, and all we need now is to finish your work on canon and fugue. So don't start composing just yet!'

Anton made his way back to his home in Linz. As he opened the door to his apartment, he saw a letter on the floor so immediately picked it up and opened it. He raised his eyes and held back a tear. Then he quickly packed his small case, ran to the Domgasse, and hailed a cabriolet.

***

Three quarters of an hour later, he opened the door to the family home in Ebelsberg and rushed in. 'Where is Mama? How is she?' he said to Maria Anna, who exploded in tears on seeing him.

'Very ill, Anton. Wherever have you been? We've tried for two weeks to contact you,' she said, just about able to speak.

'I've been to see my teacher, Simon Sechter, in Vienna.'

'Oh, him.'

'Yes, I arrived back in Linz less than an hour ago. How is Mama?'

'I'm sad to say she is at the point of dying. If she is still alive, you will see her. Come into her room now.'

'Mama, Mama, I'm so sorry you are ill,' he said.

'I've hung on to see you, Anton, but now I am going to die. Look after them, won't you?'

'You are ill, Mama, but you are still very much alive. Do not give up hope. Have you seen the doctor?'

'Yes. Please don't speak much longer. I'm too weak.'

'Is there anything you need?'

'No.'

'Try to sleep, Mama. We will watch over you.'

Anton could see she was extremely ill, so concocted a plan. 'We must not let her die alone. I will stay with her all night. Ignaz can watch Mama tomorrow night. You two girls can take over tomorrow during the day.'

'I'm happy with that, Anton,' said Ignaz. 'I agree we share the night duties between us two. Could you, Josefa and Maria Anna, look after our needs for food?'

The sisters agreed. By sheer willpower, and with the light from a single candle, Anton stayed awake all night. While he slept until lunchtime, Ignaz took over.

'I'm going to speak to our local photographer, Josefa,' said Anton.

'Why?'

'I want a picture of Mama, hopefully, before she passes.'

'That's in poor taste, Anton. You can't do that,' said Josefa.

'I disagree. A picture to remember Mama by is all I want. I shall hang it in my room in Linz so I can see her whenever I want to. I can speak to her if I need to.'

'I'm not sure I understand you, Anton,' said Maria Anna. 'But go ahead, if that's what you want.'

'I will. It's a pity we didn't get some photographs of Mama when she was well.'

Within an hour, Anton was taking the photographer into their mother's bedroom. 'What's going on?' said Ignaz, as quietly as he could.

Anton explained.

'I don't like the idea at all,' said Ignaz.

'I'll go then,' said the photographer.

'No. Stay, please. I'm going to have a photograph, Ignaz, like it or not. We have not got a picture of Mama and I am going ahead. I decide as I am the head of the family now.'

Ignaz just stared at Anton, without saying a word.

'Shall we wake your mother?' said the photographer.

'No,' said Anton.

With the photograph taken, the photographer left the house.

'Now look what you've done,' said Maria Anna. 'The flash has woken Mama.'

Their mother started groaning, but with her eyes still closed. Then she fell back into unconsciousness. Unexpectedly, Mama survived Ignaz's night shift and the following day. Anton took over that night.

'Anton,' said mother, at about 2 o'clock in the morning.

'You are awake, Mama,' he said, with a startled note in his voice. He held her hand. 'Is there anything I can get you?'

'It's time for me to go. Goodbye, my son.' Then silence. Anton tried to suppress his tears, but failed. He stood and leant over Mother and closed her eyelids. Half sitting in his chair and half leaning on the bed, he rested until morning but did not sleep. It was pointless to wake the others to tell them the sad news.

As he walked into the kitchen, Maria Anna was preparing breakfast. 'How is Mama this morning? About the same?'

Anton put his arm around her. 'I'm afraid she passed away in the night.' Maria Anna started crying and hugged Anton, who could not stop his own tears from flowing. Josefa and Ignaz appeared and cried as soon as they heard the tragic news.

'I have to see her,' said Ignaz.

'So do I,' said Anna Maria.

'I prefer to remember her alive,' said Josefa.

The three of them went into the bedroom to see mother's motionless, grey body. They each leant over and kissed her face. Anton pulled the sheet over her. They each made the sign of the cross and left the room.

'What do we do now, Anton? You are the head of the family,' said Maria Anna.

'Ignaz, will you go to the doctor and ask him to come to certify her passing?'

'I will. I'll have some breakfast and go.'

'After the doctor has been, we'll get the undertaker to come,' said Anton. 'I have one question.'

'What's that?' said Josefa.

'Where should Mama be buried? Here or in Ansfelden, with Papa?'

They agreed to have her buried in Ansfelden, and to have the funeral there.

Anton went to the village undertaker. He had never felt worse. He loved his mother, and she loved him. She was his strength and constant support, encouraging him to press on with his career, even when he doubted the direction he had set for himself. He could not believe he was about to speak to an undertaker about her. Tears ran down his face. He dried them with a handkerchief before entering.

'What can I do for you, mein Herr?' said the ginger bearded undertaker, without getting up from behind his desk.

'I am here because my mother passed away this morning, so I need your services for her burial, please.'

'Sorry to hear that,' he said mechanically, as if this was just another funeral, which it certainly wasn't to Anton and his siblings.

'There are plenty of vacant funeral times in the Ebelsberg church. Any particular day?'

'We want her buried in Ansfelden, not here.'

'I'm not sure about that. You may need an Ansfelden undertaker.'

Anton could feel his blood pressure rising at the insensitivity and obstructiveness of the man. 'Listen to me,' he said. 'You undertakers all know each other. You are all in that trade. I want you to take on the work. If you involve an undertaker from elsewhere, that is up to you. Ask your boss if you are incapable of deciding yourself.'

'Sorry, mein Herr. I didn't mean to upset you at this distressing time. Of course we will take on the job. I will go to Ansfelden to arrange the funeral.'

'Go there. It's only ten kilometres. Come back with some options.'

'I will. Certainly. While you are here, may I ask you about other needs?'

'Go ahead.'

'What sort of coffin would you like? They range from oak with brass handles, which is the most expensive, to a soft wood with iron handles.'

'I'll have the oak one.'

'Flowers?'

'I want plenty of the best flowers on the coffin and beside it.'

'Anything you'd like to specify in the service?'

'Yes. I want the normal service with a eulogy, but instead of the usual Mass, I want the choir and organist to play my *Requiem Mass*.'

'You compose then?'

'Yes. This is one of my works.'

'Do you have the performing parts?'

'Yes, of course.'

'Could you bring them along, please? They will need them for the rehearsals and the service.'

'I've brought them.' Anton placed the contents of a bag on his desk. 'Here they are.'

'Oh… Thank you.'

The funeral took place almost as Anton had planned. His major surprise was the large number of people who attended. He recognised many of their mother's friends from Ebelsberg, including people she had worked for while supplementing her husband's meagre pension. Anton's old friends from St Florian were there, including Michael and Elise Bogner, Provost Mayer and Jodok Stülz. Most of his new friends who had travelled from Linz, Irene Pascal, the von Mayfields, Karl and Nora Zappe and one of his oldest friends, August Dürrnberger came, too. So, of course, did Rosalie and Johann.

'Thank you so much for coming, August,' Anton said, as they were all waiting outside the church. 'I can't tell you how much I appreciate your attendance.'

'It was my duty, Anton. I owe it to you, my friend. I could not let you go through this without my company and sympathy.'

'I feel exactly the same,' said Irene. 'I wanted to be here in your hour of need. I also want to meet your sisters and brother.'

'Let me introduce you.' Irene met each, explaining she was first their brother's landlady when he was at the teacher training college, and had since provided him with the occasional meal.

Ignaz looked askance at Anton, as if to suspect there was more in the relationship between Irene and Anton than she had described. Anton noticed his odd glance, but ignored it, knowing their friendship was innocent.

The service was a highly emotional affair. The priest received the coffin at the church entrance. Anton, holding Maria Anna's hand, followed. She was

171

flooding with quiet tears. Then came Ignaz who had his arm around Josefa, who was also gently crying. Rosalie and Johann brought up the rear of the family members. The pall bearers gently placed the coffin on a catafalque in front of the altar. This was an upsetting moment for all the family, except Maria Anna, who was too young then, because they remembered their father's coffin being placed in exactly the same place, some twenty years before.

The priest began with the opening prayer. He then stressed the productive life of their mother and how friendly she had been to the community in Ansfelden, and how well she had looked after her family since her husband had passed away.

A man Anton didn't recognise stood to conduct his *Requiem Mass*. The priest could not find three trombonists, so only one played, and there were no string or horn players. A local musician played the organ. This was the first time the *Requiem* had been performed without Anton playing in it. He hadn't felt so sad for many years. Not only was it being played to honour his mother, it brought back memories of its first performance at the anniversary of his friend Franz Sailer's death. He could hold back his tears no longer.

Anton was still in tears as he delivered the eulogy. He stuttered and took his handkerchief out to wipe his eyes. At least he didn't have to read from a script. He said he and his sisters and brother did not know how they were going to live without their mother. Still finding it difficult to speak, he reassured the congregation they would cope, but did not yet know how. What a wonderful, caring mother she had been to them, he said, and how well she had looked after their father, towards the end of his life, when he became so ill.

By then, he had gained control of his emotions. 'I must tell you about my first visit with my mother to St Florian. I'll never forget when Prior Arneth asked me what instruments I played and what I'd composed, she told me to "be quick. The father hasn't got all day." The prior looked at me as if to say, "Just say what you want to tell me".' Many in the church laughed, which brought some welcomed levity to the service.

Anton had arranged for the wake to be held in the one tavern in Ansfelden. It could barely cope with the number of people there. Anton was sitting at a table, talking to Rosalie and Johann about the service, when Anton Storch approached him.

'This may not be the best time or place, Anton, but I have some news and a request for you.'

Anton stood up. The two of them moved a few paces away. 'Go on.'

'I am leaving my post as choirmaster and taking up a similar responsibility for the Vienna Male Voice Choir. I thought you ought to know, mainly because you are probably the obvious candidate for the job.'

'I couldn't possibly take it on without giving up my post as Cathedral Organist!'

'If I were you, I would ask Johann Schiedermayr. As your boss, he may assist. Obviously, there's no point in applying if he can't agree.'

Anton became quite interested in the idea. It was in the back of his mind as he spoke to the other mourners in the tavern. As he did, he noticed there were people there he didn't know, who were gladly ordering their drinks at the family's expense. He spoke to Ignaz about it.

'It's time we brought this to a close, Ignaz. Could you hit a stein glass with a spoon to quieten them down? I'll make an announcement to stop the wake now.'

'Good idea, Anton. I don't know those people either!'

They did as agreed, and Anton spoke.

'Thank you so much everybody for coming to this event to celebrate our Mama's life. We in the family are so grateful to you. We would now like to close here and depart. So thank you again for coming.'

Anton, Josefa, Maria Anna, and Ignaz said their goodbyes and made their way back to Ebelsberg. Rosalie and Johann did likewise and headed home.

***

He was soon back in Linz carrying out his duties. He also had a set of exercises from Sechter, the ones on canon and fugue, to complete. Much to his relief, this was the last section of the course. He was dying to begin composing again.

Soon after his return, and just after he had completed a practice session in the Cathedral, Johann Schiedermayr approached him.

'I'm so sorry to hear about your mother, Anton. I'm sorry I couldn't attend the funeral. I had so many commitments, but I understand August Dürrnberger attended, so at least someone from here went.'

'Thank you, Johann. It's kind of you to say. Yes, it was wonderful to see August there. I've known him for nigh on twenty years and we are good friends.'

'I hope it all went well, Anton.'

'Yes, until the wake. I had to close it because there were people there we didn't know, taking advantage of us by buying drinks at our expense. Those we knew wouldn't dream of such a thing.

'While you are here, Johann, I have a question for you. Anton Storch tells me he has accepted the job of choirmaster for the Male Voice Choir in Vienna. He thinks I should apply when his post is advertised. I wondered what your view would be. I would continue with my organ playing duties, here and at the parish church. The only thing which would suffer is my practicing. What do you think?'

'Actually, I know Storch is leaving. And I don't know what Bishop Rudigier would think. He is a great admirer of your organ playing and likes to listen to your practicing, in private, when the Cathedral is closed. Presumably, he would miss that. Given the assurances you have made, and the agreed terms of your contract, I would wholeheartedly support you applying for the job. I'll tell him what I think and let you know what he says. If you see him before me, you can ask him.'

It disappointed Anton that Johann did not see the Bishop for weeks, but the post had yet to be advertised, so the situation had not become urgent. Meanwhile, Anton returned to Vienna, having sent off the exercises on canon and fugue, for his final examination with Simon Sechter.

'Congratulations, Anton! I'm totally satisfied with your work, not only what you completed on canon and fugue, but the written exam you've just finished. You were such a dedicated student, I'm going to write a fugue and dedicate it to you!'

'I'm honoured, Simon. So which number fugue will that be?' They both laughed.

***

'Yes, Bishop Rudigier agrees you can apply,' said Johann Schiedermayr, the day after Anton's return from Vienna. 'He makes only one stipulation, which is that the choir should sing more often at our Cathedral.'

'If I get the job, we will. If he's happy, we can use the Cathedral for practice.'

'You or I can ask him.'

Not many weeks later, Anton was for the first time standing in front of the choir telling them his ambitions for the group. He said he wanted to improve the standard of its performing. So he told them, once they reached the highest possible level, he would enter them in various competitions, something they had never experienced before. From their reaction, he could detect their delight at what he had said. He would use on them the techniques he developed when he managed the choirs at St Florian.

'I would now like you to sing this Mass you are all familiar with. The parts are on your music stands. Please start at my count of three. I shall come around and listen to each of you singing. But just keep singing as I am coming close to you. One... two... three... '

He gradually worked his way through the choir, singer by singer. He didn't say a word but smiled at each individual member, whether or not their voice impressed him. Once he'd listened to them all, he went up to the rostrum and knocked his baton on the stand.

'I have to tell you, you are brilliant singers and I wish I was still a singer, too! Well, I am, but I wish I could sing with you!' All of them laughed. He knew from that moment he could mould them, like a potter moulding clay.

Over the months, he took great strides in working with the choir. He took care to form good relationships with each of them and to treat them firmly. With any new piece, he would ask them what they thought of it before they started rehearsing, always asking whether the tempo he suggested would suit them. He would work through the text of a new piece with them, telling them what sections he wanted louder or softer, and ask them whether they agreed with him. Part of his training was to encourage them to look at him and to follow accurately the rhythm of his movements as he conducted. And he praised them. After about three months, he told them how good they had become and that their performance had improved so much that they could compete with other top level choirs.

'I have something important to tell you. We will be holding a concert in the Cathedral in May to celebrate the sixteenth anniversary of our choir. The main work will be one of Antonio Lotti's Masses, which is not long, but a difficult work to perform. I have written a new, renaissance sounding, piece for the concert, vaguely in the style of Lotti's work. It is an *Ave Maria* for a soprano, two altos, two tenors and two basses. So I'm looking for seven volunteers to perform it. The concert will be in front of a large audience in the Cathedral, including Bishop Rudigier. So who would like to sing in it?'

A forest of arms was raised. Virtually everyone volunteered.

'Oh no!' he said. 'Now I will have to conduct some auditions! I will start with the ladies, first for the soprano part.'

It took him a whole day. He listened closely to the voices of nearly sixty volunteers. He wrote the names of those he tested, with an indication of their quality of voice.

'I have completed the auditions, and can now announce the results.' He read out the seven names. 'I propose a list of one for each voice as a reserve, in case of illness or other form of absence.' He read out four other names. An enormous round of applause greeted the result. Anton was delighted. He wondered if selecting so few from such a large number would cause some dissent.

'I have another interesting announcement. I've entered our choir into a competition in Krems. It will be on the twenty-ninth of June, and at the first German Austrian Singing Festival. I hope you are all available to go.'

'What wonderful news, Anton,' said a tenor. 'We've sung at St Florian, but that's not as far away as Krems!'

'There will not be a prize, but simply the honour of becoming better known, if we won. But the pleasure is in taking part. It will do us all the world of good, including me because I've never been seen conducting outside Linz before,' he said, chuckling. The whole choir giggled with him.

Chapter 14
1861 - 1862 Recognition

'We must work out the number of rehearsals we need for our anniversary concert and when we should hold them,' Anton said, as the choir had just completed performing a Michael Haydn Mass at the parish church. 'Should we combine the rehearsal of both works, as if we are rehearsing the whole concert, or do we practice the Lotti and the *Ave Maria* separately, on different days?'

'I think we should plan for two separate rehearsals on different days for each work. Then we could rehearse the whole concert,' said the chosen soprano soloist.

'I think we should rehearse the whole concert, with one work following the other,' said one of the men.

'Nonsense,' said the reserve alto. 'It's all very well for you, singing in only one piece,' she smiled, seeking forgiveness as if she had been too aggressive.

'I don't want to put this to a vote,' said Anton. 'The two pieces make arduous demands on all of us. So I'd prefer to rehearse them separately on different days, just to put less strain on our soloists. Does anyone object?' Anton looked around and saw no one did. 'Good. Let's start with the Lotti. I've convinced Karl Zappe to let us use his theatre, so let's meet there on Wednesday evening at seven-thirty sharp?' Heads nodded in agreement.

The choir struggled with the formidable Lotti piece but soon mastered it. They quickly became accomplished at singing his *Ave Maria*.

'Thank you, everyone. We should all be superb on the night. Good luck tomorrow!' said Anton, after the last of the full choir rehearsals. 'And our soloists will be brilliant, I'm certain.'

'Hello, Herr Bruckner. I wish you every success for tonight,' said Bishop Rudigier, when he saw Anton in the street, walking back from Mass at the parish church.

'Thank you, Your Grace. We've worked on it so hard, it should go well. The women have made a special effort, especially the soprano.'

'She has a God given voice, if she's the one I believe she is.'

'I take it you will be there?'

'Of course. I would not miss it for a king's fortune!'

'It will be my first concert as conductor and composer, so I'm more nervous than the soloists!'

'By the way, we are getting to know each other well, so please call me Franz. You will be one of a few who use my first name, but be discreet while we are in company. Then I'll call you Herr Bruckner. I will call you Anton while there are only the two of us, or with Johann. He will understand.'

'I regard that as a special privilege, Franz, and I will remember to act discreetly.'

'I have to go now, Anton. I'll see you tonight!'

The concert was to be performed in front of senior officials and dignitaries of the town, as well as some from outside. The mayor of Linz and his lady would be there, along with Johann Schiedermayr and August Dürrnberger. Anton had invited the Zappes, the von Mayfields and Irene Pascal.

Anton could not help worrying about the concert. His concerns lasted until he conducted. To his surprise, the conclusion of each piece attracted much applause and cheering. This was not what the Bishop and Johann Schiedermayr would have expected in the sacred interior of the Cathedral. He need not have felt so unsettled: the concert was a memorable success.

The Linz Daily News heaped praise on all who took part, especially upon Anton, whom they complimented as a brilliant composer of this 'profound, religiously felt, strictly contrapuntal work, which provided brilliant proof of his extensive and special aptitude for creative, ecclesiastical art.'

The Evening Post were equally fulsome: 'With this work in Linz, Herr Bruckner appeared before the public for the first time as a composer... and won a complete victory.'

'What an excellent concert,' said Johann Schiedermayr. 'The choir and soloists were superb. All credit to you, Anton. It fully justifies your appointment as choirmaster. Well done, my friend!' Anton was delighted. Johann had not praised him so highly before ... and had never before called him 'my friend'. Even the mayor and his wife congratulated him.

His friends, the Zappes, the von Mayfields, and Irene crowded around him, full of praise. He had never enjoyed such rapture. As they dispersed, Irene approached him again and invited him for a meal. 'How can I refuse, you kind lady? I just need to spend a little time with my choir.'

'I'll prepare something and see you at my house.'

'Perfect!'

Anton spoke to the choir members individually to make his praise more personal. 'It was your *Ave Maria*, that was the staggering success,' said the lady alto.

'Not at all,' said Anton. 'It was your beautiful singing, not just of my little piece, but of the Antonio Lotti. You were all brilliant.'

'How about a drink, Anton?' said a bass singer. 'The nearest tavern isn't a hundred metres away.'

'Let's round up as many as we can. I'll buy the beers!'

About thirty of them, including five of the women, were soon drinking in the Wirtshaus, one of Anton's favourite drinking dens. 'I can't thank you all enough,' he said. 'I am so proud of you all. Together, we have made our sixteenth a major event. Let's raise our glasses to our seventeenth birthday concert!' The beer flowed for an hour and the conversation became quite earthy, especially among the men. Two of them competed with each other for who could tell the crudest joke. 'Not while the ladies are with us, men. You should not speak in those terms. Oh... I've just remembered, I have a dinner engagement tonight. I must go!'

***

'I'm sorry I took so long, Irene. We went to the Wirtshaus for a celebratory drink. It turned out to be more than one.'

'You are just in time, Anton. Five more minutes and the dumplings would have been ruined!'

This was another opportunity for the two friends to have a good conversation. 'That was an incredible concert, Anton. Well done. Your time in Linz is doing your career a lot of good,' she said, as they sat in the kitchen.

'There is much truth in what you are saying. But I feel limited here. I don't have many opportunities to compose. I spend eight hours a day playing one organ or the other. And I've put a tremendous effort into honing the skills of the choir. It seems ungrateful of me to say it, Irene, but I need more, especially on composing and perhaps on conducting, too. And I'd really like a wife. I'm not at all thrilled with this bachelor life!'

'We'd really miss you if you left here, Anton. And you need to work harder to find a wife. I love you, but I'm too old for you. You need a younger woman like that Martha Knauer you fell in love with in Kronstorf.'

'Too late to go back to her. I heard she was married.'

'Yes. It's a sad story. She lived quite near here but died in childbirth, not a year ago.'

'My God, Irene. How awful. I suddenly feel I'm to blame. I ignored her and now see what's happened.'

'Don't be silly. It's not your fault. You couldn't have loved her that much.' Then she changed the subject. 'What's the next plan for the choir?'

'We're taking part in the First German Austrian Singing Festival in Krems. It's only six weeks away.'

'Great news, Anton. Good luck with it. That'll really put you on the national stage! And better luck in finding a wife. I shall look out for some prospective candidates and let you know!'

Having said their goodbyes, Anton walked back to the Pfarrgasse. He couldn't stop thinking about the tragedy of Martha. He thought he'd made a serious error with her.

***

The choir met at the theatre to discuss their approach to the German Austrian Singing Festival.

'They've sent me all we need to know about our entry. We sing two songs. We choose one and they choose the other. Shall we sing the *Ave Maria* again?'

'I don't think so, Anton. It made an enormous impact here, we know, but do we need a religious work?' said a bass member.

'Good point. Is there a song you would like to sing? It would be better if you choose!'

'We know, Anton Storch's "Forest Loneliness" so could we sing that?' said a soprano.

'A good choice,' said another.

'I don't know it at all. It will make a change for me to conduct something I don't know, but you do! I'll have to learn it! Does anyone not like the idea?' No one objected.

All seventy-eight of the choir made their way to Krems. Some travelled in groups, others individually. They each planned to stay for two nights. All of them met at the concert hall at 10 o'clock in the morning, to be given their new piece. It was a song called The Hunter's Rest by Valentin Becker.

'Has anyone heard of this song before?' asked Anton, as they were all assembled in a hall next to the tax office.

They all shook their heads. 'Here are the song sheets. Let's read them through before we rehearse.' They each took their time in studying the music. 'Would anyone like to sing it?'

Four members of the choir stood up and sang. 'Not a bad start,' said Anton. 'You kept nicely together, and I just stood here and listened!'

Within a couple of hours, they had all but perfected a performance of 'The Hunter's Rest'. They rehearsed the work by Storch and then returned to the Becker before concluding for the day.

Despite their initial nerves, the choir started well in the contest, and, to Anton's delight, continued in the same vein until they finished. They all sat anxiously to await the performances of the four choirs that followed them.

Then suddenly, not two minutes after the last of the choirs finished, the chairman announced the result. 'I and my committee award the choir from Linz "The Palm of the Evening", as winners of this competition. This is because they were above the others with the precision and delicate nuances in which they sang.' They had achieved another resounding success under

180

Anton's baton. He and the choir were overjoyed. They had, by their committed efforts, put their choir firmly on the national map. A newspaper commentary about the festival put Anton's group above the Vienna Men's Choral Society which, until then, was regarded as the best choir in Austria. So, much to Anton's satisfaction, they had beaten Anton Storch's group!

***

At dinner one evening, shortly after their Krems success, he told the von Mayfields and Irene what wonderful singers they were. He hoped he could make them more famous, not just in Austria, but internationally, over the whole of Europe. While he said these words, he thought of a new idea which he'd urgently put to the choir. But he'd have to do a little research beforehand. He would need a quick decision.

'I have an idea I'd like to try on you. There is an international singing contest in Nuremberg in July. In my view we should enter so ride on the crest of our wave of success. It's almost too late, but if we can decide tonight, I can get things moving tomorrow. I hope you are all available to go.'

A lady at the back stood up to ask a question. 'You have taken us by surprise, Anton. Who pays?'

'I've already agreed this with the choir administrators. They will pay, from choir funds, for the return journey and for accommodation. You will know we charge for performances, so we have a substantial reserve we can use. There will be a reward of a bounty if we win or come second, so there is a potential financial benefit for all of us.'

A male singer also had a question. 'How will we get there? It's a long way by horse and carriage?' Much laughter broke out.

'We go by train. There is now a steam train from Linz to Munich, which you will all know about, and a new service from Munich to Nuremberg. So transport is not an issue. Do we all approve?'

They each raised a hand. No one objected.

A leading member of the choir then spoke. 'It is my view, and I'm sure we all agree, that we are all grateful to you, Anton, for suggesting we enter this competition. You have brought our standard of singing to the top level. You must truly believe in us to do what you have done. Please join me everyone to show your appreciation.' A round of applause rang out and choristers cheered. Anton hadn't felt better since before his mother died. He had difficulty holding back his tears.

***

Being involved in an international choir competition was an incredible experience for each member. Anton regarded it as a great honour to lead them.

181

None had been to Nuremberg before. The size and beauty of this great city impressed them, as did the quality of their accommodation.

'Thank you, Anton, for providing such a comfortable place to stay,' said a soloist. 'It must have cost a small fortune for us all to be accommodated in the city.'

'Our assistant to the secretary organised it all. She is brilliant. All I asked was that we were all located as close to the concert hall as possible, in hotels and lodgings that were of high quality. Fortunately, we have made a good profit over the last few years. This is because Emperor Franz Joseph relaxed the prohibition on large societies, and choirs fall into that category.'

'I didn't know that applied to choirs,' said one of the soloists.

'Nor did I until I read it in a newspaper,' said Anton.

Choirs from many cities in Europe took part in the competition. In applying, each choir had to state which category applied to it. The Linz choir was in the 'mixed choir of mature years' category, each member being a minimum of eighteen years old. They spent the first day rehearsing two pieces the panel of judges gave them. One was a religious work by Michael Haydn and the other an aria from Mozart's 'Marriage of Figaro'.

'Now just relax,' said Anton, at the first rehearsal session. 'It's all about being here. My aim is for us to enjoy this experience, not necessarily to win. And to entertain those who will be listening to us.'

Despite his encouragement, the first rehearsal was a disaster. Many sang off key. None seemed to cope with the rhythm of either piece.

'We didn't do as well as we hoped. It's my fault entirely,' he said. 'Let's discuss the tempo. Are we attempting these pieces too quickly or too slowly? It seems we want to complete them quickly so we can stop singing.'

A woman at the side spoke. 'I think we are going too quickly. It would help if you gave us a note so we could be in tune.'

'Excellent thought. Right, let's start again on the first piece and I'll sing the beginning with you. Don't forget to look at me as I conduct. On the count of three. One... two ... three...'

Anton applauded as they completed the Haydn. He couldn't disguise his delight. He hoped they hadn't peaked too early. They sang the Mozart piece. 'Not as good as the Haydn, but we are nearly there. Well done!'

They soon discovered they were competing with six other choirs in their category. The chairman of the panel invited them to assemble as the fifth choir to perform.

Anton had never heard them sing so well. It was as if competing brought the best out of them. They were in perfect tune and kept to the exact tempo in which he conducted. The audience applauded each piece as they sang, then even louder as they finished. They waited anxiously for the two other choirs to finish.

'I'm going to announce the results in reverse order,' said the panel chairman. 'In third place in the senior mixed choir category is our local group from Nuremberg; in second place is the choir from Vienna; and the winner is... the choir from Linz.'

Anton couldn't believe his ears. He thought his choir's performance was about the same as the Vienna choir, but better than the local group. Members of Anton's choir were smiling at each other. Tears dampened the faces of some lady members.

The chairman continued. 'Could Herr Bruckner, the choirmaster of the Linz Choir, come to the stage, please? It's a pleasure for me to present you with this prize of a hundred and fifty florins.'

Anton didn't know what to say. Should he make a speech? Must he thank the organisers? Should he praise his choir?

All he said was, 'Thank you,' bowed to the panel members and then to the audience.

'We now invite your choir to join the Vienna choir to sing "Brace yourself Germany".' They did so with celebratory gusto. Again, the audience applauded wildly.

At the end of the festival, as Anton was talking to some of the choir members, one of the panel approached him. 'My name is Johann Herbeck. I am a professor at the Vienna Conservatory. I came to meet you to say I think you are an excellent choirmaster!'

'That is kind of you, Herr Herbeck.'

'I understand you are a composer, too!'

'Yes. How do you know? I didn't expect to be known in Nuremberg!'

'It's only because I am a colleague and friend of Simon Sechter. He didn't mention your work as a choirmaster but told me about your compositions. He much admires your *Missa Solemnis*! Anyway, it's good to see you. If you think I could help you in your composing, just get in touch.'

That Johann Herbeck had spoken to him surprised and delighted Anton. He immediately realised that the number of his useful contacts in Vienna was increasing, albeit slowly.

Several of his choir members came to congratulate him. Some of the women hugged and kissed him. 'It's not for you to congratulate me. It's the other way around. I congratulate you. You were brilliant. You had to be to defeat one of the two most famous choirs in the land.'

'I think we all deserve a drink,' said a tenor. 'There's a tavern near my hotel and it's only a few hundred metres away. Let's go there shall we?'

183

A mixed group of about twenty of them wandered off to the tavern. Anton, with his usual generosity, bought a round of drinks. They chatted amongst themselves until several of the men clubbed together to buy a second round. Three of them introduced Anton to a rather pretty red-headed woman, who smiled longingly at him.

'It's an immense pleasure for me to meet you. What's your name?'

'I am Olga. I'm off duty at present, but I often serve in the bar here.'

'My name is Anton. I am a member of this group of singers. Would you like a drink?'

'Yes, a glass of white wine, please,' she said, as she sat on a stool next to him.

The men who introduced her to him drifted away and left Anton and Olga alone to talk to each other. Anton was keen to take up Irene's advice to find a good woman, and he rather liked this outgoing lass. So he felt he was heading the right way. She was still sitting there when he came back from the bar with a large Sauvignon Blanc.

'So how long have you been working here?' he said. 'Do you have any other jobs?'

'Yes, I am a seamstress during the mornings and work here in the afternoons and evenings. I have a room upstairs. I've told your friends they can see it. If you'd like to come up, too, I will feed you all with some cake I made.'

Moments later, all five of them were sitting in Olga's lounge, eating her fruit loaf. Anton's comrades finished theirs and went, as if deliberately, to leave Anton alone with Olga. Anton smiled at them as they shut the lounge door.

'This is the first time for months, I could speak to a young lady on her own. Tell me more about yourself. Were you brought up around here or in another town?'

'It's lovely to speak to you, Anton. I have always lived in Nuremberg. My father is a brewer and my mother is a dressmaker. What about you?'

Anton told her about his work as choirmaster, and how well the choir had developed, and about their success at the song festival by beating the local choir.

'All credit to you, Anton. I'll be back in a minute,' said Olga. She then stood up from the sofa and disappeared.

Anton wondered what to do as she was gone for so long. Should he search for her or await her return? He sat there on the sofa, pondering. Suddenly Olga appeared. He was utterly shocked and distraught at what he saw. She was wearing a loose, short nightdress, with her shoulder so exposed her left breast was clearly visible. He stood up and scowled at her.

'Go away,' he said. 'Get out of this room.'

'Alright, I'll go!'

'Get some clothes on. You are indecent. And I'm going.'

He left the room and rushed towards the door of the apartment.

'So we fooled you, Anton! You fell for it nicely! She was more than willing to play along!' said one of his colleagues, as all three of them came out of the kitchen.

'You bastards! You're a fucking disgrace. Consider yourselves severely reprimanded. I shall soon decide whether you have a future in the choir.'

'But it was only a prank, boss,' said another.

'Yes, in the worst possible taste.' He slammed the door behind him and walked down the stairs to the bar.

'What's the matter, Anton?' said a woman chorister. 'You look furious.'

'I am. Three of our colleagues, and that woman, Olga, have totally humiliated me.'

'Tell me about it,' she said.

'Yes, tell us,' said a lady soloist.

'I'd rather not. It was so embarrassing. Let me buy you a drink and I'll go back to my lodgings.'

'I am sorry to hear that, Anton,' said the soloist.

'So am I,' said her colleague. 'We don't need another drink. Goodnight.'

It was a fair walk back to his digs, which were south of the river. He didn't have a key, so knocked at the door.

'Hello, Herr Bruckner. Are you alright?' said the landlord's sister. 'How did the festival competition go, or would it be better if I didn't ask?'

'We won, so we are all delighted. I am angry with three of my colleagues, who have caused me much humiliation.'

'I thought you looked upset when I let you in, Herr Bruckner. If it helps, would you like to tell me about it?'

'How kind of you. First, tell me your name?'

'Karla, Karla Zimmerman.'

'Yes, I knew your surname. So what happened is this...' Anton told her in full what happened. He calmed down as he told her.

'How terrible, Herr Bruckner,' she said, as she held out her arms and put a delicate kiss on his cheek.

'I'm still suffering somewhat, so I'll try to avoid travelling back to Linz with them all tomorrow.'

'Why not stay an extra night? I'm free tomorrow so I can show you around the city.'

'I'd love to do that,' said Anton, feeling less disjointed. Having cleared his mind of Olga, he detected he was being attracted to Karla. A day with her in Nuremburg would surely confirm his feelings for her.

After an erratic night's sleep, punctuated by the embarrassment of the day before, and a breakfast of two buttered rolls and a coffee, they set out on the tour.

'I must show you around our magnificent Imperial Castle,' she said. 'There is no better medieval fortress in the whole of Europe. It was the home of all our kings from the eleventh century to the sixteenth.'

Anton could not concentrate on what she was saying. He was so intoxicated with this intelligent, good looking woman, his mind couldn't focus on anything else. 'How interesting,' he said blankly.

'We'll now go to the old town hall and I'll show you the torture chamber there.'

'Good idea.'

Anton looked longingly straight into her bright blue eyes and at her luscious smile.

'Now we'll go to one of the oldest taverns in the city and have some refreshment.'

'Excellent. I'm quite thirsty now.'

They sat in the inn and enjoyed some fresh brown bread and local cheese, along with a glass each of white wine. 'So what do you think of our city, Anton?'

'I really like it. It certainly has an impressive history. But what impresses me most is you, Karla. I could easily fall in love with you.'

'You've taken me completely by surprise. I wish I could say I have the same feelings for you, but to be frank, you are not my type at all. I would prefer a businessman, not a choirmaster. Sorry!'

He didn't know how to respond to this open and frank rejection. At least he knew he needn't waste more time in trying to attract her. They continued with the walk and returned to the lodgings. Anton couldn't wait for the following morning and to return to a more familiar city.

The Linz press praised the choir for its outstanding success in Nuremberg. A journalist from a national newspaper came to the Cathedral to find Anton and to interview him. He told him he felt humbled by the way the choir had sung. With characteristic modesty, he didn't say he was the architect of their performance. He had put the Linz Choir on the international map.

**

Anton couldn't escape from his view that he was not in a post that used his full potential as a musician. He would look for something in the academic world, possibly at a university, in Austria, or abroad. He needed a further qualification in composition if a university could consider him for an important, demanding academic post. The Vienna Conservatory advertised such examinations, and he was aware of them. Any such qualification would have to include a statement of his performing ability which would be needed in any post teaching music. He could hardly use as qualifications the various documents Simon Sechter had written for him.

Simon came to stay with him at his Linz apartment for a few days, so he revealed his latest thinking to him, his revered teacher.

'Hmm. I'm not so sure, Anton. You have an important job here. You are respected and are clearly doing well.'

'You are right, but I don't want to be here for the rest of my life. I've resigned from my choirmaster post at the Linz Choir so things aren't perfect here, but have some good, trustworthy friends in this city.'

'You've resigned from the Linz Choir. Why?'

Anton explained the embarrassment he suffered at Nuremberg.

'I'm amazed!'

'They didn't want me to go, so I may go back at some point, but I've had enough of them for now. I want to concentrate on my composition and organ playing.'

'Given what you have just said, I can't see what you can lose by taking the examination for teaching counterpoint and harmony. You realised it will comprise five days of testing on these subjects and playing an instrument of your choice to show your ability in free composition and improvisation.'

'No, I didn't realise it would take that much commitment, but I'm not deterred.'

'They may let you off some of the written aspect, if you send some exercises I set you. In short, go ahead with my blessing, Anton. But don't raise your hopes too high. They may refuse to hold an examination just for your benefit.'

***

Not many days after Simon left, the von Mayfields and Irene invited him to dinner. They congratulated him for the success of the choir at Nuremberg. They asked him what his plans might be, so he explained his intentions, mentioning the problem with the choir.

'I cannot understand you, Anton,' said Irene. 'You have many friends here who, like us, admire and love you. An advanced qualification of the kind you want will not help you here. You'd have to go to Vienna or Salzburg. And start again.'

'I agree with Irene,' said Moritz. 'You are becoming well known here and have succeeded in all you have set out to do. Why throw that away?'

'I don't agree,' said Betty. 'Anton has to look at the future. He may not want to spend his life in Linz playing two organs for a living. There are few composers keener than him, or better. He's improved his skills, even having a correspondence course with a professor in Vienna. So I agree with you, Anton. Try for the diploma. You could even go before Advent if Johann Schiedermayr engages your substitute.'

So, having negotiated an arrangement with Johann, he wrote to the Vienna Conservatorium. In support of his request, and as Simon suggested, he included his reports from Simon and some examples of his compositions.

The reply surprised him by its demands. The Conservatorium wanted him to compose a new organ fugue, lasting no less than three minutes, which they would expect him to play to the examining board. This would comprise five senior individuals. The board would expect Anton to be examined for three days on various aspects of musical theory, in six three hour sessions. They would invite him to improvise on a theme the board would create and do so on an organ of his own selection. He chose the organ as he read the letter: the one at the Piaristenkirche. It told him to report to the receptionist at the Conservatorium.

He indulged in the luxury of travelling to Vienna on a Danube steam boat and stayed in a quaint hotel, close to the Conservatorium. Having slept well, after consuming a stein and a half of beer, and after breakfast and a short, nervous walk, he reported as instructed and was taken to an office near the main entrance.

'Just go straight in, mein Herr. No need to knock. They are expecting you now,' said the slim, bespectacled receptionist.

Five gentlemen were sitting behind a long table next to a tall, wide window. They had placed an empty chair a couple of metres in front. Anton immediately recognised two of the men.

'Do sit down,' said Johann Herbeck. 'We have, of course, met before.' He spoke in a friendly, but neutral, tone to admit to the others that he knew Anton, and to show his lack of bias. 'I believe you also know Simon Sechter, previously your teacher and a professor here.'

'Hello, Anton,' said Sechter.

'I should now introduce you to Otto Dessoff. Otto is a conductor with the Vienna Philharmonic and a director of the Vienna Court Opera.'

'I'm pleased to meet you, Herr Bruckner.'

'This is Joseph Hellmesberger, also a composer, He is director of the Conservatory.'

'Likewise, I am pleased to meet you, Herr Bruckner.'

'And this is Shulrat Becker, a senior administrator here.'

'Hello, Herr Bruckner.'

'As you know,' said Herbeck. 'We expect you to undertake three days of theoretical and practical examinations in music. They will be written exams. On the fourth day, we will test your ability in sight reading, general organ play, improvisation and the playing of fugues. Have you chosen an organ for your playing?'

'Yes, I would like to play on the organ at the Piaristenkirche.'

'May I ask why?'

'I have played it in the past and it is a superb instrument.'

'But it's quite a long way from here. We have an excellent organ in the Conservatory and there's one at the Imperial Court Chapel.'

'I'd much prefer the one at the Piaristenkirche.'

'Fine. We have no objection to the cab ride!'

Anton had to endure working in a small, badly lit room furnished with only a table and a chair. He was glad the table was large so he could spread out the papers they had given him. Oddly, they had not appointed an invigilator. So he worked through the examples on his own. The tests were difficult. They were clearly testing him to high academic standards. He felt mentally exhausted after three days of concentrated examinations and wondered how he would perform the following day. Drinking more than a stein of beer before bed would therefore be unwise.

The examination board had arranged the organ playing test for one o'clock in the afternoon, so Anton could relax for the morning. He ate three pork chops and drank a beer before meeting them at the Piaristenkirche.

'I'm going to ask Simon Sechter to write a theme for you to play and use,' said Johann Herbeck. 'Please write something, Simon, say of four bars.'

Simon Sechter did as asked and handed the sheet of music paper back to Herbeck, who read it. 'It's good but needs expansion... to make it more of a challenge. Could you add to it, please, Otto?'

'Let me see Simon's work.' Herbeck handed it to him.

'No, it's long enough and challenging enough as it is.'

'Give it back to me,' said Herbeck. He took up a pen and wrote four more bars.'

'How cruel!' said Otto Dessoff.

'No, I'm not,' said Herbeck, as he handed Anton the sheet of paper with the theme written on it.

Anton read it. He spent several minutes on it and thinking about how he would deal with it. He sat on the organ bench, still looking at the theme.

'He doesn't know what to do,' said Dessoff quietly.

'Yes, he does,' said Sechter.

'I'm not sure,' whispered Hellmesberger.

'He's certainly taking his time,' said Herbeck.

Anton shuffled around on the bench and played. He introduced some fragments based on each bar of the tune, then launched into an exciting, spirited fugue. This began with a statement of the entire theme in the bass, some contrasting variations which he developed into a huge, window shattering climax. It ended on an extended, powerful, church filling chord.

'Unbelievable,' said Dessoff, applauding loudly.

'What a fantastic performance,' said Hellmesberger, who also applauded.

'He should have examined us!' said Herbeck. 'We won't trouble you to play the fugue you have written for us.'

It took Anton several minutes to relax from the excited state he was in at the conclusion of his playing. 'Thank you, thank you,' he said as he soaked himself in the satisfying comments of the board.

'You are a musical master,' said Herbeck. 'All we need to do now is to prepare the diploma for you which we will post to your address in Linz. Please could you give us your permission to send a copy to the Linz Daily News?'

Anton could hardly believe what he was hearing. 'Why make so much of it?'

'It's quite normal. It was a public examination, after all. That's why we posted notices about it. Unless you object for personal reasons, we will publicise it.'

'I have no reason to object. It will help the Cathedral in Linz, as well as inform my friends there.' It would also improve Anton's standing in Linz, but modesty prevented him from saying that.

'May I ask a special favour of you?' asked Hellmesberger.

'Certainly,' said Anton.

'I am the leader of the Hellmesberger String Quartet and I wondered if you would compose a new quartet for us?'

'What an interesting idea. When would you like it?'

'Whenever you have written it, and are happy with the completed score.'

'I'll write it as soon as I can.'

Anton shook hands with each member of the board and thanked them for the time they spent examining him. He spent another night at the hotel and left the following morning by river boat to Linz.

Chapter 15
1861 - 1864 Symphony

While walking from the jetty to his apartment, he felt a tap on the shoulder.
'Hello, Anton. How are you? We haven't seen you for some time.'
'Karl, it's good to see you!' said Anton. 'I've just returned from a trip to Vienna.'
'A holiday?' said Karl.
'No, far from it!'
'Don't tell me anymore. Come for dinner with Nora and me tonight. You can tell us then. You'll meet a member of my string quartet who is also coming.'
'How kind. Much better to dine with you than to cook my own meal! When should I arrive?'
'Seven would be perfect! See you then!' Karl crossed over to the other side of the road and headed for the bakery.

As Anton opened the door of his apartment, he spotted an official looking letter on the doormat. He put down his case and opened it. The letter was from Jodok Stülz, asking if he would compose a song for St Lucy's Day. He smiled. It was the first time St Florian had commissioned him to write something, since he had become Organist at Linz.

Anton decided to dress smartly for the dinner so put on a fresh shirt and a new pair of trousers.

He knocked on the Zappes' door at exactly seven o'clock.
'Do come in,' said Nora, who immediately kissed his cheek. 'We have someone for you to meet. Come through.'
'It's the man with the baggy trousers,' said their little boy.
'And his collar is too big,' said their little daughter.
'Don't be so rude,' said Karl. 'Herr Bruckner has been here before and he likes you a lot. So treat him with respect.' The children said nothing.
'This is Otto Kitzler,' said Nora. He's a cellist in the Linz Theatre Orchestra and a member of Karl's string quartet.
'I know Otto,' he said. 'He's a member of the Linz Choir, too.'
'And I know you, of course, Anton. It was a great shame you resigned. Most of us were really disappointed. The problem was caused by the few, nowhere near the majority. I'm sorry they were so bad to you. You didn't deserve it, especially as you made us famous over the whole of Europe.'
'Yes, I was sorry to go. I've missed you, too. I liked the job. The only thing I've gained is more time to do my composing.'

'So what were you doing in Vienna?' said Karl, as they began tucking into the main course.

'I was taking an examination in counterpoint and harmony. And I had to play an instrument of my choice, the organ, of course. The aim was to become qualified to teach these subjects at university level.'

'But you are an organist and good composer, Anton,' said Nora. 'So why go through all that?'

Anton explained, saying he wanted options for his future, and he might not be in Linz until the end of his career.

'I see,' said Karl. 'You've really put yourself through the mill to learn to compose. Surely, what with your course with Simon Sechter, there's nothing else for you to do?'

'I'm lacking in two areas. They are orchestration and modern composition. The lessons from Simon were all about obeying classical rules for composing. I want to break those chains and launch into modern composition. I've reached the view that those rules are to be broken.'

'Otto may help you,' said Nora. 'He's mad on modern music. He's ripped apart many of Beethoven's late quartets, so he knows well what rules Beethoven has broken. And he's studied many modern symphonies such as Beethoven's and Schubert's. And he knows much about Wagner's operas. What do you think, Otto?'

'Anton is an excellent composer. He doesn't need my help. Do you Anton? If you do, I'll help.'

'It's an idea, Otto. I would welcome your assistance. But I can't imagine you have the time.'

'It's the least I can do. It would be a thank you for all you did for our choir.'

At lunchtime, the day after the interesting conversation with the Zappes and Otto Kitzler, Anton heard a knock on the door to his apartment. He opened it only to see Nora Zappe standing there.

'Have you seen today's paper, Anton? There is a big article there about your new qualification!'

'No!'

'Come down and I'll show you!' They dashed down to the floor below and entered the Zappes' apartment.

'It's him from upstairs with the baggy trousers,' said their daughter.

'Don't be so rude!' shouted Nora. 'I will not tolerate your rudeness to Herr Bruckner. You were rude yesterday. Do it again and I'll smack whichever one of you says it! Now apologise!'

'I'm sorry, Herr Bruckner. I won't be rude to you again, I promise,' said the girl.

'That's better,' said Nora. Anton just smiled.

He read the article in the Daily News. 'I'm amazed. They've put the full text of the diploma. Incredible! That is good for music in Linz and for the Cathedral, not just for me. Thank you, Nora, for showing me!'

***

Within days, Otto and Anton were working together. Up to then, most of Anton's fifty or so compositions had been for choirs, some with a small supporting orchestra, for soloists and for organ. But Otto took him deeply into the new world of works for full orchestra, and piano sonatas.

'I want you to have a close look at this sonata by Beethoven. It's his Pathétique. It's written in an orchestrated form and I want you to study the use of individual instruments and those in groups.'

'I can't believe it. What an amazing work,' said Anton, a few days later. 'You have inspired me to write purely for orchestra. I must! And I will!'

'Get on with it, Anton. We can perform anything you write. People already know you in Linz, and they will come to listen to any new orchestral works you write!'

'I'm excited! I can't wait!'

'I want you to look at these symphonies by Mendelssohn. You'll love them. They will show you how to use an orchestra to its best. You can write for any emotion you chose. And concentrate on the overall structure of the symphony, as well as the individual movements.'

Suddenly, a new age dawned for Anton. A fire ignited in his belly. It transformed him into a new man, a new composer. Otto Kitzler changed his life forever. He would not reject composing religious or secular works for soloists or choirs or a combination of the two, but he would focus on writing for orchestra.

Before his startling conversion, he completed the work St Florian commissioned. He called it *Afferentur regi*. The choir performed it on St Lucy's Day without Anton present. Jodok Stülz wrote to him to say how delighted he was with this beautifully written song.

Nor could he possibly refuse another important commission.

'My dear Anton, I have a request,' said Bishop Rudigier, late one evening, as Anton stepped down from the organ loft of the Cathedral. 'You may know that I have, for many years, wanted to build a new cathedral in Linz. I have at last obtained funding to start,' he said, smiling with his whole face. 'We are calling it the Cathedral of the Immaculate Conception. I therefore want you to write a cantata that we can play in the open air, to celebrate the laying of the foundation stone. The words should be entirely fitting. Could you write something, please?'

'I would regard it a great honour, Franz. Exactly when are you laying the stone?'

'It hasn't been constructed yet, but I am aiming for early May.'

'I'll make a start. You will have the manuscript by mid-March. Do you have any views on the orchestra, choirs and soloists?'

'Yes. It should be for a men's choir, male soloists, and include a military band. Otherwise, I leave it to you.'

This commission thrilled Anton more than any other. Finding the most appropriate words was the first challenge. To meet the Bishop's wishes, they had to suit the occasion perfectly. Eventually, and after spending several hours in the city library, he found a poem that staggered him. The verses by the theologian Pammesberger exactly matched. They were about both the Virgin Mary, and the laying of a church foundation stone. He silently cheered. While studying with Simon Sechter, he hardly wrote a note, so with renewed enthusiasm, spent his free time composing the piece. It was like being in another world, one of boundless creativity and a place where he could release his accumulated, unrequited desire to compose again.

Once he had completed the work, he showed it to Otto Kitzler.

'Not at all bad,' said Otto, as he read the score. 'In fact, it's good. I love the contrasts from one part to another. Superb. It flows beautifully and has a strong celebratory feel about it, which is what you want and, I imagine, what the Bishop wants, too.'

'I wondered if I'd made it too cheerful for a religious work.'

'Not at all. There are some slower, deeper parts, which give it an element of seriousness. The Bishop will like it, I'm sure.'

'I have an idea. Shall you and I play it to him? I can produce a piece for a singer, an organ and a cello. I'd play the organ and sing and you would play the cello.'

'Brilliant. Let's do it!'

Anton spent a day transposing the work and arranged a date for the Bishop to hear it. Because the organ loft in the Cathedral was so far from the chancel, they met at the parish church.

'Let me explain, Your Grace. We've made this arrangement for you hear what it's like. I've brought the full score so you can see how I've written it, hopefully as you requested.'

Otto and Anton played it, taking about ten minutes. A smiling Bishop applauded at its conclusion.

'You've composed a lovely work for the occasion, Anton. I'm grateful to each of you for your work on this version, solely for my approval. I doubt if it will ever be heard again.'

'I shall make sure it won't, Your Grace,' said Anton.

***

With every encouragement from his new teacher, Anton immersed himself in composing. He had difficulty finding time for anything else, other than his work as organist, which he dare not allow to lapse.

'I've had genuine pleasure in writing these pieces,' said Anton, handing Otto a pile of sheet music. 'They are not fit for publication but exercises, to give me practice in writing music for groups of instruments, including a full orchestra.'

'So what are they?'

'First, a string quartet. Then four pieces for orchestra, the first of which is a march. Then a march for a military band.'

'I've known no one like you, Anton. You are so enthusiastic and full of zeal,' he said, while turning the pages. 'How do you find the time?'

'I do little in the evenings, unless I'm dining with friends, so I write long into the night!'

'Leave them with me, and I'll tell you what I think.'

'Oh... and I've written these two pieces, *Der Abendhimmel* and *Das Edle Herz*, both little songs based on poems I discovered.'

'Unbelievable, Anton. Leave those, too?'

'I will!'

'How would you like to try your hand at writing a symphony? The closest you've got to one is your string quartet. You could also try an overture!'

'I'll do both,' said Anton with a broad smile.

'Nothing can counter your enthusiasm, Anton. Now I have a new idea for you. I want you to study an opera by Richard Wagner. It's called Tannhäuser, and it's outrageously modern. The music breaks many of the rules which Simon taught you. There are dissonances, enharmonics and the use of the chromatic scale all over it. I'm conducting its first performance in Linz. And there's a story!'

'Go on!'

'I thought it would be a good idea to perform this work. So I spoke to the manager of the opera house. He said he couldn't make a profit from it, so wouldn't pay any royalty fees. This annoyed Wagner, who said he wouldn't allow it on those terms. Anyway, I contacted Wagner and, after another refusal, I convinced him it would be good publicity to let us perform it. So we can! Would you like to study the score with me? I need to learn it to conduct it. We could learn together. I'm sure you would gain much from delving into it.'

'It would be an adventure for me, Otto, one I would be delighted to share!'

195

***

The arrangements for laying the foundation stone pressed ahead. Johann Schiedermayr appointed Engelbert Lanz, one of Anton's competitors for the post of Cathedral Organist, to conduct *Preiset den Herrn*, the Festive Cantata. The 13th Infantry Regiment accepted the Bishop's invitation to play in it. The Linz Mixed Choir would perform in it, as would some invited soloists. At the following High Mass, Anton would conduct Antonio Lotti's Mass, followed by his own *Ave Maria*, the exact programme he played at the sixteenth anniversary concert.

Anton and Otto watched the performance of the Cantata. They were delighted. Engelbert Lanz had rehearsed the performers virtually to perfection. Otto could detect the influence of the lessons he had given Anton.

***

Reading the score of Wagner's Tannhäuser was a revelation, an inspiration. Nothing Anton had seen before came near to it.

'So what do you think, Anton?'

'The man's a genius. There is no other way to describe him. I'm amazed that he wrote the words and the music. And what a story.'

'I'm asking you about the music and how it could influence you!'

'The music has opened my eyes. It's original. The most modern I've seen. Working with Simon, I often thought of breaking the rules he insisted I obey. What Wagner has done in this opera is to show what I have dreamed of can be successfully achieved. This work is a stimulus, not for me to follow, but for me to go my own way, and to use my own, individual style.'

'So you are saying that this opera will enrich something in your composing which is already in your toolbox.'

'Exactly that. I've already used some chromatic examples in my later works, in the sections which are not sung. In fact, I'll be more daring still in the first symphony I compose, and in the overture.'

'While we're discussing your work, I enjoyed reading your string quartet. In fact, I played the cello part of the first movement. I loved the audacity of the development in that movement. I thought the rondo was too unconventional, even for my taste! I especially liked the marches and three orchestral pieces which are richly melodic. And the two songs. Shall we see if we can get any of these works performed in Linz?'

'I think not, Otto. They are merely exercises on what I've learnt from you. I will keep them, but only for future reference.'

***

It was rare for Anton to commit himself to a specific action without telling somebody, usually Moritz, Irene Planck, or Johann Schiedermayr. This time,

196

he didn't tell a soul. There was a reason. He often thought his post at the Cathedral was too routine and insufficiently challenging. If what he was thinking of doing led to nothing, there could be no embarrassment. While in Vienna, he became attracted to the idea of being organist at the Imperial Court Chapel. So, having recently heard there was a vacancy for the chief organist post, he applied. He was delighted that he'd kept the application a secret, as he failed, even to be interviewed.

***

Anton wanted to begin the overture as soon as he could. He often spun ideas for it around in his mind. He committed himself to writing it, not only to Otto, but to the von Mayfields at another welcomed dinner they had invited him to, along with Irene.

'An overture, Anton? What made you think of that?'

'Good question, Betty. Since all those lessons with Simon Sechter, I've had further help from Otto Kitzler. He's a cellist with the Linz Theatre Orchestra and an enthusiast for studying and performing modern music. He wants me to write a modern overture and a symphony. I can't wait to get started. I especially like the idea of a symphony!'

'You're not giving up writing choral music are you, Anton?' said Moritz.

'Not at all. But I want to write modern choir music, which will be religious or secular, but the accent will be on the word modern, like Beethoven, Mendelsohn and other adventurous composers. I'm moving away from my mainly traditional approach to composing. The Bachs and Palestrinas of this world.'

'So what are you writing first, the overture or the symphony?' asked Irene.

'The overture. I've more ideas for that piece than the symphony, which I've thought little about yet.'

'When you say ideas, can you explain to us, in terms that are not too technical or sing or whistle any tunes?' said Betty.

'My idea with the overture is to make it a statement which says, "I am Anton Bruckner. This is my overture to the world. There is more to come!"'

Anton started the work on Christmas Eve. He threw himself into it, as if there was nothing more important, not even enjoying Christmas with his friends. He laboured day after day, night after night. Writing for a full orchestra gave him a sensation he had not experienced before in composing. The feeling of power. It consumed him. He thought the nearest experience was improvising on the organ at the Cathedral. He enjoyed pitching one section of the orchestra against another, like playing the strings and then the same theme or a modified one on the woodwind or brass. As much pleasure came from composing for the full orchestra, playing at once. He completed

197

the work before the end of January and made only a few changes to the manuscript. Then he was dying to write that symphony.

Writing it took much of his energy and thought. The first step was to settle on the overall structure. He would follow other modern composers and write it in four movements. Then he would decide on the mood of each movement. The first would be an allegro, the second an andante, and the third a scherzo, followed by an energetic finale. He would write each movement, except the scherzo and andante, in the classical sonata form. But he would break the rules and follow Otto's advice. The challenge would be creating the themes. Changing them, varying them, inverting them and working out the keys to play them in. Every theme would be original, the product of his mind alone.

Although he would spend the time necessary to write a full length symphony, it would be an exercise. It would be a serious attempt, but he would not want it to be performed or published. In fact, he would want none of his first symphonic attempts to be made public until satisfied he had mastered the skills of the symphonist.

Having planned the structure, he began to write down material for the first and second theme groups of the exposition. Each group would have two separate but closely related themes. The first group would open the symphony. He played it on the Bösendorfer and liked it. The first tune of the group was quiet and short. The second a louder reply. Then he created a second pair which he also tried on the piano. That too satisfied him. Then he needed to work out the dynamics and some of the instrumentation. He decided he needed at least one more group of themes which would be different in character from the first group, and which would be stated after it, but also be part of the exposition.

Anton soon realised he had taken on a major, time-consuming project. Completion of the first movement took more than a month, during which he had his work as organist to perform. One of his delights was to discuss his progress on the symphony with friends and colleagues.

'So how is it progressing?' said Irene, when she visited Anton to replace some curtains in his study.

'It is a real challenge, Irene. I've never taken on anything quite like it before. It's in four movements and two are in sonata form.'

'You've confused me already! What do you mean by four movements and sonata form?'

'The movements are the parts of the symphony. The first will start quickly, then go slowly to give contrast. A slow second movement will follow and can be sad. The third part is playful and sometimes in jest, or in the form of a dance. The fourth is the finale, usually ending on an optimistic note, but not always. Have you ever heard a symphony or a sonata?'

'Never. I've heard many religious works, including some of yours, the *Requiem Mass* and other pieces you've written, but I don't think I've listened to anything for just an orchestra or a single instrument, except when you've played the organ.'

'Now I'll explain sonata form...'

'Not now, Anton. I'm concentrating on hanging your new curtains. What are you doing for dinner tonight?'

'I'm going to the Wirtshaus.'

'I'd rather you came around to mine. I'm doing pork chops with potatoes and broad beans.'

'I accept your kind invitation.'

'Let's say seven o'clock.'

Anton continued with the symphony. He worked hard on the exposition, the recapitulation and on to the end. He read it through several times and tested it out on his piano. The trainee symphonist had used all his imagination to create what he regarded as a competently written first movement, but had yet to complete the orchestration. He had broken the rules, well and truly, in a piece that would last for about fifteen minutes.

He wondered whether to show Otto what he had written but decided he wouldn't. It made no sense to reveal the first movement, which was only a part of the whole.

Anton's release from the prison of Sechter's teaching had an inspirational effect. While only part way through his first symphony, he thought about other works he would enjoy writing. He had made no firm decisions, but while strolling through the city, humming a theme for the andante of his first symphonic attempt, he almost bumped into Bishop Rudigier.

'Oh. Good morning, Franz.'

'Good morning, Anton. You look as if you are in a dream!'

'You could say that. Several things are in my mind at present. I'm thinking of a theme I could include in my symphony and what other music I could write. Seeing you makes me wonder about a new Mass!'

The Bishop laughed. 'That's an incredible idea. I had a strange dream last night. It was that I was listening to a new Mass in the Cathedral and you had written it! It was wonderful, and I woke up with a start! So, I say yes to your new idea, Anton!'

'In which case, Franz, a new Mass it will be!'

From then onwards, he had two works on his mind, the symphony and the Mass. Single-mindedly, he concentrated on completing the symphony before he started the Mass. The theme he created while almost knocking over the Bishop was one of the simplest and most beautiful he had ever written. The problem might be working it into the movement. It was more for the second group than the first, he thought. He tested its place by playing the bars leading up to it on the piano. The contrast between the music that led to it and the first appearance of the tune was intense and, to Anton, elevated the significance and beauty of it.

Composing the scherzo seemed easier than writing either the first or second movements. He wrote a fast paced introduction which he developed, then a delightful trio which sounded like slow dance music or a song. Then he repeated the introduction, note for note. The whole scherzo had a joyful flavour to it.

His aim in the finale was to make it sound like the celebration it was. It reflected the joy he had experienced in writing the symphony. If this was the pleasure he felt in writing such a work, he would write more.

***

The Theatre Orchestra and singers, under Otto, rehearsed the Tannhäuser three times. By then they felt it was all but perfect. Anton attended the latter two.

'Well done to you, Otto, and to your choir, orchestra and soloists. That rehearsal bodes well for the two performances.'

'Thank you, Anton. Not bad, eh? Here are two tickets for you, one for each.'

In front of a full house, they performed the Tannhäuser superbly well, but it disappointed Anton. While he admired the music, he didn't like the plot and the opera seemed too long. At least with the score, he could ignore the words and just read the music, which confirmed his view that Wagner was a genius.

***

There was still work to do on the symphony before he could show it to Otto Kitzler. Within days of listening to the Wagner, he completed the orchestration. What he had written by then was a draft, which included much instrumentation but not all. So he concentrated on where he would use the full orchestra, soloists and groups of players and how they would interact. To him, the thematic material made this fairly clear, so after only a couple of weeks' further work, he completed his first symphony. He read his score through a few more times and made some minor changes.

'Well, here it is, Otto.' He handed over the manuscript.

'It will take me a few days to read it all. It's quite a size. How long is it in terms of the time to play it?'

'I would say about forty-five minutes. Not very long.'

'About right, I think. So what are you writing next?'

200

Anton told him the story of almost bumping into the Bishop.

'So a Mass then?'

'Certainly. I'm now really keen!'

'When will you start?'

'Today!'

They met again three days later. Anton could see from the look on Otto's face he would not pile praise on it.

'I've read it right through, Anton, and I've played some of it on the piano. It has some delightful parts,' he said. 'So I compliment you on your achievement. However, I have some criticism. First, I don't know why you chose F minor as the key. It seems wrong. How did you decide on it?'

'I just wanted to do something different. I looked for other symphonies in F minor and found only one: Number 49 by Joseph Haydn. Mozart appears to have avoided it, at least for symphonies.'

'Some of the thematic material is so simple it hardly justifies including in a symphony.'

'Any in particular?'

'Yes, the tune about thirty bars into the andante. It's just one note of the same length after another.'

'I'm surprised you say that. I think that is one of the nicest tunes I've written.'

'I don't agree. Finally, I think you have approached it as if you were compelled to write it, so with little inspiration.'

'Sorry, Otto, but you're wrong. I've constantly felt committed and enthusiastic about it. Of course, it was an exercise and I'm sure I could improve it. I've dedicated my time to it for the three months it has taken me to write it. We will be friends forever, but I am disappointed with your comments.'

'I can only give you an honest opinion, so there it is. I'm sorry you aren't happy with my thoughts, but I am very demanding.'

'You are! Obviously, I'll think about your comments. The one I disagree with most is the one about that tune in the andante. It recurs in the scherzo, and in a new form in the trio. I shall consider again what you say about it. You may be right about the key!'

'I think I've reached the point where you are a more accomplished composer than I am, so I think you need nothing more from me, if you agree, that is!'

'Maybe, I should agree, Otto. Thank you for all the help and tutorials you've given me, and for introducing me to Richard Wagner. It's now up to me to apply what I've learnt. I felt so good writing that symphony, I'm going to write some more.'

'We ought to celebrate your completion of my course, Anton. So I invite you to have dinner with my wife and me. Are you available tomorrow evening? I hope so. That will give me time to get some beers in!'

'Yes, I am free tomorrow. I'd be delighted to have a meal with you and your wife. It will save me from catering for myself!'

***

Anton turned his attention to the Mass. Discarding F minor, he chose D minor. This was not to admit F minor was wrong in his symphony, but simply to write in a key often used for masses. It would be a Mass in the usual six parts. He would use the techniques of composition he had used for his symphony, with drastic changes in dynamics, crescendos, and discords. The plan was to write it for a mixed choir, soloists, a full orchestra, with two each of the woodwind and brass instruments, a timpani and an organ.

'How is our new Mass progressing?' said the Bishop, at nine o'clock one night in the candle lit Cathedral, after Anton had finished playing and improvising on some themes from Bach's Toccata and Fugue in D minor. Bishop Rudigier had sat in the pews for over an hour, listening.

'I'm flattered that you are sharing ownership of it already, Franz! The next thing is you'll want to help me compose it!'

'No such thing, Anton. I only said "ours" because we both thought of the idea of you writing it at the same time!'

'I will be honoured if you continue with the "our" designation!'

'In which case I will! You still haven't told me about progress!'

'It's coming on well, I think.' He told the Bishop about the instrumentation, and that he would write the orchestral parts as if they were part of a symphony.

'I hope you see the work as glorifying the Father, not showing Him how to write a symphony!'

'You are toying with me, Franz! I hope to have the Mass completed by the middle of September.'

'You'll have to work through the night then, as we make such demands on your time here and at the parish.'

'So you say, but I'm using a means to make my work easier.'

'Really! Tell me more!'

'I shall use some material from earlier works. For example, I will quote from my *Missa Solemnis*, from a piece called *Afferentur regi* I wrote for St Florian and my setting of *Psalm 146*, which I also wrote for St Florian. They are already saving me time.'

'Don't you regard that as cheating?'

'No! I won't be quoting directly, so you will be hard pressed to recognise these sources. Let me know if you do, and I'll disguise them even more!'

'By the way, on the symphonic theme, have you finished that symphony you were working on some months back?'

'Yes, it's finished now.'

'In which case we should arrange for its performance.'

'It was only a study work, an exercise Otto Kitzler set me. So it will never be performed. I hope my next one will!'

They parted, and Anton walked home, whistling possible new tunes for the Mass as he went.

Anton completed the Mass in exactly the time he had planned and told the Bishop, who set a date for its performance: 20 November. Since Anton would himself play the organ parts, they appointed Engelbert Lanz as the conductor and the one responsible for choosing the soloists and choir, which was the Linz Mixed Choir.

The first rehearsal included a lady whom Anton knew well. 'I'm so pleased to see you Terweide,' he said, giving her a kiss on both cheeks. 'Have you come all the way from Kronstorf?'

'No! I live in Linz now with my husband, Heiner. I've only been here a year and I've joined this famous choir. I'm sorry you aren't the choirmaster any more. I've heard the story of your resignation and I don't blame you for going.'

'I have some splendid memories of our past, Terweide. Especially at the swimming session, and the curling where I couldn't stand up on the ice!'

'That was so funny, Anton. You had us in fits of laughter. But you made up for it by being a good swimmer!'

'I really enjoyed my time in Kronstorf, after the disaster of Windhaag!'

'You have done marvels since both of them. You are a composer in your own right, and the organist at the second most important cathedral in the country.'

'You are too kind, Terweide! Let me know what you think of the Mass!'

***

'This Mass is so different from any Mass I've heard or performed before that I insist on four rehearsals. So I hope you have all brought your diaries!' said Engelbert, before they started.

'Not good. Start again,' he said at the beginning of the Gloria, while hitting his music stand with his baton. 'That's much better!' So he worked his way through the score while Anton occupied the organ bench. It took a good two hours to complete the rehearsal, after which Terweide spoke to Anton.

'My goodness, that's the most striking Mass I've ever heard,' she said. 'I love the way you have brought in the orchestra and the tremendous changes in tempo and sound level. It's unique!'

'I'm pleased with it. To me, it's my first major work. I have written a number, as you know, but this is the one I'm most proud of!'

'I can understand that!'

'I just hope members of the audience don't walk out, as they did when we performed my little Mass in Kronstorf!'

'I guarantee they won't!'

Anton's anxiety was unjustified. The congregation applauded as Engelbert invited him up onto the rostrum. Anton could hardly believe his ears. This was only the second time in his life that this had happened. He bowed, not only to the audience but to the orchestra, then to the choir and shook hands with male soloists and kissed the ladies. Engelbert held his hand up high in celebration. It was one of the happiest days of Anton's life.

Once the congregation had dispersed, Terweide came to see him. 'I was right, not one of them walked out, Anton. Congratulations! You deserved every hand clap you received! You quite surprised me with that kiss! My husband was in the audience but I'm sure he won't mind!'

'It was a simple way of showing my appreciation to you for your beautiful singing. The soloists are so important in this work.'

A few days later, Irene, carrying a rolled-up newspaper, visited Anton at his apartment. 'Have you seen this? There's a wonderful review of your Cathedral concert in the Linz Daily News. They say you've got "huge potential as a symphonic composer". And they rate the D minor Mass as "being in the highest echelon of church music"! You couldn't wish for better.'

'Amazing! I'm not sure I deserve it! May I read it, please?'

'Go ahead!'

Anton read it slowly, almost as if he needed to absorb what they were saying to convince himself it was real.

'I'm pleased! Thank you so much for bringing it to me. I rarely buy newspapers, so I may have missed it completely!'

'Someone else would have told you. That's why I rushed around to see you. I wanted to be first! Do come and dine with me tonight.'

'I'd love to!'

'See you at seven o'clock. Please don't delay, drinking with the choir this time!'

'I'll be good!'

After Irene left, Anton made his way to the Cathedral to perform his day's play. The Bishop was waiting for him. A stern look on his face surprised Anton. Had he offended the Bishop? Should he have spent more time playing the Cathedral and the parish church organs? Had he delegated too much to his deputy? Surely not, otherwise Johann Schiedermayr would have told him. Then he spoke.

'Anton, I have something to tell you. I was so intoxicated by your Mass I could not pray during it. Much as I tried, I simply failed. Your Mass drastically affected me. No piece of music has ever done that to me before. It is the most powerful Mass I've ever heard. So I can say only one thing. Congratulations!'

'You really had me concerned when I saw your stern countenance, Franz. I thought I had committed a felony!'

'You did nothing wrong, Anton. It was your Mass that tore me away from God!'

***

Anton always enjoyed dinner with Irene, whom he often talked to about his inner-most thoughts on any subject, including his failures with women. It was as if she was a personal mentor on matters of deep intimacy.

'I'm so glad you liked the Mass, Irene. I had you in mind when I wrote the thing.'

'Don't be silly!'

'Well, you have been good to me, ever since you were my landlady. Goodness, it must be nearly twenty-five years ago.'

'You made me jealous, kissing that soloist. It looked as if you knew her very well.' She winked.

'I've known her for years. We first met in Kronstorf when I taught there. She recently moved to Linz with her husband.'

'So have you had any luck with the ladies, Anton?'

'I'm afraid not,' he said, looking at the table with a part frown. 'I've had several unsuccessful attempts these last eighteen months. Your advice to make more of an effort to find love has failed. So I'm in the same place: I'm too old for them. I'll keep trying!'

'I wish I was twenty years younger. I'd be with you in a trice!'

***

Johann Schiedermayr spoke to him to say that he had received dozens of requests to perform the Mass again. He said he had spoken to the director of the Illustrious Hall, who agreed it could be performed there. Anton had his doubts. The Hall had no organ which was an essential part of the Credo.

'As we speak, I've just had a thought, Johann. I can write the organ out of the Mass and replace it by strengthening the woodwind. I can add bassoons and clarinets.'

'But that will be a major job, won't it?'

'No, quite small. It will take a week at the most.'

'So, I'll get back to him and agree, as you are now happy with the idea. He will want to advertise the concert and sort out the costs. He's agreed to split the proceeds with the Cathedral.'

'Maybe a contribution to building the new one.'

'Good idea.'

The audience were delighted with the concert performance, the success of which equalled if not surpassed the one at the Cathedral. Anton had no choice but modestly to accept the adulation. The Linz and Viennese press adored it.

Chapter 16
1865 - 1866 Wagner, Berlioz and love

Anton's enthusiasm for writing symphonies boiled over with his second. He began it in the January in Linz when the weather was as cold as ever. Even though the wood fire was blazing, he sat at his desk in his winter overcoat. The thrill of writing it exceeded by far the excitement of scribbling away at his F minor Symphony. Wondering whether he should change the order of the movements presented him with a puzzle. Should the second movement form the adagio or should the third? The first would be full of energy so the strong contrast of the adagio should be second and the scherzo the third. So it would be in four movements: allegro; adagio - not andante; scherzo, and finale. He would score it for the same orchestra as he had used in the F minor and would, as before, use sonata form. This new symphony would be a wonderful and exciting opportunity for an innovation. Instead of having the conventional two different theme groups, his would have three entirely different ones. He could toy with them as he pleased, even leaving one out for the recapitulation or dropping one and introducing another. The possibilities were endless. Once again, he had to interweave his composing with his work at the Cathedral, and being entertained by his many friends.

Anton received numerous letters of praise and congratulation, usually delivered to the Cathedral, but often sent to his home in the Pfarrgasse. It was a morning in May when he picked up a letter from his front door mat. Thinking it was from an admirer, he took it into his study and put it on his desk. He left it there and went to his kitchen to prepare himself a ham and egg breakfast. During his meal, he thought he would work on the symphony before going to the Cathedral. Having gulped the dregs of his coffee, he returned to the study. He picked up his letter opener and slit it open. His mouth dropped as he read it. Richard Wagner was inviting him to Munich for the first performance of his opera, 'Tristan and Isolde'. Wagner had signed it, after saying he truly hoped he could attend. It took Anton several minutes to recover from the shock.

Why had Wagner invited him in particular? Had he invited any of his colleagues in Linz, Johann, or Otto perhaps? He would make some discrete enquiries.

The letter caused him much excitement. It was akin to a message from on high. He desperately wanted to accept Wagner's invitation. So, he spoke to Johann to ask permission to attend.

'You must go. This is the opportunity of a lifetime.' Wagner had clearly not invited him. He and Otto met at the Wirtshaus tavern for a drink, an evening or two later.

'You won't believe this, Otto.' He explained.

'What an opportunity, Anton. You've got to take it up!' So, Wagner hadn't invited him either.

Anton packed his case and headed for the railway station. Hotels abounded in Munich, so he soon found one near the opera house. He chose one named the Four Seasons, and reserved a comfortable room on the first floor, overlooking a wooded area.

He would dine in their spacious restaurant, and was soon studying the complexities of the extensive menu. Anything with ham, cabbage and dumplings, he thought. While turning the page, a tall gentleman approached him.

'Do you mind if I join you, mein Herr? I'm here for work and dislike dining alone.'

Anton looked at the stranger for less than two seconds. The balding gentleman seemed decent enough, well dressed and had a neatly trimmed, pointed beard.

'Not at all. I'd be delighted. You have asked at exactly the right time, as I've just started looking at the menu. And I prefer to dine in company, too.'

The reasonable looking stranger sat opposite Anton and started a conversation. 'So what is the reason for your visit to this great city?'

Humbly not mentioning the invitation, Anton said it was to attend the first performance of an opera by Richard Wagner.

'What an amazing coincidence. I'm here for the same opera. I know Wagner personally and have for some time.'

What the stranger had said made Anton feel easier about admitting to the invitation. 'Incredible. I've not met him and am having difficulty working out why Herr Wagner sent me a letter asking me to come.'

'I'm not surprised at all. Richard sent out several hundred to people here and in Austria, who have anything to do with music.'

'I see,' he said, not sure what to feel.

'So what is your connection?'

'I'm the head organist at Linz Cathedral and am a composer.'

'That explains it. What do you compose?'

'I've written several works but I'm most proud of a *Missa Solemnis* I wrote a good few years ago, and my Mass in D minor, which was performed twice last year in Linz. Oh, my name is Anton Bruckner. So apart from being Herr Wagner's friend, do you have connections with music?'

'My name is Hans von Bülow. I am the Court Conductor in Munich. Aren't you aware of me? I am also a composer.'

'I'm delighted to meet you, Herr von Bülow. I think I have heard of you, from Simon Sechter or Johann Herbeck in Vienna.'

'Oh, excellent. In fact, I know them both. I shall conduct this first performance.'

'What an honour!'

'For whom? Wagner or me?'

Anton slightly raised his eyebrows at von Bülow's response and laughed. Von Bülow smiled back.

'We've been talking long enough. It's time we made our selections from the menu, don't you think?' said von Bülow.

'Indeed, it is.'

The conversation paused for a few minutes. Anton fancied the boiled ham with dumplings. With a shout, and a click of his fingers, von Bülow summoned a waitress.

'I want the trout dish, and I don't know what my friend wants.'

'I'll have the ham, please, meine Fräulein,' said Anton, looking towards the waitress. Then he turned towards von Bülow. 'I'm really looking forward to the performance.'

'It's a monumental work, so I've spent an enormous amount of time on committing it to memory. We've had three rehearsals already. What are you composing at present?'

'I'm in the middle of writing a new symphony. It will be my first for public performance. I've written one before but it's only a practice exercise. I've brought my manuscript with me to work on it here. If you are interested, Herr von Bülow, you can have a look. I'd appreciate knowing what you think of it.'

'I'm surprised that you've written a symphony as a practice exercise! I'd be delighted to see your new one. Bring it down to breakfast in the morning.'

The two of them continued discussing their musical interests and their musical education. Anton told him his story.

'Interesting. So you are Austrian through to your bones!'

'You could say that!'

'I was born in Dresden and learnt much about music from Clara Schumann's father. But my parents wanted me to become a lawyer. So they sent me to Leipzig to study there. This is where I met Liszt and heard Wagner's "Lohengrin". So despite my parents, I changed course and studied music instead, in particular the piano, under Professor Louis Plaidy. My first conducting job came because of Richard's recommendation. My extraordinary career sprang from there.' To Anton's relief, he eventually stopped his monologue after revealing even more self-aggrandising detail.

'You have had an interesting life and have met many musical personalities.'

'Indeed, I have. I can introduce you to some. Anton Rubinstein is here, possibly in the same hotel as us. I know him very well, having conducted many of his concert performances.'

'I'd love to meet him. He might also be interested in my new symphony.'

'Possibly.'

They parted, agreeing to meet at breakfast, and with von Bülow reminding him to bring his symphony with him. Anton worked into the night. He could hardly stop thinking about the work. Complex and simple tunes poured into his imagination, along with their variations. By then, he had completed the first movement and was writing the scherzo, which he was making especially energetic. He put his pen down at half-past one and went to bed.

'What an interesting start,' said von Bülow, at breakfast, while looking at Anton's score. 'Not at all bad. Very modern and quite a lengthy first movement. Do I detect a third theme in the exposition?'

'Yes, you do!'

'Quite an innovation, then. I just wonder if it's too daring. Otherwise...' He turned over some more pages. 'A good scherzo, too, if rumbustious. Yes, overall, I like it. You owe it to the world to finish it!'

'I'm sure I will. It's just a matter of time!'

'We'll see if we can find Anton Rubinstein today, and show him.'

Eventually, they found Rubinstein at the opera house, practicing his piano playing. He struck the keys with his eyes closed and seemed to Anton to exaggerate his arm movements. His hair was black and thick but not long and, unlike von Bülow, he was clean shaven. He looked fit. Anton half expected to see Wagner there, but there was no sign of him or the performers. Rubinstein stopped playing when he saw von Bülow.

'Anton, I want to introduce you to another Anton, Anton Bruckner. He's the organist at Linz Cathedral and a composer, as of course are we. He's brought along what he's written of his second symphony, which will in effect will be his first.'

'I'm not sure I follow, Hans!'

'You explain, Herr Bruckner.' So he did.

'I see, so this symphony will be your first because it will be your first to be performed.'

'Correct!'

Rubinstein then stood up from the piano and shook hands with Anton, expressing his pleasure at meeting him. Anton did likewise.

'He's brought along what he's written and would like to know what you think of the thing.'

'Please, would you let me finished here first? There's a coffee shop across the road. What if I meet you there in half an hour? Oh, do you know the first performance is being delayed because Malvina Schnorr has become ill?'

'No! And I'm bloody cross. I'm the damned conductor and probably the last to know.'

'Calm down, Hans! I only learnt from Richard about ten minutes ago, and he went off to find you!'

'Oh!' he said shamefacedly, and looking away from Rubinstein. 'We'll see you in half an hour, then. If you see Richard, in the meantime, please tell him you've told me about poor Malvina. Does he know how long the delay will be?'

'I will tell him. He doesn't know how long she'll be off sick.'

Von Bülow and Anton sat in the shop, drinking coffee. Three quarters of an hour passed with no sign of Rubinstein.

'Where is he?' said von Bülow, not expecting Anton to know but expressing his frustration. 'There's only so much coffee one can drink.'

'I'll get another cup for each of us,' said Anton.

'Not for me. I've had enough.'

Anton went to the bar and bought one for himself. As he returned, Rubinstein appeared. 'Would you like a coffee?' said Anton.

'Yes, please.'

While Anton was getting another coffee, von Bülow was showing Rubinstein Anton's score. He placed the coffee in front of Rubinstein.

'As you can see, I'm looking at your symphony.' Without saying another word, he read the incomplete score, using his forefinger to beat out the rhythm as he went. Occasionally, he stopped and looked at the previous page, then resumed from where he paused. He would take a sip of coffee. Then continue.

'Would you mind getting me another cup, Herr Bruckner?'

'Not at all.'

He continued, page by page, until he had read the manuscript, up to the end of the first movement, then what Anton had written of the scherzo. He spent at least half an hour examining it.

'It's good. A truly modern work. I love its contrasts and originality, and the vastly different but related themes you've invented. You must complete it and have it performed. It's the best start to a symphony I've seen for ages!'

'I think it's a bit too daring, too modern. Audiences will struggle with it,' said von Bülow, giving a different view to what he said earlier.

'No. Music has to move on. And this man has achieved that. You are a true symphonist, Herr Bruckner.' Anton smiled at this generous compliment.

He spent the rest of the day working in the hotel lounge on the scherzo and started again the next morning. After writing for a couple of hours, he felt he needed a break, so walked the few hundred metres to the opera house. The main entrance was open, so he walked in. He would find his way to the stand, just off the stage, where Rubinstein was practicing. From there, he would explore this beautiful building. As he entered the auditorium, he could hear delightful music from the piano. Again, it was Rubinstein. He stood near and listened to the Mozart piano sonata. Rubinstein was concentrating so hard, he didn't notice Anton until he finished the third movement.

'Herr Bruckner! I'm sorry, I didn't see you!'

'In a way, I'm pleased because I could just stand here listening to your amazing playing and be sure I wasn't interrupting you!'

'It's good to see you. Have you come to explore the opera house?'

'Yes, just to see more of it.'

'I'm waiting to see Richard. We agreed to meet at two o'clock, which was about half an hour ago. If you would care to wait, I'll introduce you to him.'

'Here I am, Anton!'

Anton recognised the great man immediately from pictures he'd seen of him. His smile, on seeing Rubinstein, covered the width of his clean shaven-face.

'I'm sorry I'm so late. I've just been to see Malvina, who is really ill. It seems like influenza. She is very hoarse. It could be two weeks or more before she can sing again. So, many of you will be stuck here, I'm afraid. Who is your friend?'

'Please permit me to introduce you to Anton Bruckner,' said Rubinstein. 'He is the Cathedral Organist at Linz, and a composer in his own right. He's in the middle of writing his first symphony. I've read what he's written, and it's superb!'

'I'm pleased to meet you, Herr Bruckner.'

Anton could hardly believe he was in the presence of the great man, the Master, the most famous man in Germany. For a second, he didn't know how to respond. 'Equally, I'm delighted to meet you, Herr Wagner. I so admire your work. You are the true master of musical creation.'

'Oh, I'm flattered by your praise! I must see what you've written on that symphony. I wrote one myself, but that was over… thirty years ago! So what are you going to do for the next fortnight, Anton?'

Anton thought he'd put his question to him, so replied, 'I intend to stay in Munich.'

'That's amusing! I was addressing Herr Rubinstein. But I'm delighted you are staying. Come around every evening and you can join me and my circle of friends. That would please me immensely.'

'Thank you, but I don't want to impose.'

'You are a new symphonist. I've rather taken to you already. Come regularly to mine and we'll all have a great time, talking music, eating and drinking and we may even go on the odd late evening walk!'

'Thank you again. Yes, I'll come. My only problem is I have to return to Linz for Pentecost and for the first performance of a cantata I've written.'

'But you will come back for Tristan and Isolde, won't you?'

'I will.'

'Now you, Herr Rubinstein, you'll join us, won't you? Every evening. Like Bruckner the symphonist here?'

'I'd love to Richard. Our usual circle, plus Herr Bruckner.'

So Anton, Rubinstein, von Bülow and his wife, Cosima, and several others of high musical repute, met almost every evening at Wagner's beautiful house, which King Ludwig II, his most fervent admirer, had bought him. From the prickly attitude of von Bülow, Anton felt something odd was happening between Bülow's wife and the Master, but could not be certain.

Anton gained much from these meetings. While feeling awkward at first, in the presence of the Master, he soon felt part of the group, especially as Wagner was so congenial towards him and clearly wanted to befriend him. The conversations varied from discussion about Wagner's operas, through works of others, for example Meyerbeer, to German politics, and various sexual encounters the Master had engaged in. Anton felt embarrassed at the mere mention of such things. They raised such matters in the absence of the women who entertained themselves in another room. Anton couldn't understand how Wagner had been so successful with so many women and he had been a total failure. Could they relate to his fame? He dare not ask the Master how he'd achieved his interesting relationships. But he seemed to have failed with a number, too. His conclusion was he should continue in his own way, and not give up hope.

After a fortnight of pressing on with his symphony and enjoying the regular evening meetings and dinners with Wagner, he reminded the Master of his commitments in Linz and that he would have to leave.

'You will come back for my opera, Anton. I'd be so disappointed if you didn't. And you haven't shown me what you've done on that symphony! So you must return!'

'I will, O Master. And thank you for your delightful hospitality. Those evenings with you and your friends have been wonderful.'

Anton returned just in time for the third performance of Tristan and Isolde. He sat in the thirteenth row of the spectacular auditorium and pondered on what to expect from this opera. Would it affect him in any way? Could the techniques Wagner used help him, or would he learn nothing from it? Might it re-confirm that he was now free to be unconventional, to use discords, startling, even shocking, changes of harmony, chromaticism, striking orchestral tone and ambiguity of key?

Hans von Bülow, appeared from the wings and strutted to the rostrum. He stepped on to it, turned to face the audience, and bowed. There was no score in front of him, so he must have succeeded in committing this gigantic work to memory. He silenced the audience by hitting the rail of the rostrum with his baton. Then speedily raised it to begin.

From the very first note of the prelude, it entranced Anton. What an incredible chord, he thought, on hearing that shattering, discordant combination of four notes in the third bar. How would Wagner resolve it? Then another discord and another. The plot, despite the beautiful, sensitive and dramatic singing of Malvina Schnorr and her husband, Ludwig, as Tristan, was of no interest. He listened, mouth open, but only to the music. He had never put such an effort into analysing and dissecting the live performance of another composer's work. The miracle of this opera was that it confirmed to him he had become a free man, a free composer. He would continue to use the techniques he had learned from Otto Kitzler. They had been in his musical vocabulary from years before, but he was only just beginning to put them into practice. He would continue along this path, and the symphony would be the vehicle for his travel.

Neither Act One nor Act Two resolved that first chord. Surely, it had to be, otherwise there could be a riot, thought Anton. It was, right at the end of Act Three, at the death of Isolde.

This music had exhausted him. He took up Richard's offer of going to his abode for the regular evening meeting. He would return to his hotel first, just to clear his head of the music that still filled it, and his thoughts about his future composing. And he would take a score back with him.

'It's you, Bruckner,' said Wagner, as the maid escorted Anton into the lounge. 'It's so good of you to come back! I'm afraid you've missed the last performance of Tristan, which finished only an hour ago! And what is it, tucked under your arm, that symphony you have yet to finish?'

Much to Anton's embarrassment, he suddenly became the target of the stares of all Richard's guests. The usual band were there, von Bülow and his wife, Cosima, Rubinstein, and others whom Anton didn't know. He soon smiled when several, including von Bülow shouted welcoming greetings.

'No, I saw it. It totally enraptured me. I didn't bother with the plot but only listened to the music!'

Several there laughed. 'Do you mean to say you didn't listen to my singing?' said a woman.

'Oh, you played Isolde. I'm pleased to meet you, Frau Schnörr. I listened to your singing and the orchestral parts, but I'm not sure of the plot. I'm sure you will explain why you died in the end.'

'So how could you be enraptured, as you said, if you ignored the story?' said Ludwig Schnörr. 'So you took no notice of the words I sang either.'

'I'm just a composer, so my only interest was the incredible novelty of what Herr Wagner composed. I analysed in my head every chord and discord and was thrilled by the resolution at the end of Act Three. That music will change forever the way composers compose. It is daring, dynamic, exciting, earthshaking and totally original. Like nothing else ever written, not that I've heard, anyway. I was impressed and thrilled by Tannhäuser, but this is in a different league.'

They all applauded what Anton said. The room came alive with comments like 'I agree', 'well said', 'good thinking', and 'definitely true'.

Then Wagner spoke. 'I cannot tell you how pleased I am that you were there, Anton. And I'm even more pleased with your reaction. If no one else can understand your ignoring of the plot, I can. You didn't go, as everyone else did, to be entertained by the drama. You went to explore, dissect and evaluate my music. We have to admire Anton for that, everyone. Now let's talk about your couple of weeks in Linz. How did it go? And what's that score?'

The conversation between Anton and Wagner became separated from the talking of the rest of the group, so was more private. 'It went well, I'm delighted to say. I did my duty with the organ playing. I just avoided being double booked in Linz Cathedral and the parish church. Then I sang in the first performance of my new cantata, for which this is the score. That was an experience, and it went well,' he said, holding up the manuscript.

'Tell me more about it.'

'It's a highly patriotic work called *Germanenzug*. It's about the fate of German soldiers who die in battle and are guided to Valhalla by the Norse mythical death maidens, the Valkyries.'

'Let's sit at this table and you can show me. Interesting that you cite the Valkyries. They are important characters in an opera I've written by that name, which is one of a cycle I'm working on. I finished writing it a good ten years ago and am planning to perform the complete cycle soon. You must come to it, Anton. You'll love the music, but I'm not sure what you will think of the plot!'

Anton opened the score to the first page. 'What an unusual combination of instruments and singers. A male-voice choir, two tenors and two basses, then all brass and a euphonium. This is the work of a talented composer. It's excellent. Who wrote the words, you?'

'No, but there's a story. A poet called August Silberstein, to whom my friend, Rudolf Weinwurm, introduced me.'

'When did you write it, not alongside the symphony you are writing?'

'No! About two years ago. In fact, I should have played it last year, as an entry into a competition, but that was postponed and I ended up conducting it at the delayed competition in Salzburg. They publicised it so well that Eduard Hanslick, the critic from Vienna, attended. Disappointingly for me, it came second and, would you believe, my friend Weinwurm's piece won. Hanslick said he liked mine!'

'I can understand your dismay, but this is a superbly constructed and emotional work. I like it a great deal. So when are you going to show me what you've written on that symphony?'

'I'd much prefer not to until I've finished it.'

'But you've shown it to von Bülow and Rubinstein. Why not me?'

'But you are the Master! I don't want to inflict it on you, O Master, a half cooked piece from a beginner of a symphonist!'

The meetings with Richard Wagner had a profound effect on Anton. Not only was his path to being symphonist confirmed, he took much from him and Wagner becoming good friends. It was as if Wagner acted like a mother swan and taken him under his ample wing. The fond farewell he gave Anton would hopefully form the cornerstone of a lasting relationship.

***

Life back in Linz became increasingly hectic. Johann Schiedermayr made great demands on him as Organist, mainly because of Anton's ability and popularity, and he was working on his new symphony. Having spent much of his energy on it, he finished the first and third movements and was labouring on the second, the adagio. It was while playing in the Cathedral that Bishop Rudigier came specially to see him.

'My dear Anton, I have yet another request for you. The builders have made excellent progress in constructing the new cathedral. I was exceedingly grateful to you for writing the Festive Cantata, *Preiset den Herrn*. I would dearly like you to compose a Mass for the dedication of the Votive Chapel, which is almost complete. Could you please?'

'Yes, Franz. I would love to. Have you any thoughts about the choirs and orchestration?'

'I was thinking about something that could, like the Festive Cantata, be performed outdoors, in any weather. Maybe using the infantry band for the wind section?'

'So, not a piece for a full orchestra, as in my earlier Mass?'

'No, I think not. Could it be like a Mass from a century ago, but written in your own, inimitable style?'

'I'll take that as a commission, Franz! Thank you for asking me. I regard it as a great honour.'

Anton meant what he said. What he did not say was that this was yet another obligation, on top of the excess of work he had already committed to doing. What made matters worse was that he spent so much time alone, had to cook for himself, make his own bed and perform all the other domestic duties of living a bachelor's life.

'You don't seem your usual cheery self,' said Irene, one day when she saw Anton in the greengrocer's shop near the Pfarrgasse, while he was choosing some onions.

'There are days, Irene, when I don't know which way to turn. I seem to have too many commitments. What I really need is a woman. Someone I could love and who could happily be my wife.'

'Come to dinner at my house tonight and we can discuss some solutions. See you at seven?'

'I'd love to! Thank you.'

So he and Irene sat into the night and discussed Anton's problems. There was nothing she could do to help him, other than to talk. She realised he was overworking and not giving himself time for relaxation.

'I don't know how you can cope with all this,' she said, after he had listed his commitments and his new symphony.

'One solution might be to leave the new symphony until you've written the Bishop's Mass. I can't see any obligation to finish it, other than in your own head.'

'I must complete it before I start the Mass, Irene. You are right, though. It's in my head and I want to get out of my head and get it performed.'

'In which case you need a woman! Take my earlier advice and see if you can find someone! You know many women in the Linz Choir. Try one of them!'

Inspired by Irene's advice, Anton spoke to a choir member whom he knew well.

'Josefine, would you care to come out with me, perhaps for a drink at the Wirtshaus tavern?'

'I'd be delighted to, Anton. Say, tomorrow lunch time. I don't want to go there on my own, so where should we meet?'

'I'm playing at the parish church tomorrow morning, so how about in the chancel at midday?'

'I'll be there then.'

Josefine Lang liked Anton and admired him as a brilliant organist and composer. It seemed strange to her, a seventeen-year old, that this forty-year old man was asking her out for a drink. What could be the reason? Did he want advice about the choir, perhaps? Was he wondering about reapplying for the post of choirmaster? Surely, it could not be for any romantic reason.

'What would you like?' asked Anton, as the two of them were sitting opposite each other in a booth. 'A glass of wine, maybe?'

'I'd prefer a Pilsner. If that's alright?'

'Of course.' Anton went up to the bar and soon returned, a drink in each hand.

'Thank you. So why did you ask me out, Anton?'

He could not bring himself to lie, so told her. 'I am a highly eligible bachelor, Josefine. I am looking for a woman to love me and whom I can love. As a composer and organist, I am not poor and I have a brilliant future ahead of me. So any wife of mine will want for nothing. Nothing at all. I've known you for a long time. I like you and we have a shared interest in all things musical. I would like to meet you again. We can continue to meet until we decide whether we are in love. If so, we continue. If not, we simply go our separate ways. I apologise for the speech, but what do you think?'

Josefine took a sip of her beer and almost choked. Anton stood up, went over, and patted her on the back. 'I'm sorry, Anton, you took me by surprise. I thought you wanted to talk about the choir or a solo part I could sing, not about romance. So I don't know what to think.' The pretty, blond girl with shining blue eyes frowned and looked into her beer.

'I hope you believe I am being genuine, as indeed I am,' he said, not sure how to respond. 'All I am asking is that you think about what I am saying. You don't need to decide now whether we should meet again. Or even whether to stay with me today. Go, if you wish.' From the blank expression on her face, he felt he had lost this hand of cards. Neither spoke for a full two minutes. Then she replied.

'I do like you, Anton. And I agree you would be a good husband. But I'm only seventeen and you are a lot older. How old are you?'

'I'm forty-two in September, so not that old!'

'Hmm. I'm not sure I'm ready for marriage, but I have an idea. Let's continue to enjoy each other's company and meet again, in say a week's time.'

Anton and Josefine spent the next hour chatting, mainly about the Linz Choir, before Josefine said she needed to go shopping for her mother. They agreed to meet again, but this time in the tavern, at midday. Anton spent the week falling deeper in love with Josefine. He could speak to her father to ask for his permission to marry her. But time was on his side. He would make sure she was in love with him before he made any proposals. They met at exactly the agreed time and, as before, Anton provided the Pilsners.

'I'm so pleased to see you, Josefine. Have you had a busy week?'

'Yes, I'm training to be a cook and I'm attending our teaching college in Linz. One option is to teach cookery at junior school level, if I do well in the tests.'

This was an open opportunity for Anton to tell her about his experiences at the same college, so he did. Then he told her about the ghastly experiences of Windhaag. She laughed when he related the tale of being expected to move human manure to the fields and his outright refusal. He told her about his work in Kronstorf and St Florian. She laughed when he told her about trying curling at Kronstorf and falling over on the ice, and asked several questions about his time there. They seemed to enjoy each other's presence, far more than at their first meeting, because they were more relaxed. He saved stories about his more recent life until their next encounter. So they agreed to meet again at the same time in a week, but for only an hour, because they both had commitments in the afternoon.

The week sped by for Anton, who greeted her at the tavern with the widest smile. He hadn't been so happy for a long time and life could only improve. Josefine looked sullen and not at all happy.

'I'm afraid I have some bad news, Anton. I've discussed our relationship with my parents. We have decided that you are too old for me. So, while I would like to remain a friend, anything more cannot happen.'

Anton's ebullient smile vanished immediately, and he could only look down at the floor. He felt quite sick. He didn't know what to say. She remained silent, expecting him to respond. His feeling of rejection was hard to conceal. Then he spoke. 'I'm sorry it's worked out the way it has. I hope you will be happy for the rest of your life.'

'I'll go now, Anton. Good luck.' She then walked to the door, turned, waved to him, and went.

Anton was distraught. Somehow, by manly determination, he managed not to shed a tear, despite his dreams being instantly shattered. Contemplating his future loneliness, he sat there for a few minutes. Then went to the bar, bought himself a stein of Pilsner and ordered a ham and pickle sandwich.

'Your lady friend made a hasty exit,' said the barmaid, when she brought his food.

'She's no longer my lady friend,' he said. 'She'll never know what she's missed.'

'Best way to look at it, mein Herr. That will be one kreuzer.'

***

Disheartened though he was with yet another failure at romance, life took on a much better perspective when he visited Simon Sechter. Hopefully, he would stay with him for a few days of holiday, which even Johann Schiedermayr thought was overdue. So he wrote a brief letter, inviting himself to see him, and caught a train the following day.

'Anton, it's good to see you, my unexpected friend!'

'So didn't you receive my letter?'

'No! Come in! Come in! You've brought your travel case, so you are expecting to stay for a fortnight!'

'Not at all, but a couple of days would be nice… please!' He followed Simon into the lounge.

'You're lucky. We were going to Prague for a holiday but I became ill so we had to cancel. I'm still not fully recovered, but I'm well enough to entertain you for a few days. You'll meet my wife, Maria, this time. She's been looking after me.'

'What was the health problem?'

'I had a heart attack. I would have died, but for swift action from Maria. My doctor was here within a few minutes. He massaged my heart and got me going again.'

'What a relief, Simon.'

'Yes, it's still weak, he says, and is treating me to strengthen it.'

'I don't want to trouble you. I can easily find a hotel and visit you from there.'

'Don't be silly. I'm fine. I just have to take it easy!'

'Are you still writing a fugue a day?'

'I stopped for three days, but yes, I am now!'

'You must have been ill!'

'He was ill,' said a woman's voice from outside the room. Her curiosity aroused, she came in to see who was speaking to Simon. He introduced them.

'No, we've never met before, Maria. I think you'd gone to stay with your mother when I was here before. I spent years on Simon's correspondence course and only met him a few times!'

'I've heard so much about you, Anton. Mainly about the seventeen exercise books you sent Simon. He said he'd never have taken you on, if he knew he'd have that much marking to do!'

'No, I didn't, Maria. She is such a tease!'

'Now there are three of us for dinner, so I'll have to improvise. Dinner in an hour and a half!' She vanished.

'So what are you composing now, Anton?'

'You'll hate me for this, but I've almost finished a symphony. It breaks many, but not all, of the rules of composition you taught me.'

'Really?' laughed Simon. 'Are you expecting anyone to play it?'

'I am, and those who have studied what I've written like it, albeit in its incomplete state!'

'So, tell me more.'

Anton described what he had written so far on this symphony and said he regarded it as his first, real contribution to symphonic development. He told him about meeting von Bülow and Rubinstein in Munich, and about Wagner befriending him and admiring *Germanenzug*.

'All I can say is good luck with it. I'm sure you know what you're doing. Especially now you've shared outrageous rule breaking with your Richard Wagner.'

Anton wasn't expecting such a negative reaction, so changed the subject. 'Do you know of any musical events we can attend while I'm here, in the home of Austrian music?'

'Oh, I must tell you! Johann Herbeck played your Mass in D minor at the Court Chapel only a few weeks ago. I should have written to tell you!'

'I'm staggered, Simon,' he said, almost in tears. 'You've absolutely made my day. I didn't know he had the score, let alone the parts for the orchestra and singers. I am thrilled. He must have found out about it from the press. I'm sure there was a reporter from Vienna when we played it in the Illustrious Hall.' He hadn't felt so happy for a long time. What a contrast, he thought. From the misery of being rejected by Josefine to the elation of realising that one of his works had been played in public without him knowing.

'Yes, there is one. The Vienna Philharmonic, under Herbeck, is playing Berlioz' Damnation of Faust. I wasn't going, but if you'd like to, we can both go!'

'I'd love to go. I've heard of it, but never seen it performed.'

Anton enjoyed the Faust, but thought it not in the same league as Wagner's stunningly original creations. He soon stopped analysing the music and concentrated on following the frightening story. At the end, and after the first round of applause, Johann Herbeck went from the rostrum to bring in Berlioz himself. Anton's eyes opened wide as the applause became louder still.

Berlioz bowed to the audience. His hair was wild and wide but not overlong and his smooth-shaven face beamed brightly. Johann Herbeck grinned as he held Berlioz' hand aloft.

'Shall we try to meet them?' said Simon. 'I know the way to the players' bar. They will let me in.'

'It's you two, my friends Simon Sechter and Anton Bruckner,' said Herbeck. 'Let me introduce you to Hector Berlioz.'

As usual, when in the presence of a famous personality, Anton was initially short of words. 'I'm pleased to meet you,' was as much as could say.

'Anton is staying with me for a few days,' said Simon. 'By luck, we could come to your concert this evening. Your superb music exactly fits the mood of the characters, especially of Faust.'

'I'm so glad you liked it,' said Berlioz. 'And what did you make of it, Herr Bruckner?'

'I've never heard it before, or even read the score, but I liked it a great deal,' he said, then speaking freely. 'Is it an opera or what do you call it?'

'A good question! It can be performed as an opera, or with no acting, so it is what I call a "dramatic legend".'

'Anton is a composer in his own right,' said Simon.

'And probably the best organist in Austria, if not Europe,' said Johann.

'What have you composed, Herr Bruckner?'

'Some fifty or more pieces, ranging from several *Missae Brevis* to symphonies. I've almost finished my second symphony and I'm about to start a Mass, commissioned by the Bishop of Linz. I'm nothing like as prolific as Simon here!'

'Yes, but he is a brilliant composer,' said Simon. 'And is writing some quite radical works. His recently completed Mass, which Johann here conducted a few weeks ago at the Imperial Court Chapel, uses some original, modern techniques.'

'I wouldn't call myself brilliant for a moment, but I am trying to develop the symphony. By what you might regard as extending the sonata form.'

'How are you doing that?' said Berlioz.

'Instead of only two key theme groups, I've introduced a third. And that gives me more possibilities for developing the movement. I can drop one of them or keep all three. I'm also using chromaticism and key ambiguity and unresolved discords... and so on.'

'Amazing. I must come to a performance of one, at some point.'

'I'd regard that as the highest honour.'

The three of them adjourned to a tavern, near to the concert hall, which Johann said Schubert used to frequent.

'Let me buy the drinks,' said Johann. 'I'm the only one of us being paid!'

'You've forgotten my emolument,' said Berlioz.

'Oh, sorry! I hope the director hasn't!' said Johann, laughing.

'So what made you decide on writing symphonies?' asked Berlioz.

'You've asked me a good question! I learned a great deal about composition from not only Simon, but also from a character called Otto Kitzler, a cellist in Linz. It was him who encouraged me to pursue a more modern approach to what Simon taught, and he suggested I write a symphony.' He spoke about the one in F minor, which did not impress Otto Kitzler. Berlioz listened intently, as Anton told him what a huge thrill he had from writing it. While he regarded it only as an exercise, he said, he would specialise in writing symphonies, but not reject other types of musical composition.

'I'm staggered and delighted for you, and hope you will achieve your ambitions. You could become the Beethoven of our time. In fact, you may know that I have written four myself, and mine are not at all conventional either!' Hector told them about his, only two of which were purely orchestral, the Symphonie Fantastique and The Grande Symphonie Funebre et Triomphale. 'So we have quite a lot in common, Anton. None of my symphonies complies with what most would regard as the norm, especially my middle two. One is Harold in Italy, which is almost a viola concerto, linked to a poem by Byron. The other is Romeo and Juliet, which is mainly orchestral, but interspersed with quotations from Shakespeare.'

'I have heard none of these, but as you say, they are far from the symphonic norm. Given the chance, I will listen to them. I may even try to persuade my colleagues in Linz to perform one of them. Which one would you recommend?'

'Go for Symphonie Fantastique. If your audience like it, they may want to hear Harold in Italy. The Grande Symphonie Funebre is best played outside in the open air! Do you have military bands in Linz?'

'Yes, indeed. We have an Infantry Division. There are some wonderful bandsmen among them.'

'In that case, you might just want to get that one played first.'

'A brilliant suggestion, Herr Berlioz. Let me buy the next round, gentlemen.'

While Anton was at the bar, the three of them talked about him. 'He's wasted in Linz,' said Johann.

'I'm not so sure,' said Simon. 'He's happy there, and loves playing those two organs.'

'I disagree,' said Johann. 'He is a man of interesting contradictions. We examined him, as you know, Simon, in advanced music theory and organ play. One of the board thought he was some kind of country bumkin, with his odd, Upper Austrian accent and his simple behaviour and language. But that is not my view. From the utterly brilliant work he did on the written tests on composing and the theory, he is near to genius. And his ability at improvising on the organ has no equal, anywhere in Europe… or probably anywhere in the world. He is also an amazing choirmaster. I met him in Nuremberg just after his choir won an international competition there, thanks to him. The world of music would greatly benefit from him moving away from those two organs, to us at the Conservatorium.'

'Two organs?' said Berlioz.

'Yes, the one at Linz Cathedral and there is one at the parish church he also plays.'

Anton brought the drinks back to their table. 'I can see the crucial difference between us, Herr Berlioz. You read a great deal of literature. I have to admit, I don't,' he said.

He felt glad the three of them enjoyed each other's company. He was especially pleased that he and Berlioz had so much in common. To Anton, he seemed a modest, relaxed and likeable man, whom he hoped to see again.

Chapter 17
1866 - 1867 Bad Kreuzen

Anton finished his new symphony before making another attempt at romance. This time, he took a more business-like approach. The girl's name was Henriette Reiter. Her mother was the owner of a florist's, so she was from a middle-class background. Anton wrote to her father, asking about the family's finances, and about their eighteen-year-old daughter marrying him. His reply shattered poor Anton. He totally dismissed him, saying he was far too old for her. So he experienced another disappointing failure. He wouldn't use this method again.

***

'It is only my organ playing and composing that is keeping me sane, Nani,' he said to his sister on an overdue visit to the family home in Ebelsberg.

'What is the problem, Tonerl?'

'I am overworked. I have completely failed in my attempts at finding a wife, and I feel miserable. Something strange is happening in my head. I don't know what, but I don't feel right. Luckily, I have this Mass to write for the Bishop. If I didn't have that and my organ playing, I would have gone completely insane by now.'

'How are you looking after yourself at the Pfarrgasse?'

'Not badly, but it takes time. Buying food, cooking, washing clothing and all those sorts of things. Occasionally, I get an invitation to a friend's for dinner, mainly Irene's, but not as often as I might like, and I go to the tavern sometimes. Not just for a drink, but for a meal as well.'

'What you need is a housekeeper.'

'I don't want a stranger looking after me. That would make me worse.'

'I have an idea. I could look after you...'

'You can't do that, Sis. You have your own life to lead.'

'How many bedrooms are there in you apartment?'

'Two.'

'One for me, one for you.'

'Honestly, Sis, you shouldn't really.'

'I'm coming. Give me a few days and I'll be there.'

'Bless you, darling Nani!' He kissed her.

Within a week, Maria Anna was inspecting Anton's abode. It was in better condition than she expected. She imagined it would be an untidy mess, but he kept it in reasonable order. He said he made his bed every day and left the place in acceptable condition when he left to play at the Cathedral or the parish church. The larder was not that well stocked, but, as he said, he only bought enough food for a few days at a time. The only untidy room was his study. There were scores in piles, on the floor, on the Bösendorfer, on the corners of his desk and even on the windowsill.

'How can you work in this? There's hardly space on your desk.'

'I know where everything is, Nani. Don't worry about this room, except you can sweep the floor.'

'You can do that!'

'Alright, you win!'

Nani made life much easier for Anton. So, he could concentrate fully on his composing and his organ playing. He made steady progress on the new Mass and, by June, was over half-way through. He still felt odd.

'Nani, I think I have a problem in my head.'

'What's that?'

'I have this compulsion to count things. When I'm on my way to the Cathedral, I count the windows in the shops and houses. Yesterday, I walked around the building and counted the pews. When the Bishop asked what I was doing, I hesitated to reply. Then I told him exactly. He asked me why. I didn't lie, but told him that, as I spent so much time there, I wanted to know more detail about it. He replied that I could have worked it out by multiplying the number of rows by the number in a row. I said I wanted to be sure none was missing. He looked at me strangely and asked how his new Mass was getting on. I told him I'd written seven hundred and forty-three bars. He asked me how much I had to do. I told him I'd just started the Sanctus. He went away still looking puzzled.'

'I don't know, Tonerl. Do you have a doctor?'

'No, but I can ask Irene.'

'See how the next few weeks go? I can't see you have anything wrong, but it's a good idea to ask Irene. I must meet this paragon of a woman!'

'Shall we ask her around for dinner?'

'Yes, I can easily prepare a delicious meal for the three of us.'

So after he had played in the following morning's Mass, he dropped by to see her. 'Unusual for you to call in the morning, Anton.'

'A couple of things. First, do you know a good doctor?'

'Can you say why you need a doctor, or is it too embarrassing?'

Anton explained what he thought may be a problem in his head. He told her about his constant need to count. He said he'd stopped on his way to count the leaves on a tree and, when he got to six hundred and forty-seven, gave up to continue his walk there.

'I don't think it's anything to worry about, Anton. Maybe just try not to count. But if you need to see a doctor, you could see my doctor, whose name is Fadlinger. He lives along the road at number 12.'

'I'll try not counting first. I must tell you that my sister, Anna Maria, whom we call Nani, is my housekeeper. She's been with me for just over a week now. We would like to invite you to dinner she will prepare. When could you come? Any night in particular?'

'I'm busy for the next two nights, but how about Wednesday, at the usual time, seven o'clock?'

Nani produced an excellent meal. At first, she found it difficult to speak to Irene because she couldn't understand the nature of the relationship between her and Anton. She wondered if there was more to it than simply being friends, with Irene inviting him around for the occasional meal.

'Have you met the von Mayfields?' asked Irene, as they were about to finish eating.

'No. Who are they?'

'A married couple whom I invite to my house to dine with me and Anton. We've had some wonderful conversations together over the years. They are both interested in music and the wife, Betty, is an excellent pianist. Moritz is a high-ranking government official. You'll love them.'

'Thank you for giving Anton advice about his need to count and the name of your doctor.'

'It was a pleasure.'

'I'm trying my hardest and just walk away when I can,' said Anton. 'I don't think I need a doctor.'

'That's good news,' said Irene.

Nani softened her view about their relationship the moment she discovered Anton and Irene did not always dine in the absence of anyone else.

***

A few weeks later, Moritz von Mayfield came to see him at the Cathedral. He stood and listened as Anton played a piece of Bach and improvised on it for at least twenty minutes.

'I don't know how you do it, Anton. You are such a master of organ play. Was that a piece of Bach?'

'You are too kind to me, Moritz. Yes, it was the vivace from Bach's Organ Sonata Number 3. Well recognised, especially as I hacked it around so much!'

'"Hacked" is just not the word. You seemed to improve on the original!'

'Not at all! It's very good to see you, Moritz. Surely you haven't come just to listen to my playing?'

'No, I came to give you an invitation. The Linz Theatre Orchestra and the Mixed Choir are playing Beethoven's Ninth Symphony in a few days' time. Betty and I are going. Would you like to come with us?'

'I'd love to! May I bring my sister, Nani? She is staying with me to help with my domestic life.'

'Of course! And Betty would like to invite you to supper at our house afterwards.'

All four of them, along with Irene, whom Moritz had also invited, met in the foyer in good time for the performance. Anton didn't want to rely on the von Mayfields paying, so insisted that he buy the tickets for himself, Nani and Irene. Von Mayfield baulked at the idea, complaining that they were there at his invitation. He eventually agreed, provided they could get a box on the opposite side of the auditorium to the violins.

As expected, Otto Kitzler conducted the orchestra. The programme started with Rossini's William Tell overture, followed by Schumann's Violin Concerto, its unofficial second performance.

'Have you ever thought of composing a concerto, Anton?' said Moritz in the interval.

'No, not for a single instrument. The closest is probably my *Germanenzug*, which you have heard, where there are trombones playing solo parts, but there are singers as well, of course.'

'Would you like to write one?'

'I have no plans to. I would rather leave it to others to create a canvas upon which soloists can demonstrate their virtuosity. My obsession is with the symphony!'

'I wouldn't dismiss it completely. Imagine what you could write as an organ concerto. It would sound like heaven on earth!'

Anton listened. Beethoven's Ninth enraptured him. He had heard nothing like it before. It far surpassed Beethoven's Fourth, which he had heard here in his youth.

'So what did you make of that symphony, Herr Symphonist?' said Moritz, while they were enjoying drinks and canapes.

'It was incredible! It's a masterpiece. Its logic is clear and unchallengeable.'

'What do you mean by that, Tonerl?' said Nani.

'He uses the cellos and basses to dismiss the music of the first three movements as not good enough for the finale. He confirms this when the bass sings, "Oh friends, not these tunes…" It's wonderful and has a universal significance, especially that last movement. I see it as a challenge to compose a symphony as great, if not greater!'

'I admire your ambition, Anton. With your ability, you could well succeed. I'm dying to hear the one you've just finished!' said Moritz.

**

The year ground forward slowly for Anton, who was feeling even stranger. He had by the autumn completed the new Mass in E minor. Despite his attempts at not counting objects of various kinds, he failed. He would count the number of grains of salt he put on his vegetables. Or the number of spokes on a carriage wheel. Another obsession was attempting to count the number of notes in the manuscript score of his F minor symphony. He lost count but numbered the bars from the first until the last of the finale. Thinking how Nani might react, he said nothing to her as he didn't want to worry her.

Anton's moods swung from being deliriously happy, as he was when he wrote the last few notes of his new Mass, to being badly depressed. This was especially so when he realised he had no major compositions in mind, except another symphony, which he could not bring himself to begin. His one source of satisfaction was that the Linz Theatre Orchestra had agreed to play his Symphony Number 1, even though they hadn't decided on a date.

Christmas came and went. He performed his duties with his usual competence and enthusiasm, but behind it all was his underlying sadness of mind. It wasn't until late April that his illness became more obvious and serious.

'I hate to admit this, Nani, but I am feeling bad. I have reached the point where I don't want to go to the Cathedral and play. For the last two or three weeks, I have really had to force myself to go. It's like a walk up the side of a mountain. I even feel breathless when I get there. The salvation is going to the organ loft. I stay there as long as I can and play. That is my only actual pleasure. Even when I have to go to the parish church and play, I don't want to do so. When it's time to come home, I almost run. The only way I can stop counting people, trees, leaves, windows or anything else on my way home, is to sing my own solos or whistle tunes I have written.' Nani could see he was on the verge of tears.

'You are ill, Tonerl. There is something wrong in your head. See Dr Fadlinger. I will come with you, if you wish.'

So, accompanied by Nani, Anton explained his symptoms to the doctor. He was a young man who won Anton's trust by being sympathetic, understanding, and clearly competent. His principal expertise, the doctor said, was metal illness.

'You have a problem I'm familiar with, Herr Bruckner. It's called numeromania or arithmomania. It can be cured, you will be glad to hear. But you will have to be admitted to a sanatorium. The one I know best and recommend is in Bad Kreuzen, not that far away. There are various treatments there. One is immersion in cold water. Another is to remove you from all causes of your compulsion. So they will stop you from composing. I will write to the superintendent of the sanatorium at Bad Kreuzen to ask them to treat you. Before I do, are you willing to go there?'

'I am! I am, Doctor. As soon as possible. I don't want to get any worse. I have so many ideas for symphonies mainly, but other works, too. So I desperately need to be cured.'

There were several people to tell about his illness and where he would be treated. He had to inform Johann Schiedermayr.

'I'm really sorry, Anton. Is there nothing we can do to help you? Give you an extended period of leave?'

'That's what I'm asking for. If they accept me in the sanatorium, I could be away for months. Could you please, I beg of you, keep my position open until I return?'

'Anton, my dear friend. Of course we will. Don't worry. We will keep it open for as long as you want to return to it. We will count it as an extended period of paid leave. So you can keep you apartment in the Pfarrgasse, which your sister can continue to occupy and we will engage your deputy, Ferdinand Edelhart, or others if he's not free. You have become so well known it would be a tragedy to lose you. No one in Austria is better than you at organ play. We pray you return, Anton. Do you want to tell Bishop Rudigier or should I?'

'I will tell him if I see him. If not, please tell him for me.'

'I could see this coming, Anton,' said Irene. 'I am sorry. But you are a person with a sound mind, and I promise you will overcome it.'

'Could you please tell the von Mayfields? I don't want the embarrassment.'

'They are good friends, Anton, and you shouldn't even think of feeling awkward about telling them. I will tell them, of course.'

***

Two weeks later, he said goodbye to Nani and caught a cabriolet to Bad Kreuzen, about fifty kilometres to the east. As he approached the building, he wondered what was inside and what they would do to him. If they wanted to give him electric shock treatment, he would emphatically refuse and catch a carriage back to Linz. He hoped it wouldn't come to that. The more he looked at the place, the more forbidding it appeared. By the time he reached the front door, it seemed more like a prison.

'Welcome to the home for the insane,' said a woman, dressed as a nurse, as Anton stepped from the carriage.

'I hate to disappoint you, young lady, but I am far from insane. I am not a lunatic. I merely suffer from numeromania and I've come here for you to cure me, please. And the sooner the better!'

The woman's eyes opened wide, not expecting such a challenging reaction. A man who appeared to be a nurse then appeared. 'What is the argument about?'

Anton reacted quickly. 'I was just asking this young lady if you could quickly cure me of numeromania. From her response, I assume you can.'

'Come in and we'll see what we can do for you. There is a fee, of course, which is payable when you leave.'

The man escorted him along a dark corridor and opened the door to a room. He put his arm out to invite Anton to enter. A narrow bed and a small wardrobe were the only items of furniture. The single source of light was a small window close to the ceiling.

'This is your room,' said the man.

'I can't live in there!' The bed reminded him of the horrors of Windhaag.

'Why not?'

'It's too small. I can't see out of the window. There is no desk for me to use for reading or composing. The bed is so narrow I could fall out. And that stupid wardrobe. I can hardly hang a pair of my trousers in there, let alone my coat and my other clothes. So I refuse to stay there.'

'But you have no choice.'

'Yes, I do. I can walk out of here and they can treat me elsewhere. I am a paying customer, you know.'

'Wait here,' said the man, who went back up the corridor.

Anton sat on his case and waited. And waited. It must have been at least half an hour before the man came back. A very large, thick-set man accompanied him. Anton saw the second man as a threat. Would he lift Anton into the room and slam the door behind him or hit him into submission?

The large man picked up his case and walked back along the corridor. 'Follow me,' said the male nurse.

All three walked back to the entrance hall and took another corridor. The large man put Anton's case outside a room. The nurse opened the door.

'I hope this one is more to your liking.'

Anton walked in. The difference between the two rooms amazed him. This one was well lit from a window at the normal height. It had a light blue carpet. The bed was comfortably wide and standing against a wall was a tall, wide wardrobe, a dressing table against the other, and a desk in front of the window. A dark blue sofa stood in the corner.

'Much better. Almost perfect. A view over the lake, too!'

'This one is nearly twice the price per week.'

'That doesn't worry me.'

The male nurse took his case into the room as Anton sat on the bed. The tone of his discussion suddenly changed from its initial formality. 'We will see a lot of each other while you are here, Herr Bruckner. I'm Gert. The lady nurse who met you at the door is called Gretel. I hope we will get on well. The large man who carried your case is the porter. He does the heavy lifting. His name is Alois.'

Gert explained the routine to Anton, saying each day was almost the same as another. He told Anton the meal times and asked him to write them down. Treatment would begin an hour after breakfast and, in Anton's case, it would be submersion in cold water. He would have to hold his breath, but not for more than five seconds. The treatment would last for about ten minutes. They would treat him twice a day and would expect him to take a voluntary cold shower afterwards. The principal treatment would be the submersion. The rest of the time would be free, except while being assessed by a doctor and occasionally see a priest.

'Do you have any questions, Herr Bruckner?'

'Yes, Gert. Who gives me the water submersion treatment?'

'Gretel and I.'

'Will I be wearing clothes?'

'No. You will take them off behind a screen in the treatment room in which there is a large bath we use.'

'Will I be naked in front of Gretel?'

'Yes, but only while you get into the water. You will wrap a towel around yourself after you undress and take it off as you get in the water.'

'That is unacceptable. I won't be naked in front of Gretel!'

'She has seen many naked men in her time and it's just a job to her. She won't be embarrassed and I hope you won't be. There is no one else here, other than Gretel and I, and two other ladies, who are qualified to give this treatment. You don't have to display your private parts in front of her. Just get in, facing away from her. She is sensitive to the situation and knows how men feel about these things.'

'Alright, I'll do as you say. Another question. What do I do for the rest of the day?'

'You must relax. You can talk to other people here, choose a book from our library and read in the public lounge or go for a swim, or a walk. Or have another cold shower. You are free, but not to leave the sanatorium.'

'So it is a kind of prison, then?'

'No. Dr Fadlinger is concerned about you and does not want you roaming around here unaccompanied. I hope you are happy with that.'

'I suppose I'll have to be. When is my first submersion treatment?'

'Tomorrow morning, an hour after breakfast.'

Anton barely slept that night. Everything was new to him. He was dreading the water submersion treatment, but knew he had to endure it. To take his mind off it, he thought about his composing and what he would write next. The latest Mass of his was strange and more in the style of Palestrina than his normal work. He'd ask Bishop Rudigier to commission him for another when he returned. His over-riding ambition was to write another symphony. And Number One had yet to be performed.

'Just go behind the screen and remove your clothes,' said Gert.

Anton came from behind it, dressed only in a white bath towel.

'Now get into the bath water.'

'My God! It's freezing!' he said as he sat in the water, which almost reached his shoulders.

'After a minute or two, you'll get used to it,' said Gretel, discreetly looking away.

'The two minutes are up. Now we have to submerge you. We push you in from your shoulders, one of us on each side. Breathe in deeply and hold your breath! Now!' he said.

They each held a shoulder, forced his head under the water, and held him there. 'One... two... three... four... five,' said Gretel before they grabbed his shoulders and pulled him back into the sitting position.

'Holy shit! Are you trying to fucking drown me?' he said, as he spat out a mouthful of bathwater.

'Less of that, if you don't mind. You must not use obscenities in front of a lady. That's the first submersion. Nine more to follow.'

'I don't want any more, for God's sake.' He tried to climb out of the bath but merely slid on the sides. Water splashed over the floor.

'We are here to treat you, like it or not!' said Gert.

He had no choice. Fearing for his life, he had to submit. He reluctantly stopped struggling to get out and resumed the sitting position. By then he was used to the temperature, cold though it was.

'Now!' said Gert. They submerged him again and counted to five before straightening him up.

'I just can't stand any more of this!' he said. 'Take me out of here. I insist.'

'Sorry, Herr Bruckner. Take my advice. Just relax and let us do our job. Your reward will be a cure for your problems,' said Gert. 'We are being as gentle as we can. Don't become tense because that makes it more difficult for us and not pleasant for you.'

From that moment, Anton relaxed and cooperated with Gretel and Gert. He realised that submission was the only way forward.

'You've been so good that we've only put you under nine times and not ten!' said Gert.

'Thank you! I'm sorry I swore after the first one. I really am. It's very unusual for me to use such bad language. Please forgive me.'

'Please don't worry, Anton,' said Gretel. 'That is quite a common reaction to the first submersion, which is a shock to the body and mind.'

Anton's treatment continued. He gradually became used to it, but it could never be a pleasure. In fact, he hated it but just had to submit if he was to be cured. He took a shower, in the presence of only Gert, immediately afterwards and in the same room.

'So how are you feeling now?' said the resident doctor, after they had treated him for a fortnight.

'I still have my issues. I can't stop counting. If I go into the grounds at night, I can't stop counting the stars. Twice I've counted the logs in that pile around the back, leaves on your trees and I often count the windows in this building. When I'm asleep, I dream that someone is telling me to empty the Danube. So I don't think the cold water treatment is working. I feel I won't recover and I am condemned to this awful illness for the rest of my life. I feel I am dead as a composer and could kill myself.' He was almost in tears.

The doctor stood up and walked around his desk to give him a gentle hug. 'Please don't feel like that, Anton. We will cure you. I guarantee. It takes up to three months or more. You must have this treatment twice a day. My only advice is to do something that doesn't involve looking at objects which make you count. Ask Gert or Gretel for some paper and ink and write letters to your friends. That will help. Tell them exactly what you feel and think. They may be distressed at what they read, but it will be the truth. So tell them we will cure you. If you write a note of optimism, you'll feel optimistic yourself.'

'Thank you, Doctor. I'll take your advice.'

So Anton wrote letters. He wrote to Irene, Bishop Rudigier, Johann Schiedermayr, Weinwurm, and Moritz von Mayfield and, of course, Nani. The letters had a consistency about them. Except the one to Nani, they were virtually the same. He said he was in Bad Kreuzen because he was ill. It was not a case of laziness and the need for a holiday, but for treatment to his head. They banned him from composing, studying or playing any musical instruments. He said he had contemplated suicide but hoped he had disposed of these thoughts.

A week later, Gert and another man came to see him. Anton recognised the man. It was a priest from the Cathedral in Linz. At first, he wondered if he was even more insane and looking at an apparition.

'Hello, Herr Bruckner. How are you?'

'Not too bad. I have been worse. You are the first priest I met at the Cathedral, I think?'

'Yes, I admonished you, until I realised you wanted to see the organ!'

'So why have you come to see me here?'

'Bishop Rudigier is grateful for your letter, but what you said made him concerned.'

'Really?'

'Yes, your mention of suicidal thoughts. So he sent me here to accompany you and keep you safe.'

Tears began to trickle down Anton's cheeks. He didn't know what to say. He suddenly felt loved, not only by Irene, Nani and his other siblings, but also by Bishop Rudigier. Now the leading ecclesiast in Linz wanted to help and had sent his representative to do so. This was the last thing he expected as a response to a letter. Perhaps a sympathetic reply, but not someone actually coming to the sanatorium to 'keep him safe'. That could only mean to prevent him from committing suicide.

'That is so kind of His Grace,' he said, wiping his tears away. 'I have felt very lonely here and having someone I know to keep me company will be good for me.'

'The Reverend Father will be in the room next to yours, so will be available, he tells me, day or night,' said Gert.

'I cannot believe this is happening. It is taking human kindness to its absolute extreme. Thank you so much, Reverend. I'm sure Bishop Rudigier gave you the options of coming or not and I'm pleased you opted to come.'

The Reverend Father accompanied Anton when he felt he needed to do so. He was discreet and allowed him to take meals with other patients. Knowing he was safe in his room, he left him alone there when he wanted to be on his own.

The routine continued for another month or more until it was unexpectedly broken. One afternoon, after his period of treatment, Anton was asleep in his room when a loud knock on his door woke him up. He quickly dressed and went to the door.

'My goodness, it's you, Betty! Come in and sit in that chair. But let me hug you first!' he said, thinking she might, in her caring way, have come to visit him. He pointed to the comfortable sofa in the corner. She sat down and looked at him.

'What are you doing here? A long way to come, just to see me.'

'It's a slightly embarrassing story, but you will understand better than most. I recently became depressed and went to see my doctor, Dr Fadlinger, the same one who diagnosed you. My symptoms were feeling miserable and crying at the least little thing. So he sent me here, mainly for a break, but also for a little water treatment. Moritz has been very good. He has been very anxious about me and took time away from his work, but with me here, he is now back. He says he will pay and I'm sure he will!'

'I am sorry to hear all that, Betty. I'm improving I think. It is gradual and I'm still not that sure.'

'I need to settle in, Anton. Let's meet tomorrow, shall we, in those lovely gardens by the lake?'

'Let's do that. We can have a longer discussion then.'

***

Betty von Mayfield was sitting on a bench waiting for him. She was wearing a pretty pink dress covered in pearl sequins.

'Good morning, Anton! How are you this morning?'

'Well, but I can't cope with that dress, Betty. Could you change it, please?'

'Umm... yes, but why?'

'I can't stop counting those sequins. I'm up to sixty-seven already!'

'I'll go now. Back in five minutes!'

'That's perfect!' he said, as she reappeared in a plain yellow one. 'I'm sorry to put you to such trouble. I think I am improving, but my mind can suddenly start counting and I just can't stop unless I turn and walk away, but I could not do that to you, Betty. So asking you to change was the only solution.'

'I completely understand. So please don't worry. Tell me more about how you are getting on here. Don't look now, but I can see a man looking at us. He's dressed as a priest and he's standing outside the building by the door.'

Anton explained that Bishop Rudigier had sent a priest to look after him. Presumably, to prevent him from harming himself or committing suicide. He told her not to reply to what he had said and asked her not to react to the priest's presence and to avoid looking at him. With his hands spread out in front of him, he said he was still unsure about whether he was improving or not. Some days were better than others, and the water treatment was now part of everyday life. It was not as bad now they had subjected him to it so many times, but it was still unpleasant and humiliating, especially being seen naked by the female nurse.

'Do you mean I will be naked in front of a man?'

'I would think they will have two females in your case. If not, I would insist.'

'At least you have forewarned me!'

236

'So exactly how did you become ill and depressed? I'm still amazed to see you here! I hope you don't mind me asking.'

'Of course not, Anton. Sometimes it helps. It all began at a recital in which I was to be playing the piano. The piece was Mendelssohn's Violin Sonata in F. It is a difficult work, but that is not my excuse. I had rehearsed my part many times, but for the performance, I could not play it. My hands just would not touch the keys. I could hear the music in my head, but my hands refused to play. So I stood up and walked out crying. The recital had to be abandoned. I almost ran home. Moritz was so sympathetic.'

'That's terrible, Betty. How awful and how embarrassing.'

'I know,' she said, almost in tears. 'It didn't impress the violinist. Moritz suggested I just relax for a few days and see how I felt. He said it was because I was under pressure, but I couldn't see what, except having to play in this recital. Then, one morning, I woke up and started crying uncontrollably. Moritz wondered what was wrong. I told him I just felt miserable and down. Anyway, we agreed I should see doctor Fadlinger and here I am.'

'I'm so sorry. I quite understand. The point, I suppose, is to regain your confidence so you can play again.'

'Exactly that, Anton. I hope they have a piano here, where I can play.'

'I'm sure they have, but they don't want me playing anything, so I haven't seen it. We should tell the doctors here we think it would do us both good if we played. We could even play a four hand piece! I played some such pieces by Schubert, many years ago!'

'Either it will be good for us or drive us even madder!'

'I've always liked your sense of humour, Betty! When is your first treatment due?'

'Two thirty this afternoon.'

'I hope it goes well. I have my next session at two o'clock.'

The two of them agreed to meet that afternoon, at the same place in the garden, after each had undergone their treatment. Anton sat on the bench waiting for Betty. He'd been there for about ten minutes when the Reverend Father appeared.

'I have some interesting news for you. I received a letter from the Bishop this morning, asking how you are and whether you are improving. The news is he is offering to pay some of the cost of your stay here. All you need to do is to apply to the church authorities for reimbursement. They will decide how much to give you.'

'Why does he want to pay? He's doing enough for me by having you here to stop me from doing anything stupid and to keep an eye on me.'

'Anton, he likes you. He just wants to help you… please let me tell him you accept his offer.'

'Please, say I am supremely grateful and am honoured to accept his extraordinary kindness.'

Anton explained he was expecting to meet Betty. The priest returned to the building, leaving Anton alone on the bench. He waited another half an hour and gradually became more concerned about Betty not arriving. She had been subjected to her first immersion, so he wondered if it had caused her so much distress she didn't feel like meeting him. He would go back into the building to investigate. Realising he didn't know her room number, he went to the reception desk to ask.

'I am not at liberty to give you the room number of our clients without seeking their permission. Why do you want to know?'

'She is a close friend and has been for many years. We have the same doctor who sent us here. I am worried because she had her first immersion only a few hours ago and I want to know if she is alright. Could you please find out for me?'

'No. I cannot give you information about any of the patients here. These matters are confidential.'

'In that case, could you please locate her and tell her I am worried about her? Please also ask if she would let me know her room number so I can see her.'

Anton waited while the receptionist left to make some enquiries. It seemed odd that he needed permission to have her room number when they gave Betty his before she knocked on his door. He thought he must have given permission unknowingly when he signed the papers admitting him. Eventually, the woman returned with a plain look that showed he probably would not get what he wanted. Apparently, the doctor had told her he may not see her then, as she was exhausted and asleep. So she couldn't give permission for Anton to have her room number. He went back to his room disappointed and as worried as he was before, if not more so, about her. Perhaps she had reacted badly to her first treatment session. Rather than sit and worry about her, he wrote a letter to Bishop Rudigier to thank him for his offer to help defray his expenses. There was a gentle knocking at his door, which he recognised.

'Come in, Reverend Father. I was just writing a thank-you letter to the Bishop.'

'Oh, he will be delighted to hear from you. I just wondered if you'd heard anything about Betty von Mayfield.'

'Nothing, and I'm quite worried. Otherwise I'm fine.'

Suddenly, there was a loud knock on the door. Anton opened it.

'I can't stand that water treatment, Anton,' Betty said, with tears rolling down her face.

'Sit on the sofa and tell me.'

'I'll go now,' said the priest.

'It was hideous. Those two women almost drowned me. That gentle woman you had, Gretel was it? It wasn't her but two masculine looking ones who were clumsy and nasty. See these bruises on my shoulders. I resisted when they shoved me under and look what they did. Didn't you hear me screaming? I told them I'd never have it again, even if I was condemned to insanity.' She exploded into tears.

Anton put his arm around her and gave her a handkerchief. 'What are you going to do? Please go through with your treatment. It's the same for me. You must not resist. Just relax and let them do it. You won't be under the water for more than five seconds. Trust me.'

'I'm sure they drugged me to get me back to my room. The first thing I remember was a doctor looking over me, and checking my heart when I woke up.'

Anton continued trying to persuade her to comply with the submersion treatment. He said it was vitally important that she complied and could, if she felt like it, have a cold shower or go for a swim afterwards.

'You didn't tell me about the showers or swimming!'

'Sorry. I wasn't trying to hide anything. I have a shower after nearly every submersion.'

'In which case, let's swim tomorrow!'

They met in the morning in his room, after he had his water treatment. Betty arrived dressed in two bath towels and with bare feet. While she looked out of the window, he covered his lower half with a towel. They walked to the lake.

'I'm not sure how we are going to manage this, Betty. I have no wish to see your nakedness, good looking as you are. We should discreetly remove our towels as we slide into the water. Once we are in, up to our necks, we can speak and even splash water over each other.'

'Let's do that.'

Anton felt ashamed he had glanced at her beautiful bottom, but swore to himself he would not look again. They laughed and chatted as they swam around and threw water at each other. Neither noticed the figure of Anton's guardian as he stood for a moment to observe them before going back into the building. They could not have chosen a better time to frolic. It was the middle of a warm June when the sun was shining generously between wisps of fine cloud.

'You get out first,' said Anton, once they had been playing in the lake for long enough. 'I'll look the other way as you don your towels.'

'That sounds fine, Anton. And I'll look the other way when you get out.'

They then went to the familiar bench and sat in the sun to dry. 'Do you know, Betty, I now feel better in my head than I've felt since I came here? That was simply glorious. The best water treatment yet.'

'I feel the same. Thrilled after the trauma of yesterday. I will write to Moritz tonight to tell him. I'll mention how helpful you have been.'

'Be careful! We don't want him to think badly of us!'

'He won't, I'm sure. At least, I hope he won't!' They both laughed.

From that day on, Anton felt consistently better. He attributed his improvement to Betty, who reluctantly took his advice, to his thoughts on a new Mass, and to Bishop Rudigier. He had been so generous in offering to settle the bill, whatever that might be, and to provide his guardian angel, the Reverend Father.

Chapter 18
1867 - 1868 Vienna beckons

'Welcome home, my dear Brother. How are you feeling?'

'Honestly, Nani, I haven't felt better for at least a year now. The cold water treatment was not pleasant, but it worked!'

Over a meal, he told her the full story of what had happened at Bad Kreuzen. He told her about the amazing coincidence of Betty arriving there and that they had spent quite some time talking to each other. He did not to say they swam together naked, but told her about the priest whom Bishop Rudigier had sent to look after him. With a look of pride, he mentioned the offer the Bishop had made to help with his expense of staying there. The total bill was 225 florins for which he needed to submit a claim.

'The Bishop is so generous to you, and a good friend. So when are you starting back at the Cathedral?'

'Tomorrow. I can't wait to get back to playing that magnificent organ. They wouldn't let me play the piano at Bad Kreuzen. They wouldn't even tell me where it was!'

'And what about your composing? Did you do any there?'

'Yes, but they weren't keen on that either, so I didn't tell them. I did little, but I sketched out some parts for another Mass and some themes for a new symphony. So, I believe that helped my recovery, too. I'm ahead of myself on the new one as No. 1 hasn't been performed yet!'

Anton quickly settled back into his daily routine of playing at the Cathedral and the parish church. All his friends and colleagues were delighted to see him, especially Johann Schiedermayr. He said he had no end of arguments about who should stand in for him, when his usual deputy, Ferdinand Edelhart, wasn't available. It delighted Bishop Rudigier to see him and hear him play again at the Cathedral. The Bishop encouraged him to submit his claim to the parish council. Instead of running home, as he did when he was ill, he was often late but constantly smiling and happy. Most nights, as soon as he had finished dinner with Nani, he adjourned into his study to resume work on his new Mass, one in F minor.

Then one day in the September, he came home very early with tears pouring down his face.

'Whatever is the matter, Anton?' Believing his illness had returned and that he might need to return to Bad Kreuzen, Nani's face dropped.

'I have terrible news. My friend and teacher, Simon Sechter, has died. I learnt the sad news from Johann when I saw him at lunchtime. It's a deep tragedy. What makes it worse is he is a family man, married with a son.'

'Come into the lounge, Anton. Have a seat. I'll get you a beer. That will settle you down. I can understand you being so upset. He's the man who used to come to see you here, isn't he?'

'Yes, several times. I owe him so much. He spent five years teaching me the intricacies of classical composition. I have certificates signed by him, acknowledging the skills he gave me.' He took out a handkerchief and wiped his eyes. Just telling Nani and her sympathetic response calmed him down. She placed a half stein of beer in front of him, all of which he drank in one go. He was then back to normal, much to Nani's relief.

'Do you know when he passed away?'

'Last week, on the tenth of September, according to Johann.'

'Where and when will be the funeral? Attend, Anton. If only to support his wife. What's her name?'

'I can't remember, but it will come to me. I'll definitely go, assuming I can find out when it is.'

***

Once she was confident that both Anton and Betty had fully recovered from their illnesses, Irene organised a dinner for the two of them and invited Moritz and Nani. They savoured each other's company, having not met together since the performance of Beethoven's Ninth. They enjoyed the meal of pork, cabbage, and dumplings, which Irene prepared especially for Anton. Betty was full of praise for him and said how he had encouraged her to endure the cold water treatment at Bad Kreuzen. Likewise, he said they had helped each other, mainly by talking between treatment sessions. Their conversation continued well into the night. They talked about the Linz Mixed Choir, the progress, or rather the lack of it, being made on the new cathedral.

'I have some interesting news for you all,' said Anton, deliberately late in the evening, to limit time for argument or discussion. 'I am intending to move to Vienna.'

'Why?' said Irene. 'You are doing so well in Linz. You are so popular here. And everyone knows and likes you.'

'I don't understand you, Anton,' said Moritz. 'Your future is here. Vienna is highly competitive and political. Unless you fit in with the strongest political party or movement, they will crucify you. Or back-stab you. It's much less vicious here!'

'And what am I supposed to do?' said Nani. 'Why didn't you tell me before? I can't believe you saved it until now.'

'I'm sorry, Nani. I had no intention of upsetting you. You are a tremendous source of strength to me. I've been thinking about my future since I came back from the sanatorium. And I've only just decided. There are many hurdles to

242

cross before I go and I'm only telling you all, my best friends and sister, what my intentions are. If I go, Nani, I would ask you to come with me.'

'I'd have to think about that,' she said, looking at the ceiling.

'So what would you do in Vienna?' said Moritz. 'Assuming you find work there. You are an excellent composer, but that won't give you a living, not until you become internationally known, I think.'

'You should go there, Anton, but only if it will advance your career as a composer,' said Betty.

'You won't know this, but about six years ago, I applied for the organ post at the Chapel of the Imperial Court. I failed disastrously, but I would apply again.'

'How do you know it's still vacant?' said Irene.

'It's being re-advertised. While I love being the top organist in Linz, I am attracted by the bigger canvas of Vienna.'

The party ended at about one o'clock in the morning. They parted on good terms, even though disappointed at Anton's announcement.

'You spoilt that dinner, Anton,' said Nani, while they were walking back to the Pfarrgasse. 'Why couldn't you have left discussing your future until a better time?'

'There could be no time better than when we were all together. And I don't know what the result of my application will be. A refusal, if the previous one is any indication.'

Anton reached the point where he felt sufficiently confident in his recovery to apply again for the Imperial Chapel organist post. He wrote at the same time to the University of Vienna to ask if they would accept him as a lecturer in harmony and counterpoint. Although they had not advertised such a post, he had nothing to lose, except for a dented pride. The post as organist especially interested him, so, in the letter of application, he mentioned his experience as a teacher. He said he could also be employed in such a post or that of a secretary. His thinking was that this would put him at an advantage over other potential candidates, not that he wanted to serve in either post.

To his utter disappointment, both applications were unsuccessful. He wished he'd said nothing at Irene's party. He told no one, other than Nani, who had difficulty concealing her delight.

***

Soon after this failure, he received a letter offering him reappointment as choirmaster to the Linz Mixed Choir. Having suffered from the frivolity of some members of this organisation, he wondered if it was a prank in poor taste. He knew the efficient secretary well, so visited him.

'Hello, Matthias. I hope you don't mind me interrupting your work.'

'Of course not, Anton.'

'I have something important to ask you. It is a slightly difficult question, but I hope you understand.'

'Go on!'

'I received a letter only this morning offering me my job back as choirmaster. Do you know if it is genuine, or it is a joke? You may know, I resigned over a nasty piece of trickery.'

'I can assure you it's genuine, Anton. We would dearly like you back. Since you left, we have not done well. Various choir members have volunteered to take the lead, but no one has been as good as you. You made us famous, and we would welcome you back.'

'I would be absolutely delighted to take it. I will have to check at the Cathedral before I can accept.'

'That's excellent news, Anton!'

Anton felt overjoyed at starting again as choirmaster. He took the same approach as he had when previously in the honorary post. There were several new members, so he took great pride in getting to know them and their voices. He felt pleased that most of the new ones were women. Again, Johann Schiedermayr expected him to use the Cathedral as his primary venue for rehearsals and public playing. Recognising the major success of its first performance, he asked Anton if he would conduct the D minor Mass again at the Cathedral. Anton could not conceal his delight.

'I have some wonderful news for you. You will remember singing in my D minor Mass three years ago in the Cathedral and then in the Illustrious Hall. Well, Canon Schiedermayr has asked me if we will perform it again at the Cathedral. I have agreed on your behalf. I hope you are happy with that.' From the smiles and hand claps, the choir was as delighted as Anton. So rehearsals began. As before, Engelbert Lanz conducted the orchestra, many members of which were from the local military band, and Anton played the organ.

The performance in the January was an immense success, much to the delight of Anton, and Johann Schiedermayr. The applause was deafening and added to by unwelcomed cheering.

The reviews were excellent, but one was not.

'Moritz,' said Anton, when he saw him in the street. 'I was disappointed with your crass review in the Linz Daily. I don't want to fall out with you, but I don't believe you have understood this work. Three years ago, you said it was brilliant. And now you make spurious criticisms. When you say, "When Mr. Bruckner succeeds in refining or, rather, curbing his imagination, in avoiding over-violent cadences and strident dissonances... " I cannot think you know what the work is about. It is a modern orchestration of this most holy work. That no one has succeeded before is no reason to complain!'

'My dear Anton, I'm glad we will not be falling out over this. I'm so sorry that I have angered you. Worry not. I'll take your view to heart and write an article revising my thoughts.' Anton sensed surprise at how easy it was to change Moritz's mind.

'I would much welcome that,' he said, shook Moritz vigorously by the hand, wished him good day and walked on. He was on his way to the Mixed Choir office to speak to the secretary about future projects.

'I'm not sure if you are aware, Anton, but we have an important event this year, on the fourth of April. It will be the hundredth anniversary, not of our particular choir but of the first Linz Choir, which originated in 1768. This calls for a major concert. One that includes at least one first performance from a well-known composer.'

'I cannot agree to one of my works being performed for the first time. I'm not that well known! But thinking aloud, I could ask Richard Wagner, whom I know moderately well, if he has a new work we can play. What do you think, Matthias?'

'Unbelievable idea. How will you achieve that?'

'I'll write to him. To give him a little incentive, we should offer him honorary membership of our choral society.'

'We need council approval for that, Anton. They are meeting the day after tomorrow. I can come to see you at the Cathedral to tell you what they say, if you wish. It should be a formality.'

Anton received the approval he wanted, wrote to Wagner, and waited. While doing so, he wondered if the Master might be upset by a letter from an upstart such as him. Would it snap their friendship, such as it was? Would he say, if he responded, what a preposterous idea it was, and he simply threw out such requests?

'Here is a letter for you, Anton,' said Nani, after he returned late from the Cathedral. 'It's from Munich.'

He tore it open, just managing not to rip it apart. He quickly scanned it.

'Do I detect a sigh of relief?' said Nani.

'I could jump for joy. Richard Wagner has granted me all I asked of him. Please get me a beer. You have a glass of wine and we can celebrate!'

He desperately wanted to tell the choir what they would be playing on 4 April. So he convinced Matthias to write to them all to ask them to a meeting at which Anton would be making a special announcement. Nearly all were available on a night in February.

'I have an important announcement to make,' he said, smiling at them, as they all sat in the front theatre stalls. 'In January, I wrote to Richard Wagner to ask him if he would provide us with a new composition to play at our anniversary on the fourth of April. You all know of him as many of you played his Tannhäuser five years ago. I was overjoyed to read his response. He wants us to play the last section of the final Act of his latest opera, called Die Meistersinger, which he has all but finished. He tells me there is a bass solo and a full orchestra and a chorus of men and women. What do you think? Has anyone any questions?'

'Well done, Anton!' shouted someone from the front.

'Hear, hear!' another.

They all cheered and applauded.

'I take it we all agree to perform it! There is a fair amount to do yet. I need to write to Mainz to get a copy of the score of the last section. We'll print the parts from that. Depending on how long it is, we will almost certainly need to put something else in the programme. Oh, and Herr Wagner has accepted honorary membership of our society. He was delighted to be asked to join!'

Anton was becoming quite pleased with himself. It was only five months since his discharge from Bad Kreuzen and he felt he was coping well, considering he was under some pressure. The Wagner would take much of his time. There would have to be at least three rehearsals. There was a detailed programme to prepare. He was under even greater demand at the Cathedral and the parish church and would be conducting the rehearsals for the first performance of his Symphony No. 1 which the Karl Zappe had agreed the Theatre Orchestra would perform on 9 May. His main relaxation was the creation of his Mass in F minor, his third, large-scale version of such a work. And he still hankered for a post in Vienna.

Obtaining the last section of Act 3 of Die Meistersinger should be straightforward, he thought. He left that to Matthias who would organise the copying.

***

Anton took the opportunity to start rehearsing his No 1, while waiting for the Wagner piece to arrive. He and the Theatre Orchestra laboured in the concert venue, the Illustrious Hall, where they would premiere it.

'I'm stunned. I just don't understand why you are finding this so difficult,' he said, while standing on the rostrum with the orchestra in front of him. The faces of the musicians, especially the strings, betrayed their problems with this revolutionary composition.

'We've not played anything as impossible as this before,' said the lead viola player. 'We aren't virtuoso performers, just competent players. You'll have to change it.'

'And some of us are amateurs, so are finding it really hard,' said a cello player.

'I agree,' said the leader. 'The same goes for much of the first violin line. It's not good composing. Too much use of the chromatic scales and not enough of a definite key.'

'I'm having awful problems,' said a trombonist. 'It's nearly impossible to move the slide fast enough to get to the right note in time.'

'I cannot change the score. I could, but I won't. Let me explain. This is my first proper symphony. So if we play it badly, it will be forgotten and so will we. So I beg of you,' he said, with dampness in his eyes. 'Do your absolute best... just for me.'

They started again at the beginning of the first movement. Mistakes quickly arose. Anton hit the music stand with his baton. 'No, no! Let's leave this movement. What I suggest is you take it home and practice individually and we'll try it again at the next rehearsal.'

'You'll definitely have to make it easier,' said one of the second violins. 'Otherwise, some of us won't play in it.'

'In which case, I'll have to find replacements. There are plenty of players who would want to be in the premiere. Let's try the scherzo and see how that goes.'

An audible sigh of relief greeted the last chord of the movement. Anton applauded.

'Well done! That was brilliant! You are a wonderful orchestra,' he said, through tears of joy. They then agreed a date in the following week for another rehearsal. He would not change one note in the score. That would have meant giving in to the lack of skill in the ensemble, so out of the question. He still felt uneasy about the ability of this orchestra to premiere the work at the level he had every right to expect.

'I still haven't received the parts for the Wagner,' said Matthias when, having hunted everywhere for him, he found Anton in the Choir library.

'That's not good news. We've only five weeks left before the fourth of April.'

'I wrote to Schott, the publishers in Mainz, the day after you gave me the details and haven't heard a thing.'

'In which case, we'll need to bother Hans Richter for the score. He's a choirmaster and conductor at the Court Theatre in Munich. Wagner gave him as the alternative.'

'I'll write to Richter today.'

'Good man. I'm in the middle of preparing the programme so I'll think of an alternative, in case we don't get the score in time.'

'I'll warn the printers, so they can set aside some time to get the parts ready.'

Anton stayed there and drafted the programme. It would end with the finale of Die Meistersinger, The programme would begin with the Theatre Orchestra playing the first part of Schumann's Overture, Scherzo and Finale. It would then include some Tannhäuser, in homage to the Master. They would play more of this, if Die Meistersinger didn't arrive in time. Then there would be a brief interval. They would follow this with Anton's *Vaterlandslied*, a work he had written a couple of years before. It would be its first performance and its patriotic flavour would fit the occasion well. There would then be a second, longer interval and then Die Meistersinger.

'It's still not here,' said Matthias, when Anton walked into his office.

'No! There's only ten days to when we're supposed to perform the bloody thing!'

'There's nothing we can do but wait.'

'You are sadly right! Let me show you this draft of a programme I've put together.'

'Umm, not bad. Have you shown it to Karl Zappe? He ought to approve it before we get anything in print. We are using his orchestra and theatre!'

'I was thinking of showing him on my way home. He lives in the apartment below mine.'

'I know. He's always complaining about you playing that damn piano and keeping his kids awake.'

'Ha! Ha!'

'Here it is, Anton,' said Matthias, four days later as Anton stepped into his office. 'It arrived late yesterday afternoon. I'm taking it to the printers this morning.'

'Thank Christ! When will they have the parts ready?'

'The day after tomorrow.'

'That gives us four days to prepare the thing. It's as well we've rehearsed the other pieces in advance.'

***

Anton was staggered by the high quality of play in the first rehearsal. Maybe it was because, as he told them, they would make history in performing Wagner's piece for the first time. Their enthusiasm touched him, as did their keenness to do it justice.

As choirmaster and conductor, Anton had to grasp the words and the music and found this part of the libretto amusing. He thought it strange that Richard

248

Wagner would write a comic opera, but this one certainly was. So he had to ensure the choir and soloists sang it in such a way the humour of the piece was apparent, if not too obvious. It all ended happily, he discovered, when a protagonist, the young Walter von Stolzing, won the Meistersinger contest and the love of Eva. It made a change from the death of someone.

***

Anton continued to think about working in Vienna. By then, he had reconciled himself to the death of his friend and mentor, Simon Sechter. He thought hard about applying for his job as professor in harmony and counterpoint at the Vienna Conservatory, but was not certain about it. His supporter in Vienna, Johann Herbeck, strongly believed the post would suit Anton and no other, so encouraged him to apply.

'You must go for this post, Anton. I've convinced the authorities to set it up for you,' he said, one day when he came to see Anton.

'What would you like to drink, Herr Herbeck?' said Nani, wanting to be as sociable as possible.

'A cup of China tea, please. I'd welcome that after my arduous train journey this morning.'

'I admit, I want something different, Johann. I've had the job as organist here for twelve years. Although I love it, and am popular in it, I need something different. I can't stay here all my life, can I Nani?'

'I'm keeping out of it. You know what I think. I told you before when you applied for those other jobs there and nothing came of it.'

'This is different,' said Herbeck. 'The terms they would offer are good. Six hundred florins a year for nine lessons a week. Six lessons in counterpoint and three in the organ school. That's only nine hours at the most, plus preparation time, of course, which would be up to you. You'd have the rest of your time for composition.'

'I'm in two minds, Johann. I'm not sure about living in Vienna on that salary. Simon lived in a modest house apartment and I'm uncertain about affording even that.'

'I'll see if I can improve the deal, Anton. It will be your decision and I'm sure you'll make the right one for you!'

'Would you like to stay the night?' said Nani. 'Anton could sleep in the study and I can make up his bed for you. That'll be alright, won't it Anton?'

'Of course.'

'I'd love to stay, but I need to get back tonight. I have a meeting of the Music Society first thing in the morning.'

'I have to say, Johann, you have given me much to think about. I do want to leave the world I'm in, but I'm not sure if the world of Vienna is the one for me! I am vacillating, like a frightened ferret, wary of its new owner. But you are exceptionally kind in coming here to discuss what the Conservatorium has to offer. Please give me a little more time and I'll let you know what I decide. If you are successful in improving the offer, I'm sure that will help. I have two important performances to lead in the next five weeks. We are celebrating the Linz Choir's hundredth anniversary tomorrow and I'm conducting the premiere of my Symphony Number One on the ninth of May.'

***

Anton hardly slept the night before the anniversary concert. It was an important event and would be widely reported, certainly in Linz and possibly in Vienna and, because of the Wagner connection, even in Munich. So everything had to be right.

'This is wonderful,' said Anton to the lead tenor in the first interval, after the Tannhäuser. 'That applause was deafening. The choir deserves it! Everyone is performing so well. I'm delighted!'

'So you should be, Anton. You've done everything to make this a success. Only two pieces to go!'

Anton stood nervously on the rostrum to conduct his *Vaterlandslied*. There was something special about a first performance, which differed from a rehearsal, however well the practice went. They started the song.

If I could give you rapture,
How blessed I would stand.
You my treasured capture.
You my fatherland.

Anton's music and August Silberstein's words made this one of the most emotional pieces the audience had heard. It enchanted them and stood for an age applauding, cheering and stamping their feet. He hoped it would not overshadow the Wagner. By luck he had inserted another interval at this point in the programme. What a relief! They could talk about this and let its impact die down before the Wagner, which was intended to be the climax of the programme.

The Wagner was shorter than Anton had expected but a brilliant piece. He announced its performance to the audience and how he persuaded Wagner to allow it to be premiered in Linz. Their excitement was tangible. Its reception didn't quite rival his *Vaterlandslied* but showed great appreciation.

'How did it go, Anton?' said Nani, as he walked into the apartment.

'Extremely well. All the performers played brilliantly. My new piece almost brought the house down. I did not know how patriotic the people of Linz are.'

'I'm pleased for you,' she said blankly. 'Did you see that letter as you came in? It's on the hall table. The postmark is smudged so I can't see where it's from.'

Anton opened it. Herbeck had written to him. He quickly read it. The Conservatorium had increased the salary by two hundred florins. Anton grinned. That made the idea more attractive.

'I still don't know about moving to Vienna, Nani. Even though they are offering me more money.' He read her the letter.

'I'm getting angry with you. One minute you want to leave your life in Linz. In the next you want to stay. Only you can decide. Please make your mind up. It's beginning to cause me stress, something I don't want. It's the uncertainty.'

'I will definitely decide, Sis. I must be happy with the decision. You understand that, I'm sure.'

'Of course, and the sooner the better!' She turned around, sped into the kitchen, and slammed the door behind her.

***

He pressed on with his F minor Mass. It presented him with a glorious source of satisfaction. He had the extraordinary feeling that he was not composing it, but that a higher power was pouring it into his mind. All he was doing was placing the notes on paper as the ethereal force silently instructed him on what to write. Although he'd written seven masses up to then, he'd experienced nothing like it before.

'You're talking nonsense, Anton,' said Nani, as he attempted to explain this peculiar phenomenon. She didn't want to say it made her wonder if he was going through a renewed period of his illness.

Despite the pleasure of writing his Symphony No. 1, this Mass had generated a far greater feeling of satisfaction. He would not rush its completion as he wanted to extend the pleasure of writing it.

***

The time came for more rehearsals of the symphony, the premiere of which was only a month away. Anton had to think about managing them, especially as the first one was such a disaster.

'I would like to take a different approach to this rehearsal. Let's start with the adagio. As it's slower, I'm sure you will find it easier to play than the first movement which we started with before.'

To Anton's critical ear, it was worse than a disaster. It sounded like a catastrophe. He stopped them after about fifty bars. 'I'm sorry, my friends, but I'm sure we can do better. Shall we start again?'

'No, we can't,' said the leader.

'Why not?' said Anton.

251

'You don't appear to understand, Herr Bruckner. It is too difficult. Make it easier. Surely you can.'

'I don't agree,' said the timpanist. 'You must recognise this as a new type of symphony, written by a man who is ahead of his time. Give him respect. Play it at your level best. Please don't change a note, Herr Bruckner.'

'I don't agree with our timpanist,' said the leader of the violas, the same player who had objected so strongly to the first movement. 'The viola part is almost impossible. You have no choice but to change the score.'

'Hear, hear!' shouted most of the orchestra.

Anton raised his eyebrows and looked up at the decorated ceiling. He wasn't sure what to think or do. A solution occurred to him.

'Let's dissect the movement,' he said. 'We'll play it bar by bar and see if we can find the problem and solve it.'

They started again. 'That's fine. The introduction is fine. You played it well. Just keep going. Ah! The problem begins at bar thirty.'

'You've found it!' said the lead viola. 'Those five note phrases are too difficult for many of us. Twenty notes in a bar, even leading to a crescendo! What do you suggest we do?'

'Not too difficult. Those who are struggling go home after this and practice. Those who find it impossible just play what you can. I don't want to risk poor play when you needn't play at all, if you really believe you can't!'

'That's a perfectly acceptable solution,' said the leader.

'Does anyone disagree?' said Anton. 'Raise a hand if you do.' No hands went up.

Anton and his variegated orchestra performed the premiere on the 9 May. The Illustrious Hall was far from full. Tragically, the day before, a bridge across the Danube, close to the city, had collapsed, with several deaths and a large number injured. Many believed this unfortunate distraction had caused the poor attendance. Anton was pleased with the playing. To his relief and pleasure, the press reports were excellent. Moritz von Mayfield made up for his critical comments on the Mass in D minor by vociferously praising Anton and this 'exciting new symphony'. But Anton was more satisfied by another report.

'Let me read you this, Nani!' he said, a few days later, after making a rare purchase from a newsstand. 'It's from the New Free Press in Vienna. "A new symphony by Anton Bruckner was performed in Linz recently, and enjoyed an extremely favourable reception from a large, very select audience, and from the critics. The composer was called back to the rostrum several times. When news of Bruckner's forthcoming appointment at the Vienna

Conservatory is confirmed, we can only congratulate this educational establishment.'''

'I'm not so sure about that. Congratulations on the review itself, but isn't it going too far to say your appointment there is virtually certain?'

'That's typical of the man. It's by Eduard Hanslick who likes my music. I'm not sure where he gets the large audience from. The Hall was only half full. Mind you, if I go to Vienna, he could be a great ally. But you are right. I still haven't made my mind up. While we are on the subject, have you thought more about coming with me if I go? I would love it if you did.'

'Likewise, I haven't decided either. Why don't we jointly decide? Once you have all the facts you need.'

'A good idea. Let's do that.'

Anton thought of a tactic he used when he accepted the post in Linz. He arranged a formal meeting with Johann Schiedermayr.

'I haven't discussed this with you before, Johann, but I've been offered a post at the Conservatoire in Vienna.'

'Really? This is the first I've heard of it.'

'Please don't mistake my intentions. I've enjoyed working here in Linz and have taken out more than I feel I've given.'

'No, Anton. You've given twelve years of your life to us here and we'd hate to see you go, but please continue.'

'They've offered me Simon Sechter's post, not as a professor, but as lecturer. I haven't taken it and this is why I'm here to speak to you. You may help me decide.'

'What have you in mind, and how?'

'A move to Vienna would be an enormous change for me. I would not be a professional organist but an academic, teaching composition. So I would go from one familiar area to one which is completely new.'

'So?'

'What I would like to ask you is this. Could you do for me, in this situation, what St Florian did twelve years ago? That was to keep my job there open for two years, in case things didn't work out here as I hoped they would.'

'I wasn't aware of that!'

'No, but it's true. If they didn't agree, I wouldn't have come here.'

'Just as well they agreed then!'

'So, what do you think?'

Schiedermayr was uncertain but said he would support his case and put it to Bishop Rudigier who may not be able to authorise the request but would, if he agreed, ask the church authorities. Anton was sure the Bishop would reject the idea, not to be unkind but because he wouldn't want Anton to leave Linz.

So he almost jumped for joy when Johann told him they would give him the two years. After he finished his day's play at the Cathedral, he dashed home.

'Nani, I have some good news. The church authorities are going to keep my job here open for two years, if I accept the Vienna job. Not only that, the Bishop has secured me an excellent pension. I feel totally confident about accepting now. And I'm hugely grateful to Johann Herbeck for setting the job up for me. Have you thought more about coming to Vienna?'

'Yes, Anton. I've been pondering it. You are a large part of my life now and I don't know what I'd do if I stayed here and you went. But I have one condition. It is that we have a definite place to stay and move from here directly there. I'm not staying in a hotel or one of your friend's places!'

He kissed her on both cheeks. 'I am so grateful, Nani. I can't tell you how much. You are part of my life, too. I'll definitely find us a permanent place to live before we go.'

There was much to do before they could move to Vienna. The highest priority was to write to the Conservatorium to accept the post and to inform Johann Herbeck. The second was to find a place to live. He wanted something larger than the apartment in Linz. It was likely he would teach at his new home as well as compose and he might want to entertain guests. He didn't want to be too far from the Conservatorium either. So he wrote to his friend Rudolf Weinwurm to ask him to find a sizable apartment near his new workplace.

Days later, Anton received a telegram from Vienna. 'Nani,' she shouted to her in the kitchen. 'You'll never believe this! I've just had a message from Johann Herbeck. He says Emperor Franz Joseph has appointed me Court Organist Designate. I'm stunned!'

'So am I, Anton. That is just wonderful. Congratulations.' She hugged and kissed him.

'He says I can call myself "Imperial Court Organist" and I'm not there yet.'

'Where is the organ?'

'In the Imperial Palace Chapel which is the size of a large church. I'm sure you'll see it, while we are there. You'll love it!'

Chapter 19
1868 - 1869 Beginnings in Vienna

With the customary chaos of moving, Anton and Nani arrived in Vienna in good time for him to begin his duties at the Conservatorium on 1 October. They spent much time organising the apartment in the Währingerstrasse which Weinwurm had found for him. It was not without arguments about where various items should go. The Bösendorfer fitted well into the study which was important as he would frequently need it. The one slight drawback was that the apartment at Währingerstrasse 41 was 3 kilometres from the Conservatorium, a horsecar ride of fifteen minutes or a half hour's fast walk.

Several people were waiting in the main entrance hall of the spectacular orangey, sand coloured building when he arrived on foot, the week before his first lecture.

'Anton, it's so good to meet you here! You are perspiring! Did you walk here?' said Johann Herbeck.

'I did in fact, from Währingerstrasse.'

'Not too bad then, but far enough!' continued Herbeck. 'We have been through so much together to reach this point. I hope you will be happy in your new post and in the post of Court Organist Designate. Please allow me to introduce you to the Director of the Conservatorium, Josef Hellmesberger.'

'It's a great pleasure for me to see you again, Herr Bruckner. I shall now call you Professor! You come here with a wonderful reputation both as a composer and organist. Part of my duty is to give you a copy of the curriculum for the courses you will lecture on, but we must show you around the Conservatory beforehand, including your office, which I hope you find comfortable.'

Anton was surprised and delighted that Eduard Hanslick was also part of the reception party. His large moustache lifted as he gave Bruckner an emphatic smile. 'It's gratifying for me to see my prediction back in May has come true, and that you are now part of life in Vienna, Herr Bruckner.'

They shook hands vigorously. 'It's more gratifying for me to see you, so I can thank you face-to-face for your unstinting praise of my symphony. I cannot thank you enough. But I owe it to the determination of Johann who made your prediction come true. I did next to nothing!'

This half formal, friendly reception made Anton feel he would soon be part of the music scene in Vienna. Unlike Linz, at which Anton was then its only notable composer, Vienna was the hotbed of musical composition in Europe. Brahms, by then in his mid-thirties was becoming popular, well known and regarded by many, including Hanslick, as the successor to Beethoven. Johann

Strauss the younger, 'the walz king', was at his peak, and writing popular music, which became quickly recognised in Europe and the United States. And there was Anton's friend, Richard Wagner. Anton felt shocked to discover that, rather than being enjoyed by all as different but brilliant composers, those who supported either Brahms or Wagner were enemies of the other. The two camps could not have been more strongly opposed and irreconcilable. He had yet to hear any Brahms but inwardly vowed not to oppose him, friendly as he was with Wagner.

'I'd be overjoyed if you attended some of my lectures on the history of music,' said Hanslick.

'I certainly will,' said Anton, not then knowing he detested Wagner. 'You must give me the timetable.'

Anton's considerable experience as a teacher paid dividends at the Conservatoire. Firstly, he was confident in his ability to teach. Secondly, it enabled him to bring his relaxed, often humorous approach to his students.

'Good morning, ladies and gentlemen. You have the dubious fortune as having me as your new teacher. We will get to know each other well and I plan to make excellent composers of you all. If you fail, it could be my fault but it's more likely to be yours,' he said. 'Does anyone have any questions, so far?'

'How will you get to know us?'

'Simple. We start this way. I have a sheet of paper here with a map I've drawn of this lecture theatre. I'll ask each of you your name and I'm going to write it on the diagram. Please sit in the same place when we meet again. So names, please starting at the front row left. And tell me where you are from and why you are here.'

They obediently gave their names. 'I am Wladimir de Pachmann. I'm from Odessa and am interested in the theory of music, but I don't want to be a composer.'

'Please tell me why not. I'm sure you have a good reason.'

'I want to be a pianist. I wish to understand music theory but I'm not interested in writing music. I hope to be playing the music of others. I'm being taught by Josef Dachs.'

'Students. Wladimir here has a perfectly acceptable reason for not wanting to be a composer. Are there any others in the same position?'

Of the thirty or so students about half of them raised their hands.

'I'm surprised but pleased at the same time. We don't want too many composers but we need more instrumentalists! More names, please!'

They all called out their names and spoke about their ambitions. Some admitted they had no idea what they wanted as a career. It did not surprise him that many wanted to play a stringed instrument or the piano, but several wanted to become brass players or percussionists which did surprise him. He found it comforting that so many wanted to understand musical theory at Conservatorium level.

***

Shortly after he began teaching at the Conservatorium, Anton was having lunch with Johann Herbeck. 'How is your new job going?' asked Johann.

'I think quite well. All the students who started on my course are still with me, if that means anything.'

'Several students have said you are doing well, so that's good news for you and me, as your main supporter! I understand you are being strict.'

'You are right. I am. I won't tolerate lateness or any improper behaviour. I am following the techniques of Simon Sechter. I've told them not to compose until the course has finished and to complete all the exercises I set and submit them when they are due in or not at all.'

'That sounds totally reasonable to me. Changing the subject, you know Felix Dessoff who examined you with Simon and me a number of years ago. He's a teacher here. Well, he's also a conductor for the Vienna Philharmonic. He's a friend of Eduard Hanslick who really praised the performance of your Symphony Number One. You could ask Felix if he'd like to perform it here.'

'I like that idea, Johann. I'll ask him.'

'And what are your plans for your next symphony?'

'I'm thinking of one in D minor but I haven't started it yet. Maybe after Christmas.'

'Good luck with it. I'm sure it will be good.'

Anton's excitement at Johann's idea of his symphony being played in Vienna increased by the day. The only obstacle in seeing Dessoff was that he was on a tour with the orchestra and wouldn't return for several weeks.

Dessoff arrived even later than expected and delayed seeing Anton because he urgently needed to work on some lectures he was giving. Anton was becoming even more enthusiastic about getting the Philharmonic to perform his No. 1. He strongly believed there was no point in composing a piece like a symphony or a Mass if it was not to be performed or performed only few times before it was forgotten. So he thought the time he put into promoting his symphony was likely to be worth it. Eventually, he and Dessoff met in the student refectory.

'Show me the score,' said Dessoff.

Anton carefully lifted his original from his briefcase and placed it on the table in front of Dessoff. He turned the pages. As he did so, Anton told him

257

about its successful performance in Linz and the reviews by von Mayfield and Hanslick.

'Why can't you shut up and let me read the score? You're acting like a child.'

'Oh! Sorry!' Anton was tempted to comment on his rudeness, but could see nothing to be gained.

Dessoff continued in Anton's silence. He hummed some of it and moved his hand as if to conduct it. Dessoff read some, then missed out some pages, then started again. He looked closely at the first bars of each movement. Anton failed to interpret his expression. After about twenty minutes, he spoke.

'I'm not sure. It isn't a straightforward work to play. And it's wild, daring, and audacious.'

'That's why I call it "The Saucy Maid".'

'Weird name… How did you manage its first performance?'

'I admit it wasn't easy. The problem was many members of my orchestra were amateurs, which presumably doesn't apply to yours!'

'Of course not!' he shouted, on the verge of exploding. 'They are all highly competent professionals!'

'They asked me to change it but I refused. I'm proud of the fact I did!'

'I wouldn't have changed it either.'

'So what do you think?' Anton couldn't resist asking.

'It's savage and impudent. And too difficult. Not just for the orchestra but also for the audience. Leave me the score and give me a few days to think about it. I'll show it to a couple of section leaders. Don't be surprised if the answer is no… but it could be yes. Let's meet here at 9 o'clock on Friday morning, before classes, and I'll tell you then.' Dessoff slipped the score under his arm and went, leaving Anton sitting there. He stood up and walked back to his office, shoulders down and looking more at the floor than the direction in which he was walking.

Anton picked up his lecture notes from the desk and started thinking about how he was going to present it that day. He heard a knock and saw the door open. Johann Herbeck was standing there grinning.

'How did you fare with Felix?'

Anton told him without a hint of a smile.

'As he said, they still might play it.'

'No. He decided then. He said he'd ask a few of the leaders but the answer will be a reluctant no, believe me.'

'We'll see, Anton. That's not the main reason for coming to see you. I've read the score of your new Mass in F minor. It's brilliant. Only Beethoven's Missa Solemnis is anywhere near its equal and I want to play it in Vienna.'

'You've made me very happy, Johann,' he said smiling for the first time that day. 'Not with the Philharmonic?'

'No. With the Society of Friends of Music. I'm their chief conductor.'

'Fantastic. Let me know if I can help.'

Dessoff met Anton at the agreed time in the refectory. He approached Anton and spoke. 'No, we will not perform your symphony for the reasons I gave,' he said in the most perfunctory way. Then he walked off. It was the answer Anton expected. He'd get it performed there some time, he thought, if not by this unpleasant individual.

The attendance of so few performers at the rehearsals for his new Mass disappointed Anton and Herbeck. Neither could understand why it had generated such a lack of interest, particularly with the choir and soloists. So they left it and would start again, about a year later, once they could generate more interest in what they both believed to be one of his best works. So, while his teaching in Vienna was a success, attempts at performing his works were failing.

***

'We've had an invitation,' said Nani, when he walked in one night after an arduous day's teaching.

'Really?'

'Yes! Irene and the von Mayfields are inviting us back to Linz to spend Christmas with them.'

'Where would we stay?'

'There's not enough room at Irene's, and she's probably got students there, but I'm less sure about the Mayfields. I've never been upstairs in their house so I don't know whether they have enough bedrooms, one each for us two.'

'I don't mind if you go, and I stay here.'

'I won't accept that, Nani. If you don't go, I won't either. We could stay in the Frankfort Hotel, where they held my little farewell party.'

'I like that idea, Anton. We can come and go as we please, if we do that. I'll write and book some rooms.'

They enjoyed their time in Linz. They thrived on walking around the city. One of their first stops was at the Cathedral. Anton couldn't resist going up to the organ loft and improvising on the instrument for half an hour before they went to see Irene.

'I've missed you both,' she said. 'This place isn't the same without you, Anton. They still haven't appointed an organist at the parish church or the Cathedral. Have you played much in Vienna?'

259

'No, not much at all. I've spent nearly all my time preparing my lectures and giving them.'

'And what about your composing?'

He told her about the rejection by Dessoff of his Symphony Number One. And that he had already begun thinking about another.

'I can't understand why the Vienna Philharmonic won't play it. The Theatre Orchestra successfully performed it here, the press reports were excellent and the audience, including me, enjoyed it.'

'It's been my only real setback in Vienna. The reasons they gave were not convincing... but if an orchestra won't play a piece you've written, there is nothing you can do.'

'It must be very disheartening, especially to the composer.'

'It disappointed me at first, but I now write symphonies and will continue to do so. My ultimate aim is to get them performed, and I'm determined to do that. But if they are too difficult or too daring, that won't stop me from writing them. I don't want to be before my time, but if I am, then I'll have to accept that.'

'It would put me off writing them, but I'm glad for everyone that you won't be, Anton. So what else are you doing in the city, you two?'

'The usual domestic things for running a home,' said Nani. 'As you know, we are in the Währingerstrasse and have a large apartment there. It has three large bedrooms, a substantial lounge, Anton's study which houses his piano, and a nicely equipped kitchen. We are on the first and second floor and can see the Chemistry and Physics Departments of the University. We can also see the beautiful vineyards in the distance, and there is a pretty little park just down the road. You really must come to visit us. I'd love some female company!'

'Sounds a delightful spot, Nani. Thank you for the invitation. I will come. We'll fix a date over Christmas.'

'We'd make you more than welcomed,' said Anton. 'The weather in January won't be good, but there is a good heating system in the apartment so you won't be cold!'

'My students have gone home for Christmas, so there is plenty of room for you. Where's your luggage?'

'We're in the Frankfort Hotel, Irene. We didn't want to trouble you with accommodating us.'

'You disappoint me! You invite me to stay at yours and won't stay at mine.' Her face dropped, and she looked away from both of them.

'Are you sure about us staying here?' he said.

'Yes, of course!'

'We'll go back to the hotel and say we've changed our minds.'

Irene went up to Anton and hugged him.

He and Nani returned to the hotel. The receptionist frowned and groaned at losing two customers, one of whom he recognised. So he called for the manager who was also unhappy. Muttering under his breath, he and a porter colleague went up to the rooms Nani had reserved and brought down their luggage.

'I'm going to charge each of you for one night out of the four, Herr Bruckner. That will be three florins and six kreuzers.'

'I'm not paying that,' he said.

'In which case, I'll keep your luggage and put it in the rubbish.'

'I've changed my mind. I'll pay.'

'Here is your luggage.'

The two of them picked up a case each and walked back to Irene's. They told her the story about having to pay for a night at the hotel. She was disgusted. 'All we paid them when we had your leaving party, before you went to Vienna. You would have thought they would have been more reasonable... and generous. I suppose it's best forgotten. At least we are all together for Christmas now.'

Christmas was a major relaxation for both Anton and Nani. He would not compose, but would think of some thematic material for his new symphony. She would help Irene with the cooking and other domestics, but wouldn't have to look after Anton or their apartment. The von Mayfields soon appeared for dinner on Christmas Eve. Betty kissed Anton on the cheeks and Moritz kissed Nani.

'It's so good to see you both,' said Moritz. 'Everyone in Linz is missing you. That includes you, Nani. That's because we all know how Anton relies on you!'

'Don't be silly, Moritz. Everyone knows Anton, but few know me and I want to keep it that way!'

Anton had to explain again how he was getting on in Vienna. Nani said the Mayfields ought to come to stay. In reply, Moritz stunned them by saying they owned a property in Vienna and it would be easier for all of them to stay at their apartment there. It turned out to be about a two-minute walk from their apartment in the Währingerstrasse. It wasn't long before they all sat down for dinner. Anton raised a glass. 'I propose a toast to Irene, our hostess for three days.' They all clinked glasses.

'I thought it was only two,' said Irene, laughing.

'Really?' said Nani.

'Only joking!' said Irene.

The conversation ranged far and wide, from the political situation in Austria, which had long since recovered from the civil strife of the 40s, through the work Moritz was doing for the city and the government, to how Anton saw his future in Vienna. After dinner the three women sat in the lounge to converse, while Anton and Moritz continued talking at the dining table.

'Whatever anyone tells you in Vienna, Anton, you must continue writing those symphonies.'

'Yes, but why are you saying that?'

'Because that Symphony Number One of yours, which Dessoff is being so difficult about, has the hallmarks of a rising star. I know it was your second attempt and I'm not familiar with your first. It is not what I would call a masterpiece because it is so untamed and audacious. But it has a freshness and newness about it along with a unique style. I am quite familiar with Mozart's symphonies and Beethoven's, many of Haydn's and, of course, Mendelssohn's, and Schubert's, but that one differs massively from any of those. Your name as a symphonist will be as familiar as theirs, not this year, maybe not in ten years, but in time it will. I promise you. And I will help with reviews, if I can.'

'You are a kind and thoughtful man, Moritz. I take much from what you say. I will continue writing symphonies, as I regard it as a God given gift, which I am obliged to use to the best of my ability.'

'And don't neglect your organ playing, Anton. You are the best in Europe!'

'I love to play that instrument. It gives me immense feelings of freedom and power. So, fear not. I will continue as long as I'm physically able!'

'Good man! How are you getting on in Vienna?'

'Not too bad, but I feel like an outsider still.'

'Why's that?'

'Partly because of my Upper Austrian accent, and partly because of my clothes. It's the wide trousers and my loose fitting collar! I get some odd looks and people look askance. I've had to tolerate rudeness from Dessoff, who treats me as if I'm a child. But I won't be deterred, whatever they think,' he said, sounding less than sure.

'You have the strength of will to overcome these people, Anton. I'm certain!'

'I just hope you're right,' he said, trying to smile.

The Mayfields didn't stay the night, but returned to their house. They lived not more than a few hundred metres away, so came back for the Christmas Day breakfast, after which all five of them walked around the town for an hour. During lunch, prepared by the three women, they collectively decided it was time to exchange presents.

'I need some help to bring Moritz's present here,' said Betty.

'I'll come with you,' said Anton.

They weren't away ten minutes when they returned to Irene's with a large box which Anton managed to carry on his own. Nani gave the ladies a thick scarf each and Moritz a box of Cuban cigars. Irene gave Nani and Betty a pair of winter stockings each and Anton a book about Mexico, a country which had intrigued him since the execution of Emperor Maximilian in '67. Betty had brought a box containing several bottles of wine and some of beer. She explained that a consumable present could be very welcome at this time of the year.

It then came to Moritz's present from Betty, which Anton placed on the dining table. At first he struggled to open it. 'Take care,' said Betty. 'Its contents are delicate.'

Anton went to the kitchen for a knife. 'Let's split the box down the sides and open it that way.'

Anton used as little of the blade as he could to avoid damaging the contents. He cut the top along three edges. He could see inside but said nothing and cut the vertical edges. Then he flattened the sides onto the table to reveal Moritz's present in its incredible beauty and complexity.

'What is it?' said Nani.

'Are those planets?' said Irene.

'Yes!' said Anton

'Thank you so much, Betty. It's something I've always wanted.' He kissed her on both cheeks.

'I still don't know what it is,' said Nani.

'Nor do I,' said Irene.

'It's an orrery,' said Moritz. 'I'll turn this handle and show you how it works.' Moritz explained how the model represented the orbit of the planets around the sun. He said that Saturn took twenty-nine Earth years to go around and Neptune, which was only discovered twenty years before, took a hundred and sixty-five. 'I'm so glad that Neptune is on it... and see how quickly Mercury moves!' he said.

They all smiled and talked about this amazing piece of mechanical mastery. According to Moritz, it would keep him amused for hours. Betty grinned, knowing this would be his reaction. After the exchange of gifts, the men decided it was time to have a drink. The women opted for a small glass of local wine while Moritz poured Anton and himself a stein of beer.

'Umm,' said Anton, after taking a hefty gulp, 'I like this one. Not too strong but very hoppy.'

'I thought you'd like it,' said Betty.

'Yes, it's a good beer,' said Moritz.

'We've got plenty of it,' said Irene.

Within a couple of hours, both Anton and Moritz were incoherent, having indulged themselves to the extreme. They could hardly stand up. The women were not impressed.

'You've drunk too much, Moritz,' said Betty.

'I'm not apologising. I'm in a harmless state, so there's nothing to complain about.'

'I hope Nani doesn't complain about me.'

'I won't. I've seen you in that condition so many times, I'm used to it!'

They all laughed, except Anton, who looked towards the wall.

'We all have to attend Midnight Mass at the Cathedral,' said Betty.

'Is that compulsory?' said Anton.

'Definitely,' Irene said.

'So you've both got about six hours to sober up,' said Nani.

The men were just about clear of the effects of the beer by the time they all walked to the Cathedral. The service started. Then about halfway through the choir and organist started to play.

'My God,' said Anton, his eyebrows raised to their full extent. 'That's my Kronstorf Mass. I'm utterly staggered.' He had difficulty holding back his tears.

'That's why we had to attend!' said Betty.

***

Anton's students enjoyed his lectures, especially when he injected more of his humour. He talked about God creating Adam, then added the interval of a fifth. Then he created Eve alongside the third. He described the diminished seventh chord as the musical version of the Orient Express. Before the end of January, after one of his lectures, he started writing his new symphony, the one in D minor he'd mentioned to Johann Herbeck.

One morning in the early April, and within seconds of entering his office, there was a firm knock on his door. 'Come in! Oh, it's you Eduard! I've only just got here!'

'I've some interesting things to tell you,' said Eduard Hanslick. 'I've selected you to play in a series of competitive recitals on a newly commissioned organ in the church of St Epvre, in Nancy.'

'I'm duly flattered, Eduard, but please tell me more. I'm very busy here, of course, and I've only been teaching for less than six months.'

'I know. But if you agree to represent the Conservatorium, it will be good for you and for us. Hellmesberger has received an invitation from the church authorities asking us to send our best organist to Nancy. You know and I know it's you!'

'And?'

'You will have to compete on the new organ with organists from all over Europe. This will be on two successive days. The winner will be the one who plays the best two recitals. The audience will be important dignitaries from all over Europe. And who knows where that could lead?'

'Not another competition. I had enough of that twelve years ago to get the job in Linz Cathedral.'

'This is different, Anton. If you don't win, you just come home. It's not like applying for a post somewhere. And there would be no shame in not winning!'

'Hmm…' Anton stood up and walked towards the window. He stopped and looked out for a full minute. His eyes focussed on the distant vineyards while he pondered over Eduard's proposal. Would he be letting the Conservatorium down by refusing? Could a negative decision affect his future? Would it prejudice his new found friendship with Eduard? It could benefit him, as he said. He turned around and spoke. 'Yes, I'll go.'

Eduard rushed over and firmly shook his hand. 'Wonderful, Anton. Wonderful. I'm proud of you, my friend!'

***

'To where?' said Nani, when he explained it to her.

'St Epvre, in Nancy, France.'

'Do you want to go?'

'Yes, I do. It will benefit me and the Conservatorium.'

'When do you have to be there?'

'April the twenty seventh.'

'I'll pack for you.'

'Would you like to come with me?'

'I haven't told you this, Tonerl, but I haven't been feeling well lately. So I'll stay here, if you don't mind.'

'What has been the problem, Sis?'

'I think it's my heart. It beats very fast sometimes. I've been meaning to see our doctor.'

'I'm sorry to hear that,' he said, giving her a gentle hug. 'Please look after yourself. And go to the doctor soon! I need you!'

'Don't worry, Tonerl. I'm sure they can sort it out.'

Anton had never undertaken such a complicated journey. He travelled by train via Munich, Stuttgart and Strasbourg. Arriving exhausted, he booked himself into the Grand Hotel de la Reine, in the centre of Nancy. He thought a hotel there couldn't be that far from the church. He soon discovered it was

265

less than five minutes' walk from the magnificent, neo-gothic Basilica de Epvre. To Anton, it looked new and freshly finished. He stepped inside to look at the organ. It was a stunning instrument which he thought he could play well.

The night before the competition was due to start, he lay in bed looking at the ceiling. He felt confident that he would perform to a high standard, whatever the quality of the opposition. If there were better organists than him, he would graciously accept defeat.

He arrived at the Basilica at the appointed time, which was 10 o'clock in the morning. He was welcomed by a priest who asked him if he would listen or compete.

'I'm one of the competitors. The one from Austria.'

'Ah... Herr Bruckner, I believe. Do you have any means of identification?'

'No. All I can tell you is that Professor Eduard Hanslick wrote to someone here to say I would represent the Vienna Conservatorium.'

'That will be sufficient. Please go over there and sit with the other competitors.' He pointed to an area near the steps to the organ loft. There were already nine sitting there. Each was in discussion with another. Anton joined them and introduced himself to the one nearest to where he sat. He was from Belgium. He told Anton there were eleven competitors in all, so they weren't all there yet. Eventually, he met every one. They were from many parts of Europe: Rheims, Namur, Luxembourg, Paris, Nancy, Strasbourg, Hessen and Lunéville.

Anton listened carefully to the playing of the other competitors. The one who impressed him most was Vilbac from Paris. Anton was the fifth to climb up to the organ loft. Feeling totally prepared and confident, he played a Bach fugue followed by free improvisation, using every skill in his armoury. At the end of the contest, the chairman of the judges announced Anton as the winner of that day's event. He invited Anton to receive the applause of the vast audience. A radiant smile appeared on his face. The applause was muted, a possible sign that they expected another organist to win, the local man or the player from Paris.

For the second day of the competition, Anton made a political decision. He was aware that Emperor Franz Joseph I and Empress Elizabeth were patrons of the Basilica. He knew their family had close connections with Nancy, especially when it was the capital of the Duchy of Lorraine. So he would play the Austrian National Anthem and a series of imaginative improvisations on it. As he finished, the listeners broke into an uproar of applause and stamping. His eyes opened wide at this unwelcomed behaviour in the Basilica, which they were treating like a cheap back-street dance hall.

After the second round, the chairman of the judges, which Anton later heard was César Franck, spoke. 'It is a pleasure for me to announce that Herr Anton Bruckner of the Vienna Conservatoire has won our recital competition on the Merklin-Schüze organ. It is privilege for me to present him with this certificate.' The audience applauded with greater fervour than the day before, probably because of his performance of the National Anthem.

After the applause had subsided, he made his way back up to the organ loft to put together his papers.

'Congratulations, Herr Bruckner,' said a woman with a long green dress and decorated red hat who had followed him up the steps. 'You are the best organist I have ever heard. I'd love to hear you again.'

Anton didn't know what to say. 'Thank you, Madam. You are kind. If you wanted to listen to me again, you would have to come to Vienna.'

'Here is my card. Please write to me as soon as you plan to play a major work!'

'I will indeed, madam,' he said, not sure if he would.

As soon as the woman reached the bottom of the stairs, two more handsomely dressed ladies came up to congratulate him. One of them kissed him on both cheeks. He'd experienced nothing like it before. He responded with a grateful, 'Thank you! Thank you!'

As he reached the bottom of the steps, a gentleman approached him. 'Herr Bruckner, many congratulations on your brilliant organ playing! You made our new organ sing! My main reason for speaking to you is this. I am a director of Merklin-Shütze and I wish to invite you to come to Paris to play on the organ we have just installed in Notre-Dame Cathedral.'

'Thank you, mein Herr. I'm deeply honoured by your compliments and invitation. I would be delighted to accept, but my approved leave to come here expires on Monday.'

'But you must come, Herr Bruckner. We would be distraught by your refusal. You would light up Paris and it would be a tremendous occasion.'

'I really must go back to Vienna. I have a lecture programme to deliver and am writing a new symphony.'

'I am really going to press you. We will pay all your expenses and pay you whatever you would like, up to a reasonable amount. I am just dying for you to play at Notre-Dame.'

'You have persuaded me, Herr Director. I'm not so interested in the money which I will leave for you to decide. But I would be grateful for my expenses. I will telegram my superiors to ask them to extend my leave. Will three days suffice?'

267

'I am utterly delighted, Herr Bruckner! We will manage your visit in three days with no problem. We will book you into an excellent hotel in advance,' he said, moving closer to shake his hand. Anton retracted slightly, thinking this Frenchman might kiss him, which he believed was the national custom.

Anton sent a lengthy telegram to Johann Herbeck, telling him about his success in Nancy, asking for three days more leave, and why he needed it. His immediate, one word reply said, 'Agreed'.

The company booked him into the famous and luxurious Hotel Diesbach ou Les Polonaise. He looked around as he walked in, and placed his case next to the reception desk.

'Ah, Herr Bruckner,' said the receptionist, after Anton told her his name. 'You are the distinguished guest of the director of Merklin-Shütze, the organ makers.'

'Well, a guest. Yes,' he replied.

'We have to give you our very best, exceptional service.' She smiled at him and rang a bell, near her hand. Moments later, a young man appeared, dressed in a grey uniform, with a tightly buttoned jacket, and a round, red hat.

The manservant welcomed him with a smile and took him to the extravagant bar where he offered Anton any drink he wanted. He asked for a beer. The man raised his eyebrows, as if he expected him to order something more exotic, a glass of champagne or an expensive Bordeaux, perhaps. He waited for him to finish his beer, took him to his suite of rooms, helped him unpack his baggage and showed him around. Anton had never seen gold plated taps before or a bed so wide it could have slept four. The hotel's shameless luxury overwhelmed him.

Just as Anton was about to choose his dinner from the extensive menu, a neatly bearded, tall gentleman in a knee length-coat approached him. 'I understand you are the organist, Herr Anton Bruckner. Is that so?'

Anton hesitated for a moment, not knowing whether to admit who he was or to tell him to go away. He decided, mainly out of curiosity, to acknowledge his own presence.

'Yes, I am Bruckner.'

'Then it is a great pleasure for me to meet you, mein Herr. I am Joseph Merklin, the owner of Merklin-Shütze, the organ manufacturing company. Would you kindly allow me to join you for dinner?'

'I would be delighted,' he said, smiling. He welcomed the company of a figure as important as this man.

Joseph Merklin pulled out a chair and sat opposite Anton. A waitress brought him a menu. 'First, Herr Bruckner, I must thank you profusely for agreeing to come here to play our organ in Notre-Dame. It is a great honour for us.'

'More an honour for me,' he said, in his characteristic humbleness. 'What do you want me to play? Has anyone decided?'

'You can play anything you like. My colleagues at Nancy thought your treatment of the Bach fugue and your improvisation on themes from it was incredible. It was the best playing on one of our organs they had ever heard. So anything along those lines would be perfect.'

'Yes, I can do that. And I could add a piece I've composed, if that would be acceptable.'

'Of course. Please do!'

'Tell me. Who will be in the audience?'

'We've invited many of the dignitaries of Paris, the mayor and lady mayoress. We've asked the monarch, Napoleon III and his wife Eugenie but I doubt they will attend. Too much tension with Prussia. César Franck, Camille Saint-Saëns, Charles Gounod and Daniel Auber, our best composers, have all said they'll come.'

'Excellent. It would be good to meet them.'

They chatted about their backgrounds, Merklin's in Baden, Prussia, and Anton's. Merklin was concerned about the situation there and said he'd leave France if war broke out. They parted on friendly terms with Merklin asking Anton to appear at Notre-Dame by 10 o'clock. 'Oh, by the way,' he said, 'we are giving you 500 francs.' Anton thanked him profusely and shook his hand.

As he climbed up to the organ loft, he could see that Notre-Dame was completely full. Not only was every seat taken, there were people standing at the back and by the side chapels. He felt thrilled so many had come to hear him. They must have organised this inauguration weeks before and decided to invite the winner of the recital competition in Nancy. So he was there as the winner and not as Anton Bruckner, not that it made any difference.

He sat in front of the five manuals for a full fifteen seconds to let the audience become silent. His feet and hands then played his version of Bach's Toccata and Fugue in F Major. The sound he produced filled the cathedral with its power and energy. When he briefly stopped, the stream of notes would reverberate around this magnificent cathedral. Having played the entire piece, he launched fearlessly into his improvisation, originating new fugal structures as he went. His skills at playing this instrument were limitless, beyond incredible. The more he lost himself, the more enrapturing was his creation. His inventiveness shattered the audience to the point of exhaustion. It was as if he had them in a constrictor like grip, and wouldn't release them.

A standing ovation greeted the end of the piece. Anton stood and bowed. Looking outwards, he could see many in the audience were wiping tears from their eyes, such was the effect of his playing. He realised he had achieved a major triumph. Responding to calls for an encore, he played an improvisation on *Germanenzug*. The themes, he thought, lent themselves not only to variation but to the creation of fugues on which he could also improvise. Once more, he played at the very summit of his ability. Despite playing in this sacred place, his reception was overwhelming. He was almost in tears himself. This performance crowned the hundreds of times he had played before.

Many came up to him afterwards, some even pushing a piece of paper in his face and giving him a pen to sign his autograph. He seemed to be floating on a cloud.

Joseph Merklin shook his hand so vigorously, he thought he'd inflict damage to his fingers. 'You were wonderful, Anton. There is no other organ player in the whole of Europe anywhere near as good as you. You made our upgraded organ sound the best it ever will, unless of course you came back again!'

'You are too kind, Joseph! Thank you!'

César Franck and Daniel Auber told him how much they enjoyed his play. 'No one thinks it's possible to improve on Bach, but you proved it is,' said Franck.

'And that other piece was equally stunning,' said Auber.

***

The leave extension that Herbeck had given him finished at the beginning of the Conservatoire Easter vacation. He therefore had a short break at Wels to take up an invitation from one of his students, a certain August Göllerich.

'I wasn't sure whether you were coming, Professor! Welcome to our modest home.' The enormity of the house amazed Anton. August's father was a successful local businessman, who had amassed a fortune over the years and ploughed much of his wealth into improving the facilities of the town. 'Come and meet my parents!'

'We've heard all about your success in Nancy and Paris,' said Göllerich senior. He was tall, seemed friendly and had an upwards curled moustache, just like his smile. 'It's all over the local news and the ones in Linz! Congratulations. I am a director of our local choir and they have unanimously agreed to make you an honorary member. I'm so glad you came to our house. That has saved August from having to tell you back at the Conservatory!'

'I'm deeply honoured, Herr Göllerich. May I thank you by playing an organ concert your parish church?'

'I'm sure we would all love that,' said Frau Göllerich, who appeared in the hall and overheard them.

Within a few days, he was performing at the church. He played a distinctly different set of themes from those of Paris. He included some from his first symphony and the one he was currently writing. He ended by improvising on themes from a motet he had just finished, *Locus iste*, which had yet to have its first performance.

The congregation applauded after he had finished and a young girl came up to him while he was still at the organ. 'What lovely playing, Professor. I thoroughly enjoyed it. My name is Karoline Rabl. I live in Wels and I'm so pleased to meet you.' She held out her hand, which he took in his. His heart beat faster. He could feel it thumping on his ribs. His mind leapt into a state of excitement. No pretty blond had approached him for years. Surely, he could not be falling in love again.

He couldn't sleep that night for thinking of Fräulein Rabl. She sounded like an amiable girl who would make an excellent wife. He even thought about Nani moving back to Linz and Fräulein Rabl moving in with him. Life would be perfect with such a delightful partner. Becoming more confident, he would find out more from August.

'Tell me,' he said at breakfast, 'That girl who came up to me yesterday, Fräulein Rabl, do you know anything about her, where she lives, for example? I would like to visit her.'

August looked at him, wondering exactly what Anton had in mind. 'Yes, she's nineteen and lives with her parents in a street near here. She's a member of our choir and is a nice person. He father is a farmer whose land is right on the edge of the town.'

'If you give me her address, I'll go and speak to her.'

'Just out of curiosity, Professor, why do you want to see her, to get her to join your class?'

'No. I think I'm falling in love with her.'

August could not believe what he was hearing. He frowned, lifted his arms, and opened his hands. 'Oh, well. Good luck!' He gave Anton the girl's address.

Halfway through the morning, Anton knocked on the Rabls' front door. A large bulky man, wearing working clothes with a smoking pipe in his mouth, opened it.

'Hello,' he said. 'You are the organist we saw yesterday, aren't you?'

'I am in fact.'

'What can we do for you?'

Anton was stuck for a few seconds on what to say. 'I'd like to speak to your daughter.'

'Really?' he smiled.

'Yes. She came over to me yesterday to speak about my music and I thought it would be nice to continue the conversation.'

'Come in. I'll get her. Wait a minute.' Anton stood in the hall.

A few minutes later, the man, whom Anton assumed was her father, appeared. 'I'm sorry, Herr Professor. She's too nervous to see you. Maybe I can help.'

Anton thought again for a moment. 'To tell you the truth, Herr Rabl, I have fallen in love with your beautiful and cheerful daughter. Please, may I have her hand in marriage?'

'You must be joking!'

'No. I'm deadly serious. I am a successful member of the Vienna Conservatorium, as well as the Imperial Court Organist. So I'm not poor and I could give your daughter a wonderful life.'

'But you must be in your forties and she's not twenty yet. I'll have a word with her. Wait here. Oh, have a seat.'

Herr Rabl was back within a matter of seconds. 'The answer is no, Herr Professor. Sorry.'

A crestfallen Anton walked back to the Göllerich's house, only to be greeted by August, his student. 'So how did you get on, Professor?'

'She's not yet ready for marriage. Anyway, we parted amicably, and that is the end of that.' He managed to raise a smile, artificial though it was.

***

On his return to the Conservatorium, Herbeck, Hanslick, and almost everyone who knew about his performance in Paris, congratulated him. He had rarely felt happier and had totally dismissed the thoughts of his failure to attract Karoline Rabl. There was much more to life than love, he thought. He regarded his first year at the Conservatorium as a success, especially as his students had been so successful in their examinations.

Thinking he deserved a vacation, he went from Vienna to Linz via St Florian. He wanted to meet up with his friends and to tell them about his work in Vienna and his organ performances in France. His new symphony still needed attention, so he would use his free time in Linz to finish it. He wanted Nani to go with him but she still didn't feel well and stayed in Vienna to rest.

Joseph Schiedermayr urgently wanted to see him. 'Anton, we are consecrating the votive chapel at the new cathedral on the twenty-ninth of September and intend to play your E minor Mass, the piece Bishop Rudigier commissioned from you, some three years ago, for that very purpose. Do you think you could conduct it for us? Obviously, as the Cathedral is still being built, the Mass will be performed outdoors.'

'That will not be a problem, Johann. I've finished my teaching for this year so am a free man. I presume the Linz Mixed Choir will perform it and I will use some players from the Theatre Orchestra and some from the infantry.'

'Yes. I've already contacted the general. He's happy for us to engage their musicians.'

'Good! I have a piece of news for you. I have written a very short *Locus iste* with the dedication on mind. There is no point in playing my Festive Cantata again, so, subject to your and the Bishop's views, I would like to conduct the *Locus iste*, as a supplement to the Mass. I've scored it for soprano, alto, tenor and bass choirs.'

'Go ahead with it Anton. We don't need the Bishop's approval. It will give him a wonderful surprise. He will be utterly thrilled!'

Anton hadn't realised how many rehearsals it would take to bring the choir and instrumentalists up to the standard he had set. This dedication had to be performed to the highest professional standard, even though many of the players would be amateurs. He conducted a staggering twenty rehearsals.

Many local people attended the event, probably around a thousand. This included church officials and the press from as far away as Vienna. As usual, Anton felt uneasy about how the choir and soloists would perform. But he could applaud them all, especially the military, and the choir who sang his *Locus iste*. While the music was only a part of the ceremony, he felt he had achieved a modest success.

Anton's face lit up when Bishop Rudigier invited him to the ecclesiastical celebration lunch. This took place immediately after the ceremony, outdoors in the grounds of the new Cathedral. How different from the banquet, from which they cruelly excluded him, after the installation of Friedrich Mayer at St Florian. The Bishop made it a formal occasion, at least at the beginning. He introduced clerics from outside, and those locally, who had contributed to the success of the dedication.

'And finally, I must thank Anton Bruckner not only for conducting the orchestra and the choir, but also for composing the Mass, which he supplemented by his beautiful *Locus iste*. I'm sure both works will be played many times in the future. Could you please thank Herr Bruckner in the customary way?'

Anton expected a round of applause but smiled when they all raised their glasses, mainly of beer, and shouted, 'To Anton Bruckner!'

They all enjoyed the sumptuous meal, after which many approached Anton to congratulate him. The Bishop took him to one side.

'Anton, please come with me into our incomplete building. There is something I must show you.'

'Of course.'

The Bishop led the way into the structure which was less than half finished. There were no workmen, who had been given the day off. They cautiously stepped over loose stones and planks until they reached the steps into the crypt of the votive chapel. 'Follow me,' said the Bishop who picked up a lit candle from a small table at the entrance and sheltered the flame with his hand. Anton did likewise and both stepped gingerly to the far wall of the crypt.

'We have reserved this spot as your burial place, Anton.'

His eyebrows leapt upwards at what the Bishop said. Then he smiled broadly. 'I'm truly grateful that you have made this provision for me, Franz. And deeply honoured.'

'I know you are a firm believer. You have carried out marvels in your work here. You have provided me personally with much pleasure as I've listened to your playing. This is the least we can do for the memory of a great man.'

'I'm too modest to agree with your sentiments, Franz, but I am extremely grateful.' The Bishop was not aware that, after his demise, Anton wanted to be interred in the Monastery at St Florian. He didn't have the heart to tell him.

***

As in his first year at the Conservatoire, the term started in the October. His teaching duties for the new academic year hardly changed, but more students joined his classes, for which Anton was grateful. He was happy to present the course for the second time around, as he could use his notes from the year before. This gave him more time to work on his second major symphony, the one in D minor.

One evening in the following January, he entered their apartment in the Währingerstrasse. As he usually did, he shouted out for Nani to tell her he was home. There was no reply. He was not worried and thought she had gone from the house to do some last-minute shopping, probably for some vegetables for dinner. So he poured himself a beer and sat at his desk to resume writing his symphony. After an hour or more, he realised the shops would be shut by then so became concerned about Nani's whereabouts. He climbed the stairs to the upper floor and entered her bedroom. There she was, motionless on her bed. He felt her pulse. Nothing. She was dead. Tears streamed down his face. He did not know what to do. He suddenly remembered the von Mayfields were still at their flat, which was a few hundred metres away. Should he go there? No. He needed a doctor to attend and check Nani's condition. There was one, just along the street, the one who attended to her earlier when she had her heart problems. He'd go there.

On his way, his mind flooded with thoughts. Thoughts that he did not want to have. Where should he have her buried, here or at Ansfelden with their parents? Whom should he invite to the funeral? Should he ask their friends in Linz? Of course he should.

'You look somewhat disturbed, mein Herr,' said a middle-aged looking lady who answered the door.

'I'm almost certain my sister, Nani Bruckner, has died?'

'Where is she?'

'On her bed?'

'Is she breathing?'

'No. I'm certain.'

'I'll get my husband, the doctor.'

Within moments, he and Anton were returning to the apartment. Anton took him upstairs. He placed a stethoscope on Nani's motionless chest.

'I'm sorry, Herr Bruckner. You are right. She has passed away. I would say a heart attack is the most likely cause.'

'Do you know of a local funeral director? I feel I must start making the arrangements.'

'Yes, there are several near here. It's gone eight o'clock so I can't imagine you will get one before tomorrow. Here, I'll write the addresses of two local

275

ones on a piece of paper. The doctor handed him the two written addresses. I recommend Frier and sons. They are nearest, maybe a half kilometre away, off to your right. Do you mind having your sister's body here for the night?'

'Not at all. I shall sleep in the chair near her bed.'

'That's a nice sentiment, Herr Bruckner, but not at all necessary. I would sleep in your own bed. You will feel better rested by the morning. Do you have any friends close by?'

'Yes, a couple who have a flat, the von Mayfields.'

'I know the wife. They are a delightful couple. I'm sure they would help you. You should take a couple of days off from your work. You may know, I treated your sister for a heart problem about six months ago. She told me you are working at the Conservatoire. Is that right?'

'Yes.'

'Go there first thing and tell them what has happened. They will give you some compassionate leave.'

Johann Herbeck told him not to worry about his class because he would deal with the situation himself. Anton thanked him, not knowing whether he would take the class or find someone to stand in for him. He said he would be sure to invite him to the service, as he had known Nani well. Betty Mayfield helped Anton with the practicalities.

Nani's passing consumed Anton with sadness and guilt. He felt he had made her work too hard in looking after him. She cooked, did the washing, kept the apartment clean, did the shopping and provided a companion to speak to about anything they chose, even about his love life, or lack of one. She would criticise him when he deserved it, for overindulging in food or beer or working too hard. He believed she would have been healthier and lived longer if she had stayed in Linz.

After the service, which almost shattered Anton into pieces, Nani was laid to rest in the Währing cemetery, at which Beethoven and Schubert were also buried.

Anton found life difficult without Nani to help him. Within a few days, and with a recommendation from his friendly neighbours, he engaged Katharina Kachelmayr, or 'Kathi' as she became known to him. They agreed Kathi would cook his breakfast and clean the apartment in the mornings and, if he was composing all day, she would come back to provide him with a lunch. They would agree between them whether she should return to cook him an evening meal.

***

After several attempts to find the time, he eventually completed his new symphony, which he might even anoint as his Symphony Number Two. He wanted a colleague to have a critical look at it to give him a second opinion. While he believed it to be a solid piece of symphonic writing, he thought it didn't match the excitement and dynamism of his Symphony No 1. The most critical of his No. 1 was Dessoff, so he would ask him, despite his rudeness and forthright rejection of his earlier work. With the score under his arm, he knocked on his office door and went in.

'You've got a nerve, Anton. I could have been talking privately to one of my staff or a student, and you burst through the door.'

'Sorry, Felix. At least I didn't embarrass you by waking you up!'

Felix laughed at Anton's frivolity, apparently forgiving his transgression. 'So what can we do for you?'

'I'm taking something of a risk, Felix. It's not long since I completed another symphony. I respect your views on my Symphony No. 1, but I would much appreciate your thoughts on this one.' He took the manuscript from under his arm and waved it in front of Dessoff.

'I'd be delighted to look at it. I hope it's less wild and violent than your earlier one.'

'I think it's a calmer work and not bad. If you like it, perhaps you could consider it for performance.'

'Of course. Please leave it with me. Come back in two days' time and I'll tell you. Assuming I've found time to read the thing. Say, nine o'clock. I'm rehearsing at ten.'

Anton balked at the use of the word 'thing' but tried not to show it. He could not like this temperamental individual but had to deal with him, especially if he wanted the Vienna Philharmonic to perform his work. So he didn't feel optimistic when he knocked on Dessoff's door at the agreed time.

'Enter!... Oh, it's you, Anton.'

'Yes, you invited me back today so you could give me your verdict on my Symphony Number Two.'

'Yes. I've read it in great detail,' he said, as he picked up the score from the side of his desk. 'I have to say, I don't think it's as good as your first, which we reluctantly decided not to play.' He opened the score at the first page. 'Tell me. Where is the first theme?'

'There it is. That series of quadruplets, beginning in the first bar.'

'That's not what I call a theme. It's merely a figure. There is no tune in it. And if that's the first, where is the second?'

Anton frowned as he turned the pages. 'There it is. It starts with an exchange between the first violins.'

'But these aren't themes, either. I don't know what they are.'

The composer's face dropped. He couldn't avoid showing his disappointment. 'It may not be as good as my first, but it should be easier to play and is just as eventful. You haven't commented on the scherzo, which I think is the best movement.'

'That starts with a slide up the scale and I don't call that a theme, either.'

'I take it you have no intention of the Philharmonic playing it?'

'Sorry, but no.'

Anton was determined to have the last word. 'You just don't appreciate modern music, Felix. It's a sad reality.' He picked up his score, walked out, and almost slammed the door behind him.

Undeterred by what he regarded as Dessoff's ignorance, and still having unshakable faith in himself, he started a symphony in B flat major. He jotted eighty bars.

'Do you have a minute, Kathi?'

'What do you want?'

'To play you something I've written.'

'Oh, alright then. I'll just finish this washing up.'

'I can wait, as it's you!'

She came into his study, wiping her hands with a dishcloth. 'Go on then.' He played her the eighty bars.

'Well?'

'No, I don't like it. What is it?'

'The first part of a symphony I'm writing. I'm glad I asked you because I don't like it, either.'

He abandoned it there and then, never to write another note of it.

***

Later in the year, Josef Hellmesberger, came to see him at one of his classes, just after Anton had finished the lesson. 'I have some good news for you, on two fronts. The first is that, the Ministry of Education is donating four hundred florins to you, to encourage you in your composing. Hopefully, this will make things easier for you to spend more time writing your symphonies, which we all know are a large part of your life. What a result, eh?'

'How has that come about, Josef? I've not asked for anything. My only increase in expenses since my sister Nani passed away is the cost of my housekeeper, and I'm sure I can afford her on what I'm earning here.'

'You can blame me, Anton. I have been thinking that you deserved a financial reward. This would be for your amazing effort, and the results you have achieved from your students, since you joined us, what over eighteen months ago? So, I applied for this grant for you. Officially, it's to further your composition, but spend it as you please!'

'I can't tell you how grateful I am, Josef. Thank you so much.' This generous act improved Anton's views on Hellmesberger, whom up to then he regarded as a remote and formal leader.

'You will see the money this month in your bank account. My second point is this. As you know, we have a teacher training college attached to the Conservatorium, the St Anna's College. I'm please to say, I can offer you a teaching post there. I would very much like you to take it. That will give you an increase in salary of five hundred and twenty florins, if you accept the job, which is for a ten-month period. There are only a few lessons. Three a week. They are in the teaching of piano, organ and music theory, topics you are an expert in.'

'Doesn't that go against the purpose of the Ministry of Education grant you have just told me about?'

'Up to a point, yes. But it helps me, Anton, and it will improve your work record. It's only for a short time.'

'As it's you, Josef, I will accept. It will certainly improve my financial position!'

Anton put much thought into how he would manage the work at St Anna's. This was an advanced course in training for which he had no experience at all. So he wrote to August Dürrnberger for advice and to ask his permission to use his famous textbook. In his reply, Dürrnberger expressed his delight at hearing from his former pupil, with whom he had almost lost contact. He told him his best advice was to make the students work hard on chapters two and three of the book, which he knew was already in Anton's hands.

He made rapid progress in gaining the support and admiration of his St Anna students, all of whom were in their late teens.

'I've bought some special sweets for you today, as you are all doing so well. Please hand this bag around, Herr Piber. Don't let anyone take more than two! And when you've done, please go to the tobacconists for me, as I've run out of snuff.'

The class burst out laughing, including Herr Piber, who was the willing victim.

***

The year 1871 was an important year in London, as the national exhibition was to be held then. As part of this major event, the Exhibition Commission invited the chambers of commerce in all countries in Europe to send their best organists to play the gigantic Willis organ in the newly constructed Royal Albert Hall. Several candidates in Vienna were considered but after a competition involving two other excellent organists, Anton emerged victorious.

'Kathi, I have some important news for you. I'm going to London later this month to play an organ at a new concert hall there. The Royal Albert Hall. Apparently, commissioned by Queen Victoria. She may even be in the audience!'

'That's good news for you, Herr Bruckner, but what will I do when you are away?'

'I shall still pay you, so you don't need to worry. That is whether or not they pay me. But I understand they will, so we'll both be better off! I would like you to come in twice a week until I come back, just to keep the place tidy, and to pick up any letters from the front door.'

'That will be fine, Herr Bruckner.'

A week later, Kathi came into his study, holding a letter. 'I've just picked up this up from the hall. It's postmarked London.'

He opened it carefully and read it. It was from the Exhibition Commissioners and dated 10 July. They gave him the detailed instructions, for a series of recitals beginning on 2 August. It unexpectedly described the organ and said they would pay him a fee of £50, which would include his travel and subsistence expenses. Anton worked out that this was equivalent to 800 florins, about a year's salary.

'My goodness, Kathi. They are paying me a fortune, but that's got to include my travel expenses and hotel costs. If I make a profit, I'll give you some extra when I get back!'

'Well, don't stay in expensive hotels or travel first class. Otherwise, we'll both end up with nothing!'

'Alright, alright!'

Kathi helped him pack sufficient clothing for two weeks, telling him to use a laundry if he needed to. She waved him off on the 27 July. He checked in at Seyd's German Guesthouse, 39 Finsbury Square, on 29th, after an even more complicated journey than the one in 1869 to Paris. He could see as he walked in that it was a good, not too expensive hotel, so it would not cost him much to stay there. He noticed there was a resident barber, so, having unpacked, he found the barber shop, and had a shave and haircut.

That evening, against Kathi's advice, he took a Hackney cab to the Royal Albert Hall. It seemed to take forever. London's size and sights amazed him. The driver pointed out St Paul's Cathedral, Trafalgar Square and Nelson's Column, as well as Buckingham Palace. As the main door was open, he walked straight in.

'Excuse me, Sir, the Hall is closed at the moment. We are about to lock the doors. So please, would you leave?' said a man who appeared to be a guard.

Anton challenged the man. 'My name is Anton Bruckner. I'm due to give a recital on the Willis organ on the second of August. I just wanted to see the instrument and to become familiar with it before playing.'

'Wait there and I'll get the director.'

Moments later, a heavily bearded, tall, smiling man appeared. 'I'm so pleased to meet you, Herr Bruckner. I hope your journey from Vienna was not too arduous.'

'No, not too bad. At least I'm here a few days early. I just wanted to play the organ as a rehearsal for my recital.'

'We are closed now. The organ is steam powered, and there is none left in the tank. Could you please come back tomorrow morning? We will charge it and you can play for as long as you like. I'll be here from nine o'clock.'

Having spent what he thought was a fortune on the taxi, he would travel back to the guesthouse by omnibus. 'Could you please tell me if I can catch an omnibus back to Finsbury Square?'

'Yes, I think it's the 143,' said the director. 'The stop is on the other side of the road, in Kensington Gore. Tell the conductor, the man who collects the fares, where you want to get out.'

After a brief wait, the 143, black with yellow wheels, gently pulled by three sprightly looking mares, stopped for him to climb aboard. He told the conductor the name of the guesthouse and the bus pulled away. Eventually, having traversed what Anton thought was every street in London, it reached Finsbury Square. Anton didn't recognise the place the bus stopped, and the conductor forgot to tell him. It was about to move off when a man outside the bus banged heavily on the side where Anton was sitting.

'Get out now, Herr Bruckner. Stop the bus!' he shouted.

Anton suddenly realised he was right outside Seyd's, but baffled by the shout from outside. He thanked the conductor and stepped off.

'Thank you, Sir,' he said to the man who had knocked. 'How did you know this was where I had to get out? Especially as it's getting dark?'

'I'm the barber, Herr Bruckner. I recognised you from when I gave you a shave and haircut, earlier this afternoon. I was smoking a cheroot outside, and I caught a glimpse of you from the pavement. I assumed you wanted to get out here, so I yelled out!'

'I'm most grateful to be helped by one of my own countrymen while in this foreign city. Let me buy you a drink!'

'Maybe tomorrow, Herr Bruckner. Another gentleman has an appointment with me in the next five minutes.'

Anton dined alone that evening, unlike his time in Paris where he was in someone's company for nearly all waking hours. The menu didn't mention pork or dumplings so he settled on a pint of English beer and a plate of roast chicken breast, runner beans and boiled potatoes. He much enjoyed the beer and after a third pint went to bed. He attributed his good night's sleep, not to the ale, but to his long journey from Vienna.

He thrived on the English breakfast and took the 143 omnibus back to the Royal Albert Hall. The director met him in the main foyer and gave him a conducted tour of the instrument. 'As far as we know, it's the largest organ in the world. It has 4330 pipes, four manuals and one hundred and eleven stops! A two feet in diameter piston provides the steam pressure of one atmosphere and a vacuum on its return. We started the two steam engines early today, so there is enough in the tank for you to play for three hours. So off you go. It's yours. If you'd like to play all day, we can even arrange that!'

Anton looked enthralled by this colossal instrument. Its power and versatility staggered him. The range of notes it could produce covered the entire span of human hearing. With the director looking over his shoulder, he made himself comfortable at the console. Before starting, he located the stops and looked down to see the positions of the pedals. He adjusted the mirror so he could comfortably view the auditorium. Then he began. Rather than use items from the printed programme, he played thematic material from his symphonies and improvised on them. He became lost in his playing and created simple and complex melodies on which he could improvise or play as fugues.

The auditorium was empty when he started. However, in some mysterious way, word spread that a magician was playing the Albert Hall organ. Consequently, hundreds of people, men, women and even children, came to listen. Anton found it puzzling.

'Tell me, director,' he said, when he had a break after playing solidly for an hour and a half, 'where have all these people come from?'

'I wish I could tell you, but we often open for free attendance at rehearsals. Many would have come in hope and others probably told their friends and neighbours about your playing. They've all enjoyed it, otherwise you wouldn't have had that round of applause when you stopped. What are your plans now?'

'I'd like to have a drink and then start again. I've restrained myself somewhat because I still haven't discovered the full potential of the instrument. Another couple of hours and I should know it better. In my next session, after that drink, I shall be more experimental and stretch it to its full capacity. Is there a limit to the volume of sound I can produce?'

'No. When Willis designed it, he made sure that at maximum volume it can do no damage to the structure of the hall. It could damage a few eardrums, but that's a different matter!'

The director took Anton to a bar, opened it up, and took a couple of bottles of beer from a shelf. He carefully poured them into half pint glasses.

'I should have asked you, is a beer alright?'

'I've really taken to your English beer. I had three pints at Seyd's last night. It's not as good as our Pilsner but it's not bad at all. I'm just puzzled by these small glasses. Only women drink from these where I come from, and the men drink from glasses that are twice as big as your pints!'

'In that case, have another one before you start again. It will help you with your experimenting! You'll be less inhibited!'

'Me? Inhibited?' They both laughed.

After the session, in which he frequently used the swell pedal, pulled nearly all the stops out at once, and used the entire range of instrumental sounds, from the piccolo to the tuba, he was sure he had mastered the full ambit of tones and volumes the organ could produce. He ended by improvising on Bach's F Major Toccata, which appeared in the programme for 2 August.

With two days free, he spent some time looking around London. He fell in love with St Paul's Cathedral and would have played the organ there, given the opportunity. He joined a tour of the Tower of London and the London Wall.

Wednesday soon came around and Anton caught the omnibus back to the Royal Albert Hall. He arrived a half hour before his recital was due to start, and made his way to a collection of rooms used by members of the orchestras and soloists. The director met him there.

'Good morning, Herr Bruckner. Here is a room you can use to change if you wish.'

'Not necessary. I'm playing in what I'm wearing now,' he said, not realising that they probably expected him to play in more formal attire. 'Will anyone announce me?'

'In fact, no. The plan is that you arrive at the organ loft by noon, your scheduled starting time, bow to the audience and start playing your programme. I gave you a copy when we first met.'

'Oh, I forgot to bring it. Could you give me another copy please, just to be sure? I think I remember what it said.'

'Here you are,' he said, closing his eyes slightly.

They sat in the largest of rooms while Anton told him how much he enjoyed St Paul's Cathedral and the Tower of London.

'Don't you feel nervous, Herr Bruckner? Most performers are quite nervous before they face the audience!'

'No. I feel fine. My only anxiety was making sure I was here in good time. That's why I caught an earlier omnibus!' he laughed.

'You've got five minutes to reach the organ loft. I suggest you go now. Good luck!'

'Thank you!'

Anton raised his eyebrows at the sheer number of people in the audience. He thought there must have been at least five thousand there. A loud round of applause met his deep bow from the console. He raised his arms, gave the audience a few hand claps and sat on the bench. Unexpectedly, he had to adjust it slightly as someone had obviously played there after his rehearsals. As usual, he sat in silence for a time until in his mind he was ready to start.

He raised his hands and began playing the Bach Toccata. As he burst his way through, he couldn't help inserting his own variations. He reached the end in a little over seven minutes. The audience applauded as he launched into his improvisations. None of them had heard before such imaginative ideas and spontaneous conception. He was in that state of mind, which enabled him to be so original, in a way unique to him. Glancing in the mirror, he could see from the reaction on their faces that he had bewitched the audience. His wizardry completely overcame them.

He stood after he finished, again to be greeted by an enormous round of uninhibited applause. Having sat back down, he began playing the Handel Fugue in D minor. He timed the silences so well, the effect of the reverberation was devastating. Then he dived straight into his improvisations, creating a startling double fugue. At the conclusion, the audience not only gave him a standing ovation but applauded, cheered and stamped their feet. They seemed to enjoy this piece even more that the Bach, possibly because Handel had become naturalised as English.

Then he improvised on the E Major Fugue of Bach, this time not introducing it by playing the original. Again, they marvelled at his magical playing.

Finally, he improvised on God Save the Queen, another piece which dramatically raised the emotions of the audience.

His popularity, which he learned from people at the hotel, was at least equal to that of his audiences in France. He later discovered that, disappointingly, some of the British press did not see it that way. They complained that the management of the Exhibition Committee had advertised the need for organists too widely. There were too many foreign players, including from Vienna, Stockholm, and Brussels, so William Best, the Albert Hall's resident organist, slumbered in the dark. According to the director, some of the papers had even reported that Anton arrived on 5 August, the Saturday, and that the dates for his concerts would be announced later.

These anomalous comments didn't affect Anton in the least. He played again on all the next five days, to be appreciated just as much by those who attended.

His recitals were so popular, concert managers from all over England wanted him to play in their cities. The only invitation he accepted, and which attracted him most, was one to the Crystal Palace to play four recitals at the German Festival, for which they would pay him 10 Guineas and give him the services of a translator. He jumped at the chance.

***

Anton had agreed to play on the 19, 21, 22 and 23 August at the new venue. He had seen sufficient of London, so spent time composing a new symphony. There was something special about starting a symphony in London. This would be his fifth attempt. By then, he regarded his 'No. 2' as mediocre, nothing like as good as his No. 1. So he rejected its numbering and would call the symphony he began in London his No. 2. Using a variation on the quadruplet tune, which began the symphony he discarded, he started on the finale.

The day before his first recital, he heard a gentle knock on his room door. He was in the middle of writing a few complex bars, so ignored it and hoped whoever it was would go away. A few minutes later, he heard another knock. Frowning and with his lips pursed, he opened the door. His expression suddenly changed. A handsome, smiling blond woman in a long yellow dress was standing there.

'Good afternoon, Herr Bruckner. My name is Frau Greta Schwarzkopf, your translator. I am Austrian as well. Pleased to meet you.'

'I'm pleased to meet you, too, Frau Schwarzkopf. I feel extremely privileged to have your services.' He knew it would be improper to invite her into his room for a drink, so asked her if she would like to join him in the hotel bar. She gladly accepted.

'What would you like?' he said.

'A pot of tea, please.'

He held his hand up, and a waiter instantly appeared. He ordered the tea and a pint of English beer for himself.

'So where do you live in Austria?' he said.

'I don't. Not now. I live in London. I work for the Austrian embassy, near to the centre. In fact, I live just across the road from here and that was why the Festival organisers asked for my services. I used to live in Vienna over a bookshop on Währingerstrasse.'

'No! What an incredible coincidence! My home is above that bookshop, at number 41!'

'That is truly amazing!'

'So why did you move to London?'

'The political situation scared me. I am Jewish and could detect a rise in antisemitism in the country, which is why I left. I speak English, French, and German. I wrote to our embassy here, and it so happened they were advertising for someone with my skills to fill a secretarial post. So here I am! And what about you? I believe you are a composer as well as an organist.'

They spent the next hour or two talking about each other's backgrounds and families. Frau Schwarzkopf then decided it was time for her to go home to her husband, whom she said was also Austrian and worked at a bank in the city.

***

A couple of hours before his first recital was due, the two of them set off for the Crystal Palace. He'd never seen a building like it before. To Anton, it looked like a gigantic greenhouse, one on an unimaginable scale. It comprised a complex metal frame covered in thousands of square metres of glass. It must have been at least five hundred metres long, a hundred wide and a hundred metres tall at the centre which was much higher than each end. As they stepped inside, he stared open-mouthed at the colossal auditorium. It looked as if there were enough seats to take an audience of at least forty thousand.

'We need to find August Manns,' said Frau Schwarzkopf. 'He's the director of music here. And he conducts the orchestra.'

'There won't be an orchestra, will there?'

'Not while you are performing. As you'll see, the organ is large but not as big as the one in the Albert Hall. There's Mr Manns, over there,' she said, pointing to a short, grey-haired, grey bearded gentleman in a black, knee-length coat.

'I'm delighted to meet you, Herr Bruckner,' he said, smiling. 'Welcome to the Crystal Palace!'

Anton was delighted to be greeted by someone who also spoke German, even though Frau Schwarzkopf was with him. 'Thank you,' said Anton. 'What an incredible building! There is nothing like it in Austria.'

'Let me show you the organ,' said Manns, leading him and Frau Schwarzkopf up to the instrument, which was situated some distance behind the stage. 'I'll give you a copy of the programme. As you will see, we are performing some short pieces by Weber, Meyerbeer, Handel, Schubert and Mozart before I introduce you. That will be about an hour after we start, which is in about half an hour. Is that alright, Herr Bruckner?'

'Of course. Should I sit with the audience or are there rooms off stage for performers?'

'There is a large area at the side of the stage, if you and Greta would like to sit there. Please go to the organ bench after the Schubert songs so you are ready by the time the Mozart finishes.'

Anton sat at the organ bench in good time. For once he felt quite nervous, even though he had a clear idea of what he would be playing. Greta sat on a reserved seat at the front.

After Manns announced him, he bowed to the vast audience, sat for five seconds and started to play. The audience seemed stunned that he started by improvising on themes from the Schubert songs. Then he dived into improvising on themes from his Symphony No. 1 followed by a wild improvisation on Handel's Hallelujah Chorus. Then he played some Mendelssohn and finished with some improvisations on themes he might use in his Symphony No. 2.

He could not believe the intensity of delight at his playing. Most gave him a standing ovation, shouting, 'Bruckner, Bruckner, Bruckner!' He applauded them in thanks. Then hundreds shouted in unison and repeated, 'Watch on the Rhine'. He knew this patriotic song but just could not remember the tune. He turned to the audience, held his hands up and opened his eyes wide. Frau Schwarzkopf ran up to the organ bench and hummed it in his ear. She saved him.

He played the tune and an incredible set of improvisations, some as exciting fugues. The audience started shouting and applauding, even before he finished. As he did, he stood and bowed. Seconds later, a dozen or more enthusiastic listeners arrived at the organ bench, physically lifted him onto their shoulders and paraded him around the auditorium. He could hardly believe this kind of adulation. It enraptured him and provided him with a delightful, unforgettable moment in his life as a performer. He had never enjoyed such recognition.

The entire series of recitals at the Crystal Palace was a success. It thrilled him to know that his skills as an organist, in particular as an improviser, were so well appreciated. At his final performance there, he was again born aloft by members of the audience who virtually carried him out of the venue.

'Congratulations, Herr Bruckner,' said August Manns, as he saw him after these wild admirers placed him back onto the floor. 'You were an amazing success. You really must come back to London and perform here again, next year perhaps?'

'I'd truly love to, but I have many commitments in Vienna, not least my teaching duties at the Conservatorium, and I've recently been appointed to a temporary post at a teacher training college. Please give me your details and I'll see what I can do.'

Manns gave him a business card. 'Take this and please don't lose it. Write to me. We can adjust our programme to your convenience. Safe journey home!' They smiled and shook hands.

'I still cannot believe the reception I received,' he said to Frau Schwarzkopf, as they sat in the hotel bar, having a farewell drink.

'You deserved it, Herr Bruckner. No one has heard such brilliant organ play before and, unless, as Mr Manns suggests, you come back, they probably won't again.'

Anton thanked her, especially for humming the tune of Watch on the Rhine, and they parted with a gentle shaking of hands.

***

'Welcome home!' said Kathi, as he walked in through the door of his apartment. 'I can quickly prepare a meal for you. I've been expecting you for a few days now.'

'That is kind of you. I am hungry after all that travelling.'

'How did your recitals go?'

'Unbelievable, Kathi. Some of the audience at one of the venues picked me up, put me on their shoulders, and carried me around the auditorium. They liked my playing that much!'

'They may have just about had enough of you!'

'Not from the standing ovation and shouts of encore, they hadn't!'

'I was only teasing! I'm really glad you were so successful!'

'I was thrilled, Kathi. I have a present for you.' He smiled as he handed her a small leather wallet.

'Thank you,' she said, as she looked at it. 'What a pretty wallet. Is it from England?'

'Yes. It may have saved my life!'

'What do you mean?'

'As I was waiting at Dover for the ferry, I thought I'd go into a shop to buy you a little something. I couldn't work out what to buy, and spent too much time looking for souvenirs. Eventually, I chose this little purse. As I was struggling to pay for it, not yet sure of myself with their weird money, I heard a ship's horn. It was leaving the port, so I missed it.'

'I don't understand, Herr Bruckner. How did it save your life?'

'Well, the ship I was supposed to catch collided with another vessel in the English Channel and lots of people lost their lives. I could have been one of them.'

'That is frightening.'

'Yes, so I have to thank you and the purse.'

'I'm still in a state of shock,' she said, putting it in her pinafore pocket.

'Aren't you going to open it?'

She took it out and undid it. 'My goodness! It's full of money! You can't afford to give me all this,' she said as she finished counting it. 'It's a hundred and fifty florins!'

'It's yours, Kathi. If I hadn't bought that purse, I could be up with the angels by now!'

Although it was still the summer vacation, and few students were at the Conservatorium, Anton decided to go to his office, in case he needed to read any correspondence and to see what was happening there. Most of the letters and notes were unimportant, but one envelope was marked 'urgent'. He opened it quickly and saw it was from Josef Hellmesberger, asking him to come to his office as soon as he returned from London. What could be so urgent, especially as this was not term time? He walked to the director's office straight away.

'I'm afraid Professor Hellmesberger is on leave at present,' said his secretary. 'I think he is returning next week.'

'Do you know why he wants to see me urgently?'

'Yes, but I'm not at liberty to tell you. All I can suggest is that you call in next week, say on Monday morning when he may be back.'

Anton became concerned. What could it be that the secretary could not discuss? Could it be about his competence in teaching, playing or about the time he spent at the Imperial Court Chapel or on composing? Or the time he spent in London? Try as he did, he came to no valid conclusion. He'd have to wait. To clear his mind of it, he continued work on his new symphony, Symphony No. 2.

Filled with trepidation, Anton went to see Hellmesberger at the agreed time of 3 o'clock in the afternoon. 'First, may I congratulate you on your performances at your recitals in London, Anton? The national newspapers here and some in London, I understand, have been full of praise for you. You have been exalted by the press as the best organist in Europe and probably in the world! Well done indeed!'

'Thank you, Josef. I felt completely overwhelmed by my reception, both at the Royal Albert Hall and at the Crystal Palace.'

'You thoroughly deserved it! But that is not the main reason I wanted to see you. Please sit down because you may be shocked by what I'm going to say. But don't rush to any conclusions because I shall decide by what you tell me. I trust you completely. It is this. A girl in your class at St Anna's has accused you of improper behaviour of a sexual nature.'

'But...'

'Let me finish, please. The girl herself made no complaint, but her friend said during a lesson you called her "my dear darling". Is that so? And if so, what did you mean?'

'How ridiculous,' said Anton in a raised voice. 'I've never heard such nonsense. I used the term as a compliment. We use it in Linz as an innocent address. There was no sexual intent or implication. My behaviour is impeccable, I'll have you know. So I dismiss the claim against me and hope you do, too. In fact, it makes me angry. I no longer wish to teach a class of girls, if that's how they behave.'

'Are you sure, Anton? You will lose out financially by about two hundred florins. I totally believe you. You are an exemplary teacher and I accept that you have done no wrong. It might appear that you accept your guilt if you stop teaching the girls.'

'I am sure, Josef. To confirm my innocence, could you please provide me with a document confirming my perfect discipline in teaching?'

'I shall do that, Anton. I'll get something written straight away.'

Chapter 21
1872 - 1873 Performances

Anton soon recovered from the unjustified accusation of improper behaviour and dedicated himself to his class work, organ playing, and composition. While he still felt comfortable in Vienna, he spent as much time as he could in his favourite places in Upper Austria. He could not resist the peacefulness of the St Florian Monastery so often visited it, as well as Steyr, Enns, and occasionally Linz.

'Whatever are you doing here, Anton? Come in and have a drink at least,' said Irene, as she opened the door to him.

'I couldn't resist dropping in to see you. I'm back for a few days, mainly to renew old acquaintances. But also to escape from the relentless pace of life in Vienna... and to do some composing!'

'All my students are on vacation so you can stay here, if you wish. You haven't booked that damned hotel, as you and Nani did just a few Christmases ago, have you?'

'No, I've booked nothing yet. I've just spent a couple of days with Michael Bogner and his wife, at St Florian, and composing in the library there. He was headmaster at the school where I was a teacher before I moved here.'

'I remember him. You were good friends with both of them. Didn't you live with them?'

'Yes, I did. Well remembered. If you are happy, I'll stay with you, Irene. I'll be working quite often. Will that be alright?'

'Of course! I hope you have settled into your new life without Nani. It was so sad that she passed away so young.'

Anton's face dropped at the thought of Nani. 'Yes, I miss her and think of her a lot. Fortunately, I have a lady who comes in to do my meals, keep the place clean and helps me. Her name is Kathi. Usually, we get on well but we fall out occasionally. Sometimes she goes home in a fit of anger and I have to go and apologise before she comes back!'

Realising she had touched a sensitive nerve, she changed the subject. 'That was a wonderful Christmas we spent together, and that present Betty gave Moritz. What was it called?'

'The orrery, with all the planets moving when you turn the handle!'

'That's it! And you men got so drunk on the Pilsner, you only just sobered up in time to go to Mass!'

'Yes, thanks to you, we had a lovely time!'

'So will you be going straight back to Vienna?'

'No. I'll be calling in at one of my favourite haunts near there, Klosterneuburg.'

'I've never heard of it, but it sounds like you'll like it!'

In Linz, he spent hours working on his Symphony No. 2, but found time to visit the Zappe family. On his last night there, he dined with the von Mayfields at a dinner in his honour organised by Irene.

Klosterneuburg was about ten kilometres from Vienna and, although he had visited it only twice before, its beautiful monastery and gothic church reminded him of St Florian. The chief attraction was the three-manual organ in the church.

He sat in a hostelry in the town and consumed a grilled pork chop with beans and a half stein of beer before making his way to the abbey church, which was built next to the monastery.

Anton could see no one in the church, not even a priest. He put his baggage on a pew before looking for a person who could act as calcant. As he crossed himself in front of the altar, he heard a door close by a side chapel. A young lad appeared.

'Good afternoon,' said Anton to the lad. 'I wonder if you could help me. I hope to be playing the organ in a few moments, but I need someone to operate the pump. Could you do it for me, please? I'll willingly give you a kreuzer or two!'

'I am a regular calcant here, mein Herr. I'll do it willingly. No charge.'

Moments later, Anton was playing one of his favourite Bach pieces and following it with a string of improvisations, all of which were new to him but which flooded into his mind like a creative torrent. As far as he knew, there was no audience except the young schoolboy, but this made no difference to what happened in his mind or to how he translated it into his hand and foot movements. Having played for at least three quarters of an hour, he stepped down from the organ loft and walked towards the nave.

'That was extraordinary... phenomenal! The best organ playing I have ever heard,' said a tall, moustachioed individual, smiling generously in Anton's direction. He appeared to be in his late twenties or early thirties.

'Thank you, mein Herr. I'm glad you liked it.'

'I think I recognised the Bach!'

'You did indeed.'

As if he could detect the beer on Anton's breath, the young man offered to buy him a drink.

'That's very kind of you. I'd be delighted to accept. There is a hostelry near here.'

'I know it. Let's go.'

'Just a minute. I have to settle a debt.' Anton vanished to the back of the organ and took a four kreuzer piece from his purse and paid it to the schoolboy. The lad's eyes opened to their maximum. He wasn't expecting that much, so thanked Anton profusely.

'Let's go,' said the young man.

He bought Anton and himself a stein of Pilsner, and they stood conversing at the bar.

'My name is Anton Özelt-Newin. I believe you may also be an Anton. Anton Bruckner, I believe!'

'I cannot disagree because I am him! How do you know?'

'I knew and guessed at the same time. I remember some newspaper reports about you playing the organ in Nancy, Paris and London. The sound you've just produced had your name written all over it!'

'I'm pleased and flattered! Are you a musician, too?'

'No. I am a doctor and have a practice in Klosterneuburg.'

'Interesting. The structure of the human body has always fascinated me. It is an interesting subject. I'm too involved in music to investigate the science of medicine further.'

'We must keep in touch, Herr Bruckner. Here is my business card. I would be deeply honoured if you visited me. Please come when you feel like a break. I would bring you here for another personal recital!'

'You are kind, Dr Özelt-Newin. I do like this little town and will call on you next time I'm here.'

They parted with a handshake, and Anton left for home, leaving the doctor at the bar.

***

Not long after he returned, Johann Herbeck came to see him. 'It's time we performed that F Minor Mass of yours, Anton. I've been doing some negotiating and we can still play it in the Augustinerkirche, where we had that dismal rehearsal before.'

'How do you know it won't be as bad this time?'

'This time we can use the Imperial Court Orchestra and the Vienna Choral Society, so it will be much better.'

'That is good news, Johann.'

'And another thing, Richard Wagner is visiting in May and we are giving him a reception at the Vienna West Station, the one you use to go to Linz and back. Many dignitaries will go, including the staff from the Conservatorium, the orchestra and choir, as well as students. So you must come to see your old friend again!'

'I'd cancel everything to do that.'

***

Wagner's train pulled into the station. As he stepped out of his carriage, the mayor and mayoress of Vienna and the Minister of Education greeted him. He weakly smiled at the officials, as if he felt obliged to do so. Then he looked around at the crowd assembled on the platform. His face lit up as he saw Anton, and shouted, 'Come to me, Bruckner! He belongs to me!'

Anton could hardly believe what he heard. He obeyed the Master, who gave him a hug. 'You honour me deeply,' he said.

'Nonsense!' said Wagner. 'It's the other way around. You honour me. Come to see me again as soon as you can. I loved our time together in Munich!' A group of officials then whisked him away in a horse-drawn sedan.

Because of Wagner's spontaneous gesture, Anton felt more settled in Vienna. The effect of this public recognition by the Master, made the Viennese music circle, staff at the Conservatorium, his students and the public realise that they had a composer in their midst. This was a man whom the greatest composer of their time firmly acknowledged. He wondered if the effect might manifest itself somehow.

Johann Herbeck found the F minor Mass difficult. At the dress rehearsal with the Choral Society, he stopped after the Credo.

'Anton, I was alright conducting at the earlier rehearsals, but I want you to take over. I'm too nervous to continue!'

'What about the incidental organ parts?'

'Don't worry, I'll find someone to do that. There are many excellent organists at this church.'

'In which case, I'll conduct it. But make sure you come to listen!'

Much to Anton's delight, the Augustinerkirche was filled to capacity. People were even standing at the sides and the back. Despite performing the work in a sacred place, an enormous round of applause burst out at its conclusion. With his usual generosity, Anton turned to the orchestra and applauded them, then to the choir and lastly to the superb soloists. Good for Richard Wagner, he thought. He has made me accepted here, and this is the effect.

The press gave the performance, which was the first of his works played in Vienna, much praise. Eduard Hanslick poured unrestrained accolades on it, saying in the New Free Press that it caused a stir with its artful counterpoint and fugue work, as well as its touching and peculiar beauty. He concluded by saying it would be interesting to hear it in a good concert performance.

This June day inspired Anton to press on as rapidly as he could to finish his Symphony No. 2, which he completed on 11 September, exactly a year and a day after he started it in London. His aim was to try it out on Felix Dessoff, whom he hoped would not reject it. A few days after he finished it, he left the manuscript score with him. Anton was shrewd enough to believe that, following the much publicised success of the F Minor Mass, Dessoff may think the new symphony could make a good profit.

'Not bad,' said Dessoff, at the end of the week he took to examine it. 'It's better than your two previous attempts. It is not as rumbustious as your No. 1 and is more coherent. My decision is that the Philharmonic will play it.'

'Thank you, thank you,' said Anton, having difficulty restraining himself from giving Dessoff a hug.

'If you leave the score with me, someone here will organise the printing of the parts and we'll fix a date for the first rehearsal. Would you like to come along?'

'I must!'

Kathi was in the kitchen, preparing his evening meal when he reached home, but heard him come in. 'Is that you, Herr Bruckner?'

'It's me, alright! I've got some brilliant news!'

'What's that?'

'The Vienna Philharmonic is going to play my new symphony, No. 2!'

'Not that piece of yours I've had to put up with while you hammered it out on your piano?'

'That's the one!'

'I must admit, I did like some of the quieter tunes. Pity there weren't more of them! Anyway, who told you they are going to play it?'

'Felix Otto Dessoff, their chief conductor. I can't explain to you how thrilled I am!'

'You deserve a beer. I'll get one out of the larder.'

'Pour yourself a glass of wine.'

'No thanks. My old man will suspect something if I go home smelling of wine!'

The day soon came around for the first rehearsal. Dessoff didn't want Anton there too early, so gave him a time by which the orchestra would be fully assembled and he would be ready on the rostrum. Members of the orchestra smiled and applauded as Anton came closer to the stage. He smiled back and anticipated a successful result.

Anton soon discovered that this famous and competent orchestra failed to make sense of his symphony. The most noticeable were the first violins who simply could not play some themes or the connecting bars. His face betrayed his thoughts. The rehearsal was becoming a disaster. Half way through the first movement, Dessoff held up his hands and shouted, 'Stop, everyone. I'm not conducting any more of this!'

Two players from the string sections stood up and spoke to Dessoff. Anton could not hear what they exchanged.

He stepped down from the rostrum and, holding his hands upwards and smiling awkwardly, spoke to Anton. 'I'm sorry, but your symphony is unplayable. I'm afraid we'll have to abandon it.'

'Surely, with a bit of practice, this famous orchestra could handle it. Don't they like modern music?'

'You've missed the point, Anton. It's impossible to play. By that I mean it's too complicated, unpredictable and ridiculously demanding. If you want it performed here, you'll have to make it easier for the orchestra. Don't you understand?'

'Of course, I understand. But you are wrong. It's no more difficult than a Beethoven or a Mendelssohn,' Anton said loudly, restraining himself from shouting.

'No! You're the one who's wrong!' shouted Dessoff.

'No I'm not! I'm going,' he said, his face painfully contorted. He picked up the score from the music stand, turned his back on Dessoff, and left. What he didn't say, for fear of causing a really major rift, was he thought it was his conducting that caused the problem. Members of the orchestra played as they wanted. They seemed to ignore him. No wonder it was such a mess.

'Anything wrong?' said Kathi as he entered the apartment.

'I'm really annoyed. The rehearsal was a disaster and Dessoff is now saying the Philharmonic won't play it, because it's unplayable. I've never heard such rubbish. It was his conducting. His players didn't follow him at all. The worst thing is, he only played half of the first movement and didn't even start again or try any of the others.'

'Sorry to hear that. Can't you complain or do something?'

'No. He decides, and that's final.'

'I'll get you a beer... oh, a lady came to see if you were in. She said her name was Betty. She and her husband want you to go to dinner on Friday. I said I'd go round and tell her if you are free. She gave me her address. I suppose you know them?'

'Yes, that's Betty von Mayfield. I was in the sanatorium at the same time as her. I'm free then, so please tell her!'

'Yes, her place is on my way home. I'll call in tonight. Tell me about the sanatorium but another day.'

Anton had never visited the von Mayfields in their Vienna apartment. It wasn't far from him and overlooked one of the city's pretty lakes.

'I'm so glad you could come, Anton,' said Moritz as he welcomed him. 'Betty is in the middle of cooking us a meal. Come through and I'll get you a glass of wine.'

The quality of the decorations and furnishings of the von Mayfields' apartment seriously impressed Anton. It was less stark, and had a more homely feel about it than the one in Linz.

'It must have cost you a fortune to furnish this place,' said Anton.

'Take it from me, it did. We are thinking of moving to Vienna permanently but haven't decided yet.'

They sat down and chatted about politics and Anton's work until Betty told them she was ready to serve dinner.

'You can sit at the table now. I'll bring it in.' She returned to the kitchen and reappeared to serve them.

'I've hardly spoken to you, Anton,' said Betty, as the three of them ate. 'Did you ever get that symphony performed, the one you started in London, and labelled No. 2?'

'No. And I'm not happy about what happened.'

Anton told them the story of Dessoff first agreeing to perform it, then changing his mind after the Philharmonic had played only half of one movement.

'What did he mean by "unplayable", Anton?' said Moritz.

'Too difficult for his world-class orchestra to play!'

'That's ridiculous,' said Betty. She sipped at a glass of wine. 'I have an idea.'

'Go on,' said Anton.

'Bring the score around to me and I'll play it to you on our piano. That will tell us whether or not it's too difficult! I'm free all day tomorrow.'

'I'm teaching counterpoint to a group of trainee teachers at St Anna's tomorrow morning, then a private student at one o'clock for an hour, then I'm free.'

'See you around two thirty, Anton. Don't forget the score! You'll be here, won't you, Moritz?'

'Yes, of course.'

Moritz sat near the piano, and Anton turned the pages as Betty played. She stopped after the first movement. 'That seems highly playable to me, Anton. Let's carry on, shall we? Please get me a glass of water, would you, Moritz?'

'Of course, my love.'

She took a few sips and played the scherzo and then the trio. 'That's beautiful,' she said, half way through the trio. She continued with the adagio, then stopped for another drink. 'I do not understand these people. "Not playable" indeed!' Then she started the finale. 'Oh, Anton, you've quoted from the Kyrie of your F minor Mass. Amazing!' She continued to the end.

Anton and Moritz applauded her. She stood up and bowed to them.

'I just don't understand how they came to that conclusion, Anton. It is difficult to play, but if I can make sense of it from not having read it before, it can't be that impossible.'

'You reassure me, Betty, not that I needed it!'

'Why do you quote the Mass?'

'That is an extremely personal question, Betty, but as we are all friends, I will tell you. I secretly started writing the F minor when we were both at the sanatorium. I believe that, although I said the water treatment cured me of my mental problems, it was you and starting that Mass that really saved me. That's why I quote it... it probably prevented me from insanity.'

'We won't tell anyone, Anton. You can trust us!'

'I know.'

Undeterred, he didn't give up on the idea of a performance. He would have a word with Johann Herbeck to see if he had any thoughts.

He soon started thinking about his Symphony No 3. It would be in a different key, D minor. He started writing it during the Christmas vacation while his teaching duties were at a minimum. In his mind, this would be his most ambitious work to date. It would make a statement. He would show he could develop the symphonic form, even after Beethoven's brilliant achievements, into new and valid structures. This symphony would be the longest he had written and one of the lengthiest of all time. It would start with a strong, emphatic first theme, which would stamp its mark on the entire work. It would be a piece with sharp contrasts, beginning with the driving force of the first movement. He would compose a beautifully constructed and emotional adagio, which would have a strong and noble climax. A cheerfully dynamic scherzo would follow and lead to his best finale yet. It would compare the joy of life with sadness and pain.

***

'I'm so annoyed with Felix Dessoff,' he told Johann Herbeck as they met by chance in the Conservatorium refectory.

'What's the problem, Anton?'

He explained how Dessoff had agreed to perform his No. 2, then rejected it at the first rehearsal.

'Let me see it. I'll give you an opinion.'

'You may not know the von Mayfields, but Moritz's wife Betty played it on the piano. Admittedly, she read it from the score and could only pick out a line to play. She found it difficult but far from "unplayable".'

'I've not met her, but she is a well-known concert pianist, I think.'
'That's her.'
'I'll have a good look at it and we can discuss the options.'
'Thanks. I'm grateful.'

***

On his way home, he decided he needed a break. Vienna was suffering then from a cholera epidemic, so he had sound reasons to leave the city for a time.

'I must tell you this, Kathi, as it affects you. Now we are in the Conservatorium summer vacation, I am going on a journey.'

'Really? I thought you said you'd spend as much time as you could on that new symphony.'

'True, but I can still work on it. Let me explain. First, I want a short break in Marienbad, in Bohemia. Betty von Mayfield told me about an excellent spa there where I will stay for a few days. Then I will go to see my friend Richard in Bayreuth, which isn't far away from there.'

'You've never mentioned this Richard, before!'

'Richard Wagner. He is also a composer. Much better known than me!'

'I haven't heard of him!'

'That's because you don't go to operas! I'm going to be away for about ten days, so you needn't come around so often.'

'Thank you, Herr Bruckner. I'll pack your case. When do you intend to leave?'

'On Monday.'

***

So Anton embarked on another journey. It was much more straightforward than his complicated journey to England. On his way, he stopped for a couple of days in Karlsbad, mainly to visit a spa there but also to play the famous organ in the parish church.

As soon as he stopped playing, he heard clapping hands.

'Bravo!' said a bearded priest.

'I'm glad you liked it,' said Anton. 'I suppose I should have asked you before I asked the calcant to help me.'

'Don't worry, mein Herr. I am the master of the chapel choir, so I give you retrospective approval!'

The two of them started a conversation, during which Anton revealed he was a composer and was on his way to Bayreuth via Marienbad. He said he had the precious scores of his Symphony No. 2 and the incomplete No. 3 with him.

'Do you have the scores here?' said the choirmaster.

'Yes, they are in my shoulder bag.'

The priest read parts of them so quickly, it was as if he was scanning a book. He slowed down while reading Symphony No. 3. 'I think this is especially good,' he said, pointing to the scherzo. 'I would have the whole symphony played here, if I had that much influence!'

Anton felt flattered by the choirmaster's remarks. Apart from Kathi, who had probably suffered the sounds of it from the Bösendorfer, this was the first time anyone had commented on it.

He soon found a place to stay in Marienbad, a hotel called the White Horse. There he wrote the sketch of the last movement of No. 3. Mainly out of admiration and his natural politeness, he wrote to Wagner to ask if he could see him and to show him his latest symphonies. In his letter, he reminded him about his remarks on his composing and the encouragement he gave him to continue.

He stayed in Marienbad for a full week and thoroughly enjoyed bathing in the spa, eating at the White Horse restaurant and indulging in copious volumes of the local beer. Whether or not Wagner received the letter he didn't know, but he received nothing in reply. He was utterly determined to see Wagner, so stayed no longer in the town and made his way by train to Bayreuth. After asking several people, he found Wagner's house. He knocked on the door.

'Can I help you, mein Herr?' said a bewigged, clean shaven manservant.

'I am Anton Bruckner, a friend of the Master and want to see him.'

'Wait a moment. I'll ask if he's free.'

Moments later, he returned. 'Yes, he's agreed to see you. Could you return in about three hours?'

'Of course.'

He wandered around the streets close to the house and sat on a bench for a couple of hours working out what he would say to him. Exactly three hours after being told to go, he returned. The same manservant asked him in and ushered him into the living room where he could hear someone, presumably Wagner, playing a piano.

'Ah, the great Master,' said Anton, as Wagner walked towards the door. 'Do you remember me? I am Anton Bruckner. We last met on Vienna West Station when you picked me out from the crowd.'

'Of course I remember you. Out with it! What do you want? I'm incredibly busy right now.'

He put his shoulder bag on a table and carefully put two bundles of music paper on the table. 'I've brought my two latest symphonies to show you. I'd deeply love you to examine them, O Master, and give me your opinion.'

'I don't have the time. In a year or so, maybe.'

'O Master, I cannot wait. I am desperate for your view. With any accolade you could give them, I can get them performed, for sure. Without one, I am stuck. Please O Master, Please?'

'I am far too busy. I'll have to ask you to go!'

'Please, Master. I am not good enough to stand in your shadow. Let alone on your carpets here. Please help a modest beginner.'

'You win, you stubborn man. Come back in three days' time and I'll tell you what I think.'

Anton dropped to his knees and kissed Wagner's hand. 'I cannot thank you enough. I shall return! Many, many thanks!'

He left the house in a state of ecstasy. All he needed was an endorsement by this world renowned genius. Surely, Wagner would like these pieces, especially No. 3, in which he had quoted the 'sleep' motif from Die Walküre. His only problem was that he was running out of money. So he stayed in the cheapest lodgings he could find. The bed was so narrow it reminded him of sleeping in the hall at Windhaag. Passing the time was easy. He found a library where he could continue working on the finale of No. 3.

The three days soon passed, and he returned to the house. The manservant took him back into the living room.

'It's you, Anton!' The Master was in a better mood. 'I've hardly had time to look at them.'

'All you need is to take a glance at the major themes and that will be enough.'

'Come with me.' He took Anton into his study and picked up the score of the second symphony. 'Not bad. Hmm.' He looked as if it was too tame, but competently written.

He then picked up the third. 'Look...look here... what's that?' He carefully read on, up to about the fiftieth bar of the first movement. 'Let me have the score to study after lunch.'

'Of course. My pleasure. I have something close to my heart I want to ask you.'

'Tell me! You know how much I think of you!'

'I want in all modesty to dedicate one of these two symphonies to you... but I will not profane your name. I would not do it unless you were completely satisfied.'

'You know we are constructing a new theatre at Wahnfried. I invite you to see me there at 5 pm. We will talk over the D minor symphony once I've examined it.'

Anton walked around aimlessly, thinking and wondering what the Master would make of it. Finally, he appeared at the incomplete theatre. The amazing construction of the building fascinated him. It was going to be unique. Suddenly, he realised he had spent so much time wandering around the building, he'd forgotten the time.

'Hey, you! Herr Bruckner,' said the manservant, who had met him at the door. 'Herr Wagner is waiting for you. Come quickly.'

When he entered Wahnfried, he heard Wagner playing the trumpet theme of the first movement. He almost broke into tears. It sounded exactly as he had conceived it. Having pulled himself together, he calmly entered the room.

Wagner welcomed him with shining eyes and a smile. He stayed silent for a moment, then hugged Anton and kissed him on the cheek. 'My dear friend, your symphony is a masterpiece. It's fine about the dedication. You will give me great pleasure by dedicating this magnificent symphony to me!'

Anton could hardly contain his joy. He would remember this as one of the best days of his life. Wagner invited him to stay and gave him a tour of the Wahnfried, during which they discussed the politics and general situation of music in Vienna.

'Don't be seen to be too close to me,' said Wagner to Anton. 'I mean in the sense of a supporter of my person and music. Hanslick, the critic and professor, hates me. Brahms is not on my side either. There seem to be two distinct factions…Brahms lovers and Wagner lovers… and never the twain shall meet.'

'But Eduard Hanslick has been one of my most ardent supporters in Vienna. He thrived on the Linz performance of my Symphony No. 1. It was him who supported me going to Vienna. I like the man.'

'Be careful. He's a snake in the grass. He can bite you when you least expect it. Oh… here is my wife. Cosima, I'd like to introduce you to my great friend and composer, Herr Bruckner. He's just dedicated his third symphony to me, of all people!'

'That could be the kiss of death. You'll annoy the Wagner haters who will try to kill your career!'

Anton raised his eyebrows to the full, not so much at what she said but who she was. The last time he saw her, some eight years before, she was Hans von Bülow's wife.

'I'm delighted to meet you. I think we met before, at the first performance of "Tristan and Isolde",' said Anton.

'Quite right, I remember you now.'

'Let me get you a beer, Anton,' said Richard, moving discreetly from this potentially embarrassing introduction. 'Then I'll show you more of this incomplete creation.'

Walking around for three hours made him thirsty, so Anton drank the half stein in a few gulps. 'I'll get you another larger one, a stein?'

'Yes, please. It's all that walking.'

'Let's take our beers with us as I show you more.' They left Cosima and walked outside.

'I'm very proud of this building. King Ludwig of Bavaria donated the money for it, and I'm exceedingly grateful to him. Many of the rooms inside are virtually complete but we don't intend to move in until next year when, with luck, it will be finished.'

'It is an amazing building,' said Anton. 'Let me understand correctly. It will be your home and a theatre for performing your operas?'

'Right. And we can perform anyone else's, of course! Let me show you this special place. It is where I will be buried!'

Anton knelt at the grave site, put his hands together and prayed.

'Thank you, Anton. That wasn't necessary, but extremely considerate of you.'

They went back inside and spent the rest of the afternoon and evening chatting, drinking Richard's beer and eating various items of food that a servant brought them. By about 10 o'clock, Anton could feel he had enough to drink, so excused himself and made his way back to his modest accommodation. His head was swimming and had difficulty getting into his nightshirt, but eventually succeeded.

He woke up with a headache, which soon vanished, but he had a problem. He could not remember which symphony of the two Wagner said he could dedicate to him. Over breakfast, he tried his best to remember, but failed. So he sent a note to Wagner. It said:

Symphony in D minor, where the trumpet begins the theme?

Wagner replied:

Yes! Yes! Kind regards, Richard Wagner

So between them they solved the problem. Anton returned to the railway station only to discover he had sufficient money left for his return fare, but only if he travelled third class. So he spent the whole day without sustenance and arrived in Vienna hungry and thirsty.

'How was your time in Marienbad and your friend Richard?' said Kathi when he arrived home.

'First things first, Kathi. I must have a drink and something to eat, even if it's a small beer and a slice of bread. I haven't had food or drink for twelve hours!'

'I'll get you a drink and cook you a meal. I've got some smoked ham in the larder.' She brought him a half stein of beer, which he downed in a little over one gulp. 'So how was the trip?'

'Apart from being hungry, it's a long time since I've felt so good.' He told her the whole story, stressing the magical encounter with Wagner.

'I hope he's grateful for your dedication. He should be!'

'It's exactly the reverse, Kathi. I'm grateful to him for agreeing! And I haven't finished it yet!'

***

Anton desperately wanted to tell Johann Herbeck his news about the dedication, so went to the Conservatorium, first thing on the Monday morning. He wasn't in his office, so Anton went to the refectory and spotted him there.

'Johann, it's so good to see you. This is my first day back from Bayreuth!'

'I've got some brilliant news for you, but tell me yours first!'

Anton related the complete tale.

'What an experience! You did really well getting Wagner to agree to the dedication. He must have wanted to get rid of you!'

'Very funny! No such thing. We both got completely drunk, and I left on truly friendly terms. The only problem was I got so pissed I couldn't remember which symphony he'd agreed to. But we soon sorted that out!'

'My news is even better, I think. I've found a sponsor for a performance of your symphony No. 2!'

'Brilliant! Thank you! Who is it?'

'Would you believe, Prince Johann of Lichtenstein?'

'How did you manage that?'

'It's a long story, Anton. In brief, I asked Dessoff to change his mind. I used the argument that No. 1 was much applauded in Linz and made good money. He still flatly refused. So, off the top of my head, I asked if we could hire the Vienna Philharmonic. He laughed and said we could, but we couldn't possibly afford it. I called his bluff by saying I'd find a sponsor, so I wrote to the Prince, knowing he was a great sponsor of arts... even at the tender age of thirty-two. After two rounds of correspondence, he agreed! His private secretary wrote to say the Prince would expect a high quality performance and would pay for as many rehearsals as we needed. I still can't believe it myself!'

'I cannot thank you enough, Johann.'

'Dessoff couldn't believe it. I even had to show him the letters. Now he's on our side, realising the Prince will pay. He wanted to split the profits from the ticket sales, but I refused. That has to go to the Prince. And the Prince will pay for the tickets to be printed and the advertising. Dessoff has agreed we can use the orchestral parts already in the hands of the orchestra.'

'Just one minor issue, Johann.'

'Go on!'

'I've roughed out some changes. Not many, but the parts will need re-copying.'

'Sod you, Anton. Can't you leave it as it is?'

'No, I damned well can't. I've added trombones to two sections of the first movement. A violin solo to a part of the adagio, removed some repeats in the scherzo. I've also taken out a dissonant section in the finale and substituted a delight of a new passage. All we need is a good copyist. I have made some very clear changes on the manuscript and written some appendices for changes to the finale. Oh, and while I think of it, I've changed the order of the second and third movements. Now the scherzo comes third.'

'I can't believe this. Here we are with a sponsor willing to go ahead. And you, you stubborn bugger, want to change the bloody thing!'

'I can't help it. The version the Philharmonic have is now out of date.'

'Alright. I give in! On one condition! You begin the concert by playing an organ piece and improvising!'

'I don't call that a condition! That's an invitation. I accept!'

The two of them moved quickly to arrange for Anton's changes to be incorporated into the orchestral parts. Along with help from Dessoff, Herbeck settled on dates for three rehearsals and the concert, which would be on 26 October. Anton would conduct.

The first rehearsal was a strange affair. Many in the orchestra had found the work unplayable under Dessoff's baton, so seem to have decided to find it equally difficult under Anton's. He could see it on their faces. There were exceptions. One violinist applauded and smiled, as Anton took the rostrum. Some hardly looked at him while he conducted. For a first rehearsal, Anton thought they performed reasonably well, except a small minority who might have deliberately played badly. His aim was mainly to make allies of the players, so he would save suggestions for improvement to the next one.

As usual, Anton praised the orchestra and said he looked forward to the second rehearsal. 'Well, gentlemen, we can practice as much as we like. I've found somebody to pay for it!'

The violinist, who smiled and applauded, walked across the stage, with his instrument under his arm, and spoke to Anton, as he was about to step down from the rostrum. 'My name is Arthur Nikisch. May I compliment you on a highly original symphony? I like it. It aroused something in me. It was a pleasure to be in the orchestra.'

Anton's face sparkled. 'Thank you so much. I'm so pleased you enjoyed it!'

'I was in the rehearsal a couple of years ago and could never understand why Dessoff rejected it.'

Herr Nikisch turned and departed.

'So how did it go?' said Johann the day after.

'Reasonably well. They proved it was playable, which was what I wanted from them. It was a little untidy in places, but we'll sort that out next time, hopefully.'

He told him about the violinist, but Johann didn't know him.

The next rehearsal was a totally different experience. It was as if Herr Nikisch had spoken to his colleagues and persuaded them to be more supportive. They even greeted him with smiles as he stepped onto the rostrum.

'I'm so grateful to you all for coming today. You all did well at the first rehearsal,' he said, 'and we are going to look at some of the finer detail today.'

Anton felt satisfied with what turned out to be a thoroughly normal rehearsal. He stopped the players when he thought he had to do so and start again after delivering his instruction. He would gesture to them to slow down or speed up and diplomatically speak to soloists or section leaders about changes he wanted. They played so well at the third rehearsal, it could have been the actual performance,

Anton started the concert by playing Bach's Toccata in D Minor and improvising on it. He never tried to remember what he had played the previous time, so each one was a first performance. The audience heartily approved of his symphony. They saluted its stunning ending with loud applause and a standing ovation. The leader of the orchestra held Anton's hand high so the audience could acknowledge the composer.

'So how was the concert, Herr Bruckner?' said Kathi.

'I can't stop smiling! It went so well. That's the second work of mine performed in Vienna, and I'm totally thrilled!'

'When do you think the next one will be?'

'I don't know. The performance went so well, Johann and I may see if we can organise another concert. It could be No. 3, which I still haven't finished.'

'You'd better knuckle down and get on with it, then.'

Most of the press praised the concert highly. Hanslick was slightly critical but not vitriolic, saying Wagner's music excessively influenced the symphony. One commentator regretted there was no one there, taking down in shorthand the organ improvisation.

'I've read the press reports,' said Johann, as they met for lunch in the refectory, almost a week after the concert. 'Not bad, eh?'

'I'm so pleased,' said Anton. 'Slightly disappointed by what Eduard Hanslick says, and I don't agree with his comments about Wagner. It's my style, and I wrote it in mine alone.'

'I agree. You wonder where these comments come from. You use dissonances, powerful climaxes, and rapid key changes, as does Wagner, but you haven't copied him in any sense of the word. I'll tell him when I see him.'

'Please don't. It might antagonise him and I wouldn't want that! I've almost completed No. 3 and I'll show it to you when it's finished. By the way, did the concert make a profit?'

'Yes. We owe the Prince four hundred and fifty florins. Even Dessoff was impressed!'

'So am I!'

When he reached home, Kathi gave him a letter, postmarked Bayreuth. It invited him to be a member of the Academic Richard Wagner Society. He gratefully accepted.

He completed No. 3 on New Year's Eve.

Chapter 22
1874 - 1875 A Wagnerian

Two days later, on 2 January, he started writing his Symphony No. 4. He was feeling comfortable writing these large-scale works which, apart from Beethoven with his Ninth, no one had attempted before. Anton assumed this was because composers thought concert hall audiences would not enjoy works of this length. If so, he had shown this to be wrong from the ecstatic reception of his No. 2. It took almost exactly an hour to perform.

As the No. 2 concert made a profit for Prince Johann of Lichtenstein, he decided, despite previous disappointments, to try No. 3 on Dessoff, but keep a private sponsorship in the background. He explained his plan to Kathi.

'I wouldn't if I were you. He might agree, start a rehearsal and turn it down, like he did for No. 2. I remember the look on your face when you came home and told me. You were so miserable I had to pour you an emergency beer.'

'Don't remind me! I have no choice if I want the Phil to play it.'

So he took the huge manuscript to Dessoff. The tactic he used was to enter his office and not worry about being accused of impertinence, as he was once before.

'How can I help you, Anton? Not another of your symphonies?' he said, glancing at the massive pile of paper Anton carried under his arm.

This sounded patronising, so Anton gave a robust response. 'This is my greatest symphony so far. I don't judge it as a masterpiece. That is for others. But it is a great step forward from my Symphony No. 2, which, as you will know, was hailed as masterful by the audience and press alike.'

'Leave it with me. Come back in a week's time at say 2 o'clock in the afternoon and I'll tell you then if the Philharmonic will play it.'

***

Anton had long since exhausted the profit he had made from his visits to France and England. The work at St Anna's had lasted longer than Hellmesberger had predicted but had ended. His only sources of income were the Conservatorium and his private pupils, so he was struggling financially. He even contemplated ending his arrangement with Kathi. Therefore, in a state of financial desperation, he wrote to the University, as he had in '67, to suggest they create a lectureship in music theory for him.

His letter covered all the points he thought were in his favour: the success of No. 1 in Linz; No. 2 in Vienna, the F Minor Mass, his range of experience as a teacher at the Conservatorium; the acceptance by Richard Wagner of the No. 3 dedication; and membership by invitation of the Academic Richard Wagner Society.

***

'I agree with you, Anton. This is your best symphony by far,' said Felix Dessoff. 'The Philharmonic will play it. Congratulations!'

Knowing there were narrow bridges still to cross, Anton constrained his thanks to a few words and a handshake.

'I'll keep the manuscript, if that's alright and get the parts prepared, ready for the first rehearsal.'

'That's fine.'

***

Kathi came to prepare his breakfast the day after he saw Dessoff.

'You seem bright and jolly, Herr Bruckner. Early as it is.'

'I am, Kathi. Felix Otto Dessoff has agreed to the Philharmonic playing my Symphony No. 3!'

'We've been there before. He'll start a rehearsal, and find out they can't play it. You'll end up finding a prince to sponsor it.'

'You annoy me sometimes, Kathi. You can be such a pessimist!'

'I'm going home. I haven't come here to be insulted.' She tore off her pinafore, threw it on the floor and walked out, slamming the door behind her.

Anton rushed out of the door and chased down the road after her. 'Kathi, Kathi, please come back,' he shouted. 'I'm so sorry. I didn't mean that. I was only joking. Please come back. I need you!'

She stopped and looked at him, then turned and walked towards him. It must have been him saying, 'I need you'.

'Thank you, thank you! You don't realise how much I rely on you, Kathi. I won't say anything like that again. I am sorry.'

'Don't you dare because the next time I walk out, I won't come back, Herr Bruckner. Let's go in and I'll get your breakfast.'

'I am sorry, Kathi. No, I won't say anything like it again, not even in jest.'

'Look, there's a letter on the hall floor.' She picked it up. 'It's addressed to you,' She handed it to him, still with a mild frown on her face.

'I'll read it straightaway.' He went into his study, took an opener and slid it inside, taking care not to tear the letter. He read it. His face dropped. The university refused to create a teaching post for him. Undeterred, he immediately decided he would have another attempt. But first he would see if he could find out the exact reason for the rejection.

'You don't look as cheery now, Herr Bruckner,' said Kathi, as she put his omelette breakfast on the dining table. 'Anything you want to tell me?'

'Nothing to worry about, Kathi. It's about a professorship I could have been interested in.'

She didn't question him any further.

'I have a question to ask you, Johann,' he said, as he saw Herbeck in his office.

'Go on,' he said, staying seated at his desk.

'I haven't told you this, but I am in dire financial difficulty. I'm having to take on more private students to survive. So a about month ago, I wrote to Vienna University to ask them to create a music theory post for me. They turned me down. The letter of refusal was polite but gave no clues why they declined. You have many contacts at the university, so I wondered whether you might know and if not, could you please find out?'

'I did not know you were in such trouble, Anton. You didn't tell me you were applying.'

'I didn't think it was right to tell you. I didn't want you to think I was asking for your support. I wasn't trying to hide anything.'

'I understand, I think. I'll find out what was behind the decision. It may take time. I'll hunt you down to tell you.'

'Thank you. You are a good friend!'

'What about that Symphony No. 3. Is Dessoff interested?'

'Yes, the Philharmonic are going to perform it. They are sorting out the details for a rehearsal. I hope they don't think it's impossible to play!'

'Good luck with that one. I'm not sure Prince Johann of Lichtenstein will want to sponsor another of yours!'

***

'Another letter for you, Herr Bruckner, from Bayreuth. Your friend Richard, maybe?'

He opened it. It was not from Wagner but Cosima, thanking him, on behalf of the Master, for the signed and dedicated score of Symphony No. 3. She said that Richard had worked through the symphony with Director Hans Richter and was immensely pleased with the score itself, as well as what Anton had written on it. She invited Anton to Bayreuth in 1876 to hear the first performance of the Ring Cycle, and said Richard could thank him personally then.

'No, it's not from Richard but his wife, thanking me for the score you posted for me and inviting me to a series of operas, not immediately, but in two years' time. I'm delighted!'

'Will you go?'

'I'm not sure yet. But reply I must. I think I'll say I'll go. If anything prevents me in the meantime, I can always write again. I'm surprised the Master didn't write it himself, but there we are.'

'Maybe Cosima is acting as his secretary.'

'I think she was for a time, and that's when their affair started.'

'Affair? I didn't know it all started as an affair.'

'Yes. Right under her husband's nose. He was Hans von Bülow, the famous conductor. You may have heard of him. Anyway, the affair led to three illegitimate children. Von Bülow ignored it until the third child. He was born around the time of the first performance of Richard's opera, Tristan and Isolde, in Munich. Von Bülow conducted it. They played it before your time, Kathi, but I saw it. I detected a frosty atmosphere between the three of them then. It surprised me when I went to Bayreuth to discover the two were man and wife. I must have missed any publicity around the marriage, if there was any.'

'What a story, Herr Bruckner. I enjoy gossip like that. Please let me know of any more you come across!'

'Don't worry, I will!'

***

Johann Herbeck spoke to Anton, having explored with several of his university contacts why Anton's application had failed.

'I wish you had told me before you applied. We might have avoided your rejection by the university.'

'Really?'

'Yes. You shouldn't have mentioned your connection with Richard Wagner!'

'Why not? It was only one of the points in my case.'

'You know Eduard Hanslick is an arch enemy of Wagner.'

'I do.'

'Well, as he's a professor at the university, they consulted him. Apparently, your mention of Wagner made him see flaming red. They had to give him a glass of cold water to calm him down. Your mention of the dedication and of membership of the society set him alight.'

Anton raised his eyebrows and shrugged his shoulders. 'Are you serious?'

'Yes!'

'But he's always been supportive of my work, in Linz and here. He loved the F Minor Mass and Symphony No. 2. Alright, the symphony didn't totally convince him, but he wasn't destructive over it. In fact, up to now, I've counted him as a friend.'

'By all means, treat him as if he still is. But be wary. Now he sees you as a staunch Wagnerian. He won't promote your work. That's for sure.'

'You know what a stubborn sod, I am Johann. I won't give up, you know. I need the money!'

'I must tell you that Hanslick couldn't formally admit to his fury, so had to give some rational reasons for the rejection. He said it wasn't at all clear what you wanted to teach. He said you didn't know the scientific basis of the theory and it was like a begging letter.'

Anton boiled over. 'The man's a bloody idiot. I've spent years studying musical theory. I bet I know more about it than him!'

'No need to raise your voice with me, Anton. I tell you this not to annoy you, but to inform your next attempt, assuming you make one!'

'Sorry, Johann. I'm not angry with you and never will be. I owe you so much.'

'Changing subjects, any news on when Dessoff wants to rehearse your No. 3?'

'Not yet. I'm still waiting and I don't want to ask him!'

'Understood, and No. 4? Any progress?'

'Yes, I've finished the first movement, and started the second. I've been working on the second for about three weeks now.'

'How do you think it's progressing?'

'Very well. The work starts with the sound of a hunting call. I like what I've composed so far. It could be more popular than the other three. We'll see!'

Despite the reasons for refusing him a professorship, Anton would write to the university again. He drafted a letter but wasn't happy about sending it. Instead, he wrote to Bishop Rudigier to discuss his financial plight and to ask him for any ideas he might have for alleviating it, such as paying for a performance of one of his works. The Bishop came back with an interesting idea. He suggested Anton should seek advice from the Minister of Education, whom Anton knew from meeting him at the Vienna West Station. With unabashed brazenness, he walked into the Ministry building.

'No, I'm afraid you cannot see the Minister without an appointment,' said the Private Secretary, a thin, weak looking, clean shaven man of about thirty-five.

'How do I get an appointment?'

'You write in to ask for one.'

'Do you have a piece of paper and a pen I can use?'

'To write the Minister's postal address?'

'No. To write the letter. If you can give me what I need, I can write one now.'

'You can't do that. It's headed notepaper. You can't write to him on his own paper!' said the Private Secretary loudly.

'Why not? I can delete the heading.'

Moments later, the inner door to the Minister's office opened.

'What's going on here? Why the raised voices? Oh, it's you, Herr Bruckner! Good to see you! What are you doing here?'

'I want to see you, Minister. Your Private Secretary, rightly, says I need to write in for an appointment. We were discussing the source of some paper, so I could write to you now.'

'Don't bother with that nonsense. I've got ten minutes before my next meeting, so come in and we can talk about what you need.'

'Thank you, Minister Stremayr.'

'You sit there in that armchair and I'll sit in this one. I enjoyed the performance of your Symphony No. 2, and your spectacular organ play before it!'

'Oh. Thank you,' he smiled.

'So what do you want exactly?'

Anton explained. He mentioned Hanslick's views.

'I'd better not tell you what I think of the man, even though I'd trust you to keep it quiet.' Anton realised what he meant.

'The best advice I can give you is not to write to the university. Write to the Department of Education. Send examples of your music, but don't whatever you do, mention Wagner. Hopefully, Hanslick won't see your letter, but others of the anti-Wagner movement might. Don't write to me. Address it to the Department so the civil servants will deal with it, not me.'

'Thank you, Herr Stremayr.'

So Anton tore up the letter he had first drafted and wrote a new one. He included references to his Symphonies No. 1 and 2 but not No. 3, which was still in the hands of Dessoff.

'I'm afraid I have rather a large parcel to post for me, Kathi. Could you, please. It contains the scores of my first two symphonies. Do you think you can carry it to the post office or should I order a cabriolet?'

'That is big, Herr Bruckner!' she said as she lifted it off the kitchen table. 'Hmm... and it's heavy. I'd hate to drop it so, yes please, to the cab. I'll hand it in at the post office on my way home.'

Anton walked to the cab rank and ordered Kathi a cabriolet.

***

Just after Anton received the letter from Cosima, Felix Dessoff rudely interrupted his class at the Conservatorium. Realising that Anton was in the middle of explaining a complicated piece of theory, he sat in an empty seat at the back of the sloping array of seats.

'To what do I owe the pleasure, Felix,' said Anton, after the lesson had finished.

'The Philharmonic and I want to run the first rehearsal of your Symphony No. 3 on 10 July. Would you be able to attend? We regard it as important that you do. It looks difficult, I have to say, but many in the orchestra believe they can play it.'

'Let me look at my diary. Here it is. Yes, I can make it that day, as long as it's in the afternoon.'

'Say 2 o'clock.'

'Perfect! And thank you. By the way, will you pay me?' he said, having still not found an alternative source of income.

'Let me think about that. I thought your contract with the Conservatorium included paying for your compositions.'

Anton could feel his temperature rise at the audacity of the man. What did his contract have to do with him? He refrained from arguing the point.

'I'll investigate, Felix, but I don't believe it does. When we meet, I'll tell you. I imagine, if it doesn't, I would have a share of any profits?'

'I'll discuss this with the director, Anton. See you on the tenth, then.'

A few days later, when Anton reached home, Kathi rushed to the door with another letter from the university.

'This looks exciting, Herr Bruckner. Here you are!'

'Thank you. I'll take it into my office.'

He wondered what the Ministry of Education would say about his second letter. He skimmed it. How annoying, he thought. It was just an acknowledgement. Then he wondered how he might respond to the inquisitive Kathi. Should he tell her about the difficult financial situation he was in? No, he shouldn't. It had not reached the stage where it could affect her, so it would be better to keep it to himself. He could mention his interest in a professorship. Yes, he would do just that, but only if she raised the question.

'So you will not tell me about the letter, Herr Bruckner,' she said as he emerged from his study.

'I can tell you, by all means. For at least eight years I've been trying to convince the university they should create a professorship for me, in music theory. I teach it at the Conservatory so it would be quite easy to adapt the lectures to a university course. I've written to them about it again. The circumstances there may have changed in eight years, so they may be more receptive now. Anyway, I wrote to them a week ago, and this reply is just an acknowledgement. I was hoping for a decision but will have to wait for that!'

'Thank you for satisfying my curiosity. The only point I would make is, if you got the job and having one in the Conservatory, you would have less time for doing what you love the best, your composing, that is?'

'It depends on how many lectures they wanted and whether they could use me for planning courses and not teaching. I'd have to look at that before I accepted it. Good point though, Kathi.'

**

July 10 soon came around and Anton appeared at the Vienna Philharmonic's main concert hall at exactly 2 o'clock in the afternoon. That an orchestra was about to rehearse or play one of his works always gave him an immense feeling of satisfaction. It must have been like a mother, about to hold her new-born for the first time. He often thought of his works, particularly his symphonies, as his babies.

The orchestra was tuning their instruments, and Dessoff was standing on the podium.

On seeing Anton, he spoke. 'We are honoured today by the presence of Herr Bruckner, who, as you know, is the creator of this fine piece of symphonic writing, his Symphony Number 3. Before we start, do any of you have any questions for Herr Bruckner?'

'Why is it so long? It's going to be over an hour,' said a trombonist.

'What I am trying to do is to change the concept of the symphony. My aim is to give the audience something they can immerse themselves in for a reasonable time and take pleasure from its range of sounds and emotions.'

'An excellent answer,' said Dessoff.

'There is a lot more brass than in most symphonies I'm familiar with. Why is that?' said the lead trumpet.

'The brass is under-used in many works. I'm just redressing the balance. I hope your lungs and lips are strong!'

'I do like the climax of the slow movement, as I read it,' said Arthur Nikisch, who praised Anton before. 'What gave you the idea for that beautiful piece?'

'It's always difficult to recall what inspires a particular theme. For that one, I remembered my late sister Nani. She had been so kind to me while she lived with me and looked after me. I credit her with the inspiration and am glad you asked about it, sad though it is.'

'Just one more question?' said a bassoonist.

'Is that alright, Anton?' said Dessoff.

'Of course!'

'In the last movement, the second theme is a dance tune, played along with a sombre tune from the brass. Is there a special significance to that?'

'I'm so glad you asked. The dance tune, which is a polka, represents humour and happiness in the world. The brass chorale, sorrow and pain. When I learned of the death of an architect of the new Linz cathedral, the idea jumped

315

into my head. The poor man was lying dead in his coffin, as life was going on around him.'

'Thank you, gentlemen,' said Dessoff loudly. 'Let's begin!'

The seriousness with which Dessoff conducted surprised Anton. He struck his baton on the music stand many times to stop the orchestra and instruct them on how they should play. To Anton, the look the players gave Dessoff showed they had to obey because their jobs were in danger, if they didn't. He twice asked Anton if their method of playing was right. Only once, during the scherzo, did Anton ask for a change, namely to play it faster, to give it a greater sense of excitement. The whole exercise took just over three hours with a break after the second movement.

As soon as they finished, the leader spoke privately to Dessoff.

Anton feared the worst. Had they found this unplayable, like his No. 2? Dessoff left the rostrum and came down to speak to Anton, who could see a strained look on Dessoff's face.

'I'm sorry, Anton, but the orchestra don't want to perform it. It's too difficult even for them.'

'So that's it then,' said Anton, with his lips pursed and looking at the carpet.

'No. They may have rejected it, but, while I don't think it's a masterpiece, I am going to conduct them playing it. At its premiere. I'll let you know when it's in the programme. Not this one, next year's.'

The look on Anton's face changed rapidly. From the look of a bitterly disappointed father whose favourite child had been spurned, he smiled broadly and looked Dessoff straight in the eye.

'That's wonderful, Felix. Thank you.'

'A pleasure, Anton.' He turned and went back to speak to the leader.

***

'They are definitely going to play my Symphony No. 3, Kathi,' he said, the following morning, as she put his breakfast on the dining table.

'Really?'

'For certain. So Felix Otto Dessoff said, despite the orchestra not liking it.'

'So what happens next?'

'He will put it into the new programme. They could play it in the autumn or after Christmas. I've seen the current programme, which is full.'

'Couldn't they create an extra day in that one?'

'It doesn't work like that, Kathi. I wish it did. I'll just have to be patient!'

Anton's financial position became more of a worry. The university had not replied, other than by acknowledgement. So he had to take out a bank loan, just to survive and keep his treasured Kathi working for him.

He continued with his Symphony No. 4, the first he would write in a major key. He completed it in the autumn, when his teaching duties were at their most intense.

Shortly after New Year, he felt low and wrote to his friend Moritz von Mayfield. He shared his financial worries and said the Philharmonic had still not decided when to play his Symphony No. 3. He said he was regretting the move to Vienna where he felt vulnerable, even at the Conservatorium, and wished he could return to his old post in Linz. Having learnt that Hanslick was the destroyer of his ambitions to become a professor at the university, he regarded himself as the victim of pure malice.

Von Mayfield's reply, while sympathetic, offered no solutions, but at least Anton had put his feelings in writing and got them off his chest. He didn't mention the exchange of letters to Kathi, as he didn't want her to be upset and leave him, realising his financial state.

Anton's life took a joyful, positive turn when he heard that Richard Wagner was coming to Vienna to promote his forthcoming, but incomplete, Ring Cycle of operas. Anton could not resist going to the West Vienna Station to see him off the train. Wagner recognised him immediately.

'It's my man, Bruckner, the great composer. When are they performing that trumpet symphony, if they haven't already?'

Anton was stunned but had to reply. 'It's in the hands of the conductor, Felix Dessoff.'

'Tell him you've dedicated it to me and I expect it performed. I invite them to put it in the upcoming programme!'

'I'll write to him.'

'Good move to get a commitment on paper. I'd do the same.'

Anton sent a polite but firm letter to Dessoff, stating he was intending to explore the possibility of No. 3 being performed in Munich or Prague. He expressed a strong preference for the inaugural performance to take place on home territory rather than abroad. Dessoff's reply was curt. He said he would stick to his promise and that he would insert the symphony in the '75/76 programme.

It took until the autumn for the university to reply to Anton's second letter, actually the third, counting the one of '67. It refused his request, but thanked him for the suggestion. By good fortune, they returned the two scores he sent. He couldn't afford to get them recopied. Although disappointed, he would not give in, but write again. However, he would discuss the refusal with Johann Herbeck first.

'So another refusal. Don't you think you should abandon the idea?'

'No, I don't. I am in a state of intense impecuniosity so I desperately need more income.'

'I'll speak to Hellmesberger to see if he can increase your salary, but I don't feel optimistic.'

'Thank you, Johann, but do you think you can look into it again?'

'I probably don't need to. You wrote to the Ministry of Education, Right?'

'Yes.'

'The application, however supportive they were, will inevitably have found its way into the office of Hanslick. And he would have said no again.'

'But I didn't mention Wagner.'

'Too late. You gave that away in your first letter!'

'What do you think of this idea? Hanslick is only one of many professors there. I could write to all of them in the music faculty and ask for their support.'

'You could try, I suppose. But don't be disappointed if it doesn't work.'

So Anton wrote to all the professors in the faculties of music and philosophy, which he saw as including music, and waited. But he didn't sit on his hands. Again, he approached Felix Dessoff, this time to discuss his latest symphony.

'Good afternoon, Felix,' he said, as he met him in the Conservatory refectory. 'I'm surprised to see you here.'

'Yes, I'm seeing Professor Hellmesberger. We meet in about ten minutes,' he said, giving Anton the impression that he didn't want to talk much to the stubborn composer.

'Let me buy you something.'

'I'm fine, thank you. I've just finished a coffee.'

'I think I may have told you that I've completed my best symphony so far, No. 4. I've called it the Romantic!'

'No.'

'Well, I have, if you are interested.'

'But we haven't put your No. 3 into a programme yet and you are asking me about the next one. I'll give you credit, Anton. I've never in my life known anyone turn out these huge symphonies at the rate you do. Are you already writing your fifth?'

'Not yet, but I have some interesting ideas for it.'

'The day we put your No. 3 in our programme, you can tell me about your No. 4. But not before. There is nothing we can do about it now.'

'I'm not suggesting you put it in the programme. I'm only asking if you might be interested in it. Would you like to see the score?'

'Oh, alright then. Don't give me the original, in case I lose it. Lend me a copy.'

'I would, but I'm out of money, so I can't afford to make a copy. I trust you not to lose it.'

'No. It's a copy or nothing. I think we've agreed to leave it for now!'

'Reluctantly accepted, but as soon as you put No. 3 into your programme. In the meantime, I'll find a sponsor for the copying!'

***

'He's beginning to irritate me, Kathi!' he said, minutes after arriving home.

'Who are we talking about now?'

'Felix Otto Dessoff. The man who makes every excuse not to perform my symphonies. I've written to him about the first performance of my No. 3, which he promised.'

'Yes, I know. I posted the letter. And he gave you a blunt reply.'

'Oh! I forgot you knew. Now he doesn't want my No. 4 unless I make a copy. For no reason, he doesn't want the original. I'm getting annoyed with him.'

'Do you want my advice? I'm no expert, but I've seen what he has subjected you to. And actually the distress he's caused you. He annoys me, too.'

'Go on. Tell me. If I disagree, you won't be upset, will you?'

'Of course not.'

'I would find someone else to perform it. Dessoff cannot be the only conductor of the Vienna Philharmonic. Surely someone else could conduct it, even you, Herr Bruckner.'

'Do you know, Kathi? I totally agree with you! I won't ask him again about performing No. 3 and I won't mention No. 4 to him again, either.'

'Somehow, I thought you'd agree. You could do worse than speak to your friend Professor Herbeck.'

'I'll do that.'

'This letter arrived for you this morning. Could be from the university.'

'I'll open it in the study.' While opening the envelope, he wondered what it might say. Probably another rejection. He couldn't believe what he was reading. By a unanimous decision of the university professors, they had created an honorary post of Professor of Harmony and Counterpoint for him. It said he would receive a reimbursement of 700 florins on the second anniversary of his appointment, which would be from 8 November, 1877. After that, his salary would be 800 florins. The only disappointment was that they wouldn't pay him for two years, but at least he could repay his increasing debts then. So Hanslick must have changed his view and supported him, doubtless with great reluctance.

'Great news, Kathi! I'm overjoyed!' he said, positively glowing with excitement. 'The university has appointed me as an honorary professor. They

want me to start as soon as possible with an inaugural lecture. I'm thrilled!'
He didn't mention the lack of payment for two years or the obvious
acquiescence of Hanslick.

'Congratulations, Herr Bruckner! I'm as pleased as you are!'

Chapter 23
1875 - 1877 Popularity

'Ladies and Gentlemen,

'The top officials of the Ministry of Education and the University of Vienna, by decree, have appointed me as a lecturer on "The Theory of Harmony and Counterpoint" in the Department of Philosophy and Science. However, before I begin my lectures on these two subjects, I will, like the foreword to a printed work, mention in a few words the importance of these two subjects for our far-advanced intellectual lives.

'As you know yourselves from various sources, music has made such colossal progress within a period of two centuries, and completed its inner workings to such an extent that today, if we take a look at this rich material, we are faced with an all but finished artistic edifice. We will recognise from it that there is a certain regularity in the articulation of music, as if certain rules apply to the individual elements, as well as to the whole.

'Just as every branch of science orders its material into laws and rules, so too has musical science. I allow myself to attribute this to its artistic structure which can be dissected down to the atoms which group elements together, according to certain laws. This creates a subject for teaching which can be called musical architecture.

'In this teaching, the important chapters on harmony and counterpoint form the foundation and soul of this subject.

'After the foregoing, you will have to admit to me that in order to obtain the right and accurate appreciation of a piece of music, research must be conducted on how and to what extent these laws are complied with, and to what level the composer had used his imagination, in varying these laws.

'This makes it valid for harmony and counterpoint to have a necessary place in the far developed intellectual life where they are cultivated, where the same can be taught without the end goal of exclusively approaching the artists. This is because the artists, and rightly so, belong to the carriers of our intellectual education since we are able to give our thoughts and feelings a more aesthetic expression in music.

'After the relevant universities in Germany, France and Russia had already been recognised, the need to introduce this subject into intellectual life was also given expression.

'It would lead me too far to cite further points which indicate the importance of these subjects but I believe I must not fail to notice that through a knowledge of harmony and counterpoint one sometimes gets into the pleasant position through composition to promote the social interest which results in the desired profitable effect.

'Having spoken of the importance and significance of harmony and counterpoint, I shall now speak only briefly of the manner in which I intend to treat the subjects.

'My many years of study, and my experience, which I gained as a professor of these subjects at the local conservatoire, as well as my knowledge of the relevant literature, have led me to the decision not to bind myself to any of the works that are now available, but to give my lectures freely, and that for the reason that only for a limited time I am in a position to be able to roll out for you a clear picture from the rich and extensive material by taking out the most excellent fundamentals. My presentation will help to promote understanding and to make the letter of the theory invigorating through following the examples.

'I think of the words of Goethe:
"All theory, dear friend, is grey,
But the golden tree of life springs ever green!"

'I will reduce some of your hardships to a minimum through practical exercises, thus intimately combining theory and practice and thus taking you with safe steps through this realm of knowledge from one limit to the other. I will then guide you when you enter life's struggles with the request to use what I have learned faithfully and to think of me kindly. Although I have taken great pains to a create a nursery for these subjects at the University, I am nevertheless obliged to publicly acknowledge with gratitude the support I have received from the highly commendable college of professors in the philosophical faculty and from a prestigious ministry, to provide this form of instruction to you. I have been nurturing this idea for a long time and now it has become a reality.

'In conclusion, I would like to ask you gentlemen to address these issues with fresh minds. Please do your best to ensure that these subjects, taught here at your Alma Mater, be given due recognition and that this musical science flourishes at this university and everywhere you go.

'Thank you for your profound attention.'

Anton had worked hard in preparing this speech, his inaugural lecture, so he deserved the enthusiastic applause he received, especially from the students. It summarised what he believed for many years the university needed. Despite his continuing financial woes, he hadn't been happier for a long time. He saw himself as the leader of his students, their friend and mentor, not just a reader of lecture notes who would speak, and then vanish until the next session. He intended to be generous with his time and make himself available whenever needed.

'Well, how did your speech go down?' said Kathi as soon as he arrived home.

'Unbelievable, Kathi! The applause afterwards was overwhelming. Even the staff members applauded. But the students were in raptures. I'm going to really enjoy working with them!'

'I hope you'll still be able to write your music.'

'I'm certain I will.'

'Here's your favourite meal. I've prepared it as it's a special day for you.'

***

'I heard about your inaugural speech, Anton,' said Johann Herbeck as they met for a coffee in the Conservatorium refectory. 'Could you please let me borrow your notes? I'd love to read it. So you attracted applause from the professors and the students!'

'Yes, I couldn't believe it. I've had a less enthusiastic reception at some of my organ recitals! Yes, you can read the script!'

'Was Hanslick in the audience? He must feel defeated, having to agree to you getting the post!'

'I didn't see him, not that it means he wasn't there.'

'I take it you haven't heard from Dessoff about performing your No. 3?'

'Right. Not a word. I'm going to forget him. I don't think he will conduct it, or my No. 4. So I will have to find another conductor.'

'Let's see what happens over the next few months and then we'll discuss it further. How is your No. 5 coming along?'

'I have started it. This is going to be my most ambitious and most entertaining so far. And the longest. The first three movements build up to a huge climax in the finale, which will be my most satisfying movement so far.'

'How do you know that?'

'I've made a sketch of it. It will bring the first and second movements together.'

'Not the third?'

'No. The scherzo and trio form an interlude for the listener. I've roughed out some ideas for the third and will make it humorous, if I can!'

'You will, I'm sure. By the way, I've spoken to Hellmesberger. I'm afraid there is no more money he can pay you. Sorry.'

'Sod it! I'll have to struggle on!'

'You'll manage. You have up to now.'

'I know, but I'm not happy about it.'

***

323

'I've got a surprise for you, Kathi!' Anton said, when, a week or so after his meeting with Herbeck, she walked into his study with a cup of coffee for him before going home.

'You are full of them! Which one is it now?'

'The Vienna Philharmonic has announced they are going to conduct some test rehearsals of recent works. I was thinking of giving them No. 3 and No. 4, but they know about No. 3, so I'm giving them No. 4. We'll see what they make of that!'

'If I were you, Herr Bruckner, I wouldn't hold up much hope. Especially if that Dessoff character has anything to do with it.'

'Good advice, I think. So I'll take the score in tomorrow. They will have to get it copied if they are going to play it, and that'll save me the expense.'

Anton did as he said and, first thing the following morning, placed the score on the desk of an administrator at the concert hall.

'What are you expecting me to do with this, mein Herr?'

'It's my entry for the series of test rehearsals.'

'Oh, I see. There has been nothing as big as this, not so far.'

'Are you expecting me to take it away?'

'No. Leave it here, please.'

'Am I able to attend the rehearsal of my work?'

'Assuming they select it, you may.'

'How will I know?'

'We will write to you. Your address, please?'

It was over a month after he gave his inaugural address he heard that No. 4 had been selected for testing. They had chosen a day in December, which was convenient for Anton as term had finished by then.

'I shall keep my fingers crossed for you,' said Kathi as he left home that morning.

The conductor, a man whom Anton had not met before but who recognised him, welcomed him to the rehearsal. He listened as the Philharmonic played the first movement. Considering they had not, it seemed, attempted it before, he thought they played it well. The leader then spoke to the conductor, who left the rostrum to speak to Anton.

'I'm afraid we will not be recommending it for performance.'

'Would you mind telling me why?'

'We regard the first movement as the only one fit for playing. I'll be frank with you. The rest seems like madness put to music.'

'That's unfair,' said a member of the cello section, who had left the stage to join the discussion. 'There is nothing wrong with the other three movements.

I've studied them closely. They are all fit for play, so I beg you to have a more thorough trial of this interesting work.'

'Don't be ridiculous, Herr Popper. The rest of the symphony is idiotic!' said the unknown conductor.

'Are you calling my symphony the work of an idiot?' said Anton, his face glowing red, his arms outstretched and his hands facing upwards.

'Well... not that. But it is lacking in coherence. Impossible to understand and play.'

'That's a matter of opinion, as your Herr Popper shows. You are utterly failing to understand a modern piece of music.'

'I'm not changing my mind!' the conductor shouted.

'In that case, I'll collect the parts from your players and the score and take them with me. If you won't play it, someone else will.'

'But they are not yours to collect.'

'You don't want them, so I'll have them! Out of my way!'

Anton pushed past him, stepped up onto the stage, and collected the parts from the music stands of all the players, who blankly looked on. He was between tears of disappointment and raging anger. Lastly, he took the score from the conductor's rostrum, stepped onto the floor of the hall and walked out, without saying another word. His one thought was, 'fuck them!'

'How unkind,' said Kathi, as she put a sympathetic arm on his shoulder. 'How could they treat you like that?'

'I don't know. It's ridiculous, especially as that Herr Popper liked it.'

'I'm glad you picked up the score and the parts for the orchestra. They deserved it! What will you do next?'

'I may change it, anyway. If a symphony can't be played, it needs changing.'

'I wouldn't rush into changing it, Herr Bruckner. It could take you away from writing your next one.'

'Wise words, Kathi. I shall think further.'

***

Anton enjoyed teaching at the university. What he liked by far the most was the friendship and camaraderie of the students.

'Ladies and gentlemen,' he always said, even though it was rare for a woman student to appear. 'Today we are going to study the way Beethoven used repeated figures to build up tension in his symphonic movements,' he once said. So he made the subject of his lecture clear from the very beginning.

Using his usual method, he asked the students to introduce themselves and say their names, which Anton wrote on a map he had drawn of the lecture theatre. He asked them to sit at the same place in the next few lectures so he would recognise them.

'My name is Hans Rott. I've been studying organ playing with Herr Bruckner and I have joined this class to learn composition. My ambition is to be a composer, in the same league as Herr Bruckner.'

'My name is Rudolf Krzyzanowski. I'm from Hungary and I want to conduct and compose. I'm a student at the Conservatorium, too.'

'I am Josef Schalk. I live in Vienna and I want to be a conductor. I have learnt piano at the Conservatoire but I want to study under Herr Bruckner.'

'My name is Franz Schalk. I have similar ambitions to my brother Josef. I'm too young to be a student, but have come here with my big brother.'

'Ferdinand Löwe is my name. I am one of the youngest here, too. I want to be a conductor.'

In one lecture he delivered, while in the middle of writing the scherzo of his No. 5, he talked about humour in music. He played a piano transcription he had written of a part of Schubert's sixth symphony as an example. 'Well, it sounds funny to me, even if it doesn't to you!' They all laughed at his humour, if not at Schubert's.

'I am your elected professor,' he said, at the third or fourth of these lectures. 'So I hold a formal position here. But I am also a social person and, only if you want to accept what I am saying, I would like to meet as many of you as I can, outside of this formal setting. I would prefer to meet you in groups. We can talk about anything you wish, from music to politics, religion or other forms of art. I will refer to you from now on as "my Gaudeamus".'

It took several lectures more before the most outgoing of his students took up his interesting and unusual offer.

'Who do you regard as the best composer of our time?' said Joseph Schalk, as a group of five of them were gathered in a local inn.

'Richard Wagner. He is way in front of everybody else,' said Anton.

'Don't forget our Richard Strauss!' said Rudolf Krzyzanowski.

'How could I?' said Anton. 'He's brilliant, too!'

'What about Johannes Brahms?' said another.

'He is an accomplished composer who has written a wide range of masterpieces including his first piano concerto, the Cradle Song and, most recently, his Variations on a Theme by Haydn. I am waiting for his first symphony! But, and not everyone agrees, the best is Wagner.'

One of them asked him to explain why Wagner was so controversial. He told them about the rivalry between those who supported one and not the other. For purely diplomatic reasons, he did not mention Hanslick.

Around this time, while back at the Conservatoire, Johann Herbeck came to see him.

'Good news for you!'

Anton stood there expectantly.

'I've arranged for your No. 2 to be played here again!'

'Excellent! Well done, Johann.'

'Dessoff won't be the conductor.'

'Who will? You?'

'No! You!'

'I'd love to!'

'But I duly attached some conditions.'

'Which are?'

'You must make it shorter by at least ten but up to fifteen minutes.'

'I'd rather not play it under that constraint. It will lose its coherence, its logical structure.'

'Alright, let's say reduce it by at least five minutes, but hopefully nearer ten.'

'I'll take out five. Or near that, if it remains coherent.'

'I agree!'

What Johann didn't realise was that Anton wasn't entirely happy with the premiered version, so he had already made some cuts. He made a few more gentle excisions to the first and last movements.

***

'You look jolly, Herr Bruckner. Have you been drinking again with some of your students?'

'No, Kathi. Johann Herbeck has arranged for my No. 2 to have its second performance. That's why I'm so happy. He wants me to make it a bit shorter, but that won't be a problem.'

'What good news. Maybe my husband and I could come along to listen?'

'I'd love that. I'll get you some complimentary tickets.'

'Thank you! You are too generous!'

Several months and rehearsals later, the Vienna Philharmonic, under Anton's baton, played his Symphony No. 2. By then, the orchestra had mastered it, and Anton thrived on the excellent performance they gave. Each movement received tremendous applause from the audience, who clearly enjoyed this lengthy, but slightly shortened work. An overenthusiastic group clapped and stamped their feet at the end. The better behaved hissed them.

'So what did you and your husband think of it, Kathi?' he asked, as soon as she came in the following morning.

'Bruno liked it more than I did. It seemed more masculine than feminine, but I enjoyed those two middle pieces. I recognised some tunes, only because I heard you bashing them out on your piano!'

'I'm really pleased. You're not just saying that, are you?'

'Of course not. If I didn't like it, I'd tell you straight! It was odd to have that group stamping like mad and shouting at the end.'

'They became too keen on it! Anyway, you've made my day, and it's not 8 o'clock yet.'

'I'll sort out your breakfast!'

The press were less sympathetic, in fact downright abusive. A reporter in the Deutsche Zeitung called Anton 'one and a half fools' while another said he was 'what he eats, smoked meat, cabbage and dumplings'. Hanslick's review was equally hostile and criticised the structure of the work. Anton was unaffected by this press derision, despite the enemy, which he believed was Hanslick inspired.

'I've read some reviews, but think your Symphony No. 2 is a masterpiece. It is so original,' said one of his students. 'I wish I could write something that brilliant!'

'I totally agree,' said another. 'The reviews are totally unfair. Your symphony is too revolutionary for these ignorant individuals to appreciate. I cannot understand why they have to be so disgustingly rude.'

'I can,' said a third. 'It's pure envy and prejudice. They know they couldn't produce anything as good and they see you, Herr Professor, as a foreigner. You are from Upper Austria, aren't you? You may as well be from Sweden.'

'That still doesn't account for their rudeness,' said the one who spoke second.

'I'm grateful to you all for your support. It seems my symphonies are best appreciated by young people like yourselves. Or by older people in the audience whose minds are open to new ideas.'

The views of his students made Anton a much happier man than he would have been without them. They cheered him up and made him treasure his post as professor, even though it was still honorary. Their attitude towards his works, up to a point, made him believe he must continue writing these symphonies. He would continue if he didn't have their support, but such ardent enthusiasm helped.

***

'Kathi, could you help me pack please? The day after tomorrow, I shall go to Bayreuth to the premiere of Wagner's Ring Cycle of operas. It will be the most important musical event for many years. You remember Wagner's wife wrote to invite me?'

'Of course! You all but read me the letter… and told me the gossip about her and her affair!'

'I remember!'

'So how long with you be going for?'

'Say two weeks, no more. Luckily, there are no classes as it's the summer vacation.'

Anton travelled alone to Bayreuth and, as they invited him to stay there, made his way to Wahnfried. By then, the shell of the villa Anton had seen on his first visit had been transformed into a palatial residence, fit for a king, the king who had paid for it. Anton carried his suitcase up the wide drive and smiled as he read the motto over the door:

Here is where my delusions have found peace; let this place be named Wahnfried.

One of Richard's servants opened the gigantic door to him and showed him into an ante-room. Moments later, the Master appeared.

'It's so good to see you, my composer friend! We must play that third symphony of yours, that masterpiece,' he said, as he walked up to Anton and hugged him.

'But it's your new operas I'm here to see performed, not my symphony!'

'Have they performed it yet? Surely they have!'

'I took up your idea of seeking an agreement in writing from the Vienna Philharmonic and they've said they will put it in this year's programme. I don't actually believe them!'

'They are hoping you'll forget, but I know you won't! And how are your other symphonies progressing?'

'I've completed No. 4 and I've nearly finished No. 5. I'm thrilled with the way No. 5 is progressing!'

'Any news on performances?'

'Afraid not. They turned down No. 4 at a test rehearsal, so I've all but given up on the Vienna Philharmonic!'

'Don't give up! Keep writing these symphonies. And push to get them performed. They are the way to the future, I promise you. They are the building blocks for later symphonists to follow!'

'You are a great inspiration to me, Richard.'

'You deserve as much support as I can give you.'

He then turned to the servant, who was waiting for instruction. 'Now take Herr Bruckner to his room, please. Unpack for him and let him settle in. Once you are ready, Anton, you must come down for a beer. But we mustn't drink as much as we did last time you were here!'

'Not that much, was it?'

Anton hadn't felt this relaxed in the Master's presence since that heavy drinking session. He was soon ready and went straight back down, anticipating the beer the Master had promised.

'Ah,' said Wagner, as Anton stepped into the drawing room. 'Let me introduce you to Hans Richter. He must be totally insane as he's agreed to conduct all four of my Ring operas.'

'You've got some nerve,' said Richter. 'To whom am I being introduced?'

'This is my old friend and composer, Anton Bruckner. You will remember, he dedicated his trumpet symphony to me. Out of pure generosity. You saw the copy of the score he sent me.'

'Of course, I remember! I'm delighted to meet you, Herr Bruckner. I feel I know you through that symphony. It's one of the best and most original symphonies I've seen. You are up there with Beethoven! And I mean that. Has anyone performed it yet?'

'No,' interrupted Wagner. 'We must see what we can do to help it on its way.'

'I agree. A performance in Berlin or Munich, perhaps?'

'That would be wonderful and I should be forever grateful,' said Anton, bowing his head towards Richter, in an act of veneration.

'The crucial item on the agenda is a beer... Three steins of beer, please,' Wagner said, turning to the servant.

Anton listened carefully to all four operas of Wagner's Der Ring des Nibelungen. The music interested him far more than the struggle between the gods and the mortals. He focussed on every chord, every discord, every key change and the application of the leitmotif, a technique which Wagner himself had invented. Having enjoyed it, he felt mentally exhausted after each performance.

'What did you think of that opera?' said the gentleman who sat next to him during Siegfried and while they were leaving their seats.

'It is an incredible structure,' said Anton. 'That the man is a genius. If only I could write music half as brilliant as his, I could die a satisfied man!'

'What do you mean? Are you a composer?'

'Yes. My name is Anton Bruckner. I am only a beginner really, even though I am over fifty.'

'You are too modest, Herr Bruckner. I am aware of your music from press reports I have read. When in Vienna, I heard your F Minor Mass and thoroughly enjoyed it. It is truly a great work.'

'Well, thank you so much. Let me buy you a beer.'

They adjourned to a bar and carried on talking.

'So what are your connections with music?' said Anton.

'I do press reports and write for a music journal. I also do a modest amount of composing, but I'm not in your class, and definitely not in Herr Wagner's! So I have a certain amount of influence in musical circles, but not much. I also do some teaching.'

'Amazing! Do you know many orchestra directors? I'm struggling to get my music performed. I'm the only person who has conducted any of my symphonies, and I'm not really a conductor. What's your name?'

'Wilhelm Tappert.'

'Pleased to meet you!'

'Likewise! My turn to buy the drinks!'

They talked about their backgrounds. Each worked as a schoolteacher before they launched themselves into a musical career. They exchanged addresses and promised to keep in touch.

**

'So how did the journey go and did you like those operas?'

'Very well, Kathi. I almost missed the train at Munich because I stopped to buy some snuff. I had to run to catch it! Herr Wagner made me very welcome, and I met that Herr Richter, the conductor whom Cosima referred to in her letter of ages ago. Those operas are masterpieces. I mainly listened to the music, but I followed the stories. Would you like me to tell you the plots?'

'Not really!'

'Alright then, I won't,' he said, not betraying any disappointment for fear of causing an upset.

'Oh, there is one letter for you, postmarked Klosterneuburg. I don't recognise the writing.' She picked up the envelope and handed it to him. As usual, he took it into his study to read it.

'It's from a doctor I made friends with on a visit there a few years ago, Anton Özelt-Newin. He says he'll be in Vienna on Friday and would like to meet me, just for a beer and a chat. Shall I tell him to come here?'

'Or you could meet him at the Red Hedgehog, where you see your students?'

Anton spent the next few days completing the first draft of his Symphony No. 5 before meeting Anton Özelt-Newin at the tavern.

'It is so good to see you, Anton,' he said to Özelt-Newin. 'What brings you to the city? I'm delighted you to want to meet me!'

'I come here often to hold a clinic but, as we hadn't met since you were in Klosterneuburg, I thought I'd ask to see you again. Thanks for suggesting this tavern. Let me buy you a beer. Pilsner alright or a white beer?'

'A Pilsner is fine, Anton.'

They spent at least an hour talking. Anton told Anton Özelt-Newin about his experiences in Bayreuth and how much he had enjoyed each of the four operas. He said he was excited to finish his No. 5 and dedicate it to the Minister who helped him secure the post of lecturer. Mainly because of the excellent relationships he had with the students, he was enjoying the work even more than he expected.

'The only drawback is that it is still an honorary post, so I'm not as well off as I thought I'd be?'

'Do you need any financial help, Anton? May I assist?'

'Not really, I am just about managing, and life will improve when they begin to pay me.'

From the look on Özelt-Newin's face, Anton could see he was thinking. 'I might have an idea for you. I hope you don't mind me asking, but what is your main financial problem?'

'Two really. The first by far is the rent on my apartment in the Währingerstrasse and the second, paying my housekeeper.'

'My idea is for you to live in an apartment I own in the Hessgasse, which is quite close to where you are now. Because I admire your work and enjoy your friendship, I would not charge you a rent.'

'Anton, you cannot do that. I cannot live by charity!'

'It's not charity. It is a gift from an admirer. You will do me a favour by occupying my empty apartment. A relative left it to me recently, so it will be good to have it occupied.'

'Please tell me more!'

'All the rooms are spacious, including the kitchen. There are two bedrooms. You can organise it so you have one bedroom and a room you can use for your composing. It can easily take a desk, a piano, a library of books and scores. And there is a nice size lounge come dining room. I think you will like it. I won't be offended if you don't. It's on the fourth floor and I'm sure you are fit enough to manage the stairs...even if you've had a few beers!'

'The Hessgasse isn't far from my place. My house keeper lives in between, if I'm right. I'll take it with many, many thanks, Anton. You are an incredibly generous man.'

'So the next step is to move. Drop me a line to let me know when you want to move and I'll come in with the keys.'

Anton stood up and hugged him. His eyes were damp and didn't speak for a full minute. Then he spoke. 'I'm going to buy you a beer.' He came back with another one each.

'Good health, Anton,' he said, still almost in tears.

His one fear was whether Kathi would accept the new situation. At first, and not being a person who relished change, she was hesitant. So he took her along to the building and showed her the outside. 'Imagine the wonderful view we will have from up there, over the park and towards the city centre,' he said. 'Better than what we've got now!' He'd persuaded her.

Within a fortnight, he had moved. Kathi helped him to organise it. She chose the larger bedroom for his Bösendorfer piano, his harmonium and library of books and scores. She suggested his bedroom should contain only his bed, a wardrobe and the picture of his mother. He agreed. They soon found that the apartment suited each of them. Anton was especially pleased that Kathi liked it.

Chapter 24
1877 - 1878 Disaster strikes

On the first day of the '77 autumn term, Anton met Johann Herbeck in Anton's classroom, just before Anton was to give a lesson. He told him about his visit to Bayreuth, the Wagner Ring Cycle, and that he had moved to an apartment in the Hessgasse.

'I have some amazing news for you, Anton!'

'Go on!'

'I have been working with the directors of the Vienna Philharmonic. They've put your No. 3 into the autumn programme of the Music Society. I will have the privilege of conducting it myself on the sixteenth of December at the Society Hall.'

'Not Dessoff then?'

'No.'

'I could hug you, Johann! My greatest ambition is to have No. 3 performed and you have all but achieved it! You are a wonderful friend to me. I don't deserve you!'

'You are a good friend to me, too. But let's not get too maudlin and start planning the event.'

'May I attend the rehearsals?'

'Of course. We can use the parts Dessoff produced for his rehearsal where the orchestra didn't like it.'

'Please, no! I've made several changes. I've taken out all those Wagner quotes, except one... the sleep motif from Die Walküre in the first movement.'

'Christ, Anton. You make life difficult! Can't you leave the bloody things alone, once you've written them? You did the same with the second. Bring me your revised score tomorrow and I'll get on with getting it copied.'

'Of course.' He didn't respond to Herbeck's question.

'Once it's done, we'll start the rehearsing.'

'If you remember, most of the orchestra didn't like it. Let's hope they've changed their minds. I hope Arthur Nikisch is in it. He is a supporter and can argue our case with the others.'

'Let's hope so!'

***

'Kathi, I have some wonderful news,' he said the moment he walked in. Kathi was in the kitchen preparing his dinner.

'Come in here. I can't hear you.'

He told her about the coming performance of No. 3.

'Hmm. Are you sure?'

'Yes. My great friend Johann Herbeck has persuaded the Vienna Philharmonic to play it, with him conducting!'

'But they almost threw it out last time! What makes you so certain they won't do that again?'

'Because Herbeck is a man of tremendous influence. You'll see. Would you and Bruno like to come to the performance?'

'When is it?'

'December the sixteenth.'

'I'll ask him.'

Herbeck succeeded in his task of getting the parts printed and ready for the first rehearsal, which was to take place in late September. Anton and he discussed a tactical approach to making the orchestra accept the work they had rejected before. If any of its members reacted badly, Herbeck would accuse them of small-mindedness and of having a dangerously negative attitude to new works.

The orchestra assembled at the agreed time and began their tuning. Anton sat in the stalls, Herbeck then stepped onto the rostrum, looked at the orchestra from one side to the other and spoke,

'Gentlemen, before we start, I'd like to say a few words about the work we are about to rehearse. As you know, Anton Bruckner wrote it. In our country, he is becoming well known. He is sitting in the concert hall. Could you please stand, Herr Bruckner?'

Anton stood and nodded towards them.

'Many of you are familiar with this symphony because you played some of it at a rehearsal two years ago when you were less than keen on it, but Herr Dessoff decided to perform it. In order to make the symphony more readily appreciated and easier to perform, Herr Bruckner has made many changes. So the parts in front of you are new copies. My firm request to you all is to treat the work with an open mind. In my view, it is a masterpiece and I hope you all agree. Are there any questions?'

He looked around the players again. There were no responses.

'In which case we will begin. On the count of three. One...two...three.'

It started nicely with the series of notes played ostinato. Then the trumpeter played the theme Wagner enjoyed so much when he read the score. To Anton, Herbeck had the orchestra under firm control. Then suddenly, some players started laughing and play came to a crashing halt.

'This is a joke!' said one of the first violins. There are five notes in a bar here and it's marked as four! Ridiculous!'

Others started laughing, too. Herbeck turned towards Anton, then back to the orchestra. 'Are you people professionals or not? Can't you see the rhythm of the five notes? They go one two three; one, two with the first three played in quick succession in the time of two beats. It's obvious, isn't it? Am I right, Herr Bruckner?'

'Yes you are precisely correct. One two three; one, two. Then later one, two; one two three. A simple reversal.'

Herbeck struck the music stand with his baton. 'So now you have the explanation, we start again.'

He had regained control, much to Anton's relief, and stopped the performances in several places to instruct players, but worked through to the end. Anton admired Herbeck's supreme ability as a conductor, something to which he could never aspire. Although Anton had conducted many times, he knew he could not control an orchestra the way Herbeck could. He thought that few conductors could have brought the orchestra back from their laughing fit to total obedience.

'Thank you, gentlemen. What an excellent job you have done today. I would like to conduct another rehearsal in late October and another in the week before the actual performance in December. Thank you again,' said Herbeck. He bowed to them, left the rostrum, and came towards Anton.

'So, it all worked out in the end!'

'Superbly done, Johann! You certainly know how to control an orchestra!'

'It's many tears, and years of practice, Anton!'

***

During the following two months, Anton concentrated on revising his Symphonies No. 2 and No. 4 with the basic objective of making them less demanding on the orchestra and the audience. He also became more engrossed in his teaching at the university and socialising with his students. One evening, having explained to Kathi, he would not need a cooked meal, he dined with some of them at the Red Hedgehog. The two Schalks, Ferdinand Löwe and Hans Rott went with him.

'I don't recognise you, do I?' said Anton to a newcomer to the group.

'He's a friend of mine,' said Hans. 'He's learning to compose at the Conservatorium. That's right, Gustav. Isn't it?'

'Yes, Hans. Pleased to meet you, Herr Bruckner,' said the fresh faced lad. 'My name is Mahler, Gustav Mahler.'

'How old are you?' said Anton.

'Seventeen. My birthday is in July.'

'Who is your teacher?'

'Robert Fuchs.'

'Oh! I know him well.'

A conversation began on the forthcoming performance of Anton's Symphony No. 3. He told them he admired the conducting skills of Herbeck, who would conduct it on 16 December.

'We'll all be there, won't we, gentlemen?' said Anton.

'Of course,' said Hans.

'Alright if I come, too?' said Gustav.

'The more the merrier,' said Anton, smiling with his entire face.

'I'll come,' said Rudolf Krzyzanowski.

'I'm sorry, I'm late guys,' said Hugo Wolf. Hugo was a young songwriter whom Anton had met in Klosterneuburg, a few years before, and who often joined these student gatherings. 'I have some terrible news. Professor Herbeck has died. Apparently, of a heart attack.'

'He can't have,' said Anton, his face distorted and almost in tears. 'He's a young man. And we are supposed to rehearse again tomorrow!'

His students helped to console him. He found it almost impossible to accept what Hugo had said.

'Sadly, it is true. I spoke to a professor in the refectory, just before I came here. He was clearly upset. Apparently, Professor Herbeck collapsed in his office. His secretary tried to revive him, but in vain. By the time a doctor arrived, he had passed away. I am sorry, Herr Bruckner.'

'I'm sorry for his wife and his son, Ludwig. And for my Symphony No. 3. God knows when it will be played now. It seems to be cursed,' he said, his lips down turned and his open hands in the air.

'I'm sure they will play it,' said Hans. 'The key thing is to make sure it's still in the programme.'

'That gives me an idea. One of my students at the Conservatory, August Göllerich, has a highly influential father. He is a member of the Reich Council of the State Parliament. He may help.'

Anton bought them each a beer. They raised their glasses to Johann Herbeck.

***

The following morning, Anton told Kathi the sad news. 'I'm so sorry, Herr Bruckner. How terrible and what a shock. I really feel for his family and he was such a friend to you.'

'I know. It's a tragedy. I feel so sorry for his wife and son. I don't know if he had any other children.'

'And what about your symphony? He was going to conduct it for you, wasn't he? What will happen now? I hope it will still be played.'

'I hope so, too. I may learn today. We'll see,' he said, putting on a smile, but still in serious doubt about it being performed.

Anton picked up his briefcase and walked to the Conservatorium, looking at the ground as he went. He entered the refectory to look for August Göllerich. He wasn't there, so he headed for the lecture theatre. There were already some students sitting and waiting for a lecture to begin. He cast his eye around them, even walking down to the front to see their faces.

'Are you looking for someone, Professor Bruckner?' said a student.

'Yes. August Göllerich. Has anyone seen him?'

'No,' said another. 'He's ill at home.'

'Have you any idea when he may be back?'

'No one seems to know what's wrong with him. So no. Sorry, Professor.'

Anton decided to contact August Göllerich's father. First, he needed to work out where he should meet him. At his home in Wels or at the Estates House of Lower Austria, where members of the Reich Council met. He needed an urgent meeting, so as not to give the director at the orchestra time to remove No. 3 from the programme. First, he walked to the Estates House, which was not far from the Hessgasse. He was more likely to be there than at home in Wels, he thought.

Anton looked up at the imposing building, thinking how elegant and overpowering it was. It had a distinctly Teutonic, almost brutal feel about it. By good luck, Herr Göllerich was in and sitting at his desk, pondering over a memo.

'It's so good to see you again, Herr Bruckner. I remember the good time we had with you in Wels, and that wonderful organ recital you gave us! I'm sure you have a good reason to come to see me here. First, take a seat. So...'

Anton sat and told him about the sudden death of Johann Herbeck and the possible consequences for the performance of his No 3, scheduled for 16 December.

'The reason I have come is to ask if there is anything you can do to ensure it stays on the programme.'

'Hmm,' he said, while pacing the room. 'Who would conduct it?'

'I don't know. There are several good conductors there.'

'Yes, but this is a revolutionary symphony and you are a Wagner supporter. That means there is a reputational risk in being associated with it,' he said, his hands on his hips.

'I'm not a qualified conductor, but I have conducted many times before and am more familiar with the symphony than anyone else. I could conduct it.'

'So we have a plan. I go to the director and ask him if he can keep it in the programme and you will conduct it. Simple, eh?'

'Should I accompany you?'

'Definitely not. You either go alone or I do. I would appear to be your mouthpiece if we appeared there together… and I'm sure neither of us would want that. If you go alone, it would appear as if you were pleading with them.'

'With respect, Herr Göllerich, that's why I am asking you!'

'Excellent. Then we agree. I will go to the Music Society as soon as my secretary has arranged an appointment, hopefully tomorrow.'

'How will I know the outcome of your discussion with the director?'

'Just come to my office and ask. I or the secretary will tell you.'

'Thank you so much, Herr Göllerich. I am grateful.'

Anton shook hands with him and left. Then he walked back to his apartment in the Hessgasse wondering what the outcome of Göllerich's discussions would be. The death of Johann Herbeck deeply saddened him. Had it not been for Herbeck, he would not be working at the Conservatory or probably have his honorary post at the University. Only a few days before his passing, he showed Johann the latest version of the finale to his No. 4, and his praise had touched Anton. He said Schubert would have loved to have written it.

***

As he was going in, Kathi was in the hall on her way out.

'So, are they going to perform your symphony, Herr Bruckner?'

He told her about seeing Göllerich, and what he had promised to do.

'That sounds good to me. Let's hope he gets what you want. I've left a ham salad for you in the kitchen larder. Probably see you tomorrow?'

'Thank you, Kathi. Yes, see you then!'

Anton saw no point in going to the Estates House the day after seeing Göllerich. First, he didn't want to appear unduly anxious and, second, he wanted to give Göllerich plenty of time to meet the director. So he went on the third day, after his lectures at the University.

'Ah, Herr Bruckner,' said the fair-haired lady secretary, 'Herr Göllerich is in Wels at present and has asked me to tell you he is meeting one of the Philharmonic directors on Monday morning. He asked me to tell you he would like to see you here on Monday afternoon. Will that be alright?'

'That will be perfect,' he smiled, reluctantly accepting the delay.

It seemed he was waiting an age. The time dragged mercilessly. He found it difficult to concentrate on anything other than his lectures. The weekend was the worst he could remember. Partly because he would attend Johann's funeral on the Tuesday, something he had to do, but which he was not looking forward to. In order to take his mind off his fear that they might delete the symphony from the programme, he spent some time late into the night, playing the organ in the Piaristenkirche and walking around the city. Kathi did her best to help by cooking him some of his favourite meals.

Monday began with a lecture at the Conservatorium. Despite his anxiety over the forthcoming meeting with Herr Göllerich, it went well. The students listened intently as he explained why he thought the works of Mozart were so popular and why Bach's were less so. To illustrate his points, he played several examples on the piano and the harmonium. He stressed the conventionality of the works he quoted from and, according to the science, how they obeyed the rules, unlike some more modern music.

'Are we meeting for a drink this evening?' asked one of his pupils.

'Not tonight,' he said, wondering how he would feel after meeting Göllerich. 'Wednesday would be a better time.'

With his mind in an almost frozen state, incapable of rational thought, he walked to the Estates House and made his way to Göllerich's office. The blond secretary invited him to sit with her in the outer office, as her master was engaged in a meeting. He waited a full ten minutes. As the inner office door opened, he heard the exchange between Göllerich and the person who was seeing him.

'I'll tell him the good news,' said Göllerich.

'I hope he appreciates our flexibility,' said the man, half chuckling. Anton immediately recognised him as a member of the orchestra. It was difficult for Anton to forget him, as he was one who burst out laughing during the September rehearsal.

Herr Göllerich invited him in and asked him to sit down. 'I have excellent news for you, Herr Bruckner,' he said, still standing. 'That was a director of the orchestra. He had good news from President Dumba of the Society of Music Friends. The President has approved of you conducting your symphony on the sixteenth of December. Congratulations! I wish you well with it. The only condition is that you agree to one more rehearsal, no more than three days before what I'm sure will be an historical event.'

'Thank you, Herr Göllerich. That's brilliant news for me and my symphony,' he said, feeling a little unsure, having recognised the player and noting his position of power. 'Isn't that gentleman also one of the orchestra? I think I know him vaguely. Do you know his name?'

'Yes, he is Sigmund Bachrich. I believe he is a violinist. He has asked that you go to the concert hall office to agree a date.'

'I'll go now.'

Anton went straight to the concert hall. The secretary and he settled on Friday, 14 December, two days before the public performance.

The following day, Anton attended Johann Herbeck's funeral. Such an event is never a happy one. Johann's was particularly sad. His poor wife was constantly crying. Anton failed to comfort her, and neither did her son. She shrugged anyone off who attempted to ease her pain. Johann's tragic death at forty-six was agonisingly early. His son gave an excellent eulogy. Clearly, Johann was a much loved family man, as well as a scholar, composer, and conductor. Anton was still feeling his loss, friendship and support, and would for a long time.

The day for the rehearsal came around quickly. Not only was he busy with his teaching, he re-familiarised himself with his No. 3 to make conducting easier. The orchestra was almost completely ready when he arrived and took the rostrum. As he stood there, chatting to some members of the string sections, the latecomers took their places. He noticed Sigmund Bachrich sitting in the first violins. He spoke to the assembled orchestra.

'Ladies and gentlemen,' he said, even though there were no women there. 'First, I would like to thank you for agreeing to be members of this orchestral grouping, which will play my third symphony. It is a novel work which, I am proud to say, I dedicated to the great composer, poet, and my friend, Richard Wagner.' There were murmurings and giggling from some players. He identified Bachrich as an offender. He continued. 'I hope you will bear with me as, unlike you professional players, I am only an amateur conductor, mainly of choirs and small groups of players. However, I shall do my very best to lead you in this symphony.'

He turned to the leader of the orchestra. 'Are we ready to start?'

'Yes, let's begin. We have finished our tuning.'

'We'll start on three.' He raised his arms and brought them down on his count of 'three'. They started well. About half way through the first movement, their playing ground to a halt. Some of them, including Bachrich, started laughing. Anton challenged them.

'Why have you stopped? What is the joke? Could you share it with me?'

'This isn't a symphony,' said one of the woodwind section.

'What is it then?' said Anton.

'It's a patchwork of tunes. There is no structure and no continuity. It's a joke in itself.'

'I disagree,' said another, much to Anton's relief. So they were not all against him, he thought. 'It is a modern symphony' he continued. 'Herr Bruckner is rewriting the rules of symphonic composition. You should not be here if you can't accept progress in music.'

'That's not the point,' said Bachrich. 'We are here to entertain and this, whatever you call it, symphony or not, fails to do that. It's a hotchpotch. The

341

themes do not have even the slightest relation to each other. It has no structure. There are irrelevant blank bars and it is simply chaotic. It is not fit for an audience.'

'The fact is, it is a challenge. It is a tough work,' said a horn player. 'It is a valid piece of music, whatever you say, Herr Bachrich. So I ask everyone to continue. We must make this a work we can all play well on Sunday. It will be up to the audience to decide what they think of it.'

'Hear, hear,' called out half the orchestra.

'Thank you.' said Anton. 'I don't accept your negative comments, especially yours, Herr Bachrich. You were content with my score when Johann Herbeck rehearsed you.'

'Some of us did not attend then, including me,' said Sigmund Bachrich.

'Please, may we start again? From where you all stopped!' Ignoring Bachrich's response, he gave them the bar number.

They started before he raised his baton, but play it they did, up to a point in the slow movement when Anton stopped them. He wanted a better balance between the woodwind and the strings and the double basses to put more force into their playing. His request raised no objections, so they did as he asked them. Anton smiled broadly as they were playing the scherzo and he was setting the pace. It sounded to Anton exactly as he hoped it would, just as he had written it.

After about thirty bars into the finale, the orchestra, player by player, stopped. Not again, thought Anton.

'So what is your objection this time?' he said.

'You cannot inflict this musical rubbish on an audience,' said Bachrich. 'It's almost impossible to play that opening ostinato. It is far too fast and meaningless. Then you have a tune that sounds like a herd of elephants on a charge. That's followed by some clumsy dance tune with a tragic sounding tune on the brass in the background. It's nonsensical. Don't we all agree?' He stood up and looked around the orchestra for support.

'I definitely agree,' said a bassoon player.

'Really?' said Anton. 'I seem to have made the mistake of believing you are all professional musicians.'

'We are,' shouted another. 'The great majority of us appreciate your new symphony, Herr Bruckner. I, for one, believe it's a masterpiece. Trust the silent majority! Take no notice of Bachrich.'

'Thank you, mein Herr. In which case, shall we restart and play the finale?'

This time he started them off by looking around the orchestra, raising his baton high in the air, pausing and bringing it down quickly. He commented as they played. 'Excellent. Just the right speed', 'more volume from the clarinets', 'less heavy on the timpani' and 'again, stronger on the basses'. They fully cooperated with his suggestions, as he might have expected from this famous ensemble.

He smiled jubilantly as they finished the finale and applauded them from the rostrum. 'Well done, gentlemen. I'm absolutely delighted with where we are now. Thank you so much. I look forward to seeing you on Sunday.'

As he was closing his score, one of the viola section approached him, carrying his instrument under his arm and his bow. 'I'm sorry that some of our group could only make negative comments, Herr Bruckner. I felt ashamed of them. The one good thing is that, whatever individual members think of your symphony... which I think is a modern masterpiece... we will play it to a high professional standard.'

'Thank you, so much. I'm sorry that I'm not a better conductor, but no one else wanted to conduct it.'

'You did well, in the circumstances. And you achieved the result you wanted. I'll see you on Sunday!'

***

'How did the rehearsal go?' said Kathi as he went into the kitchen.

'Deplorable. Some comments from the orchestra were appalling. There are two camps there. One lot like my symphony and the other lot hate it.'

'Are you going to tell me more?'

'Yes, of course. I started by making a huge mistake. I shouldn't have told them I dedicated it to my friend, Richard Wagner. They hate him in some quarters and love him in others. I think the Wagner haters loathe my symphony, mainly because it's dedicated to Richard. And because they don't like modern music. You should have heard their comments on it. They were so negative. You'd think I'd written something deliberately to annoy them.'

'What did you do?'

'I asked them to explain their comments, and they struggled to. Luckily, the majority in the orchestra seemed happy with it. One of them came up to me afterwards and declared it a modern masterpiece. That made it all worthwhile!'

'So how did it all end?'

'Moderately well. I think they will be fine on Sunday.'

'Let's hope so!'

***

Anton walked from his apartment to the concert hall with the score under his arm. He wondered whether the orchestra would perform to his expectations and how the audience would react. Judging from their delight, even shouting, at his No. 2, it should attract plenty of applause, if not

343

adulation. He entered the building through the stage door and went to the conductor's dressing room. He looked at his pocket watch. There were fifteen minutes to go before the start of the symphony. Feeling a little anxious, he sat there looking through the score until there was a knock on the door.

'Time for you to go to the rostrum, Herr Bruckner,' said a smiling assistant. 'I hope it all goes well. Good luck and God be with you!'

'Thank you,' said Anton as he placed his score back under his arm. As he moved at a measured pace across the stage, he smiled at the audience. Many applauded and quite a few cheered, presumably his students, he thought.

He stepped up to the rostrum, placed the score on the music stand, the height of which he then adjusted slightly, and turned to the first page. He bowed to audience and then to the orchestra. He picked up the baton.

'All set,' he whispered to the leader, who nodded.

He raised the baton slowly, then brought it down at speed. They started.

He was delighted at the quality of the performance. This was a truly professional one in which the orchestra followed his baton with precision. He did not change the dynamics or emphasis, but simply moved his arms to the rhythm. He expected the players would follow what they agreed at Friday's rehearsal, and they did. This was no surprise, despite the outrageous views of some of them, Bachrich amongst them.

When the first movement ended and in the pause between it and the adagio, Anton detected movement in the audience. He didn't look around but thought a number were leaving.

Having looked again at the leader and received his nod, he started. Again, he admired their play. It could hardly be better. There was a minor error from one of the horns, but this he considered understandable. As he had directed, he went straight from the adagio into the scherzo, without a pause. He could not detect any movement at the end, so imagined the audience were happy.

After another short break, he launched into the finale. He thought, after a few bars, he could detect some booing. Surely, he was mistaken. Then some hissing. Then stamping. What was happening behind him? The noise became louder as some members of the audience started shouting 'rubbish' and 'terrible'. He could hardly stop for this minority, so continued. The sound of people asking those next to them to let them pass by, as they left their seats, was loud enough for him to hear, despite the continuing play. He could tell from the acoustics that the auditorium was emptying.

The audience were leaving in their droves, as if someone sounded a fire alarm. As the finale finished, there were less than twenty left in the audience.

He looked around. Tears formed as he grimaced. He turned back. The orchestra had all but vanished, too.

Anton could not help himself. 'I am totally alone,' he said out loud. 'My God has forsaken me!'

Then, much to his surprise, those left in the audience stood and gave him a standing ovation. He recognised many of them. Amongst them were his students Rudolf Krzyzanowski, Joseph and Franz Schalk, Hans Rott and Han's friend Gustav Mahler. They brought a weak smile to his face, but despite their best efforts, failed to console him.

Anton felt devastated and could not help but show it. Tears ran down his face. The thought of a similar reception for any future symphony of his leapt into his mind. Were all his creative exertions in vain? Disillusionment turned to desolation.

As he was enduring this agony, a well-dressed gentleman with a short beard approached Anton while he stood, rejected on the auditorium floor. 'Good evening, Herr Bruckner.' Anton could see nothing good in it. He looked blankly at the man, as he wiped his eyes with his handkerchief.

'My name is Theodor Rättig. I truly loved that symphony. You may not have noticed me, but I have been at all the rehearsals, including that one on the fourteenth of December when the orchestra was so rude, and the one in September. I would have thought better of Josef Hellmesberger, especially as he is the director of the Conservatorium. But I haven't come to speak about these people. I am here to make you an offer. I am a publisher and I want to publish your symphony. What do you think? Do you agree?'

Anton gradually broke into a smile. 'I would be totally delighted, Herr Rättig. This evening was a disaster until you spoke. I now feel better than I've felt all day! I will contribute financially, of course.'

'Thank you, but that will not be necessary. I will publish it at the expense of my company. It will cost you nothing.'

'I do not know how to express my appreciation. My gratitude has no bounds.'

'If you would like to give me the score, I will get it into print as soon as I can.' Anton picked it up from the music stand and handed it over. 'Thank you again, Herr Rättig.' They shook hands and Rättig left the auditorium.

***

'I'm sorry we couldn't come to your concert last night,' said Kathi as she placed Anton's breakfast in front of him. 'I assume it went well.'

'Thank you, Kathi. This looks perfect... and I'm hungry. Sad to tell you, last night was an utter disaster. I'm still feeling it.' He told her what happened, stressing the mass exodus in the finale, and saying who stayed until the end.

'Now I'm even sorrier we didn't go. At least we'd have supported you. What caused it?'

345

'It's far from obvious. It may have been the anti-Wagner movement, but I doubt it. Otherwise, more would surely have left earlier. My conducting is not good but I don't think it was that because I just kept to the agreed tempo. Nothing fancy. All I can think is that the symphony was too difficult for the vast majority of them to enjoy. There may have been a snowball effect. Once fairly large numbers went, many more followed.'

'I'm so sorry, Herr Bruckner. That is a big surprise to me.'

'Not to worry, Kathi. I'll get over it and I'll soon be writing my No. 6! It wasn't all bad news either!' He explained the welcomed approach from Rättig.

'That's good news! When will it be in print?'

'As soon as he can manage it. I left the score with him.'

The press were even more brutal than the audience, Hanslick especially. As Anton discovered, he said:

We could not make sense of his poetic intentions - perhaps a vision in which Beethoven's Ninth is joined in friendship with Wagner's Walküre - only to come to grief under its horses' hooves at the end – or to comprehend the purely musical argument.

Anton expected this brand of negativity from an anti-Wagnerite. The disappointment was that this man once claimed to be his friend. Sometimes reality was hard to digest. Other critics were equally dismissive.

***

A few months after the calamity of his Symphony No. 3, Anton was sitting in his study composing, when Kathi knocked on the door. 'May I come in, Herr Bruckner? This letter has just arrived.'

'Yes. Please bring it in. I'm not expecting anything.'

'I can't read the postmark. The inked is smeared.' She handed him the letter and turned to leave.

'Stay if you like. It may affect both of us.'

She stopped. Her face suddenly looked serious, as if she was expecting something bad. Was Anton to give the apartment back to Dr Özelt-Newin?

'Fantastic news, Kathi. They've confirmed my post as organist at the Chapel of the Imperial Court and they are going to pay me 800 florins a year. We can live like lords now!' he smiled.

'Congratulations, Herr Bruckner. I know you enjoy that post. Even better to be paid!'

'I'm so thrilled Kathi, I am going to increase yours by 200 florins! How does that sound?'

Totally out of character, she leant over and kissed him on both cheeks. 'Oh, I'm sorry, Herr Bruckner. I just couldn't help myself!' she said, suddenly looking away.

'Don't apologise. It's not every day I get kissed by a good-looking young woman!'

'May I ask what you are writing now?' she said, eager to restore her modesty.

'It's a piece called a motet which is mainly sung. I am writing it for a mixed choir, a soloist and organ.'

'Why are you writing it now?'

'It's a delightful story which I will gladly share with you. When I was in Linz, I went to see my friend, Bishop Rudigier. He asked me if I would write a piece to be played on the twenty-fifth anniversary of his appointment. For me, it's a great honour. The anniversary is on the fourth of June this year so, what with all my other tasks, I thought I'd better start it! In fact, it shouldn't take more than a day to write it!'

'Will you go to the performance?'

'Only if invited... but I'd be surprised if I'm not. I've been left out of important events before now. Much to my annoyance!'

***

Sometime later, and while having a coffee in the Conservatory refectory, Joseph Hellmesberger came to speak to him.

'I'm sure you realise I am your boss now that Johann Herbeck has sadly passed.'

'Of course. I'm sure we will work together well. But just to satisfy my curiosity, I would like to ask you a question.'

'Please go ahead, Anton.'

'You will remember, back in December, on the fourteenth in fact, you were a member of the orchestra during the final rehearsal of my Symphony No. 3.'

'Yes, I remember.'

'My question to you is this. Why did you laugh when I was conducting?'

Hellmesberger said nothing. His terrified expression was that of someone standing before a firing squad.

'I don't remember laughing.'

'Come on. Admit it. Your friend Bachrich was laughing too, as were others.'

'So what if we were?'

'Such behaviour betrays a staggering level of rudeness and puts to shame one of the most famous orchestras in Europe.'

'Alright, I admit it. I'm not sure why it happened. All I can do is to offer you my most sincere apologies. It was very childish of us. I can assure you it will not happen again.'

'It's a pity you had to lie to me, but I accept your apology. The matter is now closed. Let's talk about something else. Many years ago, you invited me to write a string quartet for the group of musicians which bears your name. Would you still be interested in such a work? If so, I have roughed out some ideas which I am happy to develop.'

'Anton, that is exceptionally good of you, especially as I did not give you the support you deserved,' he mumbled with his eyebrows lowered. 'May I tell the group what you are planning?'

'Of course. I don't know when I'll finish it. Having suffered the hideous debacle of my No. 3, I would like to take a break from symphony writing, to compose a quintet.'

'Not a quartet, then.'

'No. Something more substantial.'

Chapter 25
1878 - 1880 A holiday is due

Anton took a few days' break in Linz, mainly because of Bishop Rudigier's anniversary. While there, he would renew acquaintances and even play on the Cathedral organ, given half a chance. As usual, Kathi packed a bag for him. Unusually, she made him a picnic lunch to eat on the train.

'I've got to look after you, Herr Bruckner, especially after you gave me that big pay rise!' she said.

'No need to come here every day. I'll be at least five days, if not longer.'

Anton walked from the main station in Linz to Irene's house. He had given no notice of his visit so just turned up at her door.

'Anton, it's you,' she said before giving him a kiss. She smiled. 'What brings you to Linz? You are a Vienna man now!'

He told her about the Bishop's anniversary and the piece he composed for it.

'What about you, Irene? How are you? Are you still taking in students?'

'This is the last term they will stay here. I'd like to have more time for myself. And I've had some trouble with them paying. I'm owed about a thirty-five florins.'

'That's not good.'

'No. I'm thinking of taking them to court. Still, that's my problem, not yours. So how long will you be staying? I'd love you to stay here!'

'You are too kind, Irene. I was thinking of staying at the Frankfort Hotel.'

'Please don't, Anton. It will be my pleasure if you stay with me.'

'You've convinced me, Irene. I will, but I must pay you something, if only to help compensate for those accursed students!'

'We'll worry about that later!'

While Irene cooked them a meal, Anton went upstairs to unpack. Over dinner, he mentioned moving to the rent-free apartment in Hessgasse, and what a wonderful housekeeper Kathi still was, despite her occasional tantrums.

'And what about your composition and performances of your works?'

He told her about the symphonies he had written and the disastrous performance of his Symphony No. 3.

'I'm utterly speechless, Anton. And so sorry for you.'

'I'm over it now, Irene, but I must admit, it shook me badly. I'm writing a chamber work now, so having a rest from composing symphonies.'

'Are you not writing more symphonies?'

'Oh, yes! God put me on Earth to write them and I will until I die!'

Their conversation continued into the early hours. He told her about the confirmation of his post at the Imperial Court Chapel, the problems he had with Hellmesberger and the sad passing of Johann Herbeck. She listened intently.

The following day, Anton walked around the city. He started by visiting the site of the new Cathedral of the Immaculate Conception. They seemed to have carried out little work on it since he last saw it. He stepped across the foundations and found his way into the Votive Chapel. A choir was getting ready for a rehearsal. He sat in the pews, where about a dozen others, men and women, were already sitting, and listened. They sang his *Tota pulchra es*. There was no organ, but a young man sat at a harmonium, which Anton presumed the man would play in the actual performance. From what he heard, the scheduled performance should be brilliant. He stood up and left, pleased that no one recognised him.

He then walked to the old Cathedral. Apart from a few individuals sitting and praying, it was empty. He could not stop himself from taking the steps up to the organ loft and sitting at the console.

'Who are you?' said a young lad of about nine, who appeared behind him.

'I used to work here,' he said. 'My name is Anton Bruckner.'

The lad spontaneously took Anton's hand and kissed it. 'My father is always talking about your music and organ playing,' he said. 'I am the calcant here. Do you want to play?'

'Yes, please!'

'Give me two minutes, then you can start!'

Anton played his version of Bach's Toccata and Fugue in D Minor. He then charged into a stunning series of improvisations, a prequel as he saw it, to the Bishop's celebration. He lost himself in the power of his own creation. Piling variation upon variation, he continued for a full hour before reaching a shattering conclusion. He stopped to allow his feet and fingers to recover.

The young lad appeared. 'You are the best,' he said, and burst into tears.

Anton stood and put his arm around the lad's shoulder. He took out a handkerchief and wiped his eyes. 'Sorry I made you cry,' he said. 'We were a team. I couldn't have played at all without you!'

The lad's tears turned to laughter. 'Do you mind if I go now? My mother will wonder where I am.'

'You go, my lad. Tell your parents I wasn't as good as you hoped I'd be! Take this!' He opened his purse, took out a four kreuzer piece and placed it in the lad's open hand.

Anton waited for the lad to go before he stepped down onto the floor of the transept. As he was walking towards the main door, he heard a voice.

'Anton, it's you!'

He looked around. It was Canon Johann Schiedermayr. 'I was in the vestry and recognised your organ playing immediately. You are as good as you've ever been. Well done. We read all about your performances in London. You put us on the map!'

'Oh, thank you, Johann. It's good to see you!'

'So I imagine you've come to Bishop Rudigier's twenty-fifth.'

'Correct.'

'And you've written a deeply moving, *Tota pulchra es* for the occasion.'

'Yes, I'm pleased with it and I hope the Bishop will be.'

'He will. I'm certain. The choir has rehearsed it and we've kept him away from it so far!'

'Yes, I heard it a couple of hours ago. It sounded as I hoped it would, and they played it at exactly the right tempo.'

They stood in the Cathedral and brought each other up to date for fifteen to twenty minutes.

'Everything has been fine, except we have missed your playing, Anton. But we've had trouble at the parish church. A gang of thugs broke in one night, about six months ago, and desecrated the altar in a most disgusting way. They wantonly destroyed the main altarpiece, then stole some priceless artefacts from the vestry, including several silver communion goblets and a gold crucifix worn by the Bishop. Our problem now is, although some people saw them leaving, no one could identify them, so they are free to wreak havoc again.'

'I'm so sorry to hear that, Johann. The bastards!'

'I'm not sure about their parentage, Anton, but they cannot be Christian people.'

'I'll see you at the Votive Chapel tomorrow, Johann. I must go now.'

'For sure. You know it starts at 11 o'clock.'

'Yes, thanks.'

Anton went back to Irene's house. He felt he needed to relax before what could be a busy following day.

'Good to see you back, Anton. Have a beer and a rest. I'm busy cooking a special dinner for tonight. You will be in, won't you?'

'Yes, of course!'

Once he'd consumed his beer, Anton sat and closed his eyes. He hadn't felt more at ease for a long time.

'Wake up, Anton. Someone to see you!' said Irene, after he had been asleep for an hour and more.

He wiped the sleepiness from his face and looked up. Right in front of him were Betty and Moritz von Mayfield.

'It's so good to see you both.'

'And likewise, to see you, Anton,' said Moritz.

'Lovely Irene has invited us to have dinner with you both,' said Betty.

Anton told them about life in Vienna, its triumphs and disasters. He explained how Eduard Hanslick had changed from being an ally to an enemy of his music, presumably because he'd befriended Richard Wagner.

'I told you, Anton. Vienna is a hotbed of politics and intrigue. It's a wonder to me you can tolerate the place and the atmosphere there.'

'I have friends, Moritz. Most of them are students. Some are professors at the University and some colleagues at the Conservatorium.'

'How can you handle two jobs, Anton? You are so creative and are you still organist at the Imperial Court Chapel?'

'Sometimes I wonder myself how I cope. One thing though. I have a wonderful housekeeper who looks after me. She cooks me meals and looks after the house. Yes, my job at the Chapel is now permanent and they are paying me. So I'm not as poor as I used to be!'

'And what about performances of your works?' said Moritz.

He described the barriers he had to break through. He told them about the opposition from Dessoff and the cataclysmic performance of No. 3.

'Are you still playing with your orrery?' said Anton.

'That was one of the best Christmas presents I've ever had. I've played with it so many times, I've had to repair the turning mechanism!'

The von Mayfields stayed late enough, as far as Irene was concerned, and left for home at one in the morning.

'Sometimes they outstay their welcome, Anton.'

'At least they are good company. They enjoy your cooking and we all have a good time together.'

'That's true!'

The following morning, Anton told Irene not to prepare a meal in advance because he hoped there might be food at the celebration. He didn't know quite what to expect. On the way to the not even half built Cathedral, he wondered whether they might want him to play a part. He hoped, as no one had said anything, to be just one of the audience. By the time he arrived, at about a quarter to eleven, the Votive Chapel was already about half full. A priest took him to a seat reserved for him in the fifth row. Surely, in that position, he would just be an observer.

The priest whom Anton first met in Linz Cathedral and who guarded over him at the sanatorium oversaw the event.

'I would like you all to stand to welcome Bishop Franz Joseph Rudigier into our presence,' he said.

The Bishop entered. He looked the same to Anton as he did the last time he saw him. He had maintained his clean shaven look and short hair, ever since the first day they met.

The priest spoke about the Bishop's career. Anton was shocked to learn that he had spent time in prison for opposing new marriage laws. Then the priest led a prayer of thanksgiving, which was followed by Anton's Mass in D Minor. The choirmaster had restricted the accompaniment just to the harmonium.

Johann Schiedermayr and Ferdinand Moser, successor to Jodok Stülz as Provost of St Florian, also gave laudatory speeches. Provost Stülz had died eight years before.

Then they performed Anton's *Tota pulchra es*. This peaceful work concluded the ceremony. He hadn't expected this short piece would have such prominence.

Several priests escorted all who attended, at least seventy, out of the chapel to an outdoor meal they had set up in what would become the main floor of the cathedral. It looked an amazingly sumptuous spread. They had assembled it while the small congregation was attending the formal part of the ceremony.

'It's so good to see you, Tonerl!' said August Dürrnberger. 'What brings you here? Not just the performance of your Mass!'

'Good to see you, too, my old instructor! The Bishop invited me!'

'Go on. There's more to it than that, I'm sure!'

'You are right. There is. The Bishop commissioned me to write the piece they played at the end.'

'It was beautiful, Anton. So tell me more about life in Vienna?'

He and Anton helped themselves to a stein of Pilsner and a plate of food and sat at a table. Anton revealed his disappointing failures with Dessoff and the Vienna Philharmonic. He told him about his successes in London and France, and how much he appreciated Kathi. He described how distraught he was when almost all the audience walked out while he conducted his No. 3.

'My God, Anton. I've never heard of anything as drastic happening before!'

'Nor have I!'

'I hope you've fully recovered from it now.'

'I have. I still can't work out why it happened.'

'It sounds political to me. If Dessoff wouldn't perform it, maybe he made sure it would be a disaster if anyone else did.'

'It could be something like that. It's well known that I'm a Wagner supporter and there is a strong anti-Wagner movement in Vienna. There is no logic to that, either. The man is a brilliant composer and poet. His Ring Cycle of operas is a work of genius.'

'You've lost me there, Anton. Could you explain?'

'Before I do, let's replenish our glasses! And grab another piece of pie!'

Anton told him about the operas of the Ring. He talked about Hanslick and his opposition to his work. 'And before he knew I was a friend of Wagner, he too was a friend of mine. But sadly, no more!'

'What an appalling man. I don't know how these uncreative critics can sleep at night, after they have poured scorn on the works of you people who create music or opera.'

'I don't either. They are just unpleasant individuals. Hanslick isn't the only one!' He thought he'd stop there. 'By the way, I'm still using material from your theory of music book in my lectures at the Conservatory and the University.'

'Thank you for telling me. I'm glad it is of some use!'

'I loved that piece you wrote for me,' said Bishop Rudigier, as he approached Anton and August Dürrnberger. 'It is truly beautiful and so appropriate to be played in a Cathedral dedicated to the Virgin Mary.'

'I'm so glad you like it. Thank you for inviting me and programming my Mass into the ceremony.'

'It's a pleasure, Herr Bruckner. We so miss your organ playing, which we have sacrificed to your audiences in Vienna! I hope they are as appreciative there as we were here!'

'They are indeed, Your Grace.'

'I hope I'm not interrupting a private conversation.'

'Not at all,' said August. 'We are pleased you've joined us. And what a wonderful meal you provided for your guests!'

'So what are your career intentions, Your Grace? Will the Pope be moving you or do you think you will stay here?'

'It's interesting that you ask, Herr Bruckner. The Holy Father wrote to me about my anniversary. He said he has no plans to move me from Linz, but he would consider any request. I replied saying I am happy to serve the Diocese of Linz for as long as he is content for me to stay.'

'That's good,' said August. 'We don't want you to go!'

The Bishop laughed. 'Let's go for a beer,' he said.

The three of them topped up their glasses. By then, Anton was feeling happy and relaxed. He thought it might well be the beer that helped renew his friendships in Linz. Finding others to speak to, he struck up conversations with Karl Zappe and his wife, and Anton Storch, who had arrived from

Vienna. Talking, eating and drinking occupied him into the sunset. Then he said his farewells and returned to Irene's house.

The following day, he could hear a persistent knocking on his bedroom door. 'Wake up, Anton. You shouldn't sleep all day.'

He slowly regained consciousness. He realised he had slept naked. Looking around the room, he saw he had scattered his clothes on the floor, on the dressing table, and on the bed. Then he rubbed his head. He had a stinger of a headache. 'What's the time, Irene?'

'It's one o'clock in the afternoon. You were drunk when you got back last night!' she shouted through the door.

He dressed himself and went downstairs, expecting her to admonish him.

'Good to see you, at last,' she laughed. 'You were in a terrible state when you got back.'

'I can't remember a thing, Irene. Not from saying goodbye to all I met at the celebration. My mind is a complete blank from then. I hope I behaved myself, especially with you!'

'All you did was to give me a passionate hug and a kiss. You were in quite an excited state, but then you dashed upstairs and that was the last I heard from you until now!'

'I'm relieved I didn't hurt you or was unpleasant. Sorry for being drunk. I lost count of the number of steins of Pilsner I drank, thanks to Bishop Rudigier!'

'Don't worry, Anton. You are never unpleasant when you are drunk. I remember that Christmas with you and Moritz!'

Anton stayed one more night with Irene. He thanked her profusely for letting him stay and apologised again for his drunkenness. She laughed and kissed him on both cheeks. Then he travelled back to Vienna.

Kathi greeted him as he walked into the Hessgasse apartment at about 4 o'clock in the afternoon.

'Welcome home, Herr Bruckner. I hope you had a good time. How was the hotel Frankfort?'

'I ended up staying with my former landlady, Irene, who insisted I stay with her. So I felt I had to!'

'And the Bishop's celebration?'

'It was wonderful. I felt pleased they put my motet in pride of place, right at the end of the formal event. Then we had an outdoor party!'

'I've put a letter on your desk. It looks as if it's from a publisher. Well, it's a publisher's name on the envelope. Other than that, there's nothing more to tell you. Would you like me to prepare you a meal before I go?'

'Please don't worry, I fancy going to the Red Hedgehog tonight, just for a change.'

'See you tomorrow then.'

He went into the study to read the letter. It was from Theodor Rättig, the publisher, asking to see him about the score of his No. 3. He wrote a brief reply, giving dates when they could meet.

Anton soon returned to composing his String Quintet. He enjoyed writing it. It made such a change from writing symphonies and short religious works. He was well aware of Beethoven's late quartets and, while not attempting to compete with them, wanted to write a work of comparable achievement.

'I'm pleased to see you again, Herr Bruckner,' said Rättig, as he walked up to Anton, who was sitting at a table in the refectory. He was carrying a leather briefcase, from which he took a large publication. 'I would like to present you with this specially bound copy of your Symphony No. 3, the Wagner Symphony.'

'Thank you so much, Herr Rättig. I am so grateful to you.' He opened the volume and read the dedication to Wagner. 'I would have worded the dedication slightly differently, but it is fine. Thank you so much. You are one of the most generous people I know.' He stood up and shook hands with Rättig.

'That isn't all. Here is a copy of the piano transcription we have also published of the symphony, prepared by your student, Rudolf Krzyzanowski, and his friend Gustav Mahler. They wrote it for four hands.'

'My goodness, Herr Rättig. I am overcome with joy. I don't know what to say.' Anton looked into his coffee and had trouble suppressing a tear. 'They were among the dozen or so left after the mass exodus from the performance.'

'Yes, I know. I was also one of the dozen or so!'

'Of course, and I well remember your incredibly generous offer on the day, giving me much relief!'

'So what are your coming plans for composition?'

'I'm writing a String Quintet in F. It's coming along steadily. I shall soon embark on another symphony. My sixth.'

'Let me know if I can help you get it into print, Herr Bruckner,' he said, smiling. He turned and left the refectory.

Anton spent virtually all his free time composing his quintet. Kathi complained he spent too much time in his study and not enough relaxing. She even suggested he take a holiday. While not wishing to upset her, he pressed on with it, completing it in a little over six months, having started it in December, '78. What he didn't tell her was that he was also sketching out the scores of two highly religious works, '*Christus factus es*' and '*Os Justi*'.

He thought about when he should tell Hellmesberger about the Quintet. It was disappointing he hadn't once asked him about progress on it. What he did not want was an adverse reaction. Anton had written a modern example of the genre, which he wasn't sure Hellmesberger would like. It amused him to think the famous Hellmesberger quartet, amplified by a viola, may find it difficult but hopefully not impossible to play. He would not seek a special meeting with Hellmesberger, but tell when he next saw him at the Conservatory.

It was at least three weeks before Anton spoke to him and, much to his surprise, he asked Anton the direct question.

'How are you progressing with my quintet?' he said while seeing him walking down a corridor.

'I finished it about a month ago.'

'Why didn't you tell me?'

'Why didn't you ask?'

Anton caught him on the defensive. 'I'm sorry, Anton. I should have kept more closely involved.'

'Not a problem. You might have slowed me down. I've finished it quicker than I thought I would. Thank you for asking me as I've enjoyed writing it. It took me away from writing symphonies. And it sounds like an intimate chamber work, nothing like a scaled down piece for orchestra.'

'I'm dying to see the score. When can I?'

'I can bring it in tomorrow. It's my only copy.'

'Don't worry, I shall guard it with my life!'

Anton presented it to him, as promised.

'How long can I have it? I would like to read it thoroughly and show it to members of my quartet.'

'As long as you like. I'm writing a couple of new motets and am still revising my Symphony No. 4. So we can discuss possible changes, but I cannot guarantee I will make them quickly.'

'That makes sense. I won't keep it longer than necessary.'

'If you don't mind, could you please keep it under lock and key, in your safe, maybe?'

'That goes without saying. It will be in totally secure hands.'

Hellmesberger kept the score longer than Anton expected. It didn't worry him. He was going through a strongly creative period and didn't want to be interrupted by arguing about any changes Hellmesberger might want. After about three weeks, he invited Anton into his office.

'I want to tell you straight away what a brilliant piece you have written. It reminds us of Beethoven's late quartets but is totally different. It has your imprimatur stamped all over it.'

'Thank you, Josef,' he said, detecting from the tone of his voice that he would ask for some significant changes. He would tease him. 'You will be playing it as it is, then!'

'Well. Almost! We will play the first movement the second and the last but that curious elfin scherzo, stunning though it is, verges on the unplayable.'

'Really, even for a professional group like yours?'

'I'm afraid so,' he said, looking towards a picture on the wall to avoid Anton's testing eye. 'We wondered if you could change it to make it simpler.'

'So when do you plan to perform it?'

'Not sure.'

'In which case, I'll write a completely new movement which I may use in another work, if you aren't happy with that one either!'

'That sounds an especially elegant solution to me!'

Anton was relieved, disappointed, and challenged at the same time. That Hellmesberger's quartet was satisfied with three movements pleased him. He was less happy with their reaction to the scherzo. The challenge would be to write something new. He would thrive on it.

***

'You take no notice of me, Herr Bruckner,' said Kathi one evening, as he finished a dinner she had cooked him and was returning to his study.

'What do you mean?' he said, stopping to listen.

'I told you before, the rate you are working at the University and the Conservatory, and spending every spare moment composing, will make you ill. You don't want a heart attack and I don't want you to have one either.'

'I don't like disagreeing with you, Kathi, because I value you so much. Occasionally, creative people can't stop themselves from working every hour they can. Thank you for your concern but you need not worry. You feed me well and I sleep well. I can tell you now, I'm just about to start another symphony. My No. 6. So I could be even more active in the study!'

'Alright, have a heart attack!'

'You can't mean that, Frau Kathi!'

'No. Of course not. Sorry. I shouldn't have said that.'

'I forgive you!'

Active he was. He didn't begin then on an alternative scherzo but made a start on Symphony No. 6. He ploughed into writing it with all the energy he could muster, despite the performances up to then of only three of his symphonies. And all with him as conductor. He realised he was the type of person who no one could discourage, even after a major setback like the catastrophe of No. 3. Not always his symphonic starting point, he started with the first movement. Wisely, he did not inform the impatient Hellmesberger he had started No. 6 but merely said he hadn't begun a new scherzo.

Anton believed Kathi was right. He definitely deserved a holiday. Never had he taken a break of more than a week. His journeys to France and England didn't count. Nor did his visits to see Wagner and the Ring Cycle. So he started planning a long holiday which would start and end at St Florian, but extend as far west as Switzerland, and as far north as Munich.

'You are all talk, Herr Bruckner. You won't take a holiday! I just don't believe you!' said Kathi, in response to him outlining his plans.

'Believe what you like, Kathi. I'm going to do it. In fact, it will not be until the summer of '80 because I'm so frantically busy now and will be for some time to come. I've only just started No. 6 and I want to complete it before I go.'

She laughed. 'You'll have forgotten about it by then.'

He didn't see the point of upsetting her, so he dropped the subject.

Having spent more than six weeks on his No. 6, he decided to leave it in favour of the new scherzo and to make some further revisions to Symphony No. 4. He gave his boss priority, and spent two weeks of his spare time on the scherzo. He then took it to Hellmesberger.

'I've brought you an early Christmas present, Josef.'

'What do you mean?'

'Yesterday, I finished the new scherzo for my Quintet, or rather your Quintet!'

'Congratulations, Anton!'

'Thank you! Here it is.' He handed him the score. 'I've completely rewritten the scherzo but left the trio as it is.'

'Let me show it to the other members and I'll let you know what they think.'

'You'll notice that I've written it in the same key as the original version, but made it slower so your players will find it less technically challenging. Even an amateur quartet could play the thing!'

'Now, now, Anton! They are a serious group of professionals!'

'If they are that serious, they would be capable of playing the original! Let's see what they think of it! Have you any ideas about when to premiere it?'

'Not yet. We'll see!'

Anton enjoyed this brief exchange with Hellmesberger, from which he confidently felt he had come out on top. He didn't care which scherzo Hellmesberger's quartet wanted to play. He could use the new one for whatever purpose he chose. 'Intermezzo' he called it.

'Before you go, Anton, I have something interesting to tell you. I want to perform your Mass in D minor!'

359

'Well. I'm stunned. You are hesitating over the Quintet, but you want to perform the Mass. I have to say, I'm grateful though. Who will conduct it?'

'Could you, Anton? It will be next year on the sixth of June… '80, of course. I think we should include your beautiful *Locus iste*, and any other piece you choose.'

'Let's also play *Os justi*. That will fit well.'

'Accepted, Anton.'

'Oh, I've made some minor changes to the Mass, which we can easily incorporate into the playing parts.'

'I ought to ask you to sign a document in which you promise no more changes before the sixth of June. What you do with it afterwards is up to you!'

'I promise I won't even look at it!'

'Thank God!'

Anton sensed the thrill of his D minor Mass being performed again. He didn't ask Hellmesberger what caused the sudden desire to play it. Was it a reward for being so positive about writing the Quintet? Or had he heard about its successful performance, albeit in modified form, at Bishop Rudigier's anniversary? He would never know.

Anton could not stop fiddling with his Symphony No. 4, the 'Romantic'. Would it never satisfy him? Complex though it was, he still regarded it as a work which, could become popular. The finale of No. 4 strongly competed for his time with his No. 6, which he was dying to work on. The finale of No. 4 won.

***

'Good news, Kathi. They are going to perform my Mass in D minor at the Imperial Chapel on 6 June. I'll be conducting it. Would you and Bruno like to come? I'd love it if you did!'

'I'll ask him. I haven't heard it before but would very much like to.'

'We will be playing that motet I was writing about six months ago when you told me to go on holiday! It's called *Os justi*.'

'I'm sure I'll persuade Bruno!'

The performance of Anton's Mass would be the first of his works to be played in Vienna since the cataclysm of his Symphony No. 3, all but three years before. Since the reasons for the walkout of the audience were far from clear, he questioned what might happen on 6 June. The two major differences were all the works to be played were strongly religious and the Imperial Chapel would be the venue. Surely, no sensible audience would desert a performance there. He would find out on 6 June.

He started preparing for his holiday by writing to Ignaz Traumihler, the music director of St Florian to ask if he could stay there. Anton's love of the monastery was unbounded and he would spend as much time there as he could, not only to renew his many friendships but to play the famous organ.

As June 6 came closer, Anton's fear of what might happen increased until it reached its maximum the day before.

'Why do you look so worried, Herr Bruckner?' asked Frau Kathi.

'My concern is how the audience will react to my Mass, *Os justi* and *Locus iste.*'

'It won't be anything like what happened when you conducted Symphony No. 3, I'm sure. It's in the Imperial Court Chapel and no one will walk out, however much they dislike what they are hearing. You are becoming quite a worrier!'

'If you'd been at that terrible event, you'd be more sympathetic.'

'Are you saying I'm insensitive?'

He could detect a row in the offing, so did his best to calm her. 'Not at all, Kathi. You are the most sympathetic and sensitive person I know. All I'm saying is that it was one of the worst experiences of my life and I don't want a repeat. I cannot expect you to feel the same as I do because it was my symphony that they walked out of. I admit, I was wrong to say you'd be more sympathetic and I apologise.'

'Apology accepted, Herr Bruckner. I won't walk out! I'm grateful to you for the way you treat me. Many men don't even acknowledge their housekeeper.'

'But you are my major source of conversation, Kathi!'

Well into the night, to take his mind off the following day, he finished the new, dramatic finale of No. 4. I think that completes it, he thought, not knowing whether he would change it again.

Anton, the choir, the soloists and the organist had put a huge effort into four rehearsals. He was determined to conduct the best possible performance.

As the last note of *Os justi* faded into silence, the audience gave the performance a tumultuous round of applause. They cheered, stamped their feet and many shouted encore. From the rostrum, Anton bowed deeply to the audience, then lifted his arm towards the choir and players. They bowed, too. He wondered what to do next. Yes, he'd play an encore. '*Os justi*. Please repeat it!' he shouted to the singers and players.

Another round of applause, a more respectful one, hailed the ending. He bowed again.

Josef Hellmesberger rushed up to him on the stage. 'Congratulations, Anton. After that, I have to look up to you. You are not only a brilliant composer but you can conduct brilliantly as well.'

'Thank you, Josef. You are too kind to me!'

Anton could not have been more relieved that the performance and the reaction of the audience, not to say Hellmesberger's, had been so ecstatic. He allowed himself the thought that he and his compositions were becoming accepted in Vienna. He wondered how long it would last. Could he persuade the authorities to perform his No. 4? He wrote again to William Tappert to seek a performance in Munich, in case they refused it again in Vienna.

***

'Congratulations, Herr Bruckner,' said Kathi, as she brought in his breakfast. 'We enjoyed the performance of your Mass and your two motets. It was a lovely experience.'

'I'm so glad you liked it.'

'Like it? It completely overcame us. The best performance we've heard of your music.'

'I remember your doubts about my Symphony No. 2!'

'Only because I found it noisy in places. But this was different. The whole concert was so peaceful and beautiful! Apart from some of the audience!'

'What you are saying is music to my ears!'

'I'm glad too, Herr Bruckner! So what about this holiday you've been talking about?'

'I just need a few weeks to finish my college work and then I'll go. Probably by train. First stop St Florian.'

'I'll pack and make a sandwich you can take.'

Chapter 26
1880 - 1882 A surprise

Ignaz Traumihler welcomed him into the sanctity and peace of St Florian. To Anton, the attraction was an escape, a refuge from the pressures of Vienna and its strenuous, unreasonable politics. To be at St Florian seemed like being behind the ramparts of an impenetrable castle, a heaven on earth. He loved being there and would love it just as much, even without Vienna and its tribulations.

They shook hands at the door of Ignaz' office. 'It is so good to see you, Anton. How is life in Vienna?'

'I was hoping you wouldn't ask!'

'Sorry, I mentioned the place!'

'I'm jesting of course! I was not enjoying it but things have just taken a major step in the right direction!' Anton told him about the debacle over his No. 3 but how his D minor Mass and two motets, including *Os justi*, had triumphed spectacularly.

'I'm so pleased for you, Anton. It seems to me your struggles there are bearing fruit.'

'Let's hope so! I'm more optimistic now. The proof will be the playing of my No. 4 whenever that will be. Oh, and my Quintet!'

He told him about the Quintet and Hellmesberger's reluctance to play it.

'I must thank you for dedicating *Os Justi* to me. I don't deserve such elevation. That calming work will be played many times in the future, so you have given me a place in posterity!'

'I've brought you a copy of it,' he said as he took a small manuscript from his shoulder bag.

'You are kind, Anton. Here, let me see.' Ignaz opened it and read it, concentrating deeply. 'It's shorter than I expected it to be. Only the nine lines from Psalm 37 and the Hallelujah.'

'That's right. I could add a few lines, if you would like me to?'

'Could you please, Anton? It would be more profound then.'

'Certainly!'

'We must go for a stein of beer, Anton. Come on, leave your things here and let's go.' They walked to the Sparrow Inn, where Ignaz bought the first round.

Anton spent a full week at St Florian. While there, he added another short verse to *Os justi*. He spent much of it playing the organ, taking to the priests and singing in the choir, as well as much time at the Sparrow Inn, with whomever would go for a beer with him. Ignaz listened intently to his organ play.

'My goodness, Anton. There cannot be many organists who make up their own version of a Bach Toccata and Fugue and improvise on it for a full hour. I'm amazed and deeply appreciate it! You should write it down!'

'I've tried, but I can't. I get completely lost in the improvisation and couldn't remember what I've played if I wanted to!'

Feeling relaxed and happy with life, Anton took a cabriolet to Linz and from there travelled by train to Oberammergau, to see the passion play. It was due to be produced that year, ten years having elapsed since the previous performance. By simple forgetfulness, he had made no arrangements to stay and couldn't find anywhere vacant as so many had booked in advance. He eventually found a farmhouse, right on the edge of the town, so far from the theatre, that he had to go there by cab.

The play totally enthralled Anton. Its religiosity suited him immensely, as did the plot and the superb performance of the actors. He was, on the first day of the two-day performance, even more enchanted by a young girl who played a daughter of Jerusalem. What fascinated him most was that, while on stage, she seemed to look directly at him when he looked at her, as if there was a mutual attraction. That night, in bed, he couldn't take his mind off her. She acted well and was stunningly beautiful, at least in his image of her. He became determined to meet her and to explain his intense liking for her.

Luckily for him, she appeared on stage on the second day. He could hardly concentrate on the plot as he was working out how he could meet her. A solution dawned on him. He waited at the theatre door for the performers to emerge. Here she is, he said to himself, smiling with joy.

'My name is Anton Bruckner. I am a composer from Vienna. I was totally absorbed by your brilliant performance. So I thought the least I could do was to meet you, to tell you what a wonderful actress you are, especially for such a young person.' She looked completely puzzled by the attention of this much older individual.

'Thank you, Herr Bruckner. Pleased to meet you, too. A composer? I've never met one before. I saw you looking at me, so I spent some time looking back at you!'

'In that case, I am honoured! Would you tell me your name, please?'

'Marie Bartl.'

'Well, Marie. Would you mind if I escorted you home?'

'I'd be pleased if you did, Herr Bruckner. The streets around here can be quite dangerous for a young girl. My aunt usually meets me, but she is out with friends tonight.'

'So where do you live? You'll have to lead the way!'

'I'm staying with my aunt as my family live some distance away, and it takes too long to get here on time.'

They soon reached her aunt's house. Anton didn't know where he was and hoped he could find his way back to the farmhouse before nightfall.

'You must come in. At least, for a drink.'

She invited him to sit in the lounge while she made a cup of coffee. He wondered where this could lead. There was no doubt in his mind he was falling in love with this gorgeous girl. That he was single, he had yet to reveal, but would love to have such an attractive wife. He would have to consider his tactics.

'Here you are, Herr Bruckner,' she said, as she put the coffee onto a little table next to where he was sitting. 'So what do you do as a composer?'

He told her about the range of works he composed.

'My goodness, you write quite a variety of music from religious to not religious.'

'Yes, and I also play the organ!'

'Really?'

'Yes. Some of my admirers call me the best organist in Europe, but I'm too modest to agree with them.'

'What makes them think that?'

'It's probably because I've played in France and in London. By invitation.'

'We have a good organ in our church in Oberammergau. If we went there tomorrow, could you play it for me?'

'Yes, Marie, but only if we have the permission of the priest and there is someone there to operate the pump.'

'I could do that!'

'I don't think so. There is probably someone there who could!'

'We'll find out!'

Their conversation continued until about 11 o'clock, when Marie's aunt suddenly appeared in the lounge. 'Whoever is this gentleman, Marie?' said the grey haired lady, puzzled by Anton's presence.

'This is a composer called Anton Bruckner, Aunt.'

'Pleased to meet you,' she said, looking distinctly unsure.

'I'm equally pleased to meet you. Please, let me explain,' he said, reddening slightly. He told her how he met Marie, why he brought her home and where he was staying.

'That's very kind of you,' she said, still looking quizzically at Anton. 'It's gone 11 o'clock now, Marie. Don't you think it's your bedtime?'

The aunt eventually accepted Anton's account and asked if he knew his way back to the farm. He had to admit he hadn't the vaguest idea.

'We have a spare room so you could sleep here,' she said.

This suggestion surprised him. It seemed the aunt was beginning to like him and perhaps encouraging a relationship between him and her niece. 'But my nightshirt is at the farmhouse. So are my wash things.'

'My husband passed away a number of years ago, so you could use his.'

'In which case, I graciously accept your kind offer.'

So Anton experienced something completely new. Of all the young women he had fallen in love with over the years, he had never slept the night in one of their houses. He thought staying there might well bring him and Marie closer together.

At seven o'clock the following morning, there was a firm knock on his bedroom door. He woke up. Not wanting anyone to see him in his nightshirt, he pulled the bedclothes over himself and shouted. 'Who is it?'

'Me, Marie's Aunt. Breakfast will be served in half an hour. Would you like omelette, mushrooms and ham?'

'Yes please. I'd be very grateful.'

'Here's a bowl of hot water. I'll leave it outside your room.'

Not only had she brought the water but provided him with shaving soap and a razor, presumably last used by her husband.

Much to Anton's surprise and delight, Marie kissed him on both cheeks before they sat for breakfast. He thought, unlike most of his previous attempts with women, this one was falling in love with him. Or was he reading too much into her friendly attitude? He would wait patiently, he thought, to see how the relationship developed. The absence of her parents inspired a different approach. He would not even mention marriage and discuss it, only if she raised it.

'Are you still willing to go to the local church to play the organ, Herr Bruckner?'

'Of course.'

'Good. Let's go straight after breakfast, shall we?'

'That will be fine.'

Marie and Anton walked the few hundred yards to the church. He thought of holding hands with her, but decided against the idea, not wanting to appear too fond of her. They entered the church and Marie started searching for a priest. She found him in the confessional, so returned to Anton, who was sitting in a pew waiting.

'Sorry to interrupt, Herr Bruckner. I've found the priest who is taking a confession. I'll try him again in a minute.'

'Fine, Marie.'

After a few more minutes, Marie and the priest arrived to speak to Anton.

'This is my new friend, Reverend. His name is Anton Bruckner and he would like to play our organ. Would that be possible, please?'

'Anton Bruckner, the well-known composer?'

'I don't know how well-known he is!'

'I'm not very well known,' said Anton. 'But one day, I might be, hopefully, while I'm still alive!'

'Yes, Herr Bruckner can play, of course. The calcant is available. Give us a couple of minutes and you can start.'

'Could you lead me up to the organ loft, Marie?'

'Of course. I know exactly how to get to it. Follow me.'

As Anton was making himself comfortable at the console, he asked her what she would like him to play.

'Anything you like. But could you play something with loud parts and some which are quieter?'

'I certainly can. We'll start with something quiet.'

He played the Bach Fantasia and Fugue in C minor and improvised on it for ten minutes.

'Wonderful,' she said as he closed the piece. 'It sounds so peaceful. I've never heard it before, but I like it a lot.'

'Let's try something with more power.' He then dived into his version of the Toccata and Fugue in D minor and another set of improvisations. She smiled at him and mimicked applause as he played.

'That was wonderful, Herr Bruckner. Are you going to play more?'

'I think that's enough. I don't want us to outstay our welcome. Let's go for a coffee. Is there somewhere near?'

'Yes, I'll lead the way.'

Anton started the discussion at the café. 'So how do you see your future, Marie?'

'That's a hard question. I suppose I'll settle down and get married to some lucky chap!'

'Any idea who that could be?'

'Not at the moment. I'm only seventeen, so a few years too young to marry!'

As she had raised the subject, he thought he'd raise the question. 'Would you consider an older man?'

'That's an even tougher question! Of all the men I've met, you are the most interesting. I really like you, Herr Bruckner, but I'm not sure I would want to marry you.'

'I understand completely. I am single and have never been married. At present, I am not looking for a wife, but we could keep in contact and see how things develop between us. You are an amiable person and I like you a lot.

Liking can turn into loving! If we felt we could not become closer, we could remain just friends.'

'That sounds perfect for me, Herr Bruckner. I'll ask the waitress for a piece of paper and something to write with.'

They exchanged addresses, and Anton paid for the coffee. Marie kissed him on both cheeks before they parted. Anton found his way back to the farmhouse and knocked on the door.

'Where in hell's name have you been? We waited up half the night for you!' said the farmer.

This wasn't the reception he expected. He apologised profusely and explained what had happened.

'That's no excuse. Once you got her home, you should have come back here. Pack your things. I refuse to have you staying here another night. I'm going to charge you for the three nights you should have stayed and one more.'

'No, you're not,' said Anton. 'I'll willingly pay for the three nights but I won't accept paying a one night fine, just because you say so!'

Anton's heart was racing as he packed his case. He went back downstairs.

'If you don't pay for four nights, I won't allow you to stay here again.'

'You can shove your lodgings up your ass,' he said, paid for the three, picked up his case and left.

Soon recovering from the reaction of the farmer, he travelled via Munich and Lindau to the Rhine Falls, in Switzerland and on to Zurich. He loved Switzerland. The magnificent scenery, the sheer height of the mountains and the clean freshness of the lakes, Lucerne and Geneva in particular, completely overwhelmed him. In Zurich he thrived on playing the magnificent organ at the cathedral. At Lucerne, an admirer of his organ performance invited him to play in a recital for which he would choose the programme. He was enchanted, not only by these wonderful places and the friendly people he met, but by the thought of Marie Bartl. His conclusion was that he loved her and hoped she would reciprocate in an exchange of correspondence. He would have to be patient and not distracted from his other activities, not least from completing his Symphony No. 6.

Having visited Bern and Munich again, he returned to Vienna via St Florian to see Ignaz Traumihler again.

'So, have you had a pleasant holiday, Anton?'

He explained where he had been, the people he had met, how stunningly beautiful he found Switzerland, and about the organ recital he had given in Lucerne.

'It all sounds wonderful. I should visit Switzerland one day! And in ten years, see the passion play!'

Anton remained for only two days at St Florian. He wanted to stay longer, but he had to return to Vienna for work and resume his composing.

After more than a month away, Anton arrived home. His lonely work began on the first movement of No. 6, which he completed on 27 September, just before the start of term.

'So you're back, Herr Bruckner,' said Kathi, three mornings after his arrival. 'Good to see you. How did it all go? Oh, there are some letters for you... from Oberammergau!'

'Likewise, it's good to see you, Kathi. The holiday was wonderful. I feel completely rested. I have seen no letters.'

'I'm sorry. I put them in the front drawer of your desk.'

'Good idea,' he said, not showing he was a little cross that she hadn't left them on the hall table. 'I'll read them later.' He then told her about the Oberammergau play, the organ playing in various places and socialising with Ignaz Traumihler in St Florian. He hesitated about mentioning Marie until he had read the letters.

'I've brought nothing for your breakfast so I'll just go shopping. I'll be back in twenty minutes.'

Anton went into the study. Marie must have posted the first letter the day he left. It was short and very much to the point.

Dear Anton,
It was a pleasure to meet you in Oberammergau. I enjoyed your company and thank you for playing those lovely organ pieces in our church. I hope we meet again soon.
Yours sincerely, Marie

He smiled as he read it. It was in the right tone for him and showed her fond friendship. She was true to her word and had written to him, as promised. The second letter, much to his delight, was more effusive.

Dear Anton,
I hope my first letter arrived safely. You told me about your other travels, so I'm not disappointed you have not replied yet. I've been thinking about you a lot since you left and find that I like you very much. I am several years too young for marriage, but I may be old enough in a few years' time. I wonder if we would make a happy couple.
Yours sincerely, Marie x

Anton's face lit up when he read the last sentence and the kiss. He had been in this position many times before, when a woman of Marie's age had expressed a love for him, not long after to be bitterly disappointed. So he restrained his feelings the best he could, even though he loved her. He picked up a pen and wrote a reply. Expressing similar feelings to those of hers, he also asked what sort of couple they would make. So he would allow her to take the lead in the development of their relationship.

'Before I forget, Kathi,' he said, as she returned with a basket of food. 'Let me give you this letter. Please post it on your way home?'

She took the letter and read the address. 'Marie Bartl?' she smiled. 'Not another of your possible wives? From what you've told me, you've had several disappointments, but you manage well without one.'

For a second or two, Anton didn't know quite how to respond. Then he neutrally explained the Oberammergau connection.

'How old is she?'

She had asked the one question he hoped she wouldn't ask.

'Seventeen.'

'Far too young for you, Herr Bruckner!'

'For now, maybe. But who knows where this correspondence may lead, in two years or ten years' time?'

'I can only wish you the best, Herr Bruckner. I'd be delighted to work for the two of you! I'll post your letter!'

In the November, a few months after Anton had completed the first movement of No. 6 and had started on the second, Hellmesberger's secretary came to his office to deliver a note. Before he opened it, he wondered what brand of misery it contained that Hellmesberger wouldn't deliver in person. Then he realised the author had written his name in an exceptionally elegant, unfamiliar hand, not the scribble of his boss. He slit it open. Hans Richter wanted to see him at the Friends of Music Hall to discuss performing his No. 4. He apologised for giving Anton only one date, 17 December, '80 at noon. A wide smile broke out.

In the interim, Anton continued working on No. 6. He surprised himself by completing the slow movement in just under two months. How would he handle the coming meeting with Richter, he wondered. Would he accept any changes Richter might want to make to the score? It was Anton's symphony, and he believed it was now finished. So he would not want it changed. Nor would he want only one or two selected movements to be played. He concluded that he'd listen carefully to any suggestions Richter might make and then respond.

On the day, Anton asked a receptionist if she could tell him where Hans Richter's office was located.

'It's along that corridor and is the second door on the left,' she said, pointing. Anton followed her instruction and knocked on the door.

'Come in,' was the voice from inside. Anton entered.

'Good afternoon, Herr Bruckner,' said Richter. 'Welcome to my modest office.' Anton immediately saw it was the one previously occupied by Felix Dessoff, Richter's predecessor. 'Please sit down.'

Anton sat opposite him at his desk. 'Good afternoon to you, Herr Richter. I'm so grateful to you for offering to perform my fourth symphony, especially after the awful happenings at my third.'

'You didn't deserve that. Nor did you deserve that odd attitude of the orchestra. As you know, Richard and I read the score and thought it a masterpiece. But that was in the past. So let's talk about your fourth. First, I'll obviously need your score. By the way, let's be on first-name terms!'

'I have it in my briefcase.' He lifted it out and put it on the desk. 'Please tell me why you want to perform it?'

'A new educational institute is being formed, called the German School Association. They have asked me to hold a concert they will sponsor and have specifically asked for a new work to have its premiere there. So it will be their premiere and the new work's premiere, so to speak. The obvious choice, to me, was your fourth, so here we are!' he beamed.

'I'm so grateful, Hans. You will be the first person other than me to conduct one of my symphonies!'

'What an honour for me, Anton. Tell me, why dedicate it to Prince Konstantin of Hohenlohe-Schillingsfürst? Seems a strange but interesting dedication!'

'It's quite a story. When Prince Konstantin took over the Imperial Chapel, he wanted the repertoire changed to more modern, less dusty music. His deputy, my late friend Johann Herbeck, suggested they incorporate my D minor Mass, and the Prince agreed, so that's why I dedicated it to him!'

'I like that, Anton. Excellent decision! I'll get the orchestral parts produced and then we'll organise the first rehearsal. I'll let you know when it is and you can attend, if you wish.'

'Thank you. Yes, I'll come if I'm free. Don't you want to read the score?'

'No. I'll play it exactly as you've written it... unless we find any errors! Even then, your intentions will be clear. Do you have questions, Anton?'

'None. I only want to thank you again for choosing to perform it.'

'It's a pleasure.'

371

Anton smiled with joy and achievement. Despite his failure with Wilhelm Tappert, this was a crowning moment. It was to be performed on its merits alone. He had not spoken to anyone in the Viennese circle about performing it, mainly because he thought they would confound him by refusals, but a miracle had happened. Someone other than him would perform it and he had spent no time promoting it there, other than at that test rehearsal for recent works, some five years before. And what a farce that was.

**

'I've achieved the impossible, Kathi,' he said, as he stepped into the kitchen while she was finishing preparing his evening meal.

'Not much is impossible for you, Herr Bruckner. So what have you achieved?' she said, wiping her hands with a towel.

'My Symphony No. 4 is to be performed here in Vienna!' he said, smiling with excitement.

'What? After they turned it down at that test rehearsal. I remember how upset you were.'

'This is a completely different story.' He told her about Hans Richter and what he had said.

'Congratulations! This sounds much more like it. I like Herr Richter already. Sit at the dining table. Your dinner is ready.'

**

Richter and the orchestra set a date in January for the first rehearsal. It was not in term time, so Anton went along.

'I'm glad you could make it,' said Richter, who came down from the stage to meet Anton in the auditorium. 'Would you mind if I introduced you to the orchestra?'

'Not at all,' said Anton. 'I can see some members I recognise already. Arthur Nikisch and Herr Popper. I think his first name is David.'

'Yes, you are right. It's good you know some. I'll introduce you and then we will begin.'

'Thank you, Hans.'

Richter stood on the rostrum and banged his baton on the music stand. 'Good afternoon, gentlemen. We are rehearsing one work, today. Anton Bruckner's fourth symphony. We will play it at the German School Association concert in February. Many of you will have seen Herr Bruckner sitting in the fifth row of the auditorium.' He turned to face Anton. 'Welcome to this rehearsal, Herr Bruckner. We are deeply honoured by your presence.' He turned back to the orchestra. 'Now let's begin.'

On Richter's count of three, they started. It opened with the tremolo on the strings. Then a four note horn call, a reveille, introduced the first theme group.

Anton could feel the hairs rising on his neck at the sounds he had created. No other symphony started like this one. Then the next theme of this group, an emphatic statement of his one, two; one two three rhythm, which led into the second, song-like group. A variation on a theme from the first group began the third. Richter stopped abruptly at a point in the development. 'No! No! No! That brass chorale is too laboured. Follow my conducting, if you will! Start again at the beginning of the chorale. That's better! Well done!'

Anton admired the way Richter combined criticism with praise. The rehearsal took about an hour and a half, after which the orchestra applauded their conductor. Richter beckoned Anton, who stood up and bowed. The orchestra, much to Anton's surprise, were just as enthusiastic as they applauded him. What a contrast with their reaction to his No. 3 and the test rehearsal of this one.

As Richter stepped down from the platform and walked towards him, Anton took a thaler coin from his purse. 'We may need one other rehearsal, Anton, near the performance day, but that went well, don't you think?'

'They impressed me, Hans. Please take this and buy yourself a beer.' He pressed the coin into Richter's hand.

Anton smiled and looked him in the eye, only to see some tears forming. 'I shall treasure this coin as long as I live, Anton! Thank you so much!' Embarrassed by his own reaction, Richter turned and left.

***

On 21 February, Kathi entered the apartment and applauded as soon as she stepped into the hall. 'Your symphony was wonderful, Herr Bruckner!' she shouted in case he was still in his bedroom.

He emerged from the kitchen clutching a glass of water. 'Oh, I'm so pleased you liked it!'

'So did Bruno. We both loved the hunting themes. I recognised much of it from you playing it on the piano! The best part was the audience. I couldn't get over them applauding and giving you standing ovations at the end of each movement… and you had to appear on stage four or five times after each one! Bruno and I joined in, of course!'

'I felt delighted, Kathi. I regard it as my biggest triumph yet. It was a victory for me. I was nearly in tears of joy walking home. At the start, I was nervous, wondering if anyone would walk out halfway through. But the reaction of the audience … including you… at the end of the first movement put an end to that. I won't be changing that symphony again!'

'No! Please don't, Herr Bruckner.'

Anton thrived on the success of the performance. Suddenly, he felt successful as a symphonist. He had not felt happier since his time in England when they carried him at shoulder height around the Crystal Palace. He felt he could now forget about the hideous reaction to his No. 3, which he still could not fathom. His students at the University stood and applauded him as he came into his class. Hans Rott praised the complete work and especially the finale. Josef Schalk said it was a work of genius and encouraged him to continue writing symphonies. His younger brother, Franz, said he felt the same and that he would write a symphony one day.

'Congratulations on your major success,' said Josef Hellmesberger, when he saw him, just over a week later. 'Everyone loved your symphony. You have truly arrived as a composer of the genre. Everyone in the audience was ecstatic. They all loved it, except one person!'

'Let me guess, Eduard Hanslick!'

'You are right. So you haven't seen his review?'

'No!'

'He says, "We are very happy with the success of a work which we fail to understand".'

'I still fear him, but the reaction of the audience meant only he could write something as sarcastic as that. Changing the subject, when is your quartet going to play my Quintet? You commissioned it, after all!'

'Hmm… I'm still not ready, Anton. Like you, I fear Hanslick.'

'So you are not going to play it?'

'Not yet, and I'm not sure when. So please don't ask!'

Anton could not express his disappointment without offending Hellmesberger. He couldn't afford seriously to annoy him because of his position of power.

**

'I have an idea for a new religious work, Kathi, so you may be hearing some boisterous but hymn like tunes from my piano. It won't be a sign that I'm unhappy. Quite the opposite! I haven't written a large religious composition since back in the 60's and I have this sudden desire to write one!'

'So you must have finished your new symphony. I'm getting lost with the numbers!'

'You mean No. 6? I'm in the middle of the third movement but I'm going to stop there and start this new work!'

'Sometimes I don't understand you, Herr Bruckner. You've spent months on that No. 6 and now you want to stop and start something else!'

'I just have this raging, uncontrollable desire to do it. I have no choice. It's like an instruction from deep in the universe, far beyond the stars. I have to obey it!'

'Is it another Mass?'

'No. My *Te Deum*!'

'Why that?'

'I'm in the right mood to write it, Kathi. You know, the words are so bright and affirmative. And there is a St Florian connection.' He didn't trouble Kathi with the story of how St Augustine was involved with the writing of this ancient hymn. 'I feel so good after the triumph of my No 4 that I want to compose it now, after having it in my mind for years! And I must obey that voice from the end of the cosmos!'

'Sometimes you say some strange things, Herr Bruckner!'

Anton worked hard on this new work. He spent less than a day working out its structure. It would be in five sections and start with the *Te Deum Laudamus* which would begin with a dramatic, blazing celebration in C major with the orchestra and choir. It would end in a dazzling triumph with the *In Te, Domine speravi.* He soon completed the first draft of what he would regard as one of his most important, if not, the most important of his religious works. He would return to it later, but resume work on his No 6, before taking a summer holiday.

***

'Please pack a bag, Kathi. I'm going to St Florian for a week.'

'Good for you, Herr Bruckner! You deserve a break. I'll tell Bruno. I'll say we deserve a week off, too. Is it alright if I don't come to the apartment for a week?'

'Yes, Kathi. You have a good break, too.'

As he expected, Ignaz Traumihler welcomed Anton with open arms. He said he was hoping, if not dying, to hear him give a public recital on the famous St Florian organ, which was the one most familiar to Anton, of all those he ever played. Anton told him he'd be thrilled, and Ignaz arranged it for the Wednesday. Unbeknown to Anton, Ignaz had some posters printed and advertised the event in the town and elsewhere.

Anton played at his best. He dispensed with the familiar Bach pieces and played other works and improvised on them. One was *Germanenzug*, another, much to Ignaz's delight, was *Os justi*. He played pieces from his No 3 to No 6 and improvised on them. Finally, he played parts of his Mass in F minor, a piece which would always be close to his heart.

The audience applauded, stamped their feet and asked for an encore. He accepted and, from memory, played the first two parts from the sketch of his *Te Deum*, which was greeted by another colossal round of applause.

Ignaz and Anton ended the day in the Sparrow Inn. Anton told him he still had work to do on his No. 6. He said it would be an honour to finish it at St Florian.

'Tell me about it,' said Ignaz.

'It's totally different from anything I've written before. It is simple and easy to listen to. Of course, there is tension and excitement in it, but it makes fewer demands on the listener than my No. 5. That one is complex and builds up to a huge climax in the finale, but my No. 6 is different.'

'Is it in four movements, like your others?'

'Exactly. That is my ideal structure for a symphony. Nothing else works. Fewer movements and there is something missing. More and it would be extravagant and overstated. Most audiences would struggle with more than four, especially with other works in the programme!'

'Can you tell me more?'

'It's a cheerful symphony which takes off in A major, but uses other keys on the way. It starts with an enigmatic, repeated variation of my one, two; one two three figure which turns into a bright, confident, first theme. The movement rolls along happily, inverting and varying the bright starting tune, and shifts to a gently falling, quite complex second theme. Then the slow movement. I've made this quite majestic without being over heavy. A plaintive oboe picks up part of that earlier complex tune, so there is a clear connection between movements. The scherzo follows. This is much softer, less rumbustious than some of my other scherzos and has a trio, which is a dialogue between pizzicato strings, the horns and the woodwind. The last movement is also unlike any of my others. It starts with a confident, pretty downward theme which is another variation on the second theme of the first movement. Its crowning glory will be the reappearance of that cheery, bright theme which starts the symphony off. And that's the symphony in words!'

'It sounds wonderful, Anton. I'd love to hear it!'

'I played the opening theme on the organ yesterday, so you've already listened to an extract!'

'Do you have much to write to finish it?'

'No, just the last maybe fifty bars of the finale, most of which is already in my head! I'll finish it in a day or two!'

Anton fulfilled his prediction and completed it the day before he returned to Vienna.

***

'Welcome back, Herr Bruckner. I hope you had a wonderful holiday!' said Kathi, as she came in the day after Anton arrived back.

'Really relaxed,' he said. 'And you'll love to know I finished my No. 6!'

'Well done!'

'Did you have a holiday with Bruno?'

'We didn't go anywhere to stay, but we had some nice days out in the Vienna parks, did some walking up to the vineyards, and spent some time at home. Oh, and Bruno bought me a new dress!'

'You sound very relaxed! And good for Bruno!'

'Thank you. I suppose you'll start another symphony soon?'

'I want to get that Quintet performed, of course. But yes, I'm ready to start another one. I must wait for the ink to dry on No. 6 first!'

***

Anton suddenly awoke. It was a dream. He jumped out of bed and, nightshirt still on, rushed into his study. With sleepy eyes, he grabbed a sheet of music paper, dipped his pen into the ink, and started writing. That theme he heard in his dream had to be put on paper before he forgot it. Those twenty-one bars would form the opening of his Symphony No. 7. He would return it as soon as he could.

Over the coming weeks, he thought long and hard about getting his String Quintet performed. He knew many musicians and wondered if he could persuade a group of them to play it. Then, in a lightning flash, an interesting idea occurred to him. He would have to wait for the following day, when he was teaching at the University.

'Ladies and gentlemen, I have a little proposal for you. First, my head is still ringing with the praise you piled upon me over my fourth symphony, now six months ago. My new idea is this. I have spoken to you a number of times about my String Quintet in F. I'm sure you remember, I used some of the scherzo as an example. Would any of you like to form a quintet and give the work its premiere? Because Professor Hellmesberger commissioned it, I'm sure he would wish to arrange for the first performance of the whole work, so I would like you to play only the first three movements. I hope that seems reasonable. If you did, it would still be a premiere!'

Several hands went up. Anton grinned.

'I would be delighted to help,' said Josef Schalk.

'So would I,' said little brother Franz.

'I know Julius Winkler whose friends often form a quartet and play for the Academic Wagner Society,' said Josef.

'Of course,' said Anton. 'Don't they play in private in the Bösendorfer Hall?'

'They do,' said Franz. 'Sometimes I play for them.'

'So, what do we do now?' said Anton.

'I'll speak to Julius,' said Josef.

'Brilliant. I'm pleased to have such helpful students! You could point out to him they would be remembered forever. Those who play in a premiere always are!'

Days later, Josef Schalk spoke to Anton. Julius Winkler had spoken to his colleagues and said he'd enjoy playing the three movements of the Quintet at a premiere. The only issue was the cost of getting copies of the score.

'That isn't a problem,' said Anton. 'You get them printed and I'll pay. I have the master copy and one Prof Hellmesberger borrowed, so you only need three. Say four, just in case!'

'Perfect, Herr Bruckner. That will be fine.'

Anton's face became a picture of misery when he noticed Eduard Hanslick at the dress rehearsal. He could anticipate another sarcastic, damning review. So he ignored the man, and did not even look in his direction.

The Winkler Quintet's public performance of the work enraptured Anton. The competence of the individuals staggered him, as did their skills in playing coherently together. He praised Josef and Franz at the first opportunity and took them out for a couple of well-deserved beers.

Much to Anton's delight, Hanslick did not comment on the performance.

***

'There are two letters for you, Herr Bruckner. One postmarked Oberammergau and the other from Bayreuth. I hope you'll excuse my nosiness!'

'I'll open them in the study, Kathi,' said a smiling Anton, still glowing from the Quintet performance.

He first opened the one from Oberammergau. Marie said she was still unsure about a long-term relationship. She said she felt flattered that someone as famous as Anton found her attractive as a possible wife. Frustratingly for him, it said she would let him know once she had decided. He thought her letter deserved only a short reply saying he looked forward to hers. I'll send her a photograph, he thought, one that makes me look young. Mildly irritated, he believed she was a lost cause.

The second letter was from the Academic Wagner Society. It announced that the first performance of Wagner's latest opera, Parsifal, was to take place in the July of '82. He wondered why it was necessary to give so much notice.

'Everything alright, Herr Bruckner?' said the inquisitive Kathi as he went into the kitchen for a drink. She noticed the stern look on his face.

'The woman in Oberammergau still doesn't know what she wants. She says she's flattered to be attracted by a famous composer, which I'm not really, and will let me know in the future what she decides. I've more or less given up hope. Anyway, I'll send her a photograph of me looking young!'

378

'I'd send her one of you looking old. That way you might get a quicker reply.'

Anton immediately saw the funny side, and they both chuckled together.

A few weeks later, Anton received a reply from Marie. It said he was too old for her. He was neither surprised nor disappointed.

The time soon came around for Anton to go to Bayreuth to see Parsifal. He decided not to tell Wagner he was coming and booked himself into a hotel near Wahnfried. Wagner saw him before a performance. Anton's smile half disappeared when he set eyes on the master who did not look well.

He grabbed Anton's hand and said, 'Don't worry! I myself will perform the symphony and all your other works.'

Thinking he was referring to No. 3, Anton replied. 'We've performed it, O Master. The less said, the better. A tragedy of the worst kind!'

'Don't be upset. I will perform it again, here in Bayreuth!'

'You are a miracle, O Master.'

Then he said, 'Have you heard "Parsifal"? How do you like it?'

While Wagner still held his hand, Anton knelt before him and kissed his. 'O Master. I worship you!'

'Be calm, Bruckner. Goodnight!'

Chapter 27
1882 - 1884 What next?

'Welcome home, Herr Bruckner,' said Kathi, as he appeared in the hall and put down his case. 'So, how did you enjoy Bayreuth?'

'It was good and bad. I'm really worried about Richard. He looked unwell and when I challenged him, he just said he was fine. I could have stayed with him if I wanted to, but didn't want to trouble him. So I stayed in a hotel near his house.'

'Was it good?'

'It was. Not too expensive and the food and beer were good. The room was small, but there was only one of me!'

'And what about the main event, Herr Wagner's opera?'

'It was brilliant. I absolutely love the Master's music. I listened intently and did my best to follow the story, but I focussed on every note, every chord of the music, so the plot was wasted on me! Sometime, I must read it. I followed the Ring Cycle but this one defeated me! So how about you, Kathi, and Bruno?'

'We are both in good health, thank you. You are limping. What's wrong?'

'My foot is playing me up. If it's not better in a few days, I'll go to see my doctor.'

'Don't let it get worse.'

'I won't. Probably all that walking in Bayreuth.'

***

Anton was keen to get back to teaching, both at the University and at the Conservatoire. He was as interested in seeing his students again as much as teaching them. He would always be grateful to the Schalk brothers for arranging for the three movements of his Quintet to be performed. His principal activity was working on his No. 7. By the end of the summer, he had completed the scherzo and trio.

He took the score into the Conservatoire to use any free time on it. In the December, while attending to the first movement, there was a knock on his office door. He shouted. 'Come in!'

'My name is Wilhelm Jahn. I am deputising for Hans Richter at the Vienna Philharmonic.'

'I'm pleased to meet you, Herr Jahn. To what do I owe the pleasure of your distinguished company?'

'I want to perform your new symphony, your number six.'

Anton almost fell out of his chair. 'No!'

'Do you mean you don't want us to play it?'

'No! No! It was my reaction! I am so surprised and totally delighted.' He walked over to Jahn and shook his hand vigorously.

'That's enough,' said Jahn, as he escaped from Anton's vice like grip. 'Your fourth symphony was such a success, we thought we should play the sixth as soon as we could. So we would like to play it in February, if you are happy with that.'

'Herr Jahn, I'm totally ecstatic. I do not have the score with me, but can get it for you.'

'Could you bring it to the concert hall tomorrow afternoon and leave it in reception?'

Anton thought about security. He didn't have another copy, but took a chance. 'I'll deliver it at, say, two o'clock, before my afternoon lectures.'

'I'll make sure the receptionist is there at two.'

***

He couldn't wait to get home.

'Some brilliant news, Kathi. The Philharmonic are going to play my sixth symphony.'

'Really? That's wonderful news, Herr Bruckner. How do they know about it? I don't remember you promoting it with them. Or did you today?'

'I don't know either. All I can think is that they must have found out from one of my students or from Professor Hellmesberger. I must have told him about it. The puzzle is why they chose that one and not my fifth.'

'You'll have to ask! When are they going to play it?'

'Sooner than you would think. In February, next year.'

Anton left the score at reception.

***

Late in the January, Anton came home from the university wanting to start on the adagio of No. 7 but wondered why he felt so sad. Then he realised. In the back of his mind was the thought that the Great Master, his friend Richard, would soon die. Suddenly, in one of those rare moments of creation inspired by sorrow, the first principal theme, in C sharp minor, came into his head. He almost tore a sheet of music paper in his rush to write it down.

Then another related idea struck him. While in Bayreuth listening to the premiere of Der Ring des Nibelungen, Anton had noticed the sound of an instrument he had never seen or heard before. It was a combination of a tuba and a French horn and produced a sound, somewhere in between but nearer the sound of the horn. According to those he asked about it, Wagner himself had commissioned the instrument for Der Ring to sound between a trombone and a French horn. It was called a Wagner tuba. In homage to his friend,

381

Richard, and as a symphonic innovation, he scored the first phrase of the C sharp minor theme for this instrument. So he had started the adagio.

***

Within a few weeks, he was sitting in the auditorium listening to the rehearsal of No. 6. He felt anonymous, as Jahn knew he was there, but didn't tell the orchestra. This wasn't the way Richter treated him at the rehearsal of No. 4. Jahn's style of conducting was different from Richter's. He seemed abrupt when asking the orchestra or an individual member to change something. Even when they re-played with perfection, he didn't utter a word of compliment.

He felt moderately pleased with the rehearsal. If he'd been conducting, he would have played the work just a little faster. Jahn stepped off the rostrum and walked straight into the wings. Anton half thought he would say something to him before he left. He stood up to leave when Jahn dashed over to see him.

'I hope you liked what you heard, Herr Bruckner. Any comments?'

'No, it was a fine rehearsal. I would have played it slightly faster, but it was coherent. I liked it.'

'Good. We will play it next week, on the eleventh of February. I hope we see you then!'

'You will indeed! Usual start time? 7.30?'

'Yes.'

He went home and continued working on the adagio of No. 7. The rehearsal gave him the inspiration for the second major part of the movement, the moderato theme in F sharp major. As he penned it, he knew he was writing a tune of shattering, uncompromising, ethereal beauty. He meant it to transcend all emotion. It was not sad, not happy, and represented nothing the human mind could describe or feel. It had a purity of its own. He worked it into a breath-taking climax, heralded by the Wagner tubas.

***

He sat in the front stalls. Jahn started Symphony No. 6, not at the beginning but with the second movement, the adagio. Anton had trouble controlling his anger. After Jahn had rehearsed the whole thing, he reasonably expected the complete work to be played. It was not possible, he thought, to see the logic of the structure without the first movement, which contained its main theme and the complex second motif, both of which were integral to the whole work. Though disappointed not to hear the entire work, it thrilled him that Jahn was at least conducting a partial performance.

His delight turned to ecstasy when he heard the reaction of the audience, which gave a colossal round of applause. Jahn signalled for him to come to the stage. He stood there and bowed as members of the audience stood to give him a standing ovation. To his amazement, he saw Johannes Brahms amongst those on their feet and clapping. Hanslick sat there, expressionless and immobile, just like a stiff corpse.

'Congratulations, Herr Bruckner,' said Jahn. 'You received an amazing and justified reaction. I've admired your works for many years, and I'd like to play another one soon. Is there one you would especially want me to play?'

'My fifth,' said Anton, surprised that Jahn was so aware of his compositions and enjoyed them. 'It has never been performed, so it would be a premiere!'

'I'll tell you when I want the score.'

'That will be fine.'

Just as Jahn finished talking to Anton, Arthur Nikisch arrived to speak. 'It is so good to see you, Herr Bruckner. That is a beautiful slow movement. You can certainly write an adagio. Just like Wilhelm Jahn, I would love to conduct one of your symphonies, the next one you compose, perhaps. You know I'm a conductor with the Leipzig Opera now, so no longer a violinist here!'

'No, I didn't know, Arthur. Congratulations. I didn't think I'd seen you here recently.'

'Let me know about your No. 7, Herr Bruckner. I am a great promoter of new ideas in music! I won't promise, but a premiere in Leipzig is a strong possibility.'

Anton gave Nikisch a hug. 'I couldn't resist that,' he said, a little sheepishly. Nikisch smiled, his moustache curling, right up to his ears.

This concert confirmed he was becoming a part of the musical establishment in Vienna, whether Hanslick liked it or not. As he walked home, he wondered where this could lead. It would bring him great joy if his symphonies could be included in Vienna's concert repertoire, alongside the works of Mendelssohn, Schumann or Beethoven, and regularly played abroad, in England or in the United States. There is no harm in dreaming, he thought.

***

'How did last night go?' asked Kathi, as she put his breakfast on the table. 'I'm sorry we couldn't come.'

'I started off being quite angry. They did not play the whole symphony, which they rehearsed, but only the two middle movements. I have to admit, they performed well, and it got the most astonishing reception. Herr Jahn called me onto the stage, and the audience gave me a standing ovation, even Herr Brahms! I felt overjoyed, I can tell you!'

'Oh, I'm so pleased, Herr Bruckner.' She hugged him. 'You are becoming well known for your symphonies. You deserve some fame!'

'Thank you, Kathi.' He told her about Jahn wanting to perform his No. 5 and Nikisch's interest in playing No. 7 in Leipzig.

'You've had this before. Don't get too excited! But if the man from Leipzig is keen, you'd better get on and finish it!'

***

Anton's joy lasted three days. He was in the Conservatorium looking over some lecture notes when one of his students knocked on the door.

'Enter! What can I do for you, mein Herr?'

'Professor Bruckner. I have some terrible news which I have to report to you. Your colleague and friend, Richard Wagner, had died. He died in Venice, yesterday.'

Anton exploded into tears. 'Thank you for letting me know,' he said, wiping his eyes with his handkerchief. To spare Anton any further embarrassment, the student turned and vanished.

His first thoughts were for the beloved Cosima. So he immediately wrote to her, saying,

Dearest Cosima,

I am deeply moved by the passing of my great friend, Richard. I beg to be permitted to express my deepest condolence to your ladyship and to the whole honoured family on the occasion of the unspeakable loss of the phenomenal artist, etc, etc. May he rest in peace.

Yours ever, Anton Bruckner

14 February 1883

As he wrote it, he could feel tears running down his face. He wondered whether he had found the most fitting words, but would sign it regardless and post it to Bayreuth that day. Words had a way of defeating him, while musical notes did not.

'Why are you looking so sad?' said Kathi as he walked in that evening.

'I don't know how to say this without choking on tears, but I shall try to, anyway… my friend Richard died yesterday and I heard today.'

'What dreadful, tragic news, Herr Bruckner. That man had been a godsend to you. Where others have failed you, he has given you support. He has shown your works to other colleagues of his, so has promoted your work. And you've never asked him for anything, except to let you dedicate your symphony to him.'

'I rushed out a letter of condolence to his wife. It was a poor letter. I wish I'd included your words about him, which are much better than mine.'

'Don't worry, Herr Bruckner. Frau Wagner will be pleased to have a letter from you.'

'I will use my musical skills, for what they are, to make my No. 7 a memorial to him.'

'My advice would be to let Frau Wagner know about it. That will be better than any letter of condolence, however well written.'

'That's an excellent idea, Kathi. I'll do just that.'

Anton continued with the adagio of No. 7. Giving the moderato theme the prominence it deserved, he reached the climax of the movement. As a special tribute to the Master, using an instrument he'd never used previously, he included a spectacular cymbal crash at the summit. He wrote a sombre, overwhelming coda, the beginning of which he scored for tuba and horns. He referred to it as 'funeral music for the Master'.

Anton coped with his friend's passing by composing or teaching at the university. After one of his classes, he had an unexpected conversation with Ferdinand Löwe and Josef Schalk.

'We need your permission to go ahead with a new project?'

'And what might that be?'

'We do not have the means to organise an orchestral performance,' said Ferdinand. 'But we have been writing your Symphony No. 3 for two pianos. Could we please have your permission to finish it and play it at the Bösendorfer Hall? We will worry about the costs and share the profits with you.'

'Gentlemen, you are my exceptionally beloved students and becoming my distinguished friends! Certainly, you can have my permission! I don't want a share of the profits, but may I make a simple request? It is that I can attend and have some complimentary tickets.'

'We'd be delighted to agree, Professor,' said Josef.

The reception of the performance, which took place in the May, was a dramatic contrast to the catastrophe of 16 December 1877. The work was just as long as the original symphony and every member of the audience, of about six hundred, stayed until the last note. Their applause was deafening. Ferdinand signalled for Anton to come to the stage. As he stood there bowing, the audience cheered and stamped their feet. He walked into the wings. They applauded again, so he had to reappear. He bowed to Ferdinand and Josef and applauded them. They applauded him. He failed to understand how this simple interpretation could attract such an ovation when the audience detested the original.

What had changed in the five, coming up to six years? Surely it was not because this version was easier on the ear. It was probably more difficult.

385

There was no change except his symphonies were becoming more accepted by the public. Apart from his students and their friends, the premiere of No. 3 was an unbearable shock to the psyche of the Viennese audience. However, with the successful performance of No. 4 and the two movements of No. 6, they were finding his symphonies worthwhile. Another factor was the absence of the enemy. Hanslick was not there, so he could not write a poisoned review.

***

Anton did not attend Wagner's funeral but felt an inner compulsion to visit his grave in Bayreuth. He saw it before, while the Master was still alive. So in the August of '83, Kathi packed a bag for him with enough clean clothes for three weeks away, during which he would also visit St Florian. He took his sketch of the finale of No. 7, aiming to complete it at St Florian.

***

Anton arrived home exhausted. His legs were causing him pain. Many at St Florian had convinced him to stay and play the organ there, so he was a week later than expected. He had spent several days at Kremünster Abbey, to which the Abbott had invited him. It was another of the places he loved to visit on his holiday breaks.

'I've been worried about you, Herr Bruckner. You've been away for a week longer than you said you'd be.'

'I'm sorry, Kathi. I hope I haven't made life difficult for you.'

'No. But I've kept the larder well stocked, thinking you'd return.'

'Let me know if I owe you for any food.'

'Don't be silly, Herr Bruckner. You don't. I've taken food home for me and Bruno, so I've wasted nothing. How did your travels go?'

'As you know, the main part of the break was to go to Richard's grave, which I did.'

'What is it like?'

'It is a fitting monument to him. I prayed in front of it.'

'I hope you included me in your prayers?'

'To be honest, I didn't, but I thought of you several times!'

'I forgive you, but many wouldn't.'

'I must tell you about something odd that happened there and you can tell me if I did the wrong thing. You know that Richard's wife Cosima was always interested in my compositions, in particular my symphonies. One of Richard's servants was at the graveside. I think he was there to make sure no one chipped off any souvenirs from the monument or did anything else that was wrong. Kind of security. I asked him if he would mind telling the ladies that my Symphony No. 4 was performed in Vienna. He didn't seem to have heard me correctly, so I told him again, in just a slightly louder voice, in case he was deaf. The next thing was a tall gentleman shouted at me. He told me to be quiet at this sacred place, and no one wanted to hear anything about my symphonies. I felt bad about it, but I cannot see what I did that was wrong. Can you, Kathi?'

'Definitely not! Who was this arrogant individual?'

'I don't know. He was taller and slimmer than me and sounded important.'

'If I were you, I would forget about it. And what about your other visits?'

'I had a good time with my friend, Ignaz Traumihler, at St Florian. You wouldn't believe the number of times I played the organ there. Sometimes the Abbey was completely full of people and other times it was almost empty... when Ignaz invited a few of the teaching staff and others to listen. We also spent much time in the Sparrow Inn, drinking Pilsner. I stayed sober, by the way! Oh, and while there, I finished the last movement of my No 7.'

'So you had a good time? I'm glad you've finished that symphony. You spent enough time on it. I suppose you'll be writing another one soon!

'You'll have to wait and see! Then I went to Kremünster, to spend a few days there. I love that beautiful abbey and, as you know, I use it as a kind of refuge, an escape from Vienna!'

'Not from me, I hope!'

'Absolutely not. You are my greatest ally!'

'And I feed you!'

***

Having completed No. 7, he dedicated himself to working on the *Te Deum*. After searching frantically, he was relieved to find the sketch of it, in an untidy pile of papers on the floor of his study. He read it, played parts on his harmonium and then, drawing its threads together, transformed it into what he expected to be his greatest sacred creation. The act of labouring on the piece gave him immense satisfaction. To him, he was giving birth to this powerful child, which he hoped would make an intensely mystical impression on the listener. The majestic summit would be the last movement in which the C sharp minor theme from the adagio of No. 7 would lead to a ground shaking, scarcely credible climax. He pressed on and completed the work in the March.

Unbeknown to Anton, Josef Schalk had written a four-hand piano version of No. 7 and took it to Arthur Nikisch, who at the time was in Vienna. The quality and originality of the work amazed Nikisch, who spoke to Anton about it.

'Herr Bruckner, your student Josef Schalk said you've completed your Symphony No. 7. Well, you know I want to perform it. So I've scheduled it for the twenty-seventh of June in Leipzig. I hope you agree!'

'I'm absolutely delighted, Arthur! Let me give you the score,' he said, smiling widely, as he stood up from his desk to shake Nikisch by the hand.

'Did you know Schalk made a two-hand piano transcription of it?'

'No, I didn't!'

'That's what he showed me to entice me to perform it!'

'I can't tell you how much I owe to my students. They are among my best friends and you are, too, Arthur!'

***

'Kathi, I spoke to Arthur Nikisch today. He came to my office at the university. He is going to perform my No. 7. I'm absolutely thrilled.' He told her the details.

'You said he was keen, Herr Bruckner. What a wonderful result. So you will travel to Leipzig then?'

'I will indeed!'

Just over a week later, Anton received a letter at the Conservatorium. Anton's face dropped. He walked home with his head down.

'Why do you look so unhappy, Herr Bruckner?' said Kathi, as he stepped into the kitchen.

'They will not perform my No. 7 on the twenty-seventh of June after all.'

'Why not, in heaven's name? Those people are so untrustworthy!'

'There is a problem with the Gewandhaus concert hall. They won't play it. It's too revolutionary for them. Anyway, my new friend Arthur Nikisch is performing it in the autumn.'

'Don't believe these idiots, Herr Bruckner. He hopes you'll forget what he said and they won't perform it at all. The swine!'

'You are too negative, Kathi. You have to believe somebody.'

'No, I damn well don't!' She rushed out of the kitchen, put on her coat, dashed out, and slammed the door behind her. Anton's leg was hurting, so he could not chase after her. He had to let her go.

As he got out of bed the following morning, he wondered whether he would see Kathi again. She had gone in such a rage, her face was bright red. He made himself a cheese and cold meat breakfast, which he would have with a small glass of beer. Still in his nightshirt, he was sitting at the dining table when he thought he heard the front door open.

'It's you, Kathi and I'm undressed. I'm so sorry!'

'I'm the one who is sorry, Herr Bruckner. Please forgive me for leaving in such a huff last night. I apologise.' She started crying and put her arms around him.

'Please don't worry, Kathi. I'm so delighted you are back!' As he kissed her, he could taste her tears. 'I apologise for saying you were negative. Let's forget it, shall we?'

'Yes, I agree,' she said, smiling.

'I don't know if you are aware of this, Kathi, but on the fourth of September I shall reach the ripe old age of sixty and am going on a holiday to celebrate!'

'I had no idea, Herr Bruckner. Where will you be going?'

'I shall go to Bayreuth to visit the Master's grave again, to Munich, St Florian and to Vöklabruck.'

'Isn't that where your sister Rosalie lives? It's been some time since you've been to see her!'

'I know, but I feel a sibling duty to go.'

***

His visit to Wagner's grave caused him much sadness. He was the only person who attended then and felt an inner compunction to kiss the memorial. In tears, he did so. Then he walked to Wahnfried and knocked on the door. He told the servant that he would, if possible, like to see Cosima. The man replied that she had gone to see her father, Franz Liszt, who was unwell. He did not know when she would return.

Anton then travelled to Munich. He found a reasonably priced hotel and called on Wilhelm Tappert the next morning, to discuss again performing No. 4. Tappert was vague and non-committal about it. So, after spending a couple of days touring the sites of the city with Tappert, and playing the organ at the Frauenkirche, he made his way to Vöklabruck. He didn't want to impose himself on his sister Rosalie and family, so stayed at a guest house in the market-place.

It was raining, so he spent his first day at the lodging. He was enjoying a coffee in the lounge when two young lads appeared. They were about twelve and fourteen years of age and could have been brothers.

'Excuse us, please. Do you mind if we play the piano?'

'Oh, not at all,' he said.

The lads started playing and, for a minute or two, Anton sat and listened. Once he finished his coffee, he joined them at the piano.

'Do you play?' said the younger one.

'Yes, I do,' said Anton.

'Could you play a sonata?' asked the older one.

'I'd be delighted.' He sat at the piano, adjusted the stool and launched into Beethoven's Appassionata.

The eyes of each of the boys opened wide as they listened to him. They seemed amazed at the quality of his play. When he reached the end of the first

389

movement, they thanked him and picked up their things to creep embarrassingly away.

'No! Don't go! Let me play you some more.'

The boys sat, and, losing their shyness, obviously enjoyed listening to this virtuoso play.

That night, at dinner, the boys' father came over to the table where Anton was sitting alone.

'Thank you for entertaining my sons this afternoon. Would you care to join us for dinner?'

'Yes, please honourable Sir, I'd love to.'

He picked up his cutlery and set it on the table next to one of the boys.

'We should introduce ourselves, mein Herr. I am Ignaz von Krauss. We are here for a short holiday.'

'My name is Anton Bruckner. I'm here for a few days, too. My sister lives in Vöklabruck and I'll be seeing her most days, but I'm staying here.'

'I know your name, don't I?'

'Probably not,' said Anton. 'I'm not at all known in these parts. Some people know me in Vienna, which is where I live.'

He enjoyed his contact with this family and spent time with the lads, playing in the garden with them and swimming in the pool. The boys laughed uncontrollably when Anton jumped into the small pool from the diving board and made an enormous splash. In the evenings, on returning from Rosalie's, and after dinner, he would join the family to play music. One night he challenged them to give him a tune which he could use to improvise on the piano. His amazing, imaginative play dazzled them.

'Do come with us to the town hall, Anton,' said Rosalie, smiling on his birthday.

Anton looked puzzled. 'Why are we going to the town hall at seven o'clock at night?'

'You'll see when we get there!'

As they entered the main reception room, a choir and a small orchestra serenaded him.

'Now you know why we are here!' said Rosalie. 'There are a lot of us who want to celebrate your sixtieth birthday!' There must have been over two hundred people there. As the group of players came to the end, everyone looked at Anton and applauded.

'Speech! Speech!' they shouted in unison.

So Anton went up on the stage.

'I don't know what to say, really.' After a brief pause, he found the words. 'Thank you so much for kindly inviting me here to celebrate my birthday. I am sixty today and am feeling my advanced age. I am grateful to Rosalie for organising this event, to the choir and the orchestra for playing those celebratory songs. And I thank you all for coming along.'

He bowed to them as they all applauded.

As he stepped down from the stage, a woman he thought was in her forties approached him. 'Happy birthday, Herr Bruckner. Many congratulations! Do you remember me?'

'Only vaguely,' he said. 'Can you give me a clue?'

'I was a pupil of yours in Windhaag. My maiden name was Maria Jobst.'

'I remember you, Maria! You sang in a Mass I wrote, which we performed in the local church. Much to Herr Fuchs annoyance! I even remember your sweet voice!' He shook hands with her as she kissed his cheek.

'I'm so pleased you remember me, Herr Bruckner, from when? Forty years ago? Things have changed so much. Rosalie tells me you are a famous composer now! And I am married with three lovely children!'

'I'm just as pleased as you, Maria. And congratulations on your successful life!'

***

Anton arrived back home via a further week of organ playing and socialising in St Florian.

'Here I am Kathi. The wanderer has returned!' he said, as he stepped into the kitchen where Kathi was on her knees, cleaning the floor. 'It's good to see you.'

'Only because I'm cleaning the place,' she said, smiling with her entire face. She stood up and hugged him. 'I hope everything went well.'

'Yes, the most amazing thing was a birthday party my sister Rosalie organised for me in Vöklabruck.' He explained. 'I met a lady there whom I met at the first teaching job I had. It was lovely to see her again.'

'You didn't fall in love with her, did you?'

'No. She's married with three kids!'

'What a lovely surprise for you!' Kathi went into the lounge and returned with an item wrapped in plain paper. 'This is your late birthday present, Herr Bruckner. It is bad luck to give it before the day, so please have it now!'

'You shouldn't have, Kathi. You are too kind,' he said as he tore the paper off. 'A bottle of cabernet sauvignon! My favourite red wine! Thank you so much.' She turned her cheek towards him so he kissed her.

'Something else I should tell you.' He related the story of the two boys at the lodging house in Vöklabruck and that he played the piano there to entertain them and their family. 'The father thanked me profusely for entertaining them and asked me what they could do to help me, they had

391

enjoyed my company so much. So I said I was afraid of burglars and asked if they would check my room at night to make sure there was nobody there. So, in candle light, the boys went up to my room each night and thoroughly looked it over. They took it so seriously when it was simply a practical joke! Oddly enough, none of the family worked that out!'

'How funny, Herr Bruckner. They obviously didn't know you as well as I do!'

'And another thing. On my birthday, I started on the first movement of my Symphony No. 8.'

'I just don't know how you do it! Before I forget, here is a letter from Leipzig.'

Following his usual ritual for dealing with correspondence, he went into his study. He came out smiling, with tears running down his face. 'I've got to tell you, Kathi! Nikisch is going to play my No. 7 at the Opera House in Leipzig on 30 December, this year. I can't tell you how thrilled I am. I'm going to celebrate by having some of the cabernet sauvignon you gave me. Would you like a glass?' he said, fully expecting her to refuse, as she had on all previous occasions.

'Oh go on then. Just this once. Bruno will accept my explanation. I told him about my present for you. I'll tell him I had to sample it!'

A month or so later, Kathi picked up another letter from the hall mat, as she was coming into the apartment to make Anton's breakfast.

'Herr Bruckner, the post was early this morning. Here's a letter for you.'

'Who is it from?' he shouted from the study.

'Postmarked Linz. You'll have to open it to find out!' She knocked on the study door and took it in.

He slit the envelope open. 'I'm not expecting anything from Linz,' he said as he took the letter out and unfolded it. 'My God! I can't believe it. First Richard and now Franz,' he said, his face contorted.

'Franz?'

'Yes, Franz Rudigier, the Bishop of Linz.'

'A great friend of yours, I remember,' she said, not knowing what to say.

'He was one of the best supporters I ever had and someone I could confide in.' He thought of telling her about how he came to his aid in Bad Kreuzen but decided against it. 'He would sit for hours in the Cathedral, just listening to me at the organ. And he commissioned so many of my works. I loved him,' he said, on the edge of tears.

Kathi put an arm around him and kissed his cheek. 'I'm so sorry, Herr Bruckner. Is there anything I can do to soften the pain?'

'Not really, Kathi. But thank you for your sympathy.'

'Will you go to the funeral?'

'Difficult. It's only two weeks from now until my No. 7 is performed.' He looked at the letter again. 'No. There is no mention of a date for it. Sadly, I won't be able to go, even if I knew when it would take place. It may have been held already. And Bishop Rudigier wouldn't expect me to miss the premiere.'

'I fully understand, Herr Bruckner. I'll make you a nice breakfast.'

'You are the best.'

***

Anton made his way to Leipzig. He regarded it as one of Europe's great centres of music. Schumann and Mendelssohn had lived there, as Grieg still was. Wagner was born there and, of course, J. S. Bach was the choirmaster and organist at the Thomaskirche. Anton had provided Nikisch with the score much earlier in the year, before the performance was scheduled for the June, so he didn't have to worry about getting the parts produced. He booked into a Leipzig hotel for three nights.

It was with some trepidation that he sat through two rehearsals. He wondered whether the audience at Leipzig would be ready for one of his symphonies. Perhaps they could be better starting with No. 4. He felt more confident once he had seen Nikisch perform. There was something magical about the way he conducted. He gave the music his own interpretation, a uniqueness that he hoped the composer would readily accept. To Anton, it seemed he had studied the score in the minutest detail and appreciated all its subtlety, its key changes and tempo changes. It was as if he had collaborated with the composer to deliver this interpretation when, in fact, it was his own. Anton recognised the greatness of this young man who surely would have a successful career ahead of him.

'We have a problem, Herr Bruckner. We have no Wagner tubas, so I'm afraid I will have to use French horns instead.'

'You cannot use what you do not have,' smiled Anton.

The day of the performance dawned. Anton sat near the front and could sense the filling of the hall as members of the audience arrived and took their seats. He tormented himself, terrified about how they would react. Could this be No. 3 again, a disaster waiting to happen? No one there had, as far as he knew, heard any of his works before and, while a centre of musical culture, Leipzig audiences were known to be conservative.

He sat anxiously through to the last note of the first movement. Then the audience burst into rapturous, wild applause, more than enough to bring a smile to his face. Again, at the end of the second, the third and the fourth. His looks showed his delight and satisfaction.

As they continued applauding, Nikisch invited him onto the stage, from which he bowed deeply to the audience. The ovation became louder. They wouldn't let him go. He had to stand there for a full fifteen minutes before their applause died down.

'Congratulations, Anton,' said Nikisch, using his first name at last. 'What an immense success! You must be so proud that this totally new work was so deeply appreciated by our audience!'

'I can't tell you how much I am. Its success is due to your wonderful orchestra and your brilliant conducting! Thank you so much. I only wrote it!'

'I'll let you into a secret, Anton. A couple of nights ago, I entertained all of our fiercest critics at dinner. I gave them a talk on your symphony and explained its logic by playing the main themes to them on my piano. Their reaction then was very favourable so I expect they will give us superb reports.'

'But how could your entertaining them affect the audience?'

'Come on, Anton! They were in the audience. It only takes one man to start an ovation!'

Chapter 28
1885 - 1886 Fame at last

'Welcome home, Herr Bruckner!' said Kathi, as he opened the front door and put his case on the floor. 'You're looking cheerful, so Leipzig went well then?'

'Kathi, I couldn't believe it! My symphony had such a huge ovation, I had to stand to listen to the applause for a quarter of an hour. They clapped after each movement! My fears they would walk out were totally unfounded. My new friend, Herr Nikisch, says he wants to champion my music from now on and take it from Vienna to the rest of the world. He is going to ask Hans Richter to play it here.'

'If he does, I'll force Bruno to come with me! You are so lucky that Herr Dessoff has gone!'

'I know, Kathi. That was good luck!'

Not a week later, another letter arrived from Leipzig. It was from Nikisch and contained some newspaper cuttings. The critics were unanimous in their praise. A Cologne paper described the reaction of the Leipzig audience, saying, 'Initially surprise, then fascination, then admiration, finally enthusiasm. That was the ladder.' The Leipzig News said, 'The work evokes the greatest admiration. It has a youthful immediacy in its musical invention with a natural congeniality with Wagner and Liszt. Bruckner stands out like a giant from the world of the mediocre who parrot what others have said elsewhere.'

He read the extracts to Kathi.

'But I haven't told you the most important point he makes! It by far outweighs the press reports!'

'Well?'

'On the twenty seventh of January, he is going to play the middle two movements in a private concert for King Ludwig II!'

'You deserve it, Herr Bruckner. That symphony is going to make you famous. I'm going to tell everyone I know about it!'

'Thank you, Kathi. I don't deserve you.'

'I know!' They both laughed.

***

Kathi was right. Orchestras worldwide became desperate to perform his symphonies. In the February, his No. 3 was played in The Hague. Later in the year, it was performed in New York, then Dresden, again in The Hague, in Frankfurt and in Utrecht.

Hermann Levi, having read the press reports on No. 7, wrote to Anton to say he was going to play it in Munich. He said the performance date was 10 March and invited Anton to attend the rehearsals and the actual concert. In the letter, he said he didn't follow the finale and that the orchestra was puzzled by the work but not to worry because the performance would be a great success. He asked if, because of these issues, they could play only the adagio, an idea Anton thought utterly ridiculous, bordering on the absurd.

In his reply, Anton said he was more than pleased that Levi was to perform it, but took the risk in saying he would go to Munich only on the assumption that Levi would play the complete work.

***

Anton continued feverishly working on his No. 8, spending every spare moment on it. He focussed his efforts on the slow movement, which would be the second. His aim was to make it unique among symphonic adagios, an expression of emotional richness and contrasts. It would be the most monumental adagio ever written. The movement would be lyrical, and with its variations and different tonal textures, would be a sublime experience for the listener. His thematic material, combined with its orchestration, would, he imagined, achieve these aims. For the first time in any of his symphonies, he would use a harp. He completed the sketch of the movement on 16 February.

***

Kathi packed his case, and he set off for Munich on 7 March. His travels clashed with a performance of his Quintet in Linz, which he would have to miss.

Anton happened to be staying at the same hotel as Levi and met him at his breakfast table.

'My dear Anton, I'm so glad you could come,' he said. 'Please join me!'

'I'm delighted you are to perform my No. 7,' he said as he pulled up a chair to sit with him. 'It will be its premiere in Munich.'

'Of course, and it is an honour for me!'

'Much less of an honour than the Master inviting you to perform the "Parsifal" premiere!'

'Nonsense. You are too modest! Let's discuss the work, shall we?'

'Yes.'

'I have to say, I have the most profound admiration for this symphony. It is the finale I still find confusing.'

'So you said in your letter. What is the problem exactly?'

'I'm afraid I don't follow the logic of it. The themes in the recapitulation are all in the wrong order. And the key changes don't work!'

'With respect, Hermann, the themes are in the right order. They are in the reverse of their original statement and that it what I meant. It's the arch structure. You know!'

'But that says nothing about the key structure.'

'I can't help you there. It is what I have composed, and that's the way it will stay!' He thought of apologising for taking this stand, but decided against it.

'Could you rework it or shorten it… only the last movement?'

'I don't follow you,' he said, reddening in the face and almost choking on a bite of toast. 'In Leipzig, under young Nikisch, the orchestra didn't whinge about it… and he was happy with the structure, the key changes, and the whole bloody thing!'

'All right, Anton. You win, I hope! We will rehearse it, say two more times.'

'So with no changes!'

'With no changes. Then we'll see what the players think!'

Anton attended the final rehearsal. Despite the success of the Nikisch performance, he dreaded a repetition of the hideous No. 3 experience. He was unnecessarily concerned. Hermann Levi's familiarity with the work and his constant encouragement inspired the players to perform brilliantly. They tackled it with obvious enthusiasm.

Anton applauded from the stalls. As quickly as his ailing legs would carry him, he climbed up to the organ loft and, to thank them, improvised some well-known themes and ended with an energetic fugue.

Levi and the orchestra gave the symphony the brilliant public performance it deserved. The audience applauded after each movement. Levi invited Anton onto the stage. Smiling from ear to ear, he shook Levi by the hand, bowed to the orchestra, and then to the audience, which gave him a never ending standing ovation. Anton believed this concert outshone the one in Leipzig, both in the orchestra's quality and in the audience's reaction.

'Congratulations, Anton,' said Levi. 'I'm as delighted as you and have an idea!'

'Please tell me,' said Anton, still smiling and drying his tears of joy.

'Would you like to dedicate it to King Ludwig of Bavaria?'

'What a great idea! I'd be delighted! In January, Nikisch played the King two of the movements. So he's listened to it already.'

'I'll write to him!'

Within a month, the King had agreed.

***

Anton was so captivated by the Munich performance, he couldn't wait to tell Kathi. Having seen the press reports, he even felt the need to write to Moritz von Mayfield. He told him that the success there was the greatest in

397

his life, that he never before experienced such enthusiasm, and that the reviews were all excellent. Levi wrote to tell him he considered it the most important symphony since 1827, and called his conducting of it the pinnacle of his career.

Shortly after the Munich success, the director of the Vienna Philharmonic spoke to him in his office at the University.

'Herr Bruckner, I have a request. We have read of the stunning reception your Symphony No. 7 received both in Leipzig and in Munich. So we would like your permission to play it in Vienna in the coming concert season. Please may we?'

'Please don't. The Vienna press might have a detrimental effect on its recent successes in Germany. I'll think again in a year when, with good fortune, my name will be so well established that people like Hanslick, whatever garbage they write, will have negligible impact in Europe and the United States.'

'I see,' said the director, and he left.

***

An interesting diversion occupied Anton during the April. Bishop Rudigier's successor wrote to him to ask if he would compose two special pieces to commemorate the centenary of the formation of the Linz Diocese. He responded by writing two motets, *Ecce Sacerdos Magnus* and *Virga Jesse*. Ironically and frustratingly, they performed neither at the celebratory event.

Anton couldn't afford to waste time gloating over his success. The next important aim was to win the battle for a *Te Deum* performance. He would speak to Hellmesberger about it.

'Let's see what we can do, Anton. No promises, even so. You know you should dedicate it to the Emperor.'

'Too late. I've already dedicated it to Almighty God.'

Anton took Hellmesberger's response as less than enthusiastic. He spoke about it to the Schalk brothers and Ferdinand Löwe.

'I have an interesting idea for a new project. I'm sure I've spoken to you about my *Te Deum*. It's ready for performance. If I organised the choir, soloists and the printing of the parts, would you, as you did for my Symphony No. 3, transcribe the work for two pianos?'

'We certainly will. Do you have a copy of the score we can use while you sort out the parts?' said Josef Schalk.

'Yes, but I'll need the full score for printing the parts. Could you use the sketch? It covers the whole work.'

'We'll use that,' said Löwe. 'We'll make an equally rough version and refine it when we see the full score.'

Anton shook hands with the three of them.

He had not arranged a public performance of one of his works since his early days as a teacher. His range of contacts in Vienna had grown, so he had to make some choices. Not preparing for a full orchestral rendition, he selected a venue which would suit the use of two pianos. The small hall of the Vienna Music Society would be perfect. So he reserved it for 2 May '85. He then approached the Academic Richard Wagner Club, of which he was a member, to provide the choir and soloists. It thrilled them to become key players in the premiere of this work.

Anton attended the performance, which was in front of about five hundred. They loved it. So he relished another success.

***

'We did enjoy your *Te Deum*, Herr Bruckner!' said Kathi as she entered the apartment, the morning after the performance.

'I didn't see you there!'

'We were right at the back. We so liked it. I think it's you best work... so far!'

'I'm so pleased you liked it, Kathi. I must say, I enjoyed writing it!'

'I loved the way you go straight in at the beginning. It is such an exciting start. And that finale! It is spectacular. A climax of climaxes!'

'Thank you!'

'The soloists were excellent. Who were they?'

'They were Frau Ulrich-Linde, Emile Zips, Richard Exleben and Heinrich Gassner. I only met them at the rehearsals and they are brilliant. My student, Josef Schalk, and his friend Robert Erben played the pianos. If this work becomes widely recognised and referred to, their names will live forever!'

'They would deserve it, Herr Bruckner! They were so good!'

Again, in any spare time, he worked on No. 8. By the end of August, he had finished drafts of the scherzo and trio. He delighted in making them pure musical entertainment. He had also started on what he would regard as his best, most subtle and natural sounding finale.

Fame did not affect Anton. He regularly enjoyed dining and drinking with his students and their friends. They benefitted from his improved financial position as he, more often than not, paid for all the drinks and much of the food they consumed. One of his private students, Friedrich Eckstein, often joined them and contributed to the lively discussion which often focussed on the latest performance of one of Anton's works. Wherever in the world it may have been.

'Congratulations, Professor, on the New York performance of your third symphony,' said Friedrich.

'New York?' said Anton.

399

'Yes, I read it in the Daily News.'

'That must be thanks to Theodor Rättig, who published the score. I hope they give me some of the profits!'

'You won't be able to spend dollars here!'

'No, but I'll convert it to florins!'

'It's time you were better recognised in Vienna,' said Hugo Wolf. 'The world recognises you, but you can only give private concerts here.'

'Yes, nothing is more frustrating. In fact, I don't want my works performed here because of that rogue Hanslick. He loves his friend Brahms, but hates me. He would hang me if he could find a length of rope strong enough!'

'You will be accepted here, in time,' said Josef Schalk.

'I hope I'm still alive to see it!'

'The problem with Hanslick is he has many followers. They hate whom he hates!' said Hugo.

'You are right, Josef, I may be in the future. I'll see if Hans Richter might like to perform my No. 7. I'll choose the moment! Hanslick is less sure about irritating him! Let me buy another round.'

'By the way, Professor, do you firmly believe in God?' said Wolf. 'Such a religious work as your *Te Deum* indicates a composer of strong religious beliefs'

'Interesting you say that. I pray every day, but I'm not absolutely certain there is a God. No one has come back from heaven to tell us about it. Even so, I keep praying, if it's only for insurance!'

'Don't you believe Christ went to heaven and came back?' said Franz.

'I'm not sure about that, either! I'm happier with the virgin birth because I understand such things can occur in nature.'

By the time he left for home, Anton had had more than enough to drink. He thought he had reached his apartment, but his key wouldn't fit the keyhole. On hearing his persistent efforts to try, a neighbour came to the door.

'Good evening, Herr Bruckner. Your apartment is on the next floor up!'

'Oh bother! I am sorry. I hope I haven't disturbed you,' he just about said, slurring his speech. The gentleman neighbour took his arm and escorted him up a flight of stairs to his door.

'Give me your key and I'll open it for you.'

'No, I'll be alright.'

He tried but failed. 'Oh, yes please,' he said, then dribbling down his front.

The man let him in and handed him the key. 'Glad to read about your recent successes!'

'Oh, many thanks!'

Anton went straight into his bedroom, threw off his clothes, and slept naked on the bed.

***

'Herr Bruckner! Herr Bruckner!' shouted Kathi that Saturday morning. She expected to him to be in the study composing his No. 8, but he wasn't there or in the kitchen or lounge. So she knocked on the bedroom door.

'Herr Bruckner! Herr Bruckner!'

He woke up to her shouting. 'I'm in here, Kathi. I'll just get dressed!' A few minutes later, feeling like a scolded schoolboy, he appeared in the lounge.

'So what were you up to last night? You stink of beer!'

'I am sorry. I was with the students last night and had a lot to drink. Do we have anything for headaches?'

'If you've got a hangover, it serves you blinking right.' She was tempted to use stronger language, but he was her boss and paid her handsomely. She couldn't afford to be dismissed. 'I'll look in the pantry for some salts! Then I'll get you some breakfast. Oh, and I found these two letters in the hall.'

Anton sat at the dining table and, despite his aching head, could just about focus on reading them. The first was from Ignaz Traumihler, asking him to lead an organ recital on the 28 August which was the feast of St Augustine. The second was from the Abbott at Klosterneuburg Monastery, inviting him to the feast of St Leopold in November.

He was putting them back in their envelopes when Kathi appeared with a sumptuous breakfast of chopped ham, three fried eggs, and two fresh bread rolls. 'Here. Get that down you. That'll cure your head. And here are some salts and a cup of water.'

'Thank you, Kathi,' he said, not looking her straight in the eye. She disappeared back into the kitchen while he took the salts. She came back in just after he had eaten.

'I don't know what to do about these requests.' He told her about the letters.

'You haven't got the time. Now you are so well known, you'll get invitations from all over the place, asking you to do this, do that or the other. I'd say no to each of them'

'Difficult. I would like to agree to the St Florian one because it is a huge part of my life, but I'm less sure about Klosterneuburg.'

'Why not say yes to St Florian, then… but leave the other one until you've decided. It's not until November, so you've got plenty of time.'

'I like your thinking, Kathi. That's what I'll do.'

***

Anton was so pleased he'd accepted the one from St Florian. Not only did he feel so much at home there, they always gave him a hearty welcome and showed much appreciation for anything he did to comply with their wishes. He also had a special room there he used as a study and a place to relax. It was larger than one of the monk's cells and had a window with a view over the village.

While sitting in the library, Ignaz and Anton drew up a programme for the recital.

'Can we avoid Bach?' said Ignaz.

'Yes, I admit, I've played him to death here. What if I play some themes from my new symphony along with some Wagner? I will improvise as long as you want me to!'

Ignaz had the programme printed and distributed widely, the result of which was the Basilica was full to overflowing on the day. Anton played the main organ, starting with the principal themes from the adagio of his No. 8. Then he couldn't resist the playful tunes from the scherzo. Finally, he played a tumultuous rendering of themes from Götterdämmerung. The applause from the congregation said it all for both of them.

'Well done, Anton,' said Ignaz, as the crowds were leaving. 'You filled the place. I think many wanted to see you, now you are becoming better known.'

'Maybe,' said Anton. 'But I hope they saw me as the same person I was thirty years ago!'

Anton thought again about going to Klosterneuburg. It was only about fifteen kilometres away from the Hessgasse and he had made rapid progress on his No. 8.

'Could you please post this letter to the Abbott at Klosterneuburg, Kathi? I'm going, after all.'

'Up to you, Herr Bruckner. If you can spare the time.'

***

During the pony and trap ride to Klosterneuburg, he still wondered why he accepted, the invitation. 'I have something important to tell you, Herr Bruckner,' said the Abbott, who was inside and stopped lighting candles as soon as he saw Anton. 'We have not made it publicly known, but Emperor Franz Joseph will be attending.'

'Incredible! I'm so pleased,' said Anton. 'Will I meet His Majesty?'

'It depends on whether he makes himself available. Obviously, I shall call you if he wishes to meet you.'

He told Anton what they wanted. Then he made his way to the organ loft and placed a score in front of him. A priest would signal at the exact moment the Emperor was about to enter the Monastery, which was when he expected Anton to begin playing. As he entered, Anton was playing the Kaiserlied.

The Emperor stopped at the door and said, 'Ah, Bruckner!'

Those were the only two words Anton heard from him that day.

***

The year 1886 provided Anton with even more success abroad. His No. 3 was performed in Linz and The Hague; No. 4 in the small town of Sondershausen, Thuringia; and No. 7 in Hamburg, in Cologne, in Amsterdam, New York for the second time and in Boston and Chicago. So he was becoming widely known on the international front and reaped the benefits both financially and in the immense satisfaction it gave him.

A performance of the *Te Deum* on 10 January by the Philharmonic, under Hans Richter, was another victory in Vienna. Its reception was tumultuous.

'It was better still with the full orchestra, Herr Bruckner. So good it made me cry,' reported Kathi.

Later in the same month, the director of the Vienna Philharmonic again approached Anton about performing his No. 7. Hans Richter had offered to conduct it. Anton realised that, by then, no matter what Hanslick or his cohorts said, his global reputation would not be affected. So he consented. The director shook his hand vigorously.

***

'I have some good news and a chance to fulfil your promise!' he said when he saw Kathi that evening, while she was cooking his dinner.

'Go on!'

'The Vienna Philharmonic is going to play my No. 7 on 21 March! You remember what you said?'

'No!'

'You and Bruno would go to the performance, even if you had to drag him along.'

'You've got me, Herr Bruckner. Yes, I remember now. We will definitely come. If I make a promise, I will keep it! Oh, here's another letter for you from Munich!'

Breaking his usual ritual, he read it in front of Kathi. 'It's another trip to Munich, Kathi.'

'When?'

'Herr Levi wants to perform my *Te Deum* on 7 March and asks if I can go, so I will!'

'Unbelievable. Your works are being performed everywhere!'

'I know! All over Europe and the United States. That unpleasant critic can do me no harm now, whatever he says. Sensible people will think he's an ogre... which he probably is.'

'Yes, and he started being a friend of yours, didn't he?'

'You're right!'

403

Before he went to Munich, he resumed working on the first movement of No. 8. As in the sketch, he started with an uncertainty in its direction, and ended in a triumphant finale. He concentrated on the structure, refining its orchestration, but preserving the core themes from the initial draft, created over a year before. On 7 February, he completed writing the movement and felt pleased with it. He thought his audiences would thrive on the piece, even if orchestras might struggle.

***

Anton was touched by the enthusiasm of Levi's audience for his *Te Deum*. The orchestra, choir and soloists performed it as if it was a celebration. Again, Levi persuaded Anton to take acknowledgement from the stage.

'What a great work, Anton,' said Levi. 'You could not have had a more appreciative response. The orchestra and singers loved performing it.'

'I'm so pleased I came,' he gleamed.

'There are some people here who would like to meet you. If you have an hour to spare tomorrow morning, I can introduce you.'

'Who are they?'

'If I told you, you would not have the pleasure of being surprised! I can tell you they are not musicians!'

Anton and Levi agreed to meet these mysterious people at 10 o'clock in a coffee shop in the city centre, where the strangers had suggested. Anton wondered what special skills they might have. Would they be poets, architects, writers, sculptors or even artists? Anton could detect the strong smell of a good quality Colombian coffee as they walked in.

'We are overjoyed to meet you,' said one of them. 'My name is Hermann Kaulbach.' His faced appeared as if he'd suffered from a stroke.

'I am equally pleased to meet you, Herr Kaulbach. What is your profession? Herr Levi here has kept me in suspense!'

'We are all artists! I paint historical themes. But I also paint pictures of children.'

'How interesting,' said Anton.

'I am Paul Heyse,' said the second, a tall bearded character. 'I'm a writer of novels, short stories and dramas. As a composer, you will be more interested in my father. He was at Berlin University and was tutor to Felix Mendelssohn.'

'I so admire his music,' said Anton.

'I am Fritz von Uhde,' said the third, who possessed the widest, most grotesque moustache Anton had ever seen. 'I am a painter. Of us three, Paul is the best known. I've been a painter all my life and do a lot of outdoor work and religious scenes.'

'I'll buy the coffees,' said Levi, who went off to the counter to order.

'You have an interesting shaped head and nose, Herr Bruckner. I am about to portray the Last Supper,' continued Uhde. 'Would you like to pose as a disciple?'

'I am not worthy of being in the company of the apostles,' said Anton, his eyebrows curling. 'But there are numerous photographs of me available. If you insist, you could use one of those.'

Uhde just grinned behind his luxuriant whiskers.

They conversed about their respective careers and interests until lunchtime, when Anton bought a round of beers. They each had something to eat and carried on discussing well into the afternoon.

***

Kathi and Bruno joined in as the entire audience applauded each movement of Anton's No. 7. There was something special about listening to a piece of music written by someone you knew. Of the two of them, only Kathi had heard a symphony of Anton's before. She couldn't help comparing this symphony with the man. She failed to understand how a work like this could be the product of his mind. There must be something in his head that made him create this work of art. She could only admire it and the man who made it out of nothing. Without people like him, who produced these marvels, the world would be a poorer place.

Hanslick recognised the reaction it provoked in the audience, but reported savagely. It was unnatural, pompous, morbid, and perverted. He admitted the occasional few bars of pleasant detail, but between them, interminable stretches of darkness, boredom and over-excitement. One of Hanslick's lieutenants said, 'shivers ran down his spine when the odour of decomposing counterpoint entered his nostrils' He summarised his opinion with, 'Bruckner composes like a drunkard'.

Anton and Kathi discussed the vicious Vienna reports. They angered and disgusted Kathi, who was almost in tears. 'You don't deserve this, Herr Bruckner.'

'How does that man know about my drinking habits?' said Anton, laughing. 'But please don't let them upset you, Kathi. Critics can destroy the person they criticise but not me. They are too late! We should laugh them off!'

***

'This looks like an interesting letter, Herr Bruckner,' said Kathi, a few months after Hans Richter's performance of No. 7. 'It's from the palace.'

'You're teasing me!'

'No, seriously!'

He vanished into the study, but soon reappeared. 'It's from Franz Joseph's private secretary. They want to want to honour me with the Knight's Cross!'

'Congratulations. Herr Bruckner! Could Bruno and I come, do you think?'

'I'll ask them. I might ask if my landlady in Linz can come, Irene.'

'Good idea. You haven't mentioned her for some time.'

'Only because I haven't been to Linz!'

Anton replied to the palace, asking if he could bring some guests to the presentation. They said he could bring four. So he wrote to Irene asking if she could meet him and Kathi outside the palace on 9 July at a quarter to one. He offered to pay her train fare, and invited her, having discussed the suggestion with Kathi, to stay in the second bedroom at the Hessgasse.

'Irene, I'm so pleased to see you!' He pecked her on the cheek. 'This is my friend Kathi and her husband Bruno.' Irene already knew that Kathi was his housekeeper, but he preferred to introduce her just as a friend. They all embraced and shook hands.

'It's so good to be here, Anton. No one merits this honour more than you. Your fame is spreading!'

'Thank you, Irene.'

'I agree,' said Kathi. 'You cannot imagine the time he spends on his symphonies and his other works.'

'I went to a performance of one of Anton's masses last October. In the Cathedral. I didn't see you there, Anton.'

'No. I just couldn't spare the time.'

'You must listen to his *Te Deum*. It's wonderful,' said Bruno.

'And his fourth symphony... and the seventh,' said Kathi.

'I loved your first when they played it in Linz. That was a long time ago!'

They entered the colossal Imperial Palace, and all four sat in the main reception room. The building stunned Anton who had not before realised how massive and beautiful it was, even though he had many times played the organ at the Imperial Court Chapel which was part of the building. After a few minutes of waiting, they were ushered into a more ornate, larger room in which the ceremony would take place. They could not help noticing the deep piled, red carpet and its smell of sandalwood. Anton felt confident, knowing he was there because he earned it. He wondered who would make the presentation and smiled widely as Prince Konstantin of Hohenlohe-Schillingsfürst entered. Anton was even more pleased he had dedicated his No. 4 to him.

'My dear Anton, the Emperor has appointed me to present you with this, the highest honour he can bestow.' Anton stood to attention as the Prince pinned the insignia to his jacket.

Irene, Kathi and Bruno spontaneously but quietly applauded.

'The Emperor is going to give you an allowance of 300 florins a year and will subsidise the publication of you scores.'

'Thank you so much, Your Majesty. I cannot tell you how grateful I am to you and the Emperor. I thank you most sincerely.'

The Prince turned and left the room. A smiling, bewigged attendant escorted Anton and his friends out of the palace.

'I'd like to buy you all a drink and something to eat. There is a good restaurant near here, the Red Hedgehog.'

All four enjoyed this occasion, especially Kathi who could now put a face on Irene, whom she had not met before. This was the first time Anton had met Bruno, who showed his generosity by paying for the drinks. They vowed to meet up again, given the opportunity. Irene gladly stayed the night.

***

In the summer months, Anton worked assiduously on his No. 8. Not only did he compose on paper, aided by the use of his piano, he constantly processed the symphony in his mind. The major change he made was to alter the order of the scherzo and the adagio. Putting the adagio after the first movement, which ended in a blazing victory, seemed too much for any audience to bear. He also thought that the major climax in the adagio, for which he had used six cymbal crashes, was too dramatic to occur that early in the work. The more he thought about the symphony, he regarded the adagio as the most important movement, so thought it should be played nearer the finale. Having used the harp in the adagio when it was the second movement, he would introduce it in the trio.

***

'I have an important visit to make, Kathi. I am going to Bayreuth for the Wagner Festival and to see Cosima.'

'When will you go, Herr Bruckner? I will make the usual preparations.'

'On the first of August, so in four days' time.'

'And how long will you be gone?'

'About seven days. I'll get back as soon as I can. I've still got much to do on my No. 8.'

'I thought you'd finished it!'

'No. I've completed all movements in draft, but I've yet to finalise them. It's mainly the orchestration that's left. You could call it polishing. And making sure there are no errors in the score.'

'I see!'

Anton booked himself into the same hotel as he had used previously. He then walked to see Cosima at Wahnfried. One of her servants, who recognised Anton, answered the door.

'I'm not sure if Frau Wagner will want to see you, Herr Bruckner. She has had a recent death in her family and is very upset.'

'Can you tell me more?'

'No. It is a private matter. She's asked me to say nothing for now.'

'In which case, could you kindly ask Frau Wagner directly if she will see me? I am here for the festival, so can see her any time in the next few days.'

The servant vanished into the house and left Anton standing there in front of the open door. He soon came back.

'Frau Wagner would be delighted to see you now. Please follow me.'

Anton was much relieved that she wanted to see him. He could offer some comfort for her loss.

'Anton, I'm so pleased to see you! I imagine you are here for the annual festival,' she sobbed.

'I am indeed. It's so good to see you, too.'

'You met my father, didn't you? You won't know that he died just before midnight, last night,' she said, as tears rolled down her cheeks.

'I'm so, so sorry,' he said as he put his arm around her shoulder. As in writing the condolence letter on Wagner's death, he struggled with words. All he could think of was to speak about his own father.

'It is so sad when a father passes. I cried my eyes out the day my father died. I even passed out. It was horrible. I loved him so much.'

'It is the same for me, Anton. I can't believe he's gone,' she said, with his arm still around her. 'I would dearly like you to attend the funeral, which will be on 3 August. Would that be possible? Perhaps you could deliver a eulogy?'

'Of course, Cosima. I loved him, too,' said Anton, so as not to upset her. Although he admired much of Liszt's output, he was less sure about his personality. He remembered well the occasion when he asked Liszt if he could dedicate his No. 2 to him. As requested, he gave Liszt a copy for his approval. Liszt was so disinterested that, much to Anton's annoyance, he left the score in a hotel bedroom.

Anton enjoyed the festival. He was captivated by the playing of Tristan and Isolde, which he heard at its premiere. This was its inaugural performance in the Bayreuth Festival Theatre.

The funeral was far from a joyous occasion. Cosima was pleased that it was so well attended. Lina Schmalhausen, one of his students who helped care for him during his final days, was there. August Göllerich, the father of Anton's pupil was also present. Cosima's family sat at the front of the church.

Anton's generous 'eulogy' was to give a mighty organ improvisation on themes from Parsifal as the bearers escorted the coffin from the church to the open grave.

***

In October, Anton worked again on the newly positioned scherzo and trio. His attention focussed on the orchestration. On the twenty fourth, he wrote the word 'Finished' on the score of these movements.

Occasionally, Anton would visit the main art gallery in Vienna, not that he was a great lover of visual arts, but for a change and out of curiosity. So, before the end of the year, during a lunch break, he walked there from the university. He aimlessly strolled from gallery to gallery and could not help noticing a picture called 'The Last Supper.' He stood in front of it. Suddenly, he realised the artist had painted a picture of him, on the left hand side. He had caught him brilliantly and Anton was seriously moved. To place him alongside the disciples was an honour, in the same league as receiving the Order of the Knight Cross.

Chapter 29
1887 - 1889 Hermann Levi and Symphony No. 8

Much to his delight, Anton's symphonies were growing in popularity. They fulfilled his dream by entering the regular concert repertoire, except in Vienna. In 1887 and '88, No. 7 was performed in Berlin, twice in Dresden, in Cologne, twice in London under Hans Richter, in Budapest, again in Graz; and No. 4 in New York.

***

In the March, Josef Schalk and his friend, Franz Zottmann, met Anton for an evening meal at Gauss's expensive restaurant.

'We have a little surprise for you, Professor,' said Josef.

'Really? What's that?'

'We've written a transcription for two pianos of your Symphony No. 5.'

'That's nice,' said Anton, in a flat voice.

'Thank you,' said Zottmann. 'We have organised the date for a performance in the Bösendorfer Hall.'

'You've what?'

Josef repeated what Zottmann had said. 'We've kept strictly to the score, so have religiously followed your wishes,' he added.

'The final rehearsal will be the ideal opportunity for you to suggest changes,' said Zottman.

'No, it won't,' said Anton. 'That'll be too late. It's a complex work... so I cannot make changes at the last minute. You should have involved me in the preparation. You must delay the performance.'

'Changing the date is out of the question,' said Josef. 'The poster is already at the printers and whether we can get another date at the Bösendorfer is debatable.'

'Alright then! The concert's off,' said Anton, frowning and with his fists clenched.

'You can't possibly mean that, Herr Professor,' said Josef, 'not after all the money we've spent on it... we'd lose it if we had to cancel.'

Anton bent over the table, shaking with rage. 'I order you!'

'The concert goes ahead,' said Josef.

'In that case, Herr Schalk, I shall call the police.'

They set about each other like two fighting stags, with their antlers fully intertwined. Eventually, Anton won. The battling deer separated. Josef agreed to cancel.

***

'You look angry,' said Kathi when she saw him the following morning.

410

'I was last night,' he said, 'but I thought it had worn off by now.'

'No! You still look cross about something. Want to tell me?'

Anton told her about the temperamental exchange.

'Well, it's your symphony, Herr Bruckner. It's your God given right to have it performed as you want it performed. Mind you, those lads have been kind in writing it for two pianos. It must have taken a lot of time. So you should be grateful.'

'Kathi, I am certainly very grateful. The problem is that I wrote it for a full orchestra. Not for two pianos, however good their intentions.'

***

Anton directed five rehearsals at the Bösendorfer Hall, none of which was held in a constructive spirit, at least as Schalk saw it. Anton insisted on an exact interpretation of his symphony, the best that was possible to achieve on two pianos.

Disappointed by the result, while acknowledging they had improved, he asked for more rehearsals, but Schalk disagreed. This time Schalk won. Much to Anton's irritation, they arranged the performance for 20 April.

Along with Kathi and Bruno and several of his students and friends, including Hugo Wolf, Anton sat in the back row of the Bösendorfer Hall. As with many previous performances of his works, he wasn't sure what to expect, either from the players or the audience. He remained unhappy about their piano transcription, the orchestrated version of which he regarded as a special child.

As soon as Zottmann and Schalk played the last note of the last movement, the audience cheered so loudly, Anton could hardly believe his ears. Their reaction didn't resonate with his disappointment. It took him a minute or two to recover from the shock. Suddenly, his face lit up as if Saint Cecilia had smiled down on him. Beckoned by the two players, he walked to the front, and with his hands crossed over his chest, bowed to the audience and then to the players, again and again.

Anton celebrated by taking his friends and students, including Josef Schalk and Franz Zottmann, for a meal at Gauss's restaurant.

'It's all on me,' he said. 'Have what you like from the menu.'

'That is so generous of you, Herr Bruckner,' said Bruno.

'I agree,' said Kathi.

'First, I propose a toast to Franz Zottmann and Josef Schalk for their wonderful performance. Second, I thank them profusely for making my Symphony No 5 playable on two pianos. I could not have expected more. Their interpretation was faultless and I congratulate them.'

Zottmann and Schalk looked at each other, hardly believing what Anton was saying. Perhaps they realised he was right in pressing them to arrange it as he insisted, even though they couldn't completely satisfy him.

'My dear Professor Bruckner,' said Schalk. 'It has been a privilege for us to write an interpretation of your symphony. It is a great work and we wish to be remembered as the first two who performed it. We hope, Professor, it will soon be performed by a full orchestra.'

'Hear, hear,' said Hugo.

'I agree,' said Kathi.

They all became involved in the conversation. Kathi said she was pleased to be working for a famous composer. When Anton disagreed, she scowled at him and was on the verge of threatening to leave. Fortunately, he noticed the glare on her face.

'What I meant was that I am not famous, not that you don't enjoy working for me. I'm not good with words, so it's difficult for me to say this. I appreciate all you do for me, from keeping the apartment clean, doing my washing, cooking meals, and even posting my letters. And much more!'

'Oh, thank you, Herr Bruckner,' she said, breaking into a smile.

'So why hasn't your No. 5 been performed by a full orchestra, Professor?' said Zottmann.

'I don't know. I've asked the Vienna Philharmonic, and they half said they would. As you know, they played two movements of my sixth under Wilhelm Jahn, but completely forgot about the fifth. And they are talking about the seventh.'

'So disappointing,' said Schalk. 'But it is so good that, despite your modesty, your symphonies are being played the world over.'

'I'm so pleased,' said Anton. 'My No. 3, 4 and 7 are the ones the world has taken to and enjoy.'

'Your No. 2 is brilliant, too, Anton, but no one plays that yet, either.'

'It's time will come!' said Anton. 'As will the time when my No. 5 is played!'

'I know you are working on your eighth, Herr Bruckner. When will that be ready to be performed?'

'There is still work to do on it. I think it will be my very best. I plan to finish it by the end of August, if not before.'

Before they left the restaurant, they promised to meet again, and then went their various ways. Anton felt that his insistence on the best presentation of No. 5 they could produce had been vindicated.

***

412

'I apologise for my brief outburst last night, Herr Bruckner, but you deserved it, up to a point.'

'I agree, Kathi. I apologised for my clumsy use of language. What I said would have been clearer, if I'd thought before I spoke.'

'No matter. We have spoken to each other about it, so we can call it dealt with, Herr Bruckner. Do you agree?'

'Of course, I agree, Kathi.' He gently put his arm around her. 'I'll always treasure you, as long as I live.'

'I'll get you some breakfast now!' He took away his arm, and she went to the kitchen. 'Do you mind if I make something for myself? I was late up this morning.'

'I don't mind at all. Have what you want, if we've got it.'

He took the unusual step of laying the breakfast table for each of them. She brought in two plates of eggs, ham and German sausage. 'What are you doing laying the table, Herr Bruckner?'

'It was something to do for a change and to help,' he said, without a sign of emotion.

'Going back to last night, what a success it was for you! I even recognised some tunes. Mainly from the scherzo. It's very entertaining, especially when that tune in the middle speeds up. The best thing is you repeat it time and again. I thought that movement was the best!'

'You'll never believe what fun it was to write, Kathi.'

'I thought those lads did the whole thing proud, don't you?'

'You know I do, from what I said last night,' he said, not really believing his own words. He did not believe the piano version could match the orchestral score. Even so, he was grateful to Franz and Josef for what they did. It was better than having nothing.

***

Between March and the end of April, he worked on orchestrating the finale of No. 8. This movement, as he had originally drafted it, had to summarise and bring together the entire work. The belligerent opening theme would remain. It would remind the listener of the first movement and the second theme, as usual for him, the song theme, would relate to the adagio. The third, a march, would be a reworking of a theme in the first movement.

***

Not only were there more performances worldwide of his symphonies, there were also performances of the *Te Deum*. By far the most important for Anton was the one in the September at the Cathedral of the Immaculate Conception for the consecration of its organ. He wrote to Irene to invite her to attend as his guest.

'Thank you for inviting me, Anton. First, how long are you going to be here?' she said as she opened the door to him.

'Just one night.'

'Please stay with me! I'd love that.'

'I didn't come here to have free lodging!'

'I know, but I'd be really upset if you stayed somewhere else.'

'You've convinced me. I'll stay!'

'It will be an honour to have a famous composer sleeping here!'

'Oh, please don't, Irene. It's my music that's becoming famous. Not me! I'm the same person as I was when I first stayed with you, God knows how many years ago, over fifty.'

'Yes, I'm the same person, too, and beginning to feel my age! But I'm not too old to cook you a meal. I think I can do your favourite with the dumplings?'

'That would be a treat, Irene! Thank you.'

'I'll first have to check for the ingredients!'

Irene had everything she needed and within an hour, they were both tucking into a meal together.

'I thought you deserved that Knight of the Grand Cross Order, Anton. Well done! Who recommended you for it? Do you know?'

'Yes. My great friend and supporter, Hermann Levi, has several royal connections, including Princess Amalia of Bavaria. He told me they both put my name forward.'

'They did well for you! You've not mentioned him before.'

'I met him in Bayreuth many years ago. He recently conducted the second performance of my seventh symphony. It was in Munich. It got the most tremendous ovation. I was almost in tears!'

'Who did the first?'

Anton told her about Arthur Nikisch and the performance in Leipzig.

'What an incredible man! It must be a brilliant symphony!'

Anton escorted Irene to the Cathedral site. The basic structure of the building was complete, so it seemed a safe building to contain the complex workings of the organ to be consecrated. Anton was unsure whether they expected him to perform a role in the service until a priest approached him.

'Good afternoon, Herr Bruckner,' he said. 'We are so glad you could attend this service at which, as you know, we will perform your *Te Deum.*'

Anton wondered how he recognised him, but didn't ask.

'It's a privilege. Is it possible to meet Bishop Müller? I knew his predecessor, Bishop Rudigier, extremely well.'

'Yes, I believe so. I shall ask him now.'

414

Moments later, as Anton and Irene were about to take their places in the front pews, the Bishop appeared.

'Herr Bruckner, it is good to meet you! I'm so pleased we are performing your *Te Deum*.' They shook hands. 'Please introduce me to your companion.'

'This is Irene Planck. We have been friends for a very long time, Your Grace.'

'Good day, Frau Planck. I think I recognise you. Do you attend the Old Cathedral?'

'Oh, yes. I come to services there and often come in to listen to the organist. He reminds me of Anton.'

'I'm so pleased,' said the Bishop.

The Bishop started the service.

'We present this organ to be consecrated to the glory of Almighty God and for service in this, the Cathedral of the Immaculate Conception.'

A pastor read Psalm 150. A hymn followed. Then they performed Anton's *Te Deum*. The organist played almost right through, using the *ad libertum*, Anton suggested in the score. The Lord's Prayer ended the service.

'Your *Te Deum* is beautiful, Anton. I think it's your best religious work,' said Irene.

'Better than my F minor Mass?'

'I think so! It is so exciting!'

They parted with a hug. Anton caught a train back to Vienna.

***

He finalised his No.8 in August. He could not have been more certain that this was his best symphony by far, even better than his No. 7. It had a less real, more abstract feeling about it. 'My eighth is a mystery,' he said, more than once. He would write to Hermann Levi about it.

In a letter, dated 4 September, his sixty-third birthday, he said:

The eighth is finally ready and my artistic father must be the first to know... I would like to ask you, noble Sir, for the first performance...

Levi replied he was interested, so Anton sent him the score, along with the words:

May it find favour? My joy at the anticipated performance given by your masterful hands is indescribable.

'Herr Bruckner, here is a letter for you from Munich,' said Kathi. 'It's dated 7 October.'

'Thank you, Kathi. This is the one I've been dreaming of from Herr Levi... about my No. 8!'

'I thought I recognised the writing! I hope it is the reply you want!'

Anton took the letter and went into his study. He took his time in opening it because it could be an historical document, a certificate of his ability, of the kind he sought in his earlier days. He read it with care.

Levi said he spent many hours, even days, studying the symphony. He recognised the beauty and directness of many of the themes but could not own the symphony and perform it, as written. Therefore, some reworking was needed before he could play it. He said Anton could consider him an ass if he believed he had reached the wrong conclusion. But whatever he thought, he hoped they would remain the closest of friends.

Anton's face became distorted with fury. He didn't want Kathi to see him in a rage. So he spent some minutes in his study before coming out into the open.

'You look angry, Herr Bruckner.'

'He doesn't want to perform it. He obviously doesn't understand it. It's my greatest work and no one will convince me otherwise. He says he could be an ass, and I agree!'

'Hmm. You know I am always on your side, Herr Bruckner. Maybe there is something in what he says. He is a well-known conductor, as you are a well-known composer. I would leave it for a time and have an unbiased look at what he is saying. If you revised it, you could make it one of the best symphonies ever written, not just your best.'

'You are a wise woman, Kathi. I could not wish for a better friend than you. So I'll leave it for a time and look at it again. I won't reply until my thoughts are clearer.'

'He won't be looking for a quick reply, but you need to go back to him in a week or so.'

'I agree with that, too.'

Anton thought deeply and objectively as he could about what Levi said. Ten days after receiving the letter, he replied. He said he would study it again and do what was possible, to the best of his knowledge and belief. When it was all done, he would ask Levi to lead some rehearsals at Anton's expense and to ask Princess Amalie to attend for her opinion.

As an eminently sensible woman, Kathi didn't mention No. 8 to Anton until she thought it would cause no upset. So she left it for at least six weeks.

'What have you decided about your No. 8, Herr Bruckner? I hope you don't mind me asking.'

'Not at all, Kathi. You'll be glad to hear I've calmed down and have shrugged off my rage. I was helping Princess Amalie at the palace a few weeks ago and talked to her about it. I questioned Levi's judgement and I think... I'm not sure... but she half agreed. I've started looking over the score again and I'm beginning... just beginning... to think of revising it. I'm sorry if I didn't tell you before, but I've been making some changes to my No. 4.'

'You said you wouldn't change it! Not the version I heard!'

'Maybe that's why I didn't tell you!'

They both laughed.

'Not while you were working on the eighth?'

'Yes! My last work on No. 8 was polishing it! Don't you remember me asking for a clean duster?'

They both laughed again, but louder.

***

It was around then that the music director of the Vienna Philharmonic visited him at the University.

'My dear Anton, I have some good news for you. We are planning a concert in your honour. We want to play your fourth symphony and the *Te Deum*. Hans will conduct.'

'I'm delighted,' said Anton. 'I cannot express my joy! But I've been doing some revisions of that symphony for some time, not many, but I would like them included.'

'Oh no!' said the director. 'We want to rehearse before Christmas for a performance on the twenty-second of January.'

'I've finished it, so you can have the revised score. You can come to my apartment and collect it, if you wish. Tonight?'

'I'll do that,' he said. 'Any plans for publishing or do I have to arrange copying?'

'Yes, there are plans to get it into print, but I'm only in the middle of finding the money, so you'll have to use my revised score. You can probably get the changes copied onto the version you played before.'

'I'll see you tonight,' he said, looking at some notes on Anton's desk.

'There's a man at the door,' said Kathi after Anton had been home for no more than ten minutes. 'He said he's come to collect the score of your fourth.'

'Damn! I forgot to tell you. I'll get it. Could you give it to him, please? I don't want to see him.'

'Yes, alright.'

At first, Anton couldn't find it. He didn't panic. Eventually, he discovered it on the floor, under the side of his desk.

'Here it is. Quick!' he said.

Kathi gave the score to the director.

'That took a time.'

'I couldn't find it.'

Kathi said goodbye to the director and dashed back in.

'I'm very cross with you, Herr Bruckner. You put me in a difficult position. Why couldn't you give it to him? He seemed a nice man.'

'He's not that special. He was one of those gigglers at the rehearsals of my No 3. And he didn't want a score I'd fiddled with. That's why I left it to you.'

'Not good enough,' she shouted. 'It wouldn't have been so bad if you hadn't taken half an hour to find it.'

Anton saw no point in arguing. It had taken him no more than ten minutes, but that was a long time for Kathi, who had to wait for it.

'I apologise, Kathi. Please forgive me. I was so hungry when I came in, I forgot everything, except food. That's why I asked for some bread and cheese as soon as I walked in. I didn't have a chance to tell you the good news.'

'And what was that?' she said, still scowling.

'The Vienna Philharmonic is going to have an all Bruckner concert. They are going to play my No. 4 and the *Te Deum*.'

Her face changed to a broad smile. 'Congratulations, Herr Bruckner. They are on your side now!'

'I am beginning to believe they are, Kathi.'

The audience raved over each work. They burst into uncontrollable applause after each movement. They gave him a standing ovation at the end of the *Te Deum* and another, even more boisterous one, at the end of his No. 4. Richter invited him to the rostrum, where Anton deeply bowed to the audience and then the orchestra. He seemed to be there for an age before the clapping died down. As it did, the director presented Anton with a laurel wreath. The applause became louder again. Anton's feet were hurting him so, while the sound was at its loudest, he stumbled back to his seat in the stalls.

A handsome lady appeared in front of him and offered him her hand.

'Congratulations, Herr Bruckner! You have written two brilliant works, and I loved them both.

Anton recognised her. It was Crown Princess Stephanie, daughter of Leopold II of Belgium and wife of Crown Prince Rudolf.

Anton went to stand up.

'Please don't stand, Herr Bruckner. I just wanted to shake your hand, which I can with you seated.'

'You are kind, Your Highness. I'm so pleased you enjoyed them.'

'They are stunningly brilliant,' she said, and walked away.

Anton's face glowed with happiness. It was not often he received royal approval.

***

Anton spent hours pondering what Levi had said about his No. 8. It had to become his best, his most widely acclaimed, work. So at the end of January, he decided he would revise it. He needed to tell someone, as well as Kathi, so he wrote to Betty Mayfield saying that the eighth 'is far from done and needs major revision.' Then he wrote to Levi, saying, 'I seem to be ashamed of myself - at least this time - because of the eighth. I am the ass. I now see things differently.' He'd made up his mind.

***

Anton became aware that an important event was soon to take place in Vienna, on 22 June, '88, which he felt compelled to witness. Beethoven and Schubert had been buried in the undistinguished Währinger cemetery on the edge of the city. They were to be exhumed and reburied in the Central Cemetery, a more appropriate site for such renowned personalities.

That day, he dressed in his black, wide trousers and his overcoat, despite the heat, and walked to the cemetery. First, he laid some flowers on the grave of his beloved sister, Maria Anna, and, with a tear in his eye, kissed the headstone. He then slowly walked to Beethoven's grave and arrived as the gravediggers were removing the earth covering the coffin. As the officials were struggling to lift the deteriorating casket, a nightingale sang a sad tribute from a nearby tree. He would never forget that beautiful moment.

'Are we going to open it here or in the chapel?' said an official.

'In the chapel,' replied one of his colleagues.

'No, we're not. We're going to open it here.'

Several squabbling exchanges ensued before they settled on opening it there, mainly because it was not raining. Anton moved closer in as they inserted chisels between the lid and the shell. As they lifted off the lid, Anton leant over and peered in. He saw what remained of the genius. Deeply moved, and on the verge of tears again, he slowly edged himself away from a sight he would remember for the rest of his days. He then walked back home. He thought a sudden fault had occurred in his vision. Then he realised a lens had fallen out of his *pince-nez*. He chuckled to himself. It must have fallen into Beethoven's coffin as he was looking in. So a personal 'part of him' would accompany Beethoven until eternity.

***

419

'You seem to spend a lot of time working at home, Herr Bruckner,' said Kathi, as she came in early one morning and found him at his desk in the study. 'I suppose you are revising that No. 8 of yours?'

'Not at all. I'm much happier with my No. 4 since I revised it. So I'm making some improvements to my No. 3. I shouldn't have told my students it needed revision. They went ahead without me. So I'm ignoring what they did, if I can without offence, and working on it myself.'

'If you aren't happy with it, it makes good sense to change it. What about No. 8?'

'Once I've done what I want to on No. 3, I'll start on No. 8 again. Doing these revisions is developing my skill as a reviser! So when I start on No. 8, I will be an expert!'

'That sounds like good thinking to me.'

'I must tell you, I'll be going to St Florian again for my summer holiday at the end of this week. I'll take the symphony with me and work on it there.'

'So you're going earlier this year, then?'

'Yes, partly because of this revision.'

***

Anton was, as he expected, welcomed in St Florian, especially by Ignaz Traumihler, his friend of many years. They worked out a programme for Anton's stay. As usual, he would play some organ recitals. He said his hands were not as flexible as they used to be, so a recital of an hour at the most would suit him well.

'I hope you can still lift a stein of beer, Anton!'

'That's a different matter!'

'Let's go to the Sparrow then! I'll get Provost Ferdinand Moser to come with us, if he's free.'

The three of them went to the Inn. Ignaz insisted on buying the first round. Anton had never met Moser before but told him what support he had received more than fifty years ago from Prior Arneth, one of his predecessors.

'He was a great man,' said Moser, a tall, heavily bearded man, who spoke with an Upper Austrian accent, similar to Anton's. 'Michael Arneth had a reputation for helping people, especially if they were in any trouble.'

'He certainly helped me out when I was in trouble!' Anton told him about Prior Arneth rescuing him from the horrible atmosphere at Windhaag and getting him the post in Kronstorf.

'So you are now a well-known composer, Herr Bruckner. A writer of symphonies as well as a brilliant organist.'

'I wouldn't say that,' said Anton, looking into his beer.

'I would,' said Ignaz. 'Anton's symphonies are being played all over Europe and in America now. And he's just as good an organist now as he ever was!'

'My biggest barrier to their performance was Vienna, but I seem to be more accepted now. I had my first all Bruckner concert there back in January and they are thinking of performing my No. 7 again. We'll see!'

Anton bought the second round. He would stop at two half steins. He certainly didn't want to drink too much in front of the provost.

He took himself to his allocated study and soon settled into revising his No. 3. The most significant changes he made were to make some judicious cuts to the adagio and finale and to revise the orchestration.

People came from many towns and villages to listen to his recitals. After the last one, a lady of about his age struggled up the steps to the organ loft to speak to him.

'Herr Bruckner. I have come to see you again after many years. Do you remember me?'

'I recognise your face, but I cannot remember your name. I'm so sorry. Could you give me a clue?'

'Kronstorf!'

'You are Terweide Böhmer, the mezzo soprano! You sang in my Mass at the church there.' Anton stood up from the bench, put out his arms, and hugged her. 'How are you and how is life treating you?'

'I'm married and have a daughter and a son, both in their twenties. My name is Terweide Braun now. We have all come to see you!'

'I would like to meet your family.'

'You don't have to!'

'I know, but I'd like to!'

Much to the surprise of Ignaz, Anton spent nearly half an hour with the family, talking and laughing together.

'May I ask who those people were you spent time talking to?' said Ignaz.

'Of course. The wife is a mezzo soprano I met, when I began as a teacher at Kronstorf. I'd written my first Mass and had it played at the church there. The priest knew a mezzo we could use, and it was Terweide. She's married to a lawyer and has a son and a daughter who are both string players in the Linz Orchestra. I was amazed to see her after about fifty years! What a lovely family.'

'You must have had quite an influence on her if she was so keen to see you again.'

'She may have gained in confidence a little. She sang well for me.'

As always, Anton thrived on his stay at St Florian. While he had many friends in Vienna, he had plenty in St Florian, many of the older ones whom he had known since he was a teacher there. He found the relaxed atmosphere richly conducive to working, so pressed on with the revision of No. 3. While he was working, Ignaz called in on him.

'You are spending much time here, Anton. Are you writing a new symphony or a new religious work?'

'Neither, in fact. I'm revising my third symphony.'

'Do you have a moment to talk because I'm intrigued?'

'Of course, I love chatting about my work, especially my composing!'

'When you change one of you symphonies, would anyone know the difference?'

'It depends on what I do. If I put a cymbal crash where there wasn't one before, you would notice.'

'That's obvious! I mean, if you are just revising to make it as you want it. Say I heard the first version of that movement a few years ago, would I notice the changes you have made?'

'I haven't put in a cymbal crash, so I doubt it… unless you have an acutely sharp ear and an excellent memory for music. A member of the orchestra who played it a few years ago would probably notice. And the conductor. The point is, I want to bring my years of experience to it. I started writing No. 3 in autumn, '72 and it's now the summer of '88 so there are sixteen years of learning I am using on it.'

'But do you think you are improving it?'

'Yes, otherwise I wouldn't change it!'

'Fair point! What about other symphonies? Are you going to revise them?'

'I've revised my second and fourth. But I'm not intending to change the fifth, sixth or seventh. I may rework the first! The main one is my No. 8.'

Anton told him about his reaction to Levi's comments on it and that he eventually accepted that it needed change. 'I want to make it one of the best written, the symphony of symphonies! I'll be well practiced in revision when I turn to it.'

'I think I understand, Anton. You'll find me in the Monastery when you've finished here. Then we'll go for dinner.'

***

'You seem to have been away an age, Herr Bruckner. Have you enjoyed your stay?' said Kathi as he arrived back home.

'It was wonderful. Plenty of everything, food, beer, friendship and conviviality!'

'Not too much of the beer, I hope!'

'I was on my best behaviour, especially in front of the provost!'

'Did you finish revising your third symphony and start again on the eighth?'

'No to each of those questions! But I'm pleased with what I've done so far on No. 3. I've finished the last movement and have started on the slow movement! So not that far to go!'

'Your letters mainly arrive when you are away. Only two this time!'

He hung up his coat and opened them in front of Kathi.

'Brilliant news. The first is from the director of the Philharmonic. They want to repeat their performance of my No. 7.'

'Herr Bruckner, I could hug you!'

'You can if you wish, but Bruno may not like you to!'

'I won't until you tell me what's in the second letter!'

'I may not!' Anton opened it. 'Another performance! Karl Muck wants to play it in Graz. He did last year, but he's asking me to go this time!'

Kathi gave him a tight hug. 'You deserve that, Herr Bruckner. Many, many congratulations!'

'Thank you, Kathi!' He didn't comment on the hug, but thought it was the best he'd enjoyed for many years, even better than the one with Terweide in St Florian.

'Will you go to Graz?'

'I don't think so. If I went to all the performances of my symphonies, I'd be on the road every day from daybreak to nightfall. So I won't go. I'll write to Karl and tell him… and thank him, of course!'

'When are the Philharmonic playing your No. 7?'

'In the 89, 90 season, by the sound of it. The earlier the better, hopefully before the spring.'

'I'd love to hear it again.'

'I'll get you some free tickets in the best seats,' he said, hoping for another hug. He was out of luck.

***

His increasing acceptance, particularly in Vienna, did not change Anton, except to make him more generous. He was enjoying a drink before a meal with some friends in the Red Hedgehog when Johannes Brahms appeared with some of his friends. Most of the tables were occupied and Anton could see Brahms was struggling to find somewhere to sit, so Anton shouted to him.

'My dear Johannes, there is room on this table. Would you like to join us?'

'We'd be delighted, my dear Anton!'

'Would you all like a Pilsner?'

'Yes we would, please,' answered Johannes on behalf of them all.

'I'll order them,' said Anton, who went to the bar. A waitress brought the drinks to the table, after Anton had returned.

The conversation was chilly to begin with.

Having studied the menu, Brahms announced his choice. 'I'm going to have cabbage, dumplings and some smoked meat, my favourite! Waiter, bring me some dumplings, cabbage and smoked meat!'

'That's my favourite, too! That's the point where we two understand each other!' The effect of Anton's statement was incredible. The entire group burst out laughing and shook hands with each other. Anton had broken the ice.

They all ordered what Anton and Johannes were having and, as they were waiting to be served, started a conversation. Anton didn't want to talk about anything controversial, so they started with the acoustics of the Vienna Music Society Hall. No one liked it much. There was too much reverberation.

'It was good for my second symphony,' said Anton. 'The sound carried nicely in the silent bars!'

'It didn't help my first that much,' said Johannes.

'My songs sound good in there,' said Hugo.

Then they turned to discussing conductors. They all agreed that Hans Richter was not only a brilliant conductor but also an incredibly amiable man. Then they turned to Levi.

'I can see why you like him. He's only too keen to play your works and is a great champion of Wagner, which I am not.'

'It is good that we both write symphonies, Doctor Brahms. And people come to listen to them. Audiences can relax to your beautiful symphonies. I feel mine grip them.'

'I don't understand yours, Herr Bruckner!' said Brahms smiling.

'Really? I noticed you applauding my sixth!'

'That was different. I had to applaud because everyone else did!'

'In fact, I don't understand yours either,' said Anton, also smiling. 'But now we've met each other, we must try to be friends!'

'I'll drink to that,' said Brahms.

'We should all drink to that,' said Franz Schalk.

They all clinked glasses together. The waitress arrived with their meals and they carried on talking about music and the scene in Vienna, various personalities at the Conservatoire and the University, as well as the increasing amounts of travel all there were doing. After they finished the dish and another round of Pilsner, Brahms said his group was needed elsewhere so they left, members of each group smiling to each other as they went.

'You buggers organised this, didn't you?' said Anton, wide eyed and looking straight at Franz Schalk.

Schalk didn't know quite how to respond.

'Yes,' said Hugo. 'We thought, as did some of Brahms' friends, you two needed to meet.'

'Good idea,' said Anton. 'It worked well. The fact is we don't understand each other's works! And probably never will!'

'It doesn't matter,' said Josef. 'Your works are now performed worldwide and will continue to be.'

'Let's drink to that,' said Ferdinand.

They all clinked glasses together.

Chapter 30
1890 - 1891 Health and performances

'Good morning, Herr Bruckner! Sorry I'm a bit late!' shouted Kathi as she came into the hall. There was no reply. She entered the kitchen and started preparing his breakfast. She detected no sound from Anton.

'Your breakfast is nearly ready!' she shouted. Still no reply. She became worried and knocked on his bedroom door.

'Herr Bruckner, are you alright?'

She heard a groan from his room. Then her name, but not clearly, followed by silence. He then uttered words so unclear she couldn't understand them.

'I'm coming in. Cover yourself up.'

She went in. His head was visible above the bedclothes. He looked pale.

'What is the matter, Herr Bruckner?'

'I can only whisper. My throat hurts. I'm having trouble breathing. And I don't feel well.'

'I'm worried about you, so I'm going to get the doctor.'

'I'll be alright, Kathi,' he said, still whispering. 'I don't want Prof Schrötter. Let's see how I am tomorrow.'

'No! Not if you are having breathing trouble. I'm going now!'

Kathi put her winter coat back on and dashed out of the house. She walked as fast as she could without actually running, holding up her long dress to prevent it dragging on the road. She knocked on the Professor's door. No reply. She knocked again, but more persistently. A black woman opened the door. Her dark hair was piled high and wide on her head and was topped by a small white hat. She wore a long white dress down to her ankles. A narrow black belt accentuated her waist.

'Good morning, meine Frau. May I ask how I can assist you?' said the woman, in an educated accent.

Kathi's eyes opened wide at seeing this woman and hearing her voice. Then she hastily explained.

'I work for Herr Anton Bruckner, the famous composer. He is very unwell. I'm asking if Professor Dr Schrötter can see him as a matter of urgency.'

'Could you please tell me his symptoms?'

'Yes, but first, could you please tell me who you are?'

'Yes, I am Miss Veronica Edwards. I am Dr Schrötter's senior nurse. I am from England.'

'In which case, I will tell you. He is having trouble breathing, cannot speak properly and his throat hurts. I'm anxious because he is normally in such good health.'

426

'Where is he now?'

'In bed.'

'I'll speak to the Professor. Please come in. It's warmer inside.'

A few moments later, the Professor appeared. He and Miss Edwards, each dressed in winter coats, along with Kathi, climbed aboard the Professor's carriage and set off for the apartment in the Hessgasse. Kathi let them in and followed them. She knocked on his bedroom door.

'Herr Bruckner, the Professor is here. Can he come in? His nurse is with him.'

'Yes, of course,' he whispered.

'He may not want you in there, Miss Edwards. He won't let me see him in his nightshirt.'

'I'm here to help Professor Schrötter, Frau Kathi.'

'Come in with me,' said the Professor.

They went in. The Professor persuaded Anton out of his bed and examined him with the aid of a stethoscope.

'There are two things wrong, Herr Bruckner. Your throat is troubling you because you have catarrh. That will cure itself in a few days to a week. You can help it by taking sips of water. Veronica, go to the kitchen with Frau Kathi. Make up a salt nose rinse. You must rinse in it three times a day. I hate to tell you, Herr Bruckner, but you also have dropsy. That is an accumulation of fluid in your legs. That's why they are wide and you probably think they are heavy. I will give you some tablets which will help clear it. Stay in bed for a few days and I'll ask Frau Kathi to find something to put under your legs. They need to be higher than your heart.'

'Thank you, Professor,' he whispered. 'I'm grateful to you. May I work while I'm in bed?'

'No. Work will keep until you are better.'

'Thank you, Professor.'

Miss Edwards appeared from the kitchen with some warm salt water in a dish.

'I'll show you how to use this on your nose.' He gently pushed Anton's nose into the water and eased it out again. 'There you are. You can now do it yourself, Herr Bruckner.'

'Now?'

'No, three times a day. Again after your lunch and again before bed. Here are some tablets for your dropsy.'

'Thank you, Professor.' He turned to Miss Edwards. 'Thank you, too, nurse.'

They left Anton in his bed, and Kathi showed them out. She then knocked on Anton's bedroom door and opened it slightly to hear his whisper.

'Can I come in, Herr Bruckner?'

'Yes, I'm still in my bed.'

'Should I bring you some breakfast?'

'Yes, please, but nothing that will hurt my throat.'

Kathi brought him some scrambled eggs, bread from which she had removed the crust, and some water. She didn't want him talking too much, so refrained from asking him about what the doctor had said.

'Is there anything else you need?'

'Yes, could you fold up some blankets please to lift my legs up?'

She realised immediately that he must have dropsy.

Anton spend the next two days in bed but felt well enough to get up and dress on the third. His catarrh, as the doctor expected, had virtually cured itself and his legs were not as swollen. Having what he regarded as wasting so much time in bed, he was keen to start work again on No. 8.

The first was the one movement remaining, which he had not yet scrutinised. Even on initially examining it, he could detect something wrong with it, really wrong. He read and reread the score but could not identify the problem, so could not solve it. He spent days pondering it. Suddenly, late one night in the middle of February, as he was thinking about retiring to bed, he realised why it didn't seem right. It ended on a high note, in a positive mood. To be consistent with the rest of the movement, it had to end in despair. So, he deleted the last forty bars and, over the following week, totally reworked the ending.

Although the swelling in his legs had substantially reduced, he still found it painful to walk. So occasionally, he was late arriving at the Conservatorium or the University. He thoroughly enjoyed his lecturing and, of course, mixing and socialising with his students. He wondered if he could solve this problem. Although he had become better off financially, he decided he would not pay for a cabriolet to take him to either office. So for months he continued to walk from Hessgasse to work. He thought the three quarters of an hour walk to the Conservatorium would be good for him, despite having to cope with some pain. One evening, as soon as he stepped into the kitchen, he discussed the issue with Kathi.

'I'm not sure of the solution, Herr Bruckner. You are a senior member of staff now. You could ask the University and the Conservatorium to pay for a cabriolet.'

'Pride comes into this, Kathi. I couldn't possibly ask them.'

'In which case, have you thought of resigning from, say, the Conservatorium? You'd be better off with just the University where you are only teaching three days a week. And you have more friends there.'

'I'll have to think about that one, Kathi. It sounds too much like giving up to me.'

'The problem we both have, Herr Bruckner, is that we are getting older. I'm not as mobile as I used to be!'

'I bet if I chased you, you'd suddenly become very mobile!'

'Now! Now! No cheekiness, please!'

'No offence meant, Kathi. But if my humour was misplaced, I apologise.'

'Not at all, Herr Bruckner. We've known each other for long enough to know how far we can go with each other. You caused me no offence at all!'

Anton's health fluctuated. Some days he felt well and capable of almost anything. On others, he struggled both with walking and breathing. So, a few days later, he spoke to Kathi again.

'I've decided, Kathi. Very much based on your advice. I'm going to ask the Conservatorium for at least six months leave of absence. But I'll continue with the University. It's nothing like so far to walk!'

This decision, and bringing it into effect, took much of the academic burden from Anton's shoulders. It also made him feel better, to his and Kathi's relief and delight.

With more time for composing, he looked again at his No. 8. On 10 March he wrote, 'Entirely Finished' on the score. As he did so, he again uttered the word, 'Hallelujah!' The next step in his most important project was to fight to get it printed and performed. He didn't care who would play it. If Levi decided against it, that would not concern him. The key was for someone to agree to perform it, in Vienna or somewhere else.

Anton was so thrilled to receive the Order of Franz Joseph, he wanted to dedicate the symphony to the Emperor as a way of thanking him. Within days of writing to ask for permission, he received a letter saying the Emperor agreed and was extremely grateful and honoured. Anton then thought of seeking a publisher. In April, he contacted Hermann Levi to ask for his support in publishing it in Germany. Anton suggested using a publisher he knew of called Schott, who responded dustily that they would consider it.

Completing No. 8 made him start another project which he had been turning over in his mind since he finished revising No. 4. He would, after twenty-five years, look again at his No. 1. So the same day as he completed No. 8, he eventually, in his heaps of papers, found the score to No. 1 and read it.

***

'You may not believe this, Herr Bruckner, but here is a letter for you from the palace!'

'Really? Not another!'

'Yes. That's what it's postmarked!'

Anton opened it. 'It's from the Emperor. You won't believe this, Kathi. He wants me to play the organ at Princess Marie Valerie's wedding on the thirty-first of July.'

'Where, here, in Vienna?'

'Just a minute.' He turned over the page and read more of the letter. 'No, in Bad Ishl.'

'How are they expecting you to get there? It's at least two hundred kilometres!'

'By train, I imagine. At the palace's expense. Otherwise, I won't do it!'

'Yes, you would. Even if you paid them!'

'I must admit, it will be a great honour. You know about the Emperor's family. Isn't she involved in some scandal or other?'

'Not really a scandal. She's engaged to Archduke Franz Salvator. He's her third cousin and, according to the gossip, they've been seeing each other since they met at a ball in '86. He is the Archduke of Austria Tuscany and is a very minor royal.'

'What do you mean, a minor royal? I'm puzzled!' said Anton.

'He and his family are not rich. So he can't offer her a substantial dowry, as could others such as the Prince Royal of Portugal.'

'So her family doesn't want the marriage to go ahead?'

'Ah! That's where it gets complicated! Her brothers and sisters are against it, but the mother, Elizabeth in Bavaria, strongly supports the marriage. This is because Marie Valerie is her favourite. And she's told the others she expects them to marry into money! The whole business, it seems, has caused big trouble in the family!'

'Goodness me! I see what you mean! What a situation!'

'Anyway, the rumour is that she'll have to renounce her right to the throne before the wedding. If she doesn't, it probably won't go ahead.'

'I'm going to reply, assuming it will happen. There's nothing in the letter that raises any doubts.'

Anton replied that he would be delighted to perform at the wedding and considered it a special honour. He inquired about travel plans, specifically if he should go to Bad Ishl on his own or if there would be transport available. As he wrote, he decided not to ask about remuneration.

A few days later, he received a brief response, signed by the Emperor's Private Secretary. It said he should travel on the Royal Train, which would leave from the Vienna Central Station at 10 o'clock in the morning of 30 July, and hotel accommodation would be provided in Bad Ishl.

Kathi packed for him, having made sure his clothes were suitable for the wedding, and for travel with the Emperor. He felt well enough to walk to the station and made sure he arrived in good time.

'Herr Bruckner, we have a seat reserved for you in the Emperor's carriage. Please come this way,' said a bewigged official from the Palace, dressed in a gold braided, red jacket and tight, white trousers. Anton's eyebrows lifted and his eyes opened wide. He was not expecting to travel so near to royalty. The man put out his hand to help Anton from the platform into the carriage. 'Please follow me.'

Anton did as instructed. He couldn't believe their extravagant opulence as he walked through the royal carriages. Even the door to the toilet had a gold plated handle. He couldn't help but wonder what it was like inside. It was nothing like any train he had travelled in before. The man invited him to sit in an armchair in a thickly carpeted, luxurious room like area. A well-coiffured lady with her back towards him was already occupying a similar chair.

'I believe you have previously met,' said the escort.

As Anton approached, she spoke. 'Ah, Herr Bruckner! It's good to see you again,' said Crown Princess Stephanie of Belgium. 'We are travelling together with Prince Hohenlohe and his wife, Princess Marie zu Sayn-Wittgenstein.'

If only someone had told me, thought Anton. He was unsure of how to address these distinguished royal personages, so decided on 'Your Highness'.

'I'm more than delighted, indeed honoured, to see you again, Your Highness, so soon after meeting you at the Philharmonic's concert. I was so pleased you enjoyed my compositions.'

'That symphony totally captivated me. The tunes were rolling around inside my head for days. And your *Te Deum*! I loved the way it started. And indeed the entire work. What a beautiful piece of music.'

'Thank you again!'

'I don't know where Konstantin and Marie are! They'll miss the train if they aren't here soon.'

'Surely, the train would wait for them.'

'I'm less sure. It would wreck the schedule for the whole of Austria if it were delayed by more than a few minutes.'

As she completed her sentence, two breathless royals appeared in the coach.

'It was his fault!' said the princess, staring at the prince. 'I've never known anyone take so long to tie a bow tie!'

Anton looked upwards. He didn't expect such a demonstration of fallibility from such waited-upon royals. The newcomers took their seats as the whistle blew and the train slowly left the platform.

'You just made it!' said Princess Stephanie.

They all laughed, including Anton, who immediately felt at ease. It didn't surprise him that Prince Konstantin started the conversation.

'I am so grateful to you, Anton, for dedicating your fourth symphony, the Romantic, to me. What pleases me most is that it is a bright and cheerful work. I'm sure it will become very popular.'

'I truly hope so, Your Highness. It is being performed widely, around the world, I'm delighted to say.'

'Why did you dedicate it to him?' said Princess Stephanie.

'Because His Highness took over the Office of the Imperial Court Orchestra and had an amazing impact on the quality of performances.'

'Excellent reason,' said Princess Marie. 'I enjoyed its performance in the concert with the *Te Deum*.'

'I didn't know you were there,' said Princess Stephanie. 'I embarrassed myself by going up to Herr Bruckner after the performance and telling how brilliant his compositions are and how much I enjoyed them both!'

'I took great pleasure in your reaction,' said Anton. 'I don't think you embarrassed yourself at all!'

'Did you know Princess Marie does much promotional work for the Performing Arts?' said the Prince.

'No, I wasn't aware of that,' said Anton. 'What projects do you involve yourself in, Your Highness?' asked Anton, feeling confident enough to do so.

'Mainly in the theatres, and operas. I'm in the minority in that I have promoted some of Richard Wagner's works in Vienna.'

'That's brilliant!' said Anton. 'I love his operas, especially the music. How did you become a Wagner supporter?'

'An interesting question. As you know Cosima is a daughter of Franz Liszt. Well, my mother, Princess Carolyne, lived with Franz Liszt at Weimar after she divorced my father. That's why I'm so keen to promote Wagner.'

'So what symphony are you up to now, Anton?' said Prince Konstantin.

'It's not long since I finished my eighth.'

'Will it differ significantly from the one you dedicated to Konstantin?' said Princess Marie.

'It is a totally different symphony,' said Anton, smiling gratefully for the chance to talk about it. 'I've tried to make it as mysterious as I can from the very first notes of the first movement. It will take a grip on the listener and take him... or her... into a universe of sound they have never experienced before. The music will so entrance them, they won't want it to end… Should I continue or have I said enough?'

'No! Keep going, Herr Bruckner,' said Princess Stephanie.

'It is the first I have written with the scherzo second, so the first two movements are the major introduction to the work. The adagio, which follows, is strong and unyielding, with a variety of themes and shifts of mood, from introspection to assertiveness, from darkness to light, through contrasts, tensions and releases, ultimately leading to a transcendent sense of peace. It has the most exciting, sublime climax of any symphony I have written…' He paused.

'Carry on Anton, there is still a movement left!'

'I haven't finished describing the adagio! That massive climax, with its cymbal crash and harp arpeggio, leaves the listener wondering where they are and where the movement will end. It holds them there until the breaking out of peace at its conclusion. The finale integrates what precedes it into a vibrant whole. Its themes are mainly recognisable reconstructions of earlier statements. But there are sprinklings of independent but related new material. It captures the listener from its blazing beginning and will not put them down until it ends on a summit of glory. I have tried to make it the symphony of symphonies!'

'My God, Anton, I cannot wait to hear it! When will it be played?' said Princess Marie.

'I only wish I knew,' said Anton. 'My aim is to convince the Vienna Philharmonic to play it.'

'I'll see if I can bring some influence,' said Princess Marie.

'I would be eternally and exceptionally grateful if you could,' said Anton, smiling widely.

Well before the train pulled in to Bad Ishl station, the Emperor appeared in their carriage. Anton thought he was looking his age, even though he was younger than Anton. Anticipating his reception at the station, he was dressed in full military uniform with his medals decorating his chest. They all stood to receive him, Anton the last to rise.

'Good day to you all. I have mainly come to see Herr Bruckner about what I'm expecting of him at the wedding. First, I must thank you, Anton, for dedicating your Symphony No. 8 to me. You have made me immortal. No one will remember me, Franz Joseph I, but they will when they see that dedication.'

They all laughed.

'That assumes the symphony will outlast you,' said Princess Stephanie.

'Of course it will,' said the Emperor, removing the burden of a similar remark from Prince Konstantin and Princess Marie. 'Let me know if you want me to pay for its publication.'

'Thank you so much, Your Highness. I certainly will.'

'What I want, Anton, is for you to play the Kaiserlied, as Princess Marie Valerie is entering the church. Then lead in to Handel's Hallelujah as I escort her up the aisle. Will that be alright?'

'Of course, Your Highness. I can also improvise on the Handel, but only if you wish.'

'Brilliant. I'd appreciate that!' The Emperor said he'd see them all at the wedding, turned and left.

The princesses and the prince bade their farewells to Anton as they stepped out of the carriage at Bad Ishl and were escorted to a four horse carriage. Anton was met by the same bewigged official who had escorted him onto the train. 'Please come with me, Herr Bruckner. I have a cabriolet waiting to take you to your hotel. You'll be met in good time to take you to the church. That will be at 10.30 in the morning.'

The little town of Bad Ishl enthralled Anton. The river was wide and reminded him of the Danube as it flowed quickly, splitting the town in two. He had an early morning walk along the river bank.

Anton was looking his best as he stepped out of the hotel just before the allotted time. The cabriolet had yet to arrive. After five minutes, he was becoming anxious. Five minutes became ten. He peered at his watch. What should he do? Should he go to the hotel reception and ask them for a cabriolet or even for one of the staff to take him? Looking again at his watch, he decided. He turned to go into the hotel. Then he heard a loud voice.

'Oy you! Are you Herr Bruckner?' a driver shouted as he stopped near him.

'That's me!'

'Get in. Sorry I'm a bit late. Silly buggers sent me to the wrong hotel. We'll get you to the church on time.'

The driver whipped the horses into a gallop. Anton had never felt so thrown around in a cab before.

'Been paid, mate. Don't need nothing from you,' he blurted out, as he arrived at the church.

Anton thanked him and stepped into the magnificent building, which was almost full of guests.

A priest greeted him with an open hand. 'I'm late, Reverend. I'm playing the organ. Can someone direct me to the organ loft now, please?'

The priest turned to a colleague and echoed Anton's request. Within three minutes, Anton was sitting at the console, near to which a novice priest was standing.

'My job is to give you the signal to start,' said the novice. 'You know what the Emperor wants, don't you?'

Anton gave him a breathless nod. 'How long have we got?'

'About two minutes. No. Start now!'

Anton immediately and vigorously launched into the Kaiserlied which he knew by heart. He seamlessly attached it to the Hallelujah, improvising with his usual verve and creativity, confident the congregation had heard nothing like it before.

'You can stop now,' said the novice, who had seen another signal.

What a shame, thought Anton as he was getting into his stride.

'Should I play anything as they leave the church, even at low volume?'

'I'll ask?'

Some minutes later, the novice appeared. 'Yes, play anything you wish, but not too loud.' So he played some Michael Haydn.

'You did a wonderful job, Anton,' said Prince Konstantin, as he met Anton at the reception which was held at the town hall.

'It was a pleasure! I could have played for longer!'

He thrived on the banquet at which he was an honoured guest, so sat with Prince Konstantin and Princesses Stephanie and Marie, near the top table. Anton smiled broadly, as he heard the Emperor's speech in which he praised his organ play.

The Emperor mingled extensively with his guests and spoke again to Anton. 'Please accept this, Anton,' he said. 'A small token of my thanks and appreciation.'

'Thanking me in your father-of-the-bride speech was sufficient reward,' said a grateful Anton. 'I can accept no more.'

'You can and you will!' said the Emperor, laughing and forcing a small leather bag into his hand.

Anton would not travel back with the royal party but, because he was on leave from the university, would make the most of his time out of Vienna and take a short holiday. He wrote a brief letter to Kathi to tell her he would be away for the whole of the summer vacation. His first stop was Linz, where he called on Irene.

'What are you doing here, Anton? It's wonderful to see you. More than a day and you must stay here!' she said, as she opened the door to the weary traveller.

'I can't stay with you without giving you some form of gift!'

'Don't be silly, Anton. I want nothing of you, except your company. I'm an old woman now and suffer more from loneliness than any other malady.'

'If I can stay, I would be so grateful. I will be here for a short time, not many days, I'm sure.'

'Stay as long as you wish, my dearest friend.' She gave him an impassioned hug and a kiss on both cheeks. 'Come in before the neighbours wonder what we are up to!'

They went into the lounge.

'So tell me your news.'

He told her about his organ play at Princess Marie Valerie's wedding at Bad Ischl, the journey there with the prince and the two princesses. Then he spoke about his No. 8, his intention of making it the best symphony ever written, and the joint concert performance of No. 4 and the *Te Deum*. In a lowered voice, he told her he had not been well and was on leave of absence from the Conservatorium.

'Anton, a feature of getting older. It happens to us all. I'm not as active as I was ten years ago.'

'So what's your news, Irene?'

'I'll tell you something which will make your eyebrows rise. My neighbour next-door has a friend staying with him who knows of you but doesn't actually know you in person. He is the brother of a woman innkeeper in Neufelden, which is about thirty kilometres away. You'll never guess who the lady landlord is!'

'Go on. Don't keep me in suspense!'

'When you were the organist at Linz, you fell for a young woman called Josefine Lang. You told me you made her choke on some Pilsner. She was a member of the Linz Choir. Do you remember?'

'Clearly!'

'Well, she's the landlady! So she's married and has a young daughter. If you'd like to meet her again, we can ask the brother, Herr Lang, next door!'

'I've just got to think whether we separated on good terms… in fact, we did. So yes, I'd be delighted to see her again.'

Early the following morning, Anton was sitting alongside Fritz Lang, who was working the reins of his buggy. They were on their way to Neufelden. Anton couldn't help wondering what Josefine would look like after so many years. He knew he couldn't fall in love with her again, so the journey was simply one to reacquaint himself with an old friend.

'Guess who this gentleman is!' said Fritz, as he found Frau Josefine Weilnböck, washing some beer glasses in her public house.

'If it's my old friend, Anton Bruckner,' said Josefine. She came towards him, gave him an intense hug, and kissed him. 'It must be over forty years since we talked about getting married!' She laughed. 'Let me get you a drink. A Pilsner?'

'Wonderful!' said Anton. 'If you pour one for yourself, we can raise a glass to each other! It is so good to see you after so long!'

They sat at a table as Fritz vanished into the rear of the tavern.

'Here's to us!' said Josefine. 'So you are a famous composer now. I thought you would become famous when I heard your first symphony performed in Linz!'

'I seem more controversial than famous, Josefine. The Viennese are conservative and don't like radically novel approaches to music, the things I do. But I feel I've beaten the critics. Now my works are played all over Europe and the United States.'

'I'm so pleased for you!'

'So what made you become a public house landlady? It seems to suit you!'

'It's a long story. I did a course at the teacher training college at Linz to be a cook...'

'I remember,' said Anton, interrupting.

'I completed it and couldn't find a school job. Then I saw this advertisement for a cook to work in this inn. My parents were against it but...'

As she was halfway through the sentence, Fritz re-appeared holding the hand of a young girl.

'This is Karoline,' he said. 'Josefine's daughter!'

Anton was stunned into silence. Karoline looked just like her mother at the time Anton was on the verge of proposing to her. He could almost fall in love with her daughter, but she seemed much younger than Josephine was then.

'This is Herr Bruckner. He is a well-known composer. We were old friends about forty years ago when I was in the Linz Mixed Choir.' She didn't mention his wish to marry her.

'I'm pleased to meet you, Karoline,' said Anton. 'You must still be at school!'

'I am,' she said. 'I want to be a teacher when I leave.'

'I was a teacher once,' said Anton. 'I got on so well with my pupils. Even though I had high standards.'

'Our teacher is like that.'

'Show Herr Bruckner around the inn,' said her mother.

'Come with me, please,' said Karoline. She held his hand and led him from the bar into a room with booths and tables. Anton adored being in the girl's company, and the warmth of her hand grasping his. He kept thinking of his failed attempts at seducing her mother, but realised her daughter was equally enchanting.

'This is the private bar, we call it. My mother is a wonderful cook and serves food here. So it's like a restaurant.'

Then she took Anton, still holding his hand, into a pretty flower garden with a lawn dotted with tables and chairs.

'Would you like something to eat, Anton?' said her mother as she peered at them from the door. 'I'd love to cook you something.'

She reeled off her menu. 'I'll have some beef stew if I may. Do you have any dumplings?'

'Of course. Karoline must like you if she's still holding your hand!'

Karoline looked awkwardly at her mother and released Anton from her grip.

'We are getting on very well,' said Anton. 'I just love her company... and holding her hand!'

'I'm sure Anton would enjoy a walk around the village, Karoline. But be back within an hour.'

Karoline took Anton by the hand again and showed him around the village. He marvelled at the fast-flowing, frothing river, the bright new buildings and bustling activity in the market square. She pointed out her school, which stood next to the parish church.

'Is there an organ in the church?' said Anton, smiling.

'Yes, of course.'

'Would you like me to play it?'

'I don't see why not!'

'Could you pump the bellows?'

'Show me what to do and I will.'

Minutes later, Anton was playing with his usual verve and commitment. He started with the moderato theme from the adagio of his No. 7, then improvised on it, then some Bach. The organ completely ran out of wind just as he was about to play some Haydn. He wondered if Karoline had hurt herself pumping. Then she appeared next to him.

'Didn't you hear the clock chime? It's time we went!'

They arrived back at the inn as Josefine was dishing out a meal for Anton, Fritz, herself, and Karoline.

'We'd better eat quickly,' said Fritz. 'We need to be back in Linz before nightfall and it's nearly a thirty-five kilometre ride. We can't make the horses go faster than a trot.'

Anton was enjoying being with Josefine and Karoline, so was reluctant to leave them.

'You can stay a few nights, if you wish,' said Josefine.

'That would be lovely,' said Karoline.

'I must go. My friend, Irene, is expecting me back today. She worries about me, you know. But thank you for the offer.'

Anton and Josefine hugged each other before they parted. Karoline looked on.

'I don't know when, but I hope we meet again,' said Anton, as he climbed into the buggy.

'So do we,' said Josefine. 'Thank you for coming here.'

***

Irene was pleased Anton had returned safely from Neufelden and greeted him with open arms. He told her how he enjoyed meeting Josefine and Karoline and how Karoline reminded him of Josefine as a young girl.

'You didn't fall in love again, did you?'

'No. She was only fourteen. Too young, even for me!'

Anton stayed with Irene for almost a month, seeing old friends again and playing the organ at Linz Cathedral. He then travelled to St Florian where he continued revising his No.1. By the time he left, he was more than happy that he completed new versions of the last three movements. Socialising with Ignaz Traumihler and Provost Ferdinand Moser also occupied much of his treasured time there.

***

'Oh, you're back home, Herr Bruckner!' said Kathi as she came in, after Anton had been back for a couple of days. 'I didn't expect to see you for about a week.'

'I've been staying at various places at other people's expense, and I didn't want to outstay my welcome!'

'So how did the wedding go? I saw it in the newspapers. One of them mentioned your organ playing.'

'I had a wonderful time. They treated me like royalty and I travelled with royalty. I shared a carriage with Crown Princess Stephanie of Belgium, Prince Konstantin, and his wife, Princess Marie. I was so grateful to them for involving me in the conversation.'

Anton told her about the cabriolet turning up late, that he only just got to the church in time, the banquet and the Emperor mentioning him in his speech.

'Oh, and he gave me a leather purse I'd almost forgotten about, which I put in my case. I'll get it and see what's in it.'

Having shuffled around amongst his dirty clothing, he found it.

'Here it is.' He tipped the contents onto the dining table. 'Look at that lot, Kathi. Gold Ducats! There must be a hundred of them! They are worth at least a thousand florins. Here, ten of them must be for you!'

'Herr Bruckner, they are for you! Not me!'

'But you are so good to me! Please take them!'

'Thank you! Thank you so much.' She hugged him gratefully. 'And what about your holiday?'

He told her about his time with Irene in Linz and the journey to Neufelden to see his former flame, Josefine. 'Her daughter was totally entrancing. She was only fourteen.'

'I know what you are like with these youngsters!'

'No! Far too young for me! I spent over a month in St Florian, eating drinking and working on my No.1. I've just one movement to finish! Is there any mail?'

'Just one,' she said. 'Here it is. I can't see where it's from.'

Anton disappeared into his study and emerged in less than a minute.

'I've found a publisher for No. 8! A firm here called Haslinger-Schlesinger-Lienau. I called on them with the score, not so long ago and they say here they've accepted it. I'm thrilled. It means I can press on with getting it performed!'

'Amazing and congratulations, Herr Bruckner.'

'So I can ignore that German outfit, Schott, who said they'd look at it but clearly haven't.'

Anton thought about his future with the Conservatorium. He still had bouts of illness and was not as mobile as he used to be. He found it difficult to walk so far, there and back. So in the January, instead of asking for his leave of absence from the Conservatory to be extended, he resigned. He realised what a good choice he had made only when they told him he would receive a pension of four thousand florins a year. Thanks to financial assistance from an Upper Austrian business group, his income as a professor, and payments for performance of his works, he hadn't been this financially stable for years.

***

'You are looking very cheerful,' said Kathi, as Anton came home from the university one evening.

'I am, Kathi. My Symphony No. 8 is going to be performed in Mannheim… on the twenty-sixth of March.'

'How do you know?'

'Hermann Levi sent me a very apologetic letter. It said he couldn't play it for some daft reason, but he'd convinced a conductor in Mannheim to play it. His name is Felix Weingartner. He's only twenty-eight.'

'I wouldn't get too excited, Herr Bruckner. How do you know you can rely on this man? Have you met him?'

'I know what you are saying, Kathi, but from the tone of Levi's letter, he seems reliable. We'll just have to accept what he says until we know otherwise.'

'But you haven't got the score printed yet!'

'He's going to get it copied. He's so enthusiastic, according to Herr Levi! Weingartner has already written the programme. It's going to start with the first performance of my friend Hugo Wolf's Christnacht, then Beethoven's second, and mine will be the last work played. Fantastic!'

'I must admit, that sounds promising. I'll get you a beer!'

'Let's both have a wine!'

'No. Just one for you!'

Anton sent a copy of the score to Weingartner, who organised the orchestral parts to be prepared in Mannheim.

Achieving the first performance of No.8 was the primary aim in his life, but other activities had to be completed. He was still not happy with his revisions to the first movement of No. 1. His commitment to his teaching duties at the University was extraordinary. He was popular with the students and the staff, who recognised his ability as a lecturer, and enjoyed his growing fame.

Anton felt thrilled to hear from Weingartner that the rehearsals were going well. What troubled him was that Weingartner thought the last movement was too long and difficult to play. Anton's response was typical. He told him judiciously to cut it, insisting the score would remain as he completed it.

Then on 20 March, Anton heard from him again. This time it was to delay the performance until 2 April because Weingartner had to perform the St Mathew Passion on 27 April.

'Here's a letter for you from Mannheim, Herr Bruckner,' said Kathi, as Anton walked in from a day at the university. It's dated the ninth of April.'

'It must be to say how well... or otherwise... the performance went on the second!' Anton opened it. 'The bastard. He didn't perform it and isn't going to. Shit! Please excuse my language, Kathi, but I'm livid!'

'I didn't hear anything you should be sorry for. I would react the same! This is not the first time you've been badly let down. I really don't know what to say.'

'He says he's accepted a new appointment as conductor of the Königliche Opera in Berlin. So he didn't have time to rehearse it properly. I just don't believe his excuse. He's lying! Before he said it was too difficult and wanted to cut it. I told him he could, but not to corrupt the score. He must have found a cut version too difficult and dumped it. That's what's happened. The truth will come out, for sure.'

Anton suffered bitterly at the pen of Weingartner. Several performances of others of his works helped to relieve the pain. The new version of No. 1 was to be performed in Vienna, under Hans Richter. He learned from various newspaper reports and from his students that the revised No. 3 was played in Prague, Nuremberg and London, No. 4 in Graz and Nuremberg and No. 7 in Berlin. The *Te Deum* was also widely appreciated, especially in Europe and America. The press acclaimed him.

Not long after the stinging letter from Weingartner, Kathi brought another letter into his study. 'This one is from Berlin, Herr Bruckner.'

'My goodness, Kathi. A conductor called Siegfried Ochs is going to perform my *Te Deum* there on the thirty-first of May. He is asking me to attend. So I'll take a week off from college and go to Berlin! I'll take the score of No. 8 and see if he'll perform it!'

Chapter 31
1891 - 1892 New love and Symphony No. 8

As usual, Kathi made sure he had all he needed for his stay in Berlin. Ochs met him as he stepped off the train. Anton couldn't believe how young he was. He must have been about thirty, had a thick head of brown hair and was clean shaven, apart from a moustache which curled upwards like an avocet's beak. Ochs took him by cabriolet to an excellent hotel he had booked, the Hotel Kaiserhof.

'I'm so grateful for all you are doing for me, Siegfried. You are kind,' said Anton, while they were on the road.

'The least I could do. It is a great honour for us you accepted my invitation to the performance. I will pay the hotel bill, of course. And all your other expenses, including the train fare, and for any taxi rides.'

'May I come to the rehearsal?'

'Of course. I want you to attend the rehearsal and the dress rehearsal. Please, could you be there by 10 o'clock in the morning?'

'Definitely.'

'One other question. Could I invite myself to have dinner with you tonight?'

'Of course! You name the time.'

'Say, 7.30?'

'Perfect. I'll be hungry by then!'

Anton soon settled into the hotel. It was at least as luxurious as the one he stayed at in Paris. He was tired so laid on the bed. Within seconds, he was asleep. A hefty knock on the door woke him. He thought what a nuisance to be disturbed so abruptly, but slid off the bed and opened the door.

A young woman dressed in a chambermaid's uniform was standing there. 'Good afternoon. Herr Bruckner. My name is Ida Buhz. I am your chambermaid and assistant.'

Anton's heart beat faster at this totally unexpected and delightful interruption. He was speechless. She noticed his silence but continued.

'Would you like me to make you a cup of tea or coffee, or could I get you something from the bar?'

'A cup of coffee would be excellent, perhaps with a biscuit?'

'Of course.'

Anton watched the girl as she put some water into a small kettle and put it on the stove in the corner. He became totally intoxicated with her, partly because of her pretty face and long, light brown hair. Could he be falling in love, he wondered. Surely not. He remembered he was coming up to sixty-seven, but would still like to be married.

'Here you are, mein Herr,' she said, as she put the delicate cup of coffee and matching saucer on the table next to where he was sitting. 'Would you like me to book you a table for dinner tonight?'

'Yes, please. That would be most helpful. There will be two of us. Myself and a friend.'

'I'll go to reception and do that now.' She soon returned. 'Is there anything else I can help you with?'

'Not just now, thank you.'

'If there is anything, please pull the bell chain in the corner.'

Anton had never experienced service like this before. He knew about male butlers but not of women who combined the work of a chambermaid with assisting room occupants. What an excellent wife she would make, he thought. In his much improved financial condition, he could treat this friendly, gorgeous lass better than she could afford as a chambermaid. Kathi might disapprove, but that was another story. She was about twenty, he guessed.

Anton arrived at the restaurant just before the agreed time and chose a table next to a window. A waiter brought him a menu. He read it. The man returned to ask if he wanted a drink. Anton realised he'd been waiting for nearly fifteen minutes and Ochs had still not arrived. He chose a German white beer. About ten minutes later, after Anton had downed almost all of a half stein, a perspiring Siegfried Ochs arrived.

'I'm so sorry, Anton. The director of the Philharmonic Orchestra wanted to see me about a problem we are having with maintaining the hall. It's quite a boring one but I couldn't escape. I'm glad you've started with a drink.'

'Please don't worry, Siegfried. I guessed it would be something to do with your job. Here, have a look at the menu.' Anton waved his hand to attract the waiter's attention. He came immediately and asked Siegfried if he'd like a drink. He ordered the same as Anton.

Siegfried ordered his meal first and chose a fillet steak, only to set an example which Anton might follow. So he ordered one, too.

'Please tell me about yourself and how you became a conductor,' said Anton. In his mind, he wanted to find a subtle way to ask about performing his No. 8.

'I first wanted to be a doctor, so studied medicine and chemistry. I became so interested in music, I abandoned thoughts of becoming a doctor and studied music at the Royal High School for Music, here in Berlin. They were lacking a good choir here, so I established the Philharmonic Choral Society which is becoming very successful. I'm the director. We have a contract with the Philharmonic Orchestra and sometimes I stand in for Hans von Bülow, their principal conductor.'

'I know him well. I met him in Bayreuth at the first performance of Tristan and Isolde, which he conducted, of course.'

'I was there! It's a wonder we didn't meet then. What about you? How did you become a composer?' Anton told him about his teaching, his organ playing and his passion for composing. He said he felt compelled to write symphonies and to achieve their performance.

'My friend Levi, who is a Jew, like me, was the first to play Tristan in Munich. He told me what a brilliant success it was.'

Anton saw this as the opportunity he so dearly wanted. 'Sadly, he's let me down on my No. 8. He gave it to young Weingartner who found it too difficult and moved to conducting opera before he could perform it. Do you think you could persuade von Bülow to play it with the Berlin Philharmonic? I'd be forever grateful if you could.'

'To be honest, I think that would be difficult. Their programme goes so far into the future, it would be at least a year before they would even look at it. You could write to von Bülow and ask him.'

'I'll do that. I'm sure they've played my seventh.'

Anton felt disappointed with Siegfried's response but didn't let it spoil the meal or the conversation.

'Have a dessert, Anton.'

'Thank you. I will.'

After consuming a large portion of plum pudding each, Siegfried invited Anton to indulge in a Cuban cigar, which he willingly did. They parted after a double brandy apiece.

'See you at ten o'clock, then!'

'For certain!' smiled Anton.

As he was walking along the corridor to his room, Ida Buhz appeared from the area she was based.

'I've remade your bed, Herr Bruckner! It's better now, after you slept on it!'

'Oh, that is good of you. Thank you!'

'Would you like breakfast in your room or in the restaurant?'

Anton thought for a moment. Getting Ida to bring him breakfast would mean he would spend more time with this attractive creature.

'In my room, please.'

'What would you like?'

'Scrambled egg, toast, and a German sausage. And anything else you think I would like. And plenty of coffee!'

'At what time?'

'Say, eight o'clock?'

'Fine. I'll see you then.'

Ida knocked on his door at exactly eight o'clock. She was carrying a tray with his breakfast. He was dressed by then and asked her in. The surprise to Anton was there were two coffee cups and saucers on the tray.

'Thank you, Ida. Please leave the tray on the table.'

'Herr Bruckner, please may I have a coffee with you? I can sit on the bed.'

'Yes, we can have a coffee together, if you have the time.'

'Thank you! There is only one other occupied room on this floor, with a Do Not Disturb notice on the door. They told me on reception that you are a composer. Is that correct?' she said. She poured the coffees, handed him his, then shuffled herself into a comfortable position on the bed.

'Yes, I compose all sorts of music, but my greatest joy is in writing symphonies.'

'Do you write church music? And what is a symphony? I think I've heard the word but I don't know what it means!'

As he ate his breakfast, and between mouthfuls, Anton explained the concept of a symphony, in terms he thought Ida would understand. Then he said he wrote religious works, and mentioned his *Te Deum*.

'I'd love to hear some of your music, Herr Bruckner. In fact, I like you and think I'm falling in love with you!'

She stunned him. In a state of shock, he almost fell over. His hopes of finding a wife had suddenly increased dramatically.

Anton dived in. 'I must tell you, I'm falling in love with you, too!' He was tempted to kiss her but resisted. It was not proper and too early in the relationship. He took a sip of coffee.

'Tell me more about yourself,' she said.

He told her about the recent works he composed, his organ play, and about where he lived and worked. 'If we were married, I could afford to make you feel like a princess. You could have everything you wanted... up to a point! You would leave this menial job behind you!'

'I would love to be with you for the rest of my life.'

'I must tell you, I am sixty-seven in September, so won't live that long!' he said, taking another quaff of coffee.

'I would be with you until the end!'

'Listen, Ida,' he said, as she drank the last mouthful of hers. 'I must get ready to go now. I have to be at the concert hall by 10 o'clock. Let's meet later... when I get back.'

'I'll go now then... and be waiting for you!'

As Anton walked into the concert auditorium from a side door, he was greeted by a round of applause from the orchestra and the dozen or so people in the audience. He smiled widely, not only at their enthusiastic welcome, but because he was in love again. Ochs beckoned him to the rostrum.

'Ladies and gentlemen, it is a great pleasure for me to introduce you to Anton Bruckner, the world-famous composer. He is honouring us with his presence here, at this rehearsal, the dress rehearsal, and at the concert performance of his *Te Deum*.'

Anton listened intently. The extreme care Siegfried took impressed him. He had carefully studied Anton's score and skilfully guided the orchestra, choir and soloists to perform it, just as Anton intended.

'Brilliant. I loved it,' said Anton. 'That's exactly how it should be played.'

Siegfried invited Anton to join him for lunch. He would have much preferred to go straight back to the hotel to see Ida. However, he could not tell Siegfried about her for fear of embarrassing himself. So, with reluctance, he agreed. As soon as they finished, Anton made an excuse to leave and rushed back to the hotel as fast as his ailing legs would take him. He knocked on the door of Ida's office and waited. No reply. He knocked again. Still no reply. He took a chance and tried the door. It was locked. From what she had said that morning, he fully expected to see her. Disappointed that she wasn't there, he went to his room. The bed was made so thought she must have been there. He laid on it for an afternoon snooze. Naturally, he hoped she might appear later to straighten the bed, as she had the day before.

Anton went again to her office after he woke up. Again feeling saddened that she wasn't there, he returned to his room and dressed for dinner. Siegfried had apologised for not being able to dine with him that night, so he dined alone.

On his return, he saw his room was as he left it, so Ida could not have attended to it. He was tired so went to bed. The German white beer he had drunk and the local wine helped him to sleep. He didn't awake until gone 8 o'clock. On the way to the dress rehearsal, he couldn't help wondering if Ida had changed her mind about him. Had her parents told her that Anton Bruckner was not the man for her?

Even during this rehearsal, he couldn't stop thinking about her.

'Are you alright, Anton?' said Siegfried, after the event. 'You seem distant, as if you are composing something in your mind, and wanting to get back to the hotel to write it down!'

'Sorry, Siegfried. I didn't mean to worry you. I suffer from dropsy and my legs are troubling me a little today,' he fibbed, but didn't want to mention Ida. 'That rehearsal was perfect. I wouldn't change a thing.'

'Thank you, Anton. Let's go for a beer and a spot to eat.'

'Good idea,' said Anton, still wondering about Ida.

'So are you going to write any more symphonies?'

'Yes, I have sketched the first movement of a ninth, but my most important challenge is to achieve the performance of my eighth. I'm thinking of writing to August Manns in London. He might perform it at the Crystal Palace.'

'That would be a major achievement if you succeeded.'

'And there are other ideas. I could write to orchestra directors in Graz, Nuremburg, and Prague and, once it's in print, even in America.'

'You are clearly so enthused about it, Anton.'

'I regard it as the best of my symphonies. It is the symphony of symphonies, I think… and not wanting to sound too immodest!'

'I'm certain it will be a masterpiece, if your *Te Deum* is anything to go by, as it definitely is!'

After the convivial meal, Anton returned to the hotel. Rather than pine to himself about Ida, he drafted some letters, requesting the performance of No. 8. He would also write to Betty von Mayfield again to tell her about his recent work and his struggles over his No 8. His room had been attended to so a chambermaid had been there, if not Ida.

Anton would be returning to Vienna after the performance so this would be his last night at the hotel. He dreamt that night about Ida and he could see her in his mind as he woke up. As he opened the door to go to breakfast, he saw an envelope that had been passed under the door. He thought it must be the bill for the room, so, as Siegfried was paying, would have to give it back to the reception. His eyes opened wide as he read it, and he almost cheered. It was from Ida saying she loved him and wanted to marry him. She would see him before he returned to Vienna.

He thrived on the public performance of his *Te Deum*. Ida's proposal had suddenly brightened his outlook on life, just like the first gleam of daylight. Even if the performance had been a disaster, he would not stop smiling, but it was a huge and expected success. The audience loved it. Their jubilation overwhelmed him. They cheered and applauded. Siegfried called him to the podium. He seemed to be there forever. He was almost in tears. Dozens of the audience came up and congratulated him. It could not have been given a more enthusiastic reception.

He and Siegfried had a celebratory drink together, bid their farewells, and Anton returned to the hotel. He went straight to Ida's office and knocked on the door. She immediately opened it.

'Herr Bruckner, I am pleased to see you.' She kissed him on both cheeks. 'Did you see my note?'

'Yes. I want to marry you, too! Before we go further, I must meet your parents. When could I see them?'

'As it is the weekend, they will be home now.'

'All I need is their approval to continue our relationship, much of which will be by post!'

'They are keen to meet you. We will go now!'

Her home was only a kilometre from the Kaiserhof. Anton didn't want to walk, so they took a cabriolet. Ida explained she didn't see Anton for nearly two days because they had posted her to a different hotel to do the same sort of work.

Her parents' reaction elated Anton. They made him far more welcomed than he expected at their modest house in not the most salubrious part of Berlin.

'We would be delighted at you developing a relationship with our daughter,' said her mother, as she stood up from straightening a dirty, threadbare mat.

'I agree,' said her father. 'When will we see you again in Berlin?'

'I really don't know. Maybe when I next see Ida. In the meantime, we will write to each other.'

They parted with hugs, kisses and shakings of hands. Anton returned to the Kaiserhof for his luggage and began his journey back home.

***

'You're what? Going to get married?' said Kathi in response to his news. 'You've had so many disappointments, Herr Bruckner. What makes you think this one is any different? Honestly, I would share your joy if it went ahead!'

'Ida said she wanted to marry me before I mentioned the subject. And her family is enthusiastic about it, too!'

'How do you know?'

'I spoke to them?'

'Are they well off?'

'I doubt it. They live in a modest property in the back streets of Berlin. Everything looks worn out inside. I don't even know if her father is working.'

'So, when will you see her again?'

'I don't know yet! We will write to each other.'

'And how did the performance of the *Te Deum* go?'

'It was spectacular. I was the subject of unending adulation. I couldn't believe it. They are going to perform it again in a about month. So a highly successful visit, Kathi. For more than one reason!'

'For your sake, I hope there will be no disappointment!'

***

Later in the year, Anton was working in his office when the Vice Chancellor came to see him.

'Professor Bruckner, I have some news which may be of some interest to you. At the request of the Faculty of Philosophy, the Board of the University have unanimously decided to award you an Honorary Doctorate. May I be the first to congratulate you?'

Anton stood as the Vice Chancellor walked towards his desk. They shook hands. He was speechless. His face shone with joy. Eventually, he spoke.

'Thank you. I am thrilled, far more than any words I can express.' He spontaneously and unnecessarily bowed.

'No need for that, Professor! There will be an award ceremony on 4 July. At 2 o'clock in the afternoon.' He turned and went.

Anton's face was blank. He looked at the door. Had he just woken up from a dream? No. The Vice Chancellor had actually spoken to him. The proof was in a letter, addressed to his office, which someone had placed on his desk and which he saw the following morning.

***

'Kathi, more good news! The University is giving me an Honorary Doctorate. They tell me it's the first time they've awarded one to a musician! I cannot tell you how pleased I am. This is more than just recognition! It's an elevation beyond measure.'

'Congratulations, Herr Bruckner! When will they give you the certificate?'

'On the fourth of July. Would you and Bruno like to come to the ceremony?'

'Yes, if we are free!'

Many people attended the Senate's ostentatious meeting room, where the Vice Chancellor presented him with the honour. His students, friends and colleagues attended, including Kathi and Bruno.

'I cannot find the right words to thank you properly,' he said, wiping his eyes with a handkerchief. 'But if there were an organ here, I could express my gratitude on that,' he said, trying to reply to the presentation speech. His eyes were full of tears, which spilled down his ageing cheeks.

A month later, a huge festival to celebrate the award followed the official presentation. The Vienna choral societies and his faculty organised it. Over 3000 people attended, including his 'Gaudeamus'. After the Rector's speech, Anton's students celebrated by carrying him around the hall, while others clapped and cheered. Anton was so moved he could hardly speak.

So, a week later, after Hans Richter and the Vienna Philharmonic had played the first performance of the new version of his No. 1, he spoke from the rostrum.

'My dear friends, thank you for attending this concert and for your generous applause. The University has recently presented me with an Honorary Doctorate. As a thank you and to show my deep appreciation, I dedicate this version of my symphony to the University of Vienna,' he said, smiling and with the absence of tears. The audience applauded again and cheered him.

'Could you please post this letter, Kathi?'

She read the envelope. 'Oh, it's to Fräulein Buhz. Good luck, Herr Bruckner. I'm glad you are still writing to each other.'

Anton said he still loved her, and was looking forward to the day they would be married. After telling her about his recent successes, said he was now a doctor, explaining it was not of medicine but of music. He said he would have to burn his visiting cards and have a set printed with his new title of 'Dr'. His failure to get his No. 8 performed, he kept unsaid.

'Here's a letter from Berlin,' said Kathi, just a week after Anton had written to Ida.

He took it into his study. The letter was thin, as if Ida had little to say. Was she telling him she didn't want him anymore? He quickly opened it.

Dear Herr Bruckner,

Congratulations! Should I call you Dr? I am concerned about your health. I want to look after you, if you become ill. Have there been more performances of your symphonies?

I am so keen for us to marry!

Your ever loving Ida.

His face lit up with a smile. He could see his future life shining from this letter.

'You look thrilled, Herr Bruckner!'

'I am. She still loves me!'

His reply to Ida said he was delighted with the way their relationship was heading and nothing, including the award of doctorate, could make him happier. Knowing she was much in love with him made him more confident in telling her about the less successful happenings in his life. So he told her about his failures over his No. 8, and that he felt his health was not always as good as it could be.

Her reply, by return of post, startled him.

My dear Herr Bruckner,

I love you so much, I cannot live without you at my side. Please come to Berlin so we can discuss our wedding arrangements with my parents. They say you can stay in our house.
It is time those people in Vienna decided to play your new symphony. Could you see them and tell them?

Much love my dearest.

From Ida

So he would visit Berlin and sooner than he wanted, delighted and utterly thrilled though he was at the content of the letter. He replied that, assuming he was fit enough to travel, he would visit her and her family in the next vacation, which would be in the summer.

'So what are you working at now, Herr Bruckner?' asked Kathi, one evening before serving his dinner.

'Do you remember I attended the consecration of the organ a year or two ago at the Cathedral of the Immaculate Conception in Linz? Well, a gentleman called Richard Heuberger wants me to write a piece to celebrate the International Exhibition for Music and Theatre which he is organising. He wants it for performance on 7 May. So I thought I'd get on with it as fast as I can.'

'What has that to do with the consecration ceremony?'

'They read out Psalm 150 there, which is about how musical instruments glorify God. Well, if I put the Psalm to music that will fit well with the Exhibition, don't you agree?'

'Brilliant idea, Herr Bruckner! Don't let me stop you from working on it!'

***

The frequent performance of many of his works gave Anton enormous satisfaction. His young admirer, Gustav Mahler, was so impressed when he read the published score of his *Te Deum* he performed it. He wrote to Anton and said,

My dear Anton,

I write to tell you that last night, I conducted your Te Deum *in Hamburg with the soloists, the Philharmonic Mixed Choir and the Hamburg Philharmonic Orchestra.*

The participants and the entire audience were deeply moved by this mighty structure, and its truly sublime content. At the end of the performance I experienced what I consider to be the greatest victory for any piece I ever performed. The audience sat silently without moving and it was only after the performers and I were leaving the hall that the applause erupted.

It was a major triumph for you, my friend. Congratulations.

Gustav Mahler
15 April 1892

'Kathi, listen to this!' Almost in tears, he read her Mahler's letter.

'I say congratulations, too, Herr Bruckner. What a nice man that Herr Mahler must be!'

A few days later, Anton read in a press report that his *Te Deum* was played in Cincinnati under Theodore Thomas in front of an audience of 7,000. There were 800 singers and an orchestra of 120. It said the audience of conservative Americans was utterly stunned. He told Kathi, and they both chuckled.

***

'You seem so busy composing, Herr Bruckner. I loathe asking you, but what is happening about your No. 8?' she asked, a few weeks after he received Mahler's extraordinary letter.

'I'm glad you ask, Kathi. When I feel like composing, I have to compose. It's like an author writing. He has to write when he feels he must, and to know where he is going with words. I know where I'm going with the musical notes!'

'So where, this time?'

'I'm writing a patriotic song. So somewhere in Germany! It's a sequel to *Germanenzug*, which I think you've already heard. I'm not sure what to call it yet! Before I started scribbling it, I wrote a letter to Karl Muck, the conductor of the Graz Philharmonic, to ask him to play No. 8. So I'm far from giving up hope! Here it is. Could you post it please?'

'Of course!'

Anton surprised himself with his speed of composing. He wrote the entire piece in one day, 29 April. The score showed it was for two tenors, two basses, a choir and a brass orchestra. He called it *Das Deutsche Lied*.

Despite his declining health, he continued composing, undeterred by the failure to achieve a performance of his No. 8. During '92 he completed his *Vexilla Regis,* which was based on a hymn written in the sixth century by a

453

Latin bishop of the early church. It was a reflective piece and first performed by the Vienna Choral Society on the Good Friday of that year.

**

Anton's letters to various orchestra directors in Europe failed to generate the slightest interest in performing his No. 8. So he tried another tack. Given Weingartner's and all the other refusals, he wrote to Hermann Levi in Munich to ask him to reconsider. He made the crucial point that Richard Wagner had made a personal promise to play his symphonies so it would be in fulfilment of this pledge by the 'immortal and blessed Master' to play No. 8 in Munich. He awaited Levi's reply.

**

The summer vacation soon arrived, so an Anton in love made his way to Berlin with a hug and best wishes from Kathi. His hopes increased the nearer he was to Berlin. Ida's father, Herr Buhz, met Anton on the platform at which the train arrived.

'I'm so glad to see you, Herr Bruckner! Ida is dying to see you again. We have read about your success in many cities where they've played your music. You are world famous.'

'Oh, thank you, Herr Buhz. I'm really not that famous!' he said with modesty.

'And Ida tells me you are a doctor now!'

'Not of medicine, but of music.'

'Really? I've never heard of a doctor other than one you see if you are ill.'

'There are such doctors, I can assure you. And I am one!'

Ida was waiting at the door of their house when Anton and Herr Buhz arrived in a pony and trap. She rushed up to him, and held him tight.

'My dearest Herr Bruckner, I am so pleased to see you. You are looking so well. You are limping just slightly, I think.'

'Yes, it's gout or dropsy. It has been worse, and it has been better.' He kissed her on both cheeks. 'It's time you called me Anton. I cannot have a wife calling me Herr Bruckner!'

'From now on, I shall call you Anton, Herr Bruckner! Let me show you to your room.'

Carrying his small travel case, Anton followed Ida up the narrow staircase into one of the tiniest bedrooms he had ever seen. The bed was so narrow its occupant could not get in or out again without bumping into the wall. It reminded him again of the bed at Windhaag. A small wardrobe was squeezed between the end of the bed and the wall, next to a little window. At least there is some light in here, thought Anton.

'Where do I put my clothes, Ida?' he said, not seeing how to open the door of the wardrobe.

'The doors slide open so you don't have to pull them!'

'I see.'

'Shall I leave you to unpack, Herr Bruckner... I mean Anton?'

'Yes, please. I may have a snooze before coming down. The journey was very tiring.'

'Of course, Herr... I mean Anton!'

He was relieved at being granted some time to himself. Recognising this was a poor family, he imagined that Herr Buhz earned little money, whatever he did for a living. Full of joy, he still felt in love with Ida. He thought about why he was there. No marriage could take place on this visit. It had to be for planning purposes only. He fell asleep and woke to a knock on the door.

'Dinner is ready, Herr Bruckner!' It sounded as if it could be Frau Buhz.

He changed into a fresh shirt before going downstairs. There was no water in the room, so he couldn't wash his face.

The meal was set on a table in the kitchen. His face lit up as he saw three large German sausages, potatoes and some beans on his plate. A glass of beer stood there.

All four of them sat in front of their meal and a drink. Herr Buhz lifted his glass. 'Let's drink to the betrothed couple!' he said. Anton was less sure about the 'betrothed'. No engagement had taken place, and he hadn't given Ida a ring.

'So, let's talk about the wedding. Should it be here or in Vienna?' said Herr Buhz.

'Surely the bride would prefer it in her own city, don't you think, Ida?'

'I agree. It should be here, in Berlin.'

'There is the question of the invitations, the dress, and the wedding breakfast and so on. We will need money,' said Ida's mother.

'I'm sure I can fund it,' said Anton. 'It's the least I can do.'

'Thank you, Herr Bruckner. We are at the poor end of the people!' said Herr Buhz

'Could we go to the church tomorrow? I would love to see it,' said Anton.

'I'm working, so my wife and Ida will take you.'

After breakfast, the three of them prepared themselves to visit the church.

'Is it far?' asked Anton.

'No, about two hundred metres.'

'I can walk that.'

Anton's face dropped at the sight of the church. 'That isn't a Catholic church, is it?' he said.

'No it's Lutheran. We are Lutherans, I'm proud to say!' said Ida's mother.

'That presents a problem,' said a sad faced Anton. 'I am Catholic. Could you convert to Catholicism, Ida?'

'My husband will have a say in that!' said Frau Buhz. 'He is anti-Catholic.'

'So are all Lutherans,' said Anton.

'Let's go inside,' said Ida, trying hard not to shed a tear. She knew what her father would say. They spent some time looking around inside, pointless though it seemed to Frau Buhz. Anton thought Herr Buhz might... just might... agree to his daughter converting.

The three of them returned to the house and waited until Herr Buhz came in and hung up his coat. Anton asked him.

'Out of the question! No daughter of mine will ever become a Catholic. Not over my dead body.'

'I can't become a Lutheran,' said Anton. 'I'm so sorry, Ida. We won't be getting married.'

Ida immediately broke down in tears. Then she then left the room. Her mother followed.

'So that is the end of that, Herr Buhz.'

'I'm afraid so, Herr Bruckner.'

'I'll pack and perhaps you could take me to the station.'

'Certainly.'

'I'd like to say goodbye to Ida before I go.'

'Of course.'

Anton went to his tiny bedroom. He left the door open. A damp eyed Ida appeared. She hugged him.

'I'm sorry, Anton. I cannot oppose my father. There is nothing we can do.'

'I shall miss you, Ida. All I can say is life must go on. You are a young, personable woman. You shouldn't think again about marrying a man who is in his late sixties. I would not have been the husband you deserve. I'm sure you will find a man of your own age. So I wish you the best future imaginable.'

She kissed him and left him to pack. He never saw her again.

So, another of Anton's attempts to marry failed. He was disappointed, but not that sad. The pity was he and Ida had laboured so much on what turned out to be the impossible. On the train back to Vienna, his thoughts turned to his No. 8. His ambition to have it performed exceeded by far any wish to marry.

***

Anton smiled at Kathi as she welcomed him home.

'Well, Herr Bruckner, from the look on your face, your mission was successful!'

'In a way, it was. Ida was saved from marrying an old man like me. In another, it wasn't. I will remain single! But I'm not as sad as I might be. What I don't have I shan't miss!'

'I won't ask any more questions, Herr Bruckner. I'm just glad you are back home. Let me get you a drink. Then I'll prepare your meal.'

'Is there any post, Kathi? I'm expecting a letter from Munich.'

'No, but a man came to see you.'

'Who?'

'Just a minute, I wrote it down…'

'What did he look like?' he said.

'A large man, not fat. He had a big beard and a moustache. I noticed a coin on his watch chain.'

'That's Hans Richter! I'm as sure as I can be! I gave him the coin! It's a thaler! What did he want? Did he say?'

'No. He just said he wanted to see you. I told him you were in Berlin. I didn't tell him why. He asked me to say he wanted to see you as soon as you were available. I said I'd tell you as soon as you returned. And you'd probably either go to see him or write with some suggested dates.'

'I'll write. Could you post the letter on your way home please, Kathi?'

'Yes, of course. I'll cook your meal now.'

Anton wrote a brief letter saying he was available any day between 11 o'clock in the morning and 4 pm until term started.

They agreed to meet two weeks later at midday in the restaurant at the Music Society Hall.

'I'm so pleased to see you, Anton. How was Berlin? Come and sit down.'

'Pleased to see you, too, Hans. Berlin was fine. I went there to see an old acquaintance. So what can I do for you, my friend?'

'I want to perform your eighth symphony,' he said flatly.

'What?'

'Your eighth. I want to conduct its premiere with the Philharmonic.'

Anton could not speak. He had spent so much time pleading with conductors all over Europe to perform it. All had refused, except Karl Muck, who had yet to reply, if he was to reply at all. And here was a conductor, as well-known as any of them and better than most, who wanted to play it.

'I can't tell you how delighted I am, Hans. May I ask what has made you want to play it?'

'It's a matter of pride, Anton. I know you have attempted to get it played all over Europe and have been badly let down. So we'd like to perform it here.'

457

'Where does pride come into it?'

'We would be proud to give it the premiere… before someone else does!'

'So what next?' he said, still dumbfounded.

'I believe you have commissioned its publication by Lienau's company.'

'Yes, they finished the job in March and have at least two hundred copies. They've printed the orchestral parts, too.'

'Excellent. I'll collect it from them.'

'And a date for performance?'

'We drafted it in the programme for the eighteenth of December.'

'Could I attend any rehearsals?'

'Of course! We'll welcome you. Most will be in the mornings.'

'Could I please give you my free dates?'

'I don't see why not. We haven't agreed any rehearsals yet.'

'I'll send you them.'

They shook hands. Anton caught a cabriolet to the Hessgasse.

***

Kathi was about to go home, so he saw her just before she left.

'You'll never believe this, Kathi. Richter is going to perform my No. 8! That's what he wanted to see me about.'

'Haven't you been there before, Herr Bruckner? That Weingartner let you down. I wouldn't get too excited.'

'We'll see! He wants me to write to him with some dates for the rehearsals, which he agrees I can attend.'

'That does sound promising.'

'It's good that I no longer have to bother about a reply from Herr Levi. I can't believe he'd play it, anyway! Whatever he said!'

They both laughed.

'I'll get you a beer to celebrate. Then I'm going home!'

Almost eight weeks elapsed before the rehearsals started. They had to be delayed because Lienau's had sold many of their first print run and had to set up to produce more.

'I'm dreading the first rehearsal, Kathi. The Vienna Philharmonic have had problems with my symphonies in the past.'

'You worry too much, Herr Bruckner. It's good that they will play it. I didn't think they would. I'm glad I was wrong. Good luck and I hope it goes well,' she said, as Anton, carrying the score in his case, left to go to the concert hall for a ten o'clock start.

***

'Good morning, gentleman,' said Hans Richter, while standing on the rostrum. 'Herr Anton Bruckner needs no introduction as he is deservedly a world renowned composer. Please stand, Anton so they can see you are here!'

Anton stood and bowed to them.

'His eighth symphony is the culmination of his symphonic output. It is the most modern and incredible symphony I have ever seen on paper. Our job is to convert it from the printed page into sound. So, finish your tuning and we'll start.'

Within a few minutes, they began. Richter stopped them after about twenty bars. He was unhappy with the balance between the strings and the woodwind. They played on for a little longer. Then he held them up because he wanted more volume from the bassoons. He brought them to a halt at least fifty times in the first two movements.

'May I make a request, Herr Richter?' said one of the double bass players.

'By all means.'

'It's now past one o'clock and I think we should have a lunch break.'

'I'd lost track of time, so let's stop for an hour.'

Anton joined Hans for lunch in the concert hall restaurant. They talked about the problems the orchestra was having with the work.

'What would you say if I suggested we shorten that first movement, Anton?'

'I would simply say no. The structure doesn't permit shortening.'

'But it's taken nearly four hours to rehearse the first two movements. We'll be here all day before we finish!'

'You don't have to complete the whole symphony today. I can't see a problem in stopping after the third movement and leaving the finale until the next rehearsal.'

'But we've done nothing like that before!'

'Alright. See how this afternoon goes and decide after you've played the third movement.'

'We'll do that, Anton.'

Rehearsing the third movement proved at least as difficult as working on the first two. So Richter took up Anton's suggestion of leaving the finale to the next rehearsal.

Anton went home, uncertain about what Richter thought of how the orchestra was managing the symphony.

***

'I'm not sure how that went, Kathi. Herr Richter stopped and started the players. I dread to think how many times. It wasn't a disaster, but they didn't do well. I could tell from the look on his face at the end of the session. And they still had the last movement to play.'

459

'It will be alright on the eighteenth, Herr Bruckner. They may find it difficult now but by the time they've had the last rehearsal, they'll be fine!'

'I hope so. I really do!'

It took five more rehearsals before Richter was happy. Anton was less sure. Anton was equally unsure when the day came for the premiere. He hardly slept the night before. Despite Anton's misgivings, Hans Richter conducted a faultless, brilliant performance, of the whole work. Anton was ecstatic. Tears ran down his face. He wondered how the audience would react. They had stayed quiet to the end. After the last blazing, joyful chord, there were five seconds of silence. Then the whole audience became totally jubilant. His worries proved groundless. They applauded, cheered and stamped their feet. Richter called Anton onto the podium. He bowed to the audience and stepped down. The applause became louder. They stood and gave him a riotous ovation. At Richter's beckoning, he stepped up to the rostrum again and bowed to the audience. He did it again and again. Finally, Anton turned to applaud the orchestra, all of whom stood and applauded him. The reception of the whole audience and orchestra alike, enthralled Anton more than the performance of any other work of his. He had proved to himself, and to others, that this was his best symphony, his 'symphony of symphonies'.

***

'So, Herr Bruckner?' said Kathi, as he stepped over the threshold.

'It was miraculous. My fears were totally misplaced. I've never before had such wonderful appreciation for a work of mine anywhere,' he said.

'What did Herr Richter think?'

'He was moved by way the Philharmonic played it. He said they did it for me! The reaction of the audience delighted him. And he said my No. 8 would be remembered as one of the best symphonies of all time! So I took him to a café around the corner and I bought four dozen donuts for him and his family. He gave me a dozen to bring home. Here, you have some, Kathi, for you and Bruno!'

'Oh, thank you, Herr Bruckner! I'll get a paper bag from the kitchen. I'm so pleased for you. Congratulations!' She smiled and gave him the hug he might have expected.

'Thank you, Kathi!'

The End